Alice Hoffman

THE RIVER KING

VINTAGE

Published by Vintage 2001

8 10 9 7

First published in Great Britain in 2000 by
Chatto & Windus

Vintage
Random House, 20 Vauxhall Bridge Road,
London SW1V 2SA

www.vintage-books.co.uk

Addresses for companies within
The Random House Group Limited can be found at:
www.randomhouse.co.uk/offices.htm

The Random House Group Limited Reg. No. 954009

A CIP catalogue record for this book
is available from the British Library

ISBN 9780099286523

The Random House Group Limited supports the Forest Stewardship
Council (FSC®), the leading international forest certification organisation.
Our books carrying the FSC label are printed on FSC® certified
paper. FSC is the only forest certification scheme endorsed by the
leading environmental organisations, including Greenpeace.
Our paper procurement policy can be found at
www.randomhouse.co.uk/environment

Printed and bound by CPI Group (UK) Ltd, Croydon, CR0 4YY

TO PHYLLIS GRANN

THE RIVER KING

THE IRON BOX

THE HADDAN SCHOOL WAS BUILT in 1858 on the sloping banks of the Haddan River, a muddy and precarious location that had proven disastrous from the start. That very first year, when the whole town smelled of cedar shavings, there was a storm of enormous proportions, with winds so strong that dozens of fish were drawn up from the reedy shallows, then lifted above the village in a shining cloud of scales. Torrents of water fell from the sky, and by morning the river had overflowed, leaving the school's freshly painted white clapboard buildings adrift in a murky sea of duckweed and algae.

For weeks, students were ferried to classes in rowboats; catfish swam through flooded perennial gardens, observing the disaster with cool, glassy eyes. Every evening, at twilight, the school cook balanced on a second-story window ledge, then cast out his rod to catch dozens of silver trout, a species found only in the currents of the Haddan River, a sweet, fleshy variety that was especially delectable when fried with shallots and oil. After the flood subsided, two inches of thick, black silt covered the carpets in the dormitories; at the headmaster's house, mosquitoes began to hatch in sinks and commodes. The delightful watery vistas of the site, a landscape abundant with willows and water lotus, had seduced the foolish trustees into building much too close to the river, an architectural mistake that has never been rectified. To this day, frogs can be found in the plumbing; linens and clothes stored in closets have a distinctly weedy odor, as if each article had been washed in river water and never thoroughly dried.

After the flood, houses in town had to be refloored and re-roofed; public buildings were torn down, then refashioned from cellar to ceiling. Whole chimneys floated down Main Street, with some of them still issuing forth smoke. Main Street itself had become a river, with waters more than six feet deep. Iron fences were loosened and ripped from the earth, leaving metal posts in the shape of arrows adrift. Horses drowned; mules floated for miles and when rescued, refused to eat anything but wild celery and duckweed. Poison sumac was uprooted and deposited in vegetable bins, only to be mistakenly cooked along with the carrots and cabbages, a recipe that led to several untimely deaths. Bobcats showed up on back porches, mewing and desperate for milk; several were found beside babies in their cradles, sucking from bottles and purring as though they were house cats let in through front doors.

At that time, the rich fields circling the town of Haddan were owned by prosperous farmers who cultivated asparagus and onions and a peculiar type of yellow cabbage known for its large size and delicate fragrance. These farmers put aside their plows and watched as boys arrived from every corner of the Commonwealth and beyond to take up residence at the school, but even the wealthiest among them were unable to afford tuition for their own sons. Local boys had to make do with the dusty stacks at the library on Main Street and whatever fundamentals they might learn in their very own parlors and fields. To this day, people in Haddan retain a rustic knowledge of which they are proud. Even the children can foretell the weather; they can point to and name every constellation in the sky.

A dozen years after the Haddan School was built, a public high school was erected in the neighboring town of Hamilton, which meant a five-mile trek to classes on days when the snow was knee-deep and the weather so cold even the badgers kept to their dens. Each time a Haddan boy walked through a storm to the public school his animosity toward the Haddan School grew, a small bump on the skin of ill will ready to rupture at the slightest contact. In this way a hard bitterness was forged, and the spiteful sentiment increased every year, until there might as well have been a fence dividing those who came from the school and the residents of the village. Before long, anyone who dared to cross that line was judged to be either a martyr or a fool.

There was a time when it seemed possible for the separate worlds to be united, when Dr. George Howe, the esteemed headmaster, considered to be the finest in the Haddan School history, decided to marry Annie Jordan, the most beautiful girl in the village. Annie's father was a well-respected man who owned a parcel of farmland out where Route 17 now runs into the interstate, and he approved of the marriage, but soon after the wedding it became apparent that Haddan would remain divided. Dr. Howe was jealous and vindictive; he turned local people away from his door. Even Annie's family was quickly dispatched. Her father and brothers, good, simple men with mud on their boots, were struck mute the few times they came to call, as if the bone china and leather-bound books had robbed them of their tongues. Before long people in town came to resent Annie, as if she'd somehow betrayed them. If she thought she was so high and mighty, in that fine house by the river, then the girls she grew up with felt they had reason to retaliate, and on the streets they passed her by without a word. Even her own dog, a lazy hound named Sugar, ran away yelping on those rare occasions when Annie came to visit her father's farm.

It quickly became clear that the marriage had been a horrid mistake; anyone more worldly than Annie would have known this from the start. At his very own wedding, Dr. Howe had forgotten his hat, always the sign of a man who's bound to stray. He was the sort of person who wished to own his wife, without belonging to her in return. There were days when he spoke barely a sentence in his own home, and nights when he didn't come in until dawn. It was loneliness that led Annie to begin her work in the gardens at Haddan, which until her arrival were neglected, ruined patches filled with ivy and nightshade, dark vines that choked out any wildflowers that might have grown in the thin soil. As it turned out, Annie's loneliness was the school's good fortune, for it was she who designed the brick walkways that form an hourglass and who, with the help of six strong boys, saw to the planting of the weeping beeches beneath whose branches many girls still receive their first kiss. Annie brought the original pair of swans to reside at the bend in the river behind the headmaster's house, ill-tempered, wretched specimens rescued from a farmer in Hamilton whose wife plucked their bloody feathers for soft, plump quilts. Each evening, before supper, when the light above the river washed the air with a green haze, Annie went out with an apronful of old bread. She held the firm belief that scattering bread crumbs brought happiness, a condition she herself had not known since her wedding day.

There are those who vow that swans are unlucky, and fishermen in particular despise them, but Annie loved her pets; she could call them to her with a single cry. At the sound of her sweet voice the birds lined up as politely as gentlemen; they ate from her hands without ever once drawing blood, favoring crusts of rye bread and whole-wheat crackers. As a special treat, Annie often brought whole pies, leftovers from the dining room. In a wicker basket, she piled up apple cobbler and wild raspberry tart, which the swans gobbled down nearly whole, so that their beaks were stained crimson and their bellies took on the shapes of medicine balls.

Even those who were certain Dr. Howe had made a serious error in judgment in choosing his bride had to admire Annie's gardens. In no time the perennial borders were thick with rosy-pink foxglove and cream-colored lilies, each of which hung like a pendant, collecting dew on its satiny petals. But it was with her roses that Annie had the best luck of all, and among the more jealous members of the Haddan garden club, founded that very year in an attempt to beautify the town, there was speculation that such good fortune was unnatural. Some people went so far as to suggest that Annie Howe sprinkled the pulverized bones of cats around the roots of her ramblers, or perhaps it was her own blood she cast about the shrubs. How else could her garden bloom in February, when all other yards were nothing more than stonewort and bare dirt? Massachusetts was known for a short growing season and its early killing frosts. Nowhere could a gardener find more unpredictable weather, be it droughts or floods or infestations of beetles, which had been known to devour entire neighborhoods full of greenery. None of these plagues ever affected Annie Howe. Under her care, even the most delicate hybrids lasted past the first frost so that in November there were still roses blooming at Haddan, although by then, the edge of each petal was often encased in a layer of ice.

Much of Annie Howe's handiwork was destroyed the year she died, yet a few samples of the hardiest varieties remain. A visitor to campus can find sweet, aromatic Prosperity, as well as Climbing Ophelia and those delicious Egyptian Roses, which give off the scent of cloves on rainy days, ensuring that a gardener's hands will smell sweet for hours after pruning the canes. Among all of these roses, Mrs. Howe's prized white Polars were surely her finest. Cascades of white flowers lay dormant for a decade, to bloom and envelop the metal trellis beside the girls' dormitory only once every ten years, as if all that time was needed to restore the roses their strength. Each September, when the new students arrived, Annie Howe's roses had an odd effect on certain girls, the sensitive ones who had never been away from home before and were easily influenced. When such girls walked past the brittle canes in the gardens behind St. Anne's, they felt something cold at the base of their spines, a bad case of pins and needles, as though someone were issuing a warning: Be careful who you choose to love and who loves you in return.

Most newcomers are apprised of Annie's fate as soon as they

come to Haddan. Before suitcases are unpacked and classes are chosen, they know that although the huge wedding cake of a house that serves as the girls' dormitory is officially called Hastings House—in honor of some fellow, long forgotten, whose dull-witted daughter's admission opened the door for female students on the strength of a huge donation—the dormitory is never referred to by that name. Among students, the house is called St. Anne's, in honor of Annie Howe, who hanged herself from the rafters one mild evening in March, only hours before wild iris began to appear in the woods. There will always be girls who refuse to go up to the attic at St. Anne's after hearing this story, and others, whether in search of spiritual renewal or quick thrills, who are bound to ask if they can take up residence in the room where Annie ended her life. On days when rosewater preserves are served at breakfast, with Annie's recipe carefully followed by the kitchen staff, even the most fearless girls can become lightheaded; after spooning this concoction onto their toast they need to sit with their heads between their knees and breathe deeply until their metabolisms grow steady again.

At the start of the term, when members of the faculty return to school, they are reminded not to grade on a curve and not to repeat Annie's story. It is exactly such nonsense that gives rise to inflated grade averages and nervous breakdowns, neither of which are approved of by the Haddan School. Nevertheless, the story always slips out, and there's nothing the administration can do to stop it. The particulars of Annie's life are simply common knowledge among the students, as much an established part of Haddan life as the route of the warblers who always begin their migration at this time of year, lighting on shrubbery and treetops, calling to one another across the open sky.

Often, the weather is unseasonably warm at the start of the term, one last triumph of summer come to call. Roses bloom more abundantly, crickets chirp wildly, flies doze on windowsills, drowsy with sunlight and heat. Even the most serious-minded educators are known to fall asleep when Dr. Jones gives his welcoming speech. This year, many in attendance drifted off in the overheated library during this oration and several teachers secretly wished that the students would never arrive. Outside, the September air was enticingly fragrant, yellow with pollen and rich, lemony sunlight. Along the river, near the canoe shed, weeping willows rustled and dropped catkins on the muddy ground. The clear sound of slow-moving water could be heard even here in the library, perhaps because the building itself had been fashioned out of river rock, gray slabs flecked with mica that had been hauled from the banks by local boys hired for a dollar a day, laborers whose hands bled from their efforts and who cursed the Haddan School forever after, even in their sleep.

As usual, people were far more curious about those who'd been recently hired than those old, reliable colleagues they already knew. In every small community, the unknown is always most intriguing, and Haddan was no exception to this rule. Most people had been to dinner with Bob Thomas, the massive dean of students, and his pretty wife, Meg, more times than they could count; they had sat at the bar at the Haddan Inn with Duck Johnson, who coached crew and soccer and always became tearful after his third beer. The on-again, off-again romance between Lynn Vining, who taught painting, and Jack Short, the married chemistry teacher, had already been discussed and dissected. Their relationship was completely predictable, as were many of the love affairs begun at Haddan—fumbling in the teachers' lounge, furtive embraces in idling cars, kisses exchanged in the library, breakups at the end of the term. Feuds were far more interesting, as in the case of Eric Herman—ancient history—and Helen Davis—American history and chair of the department, a woman who'd been teaching at Haddan for more than fifty years and was said to grow meaner with each passing day, as if she were a pitcher of milk set out to curdle in the noonday sun.

Despite the heat and Dr. Jones's dull lecture, the same speech he trotted out every year, despite the droning of bees beyond the open windows, where a hedge of twiggy China roses still grew, people took notice of the new photography instructor, Betsy Chase. It was possible to tell at a glance that Betsy would be the subject of even more gossip than any ongoing feud. It wasn't only Betsy's fevered expression that drew stares, or her high cheekbones and dark, unpredictable hair. People couldn't quite believe how inappropriate her attire was. There she was, a good-looking woman who apparently had no common sense, wearing old black slacks and a faded black T-shirt, the sort of grungy outfit barely tolerated on Haddan students, let alone on members of the faculty. On her feet were plastic flip-flops of the dime-store variety, cheap little items that announced every step with a slap. She actually had a wad of gum in her mouth, and soon enough blew a bubble when she thought no one was looking; even those in the last row of the library could hear the sugary pop. Dennis Hardy, geometry, who sat directly behind her, told people afterward that Betsy gave off the scent of vanilla, a tincture she used to dispel the odor of darkroom chemicals from her skin, a concoction so reminiscent of baked goods that people who met her often had an urge for oatmeal cookies or angel food cake.

It had been only eight months since Betsy had been hired to take the yearbook photos. She had disliked the school at first sight, and had written it off as too prissy, too picture perfect. When Eric Herman asked her out she'd been surprised by the offer, and wary as well. She'd already had more than her share of botched relationships, yet she'd agreed to have dinner with Eric, ever hopeful despite the statistics that promised her an abject and lonely old age. Eric was so much sturdier than the men she was used to, all those brooders and artists who couldn't be depended upon to show up at the door on time let alone have the foresight to plan a retirement fund. Before Betsy knew what had happened she was accepting an offer of marriage and applying for a job in the art department. The Willow Room at the Haddan Inn was already reserved for their reception in June, and Bob Thomas, the dean of students, had guaranteed them one of the coveted faculty cottages as soon as they were wed. Until that time, Betsy would be a houseparent at St. Anne's and Eric would continue on as senior proctor at Chalk House, a boys' dormitory set so close to the river that the dreadful Haddan swans often nested on the back porch, nipping at passersby's pant legs until chased away with a broom.

For the past month, Betsy had been simultaneously planning both her classes at Haddan and her wedding. Perfectly rational activities, and yet she often felt certain she had blundered into an alternate universe, one to which she clearly did not belong. Today, for instance, the other women present in the auditorium were all in dresses, the men in summer suits and ties, and there was Betsy in her T-shirt and slacks, making what was sure to be the first of an endless series of social miscalculations. She had bad judgment, there was no way around it; from childhood on, she had jumped into things headfirst, without looking to see if there was a net to break her fall. Of course, no one had bothered to inform her that Dr. Jones's addresses were such formal events; everyone said he was ancient and ailing and that Bob Thomas was the real man in charge. Hoping to erase her fashion blunder, Betsy now searched through her backpack for some lipstick and a pair of earrings, for all the good they would do.

Taking up residence in a small town had indeed left Betsy disoriented. She was used to city living, to potholes and purse snatchers, parking tickets and double locks. Whether it be morning, noon, or night, she simply couldn't get her bearings here in Haddan. She'd set out for the pharmacy on Main Street or to Selena's Sandwich Shoppe on the corner of Pine and arrive at the town cemetery in the field behind town hall. She'd start for the market, in search of a loaf of bread or some muffins, only to find that she'd strayed onto the twisting back roads leading to Sixth Commandment Pond, a deep pool at a bend in the river where horsetails and wild celery grew. Once she'd wandered off, it would often be hours before she managed to find her way back to St. Anne's. People in town had already become accustomed to a pretty, dark woman wandering about, asking for directions from schoolchildren and crossing guards, and yet still managing to take one wrong turn after another.

Although Betsy Chase was confused, the town of Haddan hadn't changed much in the last fifty years. The village itself was three blocks long, and, for some residents, contained the whole world. Along with Selena's Sandwich Shoppe, which served breakfast all day, there was a pharmacy at whose soda fountain the best raspberry lime rickeys in the Commonwealth could be had, as well as a hardware store that offered everything from nails to velveteen. One could also find a shoe store, the 5&10 Cent Bank, and the Lucky Day Florist, known for its scented garlands and wreaths. There was St. Agatha's, with its granite facade, and the public library, with its stained-glass windows, the first to be built in the county. Town hall, which had burned down twice, had finally been rebuilt with mortar and stone, and was said to be indestructible, although the statue of the eagle out front was tipped from its pedestal by local boys year after year.

All along Main Street, there were large white houses, set back from the road, whose wide lawns were ringed with black iron fences punctuated by little spikes on top; pretty, architectural warnings that made it quite clear the grass and rhododendrons within were private property. On the approach to town, the white houses grew larger, as though a set of stacking toys had been fashioned from clapboards and brick. On the far side of town was the train station, and opposite stood a gas station and mini-mart, along with the dry cleaner's and a new supermarket. In fact, the town was sliced in two, separated by Main into an east and a west side. Those who lived on the east side resided in the white houses; those who worked at the counter at Selena's or ran the ticket booth at the train station lived in the western part of town.

Beyond Main Street the village became sparser, fanning out into new housing developments and then into farmland. On Evergreen Avenue was the elementary school, and if a person followed Evergreen due east, in the direction of Route 17, he'd come to the police station. Farther north, at the town line that separated Haddan from Hamilton, deposited in a no-man's-land neither village cared to claim, was a bar called the Millstone, which offered live bands on Friday nights along with five brands of beer on tap and heated arguments in the parking lot on humid summer nights. There had probably been half a dozen divorces that had reached a fevered pitch in that very parking lot and so many alcohol-induced fights had taken place in those confines that if anyone bothered to search through the laurel bordering the asphalt he'd surely find handfuls of teeth that were said to give the laurel its odd milky color, ivory with a pale pink edge, with each blossom forming the shape of a bitter man's mouth.

Beyond town, there were still acres of fields and a crisscross of dirt roads where Betsy had gotten lost one afternoon before the start of the term, late in the day, when the sky was cobalt and the air was sweet with the scent of hay. She'd been searching for a vegetable stand Lynn Vining in the art department had told her sold the best cabbages and potatoes, when she happened upon a huge meadow, all blue with everlasting and tansy. Betsy had gotten out of the car with tears in her eyes. She was only three miles from Route 17, but she might as well have been on the moon. She was lost and she knew it, with no sense whatsoever of how she had managed to wind up in Haddan, engaged to a man she barely knew.

She might have been lost to this day if she hadn't thought to follow a newspaper delivery truck into the neighboring town of Hamilton, a true metropolis compared to Haddan, with a hospital and a high school and even a multiplex cinema. From Hamilton, Betsy drove south to the highway, then circled back to the village via Route 17. Still, for some time afterward, she'd been unable to forget how lost she'd become. Even when she was beside Eric in bed all she had to do was close her eyes and she'd continue to see those wildflowers in the meadow, each and every one the exact color of the sky.

When all was said and done, what was so wrong with Haddan? It was a lovely town, featured in several guidebooks, cited for both its excellent trout fishing and the exceptional show of fall colors that graced the landscape every October. If Betsy continually lost her way on the streets of such a neat, orderly village, perhaps it was the pale green light rising from the river each evening that led her astray. Betsy had taken to carrying a map and a flashlight in her pocket, hopefully ready for any emergency. She made certain to keep to the well-worn paths, where the old roses grew, but even the rosebushes were disturbing when they were encountered in the dark. The twisted black vines were concealed in the black night, thorns hidden deep within the dried canes until a passerby had already come close enough to cut herself unwittingly.

In spite of the police log in the *Tribune*, which reported crimes no more heinous than jaywalking across Main Street or trash bags of leaves set out on the curb on Tuesdays when yard waste would not be collected until the second Friday of the month, Betsy did not feel safe in Haddan. It seemed entirely possible that in a town such as this, a person might walk along the riverbank one bright afternoon and simply disappear, swallowed up in a tangle of chokeberry and woodbine. Beyond the river there were acres thick with maple and pine, and the woods loomed darkly at night, flecked with the last of the season's fireflies.

Even as a girl, Betsy had hated the countryside. She'd been a difficult child; she had whined and stomped her feet, refusing to accompany her parents on a picnic, and because of her ill-tempered ways, she'd been spared. That day, there were seven separate fatalities due to lightning. Ball lightning had ignited fence posts and oak trees, before chasing people across meadows and fields. There had been several sightings of rocket lightning, which burst from cloud to ground in seconds flat with a display not unlike fireworks exploding in a deadly white flash. Instead of taking her place in the meadow with her parents, lying beside them in the burning grass, Betsy had been sprawled upon the couch, leafing through a magazine and sipping a tall glass of pink lemonade. She'd often imagined how the course of events might have altered if only she'd accompanied her hapless parents. They might have run for their lives instead of being caught unawares, too puzzled and stupefied to move. They might have followed Betsy's lead and been wise enough to crouch behind a flinty stone wall, which would have turned so burning hot when it took the strike intended for them that for months afterward it would have been possible to fry eggs on the hottest of the stones. Ever since, Betsy had possessed a survivor's guilt and was often in search of punishment. She raced red lights and drove with the gas gauge on empty. She walked city streets after midnight and gravitated outside on stormy days without the benefit of a rain-coat or an umbrella, long ago deciding to ignore any Samaritans who warned that such foolhardy behavior would only ensure that sooner or later she'd wind up electrified, ignited from her fingers to her toes.

Before meeting Eric, Betsy had been careening through her life with nothing much to show other than sheaves of photo-graphs, a black-and-white diary of landscapes and portraits stuffed into files and folios. A good photographer was meant to be an observer, a silent party there to record, but somewhere along the line Betsy had become a bystander to her own existence. *Just ignore me,* she would say to her subjects. *Pretend I'm not here and go about your normal routine.* All the while she'd been doing this, her own life had somehow escaped her; she herself had no routine, normal or otherwise. When she'd come to Haddan, she'd been at a low point. Too many men had disappointed her, friends weren't there for her, apartments had been broken into while she was asleep. She certainly hadn't expected any changes in her life on the day she came to take the yearbook photos at Haddan, and perhaps there wouldn't have been any if she hadn't overheard one student ask another, *Why did the chicken leave the Haddan School?* Curious, she'd eavesdropped, and when she'd heard the answer—*Because he had an aversion to bullshit*—Betsy laughed so loudly that the swans on the river startled and took flight, skimming over the water and raising clouds of mayflies.

Eric Herman had turned to see her just at the moment when her grin was its widest. He watched her arrange the soccer team in size order and then, in what he assured her afterward was the first impulsive action of his life, he had walked right up to her and asked her to dinner, not the next night or the one after that, but right then, so that neither one had time to reconsider.

Eric was the sort of attractive, confident man who drew people to him without trying, and Betsy wondered if perhaps she had simply happened to be in sight at the very moment he decided it was high time for him to marry. She still couldn't fathom what he could possibly want with someone such as herself, a woman who would spill the entire contents of her backpack on the floor of a quiet auditorium just as she was attempting to stealthily extract a comb. There wasn't a member of the Haddan faculty who didn't hear the coins and ballpoint pens rolling down the aisle and who then felt completely validated in his or her initial opinion of Betsy. Long after Dr. Jones had completed his lecture, people were still collecting Betsy's personal belongings from beneath their chairs, holding items up to the filtered light as though studying foreign and mysterious artifacts, when in fact all they'd gotten hold of was a notepad or a vial of sleeping pills or a tube of hand cream.

"Don't worry," Eric whispered to her. "Act naturally," he advised, although acting naturally was exactly what always got her into trouble in the first place. If Betsy had trusted her instincts, as Eric suggested, she would surely have turned tail and run the first time she walked through the door of the girls' dormitory where she was to be the junior houseparent. A chill had passed across her back as she stepped over the threshold, the cold hand of anxiety that often accompanies a bad decision. Betsy's cramped set of rooms at the foot of the stairs was nothing less than awful. There was only one closet and the bathroom was so small it was impossible to exit the shower without jamming one's knees into the sink. Paint was peeling from ceilings and the panes of old, bumpy glass in the windows allowed in drafts but not sunlight, turning even the palest rays a foggy green. In this setting, Betsy's furniture looked mournful and out of place: the couch was too wide to fit through the narrow doorway, the easy chair appeared threadbare, the bureau would not stand on the sloping pine floors, and instead lurched like a drunkard each time a door was banged shut.

In her first week at Haddan, Betsy spent most of her nights at Eric's apartment in Chalk House. It made sense to take the opportunity to do so now, for when the students arrived, they'd have to monitor their own behavior as well as that of their charges.

And there was another reason Betsy had avoided sleeping at St. Anne's. Each time she spent the night in her own quarters, she was wrenched from her slumber in a panic, with the sheets twisted around her and her thoughts so muddled it was as if she'd woken in the wrong bed and was now fated to lead someone else's life. On the night before school was to begin, for instance, Betsy had slept at St. Anne's only to dream she'd been lost in the fields outside Haddan. No matter how she might circle, she went no farther than the same parcels of uncultivated land. When she wrested herself from this dream, Betsy staggered out of bed, disoriented and smelling of hay. For an instant, she felt as though she were a girl again, left in someone's strange, overheated apartment to fend for herself, which was exactly what had happened when friends of the family took her in after her parents' accident.

Quickly, Betsy switched on the lights to discover that it was only a little after ten. There was a thumping coming from the direction of the stairs and the radiators were banging away, gushing out a steady stream of heat, even though the evening was unusually warm. No wonder Betsy couldn't sleep; it was ninety degrees in her bedroom and the temperature was still rising. The orchid she had bought that afternoon at the Lucky Day Florist, a bloom accustomed to tropical climates, had already lost most of its petals; the slim, green stem had been warped by the heat and was now unable to hold up even the most delicate flower.

Betsy washed her face, found a stick of gum to ease her dry mouth, then pulled on her bathrobe and went to call on the senior houseparent. She assumed people at Haddan exaggerated when they called Helen Davis a selfish old witch, the fitting owner of an ugly black tomcat who was said to eat songbirds and roses. Clearly judgments were harsh at this school, for weren't many people already calling Betsy a kook after the fiasco at the welcoming lecture? Wasn't Eric referred to as Mr. Perfect by those who failed to measure up to his standards of excellence and forever after resented him? For her part, Betsy was the last to accept anyone else's opinion, but when she knocked at Miss Davis's door no one answered, even though there was clearly someone on the other side. Betsy could practically feel Miss Davis's displeasure at being disturbed as the older woman peered through the peephole. Betsy knocked again, more forcefully now.

"Hello! Can you help me out? I just need some advice about my radiator."

Helen Davis was tall and extremely imposing, even when answering the door in her nightgown and slippers. She carried herself in the manner women who were once beautiful often do; she was standoffish and confident in equal measure and she certainly did not feel the need to be civil when an unwanted visitor came calling at such a late hour.

"My radiators," Betsy explained. Having come directly from bed, Betsy's choppy hair was sticking straight up and her eyes were ringed with mascara. "They simply won't turn off."

"Do I look like a plumber?" Helen Davis's smirk, as many of her students might confirm, was not a pleasant sight. Her disapproval could turn a person's blood cold, and there had been several occasions when a tender freshman had fainted on the floor of her classroom when asked the simplest of questions. Miss Davis had never tolerated smart alecks nor the practice of chewing gum, nor did she invite guests into her private quarters.

The administration had failed to mention to Betsy that none of her predecessors had lasted more than a year. So she dove right in, asking for assistance when anyone else would have slunk away. "You must have experience in dealing with the heating system," Betsy said. "Surely, it can't be classified information."

Miss Davis glared. "Are you chewing gum?" she asked sharply.

"Me?" Betsy immediately swallowed, but the gum clogged in her trachea. As she was doing her best not to choke, a horrible squalling creature ran by. Instinctively, Betsy drew herself against the wall to let it pass.

"Afraid of cats?" Miss Davis asked. Several junior houseparents who'd left claimed to be allergic to her pet. Although Betsy herself was not a fan of any sort of wildlife, cats included, she could tell that life at St. Anne's would be bearable only if she won Helen Davis over to her side. Eric had often made fun of Miss Davis's habit of quoting Ben Franklin whenever she wished to prove a point, and now Betsy used this information to her advantage.

"Wasn't it Ben Franklin who said the best dog of all is a cat?"

"Ben Franklin said nothing of the sort." Still, Miss Davis knew when she was being flattered, and no one ever said flattery was a crime. "Wait in the hall and I'll get you what you need," she directed.

Standing in the dark, Betsy felt an odd elation, as though she'd just aced an exam or been named teacher's pet. When Helen Davis returned, Betsy could see a slice of the apartment behind her; these quarters had remained constant for the past fifty years and included a collection of clutter that had surely taken that long to amass. In spite of the high-backed velvet love seat and a good rug from Afghanistan, the place was in serious disorder. Books were everywhere, along with half-filled teacups and forgotten crusts of sandwiches. There was the foul odor of old newspapers and cats. Helen swung the door closed behind her. She reached out and deposited a quarter in Betsy's open hand.

"The secret is to bleed the radiators. Turn the screw at the rear with this quarter and be sure to keep a pan underneath to catch the drips. After the steam's released, the radiator will cool down."

Betsy thanked the senior houseparent, then with her typical ungainliness, she dropped the quarter and was forced to retrieve it. Seeing her from this angle, crawling about on hands and knees, Helen Davis at last realized that her caller was the same individual who had made a scene in the auditorium during Dr. Jones's speech.

"You're Eric Herman's girlfriend," Helen declared. "That's who you are!"

"Hardly a girl." Betsy laughed.

"Yes, hardly. Far too old to be taken in by him."

"Oh, really?" Betsy stood, quarter in hand. Perhaps people were right about how nasty Helen Davis was. It was said she graded on a negative curve, deliberately failing as many students as possible, and that she had never once changed a grade, not even when self-mutilation or nervous breakdowns were threatened. The last houseparent to share duties with her at St. Anne's had quit midterm to go to law school, reporting back that torts and constitutional law were a breeze after dealing with Helen Davis.

"Eric Herman is the most dishonest man I know. Just take a look at his ears. A man with small ears is always dishonorable and stingy. All the great men had large ears. Lincoln was said to move his at will, much like a rabbit."

"Well, I like a man with small ears." Regardless, Betsy made a mental note to take a closer look at Eric's physiognomy.

"He's after my job," Helen Davis informed Betsy. "You might as well know right now, he's a whiner and a complainer. A man like that will never be satisfied."

"Oh, he's satisfied, all right," Betsy said, although she had already been privy to Eric's many complaints about the history department. Helen Davis, he liked to joke, ought to be fired first, then guillotined, with her head displayed on one of the posts of those iron fences on Main Street. At least then the old woman would finally serve a purpose as she scared away crows rather than students. "He's happy as a clam," Betsy reported.

Miss Davis chortled at that. "Look at his ears, my dear, they tell the whole story."

Betsy peered down the hallway; again there'd been a noise on the stairs. "What is that awful thudding sound?"

"It's nothing." Helen's tone, which had been warming as she critiqued Eric, now turned sharp. "The hour's a little late for these shenanigans, I might add."

When Miss Davis closed her door, Betsy heard the lock click shut. At least Helen Davis had bestowed a quarter; no one else at Haddan had offered Betsy so much as a helping hand since she'd arrived. Even Eric had been so busy preparing for his classes that he'd been, it was true, stingy with his time. Still, he was a good man, and Betsy could hardly fault him for being as focused as he was dependable. Tonight was hardly the time to reassess her own opinions in light of Miss Davis's observations, which were surely self-serving at best. It was most likely the emptiness of the dormitory that now set Betsy's doubts to work, but there'd soon be a cure for that. By tomorrow, the hallways would be filled with girls and it would be Betsy's job to soothe the homesick and shore up the meek and manage the wild as best she could. It would be her responsibility to make certain each and every one slept tight beneath this roof.

As Betsy returned to her apartment, she became aware of the scent of roses drifting down the stairway, richly fragrant in the overheated corridor. She found the odor in her own rooms, fainter yes, but disturbing enough so that she hurried to bleed the radiators, scalding her hands in the process. When she went back to bed she expected to toss and turn, but for once she slept deeply. In fact, she overslept, and needed to gulp down a quick cup of coffee in order to be ready for the first arrivals. It was then Betsy noticed the green vine outside her window. A few of Annie Howe's prized white roses were still blooming; they were as big as cabbages, as white as snow. In the early morning sunlight, their innermost petals appeared to be a pale, pearly green. Betsy laughed at herself then; what a fool she'd been to be nervous last night. For every odd occurrence there was a rational explanation, or so she had always believed. She tidied up, then went to get dressed, comforted by the sight of the roses. But if she'd only paused long enough to open her window she would have discovered that Polar roses have no scent whatsoever. Even the bees avoid these creamy buds, preferring thistles and goldenrod instead. Take a scissors to the stems of these roses and they'll fall apart at the touch. Try to pick one barehanded, and every thorn will draw blood.

THE TRAIN TO HADDAN WAS ALWAYS LATE, AND this day was no exception. It was a spectacular afternoon, the fields rife with late-blooming asters and milkweed, the sky as wide and as clear as heaven. In the pine trees along the railroad tracks, hawks perched in the tallest branches; red-winged blackbirds swooped across the distance. Stands of oak and hawthorn made for pockets of dark woods where there were still plenty of deer, as well as an occasional moose that had wandered down from New Hampshire or Maine. As the train passed slowly through the neighboring town of Hamilton, several boys ran alongside the cars; some waved cheerfully to the passengers on board, while others rudely stuck out their tongues and pulled their faces into freckled smirks, the grimaces of wild angels unafraid of the gravel and dust that was always stirred up as the train rolled by.

Today, there were more than a dozen Haddan students on board, ready for the start of the term. Girls with long, shiny hair and boys in freshly pressed clothes that would soon be torn and stained in soccer games congregated in the club car. Their good-natured rowdiness drifted through the train when the conductor opened the doors, but the racket didn't reach as far as the last car. There, in the farthest seat, a girl named Carlin Leander, who had never before left home, gazed out at the countryside, appreciating every haystack and fence that came briefly into sight as the train rolled on. Carlin had been planning to get out of Florida all her life. It had made no difference that she was the most beautiful girl in the county where she'd been born, with pale ashy hair and the same green eyes that had gotten her mother into trouble at the age of seventeen, pregnant and stranded in a town where a traveling carnival was considered a cultural event and any girl with a mind of her own was thought to be an aberration of nature's plan.

Carlin Leander was nothing like her mother, and for that she was grateful. Not that Sue Leander wasn't pleasant and warm, she certainly was. But to be agreeable and kindhearted was not Carlin's goal. Whereas her mother was pliant and sweet, Carlin was obstinate and opinionated, the sort of girl who went barefoot in spite of all warnings to watch out for snakes. She never paid the least bit of attention to the boys who followed her home from school, many of them so moony and stupefied by her beauty that they rode their bikes into ditches and trees. Carlin was not about to get trapped, not in a locality where the heat continued to rise after midnight and the mosquitoes were a year-round annoyance and most folks chose to celebrate a girl's weakness and ignore her strengths.

Some people were simply born in the wrong place. The first thing such individuals searched for was a map and the second was a ticket out. Carlin Leander had been ready to leave Florida since she could walk, and she'd finally managed her escape with a swimming scholarship to the Haddan School. Although her mother had been reluctant to let her go all the way to Massachusetts, where people were bound to be dishonest and depraved, in the end Carlin won the battle, using a plan of attack that included equal amounts of pleading, promises, and tears.

On this beautiful blue day, Carlin had a single battered suitcase thrown beneath the seat and a backpack crammed with sneakers and bathing suits. She had very few other belongings left at home, only some threadbare stuffed animals on her bed and an awful coat her mother had bought as a going-away present at Lucille's Fine Fashions, a fuzzy acrylic monstrosity Carlin had hidden in the utility shed, behind some retreaded tires. Carlin planned to keep her plane ticket as a souvenir, forever and ever, if it didn't dissolve first. She'd handled the ticket so many times that the print had worn off on her skin; she'd washed and she'd scrubbed, but there remained little gray flecks on her fingertips even now, the marks of her own ambition.

All the while she was on the jet traveling north, and then again as the train sped through Boston's endless construction sites, Carlin had felt little knobs of doubt rising beneath her skin. Who was she to think she could forge such a completely different life for herself? Here she was, dressed in a cheap pair of jeans and a T-shirt she'd purchased at a secondhand store, her blond hair pinned up haphazardly with metal clips that were rusty from the Florida humidity. Anyone could see she didn't fit in with the other well-dressed passengers. She didn't own a decent pair of boots, and had never had her hair cut by a professional, always snipping the ends herself when too much chlorine took its toll. She had swamp dust on her feet and nicotine stains on her fingers, and came from a universe of hash and eggs and broken promises, a place where a woman quickly learned there was no point crying over spilled milk or bruises left by some man who claimed to love a little too hard or too much.

But in spite of her history, and all she believed she was lacking, Carlin felt hopeful once they were out of the city. They passed acres of goldenrod and fields where cows were grazing. It was the season of the warbler migrations and huge gatherings skimmed over the meadows, wheeling back and forth as if of one body and mind. Carlin struggled to open the sooty window in order to savor the September air, and was caught off guard when a tall kid toting a huge duffel bag approached to help raise the jammed window. The boy was far too skinny, with a shock of unruly hair that made him seem elongated, even storklike. He wore a long, black coat that hung like a sackcloth on his spindly frame and his work boots were unlaced, leaving his feet to slop around as if they were fish. An unlighted cigarette dangled from his wide mouth. Even with the fresh air streaming in through the open window there was no way to disguise the fact that he stank.

"Mind if I sit down?" Not bothering to wait for an answer, the boy took the seat directly across from Carlin, setting his duffel bag in the aisle, unconcerned that it might cause a navigational problem for anyone wishing to pass by. He had the sort of luminous skin that can only be achieved by spending hours in a dark room while recovering from a migraine or a hangover. "God, those idiots in the next car from the Haddan School were driving me crazy. I had to escape."

Carlin noticed that he was nervous in her presence, she could tell from the flutter of a pulse beneath his eye. A very good sign, for a boy's apprehension always set Carlin at ease. She repinned a stray lock of loose hair with one of the silver clips. "That's where I'm going," she informed her fellow traveler. "The Haddan School."

"But you're not an idiot. That's the difference." The ungainly boy searched through his gear until he found a Zippo lighter. When Carlin pointed to a no-smoking sign, he shrugged his bony shoulders and lit up anyway. Carlin smiled, entertained for the first time since she'd set off from home. She leaned back in her seat, waiting for this oddity to try to impress her again.

He introduced himself as August Pierce from New York City, sent to Haddan by his overburdened father who hadn't had a moment's peace since the day Gus was born, shouldering the burden of raising his son after the death of his wife. The old man was a professor of biology with high expectations for his one and only boy; there were those who insisted upon rooting for loved ones long after they'd been thoroughly disappointed, and such was the case with Gus Pierce's father. Having failed again and again, Gus believed he owed his father one last try. Not that he himself anticipated the least bit of success. Why should Haddan be any different from the other schools he'd attended? Why should anything good ever happen to him? He had been born on the seventh day of the seventh month and he'd always had bad luck. He could cross his fingers, he could knock on wood, and he'd still hit his head upon every ladder; he'd take every wrong turn possible. While everyone else progressed on the flat, straight road toward the future, Gus fell into manholes and gutters face first, with no visible means of escape.

He viewed his own life as a prison sentence and experienced his existence much as a condemned man might have. If anything, the beauty of the world confounded him and made him more despondent. It therefore came as a pleasant surprise that a simple encounter could fill him with such optimism. He'd thrown himself into the seat across from Carlin in a fit of jitters, half expecting her to call for the conductor and have him bodily removed, and now here she was, talking to him. A sparrow flying out of his mouth would have been more anticipated than a beautiful girl such as this offering him a piece of gum. Girls like Carlin usually looked right through him; he existed in a sub-universe, a world of losers, a world of pain, located in the basement of reality, several levels beneath the realm of pretty faces and possibilities. If Carlin was leaning forward, listening to his falsified life story without laughing in his face, anything might happen: Blackbirds might turn into ginger cakes. Willow trees might burst into flame.

"Choose a number between one and twenty," August Pierce

now suggested to his newfound companion. "Don't tell me what it is." He had picked up several tricks with which to amaze, and this seemed as good a time as any to put his talents to use.

Carlin did as she was told, although her expression had hardened into a disbeliever's stare.

Gus closed his eyes and made a show of his prestidigitation, at last plucking a number from the air. "Seven," he said, triumphantly, or at least he hoped for triumph as he was attempting a ruse any beginning conjurer who knew the first thing about logic could neatly manage.

Yet for all the trick's success, Carlin was not pleased. She hated to be transparent and she certainly didn't wish to be revealed in any way. Even now, she was in the process of perfecting a story that would alter her background and create a new identity. She intended to tell people that her parents worked for the government, and although they had never settled down they had always encouraged her swimming, transporting her to races and events no matter where they might be living. A far better tale to tell than one that included a mother who worked the cash register at the Value Mart, a father she'd never seen, and the dozens of times she'd had to hitchhike to swim meets. With deception as her plan, a boy who could read her mind was a definite liability, for seven was indeed her chosen number.

"It's simple probability," Gus explained when he realized Carlin hadn't appreciated the trick. "Most people will choose either three or seven."

Carlin glared at him, scornful. Her eyes were a shade of green that could turn gray in an instant, like shallow water that mirrored any change in the weather. "I'm not most people," she told him.

"No," Gus Pierce agreed. Even a nitwit such as himself could make that distinction. "You're definitely not."

The train had begun to lurch into Haddan Station; the whistle blew long and low, rattling windows in houses closest to the train tracks, frightening crows from treetops and telephone lines. Carlin grabbed for her backpack. She had a hundred and fifty dollars in her wallet, which she planned to use toward a return ticket home in June, and no assurances of anything in between. She probably would have deserted Gus even if he hadn't pulled his stupid mind-reading stunt, and it came as no surprise to him when she hurried to get to the door before the train came to a standstill, dragging her suitcase out from beneath the seat. When Gus offered to help, Carlin appraised him carefully. Experience had taught her it was best to inform someone when she knew she'd never be attracted to him. It saved so much bother and confusion in the end.

"We might as well get this over with," she said. "I'm not interested."

Gus nodded his agreement. "Why would you be?"

He was so baffled by the notion that he might ever stand a chance with her, and so sincere, Carlin couldn't help but grin before she headed for the exit. Watching her walk away, Gus realized that her hair was the color of stars, those pale distant galaxies that are too far away ever to be charted or named. He fell in love with her in the very instant he was disclaiming his interest. When he and Carlin met next she would probably walk right past him, as though he were a piece of litter or trash. But perhaps not; strange things had been happening ever since Gus had set off for Haddan. On the shuttle from New York, for instance, the flight attendant had given him a complimentary mini-bottle of Chivas, no questions asked. In the club car, he'd requested a bag of potato chips only to have the cashier throw in a tuna sandwich on the house. Most unexpectedly and most wonderfully, a beautiful girl had not only spoken to him, she'd smiled at him. In all honesty, this was the best run of luck August Pierce had ever possessed.

As he stepped off the train, his good fortune appeared to continue. Two seniors from Haddan—Seth Harding and Robbie Shaw, good-looking, serious boys of the sort who would never associate with Gus under any circumstances—were holding up a sign with his name. When he approached, they grabbed his duffel bag and clapped him on his back as though he were a long-lost brother. Out in the sweet country air, with all that blue sky above him and the warblers chattering in every bush, Gus felt dizzy with confusion and with something that, had he been anyone else, would have been easily recognizable as joy.

"Are you sure you've got the right guy?" Gus asked as his cohorts loaded his gear into a BMW idling at the curb.

"Perfect score on your aptitude tests? Editor of the school newspaper in eighth grade at the Henley School in New York? You're the one," Seth and Robbie insisted.

Gus squeezed his long legs into the back of Seth's car even though the information they'd gathered was clearly sketchy at best, stray pieces of his autobiography garnered from his Haddan application, a portrait that carefully omitted his tendency toward depression and rebellion and the fact that he'd been suspended from the Henley School for laziness and insubordination. But what the hell, at worst he had a free lift to school, and when they passed Carlin hauling her heavy suitcase down a brick-paved sidewalk, he turned to gaze at her mournfully, wishing she'd see him accompanied by his unlikely comrades.

On the short ride to the school, Gus was informed that he'd been granted the honor of residing at Chalk House, although for his part, he could not figure out why he'd been chosen for this distinction nor could he understand what was so desirable about the dilapidated old house at which they arrived. On the outside, Chalk was no different than any other dorm on campus. A squat, boxy place, it was covered with white clapboards; there was a wide front porch, littered with Rollerblades and hockey sticks, and around back, a latticework entranceway where garbage cans were stored alongside expensive mountain bikes. On the first floor were several gracious rooms that boasted mahogany wood-work and working fireplaces, but these were always bequeathed to upperclassmen, who had already paid their dues; freshmen were relegated up to the attic. At the rear of the house, two private apartments had been tacked on. In one lived the coach, Duck Johnson, whose snoring had been known to rattle window-panes; in the other lived Eric Herman, who spent more time in his office at the humanities building than he did in his own quarters.

Because of its proximity to the river, Chalk House was by far the dampest building on campus. A film of mold coated any item left in the showers overnight, and in the evenings, snails left slippery trails along hallways and walls. Each term brought boys who couldn't resist climbing onto the roof, where they aimed their piss directly into the Haddan River from atop their perilous roost. None of these boys had ever been successful and, thankfully, none had fallen in such an attempt, but even the alumni association, never the champion of change, had agreed that the building was structurally unsound. Last spring a railing had finally been built along the roof. Still, the house was in miserable condition, with a dreadful electrical system that blinked on and off during storms and ancient plumbing that grumbled and clogged. In the rafters, on the far side of the damp plaster walls, there lived generation after generation of ill-tempered raccoons who squabbled and paced at night, so that bickering and snarling drifted into the dreams of the freshmen in the attic, and not a single one of these boys ever had a good night's sleep until their first term was over and done.

Yet no one would dare to suggest that this venerable house be torn down, and most people envied its residents. There were rumors that students could buy their way in, and suggestions that the odds of being chosen for Chalk were greatly increased if one's father or cousin had been a boarder. Indeed, there were distinct advantages for Chalk House residents. At all other houses, students had to vacuum floors and clean bathrooms, but at Chalk a maid was employed by a group of alumni; she came in every Wednesday to sort laundry and on Thursdays she made up the beds with fresh linens. Chalk boys were the first to register for courses and because the house had its own parking area, seniors were allowed to have cars on campus. Such entitlement had clearly paid off. For more than a hundred years, boys at Chalk had graduated at the top of the class, guided into a world of privilege with the help of those who had gone before them. There were Chalk alumni on most college admission committees and out in the world more alumni were eager to hire a brother who'd lived in the old house beside the river, that falling-down pile of wood and bricks where the wind rattled down the chimney and the swans always put up a good fight when chased off the porch.

The students who had not been chosen for Chalk, those boys who lived in Otto House or Sharpe Hall, felt a sort of bitterness from their very first day on campus, as if already, before anyone had seen their faces or knew their names, they had been judged lacking, fated to belong to a lower echelon where they would always be second best, chosen last for teams, never dating the prettiest girls from St. Anne's or daring to hope for a kiss under the weeping beeches. But these petty jealousies arose later on in the term; during the first weeks of school there was a sense of good fellowship as everyone settled in. The trees were still green and evenings were warm; the last of the crickets called in the meadows, a constant song most people found comforting, for it reminded them that there was still a world beyond the confines of Haddan.

Some people fit in easily at the school, but each year there were bound to be those unable to accommodate or conform, whether they were sullen or frightened or shy. In a place where teamwork and good cheer were highly regarded, loners were easily identified, and Carlin Leander was clearly among them. Although she was pretty and had quickly proven herself a worthy member of the swim team, she was moody and spent too much time on her own to be one of the crowd. As soon as practice ended, she took off by herself, like one of those bobcats people said roamed the woods, a breed too high-strung and suspicious to be among its own kind.

Such was the case with most unhappy students; they avoided even one another, so intent on their own unhappiness they failed to notice the other lost souls around them. These students often found their way to the pharmacy on Main Street. They cut classes and sat at the counter in the afternoons, ordering cups of coffee, trying to work up the nerve to buy cigarettes. They clearly had no idea that Pete Byers, the pharmacist, had never sold tobacco to a minor in his life. Anyone looking for that sort of thing would have far better luck at the mini-mart, where Teddy Humphrey would sell just about anything to a kid from Haddan; damn them but not their money as far as he was concerned. Have a good fake ID in hand and it was not Teddy's job to wonder why, but simply to sell a six-pack of Samuel Adams beer or Pete's Wicked Ale to any customer who waited in line.

Most people in town paid no attention to the Haddan students. There were new ones each year, and although every freshman class brought an aura of high hopes and even higher energy, they'd be gone in four years, the blink of an eye really, when sorted into the history of a town like Haddan. In this village most people stayed put; the farthest a resident might move was to a house around the corner when they married or, eventually and sadly, perhaps down to the rest home over on Riverview Avenue.

Every September, when the new students settled in, they came to buy boots at Hingram's Shoe Shop, then went about setting up a bank account at 5&10 Cent Bank where pretty Kelly Avon, who was always so helpful, had learned to keep a straight face whenever some fourteen-year-old wanted to deposit a check for several thousand dollars. Nikki Humphrey, who'd stayed married to Teddy from the mini-mart for far too long, never took it personally when groups of Haddan girls come sashaying into Selena's, ordering lattes and blueberry scones, expecting quick service, as if Nikki were nothing more than an automaton or a household servant. Before long these girls would be gone and

Nikki would still be in Haddan, putting all the money spent on lattes and scones to good use by remodeling the kitchen of the cute little house she'd bought on Bridal Wreath Lane after her divorce.

Some local people actually looked forward to September; they enjoyed witnessing all that youth spilling onto their sidewalks and into their stores. Lois Jeremy, from the garden club, often sat out on her gabled porch facing Main Street on Friday afternoons just to watch for those Haddan School boys and girls. It brought tears to her eyes to think of the expectations she'd had for her own son, AJ, and for a moment or two she ignored her perennial border, which she always covered with marsh grass rather than store-bought mulch to protect the bulbs from early frosts.

"Aren't they adorable?" Lois would call to her best friend, Charlotte Evans, who lived right next door and who'd had quite a year herself, what with Japanese beetles destroying half her garden and her youngest daughter going through that nasty divorce from that nice psychologist, Phil Endicott, who no one would have ever expected to be the sort of individual to have a girlfriend on the side.

"They couldn't be cuter." Charlotte had been deadheading her lilies and pulling damp leaves from between the twisted canes. She leaned on her rake to take a closer look at the Haddan boys in their khaki pants as they headed into town, and all those lovely, young girls trailing after them. The girls reminded her of her own daughter Melissa, the one who was crying all the time and taking Prozac and every other antidepressant she could get her hands on.

"I'd guess they're having the time of their lives." Lois Jeremy's lips trembled as she watched. Two girls had begun to skip, show-ing off for the boys; their long hair swung out behind them and they giggled, but their childish gait could hardly belie their wom-anly legs.

"Oh, I'd say so," Charlotte agreed, feeling slightly dizzy her-self, perhaps from all the raking she'd done or from thinking too much about Melissa's divorce. "Isn't it lovely to see people who are happy?"

Of course Mrs. Jeremy and Mrs. Evans could not be expected to guess how many girls at St. Anne's cried themselves to sleep. Unhappiness seemed to double when trapped beneath one roof. Mood swings were common; behavior marked by half-truths and secrets. One tall, dark girl named Peggy Anthony refused all solid food, choosing instead to drink only milk, supplemented by the candy bars she hid in a suitcase stored under her bed. There was a senior named Heidi Lansing who was so nervous about college applications she had pulled out half the hair on her head before she'd even begun to write her essays, and a sophomore named Maureen Brown who lit black candles on her windowsill before bed and so alarmed her roommates with the wicked conversa-tions she held in her sleep that these anxious girls had taken to spending nights in the bathroom, unrolling sleeping bags on the tile floor, so that anyone wanting to take a shower or use the toi-let was forced to step over their slumbering forms.

Carlin Leander did not cry herself to sleep or starve herself, yet unhappiness coursed through her, even when she plunged into the cold water of the pool. In fact, she hadn't much to com-plain about; she'd been granted a large airy room on the third floor and roommates who were perfectly pleasant. It was not these girls' fault that they had more than Carlin: more money, more clothes, more experience. Both Amy Elliot and Pie Hobson had filled their closets with boots and wool jackets and dresses so expensive a single one cost more than Carlin had spent on her yearly wardrobe, most of it bought at secondhand stores and at the Sunshine Flea Market, where it was possible to buy five T-shirts for a dollar, never mind the fraying seams or the moth holes.

Lest her roommates take her up as a charity case, Carlin elaborated on the story she'd come up with on the train: the only offspring of a father and mother who traveled the world, she'd far more important things to worry about than clothes. Unlike her roommates, she hadn't the chance to covet or hoard. She and her family weren't the sort of people who'd had time to gather personal effects or put down roots. They were better than that, her story implied, superior in some deep and moral way. So far, no one had challenged her story, and why should they doubt her? Truth had very little to do with a girl's image at St. Anne's; here, an individual was whoever she claimed to be. Those who had never been kissed professed to be sexually wild, and those who'd been through more boys than they cared to remember insisted they would remain virgins until their wedding day. Identity was a mutable thing, a cloak taken on and off, depending on circumstance or phases of the moon.

Carlin's only bad moments had come with the swim team, and that was because she'd been foolish enough to let down her guard. If she'd been thinking straight she would never have trusted Christine Percy, the senior who had informed her that all girls on the team were required to shave their private parts. Afterward, they had all teased Carlin, along with Ivy Cooper, the other new girl, for being so gullible. There were jokes about how chilly Carlin and Ivy would now be. Everyone had been through the same hazing; losing a little hair and a little pride was believed to strengthen team bonds. After this initiation, a girl was welcomed as a true teammate, at a celebration with some contraband wine, bought at the mini-mart with Christine's fake ID. Carlin, however, became even more withdrawn; it didn't take long before the other girls learned to leave her alone.

Each night, Carlin waited for the hour when she could flee from St. Anne's. After curfew, she lay unmoving in her bed, until at last her roommates' breathing shifted into deep, even rhythms; only then was she ready to make her escape out her window, in spite of the thorny vines that coiled up the fire ladder and left traces of blood on her fingers as she climbed to the ground. In an instant she felt free, let loose into the sweet, inky Massachusetts night, away from the steam heat and close quarters of St. Anne's. At first, she only stayed out long enough to have a quick cigarette beside the old rosebushes, damning the spiked vines as she pricked herself accidentally, then sucked the blood from her fingers. But after a while she dared to go farther, walking down to the river. One night, when there was no moon and the sky was perfectly black, the need to stray took hold. A ribbon of mist had settled onto the horizon, then flattened out to wind through the shrubbery. In the smooth still air, the edges of things melted, disappearing into the deep night, so that an elm tree might suddenly appear in the path; a wood duck might unexpectedly arise from the lawn. Although Carlin's shoes sank into the mud, she was careful to stay in the shadows to ensure that no one would catch her out after curfew.

The air was surprisingly chilly, at least to someone with thin Florida blood, and although Carlin was wearing a fleecy jacket, on permanent loan from her roommate Pie, she still shivered. In the dark, she couldn't tell east from west, and once she reached the edge of campus, she thought it best to follow the river. The evening had been leaden, with gray skies and the threat of rain, but now, as Carlin crossed a playing field and found her way into a meadow, the clouds began to clear, allowing a few pale stars to shine in the sky. She passed beneath an old orchard, where deer often congregated at this time of year. Burrs hidden in the tall grass clung to her clothes; field mice, always so bold in the hallways of St. Anne's after midnight, scurried away at her approach. For more than a hundred years, Haddan students had been following this same route, venturing beyond the riverbanks and the meadows in search of a place where rules could be broken. A passageway leading to the old cemetery had been cut through the brambles and witch hazel. Rabbits had often used this trail as well, and the impression of their tracks—two small paw prints close together, then the larger back feet swung out to land in front—had beaten down a clear path in the grass.

The first citizens to be buried in the Haddan School cemetery were four boys who gave their lives in the Civil War, and every war since has added to their number. Faculty members who preferred this spot to the churchyard in town could also be interred within these gates, although no one had asked for this privilege for more than twenty years, not since Dr. Howe had passed on at the age of ninety-seven, too stubborn to give in to death until he'd neared the century mark. This cloistered location offered the sort of privacy Carlin had been searching for; if given a choice, she preferred keeping company with the dead rather than having to put up with the girls of St. Anne's. At least those who'd passed on did not gossip and judge, nor did they wish to exclude anyone from their ranks.

Carlin unhooked the lock on the wrought-iron gate and slipped inside. She didn't realize she wasn't alone until the flare of a match illuminated not only the enormous elm in the center of the cemetery, but the figure beneath it as well. For a moment, Carlin felt her heart heave against her chest, then she saw it was only August Pierce, that silly boy from the train, sprawled out upon a flat, black slab of marble.

"Well, well. Look who's here." Gus was delighted to see her. Although he'd been coming to the cemetery since his first night at Haddan, he was nervous in the dark. There was some dreadful bird in the big elm tree that snickered and called and every time there was a rustling in the bushes Gus felt the urge to run. He had been ever alert, fearing he might have to defend himself against a rabid opossum or a starving raccoon willing to do battle for the Snickers candy bar Gus had stored in his inner coat pocket. With his luck, it was most likely a skunk lying in wait, ready to douse him in a vile cloud of scent. Expecting all of these dreadful things and finding Carlin Leander instead was more than a relief. It was bliss.

"Automatic suspension if we're caught smoking," he informed her as they inhaled on their cigarettes.

"I don't get caught." Carlin had come to perch on the marker of Hosteous Moore, the second headmaster of the Haddan School, who had insisted on swimming in the river every single morning, despite rain, sleet, or snow, only to die of pneumonia in his forty-fourth year. He had been a smoker, too, preferring a pipe, which he took daily, right before his swim.

Gus grinned, impressed by Carlin's bravado. He hadn't the least bit of courage, but it was a trait he greatly admired in others. He stubbed his cigarette out in the dirt beneath a hedge of Celestial roses. Immediately, he lit another. "Chain-smoker," he confessed. "Bad habit."

Carlin pulled her pale hair away from her face as she studied him. In the starlight, she looked silvery and so beautiful, Gus had to force himself to look away.

"I'll bet it's not the only bad habit you've got," Carlin guessed.

Gus laughed and stretched out on the black marble slab. *Eternus Lux* was engraved beneath Dr. Howe's name. Eternal light. "How right you are." He paused to blow a perfect smoke ring. "But unlike you, I always get caught."

Carlin would have suspected as much. He was so vulnerable, with his wide, foolish smile, the sort of boy who would chop off his foot in order to escape from a steel trap, too intent on his own agony to notice that the key had been there beside him all along. He was doing his best to appear casual about their chance meeting, but Carlin could practically see his heart beating beneath his heavy black coat. He was such a nervous wreck it was actually quite sweet. Dear Gus Pierce, ever cursed and denied, would make a true and faithful friend, that much was evident, and Carlin could use an ally. However strange, however unlikely, Gus was the first person she'd truly felt comfortable with since her arrival in Massachusetts. For his part, by the time they walked back along the river, August Pierce would have died for Carlin had he been asked to do so. Indeed, she had read him correctly: in return for a single act of kindness, he would remain forever loyal.

Carlin's roommates and the rest of the girls in St. Anne's

could not fathom the friendship, nor understand why Carlin soon spent so much time in Gus's room at Chalk House, where she lounged on his bed, head resting in the crook of his back, as she read from her Ancient Civilizations text for her class with Mr. Herman or made sketches for Beginning Drawing with Miss Vining. The other girls shook their heads and wondered if Carlin had any sense at all. The boys they wanted were the ones they couldn't have, the seniors at Chalk, for instance, such as Harry McKenna, who was so good-looking and smooth he could cause someone to grow weak in the knees by bestowing one of his famous smiles on a sweet, unsuspecting girl, or Robbie Shaw, who'd gone through so many coeds during his first year at Haddan he was nicknamed Robo-Robbie, for his inhuman stamina and lack of emotion.

That the girls at St. Anne's had no understanding of what should be valued and what was best cast away did not surprise Carlin in the least. She could well imagine what they might do if they ever got hold of the true details of her life before Haddan. Wouldn't they love to know that her supper often consisted of sandwiches made of white bread and butter? Wouldn't they be amused to discover she used liquid detergent to wash her hair because it was cheaper than shampoo, and that her lipsticks had all been swiped from the makeup counter at Kmart? The girls at St. Anne's would have gleefully gossiped for days had they known, so why should Carlin be influenced by their remarks? She chose to ignore Amy's nasty comments when Gus left notes in their shared locker or sent e-mails; she did not flinch when the house phone rang and Peggy Anthony or Chris Percy shouted up to tell her that her devoted slave was calling, yet again, and could she please tell him not to tie up the phone.

Carlin particularly looked forward to the messages Gus managed to sneak to her during swim practice. How he got past the matron was simply a mystery, but somehow he achieved what most boys at Haddan only dreamed about: total access to the girls' gym. He knew any number of worthwhile tricks and had inscribed a nasty message with rubbing alcohol on Amy's mirror that appeared one day when the air was especially damp. He could unlock the door to the cafeteria after midnight with a skeleton key and, once inside, manage to pry open the freezer and treat himself and Carlin to free Popsicles and ice cream bars. He could pay Teddy Humphrey at the mini-mart for a pack of cigarettes, yet walk out the door with the coins still in the palm of his hand. But the most amazing and astounding feat of all was that Gus Pierce could make Carlin laugh.

"I don't get it," Amy Elliot had said when Gus's rude remarks surfaced on her mirror. "Does he think this is the way to get people to like him?"

"My roommates don't get you," Carlin told Gus as they walked along the river on their way to the cemetery, wondering if he'd have a reaction and not surprised to find he didn't care.

"Few do," Gus admitted.

This was especially true in regard to the residents of Chalk House. Chalk was said to be a brotherhood, but as is the case in some blood families, Gus's brothers did not appreciate him. After a week they were eager to be rid of him. Ten days more and they downright despised him. As often happens in such close quarters, Gus's peers did not hold back their distaste; before long, the attic began to stink with their sentiments as they left gifts that announced their disdain: old egg salad sandwiches, decaying fruit, piles of unwashed socks.

This year there were three freshmen in the attic: David Linden, whose great-grandfather had been governor of the Commonwealth, Nathaniel Gibb from Ohio, the winner of a tristate science fair, and Gus, mistake of mistakes, whose presence testified to the fact that although an individual's statistics might look fine on paper, in the flesh they could spell disaster. As for Gus, he had come to Haddan with no appreciation for the human race and no expectations of his fellow man. He was fully ready to confront contempt; he'd been beleaguered and insulted often enough to have learned to ignore anything with a heartbeat.

Still, every once in a while he made an exception, as he did with Carlin Leander. He appreciated everything about Carlin and lived for the hour when they left their books and sneaked off to the graveyard. Not even the crow nesting in the elm tree could dissuade him from his mission, for when he was beside Carlin, Gus acquired a strange optimism; in the light of her radiance the rest of the world began to shine. For a brief time, bad faith and human weakness could be forgotten or, at the very least, temporarily ignored. When it came time to go back to their rooms, Gus followed on the path, holding on to each moment, trying his best to stretch out time. Standing in the shadows of the rose arbor in order to watch Carlin climb back up the fire escape at St. Anne's, his heart ached. He could tell he was going to be devastated, and yet he was already powerless. Carlin always turned and waved before she stepped through her window and Gus Pierce always waved back, like a common fool, an idiot of a boy who would have done anything to please her.

From the day he'd arrived in the attic, unpacking at breakneck speed, if that's what anyone could call tossing belongings haphazardly into a pile in the closet, Gus had known his arrival at Haddan was a mistake. One afternoon, Harry McKenna had knocked on his door to announce there was to be a house meeting that evening, coolly suggesting that Gus had better be there on time. Gus, who didn't appreciate the superior tone of the older boy any more than he was inspired to take orders, instantly resolved to dodge what was bound to be a boring evening, one he'd just as soon avoid.

Instead, he had met Carlin in the cemetery and together they watched Orion rise into the eastern sky, high above a line of poplars and maples. It was a beautiful night, and poor Gus sensed something that felt like hope rise within him, not that the euphoria had lasted long. Gus hadn't understood that what he'd been offered by Harry McKenna was not an invitation, but a mandate. This he realized only upon his return to his room. He'd gotten through the front door of Chalk House unnoticed, nearly two hours past curfew, and had safely made his way up the stairs, but as soon as he reached the attic he knew something was amiss. The door to his room was ajar, and even if he hadn't remembered closing it when he left, the house was much too quiet, even for such a late hour. Someone wanted to ensure that he learn his lesson and the lesson was extremely simple: Certain invitations best not be ignored.

In his room, bedding and clothes had been heaped together, then urinated upon. Lightbulbs had been removed from his lamp to be broken and sprinkled on his window ledge, where the glass glittered prettily, like a handful of diamonds displayed on the peeling wood sash. Gus stretched himself out on his mattress with a bitter taste rising in his throat and lit a cigarette in spite of the no-smoking ordinance, and watched the smoke spiral upward, toward the cracks in the ceiling. In his experience, this was what happened; an individual paid dearly for all that was sweet. Spend the evening with a beautiful girl, walk through the woods on a cool, pleasant night, lie peacefully on another man's grave to watch the three brilliant stars of Orion, and soon enough a message would arrive to remind you of what you were up against.

Gus rolled onto his stomach and stubbed his cigarette out on the floor beneath his bed. Red sparks rose up in a stream that made his eyes tear, but he didn't care; fire was the least of his problems. He was so thin that his bones pressed into the springs of his mattress. Although he was tired, he knew he wouldn't be able to sleep, not tonight and probably not on any other night. If someone were to weigh the beauty of moonlight against the depth of human cruelty, which would win? Moonlight could not be held in the palm of one's hand, but cruelty could cut deep. Who could begin to describe the color of moonlight once it had been replaced by the clear light of day? Who could say it had even existed, if it had ever been anything more than a dream?

After Gus had swept up the broken glass and washed his laundry in the bathtub, he went to check himself into the infirmary. His headache and nausea were real, as was his elevated temperature. Frankly, there weren't many at Haddan who missed him. His teachers were relieved by his absence; he was a difficult student, disruptive and challenging one moment, bored and withdrawn the next. Carlin was the only one who worried about him, and she looked for him in vain, searching the cemetery and the dining hall. When she finally tracked him down, the school nurse, Dorothy Jackson, informed her there were no visiting hours at the infirmary. And so, Carlin did not see Gus for eight days, not until he was up in his own bed, his coat wrapped around him like a blanket. In the dim light he stared at the ceiling. He had just punched a hole through the old horsehair plaster, the act of someone with no recourse other than shortsighted destruction. There were bits of plaster dusting the floor and the mattress. When she found him, Carlin threw herself down beside him on the bed to examine the results of his anger. It was possible to view the clouds through the hole in the eaves; a square of blue sky peeked at them from between the rotted shingles.

"You're insane," Carlin told Gus.

But in fact, his actions had just cause. Upon his return, he'd stumbled over the gift his brothers had left for him while he'd been in the infirmary. A bloody rabbit's foot, so fresh it was warm to the touch, had been deposited on his desk. Gus had picked it up gingerly, wrapped it in tissue, and placed this dreadful talisman into the garbage. And that was how he'd become a desperate individual, a boy who punched holes through plaster, brought low by injustice and shame.

"Did you think I was normal?" he asked Carlin. During his stay at the infirmary, he hadn't once changed his clothes. His T-shirt was filthy and his hair was uncombed. He'd often locked himself in the infirmary bathroom, where he smoked so many cigarettes there was still a film of nicotine on his skin and the whites of his eyes had a yellow cast.

"I didn't mean insane in a negative way," Carlin recanted.

"I see." Gus's mouth curled into a smile despite his despair. Carlin could do that to him, cheer him even in the depths of his misery. "You meant insane in a positive way."

Carlin propped her feet up against the wall, her long body stretched out against Gus's even longer one. She held her hand up to the sunshine streaming in through the ceiling, completely unaware that her complexion had turned golden in the light.

"What will you do when it snows?" she asked.

Gus turned his head to the wall Impossible, impossible; he was about to cry.

Carlin leaned up on one elbow to study him. She gave off the scent of chlorine and jasmine soap. "Did I say something wrong?"

Gus shook his head; there was a catch in his throat and the sound he emitted resembled the call of that dreadful crow in the cemetery; a wail so dispirited and broken it could barely begin to rise. Carlin lay flat on the bed, the beat of her heart quickening as she waited for him to stop crying.

"I'll be gone by the time it snows," Gus said.

"No you won't be. Don't be ridiculous, you big baby." Carlin wrapped her arms around him and rocked him back and forth, then tickled him, knowing it would make him laugh. "What would I do without you?"

This was exactly why Carlin had never wanted to be close to anyone. When she was younger, she'd never even asked for a dog, and was temperamentally unfit to own a pet. It was so easy to be drawn in, to care and to comfort; before you knew it, you'd find yourself responsible for some defenseless creature.

"Was somebody mean to you ?" Carlin threw herself on top of Gus. "Tell me everything and I'll make them pay. I'll defend you."

Gus rolled over to hide his face. There was a limit to how much humiliation even he could take.

Carlin sat up, her back shoved against the wall, her shoulder blades in the shape of an angel's wings. "I'm right. Somebody is being mean to you."

Down in the cellar, where tadpoles hatched in the trickle of groundwater that always seeped through the concrete no matter how often repairs were made, Harry McKenna and Robbie Shaw had drawn two orange crates close to the air vent. Both boys were good-looking, fair and rawboned, but Harry McKenna possessed a truly extraordinary face. His straw-colored hair had been clipped close to his skull, a style that showed off his outstanding features. Girls swooned when they saw him, and it was said that no one could deny him once he turned on the charm. Sitting in the basement of Chalk House, however, he was not at all pleased, and his irritation showed. His beautiful mouth was twisted into a scowl and he snapped his fingers repeatedly, as if that simple action could erase what he heard through the vent, a flattened piece of metal that ran from the rear of the closets in the attic rooms down to this cellar. Through the vent it was possible to hear nearly every word that was said up above. Even whispers resonated through the tube; a cough or a kiss could be caught and sliced apart for purposes of examination or entertainment. The older Chalk boys always listened in on the new residents, and for this practice they made no apologies. How better to know exactly who was to be relied upon and who needed to be taught a lesson still?

Pierce was proving himself to be a washout at this very moment, pouring out his heart to some girl, bellyaching like a loser. Harry and Robbie had been eavesdropping for quite some time, hunched over until Harry's long legs were riddled with cramps. Now he stood to stretch his back. Usually, he liked the benefits of his height, both with girls and on the playing field. He liked any advantage he could get and this was to be the year of his advantage. He was the senior in charge of Chalk House, and as such retained the honor of residing in what was once Dr. Howe's office, before the new administration building was built. The room's focal point was its handsome oak fireplace; tiny serrations had been carved into the side of the mantel, marks that were said to represent every woman Dr. Howe had slept with, and if the fireplace notches were to be believed, there had been quite a crowd.

Harry appreciated Dr. Howe's room, just as he valued all his many privileges. He was a boy who was grateful and greedy in equal measure. Certainly, he wasn't about to have some nitwit like August Pierce come in and ruin things. It was a cruel, cold world, wasn't it? A universe spinning through the dark, without any pledges or guarantees. A person had to take what he wanted or be left behind, flattened by circumstance. Nowhere was this more true than in the gentle Massachusetts countryside, where the weather continually proved that most circumstances couldn't be controlled. Chalk boys were certainly well aware of the wreckage that could be made of a life, an unfortunate observation made in the very first year, for these were the boys who had suffered the worst loss in the flood so many years ago. In the mayhem of the rising waters, the grades of every boy from Chalk House had evaporated from the dean's marking book. It was a thoughtful fellow from Cambridge who discovered this calamity while mopping up the dean's waterlogged office, and he ran back to tell the others what he had learned before any teachers found out.

All of their hard-earned A's in biology, their B's in Latin and Greek were gone, the letters washed away in blue pools of ink that had stained the floorboards a terrible cobalt that refused to come clean no matter how often the mop was applied. The Chalk boys wondered if the river had singled them out for torment. Why had this happened to them rather than the others? Why should their lives and careers be sacrificed? In the face of this disaster, a suggestion was proposed, a possibility voiced so humbly no one was ever quite sure whose idea it had been. *Twist fate*, that was the notion, one that was taken up immediately, by each and every boy. *Turn calamity into compensation. Take what has been denied you.*

It was a spring night, the thirteenth of May, when the boys at Chalk House changed their grades. The peepers were calling in a rush of damp music from every flooded corner of the campus; the moon floated above the library in a soot-black sky. The boys let themselves into the dean's office, where they substituted their names for those of the students from Otto House and Sharpe Hall, claiming grades they hadn't earned. The task was easily done, an elementary act of delinquency handily accomplished with a pick from the locksmith and some India ink, a simple bit of conjuring, but one so effective they decided to call themselves magicians, even though they had no true skills but one.

At the close of the term, the boys from the other houses who had once been assured an acceptance to Harvard or Yale roamed the campus, as despondent as they were confused. These students wondered what had happened to all their hours of study, for their grades had disappeared entirely, and from that day forward the term fair play was erased from their vocabularies. For those boys at Chalk who had thrown their lot in with the Magicians' Club, all that was demanded was full loyalty. If any among them did not have the temperament for cheating, no time was wasted. The others dragged boys who might be the least bit unreliable out to the meadow where the rabbits made their homes and they beat such individuals senseless. In protecting themselves and their brothers, the boys learned an important lesson about unity. Rules bound people close, true enough, but breaking rules bound them closer still.

This philosophy had been explained to Dave Linden and Nathaniel Gibb, and then to Gus when he grudgingly attended the first official meeting of the term. A circle was formed in a clearing beyond the river, although it was true that the weather had always been more foe than friend to the members of the Magicians' Club. The thirteenth of any month could be depended upon to be foul, with high snows or thunder or drenching rains. On this September meeting date, the fields were damp and the sky had turned the shade of gunmetal, with fog blanketing the fields. There were only bits of color: some green holly in the woods, a few strands of mulberry on the vine, a startled wild turkey that raced out from the underbrush in a flash of gold and red when disturbed by the intrusion. There was a chill in the air and the purple blooms of the flowering joe-pye weed had begun to turn indigo, always a sign of a cold and miserable winter to come. The boys sat around in a jumble of a ring, some lounging on the grass, others sitting on an old log that was often used to conceal contraband whiskey and beer. Those who knew what was to come and had been through it themselves were good-humored, even boisterous. But of course they'd already completed their hazing; they'd experienced the anxiety that Dave Linden and Nathaniel Gibb and even that idiot Gus Pierce, who was lying prone on his back, surely must be feeling as their induction approached.

To join, the rule was simple. An act of mayhem must be committed. Be it lawless or illicit, immoral or illegal, there was to be one hateful exploit: the single red thread that cross-stitched an individual's fate, binding him to his brothers. When told what they must now accomplish, Nathaniel Gibb and Dave Linden averted their faces and stared at the ground. Everyone knew they were hiding their tears, not that this show of emotion would be held against them. If anything, this meant they took the initiation seriously. What was far more disturbing was the lazy manner in which Gus Pierce blew smoke rings and gazed through the dark, leafy branches overhead.

There was only one way to avoid initiation and still retain membership with full privileges, and that was to perfect the trick Dr. Howe insisted his wife execute in exchange for her freedom. Who could blame Annie Howe for wanting to dissolve their union, considering those notches on the fireplace and the cruel way she'd been cut off from family and friends? But Dr. Howe was no fool; the only way he would agree to her demands was to set forth a single impossible task. She could leave anytime she wished to, all she need do was take one of her favorite flowers, those icy white roses that grew beside the girls' dormitory, and there before her husband's eyes, she must turn the bloom red.

"She killed herself instead," the older boys told whoever was not already informed of Annie's fate. "So we don't advise you to try it."

Instead, it was suggested to the new boys that they look for one of the rabbits found in the meadows and the woods. These small, shy creatures were easily caught with some patience and fishing net. All that was needed was a strong piece of wire to wrap around the front foot, and a bloody little souvenir would allow admittance to the club. The best inductees, however, were considerably more creative than this, forsaking rabbit hunts and playing a game of one-upmanship of who could execute the most original or most illegal act. Who would go down in Chalk history as the most daring was still a title ready to be claimed. One year a joker from Baltimore had used a handsaw on the dean's chair in the dining room, so that when Bob Thomas sat down to his dinner, he collapsed in a heap of splinters and beef. The previous autumn, Jonathan Walters, a quiet boy from Buffalo, had dipped into the school's computer files, searching out any college recommendations that weren't positive and altering critical passages to ensure that each letter afforded a wholehearted endorsement. There had been a wide range of induction activities, from thievery to high jinks; all that was necessary was that the deed performed would get a fellow in serious hot water if it was ever found out. That was the thread that bound them together: they were all guilty of something.

Some boys, it was true, used the initiation to serve their own twisted purposes. Three years ago Robbie Shaw climbed up the fire escape that led to the room where Carlin now slept; it was a holiday weekend and many of the students were gone, a situation Robbie was well aware of, since he'd planned his mission carefully. He told the fourteen-year-old girl he had targeted if she ever said a word about what he'd done, he'd come back and slit her throat. But as it turned out, there was no need for further coercion; the girl in question transferred to a school in Rhode Island the very next week. Robbie was criticized for going too far with his initiation, but privately his daring and his ability to choose his victim so well were applauded, for although the girl in question knew who her attacker was, she never did tell a soul.

Unfortunately, the decision to select August Pierce had not been as wise. Throughout the meeting, Gus kept quiet; it was impossible to gauge what he was feeling as he lay sprawled upon the damp grass. Afterward, he walked away without a word, and the other boys watched him carefully. There were those who would not have been surprised had Gus Pierce gone directly to the dean to report them, and still others who would have predicted that he'd hightail it to the police station in town, or maybe he'd simply phone home and beg his daddy to come and retrieve him. But in fact, Gus did none of these things. Perhaps another person with his convictions would have left that very night, simply packed his bags and hitchhiked down Route 17, but Gus was obstinate and he always had been. And perhaps he was prideful, too, because he thought he might just win at this game.

Gus had lied to Carlin about his father; the elder Pierce was not a professor, but rather a high school teacher, who on weekends performed at children's birthday parties. In spite of himself, Gus had learned quite a lot on those Sunday afternoons when he sullenly ate cake in honor of some stranger's birthday. He knew that a coin digested one moment cannot reappear in the palm of your hand seconds later. A bird pierced with an arrow cannot shake itself and then fly away. And yet, he was well aware that certain knots could be slipped open with a single touch and that doves fit quite nicely into jars with false bottoms. He had sat at the kitchen table with his father for hours, watching the same trick repeated, time and again, until what had once been a clumsy attempt was transmuted into seamless ability. Throughout his life, Gus had been taught that for every illusion there was a practical explanation, and such an education can prove worthwhile. After an upbringing such as this, Gus was aware of possibilities someone else might have overlooked, or taken for granted, or simply ignored. This much he knew for certain: for every locked trunk, there was sure to be a key.

NEEDLES AND THREAD

IN THE MONTH OF OCTOBER, when the elms lost their leaves and the oaks became yellow all at once, the mice in the tall grass beyond the river came searching for shelter. Girls at St. Anne's would often find them curled up in dresser drawers, or nesting in shoes left beneath the bed. Wasps, too, went looking for warmth, and passersby would hear them buzzing in tree stumps and fence posts. The woods were laced with an undergrowth of brambles that had previously been hidden by green leaves; rain, when it came, fell in buckets. It was the time of year when people found themselves in foul moods, plagued by headaches and bad fortune. On damp mornings, electrical appliances tended to mutiny. Cars wouldn't start, vacuum cleaners spit up dirt, coffeepots sputtered and then shut down. In the very first week of the month, there were so many people lined up at Selena's for coffees-to-go in the early, chilly A.M., and nerves were so frayed, it wasn't unusual for a fight to break out between some ordinary resident waiting on line and some obnoxious hothead, like Teddy Humphrey, whose own wife, Nikki, had been smart enough never to talk to him before he'd had his morning coffee back when they were still married, especially in the dark days of October.

One cold evening, when the swans on the river were paddling quickly to prevent ice from forming beneath them, Betsy went to dinner with Eric at the Haddan Inn. The evening was meant to be a special occasion; at last, some time alone. They'd ordered lamb and mashed potatoes, but halfway through the meal Betsy found she simply couldn't eat; she excused herself and stepped outside for a bit of fresh air. Alone on the porch of the inn, she gazed at Main Street, the white houses turning lavender in the fading light. The evening was perfect; a mockingbird perched on a fence post and sang the most beautiful song, invented or stolen, it really didn't matter, the melody was exquisite. Standing there, Betsy couldn't help but wonder if that long-ago lightning storm that had chased people over meadows and field had managed to strike her even though she'd been safe at home. Certain emotions had been burned right out of her and she'd never even missed them. Surely she had all the ingredients for happiness. What more could she want than a man she could depend on, a steady job, a future that was assured? Why was it she felt so reluctant, as though she'd been backed into this life she'd begun to lead by fear, not desire?

Thankfully, by the time Betsy returned to the table to order a raspberry trifle and cappuccino, her head had cleared. This inn was the place where she would marry next June; these were the dishes on which her wedding dinner would be served, the glasses with which they would toast their happiness.

"I'm glad we're having the reception here," she told Eric as they were leaving, but she didn't sound as convinced as she might have.

"Not too stuffy?"

"It's very Haddan," Betsy had said, and they'd both had a laugh over that, for the very word exuded a sense of order and predictability. Despite its traditional style, the inn was the nicest place in town. Rooms had already been booked for out-of-town guests, and Eric's mother, a finicky woman prey to a bad back, had asked for an extremely firm mattress. Betsy had visited the inn only days earlier to test the beds, finding the perfect model in a second-floor room, a mattress so hard that an egg dropped upon it would surely break in two.

"I wish we could stay here tonight," Eric told Betsy as they began the walk back to the school.

"Then let's. We can sneak out at midnight and check in. No one will know." Betsy ran a stick along the metal railings of Mrs. Jeremy's fence until the porch light suddenly switched on. She threw the stick away when Mrs. Jeremy peeked out her bay window, an annoyed expression on her thin face. "The kids sneak out all the time. Why shouldn't we?" By now, Betsy had come to understand why rooms at St. Anne's with fire escapes were so coveted; that pale girl, Carlin, was particularly adept at navigating the metal rungs after curfew without the slightest bit of noise.

"We're supposed to set an example," Eric reminded Betsy.

Betsy looked closely to see if he was mocking her, but no, his handsome, serious face showed only concern. He was not a man who took his responsibilities lightly, and in fact it was a good thing that Betsy returned that night. She came in from dinner to find twenty girls huddled in the dark parlor, uncertain what to do next. At St. Anne's, fuses continually blew, and no one, save for Maureen Brown with her supply of candles, had known what to do. Upon her arrival, Betsy marched over to Helen Davis's quarters, where she discovered that rather than coming to anyone's aid, the senior houseparent was sipping tea in a room illuminated by a heavy-duty flashlight, as if the well-being of their girls was the farthest thing from her mind.

A few days later there was another incident Helen Davis chose to ignore. Carlin Leander's roommate Amy Elliot was bitten by a wren that had managed to get into the house, flying above the girls' beds, crashing into ceilings and walls. Terrible luck was said to afflict anyone who suffered such a bite, with worse luck to come if the stricken party should kill the offending bird, which was exactly what Amy did. She smashed her Ancient History text atop the wren, instantly crushing its skull and spine. Within minutes, Amy's leg swelled up and turned black. Her parents in New Jersey had to be phoned, painkillers were dispensed, ice packs procured. And where had Helen Davis been while Betsy ran around like a lunatic, chauffeuring Amy over to the emergency room in Hamilton and ferrying her back ever so carefully over the rutted Haddan roads? Helen had gone back to her reading, and if she heard the wren's mate tapping against her window, she ignored it, and the sound disappeared completely as soon as she let her cat out for the night.

"Aren't we supposed to be in charge? Aren't we supposed to help them?" Betsy complained to Helen that very night. "Isn't that our job?"

It had been a trial to care for Amy, who had howled all the way to the hospital, terrified that the bird bite might cause her to lose her leg, although in the end all that was needed was antibiotics and bed rest. The evening had taken the worst toll on Betsy, for upon her return to St. Anne's she'd had to dig a grave for the battered little wren, now buried beneath some junipers. When she came to knock on Helen's door, her hands were muddy and her complexion had turned blue with the cold. Perhaps Helen Davis took pity on the younger woman because of her wretched appearance.

"They're big girls, dear. Time for them to learn a thing or two, wouldn't you say? Our job is to help them grow up, not baby them. You've been subjected to teenagers for too long." In spite of Helen's determination never to be agreeable, she found she had taken a liking to Betsy. "Schools like Haddan will drain you dry if you let them, and teenagers will do the very same thing."

There did appear to be something in the air at Haddan that caused good judgment to dissolve. Betsy had noticed that several of the girls in her care had been growing progressively wilder. More girls climbed out their windows at night than stayed in their beds, and some were so blatant in their disregard for rules that Betsy had insisted they clean the common rooms as a punishment for their late hours and careless ways. In fact, there was a reason for such bad behavior: girls at St. Anne's most often fell in love in October. Every year there was a rush of romance from the first day of the month to the last, a tumbling falling in love at first sight that occurred with such intensity anyone would have guessed no one on earth had ever fallen in love before. Love like this was contagious; it spread in the manner of measles or flu. Couples stayed out until morning, only to be discovered at the canoe shed, wound in each other's arms, Girls stopped eating and sleeping; they kissed their boyfriends until their lips were bruised, then dozed through their classes, daydreaming as they failed quizzes and exams.

Girls in love often had odd appetites, for cucumber pickles or pumpkin pie, and some of these girls were convinced that any rash acts were acceptable, if done in the name of love. Maureen Brown, for instance, did not seem embarrassed in the least when Betsy found a boy from Chalk House hiding beneath her un-made bed. There would always be girls with such unstoppable cravings they turned their backs on all reason and good inten-tions, forsaking everything but romance. Why, even Helen Davis herself had once been easy prey for love. Nowadays, people at school insisted that Miss Davis was so cold a single touch from her hand could freeze water in a glass, but this wasn't always the case. During her first year at Haddan, when she was twenty-four and the month of October was especially fine, Helen paced the hallways every night, until a path in the carpet had been worn from her tread. She fell in love with Dr. Howe in a single after-noon, long before he'd ever called her by name. That October the moon was orange, it shimmered with light, and perhaps its shine was blinding, for Helen chose to ignore the fact that Dr. Howe was already married. She should have known better, she should have held back, but before the month was done, she had agreed to meet him in his office late at night, without the wisdom to guess she was neither the first nor the last woman to do so.

Shy Helen, who had always been so serious and reserved, was now consumed by her own longings. Within this grid of passion, Dr. Howe's wife was nothing more than a woman with red hair who worked in the gardens, only a stumbling block in the path of

Helen's own resolve to win the man she loved. All through the winter, Helen ignored Annie Howe; she did not raise her eyes when they passed each other on the paths, and this was the reason Helen was among the last to know Annie was expecting a child in the spring, not that such a situation could stop Dr. Howe from straying.

Helen paid Annie no mind at all until the day in March when the roses were all cut down. She happened to be coming from the library that afternoon, carrying half a dozen books, when she noticed Mrs. Howe crouched on the ground, a pair of shears from the groundskeeper's shed in her hands. Annie had already been through most of the campus; vines and branches were everywhere, as though a storm had passed through, leaving only thorns and twisted black bark. Annie was a tall woman and in pregnancy she was even more beautiful. Her hair was the color of fire, her skin like satin, luminous and pale. But with the shears in hand, she appeared dangerous; Helen stopped, frozen in place, as Annie tore through the bare canes of the cinnamon ramblers that grew alongside the library. Helen was only a young and foolish girl, witnessing something she had neither the capability nor the experience to understand, but even she could tell that she had come face-to-face with real sorrow. Standing beside the weeping beeches, frightened for her life, Helen gleaned, for the very first time, that she might actually be the guilty party.

But for her part, Annie had no interest in Helen. Far too intent on her mission, she saw no one at all. There was no wind that day, and the aroma of cloves was powerful when Annie moved on to the scented snowbird roses that grew beside the dining hall, destroying each vine so thoroughly it would never flower again. She didn't seem to notice that her hands were lacerated and torn as she moved across the quad, in the direction of the girls' dormitory. There was the arbor Annie had commissioned the grounds crew to build, and the Polar roses she had nurtured for ten years, with no success until now. For on this raw March day a dozen white roses had bloomed months ahead of schedule, each one shivering with cool silver light. Annie began to chop at the vines, but she was careless, and before she realized what she'd done, she had clipped off the top of her ring finger. Immediately, blood began to flow. Although Helen startled, Annie herself did not even cry out; instead, she reached for one of the cut roses. Despite the thorns she held it close, letting her blood fall onto the petals. If Helen wasn't mistaken, Annie smiled as she held the one bloom that had begun to turn red.

When the swans spied their mistress there on the lawn, they came rushing to her, clucking with distress, pulling out their feathers. Their racket seemed to wake Annie from her reverie, and she gazed at the damage she'd done as though she were a sleepwalker with no idea of how she'd managed to wander so far. Her finger still bled, the blood coursing more and more thickly. Already the rose was so saturated it had begun to dissolve in her hands and she carefully put it back together again, petal by crimson petal. By then, Annie's rampage was common knowledge in Haddan. The authorities were called in by one of the faculty wives, who had run all the way to the police station, in fear for her life. Two of the three men on the Haddan force were nearing retirement, and so it fell to Wright Grey, the young lieutenant, to hurry on down to the school.

Annie had known Wright all her life. As children they'd been to school together, walking the distance to Hamilton; they'd gone swimming at Sixth Commandment Pond on hot, hazy days. Now when Wright politely asked her to accompany him to the hospital in Hamilton, Annie did as he asked. All these years later, Helen Davis can still remember how carefully Wright helped Annie from the grass; she noticed his blue eyes and his look of concern as Annie insisted he wrap his handkerchief not around her wounded hand, as he clearly would have liked to, but around the stained white rose.

In less than a week's time, Annie returned from the hospital, but she didn't look the same. Now she wore her hair in a single braid, the way women in mourning often do. She was heavier and she moved more slowly; if spoken to, she appeared puzzled, as if she had lost the ability to understand even the simplest command. Perhaps this was because she had truly believed her husband would let her go if she turned a single rose red, but he'd laughed when she unwrapped the linen handkerchief she'd borrowed from her old school friend. In time what was crimson turns black, and the petals of dried roses fade to ashes. Annie Howe might as well have given her husband a handful of soot as deliver the rose she had stained with her blood.

As for Helen, she could no longer pretend that Dr. Howe was hers, nor ignore the fact that he was a father-to-be. Now when he kissed her, it was Annie's red hair Helen thought of. When he unbuttoned her dress, she heard the swans' cry. She went out of her way to avoid him until one morning, when the sky was still dark and the girls in the dormitory were safely asleep in their beds. It was then Helen heard a tread upon the stairs. She pulled on her robe and went to the door, guessing that one of her charges needed help, but instead, she found Dr. Howe in the hall.

"Go back to sleep," he told Helen.

Helen blinked as she stood on the threshold. Was it possible for him to be standing there? Perhaps she had conjured him out of thin air and might just as easily conjure him away. But no, Dr. Howe was flesh and blood; Helen knew this because of the weight of his hand on her arm.

"Close your door," Dr. Howe said, and because of the seriousness of his tone and the lateness of the hour, Helen did exactly that, leaving herself to wonder, forever after, what would have happened if she'd disobeyed him. At the very least, she might have learned the truth.

Several hours later, two fourteen-year-old girls found Annie Howe in the attic. Their screams woke everyone in the house and so frightened the rabbits in the thickets that they were overtaken by an instinct to flee, dashing madly across the green in broad daylight, only to be scooped up by the red-tailed hawks that perched in the beech trees in anticipation of exactly such moments of panic. Annie had hanged herself with the sash from Helen's coat, left on a hook in the corridor near her back door. The coat, recently bought at Lord & Taylor, had been considerably more expensive than Helen could afford, but that didn't dissuade her from depositing it in a trash barrel behind the library that very afternoon.

Because Annie Howe had taken her own life, there was no service and no burial in either the Haddan School cemetery or the churchyard behind town hall. For weeks afterward, the house where she'd died smelled of roses, even though the weather was dismal and no flowers bloomed. The scent was in the stairwells and in the cellar and in the corners of every room. Some girls began to have migraines brought on by this odor, some became sick to their stomachs, still others burst into tears at the slightest provocation, whether it be an insult or a dashed hope. Even when the windows were closed and the doors were shut, the scent remained, as if roses had grown through the floorboards of the overheated hallways. Up in the attic, the fragrance was especially overpowering, and when several girls crept up to see the scene of the crime, they fainted dead away, then had to be carried downstairs and put to bed for a week before they regained their senses.

Only Helen Davis was resistant to the scent. When she walked through the dorm, there was only the tang of soap, the sharpness of shoe polish, the cloying fragrance of violet cologne. Helen buried her face in curtains and carpets; she went to the attic and breathed in deeply, desperate for the scent of roses, but she never did find it, not in that house and not anywhere else. Even now, when Helen approached an ordinary rosebush in the village, say a Velvet Fragrance, whose dark crimson buds emitted such a powerful perfume every bee in the county had been called forth, Helen couldn't smell a thing. She could stroll past Lois Jeremy's famed damasks, known for their lemony fragrance, and breathe in nothing but cut grass and clean country air.

In memory of the Howes' unborn child, a little stone lamb was erected in the Haddan School cemetery, and there were some women in town who still draped garlands around the statue's neck, hoping to ward off illnesses and protect their own daughters and sons. And why shouldn't such charms be possible? To this day, the scent of roses in seasons when no flowers grew continued to occur at St. Anne's, affecting only the girls who were the most sensitive and high-strung. Amy Elliot, for one, who was allergic to roses, had to be sent to a specialist in Hamilton after moving into St. Anne's and was prescribed an inhaler along with shots of cortisone. Several girls in the attic, including Maureen Brown and Peggy Anthony, went searching for the cause of the red rose-hive bumps that marked their arms. They cleaned out bureaus and rooted through closets, but in the end they found nothing but stray bits of twine and crumbs of toast left behind by the mice.

Old houses always have their flaws—radiators that bang, unexplainable odors—but they have their pluses as well. St. Anne's, for instance, was surprisingly private, the thick horsehair plaster walls serving to keep sound to a minimum. Students could throw a party on the first floor and the girls in the attic wouldn't hear a thing, thanks to the insulation and the heavy oak doors. Only a few people knew that Carlin Leander often sneaked out at night, with fewer still having any idea that Peggy Anthony rooted around in her suitcase for chocolate bars to gorge upon, and even fewer aware that Maureen Brown had a series of boyfriends who secretly spent the night. It was this level of privacy that had enabled Helen Davis to keep her illness to herself for the past two years. She suffered from congestive heart failure, and although her doctors in Boston had done their best with surgery scheduled over summer vacation and then with the prescribed course of medication, Helen's condition had grown progressively worse. Her heart, weakened by a bout of rheumatic fever in childhood, was not pumping enough blood; already, her lungs were overworked, and she coughed through the night.

At last, Helen's doctors had admitted there was nothing more to be done. In light of the finality of this diagnosis, her life had unwound, as if she herself were nothing more than a spool of thread, body and spirit combined. In all of Haddan, the only one who knew of her situation was Pete Byers, the pharmacist, and they had never once discussed the status of her health. Pete simply filled Helen's prescriptions and talked about the weather, all the time wearing the thoughtful expression he always had, no matter if a customer's ailment was cancer or a simple sunburn. Although he never said a word, Pete had taken notice of how frail Helen had become. The last time she'd come to pick up her medication, she'd been so exhausted Pete had closed up shop and driven her back to school.

Lately it had become an effort for Helen to slip on shoes or button a blouse; it was too much work to fill the bird feeder or set down a bowl of cream for the cat. Last week the most humiliating situation yet had occurred: Helen discovered she could not lift her book bag after class, she simply could not manage its weight. She'd remained at her desk, watching mournfully as the room began to clear, cursing the wreckage of her weak heart. She watched with envy as boys and girls hauled heavy backpacks over their shoulders, as though toting nothing more than feathers or straw. How could they ever imagine what it might be like to have every object suddenly turn to stone? Put a stone in the palm of a boy's hand and he'd merely toss it across the river. Give a girl a stone and she'd crush it beneath the heel of her shoe, then string the shards to wear around her neck, as though she possessed diamonds or pearls. But to Helen stone was that and nothing more; every book on her desk, every pencil and pen, the clouds, the sky, her very own bones, all of it turned to stone.

Betsy Chase might have been among those who had never guessed anything was wrong if Helen hadn't invited her in for a cup of tea. It was an invitation offered on impulse, a misguided attempt at civility that was bound to backfire, as it soon was to do. Waiting in the living room, Betsy heard the kettle whistling unattended and, when Miss Davis failed to respond, she grew concerned. She went to the kitchen, where she discovered Helen at the table, unable to rise from her chair. The room itself was a disaster, with stacks of newspapers on the floor and unwashed dishes in the sink. In spite of the daily presence of Miss Davis's cat, the mice had all but taken over; they ran through cupboards and pantries alike, as fearless as wolves. The refrigerator was all but empty; for quite some time Miss Davis had been eating nothing more than bread and butter. In point of fact, after she'd invited Betsy in and put up the water, she had realized she was out of tea as well. It served her right for being so foolish as to think she might have a guest; company, as anyone with sense could tell you, always caused trouble.

"There's nothing wrong," Helen said when she saw the worry on Betsy's face. It was pity that showed there, absolutely the last thing Helen needed.

Betsy went to turn off the kettle, and as she did she thought of Carlin Leander, the pretty scholarship girl who wore the same clothes nearly every day and never went out on weekends with the rest of the crowd. "I think you need some help around here and I know someone who'd be perfect. She needs the money, you need a strong pair of hands."

"There's nothing I want less than help." Helen felt dizzy, but with effort she managed to sound almost as ill-tempered as usual. This time around, however, she certainly wasn't scaring Betsy, who had begun to search the cupboards, at last finding something worthwhile, a jar of freeze-dried coffee.

Although the coffee Betsy fixed was awful, Helen did feel somewhat revitalized after a taste. If asked, she could probably walk to the history department and back right now. She could lift her damned book bag right over her head, couldn't she? In fact, she was feeling so much better she didn't notice Betsy sniffing around the pantry.

"Where are the roses?" Betsy asked. "They're definitely here somewhere."

"There are no roses." As usual, the scent had eluded her. Helen no longer imagined she would ever be able to experience that which had always passed her by, any more than she expected to be granted forgiveness for her youthful mistakes. "It's nothing. Some air freshener. An old sachet."

As she spoke, Helen remembered that Annie Howe had been known for a particular recipe, rose angel cake, baked only on special occasions, Easter, for instance, or to celebrate a student's birthday. Fresh vanilla beans and rose petals were added just before the tins went into the oven, and maybe that was why students all over campus were drawn to Annie's kitchen, with the more forward among them knocking at her back door to beg for a taste. These days, nobody baked anymore, let alone added roses and vanilla to the batter. People were perfectly satisfied with store-bought desserts and quick divorces and watery instant coffee. Perhaps Helen had lived too long; certainly there were days when it felt that way. So much had changed, she wasn't the same person anymore as the girl who'd come to Haddan, that foolish child who thought she knew so much. She used to work all night long; she used to wait up for the sunrise. Now she was lucky if she was able to walk from her kitchen to her bedroom without her legs giving out. She was too weak to go to the market, and could no longer carry her groceries home. Lately there had been nights when she found herself wishing for company or a hand to hold.

"Fine, if you insist," Helen Davis said. "Send the girl."

HARRY MCKENNA DECIDED HE WANTED CARLIN as soon as he spied her in the doorway to the library one rainy afternoon. In the low branches of a weeping beech, there sat a pair of phoebes, birds who mate for life and sing an uncommonly tender song. Most birds hide in the rain, but not these phoebes, and the girl with the green eyes was pointing them out to Gus Pierce, who had somehow managed to be lucky enough to be there beside her at the moment when Harry first saw her.

Carlin was laughing, unaware of the rain; her hair was damp and silvery. Harry knew right then that he had to have her, never doubting for a moment that like everything else he had ever wanted, she'd be his before long. He began to attend swim meets, watching from the bleachers, applauding her efforts with such vigor that before long everyone on the team was whispering about Carlin's not-so-secret admirer. In the dining hall, he watched from a nearby table, his interest so apparent and scorching that girls all around him wilted from the heat.

"You'd better watch out," Gus Pierce said to Carlin when he observed Harry McKenna. "He's a monster."

But of course, as soon as she heard that remark, Carlin did what any sensible girl might have done and looked for herself. She expected to find some leering creature, but instead she caught sight of the most beautiful boy she'd ever seen. Yes, she'd been aware that someone had been rooting for her at swim meets, and she'd known that someone had been following her, and she'd surely heard Amy and Pie gossiping about her Harry, how gorgeous he was, how unattainable. But Carlin had had her share of admirers and she hadn't paid the slightest bit of attention to this one, until now. She smiled at Harry McKenna for an instant, but that one look was enough to assure him that with the right amount of patience and fortitude he would get what he wanted.

Harry had always been well versed in seduction; he had a gift for such things, as though he'd been born with compliments tumbling from his mouth. Already, he'd been through the prettiest of the senior and junior girls. There were girls whose lives he had ruined, and those who persisted in calling him long after his disinterest was evident, and still others who waited steadfastly for him to return and be true. He was bored by such girls and primed for a challenge, and it amused him to wait for Carlin outside the gym. When she came out with her teammates, there he'd be, so obvious in his intentions that the other girls would elbow one another and trade jealous remarks. Before long, Carlin had begun to walk back to St. Anne's with him. They held hands before they looked into each other's eyes; they kissed before they spoke. It should not have brought Carlin pleasure to know how the other girls at St. Anne's envied her, and yet it did exactly that. Her skin flushed prettily whenever she felt their resentful eyes upon her. If anything, she had become even more beautiful. In the dark she was luminous, as though she'd been ignited by the other girls' spite and lust.

Of course, she told Harry nothing of her real background; he had no idea that she hadn't the money for a cup of coffee at Selena's, had barely enough for books, and that her wardrobe was sorely lacking. She had no decent socks, no winter clothes, no boots. She'd been forced to take Miss Chase's suggestion and had begun to work for Miss Helen Davis, twenty hours a week of shopping, cleaning, and running errands. As for Miss Davis, she found that having Carlin around was not as dreadful as she'd imagined it might be. This particular girl was quiet and quick. Unlike most of the spoiled students at Haddan, she knew how to use a mop and a broom. Carlin had begun to fix Miss Davis's supper, nothing fancy, a broiled chicken breast perhaps, prepared with lemon and parsley, served with a baked potato. There was a cache of old cookbooks in the cabinets, never used, and she began to experiment with desserts, preparing grape-nut pudding one night, cranberry-prune compote the next, graham cracker chocolate cheesecake on Fridays.

These supper were by far the most delicious meals that had been set upon Miss Davis's table for some time. She'd spent the past fifteen years eating canned soup and crackers in the evenings rather than face the ruckus in the dining hall. "I hope you don't think I'll raise your grade because of this," she said every time she sat down to her supper.

Carlin no longer bothered to remind her employer that she was not in Miss Davis's freshman class, having had the bad fortune to be scheduled into Mr. Herman's Ancient Civilizations seminar, which she found a complete bore. Still, she never replied to Miss Davis's remarks. Instead, Carlin remained at the sink washing dishes, her posture straight, her hair ashen in the dim light. She rarely spoke. She only stirred the pot of soup on the rear burner of the stove, nearly ready for the next day's lunch, and dreamed of a pair of boots she'd noticed in the window of Hingram's Shoe Shop, black leather with silver buckles. She thought about the way she'd lied to Harry McKenna, not only about her family's background, but about her own experience in matters of love. In truth, she had never even been kissed before. She'd been running from love, exactly as her mother had raced straight toward it, headlong and without any doubts. Now, her involvement with Harry had knocked the wind out of her. She had set out on a path she neither understood nor recognized, and because she was accustomed to being in control, the whole world seemed to be spinning past her.

"What's the matter with you anyway?" Helen asked one evening. Carlin had worked for her for several weeks and hadn't said more than a mouthful of words. "Cat got your tongue?"

Helen's own cantankerous cat, Midnight, was sitting on her lap, waiting for bits of chicken. The cat was ancient, and although wounded in many battles, it insisted upon going out every evening. It leapt down and scratched at the door until Carlin went to let it out. Twilight was coming earlier, and the low clouds turned scarlet at dusk.

"I'll bet you're in love." Helen was quite smug about her ability to tell which girls had been stricken each October.

"Did you want custard?" Carlin returned to the stove. "It's butterscotch."

Rather than admit she was desperate for money, Carlin told people she was helping Miss Davis in return for a community service credit. She had planned to tell this to Gus also, if she ever got the chance to talk to him, for it seemed he had begun to avoid her. If he noticed her heading toward him, he'd manage to disappear behind a hedge or a tree, skittering down a path or a lane before Carlin could catch up. He disapproved of Harry, that was the problem, and lately it seemed as if he disapproved of Carlin as well. In fact, it was a single image that kept him at bay. One afternoon, Carlin had leaned over the gate outside

St. Anne's to kiss Harry good-bye, even though she should have known better than to share a kiss over a gate, an action that it is said to cause a rift between a girl and her beloved before the day is through. When she looked up, Carlin saw that Gus was watching. Before she could call out to him, he had vanished, like those foolhardy assistants in magic shows who crawl into trunks to be dismembered and put back together again. Unlike those individuals, however, Gus had not reappeared.

People said he was taking his meals in his room, and that he no longer changed his clothes, and there were those who reported he would not respond even when called by name. Indeed, he had been cutting classes, preferring to spend his time wandering through town. He had gotten to know Haddan's topography, particularly the deserted areas beside the river, where the marbled salamanders lay eggs in the green waters of Sixth Commandment Pond. He walked the lanes, watching as large congregations of blackbirds flew overhead. Plenty of Haddan residents were enjoying the outdoors at this time of year. It was the height of the fall colors, and meadows and woods offered dizzying displays of yellow and damson and scarlet. The fields were thick with blooming redtop and ripe wild grapes; on porches and in backyards all over town there were pots of chrysanthemums and asters in shades of crimson and gold.

In spite of his rambles, August Pierce was not especially drawn to the landscape; rather, his nature walks served only to help him avoid the Haddan School. By the time other students were in morning classes, Gus was already at his regular seat at the pharmacy lunch counter, ordering black coffee. He hunched over the counter as he worked on a crossword, often staying right on through noon. Ordinarily, Pete Byers didn't care for students hanging around during class time, but he had come to appreciate Gus and he sympathized with the boy's trials at school. Pete had been privy to more personal matters than anyone else in town; he knew people's appetites and their downfalls far better than their own husbands and wives ever did, and he was quite familiar with the private lives of Haddan students as well.

People who were well acquainted with Pete knew he didn't gossip and he didn't judge. He was as pleasant to Carlin when she came looking for earplugs to prevent swimmer's ear as he was to old Rex Hailey, who'd been frequenting the drugstore all his life and who liked to chat for an hour or so whenever he came to pick up the Coumadin that would hopefully prevent another stroke. When Mary Beth Tosh's father was going through colon cancer and the insurance money wasn't on time, Pete gave Mary Beth whatever medicine was needed without any charge, happy to wait for the correct payments. In his long career, Pete Byers had seen too many people sick and dying, far more, he would wager, than those young doctors over at the health center in Hamilton ever had. These days, people never seemed to have appointments with the same doctor twice, with HMOs shuffling their patients around as if they had no more weight and importance than playing cards. Dr. Stephens, who had kept an office on Main Street for forty-five years, was a great old man, but he'd closed up his practice and moved to Florida, and even before the doctor had retired, it was Pete people came to when they wanted to talk, and as a matter of fact, they still do.

Pete had never discussed any of the information he'd been told, not even with his wife, Eileen. He wouldn't think of telling her which member of the garden club had bunions or who was trying out Zoloft for her nervous condition. Once, years ago, Pete hired a clerk from Hamilton, a fellow named Jimmy Quinn, but as soon as Pete discovered that his new assistant had taken to perusing customers' medical histories while eating his lunch, Quinn was fired, let go that very same day. Ever since, Pete has kept his ledgers under lock and key. Not even his nephew, Sean, sent up from Boston in the hopes he'd finally fly right and manage to finish out his senior year at Hamilton High, had access to the files. Not that Sean Byers was the type to be trusted. He was a dark, handsome kid of seventeen who had managed to mess up his life fairly well, at least well enough to convince his mother, Pete's favorite sister, Jeannette, to step in and take action when Jeannette had always been the easygoing type, preferring to leave well enough alone. Sean had stolen two cars and been caught with one of them. Because of this, he had been placed under his uncle's watchful eye, away from the evil influence of the city, stuck in the middle of nowhere. When Sean reported to work after a day in Hamilton High School he was always grateful for Gus's company. At least there was one other individual in Haddan who hated the town as much as he did.

"Maybe we should trade places," Sean suggested to Gus one day. It was late afternoon and Sean had his eye on a table of girls from the Haddan School, none of whom would have given him the time of day, despite his good looks. His job in the drugstore spelled instant invisibility to girls like these. "You go to the public high school and come here to wash dishes, and I'll sit in your classes and stare at all the pretty girls."

Gus's hands were shaking from his high level of caffeine and nicotine consumption. Since his arrival at Haddan, he had lost ten pounds from his already scrawny frame.

"Trust me," he assured Sean Byers. "I'd get the better part of the deal. The Haddan School would do you in. You'd be jumping out a window in no time. You'd be begging for mercy."

"Why should I trust you?" Sean laughed. He was a boy who always needed proof, particularly when it came to issues of faith. He had lived the sort of life that had soon revealed that any man who asks for undying loyalty is the man most likely to get you killed.

Gus decided to take Sean's challenge and prove his worthiness. He had ordered one of the hot rolls that had just come out of the oven, exactly what he needed for his next trick. "Give me your watch," he demanded, and although Sean wasn't so quick to hand it over, he was interested. Sean had been through a lot, yet in some ways he was an innocent, which made him the perfect mark.

"Don't you want to find out if you can trust me?" Gus asked.

The watch had been a gift from Sean's mother on the day he left for Haddan. It was the one thing of any worth that he owned, but he unhooked the band and deposited the watch on the counter. Gus made the prerequisite movements to distract his reluctant audience, and before Sean could tell what had been done, the watch was gone. Even the Haddan School girls had begun to pay attention.

"I'll bet he swallowed it," one of the girls declared.

"If you put an ear to his belly button you can probably hear him ticking," another girl added.

Gus ignored them and concentrated on his trick. "Do you think I lost your watch?" he goaded Sean. "Maybe I stole it. Maybe you made a big mistake trusting me."

Sean was now as interested in the manner of the watch's reappearance as he was in the watch itself. All his life he'd thought he knew the score. *Get the other guy before he gets you; live fast and fierce.* But now he realized he'd never thought of any other possibilities. Maybe the world was not as simple as he'd always believed. He placed both hands on the cool countertop and he didn't care which customer called for a check or who demanded a coffee-to-go. His attention was riveted. "Come on," he said to Gus. "Make your move."

Gus took a knife from the counter and cut open the roll on his plate. There, amidst the dough, lay the watch, steaming hot.

"Man." Sean was impressed. "You're amazing. How'd you do that?"

But Gus merely shrugged and went to pick up a prescription Pete had filled for him. Gus wasn't about to tell Sean the details of the trick. You had to be careful what you divulged, but now and then even the most wary had to take the leap and put his trust in someone. Like so many before him, the person Gus had chosen to confide in was Pete.

"What about my other problem?" he asked the pharmacist as he signed the insurance form for his medication. It was the thirteenth of the month and Gus had been hoping Pete might help with his problem at Chalk House.

"I'm working on it," Pete assured him. "I've got a few ideas. You know if you went to school instead of sitting here all day you'd show the other fellows how smart you are, and you'd win out. That's what I've been telling Sean."

"Have you been telling him about the tooth fairy, too? About truth and justice and how the meek shall inherit the earth?"

Gus was already convinced that the meek were not about to inherit anything in Haddan, which is why he packed a bag that evening and went down to the train station. He had no intention of participating in the barbarous rituals of the Magicians' Club. At the hour when Nathaniel Gibb was unwrapping a bloody rabbit's foot from the cotton handkerchief his grandmother had given him at Christmas, Gus was keeping an eye out for the eight-fifteen into Boston. It was a chilly evening, with frost soon to come. Waiting for the train, Gus thought about his father and the high hopes the elder Pierce still had. He thought about how many hours it took to get to New York, and how many times he'd transferred to new schools, and what a disappointment he must be. And then, before he could stop himself, he thought about Carlin Leander's silver hair and the way she smelled like soap and swimming pools. At a little before eight a police car drove by, and one of the cops leaned his head out the window to ask Gus what he was waiting for. Gus hadn't the slightest idea, and so he took his suitcase and walked back to the school, the long way, through the village. He went past Lois Jeremy's perennial garden, with its mums the size of pie plates; past Selena's, where Nikki Humphrey was closing up for the night. At last, he turned onto the path that would lead him past the weeping beeches Annie Howe had planted long ago. He did so grudgingly, returning to the place he feared most, his own room, for on this dark, blue night when the weather was about to turn, August Pierce had nowhere else to go.

IN THE MIDDLE OF THE AFTERNOON, MAUREEN Brown noticed a patch of bloodied grass in the far meadow. Intent upon searching for specimens for her biology lab, most especially the shy leopard frog, she went farther, making her way past birches and pines, at last inching along beneath thistles and thorns to the place where she found the carcass of a rabbit with one foot cut off. It was the time of year when the leaves on the wild blueberry bushes had become flame red and woody stalks of goldenrod could be found everywhere, in the fields and gardens and lanes. Deeply shaken, Maureen took to her bed after her dreadful discovery. She had to be carried up to her room on the third floor of St. Anne's, and afterward she refused to return to classes until she was allowed to drop biology. Although it was halfway through the term, Maureen was allowed to enroll in Photography 1, bringing with her a hurt expression and absolutely no talent. Due to the circumstances, however, Betsy hadn't the heart to turn her down. Eric couldn't understand her pity.

"Imagine finding something like that," Betsy said to Eric as they walked down to the pharmacy for a late breakfast on Sunday morning. "What a shock."

"It was only a rabbit," Eric told her. "When you think about it, they have rabbit on the menu over at the inn. They boil them and sauté them every afternoon and no one says boo, but find one in the woods and it's a huge event."

"You're probably right," Betsy said, even though she was far from convinced.

"Of course I'm right," he assured her. "The death of a rabbit, however sad, is hardly a federal case."

In the past few weeks, Eric and Betsy had been so overwhelmed by their duties they'd hardly seen each other. In all honesty, they both had been too busy for intimacy and it didn't seem possible to find any privacy at the school. If they were in Eric's rooms, there was always the fear that a student might knock at the door and interrupt. The few times they'd managed to get the least bit romantic, they'd been awkward with each other, like strangers who'd gone too far on a blind date. Perhaps their estrangement was unavoidable; what little energy they had was given over to students, such as Maureen, whose traumatic experience in the woods had taken up most of Betsy's week.

"Did it ever occur to you," Eric said now, "that girl of yours might be a spoiled brat?"

For a man with a doctorate in ancient history to be embroiled in the social lives of adolescents who couldn't handle the slightest mishap on their own was ridiculous, Betsy had to agree. Oh, how Eric wished he were teaching at a university, where students took care of their own petty problems and the quest for knowledge was the issue at hand. This year the most bothersome member of Eric's class was that boy August Pierce, who was clearly no student. Gus had been hanging around Eric's door for several days, obviously wanting something. At last Eric asked if there was a problem, knowing full well that with students such as Gus, there was always a problem, and that most of these difficulties were best left alone.

When Gus skipped the meeting on the thirteenth of October, there'd been quite a price to pay. When they got hold of him, they dragged him into the lounge and locked the door. Harry McKenna had held a lit cigarette to his arm, a brand to remind him that rules were rules. For days afterward, Gus couldn't get the odor of his own singed flesh out of his head; he felt as though he were still on fire, even now, beneath his sweater, beneath his coat. He had been shoring up the courage to speak to a house-parent for days. "Could I come in for a minute?" he asked Mr. Herman. "Can I talk to you privately?"

Of course the answer was no: Inviting students into one's home bred both familiarity and contempt, not at all in keeping with Haddan's code of etiquette. Gus Pierce, therefore, had been forced to trot alongside as Eric hurried to the library. The boy coughed and sputtered and began to spin some far-fetched story about his mistreatment. He hated to come to Eric like a tattletale on a playground, and Eric had no choice but to listen as the details spilled out. The sunlight was weak, yet Eric had felt a line of sweat on his forehead. No one on the faculty liked talk such as this; it was anti-Haddan, the sort of inflammatory nonsense that fueled lawsuits and ruined careers.

In point of fact, the kid claiming to be victimized was over six feet tall, not exactly the size and shape of a victim. When Gus pulled up his shirt Eric did note bruises on his back and ribs and a fresh burn Gus claimed had been recently inflicted, but what did any of this prove? Soccer could easily be the cause of such injuries, as could a wild game of football. More likely, such wounds were self-inflicted, the actions of a student whom many at school had already judged to be unstable. August Pierce was failing several of his classes; only last week there'd been a meeting wherein his teachers and the dean had discussed his wretched performance in class. Frankly, the odds were not in his favor, and several of his teachers did not believe Gus would survive the semester.

"Maybe you need to take responsibility for your own actions," Eric said. "If someone's bothering you, stand up for yourself, man."

Eric could tell the boy wasn't listening.

"I'm trying to help you here, Gus," Eric said.

"Great." The boy nodded. "Thanks a million."

Watching Gus lurch away, Eric felt satisfied that his responsibility toward the boy had been met. Certainly, he did not wish to take up Gus's case, even if the other fellows were giving him a hard time. In all probability, he deserved whatever bitter ration was dished out to him. He was annoying and exasperating. What had he expected? That his roommates would admire him, that they'd be delighted to have him among them? Eric knew a hierarchy existed at Chalk House, exactly as it had when he himself was in high school, and again when he'd joined a fraternity at college. Well, boys would be boys, wasn't that the saying? Some were bound to be evil and others bound to be good and the rest would fall somewhere in between, bending one way or another given certain circumstances or friends who led the way.

Pressure, too, was bound to affect people differently. Dave Linden, for instance, never complained about cleaning the seniors' rooms or cheating on their behalf, but he'd begun to stutter. Nathaniel Gibb, on the other hand, found himself suffering from nightmares; one night, he'd awakened to find himself standing at his window, facing the darkened quad below, as if someone with his promise might actually consider leaping from the ledge. Gus's method of dealing with the Chalk boys' offensive was to offer passive resistance. Whether they burned him or berated him, he thought only of empty space, how it went on forever and ever, how every human being was nothing more than a speck of dust. He was not in the least surprised to find that Eric Herman wouldn't help him; rather, he was ashamed of himself to have looked for help in the first place.

And so he let himself be beaten without a struggle; frankly, he did not believe a struggle would succeed. He began to avoid the Haddan campus even more than he had before, spending nearly all his time in town, going so far as to unroll a sleeping bag for the night in the alley behind the pharmacy and the Lucky Day Florist. Sean Byers often met him there in the evenings, for the boys had formed an alliance based on their mutual disdain for their surroundings. They smoked marijuana in the alleyway, breathing in the rank stench of the Dumpster along with the sweet aroma of hemp. Gus was so relieved to be away from Chalk House he didn't even mind the rats that lived in the alley, silent shadowy creatures that searched the garbage for scraps. From this vantage point, he could see Orion rise out of the east at midnight, making everything in town deliriously bright. The great square of Pegasus hung in the sky, a lantern above him as he huddled in the alley. Whenever Gus smoked pot beneath that awesome horizon, he felt shimmery and free, but this was only an illusion, and he knew it. He had grown convinced that his only method of escape was to perfect the trick no one had ever managed before. If he tried, it might be possible to succeed where Annie Howe had failed and at last turn the roses red.

It was customary for those who lived in the big white houses to place lighted jack-o'-lanterns on their front porches on Halloween night as an invitation to children who might otherwise not be allowed past the front gate. The youngest trick-or-treaters set out in the late afternoon, dressed as pirates and princesses, demanding sweets at one house before rushing on through piles of crumbly leaves to the next. The stores in town had bins of free candy inside their doorways, and Selena's was known to give out free mocha lattes. At the inn, complimentary pumpkin pie was served at dinner, and over at the Millstone, those customers who dressed in plastic masks and clown noses to celebrate the holiday were always the ones who drank so much they needed to be escorted home at the end of the evening.

In the village of Haddan, Halloween was a night that often spelled trouble. Extra police were on duty, with the usual force of eight officers supplemented by a few local men hired for the evening at an hourly rate. Often the sight of a patrol car parked on the corner of Lovewell and Main was enough of a threat to minimize high jinks and misdemeanors. Still some people were bound to go wild on this night of the year, no matter what the consequences. There were always those who wrapped toilet paper around trees, particularly upsetting to Lois Jeremy, whose Chinese cherry trees were exceedingly fragile, and others who insisted upon egging front doors and passing cars. One year, the front window of Selena's was smashed in and another year the back door to the florist's was chopped down with an ax. Pranks such as these could cause more trouble than intended: A shop owner might turn out to have a gun behind his counter, even in Haddan. A car full of teenagers might speed away, taking the turn onto Forest or Pine too quickly, with its occupants winding up in the hospital and the cartons of eggs they'd brought along forgotten and broken to bits.

There are those who will use any excuse to throw caution to the wind, especially on dark nights when goblins roamed Main Street, their hands sticky with chocolate and sugar. This year there was an east wind, always a bad omen, the fishermen say, and it went to work shaking the last of the leaves from the trees. The night was murky, with a threatening mackerel sky, but that didn't deter the boys from Chalk House, who had a party in the woods every Halloween. It was an invitation-only affair, with two kegs of beer Teddy Humphrey had agreed to supply for a surcharge of a hundred bucks, with another fifty thrown in for carting the heavy kegs into the woods.

Carlin Leander had of course been invited. She had become the girl of the moment, the beautiful girl everyone wanted to be near. True, she was maintaining an A average and was thought to be the most talented swimmer on her team, but the most important factor in her sudden rise at the Haddan School was based upon a single fact: She had Harry McKenna. She'd come out of nowhere and won him without trying, infuriating several girls who had been after him for years. Amy Elliot was so envious that she sat at the foot of Carlin's bed, begging for bits of information. Did Harry close his eyes when he kissed her? Did he whisper at such moments? Did he sigh?

Amy wasn't the only girl at St. Anne's who wished she were in Carlin's place, and there were those who had taken to copying Carlin, buying the same boots at Hingram's that she had purchased, quick to forsake their own calfskin boots purchased for three times the price. Maureen Brown had begun swimming laps on weekends and Peggy Anthony now pinned up her hair with silver clips. Only days earlier, Carlin noticed Amy wearing a black T-shirt exactly like one of her own. When the shirt in question was tossed in the laundry basket, Carlin realized it was indeed her own, and that Amy had stolen it from her bureau drawer, a turnabout that gave Carlin the greatest of pleasure, for the coveted item had cost exactly two dollars and ninety-nine cents and was probably the cheapest bit of cloth Amy had ever worn.

And yet there were times when Carlin wondered if she'd outsmarted herself. Harry was her very first love, but, every now and then, she didn't recognize him. She would spy him across the quad and blink. He might have been any one of the senior boys, waving and calling her name. Carlin was reminded of how lonely her mother often seemed, in spite of a series of boyfriends.

Much to her chagrin, Carlin understood that brand of loneliness now, for it was Gus Pierce she missed. His absence pained her; she felt it the way someone might feel a laceration or a broken bone. But what was she to do? Harry had persuaded her it was impossible to befriend Gus. Pierce was doing himself in with his bad attitude. Not a single student would sit next to Gus on those rare instances when he came to class; he stank and muttered to himself, his behavior growing more bizarre by the day. He was best avoided, for who knew where his odd ways would lead him?

On Harry's advice, Carlin hadn't mentioned the Halloween party to Gus, but being at this festive occasion without him felt wrong. She was all dressed up in an outfit she'd borrowed from Miss Davis, having a horrible time, as bored as she was guilt-ridden. A fifth of rum had been added to the punch and one of the kegs had already run dry. Maureen Brown, plastered after two cups of beer, was showing off her orange silk Halloween panties to anyone who wished to partake of the view. As far as Carlin was concerned, the whole lot were nothing more than tiresome drunks, many of them in costume, with plastic vampire teeth and black wigs and white pancake makeup, items that were always on sale at the pharmacy at this time of year.

A bonfire had been lit, and the sound of crackling wood echoed through the glen. Every shadow belonged to someone Carlin wished to avoid—that awful Christine Percy from the swim team, for one, and that horrible Robbie Shaw, who couldn't keep his hands to himself. From where Carlin stood, on the dark edges of the party, she could spy Harry, preoccupied with keep-ing the bonfire alight, hooting with his friends each time a spray of cinders shot into the sky. Harry, too, was drunk and Carlin guessed he wouldn't miss her if she slipped off for a while. She rid herself of her plastic cup of beer, which was warm anyway, and before anyone noticed, she took off in the direction of the graveyard and what she was sure would be far better company.

The vintage black dress Carlin had borrowed from Miss Davis was made of old-fashioned chiffon, and the skirt collected burrs that tore into the fabric as she made her way across the meadow. Even here, she could hear the raucous party behind her; the bonfire threw thousands of sparks into the sky. By their foul, smoky light, Carlin could see that Gus was exactly where she expected to find him, stretched out on Dr. Howe's marker. He gazed up as she approached.

"Have fun at the orgy?" he called. Aside from the sparks lighting up the sky, the night was pitch dark and Carlin couldn't make out either his expression or his intent.

"It's not exactly an orgy, just a keg of beer and some idiots dancing around a fire." The air had a bitter scent, like woodbine or damp weeds. It was late; carloads of local teenagers had already cruised down Lovewell Lane, spraying shaving cream on poplar trees and boxwood hedges.

"Are you sure you're supposed to be talking to me?" Honesty was painful, and Gus wasn't much in favor of it, but he'd been seriously hurt. True enough, Carlin had told him from the start that she'd never be his, but the fact she'd chosen Harry cut him deeply. It was as though he were bleeding anew each time he saw them together. "Maybe you'd better run along and play."

Carlin went to sit on Hosteous Moore's grave. "What is wrong with you? I came here to see you and you're attacking me."

"Aren't you afraid your boyfriend will see us together?" Gus rubbed out his cigarette and embers skittered across Dr. Howe's headstone into the tall grass, where a hedge of ballerina roses still bloomed weakly. "Bad girl," Gus chided. "I'm sure you'll be punished for not doing as you were told."

In was then, in the midst of this argument, that Betsy happened to come up the path. She had left the faculty party for a bit of air. It had been a silly event; even the costumes had been disappointing. Dr. Jones's toga had been fashioned from a bath towel worn over his suit, and Bob Thomas and his wife had come as bride and groom, decked out in their old wedding clothes, outfits that had caused everyone to point to Betsy, calling out *You're next*, as if it were the guillotine that awaited her in June rather than a lovely reception in the Willow Room. Betsy had stepped outside on the porch for only a moment, but as soon as she had, the wind seemed to be pushing her forward. She walked briskly, the sound of her breathing filling her head; she was doing her best not to be disappointed in Eric. True, he had made certain she was introduced to everyone, and he'd fetched her a drink, but when it came down to it, he'd seemed a good deal more interested in talking to Dr. Jones than to her. It was the bonfire Betsy spied first, and she thought that perhaps the woods had been set alight. Soon enough, the music and laughter assured her that it was only a party. Probably she should have gone over to break up the fun, but instead she went through the meadow and along the path, not realizing that anyone was there in the cemetery until she was almost upon them. Betsy recognized the boy as a tall, gawky freshman she'd occasionally noticed wandering through town during school hours. The angry girl who was smoking a cigarette was Carlin Leander. So many rules were being broken tonight, Betsy would have had just cause to order that both of these students be suspended immediately, had she been so inclined.

"I thought you were smarter, Carlin," she heard the boy say. "But now I see you're just like all the rest."

His words must have stung, for there were tears in Carlin's eyes. "You're just jealous because no one wants you at their parties," Carlin fired back. "No one even wants to talk to you, Gus. They won't sit next to you because you're so disgusting."

"Is that how you feel, too?" Gus said. "Friend."

"Yes, that's how I feel! I wish I'd never met you!" Carlin cried. "I wish I'd told you to leave me alone when you first started bothering me on the train!"

Gus stood up, his long arms drooping by his sides. He seemed tipsy, as though he'd been struck with a fist or an arrow. Watching him, Betsy felt a wave of sorrow; so that's what love was like, she thought, that's what it did to you.

"I didn't mean that," Carlin quickly recanted. Her words had come in the white heat of pain, twisting themselves into sharp little barbs before she'd had time to be measured or true. "Gus, really, I didn't mean it."

"Oh, yes you did." From the look on his face it was clear he could not be convinced otherwise. "You meant *every* word."

The wind from the east was getting stronger, frightening deer mice and meadow voles into hiding, causing sparks from the bonfire to rise even higher into the black sky. Already, the trout in the river had found their way to the coldest pools in Sixth Commandment Pond, and had settled there for the night, in pockets so deep the wind passed right over them.

Carlin was shivering in her borrowed black dress; she felt frozen inside and out. Gus expected too much, from her and from everyone. "Maybe it would be better if we didn't talk to each other anymore," she told him. They had both been wounded now, hurt in the way only people who care can be. "For both our sakes. Maybe we should just take a break."

"Right," Gus said. "I deeply appreciate your concern."

He turned then and fled. Even though the gate had been left open, he went over the fence, in too much of a hurry to head for the path. Luckily for Betsy he went through the trees. There was nothing for anyone to do but watch him run, like a scarecrow fleeing his field, crisscrossing in and out of the shadows, his black coat flapping behind him. He carried so much suffering that it radiated out in waves. Sorrow is like that: whenever a person runs, it comes after him; it leaves an endless trail of pain. The night was dark and the woods thick with brambles, but Gus paid no mind. Some people were fated to win and some were meant to lose, and he knew exactly who he was. He was the boy who stumbled over his own big feet, the one whose heart slammed against his rib cage as he ran away into the woods, the one she would never love.

A miserable night, but it wasn't over yet, and even a loser such as himself might still win a few rounds. Gus walked with the wind at his back, destroyed and invigorated at the very same time. So Carlin no longer wished to associate with him—in a way, that decision freed him. Now he had nothing whatsoever to lose. The hour was late, and the village had emptied, with most trick-or-treaters already home in bed, dreaming of wicked tricks and of sweets. The bands of unruly teenagers had finished their holiday handiwork, hanging old sneakers on the branches of the elms along Main Street, threading ribbons of toilet paper through the spikes of Mrs. Jeremy's fence. Candy corn had spilled onto the sidewalks, and whatever the wind didn't blow away would be greedily devoured by squirrels and wrens before long. Shutters slammed and garbage cans rolled into the gutters. In front of town hall, the statue of the eagle looked more formidable than usual, having been painted black by a gang of local boys who'd then been forced to wash their telltale clothes in the frigid waters of Sixth Commandment Pond as they tried their best to get rid of the evidence, discovering for themselves that some things can never be washed away.

In the woods, damp piles of leaves whirled up with every cold gust, frightening rabbits and foxes alike. Gus Pierce whistled as he went along, a sparse melody that soon disappeared in the wind. He thought about smoking a little weed, just to take the edge off, then decided against it. He could see the bonfire through the trees; he could hear his fellow students enjoying themselves. Because of this, he avoided the clearing as he made his way along the riverbank. He could hear wood rats nearby, a scurrying and then a splashing as they paddled in the shallows, fleeing his footsteps. Those rats were smart enough to make a trek through Lois Jeremy's garden, then cross Main Street to search the Dumpsters for food; they were far too wary ever to be trapped by the boys from Chalk House the way those luckless rabbits were every year.

Gus thought about Carlin in her black dress and how he'd made her cry. He thought about all the times he'd failed. He paid no attention to the sinking feeling he had that this might be his last chance, nor did he consider the rattle of his own destiny. He was ready to prove himself, on this night above all other nights. Throughout his life, August Pierce had been on the run, but now, at this cold and brutal hour, he began to slow down, ready to stand his ground. For the secret he'd recently discovered was that he had far more courage than he'd ever imagined, and for that unexpected gift, he thanked his lucky stars.

THE RING
AND THE DOVE

THEY FOUND HIM ON THE FIRST
morning of November, half a mile down-
river, caught in a tangle of rushes and reeds
on a clear blue day when there wasn't a
cloud in the sky. Everything but his black
coat was submerged, so that at first it appeared as if something with wings had
fallen from above, an enormously large bat
or a crow without feathers, or perhaps an
angel who had faltered, then drowned, in
the tears of this poor tired world.

Two local boys playing hooky discovered
the body, and they never again cut school
after that day. All these boys had wanted
was to catch a trout or two, when they'd
come upon something drifting in the shallow water at the bend where there was an
old stand of willows. One of the boys

guessed what they spied was only a large plastic bag drifting downstream, but the second boy noticed an object so white it was easily mistaken for a water lily. Only after being prodded with a stick did this flower reveal itself to be a human hand.

When the boys realized what they'd discovered, they ran all the way home and pounded on their front doors, screaming for their mothers and vowing that from this day forward they'd always behave. Twenty minutes later, two members of the town police clambered through the chokeberry and the holly, down to the banks of the Haddan, where they waited uneasily for the forensics team from Hamilton to arrive. Both officers wished they hadn't gotten out of bed that morning, not that either one would ever admit that sentiment out loud. These were men of duty who kept their feelings in check, not an easy task on this day. In spite of the height of the body, it was only a boy who'd been mired in a blanket of duckweed, just a boy who should have been starting his life, walking under the clear blue sky on such a rare and beautiful November day as this.

The detectives who'd been called in made up exactly one fourth of the Haddan police force and had been best friends since second grade. Abel Grey and Joey Tosh had fished from this exact spot when they were eight years old; frankly, they'd cut school plenty in their day. They could easily find the best places to dig for bloodworms, and it would be hard to total the hours they'd spent waiting for a bite from one of the granddaddy trout that haunted the deep, green center of Sixth Commandment Pond. They knew this river better than most men know their own backyards, but today both Abe and Joey wished they were far from Haddan; they would have liked to be back in Canada, where they'd spent time this past July when Joey's wife, Mary

Beth, let him take off for two weeks with Abe. On the very last day of their trip, loons had led them to some of their best fishing. There, on a silvery slip of a lake in eastern Canada, a man could forget all his troubles. But some things are not so easily put aside, the heavy pull of the water, for instance, as they reached with two long sticks to turn the body over. The color of the drowned boy's cold, pale skin. The gasping sound as they hauled him closer to shore, as if it were possible for the dead to draw one last breath.

The morning had felt all wrong from the start; these two detectives shouldn't have been assigned the case, but they'd traded shifts so that Drew Nelson could go to an out-of-town wedding and that act of fellowship had made them the guardians of this dead boy. The notion that snapping turtles or catfish might soon set to work on the remains forced them to act quickly. Both men also knew that eels had a particular taste for human flesh, and it was a relief that none had already begun to feast on the softer areas on the body, the nose and fingertips being favorite places, along with the smooth base of the throat.

When they couldn't bring him in with sticks, Joey Tosh ran to the car to get a tire iron from the trunk, and they used it to dislodge the leg that had become wedged fast beneath a rock. The sun was strong this morning, but the water was frigid. By the time the body had been brought to shore, both officers were chilled to the bone; their clothes had been drenched, their shoes filled with silt. Abe had gashed his finger on a sharp rock and Joey had pulled out his shoulder, and now all they had to show for such backbreaking work was a tall, skinny boy whose milky eyes were so unnerving that Abe went back to the car for his rain slicker, which he placed over the corpse's face.

"What a way to start the day." Joey wiped some of the mud from his hands. He was thirty-eight and he had a great wife, three kids, with another one on the way, and a nice little house over on the west side of Haddan, on Belvedere Street, a block away from where he and Abe grew up. He also had a lot of bills coming in. Recently, he'd taken a weekend job as a security guard at the mall in Middletown for the extra cash. One thing he certainly didn't need was a dead body and all the paperwork it would generate. But as soon as he started to yammer about how much he had waiting for him on his desk, Abe cut in; he knew exactly where Joey was headed.

"You're not weaseling out of doing the report," Abe told him. "I'm keeping track. It's definitely your turn."

Abe had the habit of second-guessing his friend and getting to most places first, and today was no exception. Back when they were in high school over in Hamilton, Abe had been the one all the girls had wanted. He was tall, with dark hair and pale blue eyes and a silent demeanor that could easily convince a woman he was listening to her, when he wasn't really hearing a word she said. He was even better-looking now than he had been in school, so much so that several women in town, grown women with good marriages, had the habit of sitting in their parked cars to watch when Abe took over traffic duty from one of the uniformed officers during lunch hour at the elementary school. Some women in town tended to call the station at the slightest provocation—a raccoon on the front porch that was growling and acting peculiar, or keys accidentally locked in a car—all in the hope that Abe would be sent over and they could present him with a cup of coffee to show their gratitude after he'd chased off the raccoon or unlocked the car. If, after all he'd done for them, he happened to want more than coffee, that would be all right, too. That would be just dandy, as a matter of fact, although the truth was, it was extremely difficult to get Abel Grey's attention. A woman could stand there half naked, and Abe would simply go about his business, asking which window had been broken into or where the suspicious footsteps had last been heard.

In spite of Abel Grey's good looks and the way women threw themselves at him, Joey had wound up married and Abe was still alone. In Haddan, it was common knowledge that any woman looking for a relationship was bound to be disappointed in Abe. He was too unsettled to lose his heart to anyone; he was detached at worst and distant at best, even he admitted that. He'd never once disagreed when a woman accused him of being cut off from his feelings and unwilling to commit. But here, on the banks of the Haddan, keeping watch over the drowned boy, Abe felt a wave of emotion, and that wasn't like him. Certainly, he'd seen dead bodies before; not more than a month had passed since he'd had to extricate two men from a crash over on Main Street, only to find neither one had survived. In a small town such as Haddan, police officers were often called upon to check on older residents when a ringing phone or doorbell went unanswered. On more than one occasion Abe had been the one to discover an elderly neighbor sprawled out on the kitchen floor, the victim of a stroke or an aneurysm.

Up until now, the worst death Abe had seen in his duties as a police officer was the one he'd witnessed last spring, when he and Joey were called in to assist over in Hamilton. A fellow there had beaten his wife to death, then barricaded himself in his two-car garage, where he shot himself in the head before they could jimmy open the door. Afterward, there was so much blood they had to wash down the driveway with a fire hose. One of the forensics guys, Matt Farris, who'd grown up down the street from the murdered woman, went out in the field behind the house to vomit, while the rest of the men did their best to pretend to ignore him, along with all that blood and the smell of death in the mild April air.

That incident in Hamilton had particularly affected Abe. He'd gone out and gotten drunk and disappeared for three days, until Joey finally found him out at his grandfather's abandoned farm, sleeping on the floor in a pile of hay. Considering how people say nothing ever happens in small towns, Abe had seen plenty, but the only other corpse of a teenaged boy he'd seen before today was that of his own brother, Frank. They wouldn't let him look, but he saw Frank anyway, there on the floor of his bedroom, and then, forever after, he wished he hadn't. He wished that for once he'd listened to his father and waited outside, out in the yard where the cicadas were calling and the leaves of the hawthorns were folding in on themselves, in anticipation of rain.

This boy on the riverbank was only a few years younger than Abe's brother was in that horrible year, the one Abe and Joey still didn't discuss. People in the village remembered it as the time there were no trout; a man could fish for hours, all day, if he liked, and not catch sight of a single one. Several environmentalists came out from Boston to investigate, but no one ever determined the cause. That wonderful species of silver trout seemed destined to become extinct, and people in town were simply going to have to learn to accept the loss, but the following spring, the trout reappeared, just like that. Pete Byers from over at the pharmacy was the first to notice. Although he himself was too gentle a soul to go fishing, and was known to faint at the sight of a bloodworm cut in two, Pete loved the river and walked its banks every morning, two miles out of town and two miles back. One fine day, as he headed for home, the river looked silver, and sure enough, when he knelt down, there were so many trout he would have been able to catch one in his bare hands, had he been so inclined.

"I hate waiting around like this," Joey Tosh said now as the two officers stood guard. He was tossing pebbles into the river, frightening the minnows that darted beneath the reeds. "Emily has a dance recital this afternoon and if I don't pick up my mother-in-law by three and bring her over to the ballet school I'll never hear the end of it from Mary Beth."

This particular bend in the river was muddy, with the depth of a wading pool; it wasn't a place for drowning. Abe knelt to get a better look, knees in the muck. Even with the boy's face covered, Abe knew the deceased was a stranger. If there was one thing to be thankful for, it was that he and Joey wouldn't have to drive up to some friend's or neighbor's house, maybe one of the guys they'd fished with for years, and break the news about the loss of a son. "He's not from around here."

Abe and Joey knew nearly everyone born and raised in Haddan, although with so much new construction on the outskirts of town and so many families relocating from Boston, it was definitely getting more difficult to place faces and names. Not long ago, every resident in the village was well acquainted with every family's history, which could easily work against an individual who'd been in trouble. Abe and Joey, for instance, had been wild boys. As teenagers, they'd driven too fast, smoked as much marijuana as they could get ahold of, used fake IDs to buy liquor over in Hamilton, where nobody knew them by name. Perhaps because they were the sons of police officers, they seemed fated to get into as much trouble as possible. Certainly, no one had to talk them into bad behavior; they more than willingly obliged. Ernest Grey, Abe's father, was the police chief until eight years ago, when he retired to Florida, following in the footsteps of his own father, Wright, who had been the chief before him for thirty years, and something of a local hero besides. Not only was Wright the best fisherman in town, he was renowned for his rescue of three foolish kids from the Haddan School who'd skated onto thin ice one unseasonably warm January day, boys who would have surely died had Wright not arrived with a rope and his own obstinate refusal to let them drown.

Pell Tosh, Joey's dad, was a good man as well; he was killed by a drunk driver while parked in his cruiser on Christmas Day in that same horrible year, the one they still didn't discuss, even though they were now grown men, older than Pell had been when he died. They lost Frank Grey in August, Pell in December, and after that the boys were completely out of control. Who knows how long it might have gone on if they hadn't at last been caught robbing old Dr. Howe's house at the Haddan School? When their life of crime was revealed, people from the west side felt they'd been betrayed and those on the east side felt validated. They'd never liked those boys anyway; they hadn't trusted them past the front door.

There had been a big to-do about the robbery, with resentments between townspeople and students at an all-time high. Before long, there were fights in the parking lot behind the inn, serious, bloody altercations between boys from town and Haddan boys. One night, in the midst of a particularly heated confrontation, the granite eagle outside town hall was tipped over, its left wing permanently chipped. Every time Abe drove past that eagle he was reminded of that year, and this was the reason he usually took the long way into town, down Station Avenue and right onto Elm Drive, thereby managing to avoid both the statue and his memories.

Other boys might have been sent to a juvenile detention facility, but Wright Grey spoke to Judge Aubrey, his fishing buddy, to ask for leniency. To make amends for their wrongdoings, Abe and Joey were forced to commit to a year of community service, sweeping floors at town hall and emptying trash cans at the library, which may well be another reason Abe stays away from both places. In spite of their punishment, Abe and Joey continued to rob houses the whole time they were completing their community service. It was like an addiction for them, an illegal balm that soothed their souls and kept their anger in check. Because neither one could deal with his grief, they did what seemed not only reasonable, but necessary at the time: they ignored their bereavement. They didn't say a word, and they kept on breaking the law. Abe in particular couldn't seem to stop. He wrecked cars and was suspended from Hamilton High three times in a single semester, a record that remains unmatched to this day. He and his father could not be in the same room without an argument breaking out, although both of them knew that every disagreement was based on a single shared perception that the wrong son had died.

In the end, Abe moved out to live with his grandfather, and he stayed at Wright's farm for nearly two years. Wright's house was tilted, with small twisting steps leading up to the second floor, built for a time when men were shorter and their needs less complicated. The place was far more rustic than the houses in town, with a toilet that had only recently been tacked onto the back hall, and a kitchen sink made out of soapstone that was wide enough to comfortably gut a trout or bathe a hound dog. Every spring, flocks of blackbirds roosted on the property, gorging on wild blueberries.

"How can you stand living out here?" Joey would say whenever he came to visit. He'd spend the longest time adjusting the TV antenna to try to pick up some reception on Wright's old set, never with any success.

Abe only shrugged when questioned, for the truth was he didn't like everything about his grandfather's house. He didn't like the mile and a half he had to walk to the school bus, or the canned food they ate six nights out of the week. What he did like, however, was the way dusk fell across the fields, in slats of shadow and light. He liked the sound of the blackbirds taking flight as he slammed through the back door, startling whole flocks into the sky. On mild evenings, Abe went to the meadow where a fence had been put up around a grassy area, unadorned except for some stones streaked with river mica. There was an unmarked grave inside the fence, the final resting place of someone his grandfather had known long ago, a woman who had always been searching for peace. It was peace that could be found here, both by the living and the dead, and Abe wished his brother had been buried out in the meadow as well. Their father, of course, would have never allowed that, for it would have been an admission that Frank had taken his own life. Abe's parents had insisted Frank's death was an accident.

If there were people in town who thought otherwise, then they knew well enough to keep their mouths shut. There was one bad moment at the funeral parlor when Charlie Hale, whose family had been preparing residents of the village for the journey beyond for more than a hundred years, implied that burial in hallowed ground might be denied due to the circumstances of death. It didn't take long for Ernest Grey to set Charlie straight. Ernest took him outside, out of earshot of the boys' mother, and he told Charlie precisely what he would do to any self-righteous fool who interfered with his son's final resting place. After that, the funeral went ahead as scheduled, with half the town paying their respects. All the same, it would have brought Abe more comfort to have Frank laid to rest in the meadow where the tall grass smelled sweet and clean and wild dog roses climbed along the fence. It was lonesome out in the grass, but one afternoon Abe looked up to see his grandfather by the back door, watching. It was a windy day and the laundry on the line was waving back and forth with a snapping sound, as though something had broken apart in the sweet blue air.

All during this time, Joey never questioned Abe if he put his fist through a plate-glass window or started a fight down at the parking lot of the Millstone. He didn't need to ask why. And although twenty-two years had passed since that horrible year, Abe and Joey continued to run their lives in the same guarded manner, with Abe especially firm in his belief that it was always best to leave well enough alone. *Don't get involved* was not just his motto, it was his creed, or at least it had been until now. Who knows why sorrow strikes on one day rather than another. Who can tell why certain circumstances rend a man's heart. There was no reason for Abe to unbutton the dead boy's black coat, and yet he did exactly that. He knew the body should be left untouched until the forensics team arrived, but he folded back the heavy waterlogged fabric of the coat, and then he uncovered the boy's face, in spite of those wide-open eyes. As he did so, a breeze began to rise, not that there was anything unusual about cold weather at this time of year; anyone who'd grown up in Haddan knew that a chill on the first of November meant that bad weather would surely last until spring.

"What's your guess?" Joey knelt down beside Abe. "Haddan School kid?"

Joey tended to let Abe do the thinking. With all the pressure he had at home, he had enough on his mind without cluttering it up with suppositions and theories.

"I'd say so." Close up, the boy's skin looked blue. There was a purple bruise on the forehead, so dark it was almost black. Most probably, the skull had smashed into rocks as the current carried the body downstream. "Poor kid."

"Poor kid, my ass." The forensics guys were taking their time and when Joey glanced at his watch he knew he was going to miss Emily's dance recital; his mother-in-law would bitch and moan about how he never thought about anyone but himself and Mary Beth would try her best not to accuse him of not being there for the children, which would only make him feel worse. "No one at the Haddan School is poor."

Kneeling there on the riverbank, Abe felt the cold seep through his clothes. His dark hair was too long, and now it was damp, and perhaps that was why he was shivering. He had always prided himself on being hardheaded, but this situation had somehow undone him. The dead boy was almost Abe's height, but so thin his white shirt stuck to his ribs, as if he were already a skeleton. He couldn't have weighed more than a hundred and twenty pounds. Abe guessed that he was smart, too, like Frank, who'd been the valedictorian at Hamilton High and was scheduled to go off to Columbia in the fall. His whole life was ahead of him, that was the thing; it made no sense for a boy of seventeen to take his grandfather's shotgun and turn it on himself.

Joey stood up and placed one hand over his eyes; he strained to see the road through a grove of wild olive. Still no team from Hamilton. "I wish they'd take all those Haddan kids and launch them in a rocket back to Connecticut, or New York, or wherever the hell it is they come from."

Abe couldn't help but observe that in spite of Joey's resolute family values and the advice he dispensed on how much happier Abe would be if he settled down, the same old belligerent punk endured within. Joey was a scrapper and he always had been. One hot spring afternoon when they were kids, Joey had dived into Sixth Commandment Pond, naked as the day he was born, unaware that a band of Haddan School kids had hidden nearby, waiting for the opportunity to steal his clothes. Joey was shaking with cold by the time Abe found him, but he quickly heated things up that same night. They brought along Teddy Humphrey, who would fight anyone, anytime, anyplace. Before long they had ambushed a group of Haddan students on their way to the train station; they caught them unawares and beat the crap out of them, and it wasn't until much later that Abe wondered why he and Joey hadn't really cared whether or not this was the same troop that had been responsible for the theft at the pond.

"You're still wasting your time hating Haddan kids?" Abe was amazed by how single-minded his friend could be.

"Each and every one. A little less so if they're dead," Joey admitted.

Both men recalled the way old Dr. Howe had looked at them when their robbery case came to trial, as though they were insects, nothing more than specks in his universe. Dr. Howe was ancient by then, so weak he had to be carried into the courthouse, but he'd had the energy to stand up and call them thugs, and why shouldn't he? Wasn't that what they'd been? Yet somehow they were the ones who felt violated each time a Haddan student recognized them in town and crossed over to the other side of the street. Maybe this dead boy would have done the same had he been their contemporary; maybe they would have been mere specks to him as well.

"What's your best guess?" Joey was thinking suicide, but he surely wasn't about to say the word aloud in Abe's presence. Although such incidents were rumored to happen at Haddan—a first-year student breaking under the academic rigors or collapsing from the social pressure—these matters were kept quiet, as had been the case with Francis Grey, the son of the chief of police and the grandson of a local hero as well. There hadn't been an autopsy or a medical examiner's investigation, only a closed casket. No questions asked.

"I'd say accidental drowning." Why shouldn't that be Abe's first guess? Accidents happened, after all, they happened all the time. Look away and a person might trip, he could fall down the stairs, crack his skull upon a stone, pick up a gun he thought was unloaded. It was possible to aim and fire before there was time to think. Death by misadventure, it was called. Death by mistake.

"Yeah." Joey nodded, relieved. "You're probably right."

Abe and Joey would both much prefer a simple accident, rather than a complicated mess, like the death of Francis Grey. People in town who were a mile away at the time swore they could hear the shot. They still remember exactly where they were at that moment, out picking beans in their gardens or up in the bathroom, drawing a cool bath. It was the burning, white center of August, always an unmerciful month in Haddan, and the beech trees and raspberry bushes were dusty with heat. A storm had been predicted, and it was possible to smell rain in the air; neighbors stopped what they were doing, drawn to their windows and front porches. Many thought what they heard that afternoon was thunder. The echo rose above the village for a full minute, which to some people seemed an eternity, a reverberation they continue to hear whenever they close their eyes.

Long ago, in the villages of Massachusetts, stones were set atop the graves of those responsible for their own deaths; such desperate spirits were said to walk, unable to give up the world of the living, the very world they'd denied themselves. In the towns of Cambridge and Bedford, Brewster and Hull, a stake was driven through the heart of any man who had taken his own life, and burials were hastily accomplished in a piece of farmland that was sure to be barren from that day on. There are those who believe that an individual who truly means to go through with a plan to take his own life can never be stopped. Those who live beside rivers and lakes insist it's unlucky to save a drowning stranger, convinced that in the end such a man will surely turn on his rescuer. But some men can't abide standing idly by when a body lies prone on the shore, and Abe couldn't leave well enough alone and wait for forensics. He drew up the boy's sopping white shirt and found a series of thin bloody lines along the stomach and chest. Rocks in the Haddan were sharp, and currents fast, so it made sense that a body would be battered from traveling downstream. The odd thing was, the blood still appeared to be flowing, with trickles issuing from the boy's wounds.

"What's going on?" Joey fervently wished he was someplace else. He'd much prefer to have stayed in bed with Mary Beth, but if he couldn't have that, he'd rather be out directing traffic on Route 17 than standing here with Abe.

"He's not done bleeding," Abe said.

There was a splash in the water and both men turned as if shot. The noisy culprit turned out to be nothing more than a water shrew, searching for a meal, but the little beast had done a fair job of spooking them. The shrew wasn't the only thing that had rattled them. Both men knew that a corpse didn't bleed.

"I'll bet water got under the scrapes and cuts and mixed with blood and now it's all kind of leaking out. He's waterlogged," Joey said hopefully.

Abe had heard that the blood of a murdered man will always liquefy rather than dry, and when he looked more closely he saw that several dark, oily pools had already collected on the ground. It was the scent of blood that had most probably drawn the shrew.

"Tell me I'm right," Joey said.

There was silence except for the flow of the river and the call of a wood thrush. The hawthorns and oaks were almost bare, and although there were still a few stands of flowering witch hazel, the buds were so dry they disintegrated when the wind blew. The marshy riverbanks had already turned brown, and past the tangles of mulberry and bittersweet, the fields were browner still. It was possible to taste death out here, and the taste was not unlike swallowing stones.

"Okay," Joey said, "here's another possibility. We probably shook him up when we took him out of the water. That's why it seems like he's still bleeding." Joey was always nervous around a corpse, he had a sensitive stomach and a tendency toward queasi-ness. Once, when they'd been sent to retrieve the body of a new-born baby, neatly swaddled in a towel and deposited in a trash container behind the Haddan School, Joey had fainted. An au-topsy concluded the infant was dead before birth, but the idea that someone would get rid of a newborn in such a callous way left the whole town disturbed. They never did find out who was responsible, and although Dr. Jones over at the school insisted that anyone in town could have had access to the Dumpster, the Haddan School Alumni Association bequeathed a recreation cen-ter to the village that same year.

Such donations always followed a delicate situation at the school. The addition to the town library had been built after some Haddan kids out joyriding rammed their car into Sam Arthur's station wagon when he was driving home from a town council meeting and Sam wound up in the hospital with two fractured ribs and a leg that had to be put back together again with metal pins. The new public tennis courts were the result of a drug bust that involved the son of a congressman. These gifts that had been presented to the town meant very little to Abe. He didn't use the library and one evening of Ping-Pong with Joey and his kids at the rec center was enough to give him a headache. No, Abe was far more interested in this purple bruise on the boy's forehead. He was interested in a wound that would not close.

By now, there was an odd sensation in the back of Abe's throat, as though something sharp had lodged there. It was a shard of someone's death, and it didn't belong to him but was there all the same. Already, Abe's pale eyes had taken on a vacant look, always the telltale sign that he was about to wreck another part of his life. He'd alienate the chief, Glen Tiles, by refusing to let old Judge Aubrey off with a warning when the judge was stopped on his way home from the Millstone, driving with an elevated blood alcohol level, or he'd issue a citation to the mayor for speeding when every cop in Haddan knew to let him go with nothing more than a cheerful warning. These foolhardy actions applied to Abe's personal life as well. He'd break up with some woman who was crazy about him, like that pretty Kelly Avon, who worked at the 5&10 Cent Bank, or he'd forget to pay his bills and not even notice that his electricity had been turned off until the milk in the refrigerator turned sour. If Joey hadn't covered for Abe occasionally, he would surely have been fired by now, in spite of his father's and grandfather's reputations. Today, as he had so many times before, Joey tried his best to cheer Abe out of one of his black moods. On to the next subject, and more hopeful matters.

"What happened last night?" Joey asked, knowing that Abe had taken out a new woman, someone he'd met at the scene of a traffic accident on Route 17. By now, Abe had been through most of the single women in Haddan and Hamilton alike, and they all knew he'd never commit. He had to look farther afield for women still willing to give him a chance.

"It didn't work out. We wanted different things. She wanted to talk."

"Maybe no one's told you, Abe, but talking to a woman doesn't mean you're asking her to set a wedding date. How can I live vicariously through you at this rate? I'm not getting any excitement out of your love life. Too much complaining, not enough sex. You might as well be married."

"What can I say? I'll try to have more meaningless one-night stands so I can report back to you."

They could hear sirens now, so Joey headed up toward the road in order to flag down their backup from Hamilton.

"You do that," Joey called cheerfully as he climbed the hillock.

Abe stayed beside the boy, even though he knew it was risky. His grandfather had warned him that anyone who remained with a dead body for too long ran the risk of taking on its burden. In fact, Abe did feel weighted down, as though the air was too heavy, and in spite of his old leather jacket, he continued to shiver with cold. On this first day of November, he realized just how much he wanted to be alive. He wanted to listen to the river and hear birdsongs and feel the pain in his bad knee, which always acted up in damp weather. He wanted to get drunk and kiss some woman he truly desired. This boy he stood guard over would never do any of these things. His chances had been washed away, into the deepest pools of the river, those places where the biggest trout hid, huge fish, or so people said, with brilliant fins that reflected the sunlight upward, blinding fishermen and allowing for a clean getaway each and every time.

Later in the morning, after the Haddan School had verified that one of their students was indeed missing, the drowned boy was wrapped in black plastic, then packed in ice to prepare him for the trip to Hamilton, since there weren't facilities to do a proper autopsy in Haddan. Abe left work early; he went out behind the station to watch as the ambulance was made ready. Wright's old police cruiser was parked beside the loading dock, kept mostly for sentimental reasons, although every so often Abe took it out for a spin. His grandfather liked to ride along the bumpy river road, and when Abe was growing up Wright often took his grandson along, although it wasn't always trout Abe's grandfather was searching for. He would leave Abe in the car and come back with bunches of blue flag, the native iris that grew along the banks. Those flowers had looked so small when held in Wright's huge hands, as if they were little purple stars plucked from the sky. It was almost possible for a child to believe that if these flowers were tossed aloft, as high as a man could throw, they might never come down again.

Some other big man pulling up wildflowers might have appeared to be a fool, but Wright Grey seemed like anything but. Riding back to the farm, Abe was always instructed to hold the flowers carefully and not to crush them. Every once in a while, on a hot spring day, a bee would accompany the irises into the car and they'd have to open all the windows. On several occasions the bee would stay along with them all the way home, buzzing like mad and flinging itself at the bouquet; that's how sweet those wild irises were. Wright never brought the flowers into the kitchen where Abe's grandmother, Florence, was fixing supper. Instead, he walked out behind the house, to the fields where the tall grass grew and that woman he'd known long ago had found peace. Maybe that's when Abe's suspicious nature got ahold of him. Even back then, there seemed to be a truth he couldn't quite get to, and now he wondered why he hadn't fought harder to find it out and ask the simplest and most difficult question of all: Why?

For the longest time, he had wished there was a way for him to speak to the dead. Not knowing was the thing that could haunt a man; it could follow him around for decades, year after year, until the accidental and the intentional had twisted into a single hanging rope of doubt. All Abe wanted was ten minutes with any boy who might have chosen to end his own life. *Did you mean to do it?* That's all he wanted to ask. *Did you cry out loud, your voice echoing upward through the treetops and clouds? Was it the blue sky you saw at the end or only a black curtain, falling down fast? Did your eyes stay open wide because you weren't yet done with your life and you knew how much more there was to see, years of it, decades of it, a thousand nights and days you would no longer have?*

As the drowned boy was taken to Hamilton, he would surely turn blue along the way, just as silver trout did after they'd been hooked and stowed in a tackle bag, along with empty beer bottles and unused bait. In all probability, there were no facts to go after and nothing to prove, but the boy's wounds nagged at him. Abe got into his grandfather's car, deciding to follow the ambulance, at least for a while. He did this even though he was absolutely certain his life would be a whole lot less complicated if he'd only turn back.

"Are we getting an escort?" the ambulance driver called through his open window when they stopped at the town line. Abe recognized the driver from back in high school, Chris Wyteck, who had played baseball and wrecked his arm senior year. It wasn't yet happy hour, but the dirt lot of the Millstone was already half full. If the truth be told, Abe's car was often parked among the Chevy vans and pickup trucks, a fact Joey Tosh tried to keep from Glen Tiles, as if it were possible to keep any secret in this town for long. But on this November afternoon, Abe didn't have the slightest urge to take his regular seat at the bar. Truth was funny that way; once a man decided to go after it, he had to keep right on going no matter where the facts might lead.

"You bet," Abe called to Chris. "I'm with you all the way."

As he drove, Abe recalled that his grandfather always told him that any man who took the time to listen would be amazed at all he could discover without even trying. A truly observant individual could lie down beside the river and hear where the fish were swimming; why, the trout would practically give directions to any man who was willing to study them. And because his grandfather was the best fisherman in town, and had always given out good advice, Abe started listening then and there. He thought about that dark mark on the boy's forehead, a bruise the color of wild iris, and he decided that for once in his life he'd pay attention. He'd take note of what this drowned boy had to say.

NEWS TRAVELED QUICKLY AT HADDAN, AND BY NOON most people knew there had been a death. After the initial course of hearsay and gossip, people overloaded on rumors and simply shut down. All across campus there was silence in unexpected places. In the kitchen, pots and pans didn't bang; in the common rooms, there were no conversations. Teachers canceled classes; soccer practice was called off for the first time in years. There were those who wanted nothing more than to go about their business, but most people could not so easily ignore this death. Many had encountered Gus at the school, and most had not been kind. Those who had been cruel knew who they were, and there were legions of them. Those who would not sit at his table in the cafeteria, those who would not lend him notes for the classes he missed, who talked behind his back, who laughed in his face, who despised him or ignored him or never bothered to learn his name. Girls who had thought themselves too superior to speak to him now took to their beds with headaches. Boys who had thrown volleyballs at him during phys ed class paced their rooms gloomily. Students who'd delighted in taking pot-shots at an easy target now feared that their past iniquities had already been charted in some heavenly book with a brand of black ink that could never be erased.

Gus's peers were not the only ones to feel the sting of re-morse; several faculty members were so sickened when they heard of Pierce's death they couldn't bring themselves to eat lunch, although chocolate bread pudding, always a big favorite, was served for dessert. These teachers, who'd dispensed D's, and decried the sloppy script and coffee stains that accompanied the papers Gus had written, now found that beneath the slipshod penmanship there had been a bright and original mind. Lynn Vining, who'd been looking forward to failing Gus in retribution for the series of black paintings he'd executed, removed the can-vases from a utility closet and was startled to see luminous threads of color she hadn't noticed before.

An all-school meeting had been called and in the late after-noon the entire community gathered in the auditorium to hear Bob Thomas refer to Gus's death as an unfortunate mishap, but word had already spread and everyone said it was suicide. Be-reavement specialists were stationed at tables outside the library and Dorothy Jackson, the school nurse, dispensed tranquilizers along with ice packs and extra-strength Tylenol. There was par-ticular concern for the residents of Chalk House, who had been closest to the deceased, and Charlotte Evans's ex-son-in-law, the psychologist, Phil Endicott, was brought in for an extra counsel-ing session before supper. The meeting was held in the common room at Chalk House, and clearly such an action was needed.

The freshmen who had shared the attic with Gus looked especially shaken, and Nathaniel Gibb, who was more softhearted than most, left halfway through the session when Phil Endicott had reviewed only two of the five stages of grief. At the end of the meeting, Duck Johnson advised his charges to go out and make every day count, but no one was listening to him. Because of the thin walls and ancient plumbing, they could all hear Nathaniel vomiting in a nearby bathroom; they could hear the toilet flush, again and again.

On the other side of the green, girls at St. Anne's who had never spoken to Gus now sobbed into their pillows and wished they could have altered the chain of events. Any boy who died in a mysterious fashion could easily become the stuff of dreams: a girl was free to wonder what might have happened if only she had been walking along the river on that last night in October. She might have called to him and saved him, or perhaps she herself might have drowned, pulled down in the midst of her selfless act.

Carlin Leander was disgusted by this sudden outpouring of false sympathy. She herself was boiling, a stew of fury and regret. She refused to attend the dean's assembly; instead, she locked herself in the bathroom, where she tore out her pale hair and raked at her skin with ragged, bitten-down nails. Let others think what they wanted, she knew quite well who was to blame for Gus's death. Her wretched actions on Halloween night had destroyed both Gus and their friendship and gone on to form something cold and mean in the place where Carlin's heart ought to be. To let out all that was vile within, she took a razor from a shelf in the medicine chest. A single strike and drops of blood began to form; another, and a crimson stream coursed down her arm.

All in all, Carlin cut herself six times. Her own flesh was a ledger upon which she measured all she'd done wrong. The first cut was for avarice, the second for greed, the next was for the petty delight she had taken in other girls' jealousies, then one for vanity, and for cowardice, and the last and deepest cut was for the betrayal of a friend.

On the night Gus died, Carlin had dreamed of broken eggs, always a portent of disaster. Rising from her bed in the early morning, she had gone to her window and the very first thing she saw was a dozen ruined eggs on the path below. It was only a silly prank, some local boys had egged St. Anne's, as they did every Halloween. But looking down on that path, Carlin had known that there were some things she could never put back together again, no matter how she might try. And yet once the announcement had been made she could not believe that Gus was really gone. She ran to Chalk House, half expecting to crash into him in the hall even though the place was deserted when Carlin arrived, with many of the boys wanting to avoid the confines of the house. No one stopped Carlin when she went up to the attic, or noticed when she entered Gus's room. She curled up on his neatly made bed. By then the fury and the heat had been drained away, leaving Carlin's tears icy and blue. Her cries were so pitiful they chased the sparrows from the willow trees; rabbits in the bramble bushes shuddered and dug down deeper in the cold, hard earth.

It was nearly the dinner hour when the two officers arrived. Neither man had ever been comfortable on campus and both flinched when their car doors slammed. Abe had already driven to Hamilton and back, Joey had filed their report. Now they were here to meet with Matt Farris from forensics and give the deceased's lodgings a quick once-over. Abel Grey noticed, as he had before, that tragedy tended to create an echo. Coming upon an accident on an icy road, for instance, he'd heard sounds he'd never been aware of before: leaves falling, the crunch of pebbles beneath his tires, the hiss of blood as it melted through snow. At Haddan, it was possible to hear the air moving in waves. There was the call of birds, the rustle of the branches of the beech trees, and just beyond that, someone was crying, a thin ribbon of anguish rising above rooftops and trees.

"Did you hear that?" Abe asked.

Joey nodded toward a boy racing by on a mountain bike that most likely cost a month of a workingman's salary. "The sound of money? Yeah, I hear it."

Abe laughed, but he had an uneasy feeling in his gut, the sort of apprehension he experienced late at night when he found himself looking out his window, waiting for his cat to return. He hadn't wanted the cat in the first place, it had simply arrived one night and made itself at home, and now Abe worried when it wasn't there on the porch when he got home from work. On several occasions he'd stayed up past midnight, until the damned cat had seen fit to appear at the door.

"Hey," Abe called to some kid walking by. Immediately, the boy froze. Boys of this age could always identify a cop, even the good kids with nothing to hide. "Which one is Chalk House?"

The kid directed them to a building so close to the river the branches of weeping willows trailed across the roof. When they reached the house, Abe stomped some of the mud off his boots, but Joey didn't bother. There were several more of those expensive bikes tossed down carelessly. Haddan wasn't the sort of town where bikes needed to be locked, nor front doors latched for that matter, except back when Abe and Joey were on the loose and people from the village went down to the hardware store in droves, asking for Yale locks and dead bolts.

Once the men had stepped inside the dim hallway of Chalk House, Abe's first thought was exactly the one he'd had all those years ago when they were breaking into houses: *Nobody's stopping us.* That's what had always surprised him. *Nobody's in charge.*

Matt Farris was waiting in the student lounge smoking a cigarette and using a paper cup as an ashtray.

"What took you?" he asked, something of a joke since he and his partner, Kenny Cook, were usually the ones to be late. He stubbed out his cigarette and threw the whole mess into the garbage.

"You're just on time because Kenny's not with you," Joey joked.

"Trying to start a fire?" Abe asked of the smoldering wastebasket.

"Burn the place down? Not a bad idea." Matt was a local boy, with the local prejudice against the school, and it amused him to see bits of trash simmer before he doused it all with a cup of water.

"No photographs?" Abe asked now. Matt's partner, Kenny, was the man with the camera, but he had a second job, over at the Fotomat in Middletown, and wasn't readily available for emergencies.

"The word from Glen was don't bother," Matt said. "Don't take up too much time with any of this."

Abe managed a look at some of the rooms on their way past the second floor; all were predictably sloppy, ripe with the stink of unwashed clothes. The men went on, stooping as they made their way up the last flight of stairs, trying their best not to hit their heads on the low ceiling. There was even more need to crouch when they reached the rabbit warren of an attic, with paper-thin walls and eaves so pitched a man of Abel's height had to slouch at all times. Even Joey, who was barely five-eight, quickly began to feel claustrophobic. In all those years of imagining how the other half lived, they had never imagined this.

"What a frigging dump," Joey said. "Who would have thunk it."

They'd always believed Haddan students lived in luxury, with feather beds and fireplaces. Now it seemed what they'd envied had turned out to be nothing more than a cramped attic, with floorboards that shifted with every step and pipes that jutted out from the ceiling.

As they neared Gus's room, Abe heard the crying again. This time, Joey and Matt heard it, too.

"Just what we need. Some spoiled brat in hysterics." Joey had less than twenty minutes to get home, eat dinner, placate Mary Beth for all the household tasks he'd forgotten or would forget soon, and get to his job at the mall. "We could leave," he suggested. "Come back tomorrow."

"Yeah, right." Abe took some Rolaids out of his pocket and tossed a few into his mouth. "Let's get this over with."

The nagging feeling Abe had been having was turning sour. He never could stand to hear anyone cry, although by now he should be used to it. He'd witnessed grown men sobbing as they pleaded for another chance after he'd pulled them over for a DUI. He'd had women lean on his shoulder and weep over minor traffic accidents or lost dogs. In spite of his experience, Abe was never prepared for displays of emotion, and it only made matters worse when he opened Gus's door to discover that the person in question was only a girl, one not much older than Joey's daughter Emily.

For her part, Carlin Leander hadn't heard anyone approach, and when she saw Abe, she was immediately ready to run. Who could blame her? Abe was a big man, and he seemed especially huge in the tiny attic room. But in fact, Abe wasn't paying much attention to Carlin. He was far more concerned with a bit of visual information that surprised him far more than a crying girl: the room was spotless.

Carlin had risen to her feet; she judged Abe to be a police officer even before he'd introduced himself as such, and for one stupefying instant, she thought she was about to be arrested, perhaps even charged with murder. Instead, Abe went to the closet, where he found the shirts neatly placed on hangers, the shoes all in a row. "Was this the way Gus usually kept his room?"

"No. His clothes were usually spread all over the floor."

Joey was out in the hall along with Matt Farris. When he peered into the room, he didn't like what he saw. Another rich Haddan student, that was his estimation, a pampered girl likely to burst into tears every time she couldn't get what she wanted.

"Maybe we should bring her down to the station. Question her there." Joey had a way of saying the wrong thing at the right time, and this was no exception. Before Abe could assure Carlin they'd do nothing of the sort, she darted from the room. Down the hallway she went; down the stairs two at a time.

"Brilliant move." Abe turned to Joey. "She might have known something and you had to go and scare her off."

Joey came to look in the closet; he reached along the top shelf. "Bingo." He withdrew a plastic bag of marijuana, which he tossed to Abe. "If it's there, I'll find it," he said proudly.

Abe slipped the marijuana into his pocket; he might or might not turn it in. Either way, he couldn't quite figure how in a room so neat and tidy, a bag of weed could be carelessly left behind. While Matt Farris dusted for fingerprints, Abe went to the window to see the drowned boy's view; they were so high up it was possible to spy birds' nests in the willows, blackbirds soaring above the church steeple in town. From this vantage point, the woods on the far side of the river seemed endless, acres of hawthorn and holly, wild apple and pine. No dust on the window ledge, Abe noticed, and the panes of glass weren't smudged either.

"Two scenarios." Joey had approached to stand beside Abe. "Either the kid killed himself, or he got good and stoned and accidentally drowned."

"But you're not voting for the accident theory," Abe said.

"From what I've heard, the guy was a loser." Having realized what this implied, Joey quickly backtracked, in honor of Frank's memory. "Not that only losers kill themselves. That's not what I meant."

"I wish they'd sent Kenny along." Abe was not about to discuss Frank. Not here. Not now. "I'd still like some pictures of this room, and I know how to get them."

He had caught sight of the woman with the camera on the path below, and he nodded for Joey to take a look.

"Not bad," Joey said. "Great ass."

"It was the camera I wanted you to see, you moron."

"Yeah, I'm sure it was the camera that attracted you."

As she walked across the quad, Betsy Chase was wondering if she'd been among the last to see Gus Pierce alive. She could not get past the moment when he'd scaled the cemetery fence, devastated by his argument with Carlin. Was there anything Betsy herself might have done to save him? What if she had called out as he disappeared into the woods, or if she'd gone forward into the cemetery? Might she have changed what was about to happen? Could a single word have redirected that pitiful boy's fate, much the way a single star can guide a traveler through a storm?

Betsy's camera banged against her ribs in its usual, comforting way, but she felt spacy and light-headed, perhaps the effect of crossing from the dim, shaded path into the last of the day's sunlight. In the shadows a recent death cast, even the thinnest rays could be dizzying. Betsy leaned up against one of the weeping beeches to regain her balance. Unfortunately, the swans were nesting nearby. They were such territorial creatures that anybody with sense would have known to walk on, but Betsy brought her camera up to her eye and began to focus. She much preferred to look at the world through glass, but before she could continue, someone called out to her. Betsy placed one hand over her eyes. There was a man on the front porch of Chalk House and his gaze had settled onto her.

"Is that a camera?" he called.

Well, that much was obvious, but no more obvious than the fact that his eyes were a pale, transparent blue and that he had the sort of stare that could hold a person in place, unable or unwilling to move. Betsy felt akin to those rabbits she came upon when she went walking at dusk; although it was clear they should run, they stayed where they were, frozen, even when it was clear they were in the direct path of trouble.

Abe had begun walking toward her, and so it would be ridiculous to bolt. When he took out his ID, Betsy glanced at the picture. Such snapshots were usually laughable, a portrait from the gulag or the prison farm, but this man was good-looking even in his ID photo. Best not look for too long if Betsy knew what was good for her. He was the handsomest man she had seen in Haddan, and a handsome man could never be trusted to appreciate anything as much as the reflection he saw in his own mirror. Still, Betsy couldn't help but notice a few basic facts as she scanned his ID: his date of birth, along with his name, and the color of his eyes, which she already knew to be astoundingly blue.

Abe explained what he needed and led her toward Chalk House. As Betsy walked beside him, she kept a watch on the swans, expecting them to charge, hissing and snapping at coats and at shoes, but that didn't happen. One merely peered out from the nest, while the other followed along on the path, which encouraged Betsy to quicken her pace.

"I saw Gus Pierce last night," Betsy found herself telling the detective. "It was probably right before he wound up in the river."

Abe had often noted that people gave you more information than they were asked for; without the least bit of prodding, they'd answer the exact question that should have been posed, the important detail that hadn't yet come to mind.

"He was with another student." Betsy tossed some of the crusts in her pockets onto the path, but the swan ignored her offerings and hurried after them, feet slapping the concrete. Thankfully, though, they had reached the dormitory.

"A blond girl?" Abe asked.

Betsy nodded, surprised he would know. "They were arguing in the old cemetery."

"Bad enough for him to kill himself over?"

"That all depends." What was wrong with her? She couldn't

seem to shut up, as if silence might be even more dangerous in the presence of this man than speech. "It's hard to tell how people in love will react."

"Are you speaking from personal experience?"

Color rose at her throat and cheeks, and Abe felt oddly moved by her discomfort. He stepped closer, drawn by a most delicious scent, reminiscent of homemade cookies. Abe, a man who never cared much for desserts, now found he was ravenous. He had the urge to kiss this woman, right there on the path.

"Don't answer that question," he said.

"I didn't intend to," Betsy assured him.

In fact, she had absolutely no idea what people in love might do, other than make fools of themselves.

"You're a teacher here?" Abe asked.

"First year. What about you? Did you go to school here?"

"No one from town goes to the Haddan School. We don't even like to come onto the property."

They'd reached the door, which had locked behind Abe; he pressed his weight against the wood, then ran his gas credit card under the bolt, bypassing the coded entry lock.

"Pretty good," Betsy said.

"Practice," Abe told her.

Betsy felt such a ridiculously strong pull toward him, it was as if gravity were playing a nasty little trick. It was nonsense, really, the way she couldn't catch her breath. The attraction was on the same level as wondering what the postman's kisses might be like, or what the groundskeeper who tended the roses would look like without his shirt. She and Eric would surely laugh about it later, how she'd been roped into police work by a man with blue eyes. It was her civic duty, after all. To keep matters businesslike, she'd make certain to charge the police department for film and processing.

"I see you caught yourself a photographer." Matt Farris introduced both himself and Joey when Betsy was brought up to the attic. With so many people standing around, Gus's room seemed tinier still. Matt suggested they step into the hall and let Betsy work away. "Not bad," he commented to Abe once they had.

Joey craned his neck to get a good look while Betsy set up in Gus's room. "Far too smart and pretty for you," he told Abe, "so I'm not giving out any odds."

Local people liked to joke that ninety percent of the women in Massachusetts were attractive and the other ten percent taught at the Haddan School, but these people had never met Betsy Chase. She was more arresting than pretty, with her dark hair and the sharp arc of her cheekbones; her eyebrows had a peculiar rise, as though she'd been surprised in the past and was only now beginning to recover her equilibrium. The fading light through the attic window illuminated her in a way that made Abe wonder why he'd never noticed her in town. Perhaps that was just as well; there was no point in getting worked up over Betsy, who wasn't even close to his type, not that Abe had ever found his type before. A woman with zero expectations, that's what he'd always wanted in the past. Someone like Betsy would only make him miserable and reject him in the end. Besides, it was too late for him to start any emotional attachments now; he probably couldn't if he tried. There were nights he sat alone in his own kitchen, listening to the sound of the train headed toward Boston, when he'd stuck pins into the palm of his hand, just to get a reaction. He swore he didn't feel a thing.

"Maybe I can get her number for you," Joey said.

"I don't know, Joe," Abe ribbed him back. "You're the one who seems interested in her."

"I'm interested in everyone," Joey admitted. "But in a purely theoretical way."

They were all having a good laugh over that one when Betsy finished and came to join them in the hall. Abe suggested he take the roll of film off her hands, which suddenly made her feel cautious. Perhaps it was all that male laughter, which she rightly imagined might be at her own expense.

"I develop my own film," Betsy told Abe.

"A perfectionist." Abe shook his head. Definitely not his type.

"Fine." Betsy knew when she'd been insulted. "If you want to take the film, take it. That's fine."

"No, it's okay. Go ahead and develop the photos."

"Lovers' quarrel?" Joey asked sweetly as they cleared out of Chalk House.

"No," they both answered at the very same time. They stared at each other, more confused then either one would have cared to admit.

Joey grinned. "Aren't you two peas in a pod."

But in fact it was now time for them to go their separate ways. Matt Farris headed over to the lab in Hamilton, Joey went out to the porch to use his cell phone and check in with his wife, Betsy started back on the path she'd been on when Abe had first called to her.

"You can send the prints to the station." Abe hoped his tone was one of disinterest. He didn't have to go after every woman he met, as if he were some undisciplined hound. He waved cheerfully, the good policeman who wanted nothing but justice and truth. "Don't forget to include the bill."

After she'd gone, he stood there moodily, not noticing the swan's approach until it was nearly upon him. "Scat," Abe said, to no effect. "Go on," Abe told the creature.

But if anything, the swan came closer. The Haddan swans were known for their odd behavior, perhaps because they were trapped in Massachusetts all winter, searching for crumbs outside the dining hall door like beggars or thieves. Huge flocks of Canada geese passed over the village, pausing only to graze on the lawns, but the swans were forced to stay on, nesting in the roots of the willows or huddled beneath hedges of laurel, spitting at the ice or snow.

"Stop looking at me," Abe told the swan.

From the way the bird was eyeing him, Abe thought it meant to attack, but instead it veered off behind Chalk House. Abe watched for a while before he, too, went around to the rear of the dormitory. He didn't want to think about women and loneliness; far better to concentrate on the trail that led from Chalk House's back door to the river.

When Joey was through arguing with Mary Beth about whether or not he had to be in attendance when her parents came for dinner on Sunday, Abe signaled him over. "Something's not right here."

It was watery and dank in this hollow, and although it hadn't rained for days, puddles had collected in the grass.

"Yep," Joey agreed as he slipped his cell phone into his pocket. "It stinks."

"You don't see anything?"

That they could perceive things so differently always amazed Abe. Whereas Joey's attention focused on the clouds over Hamilton, Abe was only aware of the rain in Haddan. Joey spied a car crash, and all Abe noticed was a single drop of blood on the road.

"I see that damned swan watching us."

The swan had settled on the back porch, its feathers fanned out for warmth. It had black eyes the color of stones and the ability not to blink, not even when a jet broke the silence of the darkening sky up above.

"Anything else?" Abe asked.

Joey studied the porch, if only to appease his friend. "A broom. Is that supposed to mean something to me?"

Abe led him to the dirt path heading to the riverbank. It was neatly cared for; in fact, it appeared to have been swept. When they returned to the porch, Abe held the broom upside down; a line of mud edged the straw.

"So they're neatness freaks," Joey said. "They sweep the back porch. I've seen stranger."

"And the path? Because it looks like someone swept that, too."

Abe sat on the back steps and gazed through the trees. The river was wide here, and fast. There were no cattails, no duckweed or reeds, nothing to stop an object traveling downstream.

"Anybody ever tell you you've got a suspicious nature?" Joey said.

People had been telling Abe that all his life, and why shouldn't he? In his opinion, any man who wasn't cautious was a fool, and that was why he planned to think this situation through. He, who had always made certain not to get involved in anyone else's business, was already in way too deep. After he dropped Joey off at home he found himself thinking about boys who had died too soon and women who wanted too much, and before long he had grown confused on the streets he'd known all his life. He took a wrong turn on Main and another on Forest, mistakes any man who'd been distracted by a beautiful woman might make, and before he knew it he was driving down by the bridge where his grandfather used to park, the place where the wild iris grew. After so many years Abe could still find the spot, he could still pinpoint the exact location where the river ran slowly and deeply into Sixth Commandment Pond.

IT FELL TO ERIC HERMAN AND DUCK JOHNSON to meet the boy's father at the airport that evening, a duty no one would have chosen, least of all Duck, to whom talking itself seemed an unnatural act. They set out after supper and drove to Boston in silence. Walter Pierce was waiting for them outside the US Airways terminal, and although he looked nothing like his son, Eric and Duck knew him immediately; they could feel his sorrow before they approached to shake his hand.

They carried his suitcase back to Eric's car, an old Volvo that had seen far too many miles. As they drove, the men talked briefly about the inconstancy of the weather, perfect as they left Logan, but growing gray and windy as they progressed on I93; they then discussed the brevity of the flight from New York. It was the tail end of rush hour when they left the city, and by the time they turned onto Route 17, the road was empty and the sky was midnight blue. Mr. Pierce asked that they stop in Hamilton, at the lab where the autopsy had taken place, so that he might view the body.

Although Gus would be returned to Haddan in the morning,

where he'd be cremated at Hale Brothers Funeral Parlor, his remains readied to be taken back to New York, and although Eric and Duck were both exhausted and sick of the whole affair, of course they agreed to stop. Who could deny a grieving father one last look? But for his part, Eric wished that Betsy had come along. She'd had a bit of disaster in her own life, losing her parents at such a young age. She most likely would have gone along into the lab with the elder Pierce and would have offered some consoling words, the sort survivors yearn to hear. As it was, Walter Pierce went in alone to a building that was dimly lit and understaffed and where it took several tries before the body was located.

Waiting in the parking lot, Eric and Duck grumbled and ate the tinned peanuts Eric discovered in the glove compartment, then went on to share one of the energy bars Duck always kept handy. Proximity to bad fortune made certain people hungry, as if the act of filling their stomachs could protect them from harm. Both men were relieved that Mr. Pierce didn't hold them accountable, considering they'd been the adults responsible for his son. Although Eric and Duck had shared duties as houseparents at Chalk House for five years, they'd never been inspired to communicate much with each other. Now, there was absolutely nothing to say, especially when Mr. Pierce returned to the car. They could hear him crying as they traveled the road leading to Haddan, a band of asphalt that on this dark night seemed endless. From out of nowhere, Mr. Pierce suddenly asked why this had happened to his son. His voice was ragged and barely intelligible. Why now, when the boy's life was only just beginning? Why Gus and not some other man's son? But as neither Duck nor Eric knew the answer, they didn't say a word, and Mr. Pierce went on crying all the way to town.

They took him to the Haddan Inn, relieved to at last retrieve his suitcase from the trunk and say their good nights. After they'd safely deposited Mr. Pierce, Eric and Duck Johnson went directly to the Millstone. Most people from the school opted to frequent the inn, where a martini was expensive and the sherry was forty percent tap water. So be it, people born and bred in town always said, if top dollar and bad service was what the Haddan School folks wanted, but now it was whiskey and beer Eric and Duck were after and a quiet space where no one would bother them. They needed a tonic after an encounter such as the one they'd just experienced, but their usual haunt at the inn was definitely off-limits, as the elder Pierce might decide that he, too, needed a drink, so they found their way to the Millstone, an establishment they'd always looked down upon, although they quickly made themselves comfortable at the bar.

Haddan School people rarely were customers at the Millstone, with a few exceptions, such as Dorothy Jackson, the school nurse, who was thrifty and liked the happy hour when all drinks served were two for one. Some local people took fleeting notice of the newcomers, but no one approached them.

"Too bad Gus Pierce wasn't assigned to Otto House," Eric said to no one in particular. He neither cared about nor valued Duck Johnson's opinion and therefore felt free to say whatever he pleased in the other man's presence, particularly after he'd consumed his first drink, Johnnie Walker, neat, no water, no ice. "Then he would have been Dennis Hardy's problem," he said of the geometry instructor and Otto houseparent, a man no one particularly liked.

"Maybe we should have spent more time with Gus. We should have talked to him." Duck signaled for the bartender and ordered another round. The coach was experiencing the uncomfortable feeling he sometimes had when he took a canoe out on the river early in the morning before the sun rose, a time when the birds were calling as if they owned the world. It was so peaceful at that hour Duck could feel his aloneness, a huge dark burden that wouldn't leave him be. A man by himself on the river might begin to entertain thoughts he didn't want; he might go so far as to examine his life. Whenever this happened to Duck, he'd made sure to turn around and start back to shore.

"I did talk to him!" Eric had to laugh in recalling that the boy had been as noncommunicative outside of class as he'd been in Eric's freshman history seminar, although whether or not Gus was truly in attendance depended upon one's point of view. The kid kept his sunglasses on, and several times he'd had the nerve to turn the volume of his Walkman up so high the entire class had been subjected to the driving bass line resonating from the headphones. Eric had been looking forward to failing Gus Pierce, and to some extent he now felt cheated out of doing so.

But Eric's biggest concern was the faculty committee. He worried that this Gus Pierce fiasco would leave its mark. Facts were facts: Eric was the senior houseparent and a boy in his care was dead. Not that there was anything to say that Eric, or anyone else, for that matter, had been negligent. All freshmen had a tough time, didn't they? They were homesick or overwhelmed by the workload, and of course they were inaugurated into dorm life, low men on the totem pole until they had proven themselves worthy. Hadn't Eric told the boy exactly that? Hadn't he suggested Gus take some responsibility and pull his life together?

"The father's the one I really feel sorry for." Duck Johnson was as morose as he'd ever been in his life. "The guy sends his kid away to school, and before he turns around, the kid commits suicide."

That was what everyone was saying, and even Dorothy Jackson admitted that in retrospect there'd been warning signs during his stay in the infirmary: the depression, the headaches, the refusal to eat.

"Who wouldn't feel sorry for him?" Eric agreed, in part to appease Duck, for it seemed entirely possible that after one more drink, the coach would be in tears. Eric called for a last round, even though it meant he and Duck would be late for evening curfew check-in. Still, they might as well relax. Chalk House had already had its tragedy, hadn't it? Surely statistics would keep the place safe tonight without the men's presence.

Had Duck and Eric chosen to take their drinks at the inn on this night, they might have run into Carlin Leander and been forced to report her curfew violation to the dean. But fortunately for Carlin, they were on the other side of town. The village seemed especially quiet when she set out for the inn at a little after nine. The pharmacy and Selena's were already closed and there was very little traffic, only an occasional car passing by, headlights cutting through the dark before fading to black. The branches of the oak trees on Main Street shifted in the wind; leaves fell, then gathered in unruly piles beside fences and parked cars. The streetlamps, fashioned to resemble the old gas variety that preceded them, cast long shadows that angled across the streets in yellow bars of light. It was the sort of night when anyone out walking alone would naturally quicken her pace and arrive at her destination a bit shaken, even if her visit hadn't been fueled by torment and guilt.

The lobby of the inn was deserted, except for a woman posted at the desk who was so out of sorts that when Carlin asked if she might contact a guest, the clerk merely pointed to the courtesy phone. Carlin was wearing her one good dress, a stiff blue sateen her mother had bought on sale at Lucille's. The dress was ill-fitting and so summery that even if Carlin had worn a coat rather than the light black cardigan dotted with little pearl beads she had on, she would have been shivering.

As soon as she'd overheard Missy Green, the dean's secretary, mention that Gus's father had come to town, Carlin knew she had to see him. Now, her hands were sweating as she dialed the number to his room. Fleetingly, she considered hanging up, but before she could, Mr. Pierce answered and Carlin rushed head-long into asking if he would consider meeting her in the bar. The place was empty, aside from the bartender, who served Carlin a Diet Coke with lemon and let her perch on a stool, even though she clearly wasn't of legal age. At the inn, top-notch behavior was presumed; a person with other intentions would surely be better served at the Millstone, which had lost its liquor license twice in the past several years. Darts weren't played here at the inn, as they were at the Millstone; there were no noisy feats of strength, no fried fish and chips, no ex-wives chasing a man down for al-imony past due. Admittedly, the dark booths at the rear of the bar were sometimes frequented by people married to someone other than their evening's date, but tonight even these booths were empty; any affairs that were currently transpiring in Haddan were taking place elsewhere.

Mr. Pierce had been in bed when Carlin phoned, and it was fifteen minutes or more before he came downstairs. His face had the crumpled countenance of a man who'd been crying.

"I appreciate your meeting with me, since you don't know me

or anything." Carlin knew she sounded like some chatterbox idiot, but she was too nervous to stop until she looked into his eyes and saw the grief staring back at her. "You must be tired."

"No, I'm glad you contacted me." Mr. Pierce ordered a scotch and water. "I'm happy to meet a friend of Gus's. He always acted as if he didn't have any."

Carlin had finished her soda and was embarrassed to see there was a ring on the wooden bar. She guessed the management of the inn was used to dealing with such things; there was probably a polish that got rid of the circle so that no one would ever guess there'd been a water mark.

"I think you should know what happened was my fault," Carlin said, for it was this admission of guilt she had come to announce. In spite of her shivers, her face burned with shame.

"I see." Walter Pierce gave Carlin his full attention.

"We had a fight and I was horrible to him. The whole thing was stupid. We called each other names and I was so mad I let him walk away after we fought. I didn't even go after him."

"You can't possibly have been the cause of whatever happened that night." Mr. Pierce finished his scotch in a gulp. "It was all my fault. I should never have sent him here. I thought I knew best, and look what happened." Walter Pierce signaled to the bartender, and when he had his second drink in hand, he turned back to Carlin. "People are saying that it wasn't an accident."

"No." Carlin sounded sure of herself. "He left me notes all the time for no reason. If he'd meant to do it, he would have written to me." By now, Carlin was crying. "I think he must have fallen. He was running away from me, and he fell."

"Not from you," Mr. Pierce said. "He was running away from something. Maybe it was himself."

Because she couldn't seem to stop crying, Walter Pierce reached and took a silver dollar from behind Carlin's ear, an act that so surprised her she nearly fell off her stool. Still, the trick had the required effect; the tears were confounded from her eyes.

"It's an illusion. The coin is in the palm of my hand all the time." Gus's father looked particularly worn down in the dim tavern lighting. He would not sleep that night, and he probably wouldn't for several more. "It's my second profession," he told Carlin.

"Really?"

"He didn't tell you? I teach high school during the week, but on the weekends I entertain at children's parties."

"In New York City?"

"Smithtown. Long Island."

How absolutely like Gus to have concocted a false history, exactly as Carlin herself had. They'd been lying to each other all along, and this realization made Carlin miss Gus even more, as if every untruth they had told had tied them closer together with invisible twine.

Mr. Pierce suggested that Carlin take something that had belonged to Gus, a small keepsake by which to remember him. Although she hadn't planned to ask for anything, Carlin didn't hesitate. She wanted Gus's black coat.

"That horrible thing? He got it at a secondhand store and we had a big fight over it. Naturally, he won."

The Haddan Police Department had returned the clothes

Gus had been wearing when he was found, and these items were stored in Mr. Pierce's room. Carlin waited in the hallway for Mr. Pierce to bring out the coat, which had been folded and bound with rope.

"Are you sure you wouldn't rather have something else? A book? His wristwatch? This coat is still damp. It's junk. What do you need it for? It will probably fall apart."

Carlin assured him the coat was all she wanted. When they said their good-byes, Mr. Pierce hugged Carlin, which made her cry all over again. She cried all the way downstairs and through the lobby, making certain to avert her face as she passed the nasty woman at the front desk. It was a relief to tumble down the stairs of the overheated inn and be in the chilly air once more. Carlin walked the vacant streets in the village, her steps clattering on the concrete. She passed the shuttered stores, then cut behind one of the big white houses on Main Street, traipsing through Lois Jeremy's prize-winning perennial garden before she entered the woods.

The weather had turned, the way it often did in Haddan, the temperature falling a full ten degrees. By morning, the first frost would leave an icy veneer on front lawns and meadows, and Carlin found herself shivering in her thin clothes. It made sense to stop and slip on Gus's coat, even though Mr. Pierce had been right, the wool was still damp. It was also bulky and much too large, but Carlin pushed up the sleeves and pulled the fabric in close, so that it bunched around her waist. Instantly, she felt comforted. She made less noise as she stepped farther into the woods, as though she had donned a cloak of silence that allowed her to drift between hedges and trees.

It was past eleven, and should Carlin be discovered missing

from St. Anne's she would be marked late for curfew. Her penance would consist of cleaning tables in the cafeteria all weekend, nothing to look forward to, yet Carlin didn't bother to hurry. It felt good to be out alone, and she had never been particularly afraid of the dark. These woods might be dense, but they held none of the dangers of the swampy acres she was accustomed to in Florida. There were no alligators in Haddan, no snakes, no possibility of panthers. The most dangerous creature a person might meet up with was one of the porcupines that lived in the hollow logs. Coyotes were so shy of human contact they turned and ran at the scent, and those few bobcats who hadn't been hunted down were even more timid, hiding under ledges and in caves, rightfully terrified of guns and dogs and men.

Tonight, the only animal Carlin came upon was a little brown rabbit, a jittery thing so terrified by her presence it dared not move. Carlin got down on her knees and tried to shoo the rabbit away, and at last it ran off, fleeing with such speed anyone would have guessed it had narrowly escaped being skinned and thrown in a pot. As Carlin went on, she measured her steps; she would need to get used to the way the coat whirled around her legs, otherwise she'd trip and fall on her face. The sodden fabric must have floated out like a lily pad while Gus was in the water, heavy and still. As a swimmer, Carlin was well acquainted with the properties of water—a person moved through it quite differently than she did through the air. If she'd been the one who meant to drown herself, she would have taken off the coat first; she would have folded it neatly and left it behind.

She had already passed the wooden sign that announced Haddan School property and could hear the river nearby and smell the acrid scent of its muddy banks. She could hear a splashing in the water, some silver trout perhaps, disturbed by the sudden drop in the temperature. Out on the river, wood ducks huddled together for warmth and Carlin could hear them chattering in the chilly air. Mist rose, especially from those deep pockets where the largest of the fish could be found. The silver trout were so numerous that if every one had turned into a star, the river would have been shining with light; a man out on a skiff would then be able to find his way past Hamilton, all the way into Boston, guided by a shimmering band of water.

The Haddan River was surprisingly long. It did not stop until it branched in half—one section mixing with the dark waters of the Charles, to then flow into the brackish tides of Boston Harbor, the other end meandering through farmlands and meadows in a thousand nameless rivulets and streams. Even on windy nights, it was possible to hear the current almost anywhere in the village, and perhaps that was why most people in Haddan slept so deeply. Some men in town couldn't be roused even when an alarm bell rang right beside their heads, and babies often didn't wake until nine or ten in the morning. At the elementary school, attendance records were littered with tardies, and teachers were well aware that local children were a sleepy lot.

Of course there were bound to be insomniacs, even in Haddan, and Carlin had turned out to be one of these. Now that Gus was gone, the most she could hope for was to doze fitfully, waking at two and at three-fifteen and at four. How she envied her roommates, girls who managed to sleep so deeply, without a care in the world. As for Carlin, she preferred to be out in these woods at night, although the overgrowth made for difficult going; there were nearly impenetrable thickets of woody mountain laurel and black ash, and fallen trees blocking the way. Before Carlin could catch herself, she tripped over the hem of the black coat, a misstep that pitched her over the twisted roots of a willow. Although she quickly regained her balance, her ankle ached. Surely she would pay for this foray into the woods at swim practice the following day; her time would be thrown off and she'd probably have to visit the infirmary, where Dorothy Jackson was bound to recommend ice packs and Ace bandages.

Carlin bent to rub at the pain and loosen her muscles. It was then, crouching down, still cursing the spiral roots of the willow, that she happened to see the boys gathered in the woods. Peering through the dark, Carlin lost count after seven. In fact, there were more than a dozen boys seated in the grass or on fallen logs. There was a leaden quality to the sky now, as though a dome had been clamped down hard onto the face of the earth, and the cold was surprisingly harsh. Carlin had a funny feeling in her throat, the sort of sulfury taste that rises whenever a person comes upon something that is clearly meant to be hidden. Once, when she was only five, she'd wandered into her mother's bedroom to find Sue and a man she didn't recognize in a pile of heat and flesh. Carlin had backed out of the room and fled down the hallway. Although she never mentioned what she'd seen, for weeks afterward she didn't speak; she could have sworn that she'd burned her tongue.

She had that same feeling again, here in the woods. Her own breathing echoed inside her head and she crouched down lower, as though she were the one who needed to keep her actions shrouded. She might have gone unnoticed if she had cautiously risen to her feet, quietly and safely continuing on to the school before she saw any more. Instead, Carlin shifted her weight to ease the aching in her ankle and as she did, a twig broke beneath her heel.

In the silence, the popping sound of cracking wood was thunderous, reverberating as loudly as a shotgun's blast. The boys rose to their feet in a group, faces pale in the darkness. The meadow they occupied was particularly dismal, a spot where mayflies laid pearly eggs every spring and swamp cabbage grew in abundance. Something of this desolate place seemed to have settled onto the boys as well, for there was no expression in their eyes, no light whatsoever. For her part, Carlin should have been relieved to recognize them as boys from Chalk House, and even more thankful to spy Harry among them, for she might just as easily have come upon a nasty group of boys from town. But Carlin found little comfort in the fact that these were Haddan students; the way they were staring brought to mind the bands of wild dogs that roamed the woods in Florida. At home, when Carlin went out at night, she always carried a stick just in case she happened to meet up with one of these stray canines. She had the very same thought about these boys she went to school with as she did whenever she'd heard the dogs howling in the woods. *They could hurt me if they wanted to.*

To counter her fear, Carlin faced it, leaping up and waving. A few of the younger boys, including Dave Linden, with whom Carlin shared several classes, looked terrified. Even Harry appeared grim. He didn't seem to know Carlin, although he'd told her only nights before that she was the love of his life.

"Harry, it's me." Carlin's voice sounded reedy and thin as she called through the damp air. "It's only me."

She didn't understand how truly unnerved she'd been by those staring boys until at last Harry recognized her and waved back. He turned to the others and said something that clearly set them at ease, then he advanced through the woods, taking the shortest path, not seeming to care what he stepped on or what he might break. Bare wild blueberry and the last of the flowering witch hazel were crushed beneath his boot heels; horsetails and poison sumac were stomped upon. Harry's breath rose up in cold, foggy clouds.

"What are you doing out here?" He took Carlin's arm and drew her close. The jacket he wore was rough wool and his hand had clamped down tightly. "You scared the crap out of us."

Carlin laughed. She wasn't the sort of girl to admit she'd been equally frightened. Her pale hair curled in the damp, chilly air and her skin stung. In the underbrush, one of the frightened rabbits came nearer, drawn by the tenor of her sweet voice.

"Who did you think I was? A scary monster?" Carlin escaped from his grasp. "Boo," she cried.

"I'm serious. Two guys thought you were a bear. It's a good thing they didn't have guns."

· Carlin hooted. "What brave hunters!"

"Don't laugh. There used to be bears in Haddan. When my grandfather was at school here, one came crashing into the dining hall. Grandpop swears it ate fifty-two apple pies and six gallons of vanilla ice cream before it was shot. There's still some blood on the floor where the salad bar is now."

"None of that is true." Carlin couldn't help but smile, charmed out of her misgivings about the gathering in the woods.

"Okay. Maybe not the salad bar part," Harry admitted. He'd ringed his arms around her, pulling her back to him. "Now, you tell the truth. What are you thinking, running around in the dark?"

"You and your boys are out here, too."

"We're having a house meeting."

"Right, and you're all the way out here because you're going to cut off puppy dogs' tails and eat snails or whatever it is you do."

"Actually, we're here to drink the case of beer Robbie managed to snag. I have to swear you to secrecy on this, you understand."

Carlin held a finger to her lips, an assurance that she never would tell. They laughed then at all the rules they had broken and how many consecutive suspensions could be levied against them. They had spent several nights in the boathouse, and such romantic evenings, although fairly commonplace among students, would land them in serious trouble if the houseparents ever found out.

Harry insisted on walking Carlin back to school. Although it was after midnight by the time they reached the campus, they paused to kiss in the shadows of the headmaster's statue, a bit of bad behavior they liked to engage in whenever they passed it by.

"Dr. Howe would be shocked if he could see us." Carlin reached over to pat the statue's foot, an act that some people said brought good fortune in matters of love.

"Dr. Howe shocked? You've obviously never heard the guy's history. He'd likely try to score himself and I'd have to fight him off." Harry kissed Carlin even more deeply. "I'd have to break his neck."

The leaves of the beech trees rattled like paper and the scent of the river was powerful, a rich mixture of wild celery and duckweed. When Harry kissed her, Carlin felt as though she herself were drowning, but when he stopped, she found herself thinking of Gus at the bottom of the river; she imagined how cold it must have been, there among the reeds, how the trout must have created currents as they rushed by on the way toward deeper water.

As if he knew, Harry's expression turned sour. He ran a hand through his hair, the way he always did when he was annoyed but trying his best to keep his emotions in check. "Is that Gus's coat you're wearing?"

They were standing on the hourglass path that Annie Howe had designed with lovers in mind, but now they no longer embraced. Red spots had appeared on Carlin's cheeks. She could feel the cold thing inside her chest that had formed when Gus died; it rattled and shook to remind her of the part she'd played in that loss.

"Is there a problem?" Carlin asked.

She had stepped away from him, and the chill she felt had sifted into her tone. Usually, the girls Harry went out with were so grateful to be with him they didn't talk back, and so Carlin's attitude was unexpected.

"Look, you really can't go around wearing Gus Pierce's coat." He spoke to her as he would to a child, tenderly, but with a degree of stern righteousness.

"Are you telling me what I can and cannot do?" She was especially beautiful, pale and colder than the night. Harry was more drawn to her than ever, precisely because she wasn't giving in to him.

"For one thing, the damned coat is wet," he told her. "Look for yourself."

Beads of water had formed on the heavy, black fabric and Harry's jacket had grown damp simply from holding her near. No matter; Carlin already held a fierce attachment to the coat and Harry could tell she wasn't about to back down. He also knew that the more sincere a fellow sounded in his apologies, the bigger the payoff.

"Look, I'm sorry. I have no right to tell you what to do."

Carlin's green eyes were still cloudy, impossible to read.

"I mean it," Harry went on. "I'm an idiot and I don't blame you for being pissed off. You'd be within your rights if you wanted to sue me for stupidity."

Carlin could feel the cold thing inside her beginning to dissolve. They embraced once again, kissing until their lips were bruised and deliciously hot. Carlin wondered if perhaps they would wind up in the boathouse again, but Harry broke their embrace.

"I'd better go back and check on my boys. I wouldn't want anyone to get suspended tonight. They're lost without me, you know."

Carlin watched Harry return the way they'd come, pausing to turn and grin before he stepped back into the woods. Harry had been right about one thing, the coat was sopping. A puddle had formed at Carlin's feet, there on the concrete path. The water that had collected was silvery, as if made out of mercury or tears. Something was moving within the puddle, and when Carlin bent down she was shocked to discover a pretty little minnow, the sort often found along the banks of the Haddan. When she reached for it, the fish flipped back and forth in the palm of her hand, cool as rain, blue as heaven, waiting to be saved. She really had no choice but to run all the way to the river, and even then, she had the sense that it was probably too late. She could race into the shallows wearing her good shoes, ignoring the mud and pickerelweed clinging to her dress, but the minnow might already be too far gone. One small silver fish brought her to tears as she stood there, her best clothes ruined, the water rushing around her. Try as she might, there would always be those it was possible to rescue and those whose destiny it was to sink like a stone.

WALKING ON FIRE

INDIAN SUMMER CAME TO HAD-
dan in the middle of the night when no one
was watching, when people were safely
asleep in their beds. Before dawn mist rose
in the meadows as the soft, languid air
drifted over fields and riverbanks. The sudden heat, so unexpected and so welcome at
this time of year, caused people to rise from
their beds and throw open their windows
and doors. Some residents went into their
own backyards sometime after midnight;
they brought out pillows and blankets and
slept beneath the stars, as disoriented as
they were delighted by the sudden change
in weather. By morning, the temperature
had climbed past eighty, and those few remaining crickets out in the fields called

hopefully, even though the grass was brown as sticks and there were no longer any leaves on the trees.

It was a gorgeous Saturday and time stretched out as it did on summer days. Unexpected weather often caused people to let down their defenses, and this was what had happened to Betsy Chase, who on this morning felt as though she were suddenly waking from a long, confusing dream. As she passed the old rambling roses on campus, some of which were still blooming on this mild November day, she thought of Abel Grey and the way he had looked at her. She thought about him even though she knew she shouldn't. She knew where such entanglements led. Love at first sight, perhaps; trouble, certainly. Betsy preferred the more sensible affinity she felt for Eric; she was not the kind of woman who fell hard and she planned to keep it that way. In her opinion, love that struck suddenly was too akin to tumbling down a well. She would surely hit her head if she took such a fall; she would regret it dearly.

And yet, try as she might, Betsy couldn't shake the attraction. It was as though he were still staring at her, even now, as if he had seen right through her. She tried to think of ordinary things, telephone numbers, for instance, and grocery lists. She recited the names of the girls at St. Anne's, a litany she always found difficult to recall, always confusing well-behaved Amy Elliot with uncooperative Maureen Brown, mixing up Ivy Cooper, who wept every time her grade fell below an A minus, with Christine Percy, who had yet to open a text. None of these tactics did the least bit of good. Try as she might, desire wasn't so easy to dodge, not on a day like this, when November was so very much like June anything seemed possible, even a notion as foolhardy as true love.

Work would help get rid of idle thoughts. It always did the

trick, managing to set Betsy back on track. Since her arrival at Haddan, she had been so busy with students that she'd had little time for her own photographs. The entire burden of St. Anne's rested with Betsy, since Helen Davis was hopeless in that regard, and Betsy was especially worried about Carlin Leander, who had been closest to the dead boy. Although there was some debate about whether or not Gus's death had been caused by his own hand, despair could be contagious; suicide had been known to spread through groups. There were always individuals who, already looking for a way out, came to believe they had found a door leading through the darkness. When one person walked through, the gate swung open, beckoning others to follow. This was the reason Betsy made certain to check on Carlin, for she'd heard the girl was refusing to eat and that she was skipping classes, letting her grades fall dangerously low. Often, Betsy found Carlin's bed empty at curfew, and although this was against Haddan rules, Betsy never reported these transgressions. She was well aware of the ways in which grief could affect those left behind. Would it be so surprising if one of the girls in Betsy's care took it into her head to eat a bottle of aspirin, or slit her wrists, or climb onto her window ledge? Would Betsy then be expected to follow along after such a student, inching her way along the roof, grabbing for any girl who might imagine she could fly away from her sorrows and all her earthly cares?

In all honesty, Betsy herself had had such notions after her parents' deaths. She'd been sent to live with friends of the family in Boston, and one evening, at dusk, she'd climbed out to the roof as storm clouds were gathering. Lightning had been predicted and residents were warned to stay inside, but there Betsy was, without benefit of either coat or shoes, arms raised to the sky. The rain was torrential, with winds so fierce that shingles were ripped from the rooftops, and before long gutters were overflowing. When lightning did strike, only blocks away, cleaving in two an old magnolia tree on Commonwealth Avenue that had always been appreciated for its huge, saucerlike flowers, Betsy had crawled back through the window. By then she was drenched and her heart was pounding. What had she wanted out there in the storm? To join her parents? To anesthetize her pain? To feel, for a few brief instants, the power of charting her own fate? And yet, in spite of how weary she was of this world, the very first sheet of lightning had sent her scrambling back to the safety of her room, so quick and so frantic she broke two fingers in the process, a sure sign of her attachment to the glorious world of the living.

Once again, on this oddly warm day, Betsy experienced the same charge she'd felt during that long-ago storm, as if she had not been completely alive and was slowly being shocked back, atom by atom. She unlocked the photo lab, glad to be rid of the burden of her girls if only for a few hours, in need of time alone. She had only one roll of film to develop, the one she'd taken in Gus Pierce's room, and even if the prints had not been commissioned by Abel Grey, she would have done her best. Betsy never rushed in the darkroom, knowing full well that images always profited when given extra care. Breath gave life to all that was human, but light was the force that animated a photograph. Betsy particularly wanted to illuminate this set of prints; she wanted each one to burn in Abel Grey's hand, the way his stare had burned through her. But somewhere along the developing process, something went wrong. At first Betsy thought her vision was failing; surely, it was only a matter of time until she saw straight. But soon enough she understood that her eyesight wasn't the problem. Betsy's vision was still twenty-twenty, just as it always had been, her one true gift, and perhaps this was the reason she'd always had the ability to see what others ignored. All the same, Betsy had never seen anything like this before. She remained in the photo lab for quite some time, but time wouldn't change anything. She could wait for hours or for days, but the same image would remain. There, seated on the edge of the bed, hands folded neatly in his lap, was a boy in a black coat, his wet hair streaming with water, his skin so pale it was possible to see through him, into thin air.

ABEL GREY, A MAN WHO USUALLY SLEPT LIKE a rock, unmovable until dawn, could not get to sleep when the weather changed. He felt as though he'd been set afire, and when at last he fell into an uneasy slumber, he dreamed of the river, as if perhaps its waters could cool him while he slept. His house was closer to the train tracks than it was to the Haddan, and the sound of the 5:45 A.M. to Boston often filtered through his dreams, but it was the river he heard on this night, when the weather was so warm mayflies swarmed the banks, although such insects were not usually seen until the mild, green days of spring.

In his dream, Abe was in a canoe with his grandfather, and all around them the water was silver. When Abe looked down, he saw his own image, but his face was blue, the shade it might have been had he drowned. His grandfather set aside his fly rod and stood; the canoe rocked from side to side, but that didn't bother Wright Grey. He was an old man, but he was tall and straight and he had all his strength.

Here's the way to do it, he told Abe in the dream. *Jump in head-first.*

Wright threw a rock as far as he could and the water before them shattered. Now it was clear that this silver stuff wasn't water at all, but a mirrorlike substance that stretched on and on. Wherever a man might look, he was bound to see himself, there among the lilies and the reeds. When Abe woke, he had a serious headache. He wasn't a man accustomed to dreams; he was too levelheaded and suspicious in nature to put much stock in wispy illusions or look for meaning where there was none. But today, his grandfather's resonant voice stayed with him, as if they'd recently been speaking and had been interrupted in midconversation. Abe went into the kitchen, started some coffee, and gulped down three Tylenol. It was early and the sky was perfectly blue. The big tomcat who had adopted Abe was pacing back and forth, demanding breakfast. All in all, an extraordinary day, a morning when other men might turn to thinking about fishing or love, rather than the vagaries of an unexplained death.

"You don't have to get hysterical," Abe told the tom as he opened a cabinet. "You won't starve."

As a rule, Abe had never liked cats, but this one was different. It didn't fawn over a person, arching its back and begging for scraps, and was so independent it didn't even have a name. *Hey, you,* Abe called when he wanted to get the cat's attention. *Over here, buddy,* he'd say when he reached for one of those cans of overpriced cat food he used to say only an idiot would spend good money on.

Surely, this cat had a history, for one of its eyes was missing. Whether this was the result of surgery or a badge of honor from some long-ago battle was impossible to tell. This injury was not the cat's only unattractive feature; its black fur was matted and its shrill meow brought to mind the call of a crow rather than the purr of its own kind. The one remaining eye was yellow and cloudy and could be extremely unsettling when it fixed upon someone. If the truth be told, Abe wasn't unhappy that the tom had taken up residence. There was only one troublesome sign: Abe had started to talk to the thing. Worse still, he had begun to value its opinion.

When Joey arrived to pick up Abe, as he had every day for the past fourteen years, Abe was showered and dressed, but he was still wrestling with his dream.

"What looks like water, but breaks like glass?" Abe asked his friend.

"Is this a frigging riddle at seven-thirty in the morning?" Joey poured himself a cup of coffee. When he looked in the fridge there was no milk, as usual. "It's so hot out there the sidewalks are steaming. I feel like Mary Beth is going to get after me to put the screens back in the windows."

"Take a guess." Abe got some powdered milk from the cabinet where the cat's food was stored and handed the box to Joey. "It's driving me crazy."

"Sorry, bud. No idea." Though the silverware was unwashed and the sugar only bare scrapings at the bottom of the bowl, Joey added a spoonful to his coffee and poured in the clumpy powdered milk. He quickly drank the potent mixture of caffeine and sucrose, then went to the sink to place his cup atop a pile of dirty dishes. Mary Beth would faint if she saw the way Abe kept his place, but Joey envied his friend's ability to live in a dump such as this. What he didn't understand was the addition of the cat, which now leapt onto the counter. Joey swiped at the animal with his newspaper, but it only stood its ground and mewed, if mewing was what the croaking sounds it emitted could be called. "Do you feel sorry for this disgusting animal? Is that why you have it?"

"I don't have it," Abe said of his pet, as he poured some powdered milk into a bowl, added tap water, then set the dish on the counter for the cat. "It has me." In spite of the tablets he'd taken, Abe's head was pounding. In his dream he had known exactly what his grandfather meant. Awake, nothing made sense.

"What's with you and the riddles today?" Joey asked as they went out to the car, the back door slamming shut behind them.

Joey had driven the black sedan through the car wash attached to the mini-mart on his way over and now sunlight was striking the beads of water on the roof, causing the black metal to resemble glass. Golden light streamed down Station Avenue and a bee drifted lazily over Abe's unkempt lawn, which hadn't been mowed since July. Up and down the street, people were out in their yards, marveling at the weather. Grown men had decided to play hooky from work. Women who had always been proponents of washer-dryers decided to hang their laundry out on the line.

"Will you look at this," Abe said beneath the deep and brilliant sky. "It's summer."

"It won't last." Joey got into the car, and Abe had no choice but to follow. "By tonight we'll all be shivering."

Joey started up the engine, and once they were on their way, he hung a U-turn and drove into town, making a right at the intersection of Main and Deacon Road, where the Haddan Inn stood. Nikki Humphrey's sister, Doreen Becker, who was the manager of the inn, had draped several carpets over the railing, taking advantage of the beautiful weather to beat the dust out of the rugs. She waved as they passed by, and Joey honked a greeting.

"What about Doreen?" Joey kept his eye on the rearview mirror as Doreen leaned over the railing to turn one of the carpets. "She might be the girl for you. She's got a great behind."

"That's the part you always notice, isn't it? I guess that's because they're always walking away from you."

"How did I get dragged into this? We were talking about you and Doreen."

"We went steady in sixth grade," Abe reminded him. "She broke up with me because I couldn't make a commitment. It was either her or Little League."

"You were a pretty good pitcher," Joey recalled.

Abe never took this route through town, preferring to cut across the west side on his way to work, thereby avoiding this part of the village entirely. The inn mostly served out-of-towners, Haddan School parents visiting for the weekend or tourists arriving to see the fall foliage. For Abe, the inn brought to mind the occasion of his brief and heedless involvement with a Haddan School girl. He'd been sixteen, smack in the middle of his bad behavior, in the year when Frank died. He was crazy back then, out at all hours, wandering through town in search of trouble, and as it turned out trouble was exactly what this girl from Haddan was after as well. She'd been the kind of student the school had been known for in those days, pretty and indulged, a girl who had no qualms about picking up a local boy and charging a deluxe room to her father's credit card.

Though he'd prefer to forget the incident entirely, and had never mentioned it to Joey, Abe remembered that the girl's name was Minna. He'd thought she'd said minnow at first, and she'd had a good laugh over that. Still, it had been quite some time since he thought about how he'd waited in the parking lot while Minna checked in. As they drove past the inn, he recalled how she had signaled to him from the window of the room she'd rented, confident that he'd follow her, anytime, anyplace.

"I didn't have time for breakfast," Joey said as they drove on. He reached past Abe for the glove compartment, where he kept a stash of Oreo cookies. He told people they were for his kids, but his kids were never in this car and Abe knew that Mary Beth didn't allow her children sugar. People did that all the time, and what was the crime? Most folks tossed out little white lies, as if truth were a simple enough dish to cook, like eggs over easy or apple pie.

"Let's say it wasn't suicide and it wasn't an accident, that only leaves one thing." Perhaps it was seeing the boy's open eyes that affected Abe so; you had to wonder what the synapses in the brain might have recorded, those last things the boy saw and felt and knew.

"Man, you are really into riddles this morning." It was early and the streets were empty, so Joey picked up speed; he still got a kick out of ignoring the town limit of twenty-five miles per hour. "See if you can figure out this one from Emily. What do you call a police officer with an ear of corn on his head?"

Abe shook his head. He was serious, and Joey refused to hear his concern. Hadn't that always been the way between them? *Don't ask, don't talk, don't feel anything.*

"Corn on the cop." Joey popped another cookie into his mouth. "You get it?"

"All I'm saying is that there is always the possibility of criminal intent, even in Haddan. Things aren't always what they seem."

A bee had managed to fly into the car through the open windows; it hit repeatedly against the windshield.

"Yeah, and sometimes they're exactly what they seem to be. At best, the kid had an accident, but I don't think that's what happened. I went through his files from school. He was in and out of the infirmary because of his migraines. He was taking Prozac and who knows what illegal drugs. Face it, Abe, he wasn't some innocent little kid."

"Half the people in this town are probably taking Prozac, that doesn't mean they jump in the river, or fall in, or whatever we're supposed to believe. And what about the bruise on his forehead? Did he hit himself on the head in order to drown himself?"

"That's like asking why does it rain in Hamilton and not in Haddan. Why does someone slip in the mud and crack his skull open while another man walks by untouched?" Joey grabbed the package of Oreos and smacked the bee against the glass. "Let it go," he told Abe as he tossed the crumpled bee out the window. "Move on."

When they arrived at the station, Abe continued to think about his dream. He usually did let things go; he was pleased to move on with no regrets, a trait to which most of the single women in Haddan could surely attest. But every now and then he got stuck, and that had happened now. Maybe it was the weather that was getting to him; he could hardly draw a breath.

The air-conditioning was officially turned off by town decree every year on the fifteenth of September, so the offices were sweltering. Abe loosened his tie and looked into the cup he'd gotten from the cooler in the hallway. *You can't see water, but you know it's there all the same.*

He was still mulling this over when Glen Tiles pulled up a chair to appraise next week's schedule, spread out in a heap on Abe's desk. Glen didn't like the look on Abe's face. There was trouble brewing; Glen had seen it all before. If Glen had had his way, Abe would never have been hired in the first place. For one, there was his past to consider, and second, he was clearly still unstable, in the good old here and now. He'd work overtime for weeks, then not show for the hours assigned on the schedule until Glen called him to remind him that he was a town employee, not a duke, not a prince, and not unemployed, at least not yet. You never could tell with Abe. He'd let Charlotte Evans off with a warning when she burned leaves—even though as a lifelong village resident she should have been well acquainted with the town bylaws—then he'd slap some newcomers out in one of those expensive homes off Route 17 with a huge fine for doing the very same thing. If Abe hadn't been Wright Grey's grandson Glen would already have fired him for his moody temperament alone. As it was, Glen still considered that option on a regular basis.

"I'm not so sure that boy from the Haddan School was a suicide," Abe was telling Glen, which was the last thing the chief wanted to hear on a beautiful morning such as this. Outside, those birds who hadn't migrated, the sparrows and the mourning doves and the wrens, were singing as though it were summer. "I'm just wondering if it isn't possible that someone had a hand in what happened?"

"Don't even think like that," Glen told him. "Don't start a problem where none exists."

Abe himself was a man who needed proof, and so he understood Glen's hesitancy. As soon as he wrapped up his paperwork, Abe went behind the station for the beat-up cruiser his grandfather used to drive, and headed to the river road. When he got out he could hear frogs calling from the sun-warmed ledges of rock. Trout splashed in the shallows, feeding on the last of the season's mosquitoes, wildly active in the unexpected burst of heat.

Abe liked the idea of all this life renewed on the banks just at the time when it usually faded away. Wrens fluttered past him, perching on the wavering branches of the Russian olives that grew here in profusion. In the coldest part of winter, the river froze solid, and it was possible to skate to Hamilton in under thirty minutes; a really good skater could make it to Boston in less than two hours. Of course, there was always the possibility of a sudden thaw, especially during the cold blue stretches of January and the fitful gloomy weeks of February. Disaster could strike any skater, as it had for those students from Haddan so many years ago. Abe had been only eight when it happened, and Frank had been nine. The roads were slick that day, but the air was oddly mild, as it was today; fog rose up from asphalt and ivy and from the cold, brittle front lawns. People could sense the world waiting beneath the ice; a taste of spring appeared in the form of the soft, yellowing branches of willows, in the scent of damp earth, and in the clouds of stupefied insects called back to life by the sunlight and warmth.

It was a fluke that Wright chose to ride along the river that day when the ice cracked. The old man kept his tackle box and several fly rods in the trunk, always anticipating good fishing weather, and when it came, he was ready. "Let's go looking for trout," he had told the boys, but instead what they'd found were three students from Haddan screaming for mercy and going down in the icy depths, the skates still strapped to their feet.

Abe and Frank stayed in the cruiser and didn't move a muscle, precisely as their grandfather had instructed. But after a while Abe couldn't sit still; he was the brother who could never behave, and so he climbed into the front seat to get a better look, pulling himself up to see over the steering wheel. There was the river, covered with ice. There were the boys who had fallen through, their arms waving like reeds.

He's going to be mad at you, Frank told Abe. Frank was such a good boy, he never had to be told anything twice. *You're not supposed to move.*

But in the front seat, Abe had a much better view of the proceedings. He could see that his grandfather had gotten a length of rope he kept beside the fishing rods in the trunk and was racing down the icy banks, shouting for the drowning boys to hold fast. Two Haddan students managed to drag themselves to shore, but the third was too panicked or too frozen to move, and Wright had to go in after him. Abe's grandfather took off his wool coat and threw his gun on the ground; he looked behind him before he dove in, thinking, perhaps, that this was his last view of the beautiful world. He spied Abe watching, and he nodded; in spite of Frank's warning, he didn't look mad at all. He appeared perfectly calm, as though he were about to go for a swim on a summer day when all that was waiting for him was a picnic lunch set out on the grass.

As soon as Wright dove into the water everything seemed to stop, even though the ice broke beneath him, shattering into thousands of shards, even though the drowning boy's friends shouted from the bank. Abe felt as though he himself were underwater; all he could hear was the sound of ice popping and the silence of the dark, still water, and then, with a whoosh, his grandfather was back, up through the hole in the ice, the boy right there in his arms. After that, everything was hugely loud, and there was a ringing in Abe's ears as his grandfather called for help.

Those Haddan School boys onshore were useless, too scared and cold to think, but luckily, Abe was a bright boy, or so his grandfather had always said. He had played in the cruiser often enough so that he knew how to place a call to the station asking for an ambulance and some backup. Afterward, Wright insisted that he would have turned blue on that riverbank with the foolish kid from Haddan dying in his arms, if his youngest grandson hadn't been sharp enough to call for an ambulance.

You didn't do anything so great, Frank whispered to his brother later on and Abe had to agree. It was their grandfather who was the hero of the day and for once the people at the school and the residents of the village had something on which they could agree. There was a big ceremony at town hall at which Wright was presented with an award from the trustees of the Haddan School. Old Dr. Howe himself, the headmaster emeritus, near eighty by then, sat on the podium. The family of the boy who'd fallen through the ice made a contribution to the town, funds used to build the new police station on Route 17 later named in Wright's honor. There in the crowd, Abe had applauded with the rest of the town, but for months afterward, he couldn't shake the image of his grandfather rising from the water with ice in his hair. *Didn't affect me in the least,* Wright always assured the boy, but from that day on, Wright's toes were blue, as though cold water flowed through his veins, and perhaps that was why he was the best fisherman in town, and, in Abe's opinion, the best man as well. Even now, if someone wanted to compliment Abe, all that needed to be said was that he took after his grandfather, not that Abe would ever accept such a statement as truth. He had the same blue eyes, it was true, and the height, and he chewed on his lip the way Wright always did when he listened to you, but never in his life could Abe be convinced he would be as good a man. Still, he wondered if he'd finally been given a chance at something with this boy they had found, a drowning of his own.

On this rare and beautiful day when men were leaving work early to go home and make love to their wives, and dogs were straying far into the fields, chasing after partridges and yapping with joy, Abe walked along the river. He wished that his grandfather still lived out on Route 17 and that he had the old man to guide him. He thought about the dream he'd had, and the silver river made of glass. He went over all the things it was possible to break: a lock, a window, a heart. He didn't come to it until he'd driven home, later in the day, when the sky had begun to darken in spite of the warm weather. He was parked in his own driveway, too tired and hungry and aggravated to think about riddles anymore when he finally understood his own dream. It was the truth that was always as clear as water until it had been broken; shatter it and all that's left is a lie.

PEOPLE IN THE VILLAGE OF HADDAN HAD LONG memories, but they usually forgave transgressions. Who among them hadn't made a mistake? Who had never run aground of good sense and simple reason? Rita Eamon, who ran the ballet school and was a well-thought-of parishioner at St. Agatha's, had been so drunk at the Millstone last New Year's Eve that she'd danced on the bar and flung off her blouse, but no one held it against her. Teddy Humphrey had been involved in a laundry list of mishaps, from accidentally targeting the gym teacher during archery practice back when he was in high school, to ramming his Jeep into his neighbor Russell Carter's Honda Accord after he discovered that Russell was dating his ex-wife.

Those who had called Joey and Abe hoodlums when they were young were pleased to note what upstanding citizens they'd become. Barely anyone could remember those times when the boys had ordered sodas and fries at the pharmacy with no money in their pockets, then had run for the door, half expecting Pete Byers to race after them with the hatchet he was said to keep by the register, in case of fire. Instead, Pete had merely waited for them to see the error of their ways. One morning, on the way to school, Abe had stopped by and paid off their debt. Several years later, Joey admitted he'd done the very same thing and the joke between them now was that Pete Byers was the one who'd wound up owing them money, with twenty or more years of interest tacked on.

On the second day of the heat wave, Abe was thinking about the grace with which Pete had handled that situation when he dropped by the drugstore, as he often did, for old times' sake and some lunch. There at a rear table, having tea and scones, were Lois Jeremy and Charlotte Evans from the garden club. Both women waved when they saw him. These two usually wanted something or other done for their precious club, which met every Friday at town hall, and Abe did his best to assist them. He felt particularly bad whenever he saw Mrs. Evans, from whose house he and Joey had once stolen three hundred dollars they'd found in a tin stored beneath the kitchen sink. The robbery had never been reported to the police or mentioned in the *Tribune*, and Abe later realized the money had been a secret kept from Mrs. Evans's husband, a well-known bully and bore. To this day, Abe will not write Charlotte Evans a parking ticket, not even on those occasions when her car blocked a fire hydrant or when she parked in a crosswalk. He'll go no farther than issuing a warning and telling Mrs. Evans to buckle her seat belt and have a nice day.

"Something is wrong with the safety precautions in this town," Lois Jeremy called from her table. "I see no reason whatsoever why we cannot have an officer posted outside the hall during our fund-raiser." She treated Abe as she did all civil servants, as though they were her own personal hired help. "Main Street will be a disaster if there's no one to direct traffic."

"I'll see what I can do," Abe assured her.

As a boy, Abe would take offense at the mildest slight, but he was no longer insulted when people from the east side talked down to him. For one thing, his line of work had allowed him to see behind the facade on Main Street. He knew, for instance, that Mrs. Jeremy's son, AJ, had moved into the apartment above her garage after his divorce because the police had been called in several times to quiet AJ down when he'd had too much to drink and was on a rant, scaring Mrs. Jeremy out of her wits.

Pete Byers, whose own wife, Eileen, was well known for her perennial garden, although she had yet to be invited to join the garden club, gave Abe a sympathetic look when Mrs. Jeremy was done with him.

"These ladies would be gardening if you set them down on the moon," Pete said as he placed a cup of milky coffee before Abe. "We'd look up at night and see daffodils instead of stars if they were the ones in charge."

Abe took note of the new boy working behind the counter, a dark, intense kid who had the hooded look of trouble Abe recognized.

"Do I know him?" he asked Pete Byers.

"Don't think so."

The boy was at the grill, but he must have felt the weight of Abe's gaze; he looked up quickly, then, even more quickly, he looked away. On his face was the polecat expression of a boy who knew his fate hung by a thread. He had a scar under one eye, which he rubbed like a talisman, as though to remind himself of something he'd lost long ago.

"He's my sister's boy from Boston," Pete said. "Sean. He's been living with us since the summer and now he's finishing up his senior year over at Hamilton." The boy had begun to scrape the grill, not a job anyone would envy. "He'll be all right."

Pete knew Abe was considering whether he needed to keep his eye on the boy should one of the ladies from the garden club have her car stolen or one of the houses on Main Street be broken into late one night. After he'd studied the specials board above the grill, which on this day included tuna salad on rye and clam chowder, the soup of the day for the past eight years, Abe observed the boy as he drank his coffee. The coffee tasted strange, so Abe signaled to Pete's nephew; here was reason enough to see what this kid was made of.

"What's this supposed to be?"

"It's a café au lait," the boy told him.

"Since when did the coffee here get so fancy?" Abe guessed Sean had gotten into trouble in Boston and that his worried relations had doled him out to his uncle in the country, where the air was fresh and the felonies less numerous. "What's next? Sushi?"

"I stole a car," Sean said. "That's how I wound up here." He had that edgy defiance Abe remembered so well. Anything said to him would be defined as a challenge; any answer would be a variation of a single thought: *I don't give a damn what you say or what you think. I'll live my life as I please and if I ruin it, that's my choice, too.*

"Is this an admission?" Abe stirred his milky coffee.

"I can tell from the way you're watching me, you want to know. So now you know. Actually, I stole two, but I only got caught with one."

"Okay," Abe said, impressed by the sudden integrity of such an answer.

People could be truly surprising. Just when you thought you knew what to expect from another individual, there'd be a complete turnaround; compassion would be offered when acrimony was expected, charity where before there had been only indifference and avarice. Betsy Chase had been equally surprised by the differing points of view that were held when it came to the subject of Abel Grey. Some people, like Teddy Humphrey over at the mini-mart where Betsy bought her yogurt and iced tea mix, said he was the life of the party, and that down at the Millstone there was a barstool that practically had his name carved into the wood. Zeke Harris, who ran the dry cleaner's where Betsy brought her sweaters and skirts, offered the opinion that Abe was a real gentleman, but Kelly Avon over at the 5&10 Cent Bank disagreed. *He looks great and all, but trust me,* Kelly had said, *I know from experience: he's emotionally dead.*

Betsy had not planned to refer to Abe as she ran errands in the village, but his name kept coming up, perhaps because she had him on her mind. She had been so disturbed by the photograph she'd developed, that she'd gone ahead and looked up Abe's number in the Haddan phone book. Twice she had dialed, then hung up before he could answer. After that, she couldn't seem to stop talking about him. She discussed him at the florist's, where she'd stopped to buy a pot of ivy for her windowsill, and had thereby discovered that Abe always bought a wreath at Christmastime rather than a tree. She had found out from Nikki Humphrey that he liked his coffee with milk but not sugar, and that as a kid he'd been crazy for the chocolate crullers that he nowadays eschewed in favor of a plain, buttered roll.

Although Betsy had fully expected to discover more details about him when she walked into the pharmacy to buy the *Tribune*, she hadn't expected to find the man himself there at the counter, drinking his second café au lait. It seemed to Betsy that she had summoned him by stitching together the facts of his life. By now, she knew as much about him as people who'd known him all his life did; she could even name the brand of socks he preferred, clued in by the clerk at Hingram's.

"There's no point in hiding," Abe called when he noticed her ducking behind the newspaper racks.

Betsy came to the counter and ordered a coffee, black; though she usually took sugar and cream she felt the undiluted caffeine might help her maintain some degree of prudence. Luckily, she had her backpack with her. "I've got the photos for you." She handed Abe the packet of perfectly ordinary prints she'd been carrying around.

Abe leafed through the photos, biting down on his lip, exactly as Wright used to whenever he was deliberating.

"I've got one other photograph that I took that day." Color had risen in Betsy's face. "You're going to probably think I'm crazy." She'd held the singular print back, afraid to present it, but now that she'd seen how thoughtful he was, she had reconsidered.

"Try me," Abe urged.

"I know it sounds crazy, but I think I've got a picture of Gus Pierce."

Abe nodded, waiting for the rest.

"After he was dead."

"Okay," Abe said reasonably. "Show me."

Betsy had studied the photograph, waiting for the image to disappear, but there he was still, all these days later, the boy in the black coat. At the top edges of the print, flashes of light had been recorded. These weren't errors in the developing process, which usually showed up in blotches of white, but a distinct illumination hovering below the ceiling of the room, as though a field of energy had been trapped inside. Betsy had always yearned to go beyond the obvious and reveal what others might not see. Now she had done exactly that, for what she believed she'd handed over was a portrait of a ghost.

"There was a mix-up with the film," Abe quickly decided. "Some old photograph already on the film was overlaid on top of the one you took in his room. That would explain it, wouldn't it?"

"You mean a double exposure?"

"That's what it is." She had him going for a minute there. He'd actually felt the cold hand that people say reaches out when the border between this world and the next splits apart. "It's just a mistake."

"There's only one problem with that theory. The water. He's drenched. How do you explain that?"

They both stared at the photograph. Streams of water ran down Gus's face, as if he'd risen from the river, as if he'd been held down too long and had already turned blue. There were the weeds threaded through his hair, and his clothes were so sopping that a puddle of water had collected on the floorboards at his feet.

"Do you mind if I keep this for a while?"

When Betsy agreed, Abe placed the photograph in his jacket pocket. It was his imagination, of course, but it was almost as though he could feel the damp outline of the image against his ribs. "That girl who was in Gus's room before you took the photographs, I thought I might talk to her."

"Carlin." Betsy nodded. "She's usually at the pool. I think she was Gus's only friend."

"Sometimes one is enough." Abe paid for their coffees. "If it's the right person."

They went out into the sunlight where a few bees rumbled around the white chrysanthemums Pete's wife, Eileen, had set in an earthenware pot in front of the store. Across the street was Rita Eamon's ballet school, where Joey's daughter Emily took lessons, as well as Zeke Harris's dry-cleaning shop, established more than forty years earlier. Abe knew every shop owner and every street corner, just as he knew that anyone born and raised in this village who was foolish enough to get involved with someone from the Haddan School deserved whatever consequences he received.

"We could have dinner sometime," Abe suggested. Immediately, he rethought the invitation, which sounded too serious and too formal. "No big deal," he amended. "Just some food on a plate."

Betsy laughed, but her expression was cloudy. "Actually, I don't think we should see each other again."

Well, he'd gone and done it, made a complete idiot of himself. He noticed that one of those damned swans from the school was traipsing along the sidewalk across the street, hissing at Nikki Humphrey, who had been on her way over to the 5&10 Cent Bank to make a deposit, but had become too alarmed to proceed.

"I'm getting married," Betsy went on to explain. She was smart enough to know that not everything a person might want was necessarily good for her. What if she were to sit down with a dozen chocolate bars and devour each one? What if she drank red wine until she swooned? "June seventeenth. The Willow Room at the inn."

Across the street, Nikki Humphrey was waving her hands around, trying her best to shoo away the swan. Abe should have gone over to help her out, but he remained in the doorway of the pharmacy. Plenty of people arranged weddings, but not every one went off exactly as planned.

"I'm not asking to be invited to the reception," he commented.

"Good." Betsy laughed. "You won't be."

She must be insane to be standing out here with him; she'd be better off anywhere else. But even on a beautiful day, it was impossible to predict behavior, human or otherwise. The swan across the street, for instance, provoked by the crowds and the heat, was going wild. It had scared Nikki Humphrey off the sidewalk and into the Lucky Day flower shop and was now crossing Main Street against the green light. Several cars screeched to a halt. People who couldn't see the swan leaned on their horns, wishing an official was present to direct traffic. Abe should have sorted out the mess himself—someone could get hurt with that swan flapping around in the middle of the street—yet he stayed where he was.

"You could invite me to something else," he said, as if he were a man who asked for rejection on a regular basis. "Anything other than a wedding, and I'll be there."

Betsy was unable to gauge whether or not he truly meant this declaration. She was staring at the swan, which had stopped in the middle of the road, plucking at its feathers and causing a tie-up of cars that reached all the way to Deacon Road.

"I'll think it over," she said, lightly. "I'll let you know."

"Do that," Abe said when she walked away. "Good to see you," he called, as if they were merely two people who had cordially exchanged recipes or household tips, suggesting vinegar for sunburn, perhaps, or olive oil for damaged woodwork.

Mike Randall, the president of the 5&10 Cent Bank, had come out to the street in his shirtsleeves, his suit jacket in hand. He went right up to the swan and shook his coat as though it were a matador's cape until at last the stubborn bird took flight, hissing as it rose into the air, and still sputtering angrily when it landed on the walkway in front of Mrs. Jeremy's house.

"Hey," Mike called to Abe when he caught sight of him, all moony and distracted in front of the pharmacy, standing in a square of sunlight and blinking his eyes like a lovesick boy. "What were you waiting for? A head-on collision?"

It was more like a train wreck, actually, the kind Abe had seen back when he was a kid and the train into Boston jumped the rails. For weeks afterward bits of clothing and shoes without soles could be found along the tracks. Abe had accompanied his grandfather to help search for personal items, such as wallets and keys. The accident was unavoidable and unstoppable; it had taken people unawares, so that they were tying their shoes or catching a catnap, completely unprepared for what was to come.

Late in the day, when the sky was turning inky and the last of the geese flew above Haddan traveling south, Abe drove over to the school and parked in the lot closest to the river. By then, the weather had begun to change, as everyone knew it would. Before long, all traces of the heat wave would be gone. Abe went around a mud puddle that would freeze solid by morning. He knew his way to the gym; local kids had always been envious of the basketball court and especially coveted the indoor pool. One night, when they were seniors in high school, Abe and Joey and Teddy Humphrey, along with half a dozen other guys they hung out with, spent an evening getting loaded, thinking of new ways to stir up trouble. Somehow, they'd chosen the Haddan pool as their target. They'd walked in during swim practice as though they owned the place, drunk on beer and fury, brimming with the sort of courage numbers can bring. They'd stripped off their clothes and dived right in, shouting and cursing, having a grand old time, naked as the day they were born.

The Haddan students who'd been swimming laps got out as fast as they could. Abe still recalled the look on one girl's face, the contempt in her glare. They were pigs to her, nothing more, morons who were easily amused by their own stupid stunts and would never amount to anything. One guy, Abe could no longer remember who, got up on the ladder and peed into the deep end, then was wildly applauded for his efforts. It was then Abe found himself agreeing with the girl who had considered them so disgusting.

He was the first to get out of the pool; he pulled his jeans and T-shirt over his wet body, and it was lucky for them all that he did, for someone had phoned the police and Abe was the one who heard the sirens. He alerted his friends and they hightailed it out of the gym before Ernest could walk in and blame Abe for everything, the way he always did back then.

This evening, Abe was well within his rights as an officer to come looking for Carlin at the pool, yet he felt the same trepidation he had all those years ago. He went along the tiled corridor until he reached the glass partition through which it was possible to peer down at the swimmers. The girls on the team all wore black bathing suits and caps, but he could pick Carlin out right away. It was her attitude that distinguished her from the others. She was a strong swimmer, clearly the best on the team; she had talent, but most likely it was ambition that drove her, for when other girls got out of the pool, Carlin kept on, exerting herself in a way the others did not.

The rest of her teammates were already showered and dressed by the time Carlin dragged herself out of the pool. She sat on the ledge and pulled off her goggles; her black bathing cap made her head look as sleek as a seal's. She swung her legs back and forth in the water and closed her burning eyes; her heart was pounding from exertion, her arms ached.

When she heard someone rap on the glass, Carlin looked up, expecting to see Harry, but instead, she spied Abel Grey. Carlin should have been upset to have a cop come looking for her, but actually she was relieved. Being with Harry had been difficult lately; whenever they were together, she had to hide a piece of herself: all her sorrow, all her grief. She had stopped going to the dining hall at mealtimes, in part because she had no interest in food, but also as a way to avoid Harry. Unfortunately, he still expected Carlin to be exactly as she was when he first saw her on the library steps, but she wasn't that girl anymore. Now, she was the friend left behind, the one who couldn't stop wondering what it might be like to see light filtering deep underwater, to breathe in water lilies and stones rather than air.

"Harry was looking for you," Amy would inevitably say when Carlin came in at night from walking the paths Gus had taken, along the lanes and through the alleyways. "I don't know why you treat him the way you do."

Often, when Harry phoned or came calling, Carlin would have Amy tell him she was asleep or suffering from a migraine. "You're very peculiar," Amy marveled at such times. "Which is probably why he wants you. He grew up with girls like me."

It was too much work to be with Harry, to pretend life was made up of fun and games, when it was sorrow and river water Carlin was thinking of. At least she could be herself with this cop, as cold and as distant as she wished to be.

"What do you want?" she called to Abe, her voice echoing off the tiled walls.

Abe made a talking motion with his hand as though he were throwing a shadow puppet onto the tiles.

Carlin pointed to the door. "Meet me out front."

She went to the locker room, toweled dry, then dressed without bothering to shower. She found Abe outside, waiting beside Dr. Howe's statue. It was four-thirty but the sky was already darkening, except for the farthest horizon where there was still one delirious band of blue. The weather had returned to the usual chill of November, cold enough for ice crystals to form in Carlin's wet hair. It was foolish, she knew, but in the very back of her mind, she hoped this cop had searched her out to inform her that a mistake had been made and that Gus had been found. That's what Carlin wanted to hear: it was some other ill-fated boy who had fallen in the river and drowned.

Abe patted Dr. Howe's statue on the foot. Luck in love, he'd heard, came from doing so, although he'd never put much stock in such tales. "What a creep this guy was," Abe said of the illustrious headmaster. "A real fuddy-duddy."

"Supposedly, he screwed everything he could get his hands on." The cold center that had been growing inside Carlin ever since Gus's death was rattling around in her chest. "Didn't you know? He was a womanizer."

"Dr. Howe? I thought he was a bookworm."

"Bookworms have sex. It's just lousy." Or at least this was true for Harry, who had gotten more and more selfish, until it seemed he didn't really care who he was with, as long as she was a living, breathing girl who did as she was told.

Carlin took out her cigarettes, suggesting to Abe that they walk behind the gym, so she could smoke. As he followed her, Abe recognized her coat as the same one the dead boy had been wearing when they found him.

"Smoking will slow down your swimming." In spite of Carlin's bad temper, Abe pitied her. She looked so lost inside that big coat; you couldn't even see her hands.

"Gee whiz." Carlin lit up, that cold kernel throbbing right beside her heart. "No one ever told me that before."

"Fine. If that's the way you want it, go on. Don't give a shit. You've got my permission."

In spite of Gus's heavy black coat, Carlin was shivering. "Is that what you wanted to talk to me about? My smoking?"

She was shaky, either from the exertion of swimming or because she hadn't eaten since breakfast. She simply couldn't stop feeling bad no matter how hard she tried. Every now and then she sneaked into the bathroom and took the straight razor to her arm. This cold thing inside her had taken root and changed her into a foul little girl whose hair was turning green at the edges and who wanted to hurt someone, most of all herself.

"I came to talk to you because I'm trying to figure out what happened to your friend."

Carlin let out a short, harsh laugh, then quickly covered her mouth with her hand.

"Is that funny? Did I miss something?"

Carlin blinked back tears. "He's been contacting me. Gus or his spirit, or whatever. I know it sounds stupid. I don't even believe in any of it. It's crazy, right?"

She looked so desperate then, with her pale hair and her even paler face, that Abe couldn't bring himself to tell her about the photograph in his pocket for fear she'd be even more disturbed. He couldn't tell her how many times his own brother had spoken to him; night after night, he had heard his brother's voice, and what's more, he had wanted to. Even now there were times when he said Frank's name aloud in the dark, still hoping for an answer.

"He keeps leaving me things." Carlin punctuated her words with puffs of smoke. "Stones. Water lilies. Sand. I find fish all the time, little silver ones. And that's not all. I can hear him when it's quiet. It sounds like water, but I know it's him."

Abe waited politely as Carlin wiped her eyes with the back of her hands, then lit another cigarette from the one that had already burned down to ash. Watching her, Abe was grateful he was no longer young.

"Maybe he's leaving you things and maybe he isn't, but what I'm interested in is how he died," Abe told the girl when she'd composed herself. "I just have this need to be convinced, and when it comes to Gus, I'm not convinced of anything. Too many questions, not enough answers. So maybe you can answer something for me. Did he talk about suicide?"

"Never," Carlin said. "I already told Mr. Pierce, Gus would have left me a note. Even if it was just to make me feel worse, he would have written something down."

Of course, Abe knew that not everyone discussed such plans. You could live with someone in the very next room and have no idea what he might be capable of. As for Carlin, she appreciated the fact that Abe hadn't tried to comfort her the way most people would have. He was honest, and his doubts matched her own. He took a notepad from his pocket and jotted down his phone number.

"Call me if you hear anything about your friend. If he ate corned beef hash on the night when he died, I want to know. Any detail, no matter how unimportant it seems, I'd like to hear about it. These things can add up when you put them all together. You'd be surprised."

"Okay." Carlin had discovered that she didn't feel quite as vicious anymore. Her wet hair was freezing into disorderly strands and the black coat coiled around her legs as she walked with Abe across campus.

When St. Anne's came into view, Abe could see what was surely Betsy Chase's window. In all probability, Betsy had not thought to lock her windows, not here in Haddan, where the nights were so safe. For an instant, Abe thought he saw her, but it was only Miss Davis out on the porch, trying to fill her bird feeder with seed.

"I'd better go," Carlin said. "I work for her."

In the settling darkness, the thicket of quince beside Miss Davis's door trembled as the nesting finches fluttered with anticipation. Abe could tell that Helen Davis was ill; it wasn't her age that gave her away, but how carefully she lifted each handful of seed, as if such things were too heavy for flesh and blood to manage.

"Sorry I'm late," Carlin called. She would hardly have time to fix the cheese pudding and fruit salad she'd intended to serve; Miss Davis would have to make do with sliced cantaloupe and cottage cheese.

Helen peered through the darkness. "Of course you're late if you're spending all your time wandering around with strange men." She may have been speaking to Carlin, but it was Abe she was staring at.

"He's with the police," Carlin informed Helen Davis as she went inside to get supper on the table. "I was safe the whole time."

Right away, Abe noticed there were no locks on Miss Davis's windows. He went to appraise her door. Exactly as he thought, one of those useless hook and eyes any six-year-old could get past. "Your security is practically nonexistent."

"Are you always such a worrywart?" Helen Davis was intrigued. Ridiculous, but she was actually quite breathless in this man's presence.

"No, ma'am," Abe said. "I was the guy breaking in."

"Were you?" Helen tilted her head, the better to see him through the shadows. "You don't have to worry about me. No one would dare bother me. I've scared everyone off." Helen had finished with the bird feeder, she should have gone in and had her supper, but she could not remember when such a handsome man had appeared on her back porch.

Abe laughed at Miss Davis's remarks. He liked to be surprised by people and Helen Davis had surprised him. He'd expected some snooty sourpuss, but clearly he'd been wrong.

"If anyone broke in, they'd get nothing for their efforts," Helen assured Abe.

Beyond the thicket of quince, a motionless creature lay in wait below the bird feeder.

"What do you know." Abe whistled, then turned back to Helen. "There's my cat."

"That's Midnight," Helen corrected him. "My cat."

"It looks a hell of a lot like mine. Hey you," Abe called.

The cat turned to him disdainfully and glared. A nasty disposition and one yellow eye. No mistake about it.

"Yep," Abe said. "That's my cat."

"I can see how he recognizes you. He's practically jumping for joy. He is a he, for your information."

The cat had begun to wash its paws, exactly as it did every day upon arriving home. "He lives with me," Abe insisted. "Sheds all over my furniture."

"Highly doubtful. I've had him for twelve years. I think I know my own cat."

It had been a very long time since Helen had noticed how

blue a man's eyes were, but she noticed now. Talking to a stranger on her back porch went against her nature, but she had done all manner of strange things since she'd learned she was ill. Since that time, she had melted somehow. Things she had hitherto ignored she now felt hugely; time and again, she was engulfed in waves of emotion. When she walked onto her back porch, the scent of grass could make her weep. She could see a handsome man like Abel Grey and be overwhelmed by longing. The sting of cold air was delicious. The appearance of the first star in the eastern corner of the sky was just cause for celebration. Tonight, for instance, she had observed the three bright stars of Orion rising as daylight was fading. She'd never in her life noticed such occurrences before.

The heat wave was through, the temperature was dropping, and although Helen should have been concerned about her own poor constitution, it was Midnight she worried about on nights like this. Abel Grey was also eyeing her pet with concern, as though he had equal rights to worry and fuss.

"My cat," Helen reminded him. "And I've got the vet bills to prove it. When he lost that eye the doctor said he'd had a fight with another cat, but I think it was done with malice. Whenever he sees a teenaged boy he runs, so what does that tell you?"

"That he's highly intelligent?"

Helen laughed, delighted. "Malice. Believe you me."

"There is a lot of that in the world."

There was still a stretch of blue in the dark sky and the lights around the quad had switched on to form a circle of yellow globes, like fireflies in the dark.

"Think what you'd like," Helen said, as they said good night, "but he's not your cat."

"Fine," Abe conceded as he set out for his parked car. He waved as he crossed the green. "You tell him."

WHEN FRIDAY CAME AROUND AND THE WEEK-end stretched out ahead without plans or responsibilities, Abe was not among those who headed to the Millstone to get hammered in order to forget that Monday was only two days away. He wasn't fit company, that much was obvious, and even Russell Carter, the mildest among their group of friends, had noted Abe's bad temper when they'd gotten together to play basketball at the elementary school gym the previous night.

"I don't know." Russell had shaken his head. Abe was cursing every missed layup. "You're not yourself tonight, Abe."

"Yeah, well, who am I?"

"Maybe you're Teddy Humphrey, man of a thousand altercations. No offense," Russell had added.

Whoever he was, Abe had stopped off at the mini-mart attached to the gas station after work on Friday, where he bought a six-pack of Samuel Adams beer. His plan was to study the autopsy report on the Pierce kid, then go out and get some dinner. He was alive and well, happy enough to have a free evening with one beer started and five more waiting, but the more he looked over the report, the more the details troubled him. The contusions on the boy's forehead and along his back had been assessed as injuries incurred while traveling with the river's current. His health had been excellent, although his toxicology report had been positive for THC, noting that he had smoked marijuana within forty-eight hours of his death.

There was a sense of certainty to such official reports that irked Abe; facts always gave him pause, as so much depended on who the fact finder was and what his point of view happened to be. One detail in particular bothered him all the way through his second beer, so much so that he took the rest of the six-pack into the kitchen and telephoned his father down in Florida. Ernest Grey knew the Haddan River as well as anyone, he was the sort of man whose friends liked to joke would one day have to be surgically separated from his fly rod. In Florida he had bought himself a boat, much to Abe's mother's dismay, and had begun fishing for marlin. Still, there was no substitute for trout and Ernest continued to miss the Haddan River. One year, when he wasn't much more than a boy, Ernest had reeled in the biggest silver trout ever recorded in the county, a catch that had been mounted and was still displayed in town hall, right over the doorway that leads into traffic court.

Abe first spoke with his mother, Margaret, always the far easier task, for when his father took the receiver there was inevitably an uncomfortable silence between them. But the strained tenor of the conversation changed as soon as Abe mentioned that a boy from the Haddan School had drowned.

"That's a terrible situation," Ernest said.

"What bothers me most is that they found fecal matter in the lungs."

"Are you saying it's human waste?" Ernest was really interested now.

"Human as can be."

Abe started in on his third beer. He felt he was entitled to that at least; it was Friday and he was alone. Soon enough, the cat would arrive at the back door, clawing at the screen, happy as hell to be home, in spite of what Helen Davis believed.

"What that autopsy's telling you is impossible," Ernest said with complete certainty. "You won't find anything like that in the Haddan. We had an environmental study done back when the trout stopped running. That was when the town passed the strictest sewage laws in the Commonwealth." Neither man mentioned what else had happened that year, how their lives fell apart for reasons they still didn't understand, how the universe had exploded right under their roof. "A couple of folks over on Main Street had to install completely new septic systems," Ernest went on. "Cost a fortune and they weren't too happy about it. Paul Jeremy was on his last legs then and he raised holy hell, but we went ahead with it for the sake of the river and it's been running clean ever since. So don't tell me there's human shit in the Haddan, because there's not."

Abe thought this information over, then he called Joey, asking him to meet him at the pharmacy, pronto.

"This better be good," Joey said when he got there. He ordered coffee and two jelly doughnuts without bothering to take off his coat. He didn't have time to make himself comfortable; he wasn't staying. "Mary Beth and I were supposed to spend a little quality time together once the kids were in bed. She's so pissed at me for never being home that I'm not even allowed in the doghouse anymore."

The dog was a little terrier Joey hated, a present for Emily's last birthday, and it lived, not in the yard or in a doghouse, but on Joey's favorite chair.

"What if something was wrong with the autopsy report?" Abe said, his voice low.

"Such as?"

"What if he hadn't drowned in the Haddan River?"

"You just need one thing to convince me," Joey said. "Proof."

"I don't quite have that, yet."

"What do you have, buddy? Nothing?"

Abe placed the photograph of Gus on the counter.

"What's this supposed to be?" Joey asked.

"I don't know. A ghost?"

Joey laughed so hard they could hear him over in the notions aisle. "Yeah, right." He slid the photo back across the counter. "And I'm the reincarnation of John F. Kennedy." He bit into a jelly doughnut. "Junior."

"Okay. What do you think it is?"

"I think it's a damn bad photograph. I think you'd better hope that gal over at the school you've got your eye on is better in bed than she is with a camera."

"Maybe the image on that photograph is caused by a field of energy left behind by the deceased." Abe was refusing to let this go. He remembered old-timers down at the station insisting that murdered men could get stuck somewhere between this world and the next. They were probably just trying to scare Abe when they told him that whenever the wind came up it was one of these dead men, rattling at the doors, stranded here among the living.

"You're kidding, right?" Joey said. "Tell me you don't believe in this crap."

"You don't seem to have a better explanation."

"That's because there is none, Abe. You want to believe that someone who dies lives on in some way, I understand that—hell, I've lost people, too. But if you want to convince me of something, give me proof. Something I can see, touch, feel. Not ghosts."

Joey had had the very same reaction back in the old days when Abe told him he heard Frank's voice. As soon as he had seen the look on Joey's face, Abe had known he'd better shut up. He was feeling that same way now.

Joey still had time to stop at the mini-mart, pick up a bottle of wine, and try to get back in Mary Beth's good graces, so he said his good-byes, leaving Abe to get the tab. After he'd gone, Abe had another cup of coffee, while Pete Byers looked in the back room for one of the sterilized jars that customers used to bring urine samples to the health center in Hamilton. Abe had had too much to drink and now his head was aching. That pounding in his skull, however, didn't stop him from setting off once he had the glass jar from Pete. It was a blustery night, with fast-moving clouds illuminated by moonlight. On nights like this Frank could never sit still. People said he was restless, he had too much energy, but in recent years Abe had wondered if it might have been something more: a fear of the dark, and of himself, and whatever it was that was going on inside his head. When they were kids playing hide-and-seek, Frank had always carried a flashlight and he never ventured far into the woods. Once, Abe had come upon his brother in the backyard, looking up at the thousands of stars in the sky as though he were already lost among them, without any hope of finding his way back home. Never had Abe seen such loneliness, even though Frank was only steps from their own back door.

Thinking about such matters almost caused Abe to miss the first side street that would lead him to the river road. He parked on a sandy embankment, then walked along until he passed onto Haddan School property, even though he knew Glen and Joey never would have approved. He wanted a spot close to where

Gus might have first made contact with the river, and therefore made his way to the reedy area nearest Chalk House. Abe didn't feel like a trespasser; no sweaty hands, no butterflies in the gut. He had spent more time on this river than most men spent in their own living rooms, and could still recall a canoe trip with his father and grandfather at a time when he hadn't been more than three or four. There had been bowers of green leaves overhead and the slapping sound of water as they moved downstream. Whenever he had tried to speak, the men hushed him, warning that he'd scare the fish away. They were out on the river so long that day, Abe fell asleep in the bottom of the boat and awoke with dozens of mosquito bites. No one would believe him afterward when he swore he'd heard the fish swimming below them as he slept.

Abe had come to the old flat rock he and Joey used for diving in summers past, sneaking here whenever school wasn't in session and there was no one who might catch them on private property and call their parents to complain. There were more reeds than Abe recalled, and thickets of thorn bushes grabbed at his pant legs. Nonetheless, he went out onto the rock; his boots got wet and he knelt down and before long his jeans were soaked. He scooped water into the sterile jar, then closed it tightly, returning the jar to his jacket pocket.

By now, the night was so chilly Abe could see his breath in the air. Soon, a film of ice would form in the shallows, a layer so thin it might remain invisible unless stones were thrown. Since Abe had already come this far, he kept on, past the boathouse. Funny how people can keep things from themselves, but he truly didn't know where he was bound until he was standing outside St. Anne's. The hedges were rustling in the wind, and the thin, moonlit clouds raced by up above. He could see Betsy clearly through the window. She wore a cotton robe and her hair was wet from the shower; she sat in a frayed upholstered chair, her bare legs curled up beneath her, as she looked over her students' portfolios. A lamp inside the room cast a faint light so that looking inside was like peering into an Easter egg in which a scene had been designed, there for anyone to hold in his hand and view whenever he pleased.

Watching her this way, Abe felt completely reckless, exactly as he had all those years ago when he was robbing houses. Once more he was the victim of desire and circumstance. He could hear the sound of girls' voices from inside the dorm; he could smell the river, a pungent mixture of mold and decay. He moved a vine that blocked his vision. The difference between now and then was that now he was a grown man who made his own decisions, not a boy breaking into the headmaster's house. No one forced him to remain outside Betsy's window; there was no lock and key. A rational man would have turned and run, but this night had nothing to do with reason. Whenever Abe made an arrest he always tried to figure out the offender's motives. *What were you thinking, man?* he'd said time and time again as he waited for the ambulance with some teenaged boy who'd crashed his father's car, or as he drove to the jail in Hamilton with men who had slapped their wives around once too often or too hard. Most recently, he'd confronted a couple of kids who'd been caught stealing cartons of cigarettes from the mini-mart. *What were you thinking?* he'd asked as he peered into their backpacks. The boys had been terrified and they hadn't answered, but here at last was Abe's answer: they weren't thinking at all. One minute they were standing in the dark with no intention of doing anything out of the ordinary, and the next they were acting on instinct, barreling ahead with no thought in their heads other than *I want* or *I need* or *I've got to have it now.*

It was always possible to go back and consider the path not taken; in retrospect, bad decisions and mistakes leapt out so that even the most irrational individual would eventually see the failure of his ways. Later, Abe would wonder if he'd have been so irresponsible if he hadn't started in on that six-pack so early in the day, or if he hadn't stopped at the pharmacy, or if he'd held off going to the river to collect water. One alteration of his conduct might have prevented all the rest, a road strewn with poor choices that had led him to her window and kept him there now.

He thought about the boy who had died, gone so early he would never spy on a woman like this, all tied up in knots, caught up by his own appetites. Gazing into the yellow light, searching Betsy's beautiful, tired face, Abe could feel his own hunger; it was bitter and he hated himself for it, but it couldn't be denied. If he stayed any longer he might circle around to the rear of the building in order to watch her get ready for bed, and then who would he be? The sort of man he'd dealt with a hundred times before, whether it was at the scene of traffic accidents or in the parking lot of the Millstone, a man who was already out of control.

As he forced himself to turn away, Abe thought about all the times he hadn't cared; the girls in school he had kissed so thoughtlessly, the women he'd gone swimming with in the river on hot summer nights. There'd been far too many of them; why, there'd even been something with Mary Beth one New Year's Eve when they'd both had too much to drink, a heated, overwrought incident they both politely chose to forget. He had not cared about a single one of these women, an accomplishment for a man as wary as Abe, something of which he'd been proud, as if he'd won a point of honor by not loving anyone. And so it came as a great surprise to find he could want someone as much as he wanted Betsy. He had thought he could walk through life without any pain; he'd thought solitude would comfort him and keep him safe all the rest of his days, but he was wrong. His grandfather always told him that love never arrived politely, knocking on the front door like a kindhearted neighbor, asking to be let in. Instead, it ambushed a man when he least expected it, when his defenses were down, and even the most obstinate individual, no matter how bullheaded or faithless, had no choice but to surrender when love like this came to call.

THE VEILED WOMAN

AT THE END OF THE MONTH, A
cold rain began to fall at a steady pace, hour
after hour, until its rhythm was all anyone
could hear. This was no ordinary rain, for
the rainfall was black, a rain of algae, an
odd phenomenon some of the older residents in town recalled from the time when
they were children. Mrs. Evans and Mrs.
Jeremy, for instance, had played out in a
black rain when they were girls and were
rightfully punished by their mothers when
they flounced home in wet, sooty dresses.
Now, the two neighbors stood beneath the
shelter of their front porches and called to
each other, noting how lucky they were that
it wasn't spring, when their gardens would
be ruined by this strange substance, the

hollyhocks and delphiniums slick with black gunk, the leaves turned dark as coal.

People donned raincoats and hats and ran from their cars into houses or stores. Rugs were set out by back doors, but despite any precautions, black footprints were tracked across floorboards and carpets; dozens of umbrellas were ruined and had to be tossed out with the trash. At the Haddan School, the features of Dr. Howe's statue turned moody and dark, and those who approached him walked on quickly, their feet slap-dashing through puddles that seemed to be made out of ink. Betsy Chase may have been the only one in town who used the black rain to her advantage; she decided to send her students out to photograph the village in the midst of these strange circumstances. Although most of the prints that were later developed were nothing more than murky splotches, there were a few memorable images, including Pete Byers sweeping black rain off the sidewalk, Duck Johnson shirtless and grim as he hosed off canoes at the boathouse, and two black swans, hiding beneath a wooden bench.

When the rain finally stopped, the gutters flowed with algae and the town stank of mildew and fish. There was some flooding in the usual places: the hollow around town hall, the backyards of those who lived closest to the railroad tracks, the dank cellar of Chalk House. A hydraulic pump was brought in and while people fussed about how to best siphon out the muck that had collected in the basement at Chalk House and worried about what the next serious storm's effect would be on the structural integrity of the building, Betsy took the opportunity to go up-stairs to the attic, to Gus Pierce's room, empty now, save for the desk and the bed. The windowpanes were splattered with black algae and only a faint, fish-colored light streaked through. Rain had seeped beneath the window, darkly staining the sash. In spite of the dim lighting, Betsy shot a roll of film, recording every angle of the room.

Once in the darkroom, Betsy was prepared for any oddities that might surface, but the film yielded only ceilings and doors, white walls and the single bed, unmade and unremarkable. That evening, when she met Eric for supper, Betsy was still wondering what she had done differently with that first roll of film. She found herself disappointed that another image had not appeared.

"Do you ever think about what comes after?" she asked Eric at dinner. Because of the season, the kitchen was serving turkey soup and potato-leek pie. The dining hall had been decorated with pilgrims' hats, which swung from the ceiling on strings.

"Chair of the department," Eric said without hesitation. "Eventually a university position."

"I meant after death." Betsy stirred her soup. Bits of carrot and rice rose to the surface of the cloudy broth.

"Luckily, we can both be buried in the Haddan School cemetery."

Betsy thought this over, then pushed her bowl away.

"How did you know I was the right person for you?" she asked suddenly. "What made you so sure?"

Before Eric could answer, Duck Johnson ambled over to join them, his tray loaded down. "Are you going to eat your fruitcake?" he asked, always hungry for more.

"Guess who was invited to Bob Thomas's for Thanksgiving?" Eric announced as he passed on his portion of dessert.

"Congratulations." Duck nodded cheerfully. "Atta boy."

Only the chair of each department was invited to the dean's

dinner; this year, when Helen Davis declined, Eric had stepped up to take her place. This arrangement, however, was news to Betsy, who had been planning a trip to Maine over the long holiday weekend. It would be good to escape, not just from the school, but from any possibility of running into Abel Grey as she went about her errands in the village.

"We can go to Maine anytime," Eric assured her.

Betsy wished she wasn't reminded of Helen Davis's warning. Nonetheless, who didn't have doubts every now and then? Every couple needn't always agree or spend every moment in a delirium of happiness. Look at Carlin Leander, who should have been pleased that Harry McKenna was so enamored of her. The other girls at St. Anne's followed him across campus like a flock of trained birds, but Carlin had begun to avoid him. She could feel Gus's disapproval whenever she was with Harry and in time she began to notice the traits Gus had warned her about: the smile that could be turned on and off at will, the selfishness, the certainty that his own needs were at the very center of the universe. She pulled farther and farther away from Harry. If he brought her chocolates, she said she could not stomach sweets. If he came to call, she sent one of her roommates to inform him she was already in bed, far too tired or sick to see anyone at all.

Harry, always so accustomed to getting whatever he wanted, only wanted her more when she withdrew.

"He's worried about you," Amy Elliot told Carlin, for Harry had begun to confide in Amy, a good listener when it served her purposes. Amy had a little girl's voice that belied her determination to get what she wanted, which in this case was Harry. Since Carlin already had him, Amy had begun to take on her roommate's style, in the hopes that some of Carlin's luck would rub off. She wore a silver clip in her hair, and her brand-new black woolen coat echoed the lines of Gus's old coat. "What's wrong?" Amy asked. "Because if you don't want Harry anymore, believe me, there are plenty of us who do."

Girls like Amy believed they'd be granted whatever they wanted, if they only crossed their fingers or wished upon stars, but Carlin knew better. She carried her grief with her; she couldn't let it go. Betsy noticed this phenomenon when she photographed the swim team for the alumni newsletter. As she developed that particular photograph, Betsy began to wish Abel Grey were beside her, so he might see for himself what had begun to appear in the tray of developing fluid. If anything, love was like light, illuminating what no one would have ever guessed was there in the darkness. Carlin Leander was at the far end of a line of smiling girls, her grim expression separating her from the group. Her arms were crossed and a frown tilted her mouth downward, but even though she stood apart from the others, Carlin wasn't alone. He was right there beside her, leaning up against the cold, blue tiles, made out of equal parts liquid and air, a fish out of water, a boy with no earthly form, drowned both in this life and the next.

WHEN MATT FARRIS FAXED OVER THE REPORT from the lab the results were exactly as Abe's father had predicted. The water was clean and clear, with only trace amounts of fish eggs and algae, nothing more.

"Don't bother me," Joey said when Abe approached him with the report. "I'm writing up our monthly expenses."

Abe stood there, shirttail out, with an expression that might lead a person to believe he'd never heard of monthly expenses before. Ever since the night he'd looked through Betsy Chase's window, he had been preoccupied and more than a little confused. He'd forgotten to take out the trash so often it was piling up in his back hall; he hadn't once checked his mail, so that stray bills and circulars had begun to overflow from the delivery box beside his door. This morning, he had mistakenly taken one of his grandfather's old suits from the back of the closet. Once having settled the jacket onto his lanky frame, he was surprised to find that it fit. He hadn't thought he was as tall as his grandfather, but it turned out that he was, and because he was late, he'd worn the suit to work.

"Nice suit," Joey noted. "It's just not you."

Abe placed the lab report atop the set of figures Joey was working on. Joey looked at the printout, then sat back in his chair.

"So?"

"So there's human excrement in the kid's lungs, but none in the Haddan River."

"I repeat." Joey gulped down some cold coffee and shivered at the bitter taste. "So?"

"Does it make sense to you?"

"Not any more than the fact that I have to work as a security guard all weekend to bankroll a trip to Disney World. Nothing makes sense to me. Why should this? It doesn't mean a thing."

"You asked for proof. Here it is. He didn't drown in the Haddan."

Joey was looking at his old friend as though he were a crazy man, and maybe he was. Certainly, everything Abe had done in the past week would back up that assessment.

"You know why you think that? It's all because you haven't gotten laid in a really long time and you have nothing else to do with your mind other than come up with these preposterous scenarios based on nothing." Joey tossed the report back to him. "Let it go."

Abe wished he could simply file the lab report and stay out of affairs that weren't his business, but that wasn't the sort of man he was. At a little before noon, he went in to speak to Glen Tiles. It was bad timing on Abe's part. Glen had high blood pressure and his wife was starving him with his best interests at heart; set out on his desk were a container of cottage cheese and a lone apple. Abe should have known that mealtime wasn't the best hour to approach the chief, but he did so anyway. Glen surveyed the lab report, then gazed at Abe. "You want me to read about shit while I'm having lunch?"

"I want you to read about the lack of shit."

Abe sat across from Glen, watching him read. When he was done, Glen handed the report back and immediately started in on his cottage cheese.

"I don't think the kid drowned in the Haddan River," Abe said.

"Yeah, Abe, maybe he was an alien. Did you ever think of that?" Glen ate like a famished man. "Or maybe this is all a dream. Maybe it's my dream and you're not really here at all, you're just a participant in my dream. Which means I could make you do anything I want to. I could make you stand on your head right now and cluck like a chicken if that's what I wanted to do."

"He could have been killed somewhere else, then thrown into the river," Abe persisted. "I've talked this over with Ernest. You know he'd be the last person to agree with me, but even he thinks something's not right."

"That doesn't surprise me. Your father has grasped at straws before." There was an awkward silence, and in the end, Glen had no option but to apologize. "Sorry," he said. "That was out of line."

"This isn't about Frank, you know. This is Gus Pierce, dead with shit in his lungs in a river that has been clean for more than twenty years. It's probably the cleanest water in the whole damned Commonwealth."

"You may not be satisfied, Abe, but the Haddan School is very happy with our investigation. In fact, they sent a letter commending us, and what's more, the alumni fund made a donation to the benevolent association. They think we did a good job and I agree. The kid drowned in the river. End of story."

Abe folded the report in half, stowing it in his jacket pocket, alongside the photo of the dead boy. "You're wrong on this one. You're wrong all the way around."

"Is that Wright's suit you're wearing?" Glen called when Abe was leaving. "Because, man, it's way too big for you."

Abe went over to the mini-mart, where he picked up some lunch, then he kept on driving. He didn't have to think when he rode around Haddan, he knew it so well he might as well have dreamed the town. He could eat a sandwich, think about sex and murder, and navigate the streets all at the same time. He went out to Route 17 to consider his options, heading to his grandfather's house on instinct. Along with Wright's suit, he'd found a thin, black tie in the back of his closet, which he realized was choking him; he loosened it and undid the top button of his shirt, breathing a little easier at last.

This was the section of Haddan that had changed the most since Abe was a boy. Nowadays there were houses where there had only been fields, and a Stop & Shop market where Halley's farm stand once sold yellow beans and cabbages. The rutted dirt road where Abe used to catch the bus to the high school had been paved, but at least the fields outside his grandfather's farm were still the same. The deed was in Abe's name and he couldn't bring himself to sell the place to any of the developers who routinely put their feelers out, tracking him down and offering continuously escalating sums. Once he got to the property, Abe pulled over to finish his lunch and watch the songbirds that flew so low across the meadow their wings grazed the tall grass. On this day, Abe felt he was alone in the world. He had lived in the village all his life, had grown up with Joey and Mary Beth and Teddy Humphrey and all the rest, yet there wasn't a single one among them whose counsel he cared to seek. He wished he could talk to his grandfather, that was the problem. A man could confide in Wright Grey. What you told him stayed put—he didn't like people who aired their personal affairs in public or complained about their fate—and he certainly knew how to listen.

Abe got out of the car and walked toward the field. The meadow grass, although brown, smelled sweet. The whole world seemed like a mystery to Abe at that moment, and he thought about all he hadn't yet done. Wanting Betsy had unleashed a hundred other possibilities, and now he was a man at the mercy of his own longing. It was cold and Abe wasn't wearing a coat; the wind blew right through his grandfather's suit and Abe could feel it on his skin just as sure as if he'd been naked. There was a fence separating the road from the field, but Abe climbed to the other side. The grass reached his waist here, still he lay down in it, flat on his back. He looked up at the clouds and the sky above him. He could hear the north wind here, but he couldn't feel it; it passed right over him. Abe felt lucky somehow, for the first time in a very long while. Nobody in the world knew where he was, but he was here in the grass thinking about love and how he had blundered into it, kind of late in life, and how grateful he was, how completely and utterly surprised.

It wasn't the season for love; the days were dark and nothing grew save for a few renegade cabbages left from the days when Haddan was still mostly farmland. Hingram's Shoe Shop already had a display of winter boots in its front window, and all along Main Street the gardens were bare, with burlap hoods covering the most delicate plants, the rhododendrons and pink azaleas that were so susceptible to frost. With the long holiday weekend stretching out, the village grew quiet. Most Haddan School students had gone home for Thanksgiving and only a few remained, including Carlin Leander, who had decided against going to Connecticut with Harry in order to have dinner with Helen Davis. As for Harry, he didn't like this choice one bit; he begged and he pleaded, but Carlin would not change her mind, and in the end Harry brought Amy Elliot and Robbie Shaw home for the holiday.

By Thursday morning, there was no traffic on Main Street and the shops had all closed down, except for the mini-mart, which stayed open until midnight. Ever since his divorce, Teddy Humphrey no longer celebrated holidays. Instead, he was a guardian angel of sorts, ready and waiting should anyone run out of vanilla, or butter, or eggnog, all of which were readily available at twice the usual price.

Abe wore Wright's suit to Thanksgiving dinner at Joey and Mary Beth's, in spite of the fact that he always got down on the floor to play with five-year-old Jackson and three-year-old Lilly, and usually wound up with clay or chalk in his hair. Mary Beth's whole family was there, her parents and her two brothers and a cousin from New Jersey, a pretty blonde, recently divorced, who Mary Beth had thought would be a perfect match for Abe.

"I'm not interested," Abe told MB as he helped her load platters with turkey and the cranberry-apple stuffing that was her Thanksgiving specialty.

"Come on. You're always interested," Mary Beth joked as she finished carving the turkey. When Abe didn't laugh or kid her back, she held the knife in the air and studied him. MB was pregnant again, but she looked the same as she had when they were in high school, with her dark hair pulled back into a ponytail and her face fresh, without any makeup. "You've already got someone," she declared.

"You're wrong about that, Miss Mind Reader," Abe told her.

When dinner was over, the finale of pumpkin pie and vanilla ice cream was perfectly timed to coincide with the kickoff of the third televised football game of the day. While seconds of dessert were being served, Joey asked Abe if he wanted to get some fresh air. Abe assumed they were going for a walk and he hadn't expected Joey to head for MB's old station wagon. He got in amiably, scooping stray potato chips and raisins from the passenger seat. Joey put the car in gear and turned onto Belvedere Street.

"We're going to buy beer," Abe guessed, wishing he had thought to bring some along to dinner, but they passed the minimart without pause, not stopping until they reached the Haddan School. They parked in the lot between the dean's house and the headmaster's house, now inhabited by old Dr. Jones, who had inherited the place from Dr. Howe in a long line of illustrious educators reaching back to Hosteous Moore. "Don't tell me we're robbing the headmaster's house again."

"You could put it that way." Joey left the car running and got out, leaving Abe to think things over. Mary Beth's heater was on the fritz and before long Abe's breath had fogged up the windshield. He turned off the ignition, then climbed out to stretch his legs. The trees were bare and there was a coating of ice on the path Joey had taken to the dean's back door. This area was reserved for faculty housing, cottages set out in a row for married staff and their families. Bob Thomas's was the first and the largest of these, a two-story Victorian with a double chimney and a wide back porch where the dean and Joey stood talking.

Bob Thomas was a big man who enjoyed his dinner; he'd come to the porch without the benefit of a coat or a hat, while inside his house the festivities went on without him. Abe ambled closer, positioning himself beside a boxwood hedge where nuthatches were roosting, beating their wings to keep from freezing. He could see through the dining room window; quite a crowd had gathered. The meal had been cleared away, but guests were still enjoying the rum-enhanced eggnog and mulled wine.

Abe couldn't help but see Betsy; she and some man were there together. Abe figured this was the fiancé, for certainly, Betsy's companion looked as if he'd stepped out of an alumni bulletin. Crouching beside the boxwood in his grandfather's old suit, in need of both a haircut and a shave, Abe felt himself burn with shame. What had he been thinking? If he knocked on the kitchen door, they'd surely slam it in his face. To be honest, he wished Betsy and her perfect fiancé a miserable holiday. He hoped they choked on the petit fours Meg Thomas was now serving, sweet concoctions of chocolate and marzipan that could easily stick in a person's throat.

Abe waited in the fading light for Joey, his ill temper rivaling the disposition of those miserable Haddan swans. Just his luck, the pair nesting close by seemed interested in him; one had already begun to advance across the frozen grass.

"Don't come near me," Abe warned the swan. "I'll cook you," he threatened. "I will."

At last, Joey finished speaking with the dean. When he returned, he was as jolly as Abe had ever seen him. Abe, on the other hand, felt his evil mood taking a turn for the worse. The sun was setting and crimson clouds fanned out across the hazy sky. That swan was still eyeing him and Abe knew from experience that these birds weren't afraid to attack. He had been on duty on one such occasion, when a big male swan had wandered onto Mrs. Jeremy's property. Her son, AJ, had tried to chase it off only to wind up with a dozen or more stitches in his forehead.

"None too soon," Abe said as Joey reached him.

Joey's color was good; he'd been invigorated by the cold air and the business he'd completed. He had an envelope in hand that he smacked against his open palm. "This will cheer you up."

All over Haddan, people were finished with dinner; as for Abe, he wouldn't be able to eat another thing for twenty-four hours. It wasn't only Mary Beth's menu that had done him in, it was the queasiness he'd begun to feel when he spied the envelope in Joey's grasp.

"The town's gotten plenty from the school, why shouldn't we get something back?" Joey said. "Hell, they treat us like we're their personal security department, they can damn well pay us for our services."

Abe truly did feel ill. He wasn't used to rich food and even richer rewards. He liked things simple and plain and within the limits of the law. "Don't show me what's in that envelope. Put it away, man, otherwise I'm going to have to go to Glen on this."

"You think he doesn't know?" Joey laughed when he saw the look on Abe's face. "Wake up, friend. This has been going on for years. Since before your father retired. These services went on right under his nose, and he never knew the first thing about it."

"What exactly are our services?"

"We don't go digging around where we don't belong, and that means when some Haddan kid kills himself, we let it be."

Joey got into the car and started it up. The idling station wagon sputtered and exhaust spiraled into the air. When Abe didn't move, Joey rolled down his window.

"Come on. You're not going to be self-righteous like your old man always was, are you? That's why Glen kept you out of this in the first place."

Abe decided he didn't need a ride, not now. It was better to walk off a big meal; the exercise would do him good. When he started off, Joey shouted out for him and honked the raspy horn, but Abe continued on across the frozen grass. He left the campus, then turned onto Main Street. There were vines of woodbine and bittersweet twisted along the black wrought-iron fences and a glossy hedge of holly that was over six feet tall in Mrs. Jeremy's garden. If today's circumstances had been different, Abe would have stopped by to make certain that AJ was safely passed out in bed, but this was one holiday when Mrs. Jeremy would have to take care of her own family business.

It had been a long while since Abe had been through the east side on foot, and he was as uncomfortable as he'd been back when he was a boy. The rattle of a trash can, the bark of a dog in someone's yard, the slightest bit of noise and he was ready to run.

There had always been divisions in Haddan, lines drawn between the haves and have-nots, and maybe some payment was long overdue. Who was Abe to judge Joey, or anyone else for that matter? He himself hadn't always been on his best behavior, but even when he was the one breaking the law he'd known the difference between right and wrong. He thought of his grandfather, who'd truly believed a man's highest calling was to serve his fellow citizens. Wright had plunged into the frozen river when most men would have been too concerned for their own welfare ever to have left the shore.

As Abe walked home, he felt he, too, was stranded on that shore, unable to commit to a leap, as if the black Haddan mud were quicksand, pulling him down. The queasiness he'd begun to feel was growing worse, just as it had back when Frank died. It was the sense that he hadn't really known his brother and that they'd all been living a lie that had been most disconcerting. Abe had always admired his brother, but had he ever understood him? The smartest boy who'd ever attended Hamilton High, who faithfully washed their father's car on Saturdays and stayed up all night studying, was the same person who walked up the stairs and shot himself on that hot August day when Sixth Commandment Pond was perfect for swimming. How could he have given it all away, that dusty, torpid afternoon when they could have been fishing in one of the secret places their grandfather had shown them, the rocky ledges that overhung the deep cool pools where the biggest trout could be found.

It was Frank who came down for breakfast every morning and Frank again who kept the shotgun under his mattress in the hours before his death, one and the same, just as Joey was not only the man who accepted a bribe, but the boy who stood beside Abe at Frank's memorial service. It was Joey who'd walked all the way to Wright's farm on days when it was so cold ice formed inside his gloves and he needed to stand in front of the oven to defrost himself. Once again, Abe had taken for granted that he was privy to all there was to know about a person, just as he knew the village itself, but as it turned out, he'd been wrong yet again. It was as if someone had taken all the streets in town and thrown them sky high, letting them fall wherever they might, in a jumble that was unrecognizable.

Abe crossed the railroad tracks, taking Forest Street for a while before turning onto Station as dusk began to fall, like a curtain of soot. It was an especially dark sky on this holiday evening and people cherished the pleasures and warmth of their homes. Abe could see his neighbors through their front windows. He passed by Pete Byers's place and Mike Randall's neat cottage, far too small for his five children, but well kept up, with a new porch and fresh paint. He saw Billy and Marie Bishop at their big oak table, surrounded by half a dozen grandchildren. When he reached his own house, there was the cat, waiting, and he knelt to scratch its ears. Why, even this creature had a secret life, spending afternoons in the sunny window of the Lucky Day Florist, sharing lunch with Miss Davis.

"I hope you had your turkey someplace else," Abe told the cat.

Abe knew how easy it was to break into a house, and that was why he never bothered to lock his own door. He had nothing worth stealing, anyway; his TV was on the blink and the last time his VCR quit working he'd brought it to the appliance shop in Hamilton and never bothered to return for it. Even his doorbell was busted, which was why Betsy Chase had to pound on the door when she arrived.

It had been a day of surprises for Abe, but Betsy's appearance was the only pleasant one. He had been ready to have a few drinks and crawl into bed, defeated and disgusted by the day's events, but here was absolute proof that whenever a man thought he knew what his future would bring, something was bound to amaze him. He stood there looking at Betsy the way he had when they'd first met, causing the color to rise in her face. Every time she saw him she became flustered, as if she had no more sense than the girls from St. Anne's.

"I thought I saw you over at the school," Betsy said, but that was a lie; in fact, she was certain of it. She'd seen him through the dean's window, there beside the boxwood, wearing the same dark suit that still hung on his angular frame.

Abe swung the screen door open to allow Betsy into the hallway. She had left her coat in her car parked in his driveway, and was wearing an outfit that had seemed well suited to the occasion of a dinner at the dean's house, a black dress and a good pair of heels. Now, however, she felt awkward in these clothes, as if she were a stranger to herself. The hallway was so cramped they were forced close together. As if that weren't difficult enough, her shoes were killing her; she thought she might actually topple over. She was probably crazy to have come, subject to the green river light that always confused her at this hour.

"I brought over some photographs," she told Abe in a businesslike tone. She tapped on her camera bag, which was draped over one shoulder.

When they went into the kitchen, Abe realized what a mess

his place was, with dishes stacked in the sink and newspapers on the floor. A basket of laundry had been left on a chair, unwashed and forgotten; Abe removed it so that Betsy could sit at the table. As she did, she pointed to the countertop where the black cat was parading back and forth, mewing at the cabinet where the canned food was stored. "That's Helen Davis's cat."

"Nope." After getting two beers from the refrigerator, Abe took the chair across from Betsy's. "It's mine."

"I see it all the time on campus." Betsy started in on her beer, not that she wanted it, and she drank too fast, agitated in Abe's presence. His eyes were not unlike the ice that had recently formed in the shallows of the river, fluid and pale. Looking into them, Betsy had the sense that she could fall right through and keep on falling. She quickly took out her folder of prints. "I wanted to know what you thought of this."

Abe began to look them over, distracted at first, then more interested. After developing the prints of the swim team, Betsy had gone on to take a series of photographs. In each there was a shadow behind Carlin, the unmistakable shape of a tall boy.

"You're good." Abe fixed Betsy with those pale eyes of his. "These look real."

"They are real. It only happens when I use high-speed film. And when Carlin is around."

In one of the prints the shadow's features were particularly clear: a wide mouth, a broad forehead, the sorrowful expression of the denied and the lovelorn. Even in the haziest of the images, the shadowy figure appeared to be soaking wet; there were pools of water in every picture, on furniture and floors alike. Abe returned the photographs to the folder. "The girl told me he's leaving her things. Maybe he's got some need to communicate, so he's hanging around. Sort of the way you're hanging around me," he added.

"Oh, don't you wish." Betsy laughed and held up her hand, displaying her engagement ring to remind him of her situation.

"You keep showing me that ring, but here you are." Abe moved his chair closer to hers.

Instantly, Betsy stood and collected her photographs. "You're kind of an egomaniac, aren't you? I thought you were interested in Gus Pierce."

She had already started for the hallway and Abe followed along. "I am interested," he told her.

"In the photographs?"

"I'm more interested in you."

Betsy shifted her camera bag, so that it was directly between them, in self-defense, in self-denial. What was her situation, exactly? It was only days ago that she'd settled the dessert problem for her wedding with Doreen Becker at the inn. Doreen had been pushing the white ladyfinger variety, insisting that chocolate wedding cakes such as the one Betsy preferred always brought bad luck. It was said that several divorce lawyers in Hamilton ordered similar cakes delivered to churches and halls to ensure their continuing brisk business.

"Do you tell every woman you bring back here that you're interested?" she asked Abe now, realizing as she did that she didn't like the idea of other women being here with him.

"I don't bring anyone here," Abe said. "Let's not forget, you came here all by yourself. And I'm glad that you did."

And because she knew this to be true, it was Betsy who

kissed him first, there in the dark hallway. She meant for it to be just that once, but that's not what happened. Later, she would tell herself that she got swept up, she didn't know what she was doing; it was the beer she'd gulped down or her unpredictable reaction to holidays. No matter what the reason, she kissed him for a very long time, too long, even though she knew she was making a major mistake. She was reminded of lightning, the way it struck so suddenly a person never had time to get out of range until it was over and the damage had already been done.

Betsy told herself it would only be one night, just a few passionate hours, erasable, forgettable, surely not meant to hurt anyone. She didn't stop him when he pulled off the black dress she'd so carefully chosen for the holiday. It was thoughtless, and heedless, but she didn't care. What was desire anyway, when examined in the clear light of day? Was it the way a woman searched for her clothes in the morning, or the manner in which a man might watch her sit before the mirror and comb her hair? Was it a pale November dawn, when ice formed on windowpanes and crows called from the bare black trees? Or was it the way a person might yield to the night, setting forth on a path so unexpected that daylight would never again be completely clear?

AT THIS TIME OF YEAR, THE LUNCH COUNTER at the pharmacy offered its famous Christmas muffins, an item added to the specials board every year between Thanksgiving and New Year's, expertly baked by Pete Byers's wife, Eileen. This local treat, reminiscent of ginger cake, only richer and more dense, had become so desirable that several residents of the largest houses on Main Street, well-dressed women who ordinarily wouldn't be caught at the lunch counter, arrived early in the mornings to buy half a dozen or more at a time.

Although the lunch counter was crowded with Haddan School students in the afternoon, the mornings belonged to local residents. People discussed both old news and current events over coffee for hours, and by noon everything from wedding announcements to nervous breakdowns had been hashed over. It was here people began to wonder if something had happened to Abel Grey. He was never at the Millstone anymore, where he'd been a regular ever since he'd reached legal age, and several women he occasionally dated—Kelly Avon, for instance, from over at the 5&10 Cent Bank—hadn't heard from him in weeks. Doug Lauder and Teddy Humphrey, with whom he often played pool on Saturday nights over in Middletown, had started to worry, and Russell Carter, who reported that Abe had stopped showing up to play basketball, was so concerned he phoned down to the station to make sure Abe was still alive.

As single men, these fellows had always depended on Abe's availability to play cards or agree to a fishing trip on short notice; now they couldn't get ahold of him anymore. They had no idea that Abe could be found lying in the tall grass thinking about fate or that he'd been so shaken up by love he had lost the ability to tell time. He, who had always prided himself on being punctual, was showing up not just at the wrong hour, but on the wrong day, arriving to direct traffic outside town hall on Thursday mornings when everyone knew the garden club didn't meet until Friday afternoon.

Abe's neighbors began to guess there was a woman involved when they noticed him out on his porch late at night, gazing at stars. They figured they had his number when he came into Selena's Sandwich Shoppe whistling love songs and completely forgetting what he planned to order, when he'd asked for a turkey on rye for the last nine years. Some of the ladies from Main Street, to whom Abe had always been so helpful, patted him on the back when they saw him, pleased that at last he'd found love. Certainly, it was high time. Because of the lack of single men in Haddan—and no one counted Teddy Humphrey as such, since every time he got good and drunk, he begged his ex-wife, Nikki, to take him back—there were several women who were disappointed to hear that Abe was no longer available. A few, like Kelly Avon and Mary Beth's cousin, the one who'd been unsuccessfully set up with him at Thanksgiving, tried to get the truth out of Joey Tosh, who insisted that his lips were sealed, although when it came right down to it, even Joey didn't know much.

Since their disagreement on Thanksgiving, Abe had avoided his old friend. He drove himself to work in his grandfather's cruiser and asked for assignments no one else wanted, traffic, for instance, and domestic disputes, to ensure he'd be working alone. When both men happened to be at the station at the same time, Joey busied himself with paperwork or with the *Haddan Tribune*. He had a shielded look that was impossible to read, the same expression he'd had when Mary Beth was first pregnant with Emily and they'd decided to get married without telling anyone.

Now and then, Abe caught Joey staring and one morning Joey stopped at Abe's desk. "Man, you're the early bird these days."

Funny that Abe had never even noticed that when Joey was upset he pulled at the right side of his face.

"You keep it up, you're going to make the rest of us look bad."

Abe sat back in his chair. "Is that what you're worried about, Joe? Looking bad?"

"That was my mistake on Thanksgiving. I shouldn't have brought you with me. I should have kept you out of it, like everyone said to."

"Yeah? I thought your mistake was taking the money."

"You're just pissed because I disagreed with you about the Pierce kid. You want me to say he was murdered? Fine, he was murdered. And maybe Frank was, too, while we're at it. Maybe somebody climbed up through his window and shot him. Is that what you want to hear?"

"If that's what you think I want, then you don't know me."

"Maybe I don't." Joey was looking his age and he seemed tired, even though Abe had heard he'd quit his second job at the mall. "Maybe I don't want to."

That was the way they left it, with the distance between them,.as if they hadn't been best friends their whole lives long. Now when people asked Joey where his buddy was, and why Abe could no longer be found at the Millstone on Saturday nights, Joey just shrugged.

"I'm not his bodyguard," he'd say when asked. "Abe goes his way and I go mine."

Joey would never have known that Abe was involved with someone if Mary Beth hadn't informed him of the situation. She and Kelly Avon had sat down at Selena's with a list of every unmarried woman in the village, thereby determining that the person in question wasn't anyone they knew. People in town wouldn't have figured Abe to go and find himself someone from the Haddan School. That's the way things were in the village still, after all these years: it was fine for the people of Main Street to do as they pleased, and a few had gone so far as to send their sons and daughters to the Haddan School, but expectations were different for anyone from the west side. Though they owned the stores and supplied the other residents with their shoes and chrysanthemums and cheese, people were expected to stay on their own side of town when it came to personal matters. And if Joey might have predicted Abe would get involved with that teacher from Haddan, he would never have guessed how often Abe went to see her, always late at night, after curfew, when the girls at St. Anne's were asleep in their beds and the hallways were silent and dark.

Abe had become so familiar with this route that he no longer stumbled over the frayed carpet. He had learned to expect stray umbrellas and Rollerblades inside the doorway and was accustomed to the rushing sound of steam heat rising from the old metal radiators, as well as the scent of bath oil and musk, fragrances that might have caused a less experienced man to lose his bearings. Abe usually parked down by the river and walked the rest of the way, so that no one would notice his grandfather's car, not that anyone attended to who was going in and out of the dorm. There was absolutely no security in the building, all Abe had to do was jiggle the knob and push his weight against the door and he was in.

Each time they were together, Betsy promised it would be the last. But this was a pledge she made to herself after he'd gone, and it was a rather flimsy pact. While Abe was beside her, she wanted him far too much to let him go. It was Abe who usually realized he had to leave, quickly, before the bells rang and the girls at St. Anne's were awakened to find him in the hallway, shirttails out, boots in hand. How could Betsy let him go? Every time the wind tapped at her window glass, she wished that it might be him. She could hear him sometimes, out by the roses, watching her before he let himself in the front door, and the knowledge that he was there in the garden made her so light-headed she was willing to take risks she could not have imagined before. In time, she found that what happened between them at night was spilling into her daylight hours. While she taught her classes, while she showered, while she made coffee or kissed the man she was to marry, it was Abe she was thinking of.

It was nearly the end of December when Betsy realized how dangerous a game she was playing. She knew then she would have to end it immediately. It was a cold morning and they'd stayed in bed too long, sleeping past the bells; by the time they awoke it was after nine. Snow had begun to fall, and a silvery light coursed through the window; perhaps this pale sky was the reason they'd been so reckless, for the girls in Betsy's care were already dressed and on their way to classes. Betsy could hear the front door open and close as she lay there beside him. She recognized the sound of Maureen Brown giggling as the girl leaned over the porch railing to catch snowflakes on her tongue, and that awful Peggy Anthony's high-pitched wail as her leather boots skidded on the icy steps. How easy it would have been for Abe and Betsy to be caught on this morning. Say Peggy Anthony broke her leg on the icy stair. Say Amy Elliot had one of her allergic reactions and came pounding on the door. How long would it take for the news to drift to Chalk House? Fifteen seconds? Twenty? How long exactly, before Betsy ruined her life?

She had never told a lie in her life before this. She had never believed herself capable of such subterfuge, making up excuses not to see Eric, her deceit forming with such ease she surprised herself. All that she'd wanted, the security of her life here in Haddan, would be undone by her own hand, unless she stopped now. She called a locksmith that same afternoon. After the new electronic lock had been installed on the front door, Betsy insisted upon a house meeting. Her girls were told in no uncertain terms not to give the code to either boyfriends or deliverymen. Betsy then had a dead bolt placed on the door to her own quarters as well, one that the locksmith had assured her was impenetrable, except to the most experienced thieves, the sort who would stop at nothing to get what they wanted.

Abe came back the next night, an inky blue night, as deep and immeasurable as the farthest reaches of heaven. Betsy heard him in the garden, but instead of going to the window to wave, she drew the curtains. She imagined his confusion when he found that the old lock had been replaced; it was an act not only of self-preservation, but of cruelty, as well. Betsy knew this, but she couldn't bring herself to face him. So she let him stand out there on the porch until, at last, he went away. Afterward, she did her best to avoid him. If a man even reminded her of Abel Grey, if he was tall or had blue eyes, Betsy went the other way, ducking behind hedges, fleeing the mini-mart before her purchases were rung up. She wouldn't even go to the pharmacy for fear she might run into him. She spent every night with Eric, as if he were the remedy, the cure for a bothersome ailment, no different than a fever or a cold.

Abe, however, was not so easy to dismiss. He had never envisioned himself as a man in love, but that was what he had turned out to be. He tried his best not to think about Betsy. He spent his days immersed in his job, gathering as much information about Gus Pierce as he could, telephoning the boy's father in New

York, going over his various school records, searching for a key to Gus's intent. Why people did the things they did, whether it be on impulse or a premeditated act, was always a puzzle. The boy in the water, the shotgun hidden in his brother's room, the locked door at St. Anne's. In the evenings Abe left his files and drove past the school, far more wounded than he'd ever imagined he'd be. When Kelly Avon suggested they meet down at the Millstone, he declined; he remained in his parked car, there on school property, where he didn't belong.

The holiday season was approaching and luminous silver stars had been affixed to the stoplights to celebrate the season. At the Haddan School, white lights decorated the porch balustrades. On the night when Abe finally decided to confront Betsy, he knew it was a bad decision. A light snow had begun to fall; it was just after supper and the campus was bustling. Abe was bound to be seen, not that he cared. He thought about all the times he'd been called in to settle altercations he hadn't understood: the heated fights of divorcing husbands and wives, the battles between brothers, the agony of thwarted lovers who had slit their exes' tires in the parking lot of the Millstone. All of them had been people whose love for each other had turned sour, deteriorating into a need for revenge or justice and a desire to hurt whoever had wronged them. Now Abe knew what those people were after; it was somebody's love they wanted, and they went after it the only way they knew how, exactly as he meant to do here tonight.

Two girls were sitting on the porch steps, letting the snow fall down on them. Abe had to lurch over them in order to get to the door.

"The combination is three, thirteen, thirty-three," one of the girls on the porch told him, forgetting Betsy's demand for security and caution.

Abe punched in the code and let himself in. It was the free hour between supper and study hall, when most students had their radios blaring and the TV in the lounge was turned up. Abe bumped into one girl who was toting a bag of laundry and almost tripped over another who sat squarely in the hallway, nattering away on the pay phone, unaware of anyone who passed by. St. Anne's seemed a very different place from the dark, silent house Abe was used to when he arrived in the middle of the night, not that the crowded corridors stopped him from going on to Betsy's quarters.

A dead bolt wasn't always as invincible as locksmiths would have a buyer believe, not if a thief came prepared. Abe had brought along a small screwdriver he most often used to tighten the loose rearview mirror of his grandfather's cruiser; in no time he had pried open the dead bolt, hoping that Betsy hadn't paid much, since it was fairly worthless in warding off any serious criminal intent. Going into her rooms uninvited, Abe had the same itchy feeling he used to have as a kid. He was breathing hard, not quite believing what he'd done, his hands were shaking, exactly as they had whenever he broke into a house. What he needed was a cold beer and a friend to set him straight, but as he had neither, he went on, into her bedroom. He ran his hand over the lace runner on top of the bureau, then approached the night table. Betsy had every right not to see him anymore. Hadn't he done the exact same thing dozens of times, not bothering to call some woman who'd made it clear she was interested, not even having the decency to explain himself? He held the earrings Betsy had left on the bureau, uncertain as to whether he wanted to understand her or punish her. Either way, he was not really surprised when he heard the door open. With his run of bad luck, he'd expected as much.

Betsy could tell Abe was there right away; she knew it the way people say they know they are about to be hit by lightning, yet remain powerless to run, unable to avoid their fate. She panicked, as anyone might have when disparate parts of her life were about to crash into each other, certain to leave a path of anguish and debris. It was true that devotion could be lost as quickly as it was found, which was why some people insisted that love letters always be written in ink. How easy it was for even the sweetest words to evaporate, only to be rewritten as impulse and infatuation might dictate. How unfortunate that love could not be taught or trained, like a seal or a dog. Instead, it was a wolf on the prowl, with a mind of its own, and it made its own way, undeterred by the damage done. Love like this could turn honest people into liars and cheats, as it now did to Betsy. She told Eric she needed to change out of her clothes, but it wasn't the blue wool outfit she had worn to the dean's for dinner that made her feel faint in these overheated rooms.

"Can you open a few windows, too?" Betsy called as she went on to the bedroom, making sure to close the door behind her. She was burning hot and overwrought; she should not have had that drink at the dean's house after the dinner to which Eric had insisted they go. She was dressed in unfamiliar clothes, with the unfamiliar taste of whiskey in her mouth, so that it seemed as though she were the stranger here and Abe, there at the edge of her bed, was the one who belonged.

By now the snow outside was falling harder, but that didn't stop Betsy from going to raise her bedroom window. The falling snow began to drift onto the carpet, but Betsy didn't care. She had a prickly sensation up and down her spine. How well did she know this man in her room? How could she know what he might be capable of?

"If you don't change your clothes he'll wonder why you lied to him," Abe said.

The only illumination came from beyond the window, due to the streetlamp and the brilliance of the snow. In such light everything appeared distant; it was as if Abe and Betsy and whatever had been between them had already moved into the past. "He'll wonder what else you lied to him about."

"I haven't lied to him!" Betsy was grateful for the cold air coming in through the window. She was burning with shame, the penance of her own deception. Although she had been the one to refuse him, she still remembered what it was like to kiss him, how such a simple act could turn her inside out.

"I see. You just didn't tell him the truth." Abe would have laughed then, if he found such matters amusing. "Is that what you did when you were with me? You sidestepped the truth? Is that what happened between us?"

They could hear Eric in the kitchen, putting up the kettle, opening cabinets as he searched for sugar and cups.

"Nothing happened." Betsy's mouth burned. "There was nothing between us."

It was the one answer that could drive him away, and this was Betsy's intent. Abe went out through the window; he banged his bad knee against the window frame, collecting a bruise that would ache for days. The campus was already covered with two or three inches of new snow, and the falling flakes were large and swirly, the mark of a storm that would last. By morning, traffic

221

would be a mess; a heavy snowfall in Haddan never went by without at least one bad accident, usually up by the interstate, and one local boy injuring himself on a makeshift sled or a borrowed snowmobile.

The snow was blinding as Abe walked away from St. Anne's; all the same, he was reminded of the hot afternoon when his brother died. He'd recognized the same thing then, how quickly the future could become the past, moments melting into each other before anyone could reach out and change them. He'd gone over how it all might have happened differently if he'd run up the stairs. If he'd knocked on the door, if he'd barged right in; how it might have changed had he denied his brother's request that morning and refused to go along to their grandfather's farm. It had been the sort of summer day that shone and glittered in the dusty sunlight like a miracle, all blue heat and endless white clouds, stifling hot, so quiet Abe could hear himself breathing when Frank hoisted him up so Abe could climb through the window to get the gun.

Afterward he'd had to do it again and again, compelled to repeat his thievery. At least these acts had stopped him from thinking, but now he was done with breaking into other people's houses. It had never done any good anyway, he'd carried his pain around inside him; it was still here on this snowy night. Maybe that was why he decided to leave his car where it was, parked by the river, and walk home. Once he started, he just kept going, past his house and halfway to Hamilton, not returning until sometime near dawn when he hitched a ride back with a plow Kelly Avon's little brother, Josh, was driving.

The next day he went walking again, even though he was supposed to show up for work, and Doug Lauder, a patrolman who grumbled under the best circumstances, was forced to take his shift, stuck directing traffic outside town hall until his toes turned blue. Before long, people in town noticed that Abe had quit stargazing. Why, he didn't even look up anymore as he walked through the village. He no longer whistled and his face was grim and he'd taken to being out at hours when decent people were all at home in bed. Several old-timers in town, Zeke Harris at the dry cleaner's, and George Nichols over at the Millstone, remembered that Wright Grey had done the very same thing for a while, walking so many miles he'd worn down his boots and then had to take them into Hamilton to be resoled.

Now it seemed that Abe had inherited this trait. Even when the weather took a turn for the worse, with ragged sleet and cold, blue ice, Abe kept at it. People would glance out their windows and there he'd be, on Main Street or on Elm, or over by Lovewell Lane, without even a dog as an excuse to slog through the slush. He had decided he would go on walking until he could figure things out. How was it, he wanted to know, that things could turn so quickly from love to locked doors? This was why he had resisted commitments for so long; he wasn't constitutionally fit for love. He had fallen into it headfirst, just like those fools he'd always made fun of, Teddy Humphrey, for instance, who was so driven he didn't care if he looked like an idiot; he'd park outside Nikki's house and blast his car radio, hoping all the songs of heartbreak he played would remind her that love that had been lost could also be found.

Abe pitied Teddy Humphrey, and now he pitied himself as well. Some days, he had a terrible feeling in the center of his chest that simply wouldn't go away. He'd even gone over to the clinic in Hamilton to have it checked out, knowing that Mrs. Jeremy's son, AJ, had been walloped with a heart attack two years earlier at the age of thirty-seven, but the nurses insisted nothing was wrong. *Get yourself an antacid,* they told him. *Stop drinking so much coffee. Stop walking in such bad weather, and make sure to wear gloves and a scarf.*

Abe went directly from the clinic to the pharmacy. "What's the difference between love and heartburn?" he asked Pete Byers, who was the one person in town who surely knew about such matters.

"Give me a minute." Pete, always a thoughtful man, assumed he'd need time to think it over. It seemed like a difficult riddle, but as it turned out, the answer didn't take long. "I've got it," he declared. "Nothing."

On that advice, Abe bought some Rolaids, which he swallowed right down, along with most of his pride. No wonder he hadn't trusted anyone before; you never could tell what people would do, one minute they'd be smiling at you and the next they'd be gone, without so much as an explanation or a civil good-bye. There wasn't a grown man on this planet who wound up with everything he wanted, so who was Abe to complain? He was still here, wasn't he? He woke every morning to see the sky, he drank his coffee, scraped the ice from his front steps, waved to his neighbors. He wasn't a boy who'd been cheated, who never got the chance to grow up and make his own decisions, right or wrong. The difference between tragedy and simple bad luck, after all, could be easily defined: it was possible to walk away from one, and that Abe would do, no matter how many miles it took or how many pairs of boots he wore through.

THE WATCH
AND THE LOAF

SNOW FELL ALL THROUGH DE-
cember, covering the Christmas tree in
front of town hall with a blanket of white
that would not melt until the tree was taken
down, as it was every year, on the Saturday
after New Year's. This was the season when
the north wind slammed around town, tossing garbage cans into the street, shaking
store awnings. The days were so short they
were finished by four, at which point the
sky turned black, and evenings were cold
enough to freeze a person's breath in the
crystal-clear air. There seemed to be handfuls of stars tossed right above the rooftops
in Haddan, keeping the town still alight at
midnight. Some people joked that it would
make sense to wear sunglasses after sun-
down, that's how bright the snow was; it

shone in the starlight, causing even the most serious people to put aside all caution and restraint and jump into the biggest of the drifts.

The boat shed at the Haddan School was unheated and drafty; it overlooked a bend in the frozen river, and although the building was closed until spring, that didn't mean it went unused. On Friday nights kegs of beer were set up beside the tarp-covered kayaks and canoes, and several girls in the freshman class had already lost their innocence there beside the sculls. Although she was embarrassed to be like so many others, Carlin had spent a good deal of time in the boathouse with Harry, but by the end of the semester, all of that had changed. Now whenever she was with Harry, she would discover a stone in the pocket of Gus's coat;'some were black and some were white and others were a crystalline blue-gray, the color of the ice that formed in the shallows of the river. The floor of Carlin's closet was now covered by a collection of such stones; they rattled every time she reached for her boots, and soon she noticed the stones turned clearer as the hour grew later, so that by midnight they were transparent, nearly invisible to the naked eye.

When it came time for winter vacation, a group had arranged a week-long trip to Harry's family's place in Vermont. It was assumed that Carlin would be going with them, and she didn't let on that she was staying behind until the day before they were to leave.

"You're not serious." Harry was deeply annoyed. "We made all the plans and now you're not going?"

They were his plans actually; still Carlin did her best to explain how difficult it would be for her to leave Haddan. Miss Davis could no longer rise from her chair and was often too tired for dinner, falling asleep at the table, her untouched plate before her. Miss Davis had been so grateful at Thanksgiving that Carlin didn't feel she could leave her employer alone for the holidays.

"I don't care," Harry said. "I'm selfish and I want you there with me."

But Carlin could not be convinced. At five the next morning she was in bed when she heard Amy leave. The van Harry had hired was idling in the parking lot, headlights cutting through the dark, and when Carlin listened carefully, she recognized the voices of the lucky few Harry had invited along on the ski trip. She kept her eyes closed until the van pulled out of the lot; the rattle of the engine drew farther and farther away as it turned onto Main Street, passing the fences decorated with white lights, and the brilliant tree outside town hall, and the graveyard behind St. Agatha's, where so many had already deposited wreaths to mark the season.

On the first day of vacation, St. Anne's was deserted, save for the mice. All of the girls had gone off with family or friends, and in the emptiness left behind there was a moment when Carlin felt lost. She went to the pay phone and called her mother, Sue, who cried and said it just wasn't Christmas without Carlin home to celebrate. As much as she loved her mother, by the time they were through talking, Carlin was glad enough to be in Haddan. Sue Leander had sent Carlin a present of white musk cologne, which Carlin rewrapped and presented to Miss Davis.

"You must think I'm trying to catch myself a man," Miss Davis said when she saw her gift, but she was persuaded to try out a dab or two on her wrists. "There," she proclaimed. "I'm a knock-out."

Carlin laughed and set to work on the dressing for the goose, which she'd had delivered from the butcher in Hamilton. As it turned out, Carlin was a good cook. She, who'd been raised on frozen dinners and macaroni and cheese, could now julienne peppers and carrots in seconds flat; one afternoon she made a vegetable soup so delicious that when the aroma drifted through the dormitory several girls came down with a bad case of homesickness and they cried themselves to sleep, dreaming of their childhood homes.

"Pecans in the stuffing?" Miss Davis sniffed, as she peered over Carlin's shoulder. "Raisins?" Her voice was grave with mistrust.

Carlin held the goose up by the neck and asked if perhaps Miss Davis would like to take over. The goose looked rather naked and strange to Miss Davis's eyes and, truthfully, the notion that she might fix anything more complicated than a cheese sandwich was far-fetched at best, while the idea of her taking a dead goose in hand was nothing short of ludicrous. Quickly, she reconsidered. When all was said and done, pecan dressing would be fine.

Helen hadn't wanted to like this girl who worked for her; it was foolish to begin attachments now, when it was far too late for such things. She would never have admitted how glad she was that Carlin had stayed for the holiday. The girl was good company and had an exceptional talent for solving problems that seemed insurmountable to Helen, arranging, for instance, for a cab so that Helen could attend mass at St. Agatha's instead of going to the services led by Dr. Jones in the school chapel. Having been raised Catholic, Helen had always wished to go to St. Agatha's but she'd feared local parishioners would be unfriendly to an outsider, particularly a lost soul such as herself, who hadn't been to a proper mass for so long. As it turned out, the congregation had welcomed her warmly. Pete Byers helped her to her seat, and afterward some nice young man named Teddy had driven her back to St. Anne's. When she arrived home, she found that Carlin had set out a real Christmas dinner, which brought to mind the holiday meals Helen's own mother used to serve, with dishes of candied yams and brussels sprouts, and of course the goose with its lovely stuffing.

Halfway through dinner, Helen Davis gazed out the window and saw that handsome man again. Abel Grey was standing by the rosebushes, even though it was snowing. He was just about the best-looking man Helen had ever seen, and she thought now that she should have found herself a man like that back when she was young, rather than moping around after that worthless Dr. Howe.

"Look who's here," she said to Carlin, and she quickly sent the girl to fetch him. Carlin ran through the falling snow, the black coat flaring out over a white apron and her good blue dress.

"Hey," she called to Abe, who didn't seem happy to have been discovered. "Miss Davis wants you to have dinner with us. You might as well, since you're lurking around here anyway."

Carlin jumped up and down to keep warm, but at least the boots she'd bought at Hingram's were doing the job, and Gus's coat was a blessing in weather such as this. Those big snowflakes were still falling, and Abe's hair had turned white. He looked sheepish under all that snow, the way any man would be who'd just been caught peering through windows.

"I'm just out for a walk," he insisted. "I'm not lurking."

"Miss Chase went to a hotel in Maine with Mr. Herman. So you might as well have your dinner with us."

Abe had already had his Christmas lunch at the Millstone—two drafts, a burger, and a large order of fries.

"Come on," Carlin urged. "I'll pretend I never saw you sneaking out St. Anne's at three in the morning and you can pretend you're polite."

"What are you having for dinner?" Abe asked grudgingly.

"Goose with pecan stuffing and candied yams."

Abe was surprised. "You cooked all that?" When Carlin nodded, he threw up his hands. "I guess you talked me into it."

By now, the light had already begun to fade. Abe hadn't really expected Betsy to be home, nor had he planned what he might say should she be there. Would he have begged for her to reconsider? Was he that far gone?

As they approached St. Anne's, Helen Davis opened the back door; when she saw Abe she waved.

"I think she's got a crush on you," Carlin confided.

"I'm sure she'll dump me before dinner's over." Abe waved back. "Hey there, Helen," he called. "Merry Christmas!" The black cat slipped out onto the frosty porch. "There's my buddy." Abe clucked as if calling chickens, but the cat ignored him and went instead to rub against Carlin's legs.

"Pretty boy." Carlin leaned down to pat the cat's ears.

"Again your cat has failed to recognize you," Helen noted as they all traipsed into the kitchen, cat included. Helen had placed a cover over the yams and she'd shoved a plate atop the bowl of vegetables to keep them warm. A few small exertions and those brief moments on the porch had left her exhausted. Standing there at her own dinner table, holding on to the back of a chair, Helen seemed likely to topple over, exactly like Millie Adams over on Forest Street, who had been ill for years before she passed on, so weak that Abe often stopped by on his way home from work to make certain that Millie had made it through the day. Now, Abe helped Miss Davis to her chair.

"How nice that you happened to be passing by," she said. "Just in time for dinner."

Still wearing the black coat, Carlin hurried to the cupboard for an extra plate. "He was lurking."

"Lurking," Miss Davis said, pleased.

"I was walking." Now that he saw the food before him, Abe rubbed his hands together like a starving man.

Carlin was searching through the cutlery drawer for silverware with which to set another place when she felt something move in her pocket.

"Take off that coat and sit down," Helen Davis instructed. "We can't very well eat without you."

Carlin put down the silverware. She had a funny look on her face. She had forgotten the cranberry relish, but she didn't move to rectify that mistake. Midnight leapt onto Helen's lap and began to purr, low down in the back of its throat.

"What is it?" Helen said to the silent girl.

The worst part of caring about someone was that sooner or later you were bound to worry, and to take notice of details that wouldn't otherwise be apparent. Helen, for instance, now saw that Carlin had grown pale, a wisp of a thing wrapped up in that old black coat she insisted on wearing.

"What's wrong?" Helen demanded.

Carlin reached into her pocket and brought forth a small fish, which she placed upon the table. Helen leaned forward for a better look. It was one of those silver minnows found in the Haddan River, small and shimmering and gasping for breath. Helen Davis might have dropped the little fish in a tumbler of water had Midnight not pounced on it and eaten it whole.

In spite of herself, Carlin laughed. "Did you see that? He ate it."

"You bad, bad boy," Helen scolded. "You rascal."

"I told you Gus left me things," Carlin said to Abe. "But you didn't believe me."

Abe leaned back in his chair, baffled, but Helen Davis was far less surprised. She had always believed that grief could manifest itself in a physical form. Right after Annie Howe's death, for instance, she had been covered by red bumps, which itched and burned into the night. The doctor in town told her that she was allergic to roses and must never again eat rosewater preserves or bathe in rose oil, but Helen knew better. She'd had nothing to do with roses. It was grief she was carrying around with her, grief that was rising up through the skin.

Recalling these times caused Helen immeasurable pain, or maybe it was her illness that was affecting her so. It was so awful that she doubled over and Carlin ran to get the tablets of morphine hidden in the spice cabinet.

"There's nothing wrong with me," Miss Davis insisted, but she gave them no further argument when they helped her to her room. Afterward, Carlin put up a plate for Miss Davis for tomorrow's lunch, then she ate her own dinner between bouts of cleaning up. Abe bolted his food, then checked to ensure that Miss Davis was sleeping. Thankfully, she was, but Abe was disturbed by how lifeless she appeared, pale as the deepest winter's ice.

When Carlin and Abe left Miss Davis's, the air was so cold it hurt a person's throat and lungs just to breathe; the sky was alight with constellations swirling through the dark. It was possible to see the Pleiades, those daughters of Atlas placed into the Milky Way for their own protection. How lovely it was with no people in sight and only the stars for company.

"How come you're so rarely lurking around anymore? Doesn't Miss Chase miss you?"

"She's got a fiancé." Abe had learned the constellations from his grandfather and as a child he'd gone to sleep counting not sheep but all the brilliant dogs and bears and fish that shone through the window.

"That didn't stop you before," Carlin reminded him.

"I guess the better man won." Abe tried to smile, but his face hurt in the cold.

"I'm in Mr. Herman's history seminar. Believe me, he's not even the second-best man."

The snow had stopped; it was the brilliant sort that made every step squeak.

"Christmas." Abe watched his own breath form little crystals. "What do you think Gus would have been doing right now?"

"He'd be in New York," Carlin said without hesitation. "And I'd be with him. We'd eat too much and see three movies in a row. And maybe we wouldn't come back."

"Gus couldn't have put that fish in your pocket. You know that, don't you?"

"Tell that to your friend." Carlin nodded to the cat, which had followed them from Miss Davis's. "He has fish breath."

Later that night, Carlin was still thinking of Gus as she went into the gym, using the key every member of the swim team was granted. She switched on the emergency lights in the entrance-way, then went to the locker room and changed into her suit, grabbing for her cap and goggles. Abel Gray didn't want to believe the fish at Miss Davis's dinner had come from Gus, but Carlin knew that some things never disappeared completely, they stayed with you for better and for worse.

Down at the pool, light reflected from the glassed walkway, and that was bright enough. The water looked bottle green, and when Carlin sat on the edge and swung her legs over, she was shocked by how chilly it was. Clearly, the heater had been turned off for the holidays. Carlin eased into the water, gasping at the cold. Her skin rose in goose bumps; her goggles steamed up the moment she slipped them on. She set about doing laps, using her strongest stroke, the butterfly, falling into her rhythm naturally. It brought relief to swim; Carlin felt as though she were out in the ocean, miles from land and all the petty concerns of humankind. She thought about the stars she had seen in the sky, and the snowflakes that had dusted the stone walkways, and the New England cold that could cut right through a person. By the time she was done, the action of her stroke had created a current; little waves slapped against the tiles. With her elbows resting on the edge of the pool, Carlin removed her goggles, then pulled off her bathing cap and shook out her hair. It was then she saw that she wasn't alone.

There was a greenish mist of chlorine rising from the surface, and for a moment Carlin thought she'd only imagined a figure approaching, but then the figure took a step closer. She pushed herself away from the edge; as long as she stayed in the center of the pool there was no way anyone could catch her, if catching her was what this individual was after. Whoever it was, he'd never be as fast as Carlin was in the water.

She narrowed her eyes, already burning with chlorine, and tried to make out his face. "Don't come any closer!" she commanded, and then was somewhat surprised when he did as he was told. He crouched down on his haunches and grinned, and that was when she saw who it was. Sean Byers from the pharmacy. Carlin could feel her heartbeat slow down, but the funny thing was, her pulse was still going crazy. "What do you think you're doing here?"

"I could say the same to you." Sean took off his watch and carefully placed it into the front pocket of his jeans. "I'm here two or three times a week, after closing. I'm a regular. Which is more than I can say of you."

"Oh, really? You swim?"

"Usually in Boston Harbor, but this does fine. No shopping carts or half-sunk boats to dodge."

Carlin continued to tread water; she watched as Sean took off his jacket and tossed it on the tiles. He pulled off his sweater and his T-shirt, then gave Carlin a look.

"You don't mind, do you?" he asked, one hand poised by his fly. "I wouldn't want to embarrass you or anything like that."

"Oh, no." Carlin tilted her head back, challenging him. "Go on. Be my guest."

Sean pulled off his jeans. Carlin couldn't help herself, she looked to make sure he was actually wearing a bathing suit and was amused to see that he was. Sean let out a holler as he jumped into the far end of the pool.

"You're a trespasser with no legal rights," Carlin said when he swam over. "I hope you know that." In the deep end, the water was so black it appeared bottomless.

Sean's face was pale in the dim light. "There's nothing to do in this town. I had to find some way to occupy myself. Especially with Gus gone. You're a good swimmer," he noted.

"I'm good at everything," Carlin told him.

Sean laughed. "And so modest."

"Well? Do you think you can keep up with me?"

"Definitely," he said. "If you slow down."

They swam laps together and Carlin didn't change her pace to suit him. To his credit, Sean managed to do fairly well; he hadn't been lying, he really was a swimmer, and although his stroke was awkward and wild, he was fast and competitive. It was lovely to be in the dark, alone, yet not alone. Carlin could have gone on this way forever, had she not noticed flashes of reflected light glittering before her. She stopped to tread water, thinking her vision would clear, but they were there, a stream of tiny minnows.

Sean came up beside her. His wet hair looked black and his eyes were black as well. He had a scar beneath his right eye, an unfortunate reminder of the car he'd stolen, the one that had wound up crashed on a side road in Chelsea and had landed him in juvenile court and then in Haddan. In spite of his injury, he had a beautiful face, the sort that had always brought him more fortune than he deserved. In Boston, he was known for his daring, but tonight, he felt uneasy. The pool was much colder than usual, but that wasn't the reason he'd begun to shiver. There was some movement grazing his skin, fin and gill, quick as a breath. A line of silver went past him, then circled and came back toward him.

"What are those?"

Sean had been wanting to get Carlin alone since the first time he saw her, but now he was far less sure of himself than he'd thought he'd be. Here in the water, nothing looked the same anymore. He would have sworn he saw fish darting through the pool, as ridiculous a notion as if stars had fallen from the sky to shine beneath them, giving off icy white light.

"They're only minnows." Carlin took Sean's hand in her own. His skin was cold, but underneath he was blistering. Carlin made him reach out along with her, so that the fish floated right through their fingers. "Don't worry," she said. "They won't hurt us."

PETE BYERS COULDN'T BEGIN TO COUNT THE times he'd hurried to his store during snowstorms, called there by frantic mothers whose babies were dehydrated and burning up with fever, or by old-timers who'd forgotten to pick up a much-needed medication without which they might not make it through the night. He opened when necessary and closed down when appropriate, locking his doors, for instance, to honor Abe Grey's grandfather when Wright was laid to rest. On that day, there was a funeral procession that reached from Main Street to the library; people stood on the sidewalks and wept, as if one of their own had passed on. Pete also came in after hours on the day Frank Grey shot himself, to fill a prescription for tranquilizers to ensure that Frank's mother, Margaret, would finally get some sleep.

Pete had told Ernest Grey it would be no bother for him to drop the prescription by the house, but Ernest must have needed to get out, as he insisted on coming down himself. It was late, and Ernest had forgotten his wallet; he went through his pockets, pulling out change, as if Pete wouldn't have trusted him to make good on whatever he owed. Then Ernest sat down at the counter and cried, and for the first time, Pete was grateful he and

Eileen had never had children. Perhaps what people said was true, that any man who lived long enough would eventually realize that the way in which he was cursed was also the blessing he'd received.

Since the town had changed so much in recent years, with so many new people moving in, it was difficult for Pete to know everyone by name, which meant service wasn't what it once was. But towns don't remain the same, they go forward, like it or not; there had even been talk about building a town high school, out near Wright's old farm, for there would soon be too many students to send to the Hamilton school district. It wasn't the way it used to be, that much was certain, back when a person would meet the same people at the Millstone on a Saturday night as he'd see at St. Agatha's on Sunday morning, knowing full well what there was to confess and what there was to be thankful for.

Lately, Pete had been puzzling over the issue of confidentiality, and it was this topic he was contemplating when Abe came in for lunch on the Saturday after Christmas. The few regular customers—Lois Jeremy and her cronies from the garden club, and Sam Arthur, a member of the town council for ten years running—all cried out a greeting to Abe.

"Happy holidays," he called back. "Don't forget to vote yes on the traffic light by the library. You'll save a life."

Anyone looking closely would be able to tell that Abe hadn't been sleeping well. Over this holiday break, he'd gone so far as to phone half a dozen hotels in Maine, like a common fool, searching for Betsy. At one hotel, a party named Herman had been registered, and although it turned out to be a couple from Maryland, Abe had been distressed ever since. Sean Byers, on the other hand, looked just fine. He was whistling as he filled Abe's order, which, like everyone else in town, he now knew by heart—turkey on rye, mustard, no mayo.

"What are you so happy about?" Abe asked Sean, who was practically radiating good cheer. It didn't take long for Abe to figure it out, for when Carlin Leander came into the pharmacy Sean lit up like the Christmas tree outside town hall.

Carlin, on the other hand, was cold and bedraggled; she had just been at the pool and the ends of her hair were a faint, watery green.

"You went swimming without me?" Sean said when she approached the counter.

"I'll go again," Carlin assured him.

When Sean went to get Sam Arthur's bowl of chowder, Carlin sat beside Abe. It was because of a call from Carlin that Abe was here today, and although she hadn't said what the reason was, Abe grinned as he nodded toward Sean. Love was often the explanation behind most emergencies.

"Who would have guessed."

"It's not what you think. We just go swimming. I know it would never work out—you don't have to tell me not to get my hopes up. I'm not that stupid."

"That's not what I was going to say." Abe pushed his plate away and finished his coffee. "I was going to say good luck."

"I don't believe in luck." Carlin checked out the vinyl-covered menu. For the first time in days the idea of food didn't make her queasy. She was actually considering a mint chocolate chip ice cream soda. Beneath Gus's old coat, she was wearing jeans and a ratty black sweater, but as far as Sean was concerned, she could not have looked more beautiful. He stared at her while he fixed a raspberry lime rickey for Sam Arthur, who was there to pick up his insulin and would have been better served had he ordered a sugar-free cola.

"What's the other guy in your life going to think if you get involved with Sean Byers?" Abe asked.

"Harry?" Carlin had refused to think past vacation. Every night when she met Sean at the pool, it seemed as if they would have the school to themselves forever. Some other girl might have been frightened of staying on the deserted campus, but not Carlin. She liked the way her footsteps echoed, she liked the silence that greeted her in the hallways and on the stairs. All of the windows at St. Anne's were coated with blue ice and when the wind blew, icicles were shaken down from the roof with a sound that brought to mind broken bones, but Carlin didn't care. She was happy, but happiness can often be figured in minutes. First there were seven days before school began anew, then six, then five, then Carlin stopped counting.

"I can handle Harry," she said to Abe now.

"No," Abe said. "I meant the other guy. Gus."

Lois Jeremy stopped by on her way to pay her check; she wagged her finger at Abe. "You weren't posted outside town hall when we had our last meeting." She treated Abe, along with all the members of the Haddan police force, as though they were her own personal employees, but at least she was polite to the hired help.

"No, ma'am. But I'm hoping to be there next time."

"I can't believe her." Carlin was livid. "She treated you like a servant."

"That's because I'm at their service." Abe saluted as Mrs.

Jeremy and Charlotte Evans left, and the two women chuckled as they waved good-bye.

Carlin shook her head, amazed. "You've lived here so long you don't notice when someone's a snob."

"I notice, but if you care about what other people think, you're a goner. That's the lesson you learn in Haddan." Abe reached for his coat. "Thanks for calling me down here. I'm assuming you're paying my tab, especially now that you have this relationship with Sean. He'll probably give you a discount."

"I called you because I found something." Carlin opened the black coat to reveal an inside breast pocket, one she hadn't known existed before that morning. She took out a plastic bag of white powder.

Once again, Abe felt that his drowned boy wasn't at all like the Haddan student his grandfather had pulled from the river. This one kept on drowning, and any man foolish enough to get too close might be pulled down along with him.

"I wasn't going to show it to you, but then I realized Gus can't get into trouble. I don't even think it's his because I would have known if he was involved with this sort of drugs."

But Abe wasn't so sure. It was astounding how thoroughly someone you cared for could deceive you and just how wrong you could be. Back when Abe was a boy, he was the one who had liked gunplay a little too well. Whenever Wright had taken them to Mullstein's field for target practice, Frank sat on a bale of hay with his hands over his ears while Abe fired away; he'd shoot anything, even Wright's big, old twelve-gauge, the one they stole, a gun so powerful that after he pulled the trigger, Abe was often left flat on his back looking up at the clouds in the sky.

Abe opened the bag, but as he was about to test for the bitter edge of cocaine, Pete Byers stopped him.

"I wouldn't eat that stuff, son," Pete said. "It will burn right through your trachea."

Abe thought of all the things the powder might be: baking powder, arsenic, chalk dust, angel dust, cake mix, heroin. Sam Arthur was getting ready to leave, chatting with Sean about the lack of team spirit on the Celtics, mourning the days when Larry Bird could always be depended upon to pull a win out of a hat. The sky had been threatening snow all morning, but only a few flakes fell, just enough to cover the icy roads and make driving treacherous.

"If you know what this is, Pete, I need for you to tell me," Abe said.

People had a right to their own business, didn't they? Or so Pete had always believed. Take the case of Abe's own grandfather, who stopped taking his medications at the end of his life, simply refusing to come into town to pick up what the doctor ordered. One night Pete drove out to the farm; he knocked on the door with the nitroglycerin tablets that had been sitting on the counter in the pharmacy for days, but Wright hadn't invited Pete in with his usual hospitality. He'd merely looked through the screen door and said, *I've got a right to do this,* and Pete found he had to agree. Once a man began drawing the line, judging right and wrong, he'd need the stamina of an angel on earth, dispensing the sort of wisdom Pete Byers knew he didn't possess.

It had been difficult all these years, never divulging a confidence, lying beside Eileen in bed with a headful of information he could never discuss. When they went to the inn for the New Year's dance at the end of the week, he'd know which waitresses were using birth control pills, he'd be aware of how Doreen

Becker had tried nearly everything for that rash she had, just as he knew that Mrs. Jeremy's son, AJ, who always went to the inn to pick up platters of cheese and shrimp for his mother's yearly party, had begun to take Antabuse in yet another attempt to curb his drinking.

All this knowledge had turned Pete into a man who didn't comment on much of anything. Frankly, if he heard that aliens had landed in Haddan and were eating the cabbages out of the fields and getting ready for battle, he would simply have told his customers they had better stay at home, doors locked, and take care to spend as much time as they could with those they loved best. All Pete knew was that people deserved privacy; they had a right to meet death as they saw fit and they had a right to live their lives that way, too. He had never discussed a customer or a friend's personal life, at least not until now. He pulled up a chair and sat down; he had a right to be tired. He'd been standing for the best part of forty-five years, and he'd been keeping quiet that long, as well. He sighed and shined his glasses on the white apron he wore. Sometimes a man did the wrong thing for the right reasons, a decision often made on the spot, much like diving into a cold pond on a broiling August day.

"Gus used to come in here every afternoon. He told me the boys he lived with were making his life miserable. One time I suggested some medication, because he couldn't sleep. The worst thing was some kind of initiation he had to go through to be part of the house where he lived. He said they gave him a task they thought no one could complete. They wanted him to turn white roses red."

"That was the initiation?" Abe was confused. "No drinking until he dropped? No blindfolds and nights of terror?"

"They chose an impossible task," Carlin said. "That way he would fail and they could be rid of him."

"But it wasn't impossible." Pete held up the packet of powder. "Aniline crystals. It's an old trick. You sprinkle them on white roses, turn around for a minute, use a mister to add some water, and there you have it. The impossible's done."

Later, as Carlin walked back to school, she stopped at the Lucky Day flower shop. The bell over the door rang as she entered. All the while Ettie Nelson, who lived half a block down from Abe on Station Avenue, waited on her, Carlin thought about the many forms cruelty could take. She had a list too long to remember by the time she had chosen half a dozen white roses, gorgeous, pale blooms, the stalks of which were crisscrossed by black thorns. An expensive choice for a student, which was why Ettie had asked if the bouquet signified a special occasion.

"Oh, no," Carlin told her. "Just a gift for a friend."

Carlin paid and went outside to find that the sky seemed to be falling. The snow was coming down hard; the sky was misty and gray, with endless banks of dense clouds. The roses Carlin had chosen were as white as the drifts that were already piling up on the street corners, but so fragrant that people all over town, even those who fervently hoped for the return of good weather as they shoveled out doorways and cars, stopped what they were doing in order to watch her pass by, a beautiful girl in tears who carried roses through the snow.

ON THE FIRST DAY OF THE NEW YEAR, WHEN midnight was near, the van Harry had rented pulled into the parking lot at Chalk House. Carlin might not have been aware of anything, for both the engine and the lights were cut before the van glided into the icy lot, but her sleep was disrupted when Amy turned the doorknob with a click and a clatter, then stole into their room with what she surely believed was caution. Pie had returned earlier in the day, but she was such a deep sleeper she would never have noticed that Amy carried the scent of deception with her, or that as she stripped off her clothes and hurried to bed it was possible to see love bites on her shoulders and throat.

"Have fun?" Carlin called, in a hoarse, chilly whisper.

She could see Amy startle, then pull the blanket up to her neck. "Sure. Tons."

"I didn't know you could ski. And I thought you hated cold weather."

Carlin had sat up, leaning against the headboard for a better look. Amy's dark eyes shone, wide awake and anxious. She forced a loud yawn, as though she couldn't keep from falling asleep. "There's a lot you don't know about me."

Amy turned her face to the wall, assuming Carlin couldn't perceive betrayal from the back, but such things are infinitely easy to read. Carlin supposed she should be grateful to Amy for making it easier to break up with Harry, but as it turned out she was out of sorts in the morning, the way anyone duped into giving her love away might have been. Harry, on the other hand, acted as if nothing between them had changed. When they met crossing the quad, he grabbed Carlin and hugged her, not noticing her hesitancy.

"You should have come with us." Harry's breath billowed out in the cold. He seemed revitalized and more sure of himself than ever. "The snow was great. We had a blast."

Perhaps Harry planned to have them both. It wouldn't be difficult to go behind Carlin's back and assure Amy he was trying his best to end it with Carlin, then drag their breakup out for months. He could tell Amy he was a gentleman, and as such, never did like to break anyone's heart unless it was absolutely necessary.

"I've got something for you," Carlin told him as she ducked his embrace. "Come to my room later. You'll be surprised."

She left him there, curious and more interested than he was in most things. That's what had intrigued him in the first place, wasn't it? How different she was from the other girls. How difficult to second-guess. He'd have to do some sweet-talking to explain to Amy why he was seeing Carlin, but Carlin had faith that he'd manage to spin a believable tale. A good liar always found excuses, and it seemed clear that for Harry such things came far easier than the truth.

He arrived before supper, throwing himself onto Amy's bed, where, unbeknownst to Carlin, he'd spent quite a lot of time, making sure to keep track of the hours Carlin spent at swim practice while he seduced her roommate, not that the assignment had been a chore. Harry fancied the idea of having had two girls in the same bed and he pulled Carlin toward him. Again, she drew away.

"Oh, no. I told you, I've got something to show you."

Harry groaned. "This better be good," he warned.

He hadn't even noticed the white roses, there on the bureau in a vase borrowed from Miss Davis. He leaned up on his elbows when he spied the flowers.

"Who sent those?"

By now, the roses were limp and imperfect, with the edges of the leaves turning brown; still, in Miss Davis's lovely cut-glass vase the bouquet was impressive, the gift of a rival perhaps.

"I bought them for myself. But now I've changed my mind. You know how it is when you decide you want something new." She took the black coat from a hook in the closet and slipped it on. "I realize I want red roses."

There was a flicker of distrust behind Harry's eyes. He uncoiled himself now, the better to watch Carlin's display. He didn't like being tricked, still he'd been well brought up and the smile he bestowed on Carlin was not without appeal.

"If you want red roses, I'll get them for you."

"Get them for Amy," Carlin suggested.

Harry ran a hand through his hair. "Look, if this is about Amy, I admit it, I made a mistake. I figured she was your friend, I didn't expect anything to happen, but she was all over me, and I didn't say no. If you had gone to Vermont, none of it would have happened. Amy is nothing to me," Harry assured her. "Come on over here and let's forget all about her."

"What about the roses?" Carlin kept her distance. She had been spending so much time in the water that the white moons of her cuticles had turned faintly blue; her complexion was so pale she looked as though she'd never seen sunlight. She turned her back and took the packet of aniline from the inner coat pocket. There was a lump in her throat, but she forced herself to face Harry. There were only enough crystals to cover one flower, but even before she could add water, as Pete Byers had instructed, the single rose began to turn color, one vivid bloom, scarlet amongst the rest.

Harry applauded, slowly. His smile had broadened, although Carlin knew it was not an expression that necessarily revealed what he felt inside.

"Congratulations," Harry said, impressed. "Who would have thought a little bitch like you would have so many tricks up her sleeve?"

Harry had left Amy's bed and was already pulling on his jacket. He'd always known when it was time to leave and when he'd gotten as much as he could out of a situation.

"I learned the trick from Gus," Carlin said. "But of course, you've seen it before."

Harry came close enough for Carlin to feel him, his body heat, his warm breath. "If you're implying I had something to do with what happened to Gus, you're wrong. I wouldn't have wasted my time on him. I just don't think it was that great a loss, and you obviously do, and that's the difference between us."

When he'd gone, Carlin took the roses, wrapped them in newspaper, and threw them in the trash. She felt disgusted with herself for having been with Harry, as though she'd been contaminated somehow. She went up to the bathroom and locked the door, then sat on the rim of the tub, letting the hot water run until the room was steamy. She felt filthy and stupid; all those hours she'd wasted with Harry, time that would have been much better spent with Gus. She couldn't bear it, truly she couldn't, and that was why she reached for one of the razors kept on the bathroom shelf. But how many times would she have to cut herself to feel better? Would twelve strikes be enough, would fourteen, or a hundred? Would she only be happy when the bathroom tiles ran red with blood?

The razor should have been cold in her hands, but it was burning, leaving little hot marks in her skin. She thought about

Annie Howe's roses and how hopeless it was to make a strike against yourself. In the end, she did the next best thing. She chopped off her hair without even bothering to look in the mirror, hacking away until the sink was filled with pale hair and the razor was dull. This act was meant to be a punishment, she'd thought she'd be ugly without her hair, to match the way she felt inside, but instead she felt astonishingly light. That night, she climbed out to her window ledge, and as she perched there, she imagined she might be able to fly. One step off the rooftop, one foot past the gutter, that's all she need do to take off with the north wind that blew down from New Hampshire and Maine, bringing with it the scent of pine trees and new snow.

From then on, she sat out on the ledge every time Harry came calling for Amy. Poor Amy, Carlin pitied her. Amy thought she had won an exceptional prize, but each day she would have to worry that someone prettier and fresher would catch Harry's eye, and she'd bend herself around him, like the willows beside the river must in order to survive along the banks.

"He's mine now," Amy gloated, and when Carlin replied that she was welcome to him, Amy refused to believe that Carlin hadn't been torn apart by their breakup. "You're just jealous," Amy insisted, "so I refuse to feel sorry for you. You never appreciated him in the first place."

"Did you do that to your hair because of Harry?" Pie asked one night as she watched Carlin run a comb through her chopped-up hair.

"I did it on impulse." Carlin shrugged. She did it because she thought she deserved to be torn apart.

"Don't worry," Pie said to Carlin, her voice sweet with concern. "It will grow back."

But some things weren't so easily repaired; at night Carlin lay in bed and listened to the wind and to the sound of her roommates' quiet breathing. She wished that she was still the person she was before she came to Haddan, and that she, too, could sleep through the night. Whenever she did fall asleep, during the gray and freezing dawn, it was Gus Carlin dreamed of. In her dreams, he was asleep underwater, his eyes wide open. When he arose from the water to walk through the grass, he was barefoot and perfectly at ease. He was dead in her dream and he carried with him the knowledge of the dead, that all that matters is love, here and beyond. Everything else will simply fall away. Carlin could tell he was trying to get home; in order to do so he needed to climb a trellis covered with vines, not that this obstacle deterred him. Though the vines were replete with thorns, he did not bleed. Though the night was dark, he found his way. He climbed into his attic room and sat on the edge of his unmade bed, and the vines came in after him, winding along both the ceiling and the floor until there was a hedge of thorns, each one resembling a human thumb, each with a fingerprint of its own.

Was it possible for the soul of a person to linger if it so desired, right at the edge of our commonplace world, substantial enough to move pots of ivy on a windowsill or empty a sugar bowl or catch minnows in the river? *Lie down beside me,* Carlin said in her dream to whatever there was left of him. *Stay here with me,* she begged, calling to him in whatever way she knew how. She could hear the wind outside, rattling against the trellis; she could feel him beside her, his skin cool as water. The hems of her bedsheets grew muddy and damp, but Carlin didn't care. She should have followed him over the black fence, into the woods and along the path. Because she had not, he was with her still, where he would remain until the day she let go.

VERY FEW PEOPLE IN TOWN REMEMBERED AN-
nie Howe anymore. Her family's acreage had been sold off in parcels and her brothers had all moved west, to California and New Mexico and Utah. Some of the older residents in the village, George Nichols at the Millstone, or Zeke Harris from the dry cleaner's, or even Charlotte Evans, who hadn't been much more than a child when Annie died, recalled spying her on Main Street, certain that they would never again see a woman as beautiful as Annie, not in this lifetime or in the next.

Only Helen Davis thought about Annie. She thought of her daily, much the way a devout person might utter a prayer, words summoned forth without design. Therefore, she was not in the least surprised to smell roses one cold morning at the very end of January, a day when ice coated every growing thing, lilacs and lilies and pine trees alike. Carlin Leander also noticed the scent, for it overpowered the caramel aroma of the bread pudding she had in the oven, in the hopes that dessert might tempt Miss Davis's appetite. Miss Davis had gone to bed the previous Sunday and simply hadn't gotten up again. She had missed so many classes a substitute had been hired, and the members of the history department grumbled about the extra work they were forced to take on in Miss Davis's absence. Not one of them, including Eric Herman, knew that the woman they'd feared and disliked for so many years now had to be carried to the bathroom, a task that all but defeated Carlin and Betsy Chase working together.

"This is so embarrassing," Miss Davis would say each time they helped her to the bathroom, which was the reason Betsy had not told Eric how dire the situation was. Some things were meant to be kept concealed from public view, and that was why every time Betsy and Carlin stood outside the open bathroom door, they kept their eyes averted, trying their best to offer Helen a bit of privacy. The time for privacy, however, was over and with it the pretense that Miss Davis's health might improve. Yet when Betsy suggested a trip to the hospital or a call to the Visiting Nurses' Association, Miss Davis was outraged. She insisted it was only the flu that had her down, but Carlin knew the real reason she demurred was that Miss Davis would never tolerate being prodded and poked and kept alive past her time. Helen knew what was coming for her, and she was ready, except for one last act of contrition. In hoping for forgiveness, even those who are failing may hold on to the material world, they cling to the edges until their bones are as brittle as wafers and their tears have turned to blood. But at last what Miss Davis had been waiting for had arrived on this cold January afternoon, for it was then that she breathed in the scent of the roses, and the fragrance was so strong it was as if the vines had grown up through her bedroom floor to bloom and offer her absolution for all she had done and all she had failed to do.

Helen looked at the window to see the garden exactly as it had been when she first came to Haddan. She, herself, had always preferred red roses to white, especially those gorgeous Lincolns, which turned a deeper shade with each passing day. She did not panic the way she had feared she might when her time came. Although she was grateful for her life, she had been waiting to be forgiven for such a long time she'd thought she might never experience what she wanted most of all, and now here it was, all in a rush, as if grace and mercy were flowing through her. Things of this world fell into their proper place and appeared to be very far away: her hand on the pillow, the girl coming to sit beside her, the black cat at the foot of her bed, curled up and sleeping, breathing in, breathing out.

Helen felt a sweetness rising within her and a vision so bright she might have been gazing upon a thousand stars. How quickly her life had gone by; one moment she had been a girl taking the train to Haddan and now here she was in her bed watching dusk fall through the window, spreading out across the white walls in pools of shadow. If only she'd known how short her time on earth would be, she would have enjoyed it more. She wished she could let the girl beside her know as much; she wanted to shout, but Carlin had already gone to dial 911. Helen could hear her asking for an ambulance to be brought around to St. Anne's, but she paid little attention to Carlin's distress, for Helen was now walking to school from the train station, suitcase in hand, on a day when all the horse chestnut trees were in blossom and the sky was as blue as the china cups her mother used to set the table for tea. She had come for the job at the age of twenty-four, and all things considered, she had done well. The girl fussing about seemed silly and Helen wished she could say so. The panic in the girl's voice, the sirens outside, the cold January night, the thousands of stars in the sky, the train from Boston, how her heart had felt that day when her whole life was about to begin. Helen signaled to Carlin, who at last came to sit beside the bed.

"You're going to be fine," Carlin whispered. This was not at all true and Miss Davis knew it; still she was touched to see that the girl had turned pale, the way people did when they worried, when they truly cared.

Don't forget to turn off the oven, Helen wanted to tell the girl, but she was watching the roses outside her window, the gorgeous red ones, the Lincolns. There was the lovely sound of drowsy bees, the way there had been every June. Each year at that time, the campus had exploded into bands of red and white, ribbons of peach and pink and gold, all because of Annie Howe. Some people said bees came from all over the Commonwealth, beckoned by the roses at Haddan, and it was well known that local honey was uncommonly sweet. *Don't forget to enjoy this life you're walking through,* Helen wanted to say, but instead she held on to the girl's hand and they waited together for the paramedics to arrive.

This was a volunteer crew, men and women called away from their dinners, and as soon as they walked into the room, they all knew no lives would be saved tonight. Carlin recognized some members of the team: there was the woman who ran the dance studio, and the man who worked at the mini-mart, along with two janitors that Carlin had passed many times but had never paid much attention to. The woman from the dance studio, Rita Eamon, took Helen's pulse and listened to her heart while a canister of oxygen was wheeled in.

"It's pulmonary edema," Rita Eamon told the others before turning to Helen. "Want some oxygen, honey?" she asked Helen.

Helen waved the offer away. There was blue sky above her and all those many roses, the ones that gave off the scent of cloves in the rain and the ones that left a trace of lemon on your fingers, the ones that were the color of blood, and those that were as white as clouds. Cut one rose, and two will grow in its place, gardeners say, and so it had happened. Each one was sweeter than the next and as red as gemstones. Helen Davis tried to say, *Look at these,* but the only sound she could force out led them to believe she was choking.

"She's passing on," said one of the volunteers, a man who'd been doing this job long enough so that he did not flinch when Carlin began to cry. He was one of the janitors, Marie and Billy Bishop's son, Brian, who had worked at Haddan for quite a while and who had in fact fixed Miss Davis's refrigerator some time ago. People said Miss Davis was nasty, but Brian never saw any evidence of that; she'd had him sit at her table when he was through working, which was more than anyone else at the school had ever done. She'd given him a glass of lemonade on that hot day, and now Brian Bishop returned the favor. He took Miss Davis's free hand and sat across from Carlin as if his own dinner wasn't cooling on his table at home, as if he had all the time in the world.

"She's going easy," he told Carlin.

Someone from the rescue crew must have turned the oven off when they went into the kitchen to phone the police station and report a death on campus, because hours later, when Carlin remembered the bread pudding and hurried to retrieve the pan, the pudding was perfectly done, the syrupy topping bubbling and warm. At the president's house they knew something was wrong when the ambulance pulled up. Dr. Jones called Bob Thomas, who went out to the ambulance to ask what was going on and was surprised to find he recognized the fellow at the wheel from somewhere; although Bob Thomas couldn't quite place him, the driver, Ed Campbell, was a member of the grounds crew and had been mowing the lawns and salting the paths at the Haddan School for more than ten years. It was a gloomy evening, and bad news hung in the air.

Bob Thomas waited until the hospital in Hamilton called to notify the school that the death certificate had been signed, then he asked the janitor on duty to ring the chapel bells. When the community gathered in the dining hall, Helen Davis's passing was announced. She had been at school for so long no one could quite imagine it without her, except for Eric Herman, who had been waiting for more years than he'd like to count to take her place as the chair of the department.

"If she was that ill, it's better this way," Eric said when he saw how upset Betsy had become.

But his words weren't any comfort. Betsy felt as if something had been tossed down a well, something precious and irretrievable; the world seemed much smaller without Miss Davis as a part of it. Betsy excused herself and walked back to St. Anne's; the sky was black and starry, as cold as it was deep. A north wind was shaking the trees, but in the arbor behind St. Anne's a pair of cardinals slept in the thicket, one gray as the bark, the other red as the deepest rose.

Carlin was still in the kitchen, cleaning up. She'd tied one of Helen Davis's white aprons around her waist and was arm-deep in soapy water, crying as she scrubbed the pots. She had already consumed three glasses of the Madeira stored in the cabinet under the sink and was extremely tipsy, with a pink cast to her skin and her eyes rimmed red. For the first time the black cat hadn't begged to be let out at dark, rather it perched on the counter and mewed uncertainly. When Betsy came in, she draped her coat over a kitchen chair and examined the half-empty bottle of Madeira.

"You can turn me in if you like." Carlin dried her hands and sat across from Miss Chase at the table. "Of course, I never turned you in for having men in your room."

They stared at each other, dizzy from the scent of roses, their mouths dry with grief. Betsy poured herself a glass of wine and refilled Carlin's empty glass as well.

"It was just one man," Betsy said. "Not that I need to explain myself to you."

"Miss Davis had a crush on him. She invited him to Christmas dinner. It's none of my business, but in my opinion, he's definitely the better man."

The Madeira had a heavy, bitter aftertaste, perfectly suitable, considering the circumstances. A few nights earlier, Betsy had gone to the phone booth at the pharmacy and called Abe, but as soon as he'd answered, she hung up, completely undone by the sound of his voice.

"It's all over now, and I'd just as soon nobody knew about it."
Carlin shrugged. "It's your loss."

"What is that I smell?" Betsy asked, for the scent of roses was everywhere now. Surely, the fragrance was too floral to be wafting over from the bread pudding set out on the table. Betsy was surprised to discover that Carlin was such a good cook; she didn't think anyone made desserts from scratch anymore, not when there were instants for just about everything other than love and marriage. She gazed out the window, and seeing the cardinals perched there she grew confused; for a moment she believed them to be roses.

They let the cat out when it mewed at the door, then locked up, even though there was nothing to steal. In only a few days the maintenance crew would have the place down to bare wood and walls, carting the furniture down to the thrift shop at St. Agatha's and toting boxes of books to the secondhand store in Middletown. By now the odor in the apartment was so strong that Carlin had begun to sneeze and Betsy felt bumps rising on the most tender areas of her skin, the base of her throat, the backs of her knees, her fingers, her thighs, her toes. The scent of roses was seeping into the hallways, winding up the staircases, streaming beneath closed doors. That night, any girl who had something to regret tossed and turned, burning up while she slept. Amy Elliot, with her terrible allergies, broke out in hives and Maureen Brown, who could not abide rose pollen, awoke with black spots on her tongue that the school nurse diagnosed as bee stings, although surely such an affliction was impossible at this time of year.

A funeral mass was said at St. Agatha's early Saturday, the last cold morning of the month, with several townspeople in attendance, including Mike Randall from the bank, and Pete Byers, who'd ordered the flowers from the Lucky Day and who sat in the first pew alongside his nephew and Carlin Leander. Abe came in toward the end of the service, wearing his grandfather's old overcoat, for lack of something of his own that might be appropriate for such an occasion. He stayed in the back row, where he was most comfortable, nodding a greeting to Rita Eamon, who had come to pay her respects, as she did with every 911 patient the rescue team was unfortunate enough to lose. He waved to Carlin Leander, who looked like a pixie from hell with her hair all chopped off and the worn black coat, which was coming apart at the seams.

After the service, Abe waited outside in the raw January air, watching as parishioners left the church. Carlin had wrapped a green woolen scarf around her head, but when she came down the steps, she looked chalky and chilled to the bone. Sean Byers was close beside her; anyone could judge his attachment from the look on his face. To see a wild boy so concerned made people passing by pity him and envy him at the very same time. Pete had to drag the boy back toward the pharmacy to get him away from Carlin, and when at last he had, Carlin went over to Abe. Together, they watched six strong men from the funeral parlor carry out the coffin.

"You're not going to break Sean Byers's heart, are you?" For Abe could still see the love-struck boy looking over his shoulder as he followed his uncle down Main Street.

"People break their own hearts, if you ask me. Not that it's your business."

It was a good day for a funeral, brutal and cold. The burial was at the school cemetery and Carlin and Abe set off in that direction. Carlin didn't mind being with Abe; it was almost like being alone. She didn't have to be polite to him, and he clearly felt the same way. When the scarf on her head slipped back he nodded toward what she'd done with the razor. "Walk into a lawn mower?"

"Something like that. I mutilated myself."

"Good job." Abe couldn't help but laugh. "If Sean Byers wants you when you look like this, he'll take you any way."

"He didn't even notice," Carlin admitted. "I guess he thinks my hair was always this way."

They passed the Evanses' house, and Abe waved to Charlotte, who was peeking out her front window, curious to see who was walking along Main Street on such a dreadful day.

"Why did you wave to her?" Carlin shook her head. "I wouldn't bother."

"She's not as bad as she seems."

"Some people are worse than they seem. Harry McKenna, for instance. I think he's guilty of something. If nothing more, he knows what happened to Gus. It's disgusting how he gets to go on with his life as though nothing happened."

"Maybe." They had cut through Mrs. Jeremy's yard in order to take the fastest route to the far meadow. "Maybe not."

Now they made their way through the tall, brown grass, taking the path where the thornbushes grew. The gravediggers had been at work earlier, for the earth was frozen and it had taken three men quite some time to break ground. A small number of mourners had gathered at the graveside; faculty members who felt it was only civil to pay their respects. A pile of dirt had been deposited outside the fence and icy clods littered the path.

"I've been thinking about leaving Haddan," Carlin told Abe.

Getting out of Haddan seemed like a fine idea to Abe, especially as he was forced to watch Betsy, who was standing between Eric Herman and Bob Thomas. She had on the black dress she'd worn when she'd come to his house and stayed the night, but today she wore sunglasses and her hair was combed back and she looked entirely different than she had on that night. The priest from St. Agatha's, Father Mink, a large man who was known to cry at funerals and weddings alike, had arrived to consecrate the ground, and the circle of mourners stepped back to accommodate his girth.

Abe watched as those in attendance bowed their heads in the pale winter light. "Maybe I should be the one thinking about leaving."

"You?" Carlin shook her head. "You'll never leave here. Born and bred. I wouldn't be surprised if you got special permission to be buried right in this cemetery, just to stick it to the Haddan School."

There was no way Abe was going into that cemetery, not today and not when he was ready for his final resting place. He preferred to meet his maker out in the open, as the woman buried out at Wright's farm had, and he'd pay his respects right out here in the meadow as well. "I bet I'm gone before you are."

"I don't have to make bets," Carlin said. "Miss Davis left me money, enough to cover all of my school expenses."

The instructions in Miss Davis's will were absolutely clear. Her savings, wisely invested by that nice Mike Randall over at the 5&10 Cent Bank, were to be used in a fellowship program for students in need, providing funds each semester that ensured the recipient would not have to work and would also be free to travel during vacations. Miss Davis had stipulated that Carlin Leander was to be the first beneficiary of this award; all of her expenses would be seen to until the last day of her senior year. If she wanted clothing, or books, or a semester in Spain all she must do was write up a request and present it to Mike Randall, who would process the check and forward any cash that she needed.

"I have nothing to worry about financially." Carlin secured the green scarf around her throat. "If I stay."

Last week Carlin had turned fifteen, not that she'd told anyone, or felt she had anything to celebrate. Today, however, she didn't look more than twelve. She had the blank expression of disbelief that often accompanies the first shock of bereavement.

"You'll stay." Abe was looking at the little stone lamb, which had been festooned with a garland of jasmine.

"Miss Davis told me that people bring flowers here for luck," Carlin said when she noticed his gaze. "It's a memorial for Dr. Howe's baby, the one that was never born because his wife died. Every time a child in town is sick, the mother presents one of those garlands to ask for protection."

"I never heard that one, and I thought I'd heard them all."

"Maybe you never had anyone to protect."

When Carlin went on to the cemetery for the service, Abe stayed where he was for a while, then turned and retraced their path through the meadow. Father Mink's voice was harsh and mournful and Abe had decided he would prefer to hear birdsongs in memory of Miss Davis, who, no matter how ill, had always made certain to set out suet and seed.

His ears were ringing with the cold and he still had to get back to the church, where he'd parked his car, but he found himself heading in the opposite direction. It made no sense, he should have stayed away from the school, and yet he kept on through the meadow. It was a long, slow trek and he was freezing when he finally reached the quad. There were starlings perched in the trees, and because of the thin sunlight, the rose trellis outside St. Anne's was filled with birds. Abe couldn't see them, but he could hear them, singing as if it were spring. He recognized the chirrup of cardinals as well, and the black cat also heard the call. It was poised beside the trellis, head tilted, mesmerized by the pair of birds nesting there.

There might be another black cat with one eye in Haddan, but it wouldn't be wearing the reflective collar Abe had sprung for at Petcetera in Middletown Mall last week. Helen Davis's cat and his were definitely one and the same. If it hadn't shown up at his door, Abe would have been happy to be alone, but now things were different. He'd gotten involved, buying collars, worrying. Now, for instance, he found he was actually pleased to see the wretched creature, and he called to it, whistling as he would for a dog. The birds flew away, startled by the tinkling of the bell on the new collar, but the cat didn't glance over at Abe. Instead, it walked in the direction of Chalk House, navigating over ice and cement, not stopping until it crossed the path of a boy on his way to the river where a free-for-all game of ice hockey would soon begin. It was Harry McKenna who gazed down at the cat.

"Move," he said roughly.

Harry had always felt the need to excel. It made perfect sense that he'd surpassed those fools who'd thought themselves so brave, trapping helpless rabbits on the night of their initiation. He had chosen the black cat instead, and therefore had in his possession a souvenir far more original than a rabbit's foot, a memento he kept in a glass tube taken from the biology lab. By now, the yellow eye had turned as milky as the marbles Harry used to play with; when he shook the tube, it rattled like a stone.

On his way to play hockey, Harry knew he was finished with Haddan; he was as sure of it as he was certain whatever team he played on would win. The future was all he was interested in. He'd been granted early admission to Dartmouth, yet he sometimes had nightmares in which his final grades rearranged themselves. On such occasions, Harry awoke sweating and nauseated, and not even black coffee could separate him from his dreams. On these mornings, he grew nervous in ways that surprised him. The slightest thing could set him off. The black cat, for instance, which he came upon every once in a while. Although impossible, the cat seemed to recognize him. It would stop in front of him, as it did on this January afternoon, and simply refuse to move.

Harry would then have to shoo it away, and when that wasn't effective, he'd threaten it with a well-aimed book or a soccer ball. It was a disgusting animal and Harry felt he really hadn't done it much harm. Its owner, that nasty old Helen Davis, had spoiled it more than ever after the incident. The way Harry saw it, the cat should probably be grateful to him for ensuring it be granted a soft life of pity and cream. Now that Miss Davis was gone, the cat would probably follow her lead and good riddance to both of them, in Harry's opinion. The world would be a better place without either one.

The black cat did seem to have a surprisingly long memory; it peered up at the boy through its one narrowed eye, as though it knew him well. From where he stood, Abe could see Harry chase off the cat with a hockey stick, shouting for it to stay the hell away, but the cat didn't go far. Cruelty always gets found out in the end; there's simply no way to run from all that you do. Frail and inadequate although this evidence might be, it was all the proof Abe needed. On this cold afternoon when the starlings had all flown away, he had found the guilty party.

THE
DISAPPEARING BOY

WHAT THEY HAD PLANNED WAS
very different, but plans often go awry.
Look at any house recently built and it will
always be possible to spy dozens of errors,
in spite of the architect's care. Something is
bound to be off kilter: a sink installed on
the wrong wall, a floorboard that squeaks,
walls judged to be plumb that simply do not
meet at the proper angle. Harry McKenna
was the architect of their plan, which,
when it began, consisted of nothing more
than intimidation and fear. Wasn't that the
root of all control, really? Wasn't it the force
that obliged even the most unruly to adhere
to rules and regulations and join in the
ranks?

August Pierce had been a mistake from
the start. They'd seen it before. Boys who

liked to play by their own rules, who'd never been members of any club; individuals who took some convincing before they learned there was not just strength in numbers, but lasting power as well. That was what pledging was all about, learning a lesson and learning it well. Unfortunately, Gus never cared about such matters; when forced to attend meetings, he wore both his black coat and an expression of disdain. There were those who claimed he kept a set of headphones on, hidden by the collar of his coat, and that he spent his time listening to music instead of jotting down the rules the way other freshmen did. And so they set out to teach him his place. Each day they piled on both work and humiliation, forcing him to clean toilets and sweep the basement floor. This hazing, meant to initiate him into a code of loyalty, backfired; Gus dug in. If an upperclassman demanded he return trays in the dining room or collect dishes, he simply refused, which even the freshmen at Sharpe Hall and Otto House knew wasn't done. He would not share homework or notes, and when he was told his personal hygiene did not live up to Chalk standards, he decided to show them what filth really meant. From then on, he would not change his clothes, or wash his face, or send his laundry out on Wednesdays. His hygiene suffered further when several boys thought it would be a good lesson to turn off the water while he was in the shower. The upperclassmen waited for him to tear into the hallway, shampoo burning his eyes; they had their towels twisted for strategic hits on his bare flesh. But Gus never came out of the bathroom. He stood in the shower for a good half hour, freezing, waiting them out, and when they finally gave up, he finished washing at the sink and refused to shower from then on.

Despite this harassment, Gus had discovered something

about himself that he hadn't known before: he could take punishment. To think that he of all people had strength was laugh-out-loud funny, although when it came down to it, he might just be the strongest man in town, for all he'd survived. The other freshmen at Chalk wouldn't consider saying no to their elders and betters. Nathaniel Gibb, who had never had anything to do with alcohol before, had so much beer poured down his throat through a tube that farmers on Route 17 used to force-feed geese and ducks, that he'd never in his life be able to smell beer without vomiting. Dave Linden also refused to complain. He swept out Harry McKenna's fireplace every morning, even though soot made him sneeze; he ran two miles each day as the seniors insisted, no matter how dreadful or damp the weather, which was why he'd developed a rumbling cough that kept him up far into the night, leaving him to sleep through his classes, so that his grades fell dramatically.

It was odd that no one had figured out what was going on at Chalk House. The nurse, Dorothy Jackson, never suspected anything, in spite of the alcohol poisoning she'd seen over the years, and all the freshmen plagued by insomnia and hives. Duck Johnson seemed easy enough to fool, but Eric Herman was usually such a stickler, how was it that he hadn't noticed something amiss? Was he only concerned if his own work was interrupted? Was silence all he asked for, damn what else happened on the floors above him?

Gus had expected some measure of assistance from those in charge, and when Mr. Herman refused to listen he went to speak to the dean of students, but soon enough he understood he wouldn't get far. He'd been made to sit waiting in the outer office for close to an hour, and by the time the dean's secretary, Missy

Green, had ushered him in to see Thomas, Gus's hands were sweating. Bob Thomas was a big man, and he sat impassively in his leather chair as Gus told him about the nasty traditions at Chalk House. Gus sounded pitiful and wheedling even to himself. He found he couldn't bring himself to look Thomas in the eye.

"Are you trying to tell me that someone has assaulted you?" Bob Thomas asked. "Because, the truth is, you look fine to me."

"It's not like being beat up on the street. It's not an all-out attack. It's the little things."

"Little things," Bob Thomas had mused.

"But they're repeated, and they're threatening." To himself he sounded like a spineless tattletale from the playground. *They threw sand in my face. They didn't play fair.* "It's more serious than it sounds."

"Serious enough for me to call a house meeting and have all your fellow students hear your complaints? Is that what you're telling me?"

"I thought this charge would be anonymous." Gus realized that he stank of nicotine and that he had half a joint hidden in his inside coat pocket; in stepping forth to make this accusation, he might be the one who was expelled. Definitely not what his father had in mind when sending him to Haddan.

"'Anonymity most often points to a lack of courage or a flawed moral compass.' That's a quote from Hosteous Moore from the time he was headmaster here and it's a sentiment I second. Do you want me to go to Dr. Jones with this information? Because I could. I could interrupt him, even though he's at an educators' meeting in Boston, and I could bring him back to

Haddan and I could tell him about these little things, if that's what you want me to do."

Gus had been the loser in enough situations to know when a fight was pointless. So he kept his mouth shut; he certainly didn't tell Carlin anything for if he had, she would surely have gone running to Dr. Jones, probably more indignant about all those rabbits killed over the years than anything else. She would have wanted to do his fighting for him, and Gus could not have tolerated that. No, he had a better plan. He'd managed to best the Magicians' Club. He would complete the impossible task Dr. Howe had long ago set forth for his wife.

It was Pete Byers who told him it could be done. Pete knew a bit about roses because his wife, Eileen, was a superior gardener. Even Lois Jeremy phoned every now and then for advice concerning a no-pesticide method to remove Japanese beetles (a spray of water and garlic was best) or a remedy that would remove toads from her perennial beds (welcome them, was the answer, for they'll eat mosquitoes and aphids). In June, blooms of the spectacular Evening Star grew right outside the Byers's bedroom window with a silver color that made it appear the moon had been caught in their backyard.

Pete was merely a helper in the garden, there to spread mulch and plant seedlings. Thumbing through a horticulture magazine only days earlier, trying to figure out the fertilizer situation, he'd been amazed to discover that a piece Eileen had submitted on her favorite topic, white gardens, had been published. That she'd done so without telling him had shocked Pete; he'd never thought of Eileen as having secrets, as he did. He'd read the article carefully and so he remembered how Eileen had noted that

Victorians often filled their gardens with white flowers precisely because they liked to amuse one another with the exact trick the boy had been searching for.

Gus let out a whoop when he heard the transmutation was far from impossible; he leaned over the lunch counter to grab Pete and give him a bear hug. Each day afterward, Gus stopped by to check if his order had arrived, and at last, on the day before Halloween, Pete handed him the aniline crystals.

That night, Gus went to the graveyard to calm his nerves and think about all the magicians he'd seen with his father. What they'd all had in common, the mediocre and the transcendent alike, was confidence. Up in the tall elm, the crow called out its disapproval at Gus's slouching figure. A bird such as that was far better at sleight of hand than Gus would ever be, swift as a thief. Still, Gus knew the most important attributes were always invisible to the naked eye, and he was practicing silence and patience when Carlin Leander, who'd been avoiding him for weeks, came walking along the path.

Gus should have remained silent, but instead he let his pain out in a blast of anger. After they'd argued, and he'd climbed over the iron fence, an odd calm came over him. It was after midnight when he returned to Chalk House, and the others were waiting. It was the hour of tricks and deep resentments, the time of night when people found it difficult to fall asleep even though the village was quiet, except for the sound of the river, which seemed so close by anyone from out of town might have imagined its route followed Main Street.

Gus went to Harry's room on this, his pledge night. The boys formed a circle around him, certain that by morning Gus Pierce would be gone; his initiation a failure, he'd either go of his own free will or be expelled when the proper authorities found the marijuana Robbie and Harry had stashed on the top shelf of his closet. Either way, he'd soon be consigned to the evening train and Haddan history. But before he left, they had a surprise waiting for him, a going-away present of sorts. They had no idea that Gus had a surprise of his own. Although Harry's room was overheated, Gus wore his black coat, for the white flowers he'd bought at the Lucky Day were concealed within. He believed his father would have been proud of his style, for he had rehearsed until he was able to pluck the roses from his coat with a flourish worthy of a professional. The blooms were luminous in the darkened room, and for once those idiots Gus had to live with, those fools who took so much pleasure in humiliating him, fell silent.

It was a long and beautiful moment, quiet and sharp as glass. August Pierce spun away from his audience, quickly sprinkled the aniline over the flowers, then he wheeled back to face his tormentors. There, before their eyes, the roses turned scarlet, a shade so alarming that many in the room thought immediately of blood.

No one applauded; not a single word was said. The silence fell like a hailstorm, and that was when Gus knew he had made an error, and that success was the last thing he should have tried to achieve. In the light of Gus's small triumph, something poisonous had begun to move through the room. If Duck Johnson really considered that night, he might recall the quiet in the house; he would remember there had been no need to announce curfew, and although that was rather unusual, he was ruminating about problems with the crew team—lack of leadership, lack of spirit—and he took no notice. Eric Herman heard them later on, there were footsteps in the hallway and urgent, hushed voices; if pressed he would have to admit he felt annoyed, for there never seemed to be peace and quiet at Chalk House, even after midnight, and he had work to do. Eric turned up his stereo as he graded papers, grateful to at last hear nothing but cello and violin.

Two boys held their hands over Gus's mouth, and although he could not shout, he managed to bite down on someone's fingers, hard enough to break the skin. They dragged him down the hall and into the bathroom, no doubt the commotion Eric had heard before he put on his headphones. The boys at Chalk weren't about to allow Gus's success to alter their plans for a send-off. They had all used the toilet in preparation and it was filled and stinking as they lifted Gus up and plunged him into the bowl headfirst. They were all supposed to be silent; it was a vow they had taken, but several of them had to cover their mouths and hold back their nervous laughter. Gus tried to get away at first, but they jammed his head down lower. There was a snicker when he started thrashing his legs around.

"Look at the big shot now," someone said.

Gus's legs were soon jerking weirdly, as if he had no control, and he actually kicked Robbie Shaw in the mouth. Filthy water spilled onto the tiles and when Nathaniel Gibb gasped at the brutality, the sound echoed with a high-pitched metallic ring. Some actions, once begun, have nowhere to go but all the way to the end, like a spring that has been wound up tightly and set. Even those who offered an unspoken prayer could not back down; it was far too late for that. They kept his head in the toilet until he stopped struggling. That was the point, wasn't it? To get him to give up the fight. Once the battle was over, he seemed like a rag doll, all batted cotton and thread. They'd meant to scare him and reduce him to his rightful place, but what they got when they pulled him out was a boy who'd already begun to turn blue, suffocated in their waste and venom, unable to draw a breath.

Some of the older fellows, tough, competent students who played vicious games of soccer and sneered at whoever they considered to be weak, panicked immediately and would have run off had Harry McKenna not told them to shut up and stay where they were. There was a purple bruise on Pierce's forehead where he'd hit his head against the inside of the commode; he'd lost consciousness early on in this game and therefore hadn't fought back as they'd expected him to, at least until the very end when the struggle was involuntary and already impossible to win.

Harry pounded on Gus's back, then turned the body faceup and called Robbie over. Robbie had been a lifeguard for the past two summers, but he could not be persuaded to put his mouth to Gus's, not after Pierce had been soaked in all that excrement. In the end, Nathaniel Gibb frantically tried mouth-to-mouth resuscitation, trying desperately to pump air back into Gus's lungs, but it was too late. There was water and waste all over the floor as moonlight poured through the window illuminating what they'd wrought: a six-foot-tall dead boy, sprawled upon the tiled floor.

Two of the most practical fellows ran to the basement for buckets and mops and did their best to clean and disinfect the bathroom floor. By then, the older boys had carried Gus Pierce out of the house. Dave Linden was instructed to sweep the path behind them to clear their tracks away as they proceeded in silence, out the back door and down the path to the river. They trod along through the woods until they found a spot where the bank sloped gently. The area smelled faintly of the violets that bloomed there in spring, and one of the boys, suddenly reminded of his mother's cologne, began to weep. This was the place where they laid the body down, quietly, slowly, so that several green frogs asleep in the grass were caught unawares and crushed beneath the unexpected weight. Harry McKenna knelt over the corpse and buttoned the black coat. He left the eyes open, as he imagined they would be had someone chosen to walk into the river on a clear, moonlit night with the intent of drowning himself. Then came the end of the journey. Gus was hauled down the bank to the shore that rolled easily into the dark water. The boys maneuvered him past the reeds and the lily pads until they were knee-deep, floating him between them like a black log, and then they let him go, all at once, as though they had planned it. They released him to the current and not one of them stayed to watch where it would take him or how far downstream he would have to travel before he found a place to rest.

THE BOYS FROM CHALK BEGAN TO FALL ILL during the first week of February. One by one it happened, and after a while it was possible to predict who the fever would afflict next simply by looking into an individual's eyes. Some who'd been stricken were so lethargic they could not rise from their beds; others could not get a single night of sleep. There were boys whose skins crawled with an unforgiving rash and those who lost their appetites completely, able to digest only crackers and warm ginger ale. Attendance in classes fell to an all-time low, with morale lower still. Aspirin disappeared from the infirmary shelves, ice packs were called for, antacids swallowed. Those most affected were the new boys up in the attic, who suffered in silence, lest they call attention to themselves. Dave Linden, for instance, endured debilitating migraines that kept him from his studies, and Nathaniel Gibb experienced a constant tightening in his chest, and though he never complained, there were times when he had to struggle for breath.

The school nurse admitted that she'd never seen anything like this current scourge; she wondered if perhaps a new strain of Asian flu had befallen these boys. If so, those who'd taken ill had no choice but to wait for their own antibodies to restore them to health, for surely, no medicine that had been doled out had done the least bit of good. In fact, the epidemic had not been triggered by a bacterial infection or a virus. The blame for the outbreak rested squarely with Abel Grey, for in that first week of the month, as the afternoon sunshine encouraged stone flies to bask on warm rocks along the riverside, Abe stationed himself on the Haddan campus. He didn't speak to anyone or approach them, but his presence was felt all around. In the morning, when boys raced down the steps of Chalk House, Abe would already have made himself comfortable on a nearby bench, eating his breakfast and scanning the *Tribune*. He was posted at the door of the dining hall at noon and could be found there again in the evening at supper. Every night, after dark, he parked in the lot beside Chalk House, where he listened to his car radio as he ate a bacon cheeseburger picked up at Selena's, trying his best not to get any grease on Wright's coat. Each time a boy left the house, whether going for a run or hurrying to join friends in a game of hockey, he'd be confronted with the sight of Abel Grey. Before long, even the most self-confident and brashest among them began to have symptoms and fall ill as well.

Guilt was a funny thing, a fellow might not even notice it until it had already crawled inside him and set up shop, working away at his stomach and bowels, and at his conscience, as well. Abe was well acquainted with the need for contrition, and he kept watch for the ways in which it might surface, singling out several residents who seemed more nervous than most, trailing along as they went to class, keeping an eye out for the warning signs of remorse: the flushed complexion, the tremors, the habit of looking over one's shoulder, even when no one was there.

"Do you expect someone to come to you and confess?" Carlin asked when she realized what Abe was doing. "That's never going to happen. You don't know these boys."

But Abe did know what it was like to hear the dead speaking, placing blame on those left behind for all they had or had not done. Even now, when he drove past his family's old house he sometimes heard his brother's voice. That's what he was looking for here at the school: the person who was trying his best to run away from what was inside his own head.

As he kept his vigil at the school, he also had the pleasure of observing Betsy Chase. For her part, Betsy did not seem pleased by Abe's presence on campus; she kept her eyes lowered and if she spied him, she turned on her heel and changed direction, even if that meant she'd be late to class. Abe always felt a combination of turmoil and joy when he saw her, even though it had become clear he was unlucky in love, not that good fortune appeared in his card playing during poker games at the Millstone, although by rights, he should have been dealt all aces, all the time.

One morning, when Abe had been at Haddan for more than a week, Betsy surprised him by veering from her usual route and walking directly toward him. Abe had been keeping watch from a bench outside the library after phoning down to the station to ask that his schedule be changed yet again. He could tell that Doug Lauder, who'd been covering for him, was starting to get annoyed, although Doug hadn't complained enough to prevent Abe from being here at the school, drinking a café au lait he'd picked up at the pharmacy. Although shoots of jonquils had appeared in the perennial beds and snowbells dotted the lawns, the morning was raw and steam rose from Abe's paper cup. Gazing through the haze, he thought he was imagining Betsy when she first began to approach, in her black jacket and jeans, but there she was, standing right in front of him.

"Do you think no one notices that you're here?" Betsy lifted one hand to shield her eyes; she couldn't quite make out Abe's expression in the thin, glittering sunlight. "Everyone's talking about it. Sooner or later they'll figure it out."

"Figure what out?" He stared right at her with those pale eyes. She couldn't stop him from doing that.

"You and me."

"Is that what you think?" Abe grinned. "That I'm here for you?"

The sunlight shifted and Betsy saw how hurt he'd been. She went to sit at the far end of the bench. How was it that whenever she saw him she felt like crying? That couldn't be love, could it? That couldn't be what people went searching for.

"Then why are you here?" She hoped she didn't sound interested, or worse, desperate.

"I figure sooner or later someone will tell me what happened to Gus Pierce." Abe finished his coffee and tossed the cup into a nearby trash can. "I'm just going to wait until they do."

The bark of the weeping beech trees was lightening, green

knobs forming along the sweeping branches. Two swans advanced toward the bench warily, feathers drooping with mud.

"Shoo," Betsy called out. "Go away."

Spending so much time on campus, Abe had become accustomed to the swans and he knew that this particular pair were a couple. "They're in love," he told Betsy.

The swans had stopped beside the trash barrel to bicker over crusts of bread.

"Is that what you call it?" Betsy laughed. "Love?" She had a class to teach and her hands were freezing but she was still sitting on the bench.

"That's exactly what it is," Abe said.

After he left, Betsy vowed to keep away from Abe, but there seemed no way to avoid him. At lunch, there he was again, helping himself to the salad bar.

"I've heard that Bob Thomas is furious that he's hanging around," Lynn Vining told Betsy. "The kids have been complaining to their parents about a police presence on campus. But, God, is he good-looking."

"I thought you were crazy about Jack." Betsy was referring to the married chemistry teacher Lynn had been involved with for several years.

"What about you?" Lynn said, not mentioning that she'd been unhappy for some time, having realized that a man who was willing to betray one woman wouldn't mind betraying another. "You can't take your eyes off him."

As for Abe, he sat at a rear table in the dining hall, eating his salad, watching the boys from Chalk House. All he needed was for one boy to confess an involvement and he hoped the others would fall into place, each one scrambling for immunity and understanding. He believed he'd found the signs he'd been searching for in Nathaniel Gibb, whom he followed when the boy dumped his uneaten lunch in the trash. All that afternoon he trailed Nathaniel, stationed outside his biology lab and his algebra classroom, until at last the beleaguered boy wheeled around to face him.

"What do you want from me?" Nathaniel Gibb cried.

They were on the path that led along the river, a route many people avoided due to its proximity to the swans. Nathaniel Gibb, however, had more to fear than swans. Lately, he had begun to spit up blood. He had taken to carrying a large handkerchief with him, a rag that both shamed him and reminded him of how fragile a body could be.

Abe saw what he'd been looking for, that line of fear behind the eyes. "I want to talk to you about Gus, that's all. Maybe what happened to him was an accident. Maybe you know something about it."

Nathaniel was the sort of boy who had always done what was expected of him, but he no longer knew what that meant. "I don't have anything to say to you."

Abe understood how difficult it was to live with certain transgressions. Own it, and the pain ceases. Say it out loud, and you're halfway home.

"If you talk to me, no one will hurt you. All you have to do is tell me what happened that night."

Nathaniel looked up, first at Abe and then, beyond him. Harry McKenna was horsing around on the steps of the gym along with some of his buddies. The afternoon was filled with streaky, yellow light and the chill in the air remained. As soon as Nathaniel saw Harry he began to cough his horrible cough, and before Abe could stop him, he turned and ran down the path. For a while Abe jogged after him, but he gave up when Nathaniel disappeared into a crowd of students.

That evening Abe could feel trouble coming, just as he always could when he was a boy. And sure enough, the very next day, as Abe was about to leave his post at the school to run over to Selena's to pick up some lunch, Glen Tiles and Joey Tosh pulled up next to Wright's old cruiser in the parking lot of Chalk House. Abe went over and leaned down to talk to Glen through the window.

"I see you're creating your own schedule these days," Glen said.

"It's just temporary," Abe assured him. "I'll make up any hours I've missed."

Glen insisted on taking Abe out to lunch, even though Abe assured him that it wasn't necessary.

"Yes it is." Glen reached to open the rear door. "Get in."

Joey did the driving, one hand on the wheel. His expression was guarded; he didn't look away from the road, not once. They drove all the way to Hamilton, to the Hunan Kitchen, where they picked up three orders of General Gao's chicken to go, in spite of Glen's restricted diet, then ate in the car, on a street facing the Hamilton Hospital. Such a lunch guaranteed privacy, as well as indigestion.

"Did you know the Haddan School has made a contribution that will let us start construction for a medical center in Haddan?" Glen said. "There's a party to celebrate next weekend, and let me tell you, Sam Arthur and the rest of the councilmen will be pissed as hell if anything goes wrong between now and then. It would save lives, you know, Abe. Not having to come all the way to Hamilton in an emergency alone would make it worth it. It might have been possible to save Frank, if we'd had a decent facility in town that had been prepared to deal with gunshot wounds. Think about that."

Abe deposited his chopsticks into the container of spicy chicken. He felt a tightness, as though a band were being pulled around his chest. He used to feel this way when he couldn't please his father, which, it turned out, had been most of the time.

"So all we have to do to get the medical center is to look the other way when some kid is killed?"

"No. All you have to do is stay the hell away from the Haddan campus. Bob Thomas is a reasonable man and he made a reasonable request. Stop harassing his students. Stay off the grounds."

They drove back along Route 17 in silence. None of the men finished the food they'd traveled so far to obtain. Abe was let off by his car in the lot of Chalk House, where there was a thin scrim of ice over the asphalt. Joey got out of the car, too.

"If you keep bothering the powers that be at the school, we'll all suffer," Joey said. "The way I see it, money coming from the Haddan School is owed to this town. We deserve it."

"Well, I disagree."

"Fine. Then you do it your way and I'll do it my way. We don't have to be fucking identical twins, do we?" Joey was already on his way back to the car when Abe called after him.

"Remember when we jumped off the roof?" Abe had been thinking about that time ever since they passed the turnoff to Wright's house on Route 17.

"Nope."

"Out at my grandfather's place? You dared me and I dared you and we were both stupid enough to go for it."

"No way. Never happened."

But it had, and Abe recalled how blue the sky had been that day. Wright had told them to mow the back fields where the grass was nearly as tall as they were, but instead they'd climbed onto a shed, then made a leap for the roof of the house, clutching onto the gutters and pulling themselves over the asphalt shingles. They'd been twelve, that reckless age when most boys believe they will never get hurt; they can jump through thin air, shouting at the top of their lungs, waking all the blackbirds in the trees, and still land with only the wind knocked out of them and not a single bone broken. Back then, a boy could be as certain of his best friend as he was of the air and of the birds and of the everlasting that grew in the fields.

Joey wrenched the door of his car open and shouted over the idling motor, "You're imagining things, buddy. Just like always."

After they'd pulled away, Abe got into his car and drove over to the Millstone. It was still early and the place was empty and maybe this was the reason Abe felt as though he'd entered a town he'd never been to before. For one thing, there was a new bartender on duty, someone George Nichols must have hired who didn't know Abe by name and who wasn't familiar with the fact that Abe preferred draft beer to bottled. George Nichols had inherited the place and was already considered ancient when Joey and Abe first tried out their fake IDs. He'd busted them several times, phoning Abe's grandfather whenever he caught them hanging out in the parking lot, where they would plead with the older guys to buy them drinks. When Abe was living with his grandfather he'd wasted one entire week of summer confined to his room after George Nichols discovered him in the men's room of the Millstone with a contraband whiskey sour. "You're not devious enough to get away with this sort of thing," Wright had told Abe back then. "You're going to get caught each and every time."

But what about the boys who didn't get caught, that's what Abe wanted to know as he fished peanuts from a bowl on the bar. Those boys who were so guilt-ridden they broke out in hives or started spitting blood, but who managed to get away with their wrongdoings, how did they live with themselves?

"Where's George?" Abe asked the new bartender, who hardly looked of age to drink himself. "Out fishing?"

"He's got some physical therapy appointments. His knees are giving up on him," the new bartender said. "Decrepit old bastard."

When Abe got up from the barstool his own knees didn't feel so great. He went out and blinked in the sunlight. He couldn't shake the feeling of being a stranger in town; he made two wrong turns on his way to the mini-mart and couldn't find parking on Main Street when he went to pick up one of Wright's sport coats at the dry cleaner's. Why, he didn't even recognize anyone at the cleaner's, other than Zeke, another old-timer who had a fondness for Abe due to the fact that his grandfather had stopped the town's only armed robbery on record thirty-five years earlier in this very establishment. That there had been only fourteen dollars in the cash register didn't matter; the robber had a gun pointed straight at Zeke when Wright happened to walk through the door, arriving to pick up some woolen blankets. For this reason Abe was given a twenty percent discount to this day, though in fact he rarely had anything to dry-clean.

"Who are all those people?" Abe asked, when the line of customers before him had thinned out and he could pick up Wright's coat.

"Damned if I know. But that's what happens when a town starts growing. You stop knowing everyone by name."

But for now, it was still Abe's town and in his town it was not against the law for a taxpaying citizen to wander across Haddan School grounds. If there had been such a law, local people would have been incited to riot before the ink on the edict had dried. Imagine Mrs. Jeremy's son, AJ, being kicked off the soccer field when he arrived with his golf clubs to work on his short game. Imagine the yoga club, meeting on Thursday mornings for more than ten years, thrown off the quad as if they were common criminals rather than practitioners of an ancient discipline. Abe was pushing his luck, he knew that, but all he needed was a little more time before Nathaniel Gibb broke down. He began to track the boy again.

"Just talk to me," Abe said as he trailed after Gibb.

By now, Nathaniel was panicked. "What are you trying to do to me?" he cried. "Why won't you leave me alone?"

"Because you can tell me the truth."

They were on that same path beside the river where before long fiddlehead ferns would unfold; there really was nowhere for Nathaniel to run.

"Just think about it," Abe went on. "If you meet me here tomorrow and tell me you don't want to talk, then I won't bother you anymore." It was the time of year when those Haddan boys had needed to be rescued by Abe's grandfather, the season when the ice on the river appeared thick to the inexperienced passerby, but upon closer inspection the surface revealed itself to be clear rather than blue, the way river ice is right before it begins to break apart.

"It wasn't me," Nathaniel Gibb said.

Abe did his best not to react; he was not about to scare this boy off, even if his head did feel as if it were about to explode. "I know that. That's why I'm talking to you."

They arranged to meet early the next day, at an hour when the blackbirds were waking and most students at Haddan were still asleep in their beds. The sheen of spring was everywhere, in the yellowing bark of the willows, in the cobalt color of the morning sky. Though the season would soon change, it was brisk enough for Abe to keep his hands in his pockets as he waited. He waited for a long time, there on the path to the river. At eight o'clock, students began to appear, on their way to breakfast or the library, and by nine most classrooms were full. Abe walked over to Chalk House, tinkered with the lock—an easy push-button type any rookie could get past—and let himself in. There was a directory in the hallway. Abe was not surprised to see that Harry McKenna had what appeared to be the best room, nor was he surprised that Gibb's room was up in the attic.

"Hey, there," Eric Herman called when he saw Abe on the stairs. Eric had just finished compiling his exam for the following week's midterm and was rushing off to class, but he took the time to stop and look Abe over. The dean had made an announcement asking to be informed if anyone who didn't belong was found on campus. "I think you're in the wrong place."

"I don't think so." Abe stayed where he was. He'd never before been face-to-face with his rival. What had he imagined? That he'd challenge Herman, that a fight would result, with punches aimed to inflict the most damage? What he found was that he merely felt he and Eric Herman had something in common, they were both in love with Betsy. "I'm looking for Nathaniel Gibb."

"You're out of luck. He's in the infirmary."

Abe could tell from the way Eric was glaring at him that he wouldn't get any more information out of him, but fortunately Dorothy Jackson was a regular at the Millstone, and much friendlier when Abe approached her; in spite of the dean's warning not to speak to Abe, the nurse let him visit the infirmary.

"He's had a bad accident at hockey practice. Five minutes," she granted Abe. "No more."

Nathaniel Gibb lay on his back on the cot nearest the wall. Both his arms had been broken. He'd been driven by ambulance to the hospital in Hamilton where X rays were taken and casts had been fashioned, and now he was awaiting his parents, who were on their way from Ohio to bring him home. For months, he would have to be fed and dressed, as though he were an infant once again, and it was somehow fitting that he had also lost the ability to speak. Whether this development had been caused when he bit down on his tongue, nearly severing it as the group of boys at hockey practice rammed him into the wall, or whether the words had simply been scared out of him really didn't matter. He could not speak to Abe.

"I don't know what you want from this boy," Dorothy Jackson said when she brought up a glass of ginger ale with a straw. "But he probably won't be able to talk for a month. Even then he'll need speech therapy for some time."

Abe waited for the nurse to leave, then went over to Nathaniel and lifted the glass so that the boy might quench his thirst. But Nathaniel wouldn't even look at him. He would not drink even though his tongue, stitched together at the emergency room by a resident who had never before performed the procedure, was throbbing.

"I'm sorry." Abe sat down on a nearby cot. He was still holding the glass of ginger ale. The infirmary smelled of iodine and disinfectant. "I was probably wrong to get you involved. I hope you can accept my apologies."

The boy made a guttural sound that might have been a laugh or a snort of contempt. Nathaniel peered over at Abe, hunched on the metal cot across from his own. Sunlight poured in through the windows and the dust motes whirled into the shape of a funnel. In only a few hours Nathaniel Gibb and his belongings would be loaded into his parents' car, ready to drive far from this place. Here was one boy who would never again have to set foot in Massachusetts or go through another of its wicked winters. He would be miles away, safe in his home state, which is why he forced himself to open his mouth and move his tortured tongue, straining to utter an initial, the letter of the alphabet that hurt him most to recite, a clear and single *H*.

BY THE FOLLOWING MORNING ABE HAD BEEN released from duty, the first officer in Haddan ever to be asked for his resignation. Abe wasn't even dressed when Glen Tiles arrived on his front steps to tell him the news. What had he expected, really? A dozen or more of the staff at Haddan had seen him stalking students, helping himself to food in the dining hall, bothering the faculty with questions. And then there'd been Eric, who'd wasted no time in contacting the dean.

"You had to push it," Glen said. "You couldn't take my advice. I had the attorney general's office call me on this, Abe. Somebody over there is an alum."

The two men stood there facing each other in the cold, bright light. They had measured each other against Wright's legacy, and neither believed the other would ever come close to the old man's stature. At least now they wouldn't have to see each other every day. By lunchtime, everyone in town knew what had happened. Lois Jeremy and her friend Charlotte Evans had already mobilized, but when they tried to reach Abe to inform him they had started a petition to have him reinstated, he didn't answer his phone. Over at Selena's, Nikki Humphrey made up the sandwich Abe usually ordered for lunch and had it waiting for him, but he never showed up. He didn't even bother to get dressed until sometime past noon. By then, Doug Lauder had been told that he was being promoted to detective, and truthfully, Doug deserved it; he was a decent guy and he'd do a good job, although the job would never mean as much to him as it had to Abe.

Toward the end of the day, Abe went out for a drive. He still had Wright's old cruiser, and he figured he might as well make use of it in case they came to repossess it. He spotted Mary Beth in the park with her children. Even though the new baby was due in a few weeks, MB still looked great, and both girls on the swings, Lilly and Emily, the eldest, resembled their mother, with dark hair and wide-set hazel eyes. Abe knew nothing about children, but he knew they had big expenses, and that Joey would want to provide them with all that he could and more. It was the more that was the problem. Abe got out of the cruiser and went to greet Mary Beth.

"Hey, stranger," she said, hugging him.

"You look great."

"Liar." MB smiled. "I'm a whale."

A person could really learn to hate February living in this part of the world, although the kids surely weren't bothered by the gloomy weather; they screamed with glee as they went higher and higher on the swings. Abe remembered exactly what that felt like—no fear. No thought of the consequences.

"Not so high," Mary Beth called to her children. "I heard about what happened at work," she said to Abe. "I think it's just crazy."

Joey and MB's son, Jackson, was a maniac on the swings; he went as far into the sky as possible, then came rushing down to earth, breathless and hollering out loud. Joey was crazy about this kid; on the day he was born, Joey had thrown open the doors of the Millstone, inviting everyone to have a drink, charged to his tab.

"I heard about it from Kelly Avon. Joey didn't even tell me. What's happened between you two?" Mary Beth asked.

"You tell me."

Mary Beth laughed at that. "Not possible. He talks to you more than he talks to me."

"Not anymore."

"Maybe he just grew up." Mary Beth put one hand over her eyes in order to keep watch over her children in the dwindling sunlight. "Maybe that's what happens with friendships. I think he sees the kids getting older and he wants to spend more time with them. If this was before, he'd be planning a fishing trip with you over the Easter break, now we're all going to Disney World."

A vacation such as that was an expensive proposition for Joey, who in the past had often needed to borrow from Abe to pay off his monthly mortgage payment. As he thought this over, Abe noticed that Mary Beth's wreck of a car had been replaced by a new minivan.

"Joey surprised me with that," Mary Beth said of the van. "I've been driving around in that old station wagon for so long I thought I'd be buried in it." She took Abe's hand. "I know it's not the same between you, but that won't last."

She'd always been generous about their friendship; she'd never complained about including Abe in their lives or griped about the time Joey spent away from her. She was a good woman who deserved a minivan and a whole lot more, and Abe wished he could be happy for her. Instead, he felt as though they'd both lost Joey.

"I hope you're going to fight to get reinstated," Mary Beth called when he headed back to his car, even though it was clear to them both that it would be pointless for him to do so.

Abe drove to the school out of habit, like a dog who insists on circling the same plot of land, certain there are birds in the grass. Because he stood a good chance of being arrested if caught venturing onto private property, Abe parked down by the river and walked the rest of the way. He could feel his heart lurching around in his chest, the way it used to when he and Joey took this route. They didn't have to talk back then; they knew where they were headed and what they meant to accomplish. He went past the place where the violets grew in spring and along the dirt trail to the rear of Chalk House. He didn't even know what he wanted until he came to a window through which he could see Eric Herman's living quarters. He could feel something fill up his head, blood or lunacy, he wasn't sure which. He was wearing gloves, because of the chill in the air, or maybe a break-in was what he'd intended all along. Either way, he didn't have to protect himself when he put his fist through the window, shattering the glass, then reached in to unhook the latch.

He pulled himself over the ledge; it wasn't as easy as it once was, he was heavier, for one thing, and there was his bad knee to think of. He was breathing hard by the time he was in Eric's living room. He brushed the glass off and began to take a look around. A thief could decipher a great deal from observing a person's lodgings, and Abe could tell that Betsy would never be happy with the man who lived there. He could not imagine her in this tidy room, beneath the sheets of the perfectly made bed. Even the refrigerator revealed how wrong Herman was for Betsy; all he had was mayonnaise, bottled water, half a jar of olives.

Whenever Abe burglarized a house he could always sense where he would find the best loot, he had a natural ability to zero in on treasures, and as it turned out he hadn't lost that knack. There it was, in the living room, the midterm for Eric's senior history seminar, five pages of questions on Hellenic culture. A typed class list had been paper-clipped to the exam. Quickly, Abe looked down the page until he found what he was looking for. Harry's name.

He rolled up the exam and kept it inside the sleeve of his jacket as he went through the door that opened into the hallway of the dormitory. It was the dinner hour and except for a few boys who were ill, no one was around. It was easy enough to walk down the hallway, and easier still to discern which room was Dr. Howe's old office: there was the mantel into which so many lines had been carved, there were the golden oak floors, and the woodwork that was dusted by the hired maid every other week, and the desk, into which Abe deposited exactly what Harry McKenna deserved.

CARLIN WAS ON HER WAY HOME FROM A SWIM meet in New Hampshire when she felt him beside her. She had claimed a double seat on the bus for herself, throwing down the black coat, not wanting to be forced into making polite conversation with any of the other girls on the team. It was just as well that the seat next to her was vacant, for now there was room for what was left of August Pierce to settle in beside her, drop by watery drop.

Although Carlin had performed well at the meet, it had been a generally disappointing evening and the bus was quiet, the way it always was after a defeat. Carlin hadn't even bothered to shower before she dressed; her cropped hair was wet and smelled of chlorine, but the droplets of water that now rolled down the plastic seat weren't from her hair, nor from her soaking bathing suit, stowed away in her gym bag. Carlin glanced to see if a nearby window had been left ajar, for there was a fine drizzle falling outside, but all the windows were shut and there were no leaks in the roof of the bus. The liquid Carlin noticed wasn't rainwater; it was murky and green as it spread out over the seat, a watermark that had both weight and form. Carlin could feel her heart racing, the way it did when she pushed herself to the limit during a race. She looked straight ahead and counted to twenty, but she could still feel him beside her.

"Is that you?" Carlin's voice was so small no one on the bus took notice; not even Ivy Cooper in the seat right behind overheard.

Carlin moved one hand to touch the black coat. The fabric was soaking and so frigid to the touch she immediately began to shiver. She could feel the cold moving up her arm, as if ice water had been added to her veins. The bus had already entered Massachusetts and was headed south on 93, toward the Route 17 exit. Outside, it was so dark and damp everything disappeared into the mist, fences and trees, cars and street signs. Carlin reached her hand into the pocket of the black coat to find it had filled with water. There was silt there, too, in among the seams, the grainy mud from the bottom of the river, along with several of the little black stones so often found when the bellies of silver trout were slit open by fishermen's knives.

Carlin glanced across the aisle to where Christine Percy was dozing. In Christine's hazed-over window, she could see Gus's reflection. Inside the black coat, he was as pale as tea water, so translucent his features evaporated in the glare of oncoming headlights. Carlin closed her eyes and leaned her head against the seat. He had appeared beside her because she had wanted him to. She had called him to her, and was calling him still. Even when she fell asleep, she dreamed of water, as if the world were topsy-turvy and everything she cared about had been lost in the deep. She plunged through the green waves with her eyes wide open, searching for the world as she'd known it, but that world no longer existed; everything that had once been solid was liquid now, and the birds swam alongside the fish.

It was not until the bus pulled into the parking lot at Haddan, gears squealing, engine straining, that Carlin awoke. She came back with a start, arms flailing, the way the girls on the team had been taught a drowning person's might, and a wave of panic moved through the bus. At that point, Carlin was making a gurgling sound in the back of her throat, as though she were already past any rescue, but thankfully, Ivy Cooper had a cool head; she quickly handed Carlin a paper bag, into which Carlin breathed until her color returned.

"You're freezing," Ivy said when their hands touched as Carlin gratefully returned the paper bag. "Maybe you were in the water too long."

Carlin reached for her black coat and her gym bag, ready to rush off, then realized that most of the girls had turned their attention to a car parked on the grass in front of Chalk House. In spite of the drizzle and the late hour, Bob Thomas was out there along with some other man none of the girls recognized.

"What's happening?" Carlin asked.

"Where have you been?" Ivy Cooper stood beside her. "They're kicking Harry McKenna out of school. They found a midterm exam in his room. There was a hearing last night, and he couldn't talk his way out of it. I heard he broke into Mr. Herman's quarters to get the exam. He smashed the window and everything."

Sure enough, the trunk of the parked car was filled with suitcases and a heap of possessions tossed in hurriedly. Everything Harry owned was there, his sweaters, his sneakers, his books, his lamp. Some of the girls from the swim team had begun to file out of the bus and were already running through the rain toward St. Anne's, but Carlin stayed where she was, gazing out the window. At last Harry came out, as though he were in a hurry to get somewhere. He was wearing a sweatshirt with a hood, so that it wasn't possible to see his fair hair, or even to manage a good look at his face.

He flung himself into the passenger seat of his father's car, then slammed the door shut. Carlin got off the bus, the last to leave. She could still see Harry from where she stood in the parking lot, but he didn't look at her. The dean and Harry's father didn't bother to shake hands; this was not a friendly parting. Dartmouth had been informed of Harry's expulsion and his admittance there had been retracted. He would not be attending college in the fall, nor would he graduate from high school this year, as he'd been asked to leave before the end of the semester. Carlin followed along behind Harry's father's car as it slowly traversed the speed bumps in the parking lot, then turned onto Main Street. She walked along through the rain, which was falling harder now, hitting against the roofs of the white houses. The car was a luxury model, black and sleek and so quiet most people in town didn't even notice it on the road. Once it had passed the inn, the car began to pick up speed, splashing through the puddles, leaving a thin trail of exhaust that drifted down the center of town.

It was after curfew when Carlin sneaked into her room, and although the hour was late, Amy Elliot was up in bed, sobbing.

"Now are you happy?" Amy cried. "His life is ruined."

Carlin got into bed, fully dressed. She wasn't happy at all; Harry's departure wouldn't bring Gus back. Gus wouldn't rise from the river in the morning to retrace his steps; he wouldn't wake in his bed, ready for school, eager for his life to go on. When the morning did come, Carlin didn't attend classes. It was the harsh end of the month and torrents of rain were now falling, none of which prevented Carlin from going to the bank to speak to Mike Randall, then taking the bus to a travel agency in Hamilton where she used her funds from Miss Davis to buy a plane ticket. She rode the bus back to Haddan late in the day, going directly to the pharmacy, where she sat down at the counter. By then it was after three and Sean Byers had reported for work. He was at the sink, rinsing out glasses and cups, but when he saw Carlin he dried his hands and came over.

"You're drenched," he said, his voice a mixture of longing and concern.

Puddles of water had collected on the floor around Carlin's stool and her hair was plastered against her head. Sean poured her a hot cup of coffee.

"Do you ever feel like you want to go home?" Carlin asked him.

Although the pharmacy was usually busy at this hour, the heavy rain seemed to be keeping people off the streets and out of the stores. Sam Arthur from the town council was the only other customer in the place; he was going over the plans for the ground-breaking celebration for the new medical center, muttering to himself and enjoying a strawberry milkshake, an item that was definitely not on his diabetic diet plan.

"Is that what you're thinking about doing?" Sean asked. He hadn't seen Carlin much since Christmas vacation, at least not as much as he would have liked. He still sneaked into the pool, late at night, hoping that she'd be there, too, but she never was. It was as if the time they'd had together existed separately from the rest of their lives, like a dream that's in danger of dissolving as soon as the dreamer awakes. "You're running away?"

"No." Carlin was shivering in her wet clothes. "I'm flying." She showed him the one-way ticket.

"Seems like you've already decided."

"They kicked Harry out of school," Carlin told Sean.

"Nah. Guys like that never get kicked out of anything."

"This one did. Late last night. He was expelled for cheating."

Sean was gleeful. He did a little victory dance, which made Carlin explode into giggles.

"You're not pretty when you gloat," she told him; all the same, she laughed.

"You are," Sean said. "I just wish you weren't such a coward."

A group of ravenous Haddan students had braved the rain on a mission for hamburgers and fries and Sean was called to take their order. Carlin watched as he tossed meat patties onto the grill and started the fryer. Even here in the pharmacy, Carlin felt as though she were stuck underwater. The world outside floated by—Mrs. Jeremy with her umbrella, a delivery truck of hibiscus pulling up to the Lucky Day, a gang of kids from the elementary school racing home in rain slickers and boots.

"I'm not a coward," Carlin told Sean when he returned and refilled her cup with steaming black coffee.

"You're letting them chase you off. What do you call it?"

"Wanting to go home."

Because of his extremely dark eyes Sean Byers had the ability to hide most of what he felt inside. He'd always been a good liar; he'd talked himself out of situations that would have landed anyone else in jail, but he wasn't lying now. "This is what you always wanted. Why would you leave if you weren't being chased off?"

Carlin threw down some money to pay for her coffee, then headed for the door. The potatoes in the fryer were sizzling, but Sean followed her anyway. He truly didn't care if the whole place burned to the ground. The rain was falling in such torrents that when it hit against the asphalt it sounded as if guns had been fired or cannons discharged. Before Carlin could plunge onto the sidewalk, Sean pulled her back beneath the pharmacy awning.

He was crazy about her, but that's not what was at stake here. The rain was coming down harder, yet Carlin could hear Sean's heart beneath the fabric of his shirt and the rough white apron he wore. All the world out there was liquid, all of it enough to pull her down, and so, for this brief time she held on tight and did her best not to drown.

A TENT HAD BEEN SET UP IN THE FIELD BEHIND town hall and above it a flag had been raised to wave in the wind so that no one in town would fail to notice the ground-breaking celebration. The Becker construction company had been retained by the town council and Ronny Becker, Doreen and Nikki's father, had already bulldozed a level area that allowed the tent to be set up on flat ground; it certainly wouldn't do for any of the older guests such as Mrs. Evans, who'd recently been in need of a cane, to tumble over the ruts and break a hip or a leg.

The Chazz Dixon band played that afternoon, and two dozen of Mr. Dixon's violin and flute students from the elementary school were allowed to miss their last class in order to attend. Thankfully, even though it was the rainy season, the afternoon was clear and sunny with a brisk, rather enjoyable west wind. Just to be safe, portable heaters had been set up inside the tent, to ensure that those in attendance could enjoy the salmon sandwiches and cream cheese puffs that the staff of the Haddan School cafeteria served on large silver trays. It came as no surprise to anyone that while people from town tended to congregate over by the bar, the staff and faculty of the school gathered around the hors d'oeuvres table, gorging on deviled eggs and clam cakes.

A motion had already been passed by both the board of trustees at the school and the town council to name the health center after Helen Davis and a bronze plaque with her name etched upon it had been set into the cornerstone. The dean had asked Betsy Chase to commemorate the occasion with a photograph, and she was there to preserve the moment when Sam Arthur shook hands with Bob Thomas, each man standing with one foot balanced on the cornerstone. Betsy was then asked to photograph the doctors who'd been wooed away from an HMO in Boston, along with the center's new administrator, Kelly Avon's cousin, Janet Lloyd, who was delighted to be moving back to Haddan after eight years of exile at Mass General.

On the way over, Betsy had noticed the cruiser Abe drove, one of dozens of cars left at the curb along Main Street, where the no-parking signs had been covered with burlap hoods. In spite of herself, Betsy found herself looking for him, but the place was crowded, filled with people Betsy didn't know, and she didn't see Abe until the Chazz Dixon band was playing its final set. He was standing beside the makeshift cloakroom, a direction Betsy needed to go toward anyway, in order to retrieve her coat.

"Hey," she said as she approached. "Remember me?"

"Sure I do." Abe raised his drink to her and said, "Have fun," then quickly moved on. He had decided that he was finished getting hit over the head with rejection, so he made his way to the bar to get himself another beer. In spite of all the initial hoopla, people were managing just fine without Abel Grey on the police force. Mrs. Evans, for instance, had taken to phoning Doug Lauder about the raccoon that came into her yard to eat her birdseed and rattle her trash cans. A new uniformed cop had been hired and in the mornings he could be seen at the crosswalk in front of the elementary school. On days when the garden club met, he was posted outside town hall, directing traffic and gratefully accepting the thermoses of hot chocolate Kelly Avon had taken to delivering. Residents who had invited Abe into the most personal moments of their lives—Sam Arthur, for instance, with whom Abe sat vigil when his wife, Lorriane, was in that head-on collision while visiting their daughter in Virginia, and Mrs. Jeremy, who had wept while Abe talked AJ out of jumping out a second-story window one horrible spring night, a leap that probably wouldn't have done any more than rattle a few of AJ's bones considering how drunk he'd been—now seemed startled when they ran into him, embarrassed by all the secrets he'd once been privy to. Actually, Abe himself didn't feel that comfortable with most people, what with Joey and Mary Beth clearly avoiding him and all those busybodies from Haddan School who'd reported him for harassment keeping an eye on him.

The only reason he'd shown up at the festivities was to pay his respects to Helen Davis. He'd already had two beers in honor of her memory and he figured a third wouldn't hurt. He'd have a couple of drinks and get out, no damage done, but when he turned he saw that Betsy had also come to the bar. She was asking for a glass of white wine, and looking his way.

"There you go, following me again," Abe said, and he was surprised when she didn't deny it. "Give her the good stuff, George," Abe told the bartender, George Nichols from the Millstone.

"The school's footing the bill," George said. "Trust me, there is no good stuff."

"I heard you got fired," Betsy said as she moved aside to let AJ Jeremy get to the bar.

"I prefer to think of it as a permanent vacation." Abe looked past AJ and signaled for George Nichols to add only a small amount of vodka to the double vodka tonic AJ had ordered. "Looks like they roped you into being the inquiring photographer," he said when Betsy stepped back to take a shot of Chazz Dixon, wailing on his saxophone with a fervor that shocked many of his music students. Betsy turned and found Abe in her viewfinder. Most subjects were shy, they tended to look away, but Abe stared back at her with an intensity that flustered her and made her snap his picture before she was ready. It was those blue eyes that were to blame, and had been from the start.

"My turn," Abe said.

"You have no idea how to take a decent picture." Betsy laughed as she handed over the camera.

"Now you'll always remember this day," Abe told her after he'd taken her picture. "Isn't that what they say about a photograph?"

It was a big mistake not to just walk away from each other and they both knew it, but they stood together awhile longer and watched the band.

"Maybe you should hire them to play at your wedding," Abe said of the musicians.

"Very funny." Betsy drank her wine too fast; later in the day she'd have a headache, but right now she didn't care.

"I don't think it's funny at all." He was reaching toward her.

"What are you doing?"

Betsy was so certain that he was about to kiss her, that she found it difficult to breathe. But instead, Abe showed her the quarter he'd pulled from behind her ear. He'd been practicing, and although the trick still needed work, in his many free hours he'd discovered that he had a gift for sleight of hand. Already, he'd finagled close to a hundred bucks out of Teddy Humphrey, who still could not figure out how Abe always discerned which card Teddy picked from the deck.

"You're good at that," Betsy said. "Just the way you're good at breaking into places."

"Is this an official investigation or a personal accusation?"

Betsy swayed to the music. She refused to say more, even though as soon as she'd heard about the robbery at Eric's, her first thought was of Abe. Even now she wondered if the student they'd expelled, Harry McKenna, might have been innocent of that particular crime. "I think it's too bad Helen Davis couldn't be here."

"She would have hated it," Abe said. "Crowds, noise, bad wine."

"They've found someone to take her place." As the new head of the department, Eric had been on the hiring committee. A young historian fresh out of graduate school had been chosen, someone too fresh and insecure to question authority. "They wasted no time replacing her."

"Here's to Helen." Abe raised his beer aloft, then finished it off in a few gulps.

Betsy had a dreamy look on her face; lately she had been especially aware of how a single choice could alter life's course. She wasn't used to drinking wine in the afternoon, and maybe that was why she was being so chummy with Abe. "What do you think Helen would have changed if she could have chosen to live her life differently?"

Abe thought this over, then said, "I think she would have run off with me."

Betsy let out a yelp of laughter.

"You think I'm kidding?" Abe grinned.

"Oh, no. I think you're serious. You definitely would have made an interesting couple."

Now when Abe reached for her he really did kiss her, there in front of the Chazz Dixon band and everyone else. He just went ahead and did it and Betsy didn't even try to stop him. She kissed him right back until she was dizzy and her legs felt as though they might give out. Eric was over by Dr. Jones's table with the rest of the Haddan faculty and might easily have seen them had he looked behind him; Lois Jeremy and Charlotte Evans were walking right past, chattering about the good turnout, and still Betsy went on kissing him. She might have gone on indefinitely if the drummer in the Dixon band hadn't reached for his cymbals and startled her into pulling away.

Some of the crowd had decided to create a dance floor, up beyond the coatroom, and several locals were letting loose before the band packed up. AJ Jeremy, who had managed to get looped despite his mother's watchful eye, was dancing with Doreen Becker. Teddy Humphrey had taken the opportunity to ask his ex-wife to accompany him to the dance floor, and to everyone's surprise Nikki had agreed.

"Well," Betsy said, trying to compose herself after their kiss. Her lips were hot. "What was that for?"

She looked up at Abe but she couldn't see his eyes. So much the better, for if she had she would have known exactly what the kiss was for. At least she was smart enough not to watch when Abe walked away. She told him once there had never been anything between them, now she just had to convince herself of the very same thing. She ordered herself another glass of wine, drank it too quickly, then got her coat and buttoned it against the changing weather. Above the tent, the flags snapped back and forth in the wind, and the late afternoon sky had begun to darken, with clouds turning to black. It was the end of the celebration, and by then Eric had found her.

"What's wrong?" he asked, for her face was flushed and she seemed unsteady. "Not feeling well?"

"No, I'm fine. I just want to go home."

Before they could leave there was the sound of thunder, rolling in from the east, and the sky was darker still.

"Bad timing," Eric said. Through the fabric of the tent they could see a fork of lightning. "We'll just have to wait it out."

But Betsy couldn't wait. She could feel little bits of electricity up and down her skin each time the sky was illuminated, and before Eric could stop her, she dashed out of the tent. As she made her way along Main Street, the sky rumbled, and another line of lightning crossed the horizon. The storm was moving closer, and there were several large oak trees on Main Street and on Lovewell Lane that were particularly susceptible to a strike, but that didn't stop Betsy on her way back to the school. Before long, fat raindrops had begun to fall, and Betsy stood with her face upturned. Even with the rain washing over her, she continued to burn; she hadn't talked herself out of anything.

Bob Thomas had asked her to rush the photographs, so she went directly to the art building. She was happy to be working, hoping she might keep her mind off Abe, and as it turned out, the photographs she'd taken that afternoon were quite good. One or two of the prints would make their way to the front page of the Sunday edition of the *Haddan Tribune*—the one of Sam Arthur and Bob Thomas shaking hands and another of Chazz Dixon wailing away. It was amazing how the lens of a camera could pick up information that was otherwise invisible to the naked eye. The suspicion on Sam Arthur's face, for instance, when he gazed at the dean; the sweat on Chazz Dixon's brow. Betsy had assumed she'd be most rattled by the photograph of Abe, but in fact he had moved and the image was blurry. It did him no justice at all. No, it was the photograph Abe had taken of her that turned out to be the most disturbing. Betsy let that print sit in the developing vat for quite some time, until it was over-developed and streaky, but even then, it was impossible to ignore what this picture revealed. There, for all the world to see, was a woman who'd fallen in love.

THE ARBOR

IN THE PEARLY SKIES OF MARCH
there were countless sorrows in New England. The world had closed down for so
long it seemed as though the ice would
never melt. The very lack of color could
leave a person despondent. After a while
the black bark of trees in a rainstorm
brought on waves of melancholy. A flock of
geese soaring across the pale sky could
cause a person to weep. Soon enough,
there would be a renewal, sap would again
rise in the maples, robins would reappear
on the lawns, but such things were easily
forgotten in the hazy March light. It was
the season of despair and it lasted for four
dismal weeks, during which time more
damage was done in the households of

Haddan than the combined wreckage of every storm that had ever passed through town.

In March, more divorces came before old Judge Aubrey and more love affairs unraveled. Men admitted to addictions that were sure to bring ruin; women were so preoccupied they set fire to their houses accidentally while cooking bacon or ironing tablecloths. The hospital in Hamilton was always filled to capacity during this month, and toothaches were so commonplace both dentists in Hamilton were forced to work overtime. Not many tourists came to Haddan during this season. Most residents insisted that October was the best month to visit the village, with so much marvelous foliage, the golden elms and red oaks aflame in the bright afternoon sunshine. Others said May was best, that sweet green time when lilacs bloomed and gardens along Main Street were filled with sugary pink peonies and Dutch tulips.

Margaret Grey, however, always came back to Haddan in March, despite the unpredictable weather. She arrived on the twentieth of the month, her boy Frank's birthday, taking a morning flight up from Florida and staying overnight with Abe. Abe's father, Ernest, could not be asked to accompany her; Margaret wouldn't have expected her husband to face the cemetery any more than she would have insisted Abe pick her up at the airport in Boston. She took the train up to Haddan, looking out at the landscape she once knew so well; it all seemed terribly unfamiliar, the stone walls and the fields, the flocks of blackbirds, the multitudes of warblers who returned at this time of year, marking Frank's birthday by swooping across the cold, wide sky.

Abe waited for his mother at the Haddan train station, the

way he did every year. But for once he was early and the train was late, held up outside Hamilton by a cow on the tracks.

"You're on time," Margaret commented when Abe came to give her a hug and collect her suitcase, for he was notoriously late on the occasion of these visits, postponing the sorrow that inevitably accompanied the day.

"I'm unemployed now," he reminded his mother. "I've got all the time in the world."

"I recognize this car," Margaret said when Abe led her over to Wright's cruiser. "It wasn't safe to drive twenty years ago."

They stopped at the Lucky Day Florist where Ettie Nelson hugged her old friend and told Margaret how jealous she was of anyone who lived in Florida, where it was already summer when here in Haddan they still had to struggle with dreadful blustery weather. Abe and his mother bought a single bunch of daffodils, as they always did, although Margaret stopped to admire Ettie's garlands.

"Some people swear by them," Margaret said of the garlands. Some were fashioned of boxwood and jasmine, others of pine boughs, or of hydrangeas, twisted together in a strand of heavenly blue. "Lois Jeremy's boy, AJ, nearly died of pneumonia when he was young, and Lois went out to the Haddan cemetery day after day. There were so many wreaths around that lamb's neck you would have thought it was a Christmas tree. But maybe it worked—AJ grew up strong and healthy."

"I don't know about the healthy part," Abe said as he thanked Ettie and paid for the flowers. "He's a bully and a drunk, but maybe you're right. He's definitely alive."

Frank was buried in the new section of the church cemetery.

Each September, Abe put in chrysanthemums at the base of the memorial and in the spring he came to weed around the hedge of azaleas that Margaret had planted that first year when every day hurt, as if sunlight and air and time itself were the instruments of heartache and pain. Today, as he watched his mother place the daffodils at the graveside, Abe was struck by what a short time Frank had had on this earth, only seventeen years. Abe himself might have had a son that age if he'd ever managed to settle down.

"I should have known it was going to happen," Margaret said as they stood together. "All the signs were there. We thought it was a good thing that he locked himself away from other people. He was studying so hard and doing so well."

Abe's parents had always seemed to agree that what happened that day had been an accident; a boy who didn't know any better playing around with a shotgun, a single instant of misfortune. But clearly Margaret had come to believe this hadn't been the case, or maybe she just hadn't the heart to admit her doubts before.

"When you look backwards everything seems like a clue, but that doesn't mean it is," Abe told her. "He had French toast for breakfast, he washed the car, he was wearing a white shirt. Does any of that matter?"

"He'd be thirty-nine today. The same age as AJ Jeremy. Both of them born on the day before spring," Margaret said. "That morning I knew something was wrong because he kissed me, just like that. He put his hands on my shoulders and kissed me. He didn't even like to be hugged when he was a baby. Frank wasn't a people person that way. He was always going off on his own. I should have known then and there, it was so out of the ordinary. Kissing wasn't his way."

Abe bent to kiss his mother's cheek.

"It's your way," she said, and her eyes filled with tears.

There are secrets kept for self-interest and those kept to protect the innocent, but most spring from a combination of the two. For all these years Abe had never told anyone about the favor he did his brother. He kept his promise, just as he had on that hot summer day. It was so rare for Frank to take an interest in Abe or include him in his life, how could Abe have denied him anything he might want?

"I went with him to get the gun." This is what Abe had wanted to tell his mother since that hot afternoon, but the words had stuck in his throat, as if each one had been fashioned from glass, ready to cut at the slightest admission. Even now, Abe couldn't look at Margaret. He couldn't abide the expression of betrayal in her eyes that he'd imagined since Frank had died. "He said it was for target practice. So I did it. I climbed through the window and got it."

Margaret's mouth was set in a thin line when she heard this information. "That was wrong of him."

"Of him? Don't you hear what I'm telling you? I got the gun." He clearly recalled the look on Frank's face when he crouched down so that Abe could climb on his shoulders. Never had Abe seen such certainty. "I helped him do it."

"No." Margaret shook her head. "He tricked you."

Above them in the sky, two hawks glided west, cutting through the canopy of rolling clouds. The weather had turned nasty, the way it often did on Frank's birthday, an unpredictable day in an unpredictable month. Margaret asked if they might go

out to Wright's farm. She had always believed that kindness be-
got kindness but that truth was more complex, and that it
brought to an individual whatever he wished to take. Truth was a
funny thing, difficult to hold on to, difficult to judge. If Margaret
hadn't been the one to be with Wright Grey on the last day of his
life she would never have known that her husband, Ernest, was
not Wright and Florence's natural son.

"Don't be silly, Pop," she had said to Wright when he told her.

She'd been young and nervous around death and she remembered wishing Ernest would hurry up and relieve her. When she
heard his car pull up she was grateful.

"I found him," Wright had insisted. "By the river. Under some
bushes."

Margaret had stared at the window to where Ernest was taking a hospital bed from the trunk of his car, in the hopes of making his father's last days more comfortable. While Ernest set up
the bed in the front parlor, Wright told Margaret how he'd discovered the baby most people in town believed never took a single breath. That child had in fact been born and lived on, left by
his mother in the care of the swans, tucked into the roots of the
willows and kept out of sight until Wright had come searching
for Dr. Howe. Wright had wanted to dole out some measure of
punishment, for all the mistreatment Annie had suffered, but he
never did thrash the headmaster as he'd set out to, even though
he believed Howe deserved it, for he had been distracted by a
trail of tears and blood that led to the willow where the child had
been hidden from his father.

The very next morning, Wright walked all the way into Boston
with the infant tucked inside his coat. He was a man who'd always held himself accountable, even when the accounts weren't

his. He passed through towns he'd never been to before and villages that consisted of nothing more than a post office and a general store. At last he reached the city limits; at an embankment of the Charles River he spied a young woman and because of the kindness that showed in her face he immediately knew she was the one he would marry. Wright approached her slowly, so he would not frighten her away. Annie Howe's baby was warm and safe inside his coat, sucking on a rag dipped in store-bought milk. Wright sat down beside Florence, who was good-natured and plain and who'd never before had a handsome man look at her, let alone pour out his heart to her. They raised the child as if he were their own, because that's what he'd become. They hoped that the boy would never know grief or loss or sorrow, but such things are part of the natural world; they can't be escaped or denied.

Margaret Grey had married a boy most people believed had never been born, so she knew that anything was possible. "Maybe I should have bought those garlands, the way Lois Jeremy did," she said to Abe as they drove out to the farm. "Maybe things would have been different then."

Margaret thought of all that she knew for certain, that day would always follow night and that love was never wasted, nor was it lost. On the morning when it happened, Frank had gone to the market to pick up milk and bread and Margaret had watched him all the way down the road. People always say that anyone who's watched until they disappear out of sight will never be seen again, and that was exactly how it had happened. There wasn't a thing to be done about it, not then and certainly not now. If she had placed a thousand garlands around the lamb's neck, it might not have kept him from harm.

When they reached Wright's house, Abe opened the passenger door and helped his mother out. Some people were lucky with their children and some people were not, and Margaret Grey had turned out to be both. Abe was so tall and strong he surprised her. People said he would come to no good, but Margaret had never believed that, which was the reason she finally told him who his grandparents were. He didn't believe her at first, he laughed and said that there wasn't a person in town who hadn't told him how much he resembled Wright. But of course, it was possible for both things to be true and to belong most of all to those who loved you.

The deed to Wright's house was in Abe's name. He still had a few developers who came sniffing around, including some fellow from Boston who wanted the acreage to build a mall like the one over in Middletown, but Abe never returned their calls. Route 17 was getting so built up that it seemed as if they were pulling into a different time when they turned onto the dirt road that led to Wright's place. There were dozens of robins, returning from wintering in the Carolinas, and they perched in the apple trees that grew near Annie's grave, the one in the meadow, to which Wright used to bring the flowers he picked by the river. Because of the circumstances of her death, Annie had not been allowed a burial at the Haddan School cemetery, where her husband was later put to rest, or in the churchyard. Wright had been the one to retrieve her remains from Hale Brothers Funeral Parlor, and he and Charlie Hale had dug the grave themselves on a windy day when the dust was flying everywhere and there wasn't a cloud in the sky. Love someone and they're yours forever, no matter how much time intervenes, that's what Margaret Grey knew. The sky will always be blue; the wind will always rise up across the meadow and thread its way through the grass.

IN APRIL, PEOPLE HEARD THAT ABEL GREY WAS planning to leave town, not that they believed the rumors. Some people are predictable; they never wander far. Neighbors begin to set their own lives by the clockwork of such individuals and they want to keep it that way. As far as anyone knew, the only times Abe had ever left town were on those occasions when he'd gone fishing with Joey Tosh or when he'd visited his parents in Florida. People believed he'd no more move away from Haddan than he'd dance through the streets naked, and one or two of the boys at the Millstone put money down, with serious odds, betting that Abe would remain in his house on Station Avenue until the day they came from Hale Brothers to carry him to his rest.

And yet facts were facts. A man who's about to leave town always leaves a trail as he finishes up his business, and such was the case with Abe. Kelly Avon reported that he had closed out his bank account at the 5&10 Cent Bank, and Teddy Humphrey witnessed him searching through the recycle bin behind the minimart for cardboard boxes, always a sign of a move to come. Every morning, people at the pharmacy discussed whether or not Abe would go. Lois Jeremy was of the mind that Abe would never leave the town where his brother was buried, but Charlotte Evans wasn't so sure. A person never could tell what was inside somebody or what they might do. Look at that nice Phil Endicott her daughter was married to, how his personality had changed so completely during the divorce proceedings. Pete Byers, who never gossiped in his life, now looked forward to contemplating the direction Abe's future might take every night at dinner. He'd begun to close the pharmacy early in order to get home and discuss the possibilities with his wife, Eileen, who he'd recently discovered had a great deal to say, having saved up twenty years' worth of talk, so that the two of them were often up all night, whispering to each other in bed.

Betsy Chase heard about Abe when she was at the Haddan Inn meeting with Doreen Becker, going over the final plans for her wedding reception. It was the first day of spring vacation, and Betsy had taken the opportunity to deal with the details of her personal life. She had already let Doreen know that she didn't want to hire the Chazz Dixon band, not that they weren't terrific musicians, when Doreen's sister, Nikki, phoned to inform Doreen that Marie Bishop had told her that she could look out her living room window and see Abe packing up his car, that old cruiser of Wright's no rational man would have bothered to keep.

The inn was overheated, and maybe that was why Betsy felt faint when she heard the news of Abe's leaving. She asked Doreen for a glass of water, which did no good at all. In the hedges outside, a starling sang sweetly, the first strains of its spring song, a trilling that was a lullaby to some ears and a restless call to others. Mrs. Evans's and Mrs. Jeremy's perennial gardens were filled with jonquils and tulips, and the oaks along Main Street had clusters of fresh, green buds. It was a beautiful day, and no one thought anything was amiss when they saw Betsy walking down Main Street later on. By now they were used to her wandering through town, asking directions, and making wrong turns, until at last she found her way.

People who thought they knew her, Lynn Vining and the rest of the art department, for instance, would never have predicted that Betsy would leave the way she did, with a hasty grade sheet drawn up for her classes and a call to a storage company to come for her furniture. Lynn herself was forced to serve as St. Anne's houseparent for the rest of the year, a job that gave her a continuous migraine. No wonder that afterward Lynn told anyone within earshot that she now believed it was impossible ever to divine a person's truest nature. Eric Herman, on the other hand, was not really surprised at Betsy's sudden departure. He had seen the way she'd looked at lightning, and to his closest friends he admitted he was relieved.

The black cat was already pacing on the other side of Abe's door, begging to be let out, when Betsy arrived. As it happened, neither Betsy nor Abe had much to pack. They threw their belongings into the trunk of Wright's old car, then had coffee in the kitchen. It was close to noon by the time they got going, time enough for anyone with doubts to back out. Since Abel Grey was the sort of man who liked to tie up loose ends, he rinsed out his coffeepot before they left, and emptied the containers of milk and orange juice so they wouldn't spoil in the refrigerator. For the first time in his life, he had a clean kitchen, which made it all the easier for him to leave.

He tried his best to get the cat to go with them, but cats are territorial creatures and this one was especially stubborn. It could not be coaxed into the backseat, not even with an opened can of tuna fish. Despite this bribe, the cat gazed back at Abe with such disinterest that Abe had to laugh and give up. When they were set to leave, Abe crouched down on the pavement to pat the cat's head, and in response the cat's one eye narrowed, with disapproval or pleasure, it was impossible to tell. In truth, this cat was the individual in Haddan Abe felt sorriest to leave, and he waited for a while in the idling car with the back door open, but the cat only turned to trot down the street, never once looking back.

They drove out of town, past the new housing developments, past the mini-mart and the gas station and the fields of everlasting. They went on until they reached the road that led to Abe's grandfather's house. The day was so bright Betsy thought about putting on sunglasses, but the sky was too beautiful and too blue to miss. In the woods, the violets were blooming, and hawks swooped above the meadows. They got out when they reached the farm, slamming their doors shut, so that the blackbirds took flight all at once, weaving above them as if cross-stitching themselves onto the sky. Bees were rumbling around the lilacs beside the porch and although the farm was miles from the marshy banks of the river, there was the call of spring peepers. Abe went out to pay his last respects with a bunch of wild irises he'd stopped to pick alongside the river road. Aside from the fence, no one would have any reason to believe this was anyone's final resting place; it was just another stretch of land where the grass grew high and turned yellow in the fall.

Watching him, Betsy ignored the urge to reach for her camera, and instead she stood there and waited for him to come back to her. The grass he walked through was new and a sweet smell clung to his clothes. There was blue dye on his hands from the wild irises. These were the things Betsy would always remember: that he waved to her as he made his way back through the field, that she could feel her own pulse, that the color of the sky was a shade that could never be replicated in any photograph, just as heaven could never be seen from the confines of earth.

For a time they stood looking at the old house, watching as

the shadows of clouds settled onto the fields and the road, then they got back into the car and drove west, toward the turnpike. It was days before anyone realized they were gone, and Carlin Leander was the first to know they'd left town. She knew long before Mike Randall at the 5&10 Cent Bank received a notice to sell Abel's house and wire him the money, before the Haddan School understood it would be necessary to find someone to take over Betsy's classes. She knew before Joey Tosh used his key to check inside Abe's house, where he was surprised to find that the kitchen was tidy and neat, as it never had been before.

Carlin had traveled home for the Easter break, as most students did, the difference being she had no definite plans to return to Haddan. Sean Byers had borrowed his uncle's car to drive her to Logan Airport and he'd noticed that she had more luggage than most people had when they were going away for only a week. She had packed a tote bag of books and brought along the boots she'd bought at Hingram's, even though there'd be no need for such things in Florida. In spite of his fears that she might not return, Sean kept his mouth shut, which wasn't easy for him. His uncle Pete had taken him aside that morning and told him that when he got older he'd understand that patience was an unappreciated virtue, one that a man would do well to cultivate even when he was the one who was being left behind.

And so, instead of going after her, Sean had sat in his uncle's parked car and watched her leave. He was still thinking about her when she walked out into the bright, humid Florida afternoon, instantly dizzy in the heat.

"Are you crazy, girl?" Carlin's mother, Sue, asked, as she greeted Carlin with a huge hug. "You're wearing wool in April. Is that what they taught you up in Massachusetts?"

Sue Leander was polite about Carlin's cropped hair, although she did suggest a visit to the hair salon up on Fifth Street, just to give her daughter's new hairstyle a little oomph with a perm or body wave. As soon as they got home, Carlin stripped off the sweater and skirt she'd bought at the mall in Middletown in favor of shorts and a T-shirt. She went to sit on the back porch, where she drank iced tea and tried to become reacclimated to the heat. She'd been cold for so long she'd gotten used to it somehow, that crisp Massachusetts air that carried the scent of apples and hay. Still, she liked hearing her mother's voice through the open window; she liked seeing the red hawks circle above her in the white-hot sky. When she told her mother she wasn't sure about going back, Sue said that would be just fine, she wouldn't be letting anyone down, but Carlin knew that she and her mother had always seen things differently and that the only one who might be let down by such a decision was Carlin herself.

One afternoon, the postman brought Carlin a package, mailed from the post office in Hamilton. It was a Haddan School T-shirt, the sort they sold in the notions aisle of the pharmacy, along with a Haddan coffee mug and a key ring, all of it sent by Sean Byers. Carlin laughed when she saw the gifts. She wore the Haddan shirt when she went out with her old friend, Johnny Nevens.

"Boola boola," Johnny said when he saw the shirt.

"That's Yale." Carlin laughed. "I'm at a boarding school. Haddan." She pointed to the letters across her chest.

"Same difference." Johnny shrugged. "Little Miss Egghead."

"Oh, shut up."

Carlin slipped on a pair of sandals. For the first time in her life she was worried about the snakes her mother always said came out after dusk, searching for insects and rabbits.

"I don't get it," Johnny said. "All these years you've been telling me how smart you are, and now that I'm finally agreeing with you, you're pissed."

"I don't know what I am." Carlin raised her hands to the sky as though pleading for answers. "I have no idea."

"But I do," Johnny told her. "And so does everybody else in this town, so you can relax, smarty-pants."

They went over to the park on Fifth Street, the only hangout in town other than the McDonald's on Jefferson Avenue. It was a gorgeous night and Carlin sat on the hood of Johnny's car and drank beer and looked at stars. She'd spent the past few months tied up in knots, and now she felt herself get loose again. The cicadas were calling as if it were already summer, and there were white moths in the sky. The moonlight was silvery, like water, pouring over the asphalt and the streets. People were nice to Carlin and several girls she'd known in grade school came over to tell her how great she looked, in spite of the haircut. Lindsay Hull, who had never included Carlin in anything, went so far as to invite her to the movies on Saturday with a group that went to the mall together on a weekly basis.

"I'll call you if I'm still in town," Carlin told Lindsay.

She wasn't certain if she was looking for a way to get out of the invitation or if in fact she had not yet made up her mind whether or not to stay. Later, she and Johnny drove down to the woods, to the place where they had once had the misfortune to confront an alligator. They were just kids and to Johnny's enduring humiliation, he'd been the one to run. Carlin, on the other hand, had hollered like a demon until the alligator turned tail and headed back to a pool of brackish water, moving quicker than anyone would guess a creature that big could manage.

"Man, you stared him right in the eye." Johnny was still proud of Carlin's long-ago encounter. He talked about her at parties, referring to her as the girl who was so willful and mean she could scare a gator back into the swamp.

"I was probably more terrified than you were." The night was darker here than it was in Massachusetts, and much more alive, filled with beetles and moths. "I was just too stupid to run."

"Oh no," Johnny assured her. "Not you."

All that week, Carlin sat in front of the TV, addicted to The Weather Channel. The sky in Florida was clear, but in New England a series of spring storms had passed through and Massachusetts had been hit especially hard. Sue Leander appraised her daughter's expression while she took in this news, and Sue knew then and there that Carlin would not be staying. In the end, Carlin went back to school a day early, arriving on the empty campus after the worst of the storm damage had already been done. She had sprung for a taxi from Logan, using money from the travelers' fund Miss Davis had arranged. It was a luxury Carlin hardly enjoyed once they arrived in Haddan and she saw how much devastation there had been in her absence. Streams that had been running high from melting snow had overflowed and the fields were now green with water rather than cabbages and peas. Several silver trout had been stranded on the road, their luminous scales crushed into the blacktop, and anyone traveling this route needed sunglasses, even on the cloudiest of days.

"Spring squalls are the worst," the taxi driver told Carlin. "People are never prepared for them."

They had to bypass Route 17 entirely, for a five-foot-deep puddle had collected beneath a highway bridge. Instead, they drove along the long, loopy road that passed farm stands and several of the new housing developments. There was still a bite in the damp, green air, and Carlin slipped on Gus's overcoat. She'd brought it with her to Florida and kept it in her closet until her mother had complained of water seeping onto the floor. Carlin had thought she'd leave what had happened behind when she left school, but in Florida she had continued to find black stones, on the back porch, in the kitchen sink, beneath her pillow. She felt Gus's presence whenever she stepped out of the sunlight, like a splash of water. Every morning, she had awoken to find that her sheets were damp, the fabric gritty, as if sand had drifted over the cotton. Carlin's mother blamed the humid air for soaking the bedclothes, but Carlin knew that wasn't the cause.

When at last the taxi drove through the village, Carlin took note of the storm damage. Several of the old oaks on Main Street had been split in two and the eagle in front of town hall had been permanently tumbled from its bronzed perch. Some of the big white houses would have to be reroofed, but the Haddan School had been hit with the most severe damage, for the river had risen four feet above its highest level, flooding the buildings, which had fortunately been emptied of residents during spring break. Now, the sopping carpet in the library would have to be torn up and removed, and the parking lot behind the administration building was still being drained with a sump pump belonging to the department of public works. Worst affected had been Chalk House, built so perilously close to the river. The house had tilted and lurched as the river rose; at last whole sections of the foundation were swept away. When Billy Bishop, the town building inspector, was called in, he announced there was nothing to do but take the whole mess down before it fell down. It was an emergency situation, with the real possibility of structural collapse, and the house was razed during vacation. Two afternoons and some bulldozers did the trick, and people from town not only gathered to watch, they applauded when the timbers came crashing down, and several local children swiped bricks to keep as souvenirs.

Students returning from the holidays came back to a hole in the ground, and although several boys from Chalk House did not return after vacation, stricken still with that dreadful flu, those boys who did come back were sent off to live with local families for the rest of the year, until a new dormitory could be built. Some of these boys grumbled about their new circumstances, and two were so offended by their lodgings they left school, but the rest settled in, and Billy and Marie Bishop grew so fond of their boarder, Dave Linden, they invited him to spend the summer with them and in return, he mowed their front lawn and clipped their hedges for the next three years.

Without Chalk House in the way, Carlin now had a view of the river. She was up in her room admiring the expanse of water and willow trees, when the black cat climbed the trellis to her window ledge. It was the hour when the sky turned indigo and shadows fell across the grass in dark pools. Carlin could tell from the way the cat came inside and the proprietary manner in which it settled on her blankets that it had come to stay. Cats were sensible that way: when one owner left, they made do with whoever was at hand, and sometimes the situation worked out just fine.

When the cat moved in, Carlin knew that Abe had left town, and after going downstairs to find there was no answer at Betsy's door, she was pleased to discover that Miss Chase had changed her mind. Not long afterward, the photograph Betsy had taken in Gus's room arrived in the mail. For quite some time, Carlin kept it in a silver frame beside her bed, until the image began to fade. She still thought about Gus when she swam laps in the pool and once she felt him there beside her, matching her strokes, cutting through the water, but when she stopped to tread water she found she was alone. In time, the weather grew too warm to wear his coat, and nothing surfaced in the pockets anymore, not silver fish or black stones.

In the height of the fine weather, Carlin began swimming in the river, at the hour when the light was pale and green. There were days when she swam all the way to Hamilton and when she made her way back to Haddan, the sky would already be dark. But soon enough dusk held off until seven-thirty, and in June the evenings were light until eight. By then, the fish had grown used to her, and they swam along beside her, all the way home.

RAY MEARS

My Outdoor Life

HODDER

First published in Great Britain in 2013 by Hodder & Stoughton
An Hachette UK company

First published in paperback in 2014

1

Copyright © Ray Mears 2013

A CIP catalogue record for this title is available from the British Library

ISBN 978 1 444 77821 2

Printed and bound by Clays Ltd, St Ives plc

Hodder & Stoughton policy is to use papers that are natural, renewable
and recyclable products and made from wood grown in sustainable forests.
The logging and manufacturing processes are expected to conform to the
environmental regulations of the country of origin.

Hodder & Stoughton Ltd
338 Euston Road
London NW1 3BH

www.hodder.co.uk

I dedicate this book to my mother, Dorothy, and to my late father Leslie John Mears. Without their love, support and patient encouragement, none of what follows would have taken place.

Contents

Introduction

For over thirty years now, I've been exploring the world through the eyes of bushcraft – writing books, making documentaries, giving lectures and training – all of which has literally taken me around the world several times over. My sole focus has been to tell the story, to all who want to listen, of the natural world – stories of the forest, the Arctic, the deserts, and all their inhabitants. My love and passion for bushcraft has grown and become my life, so with 2013 marking the thirtieth anniversary of Woodlore, the organisation I established to help thousands of people to a greater understanding of the world around us, I've decided that the time has come for me to tell my own story – how I started, what has inspired me, and what I've learned along the way. There have been some extraordinary, and heart-rending moments – like surviving a devastating helicopter crash, losing two people who were very dear to me, and tracking one of the most dangerous men in British criminal history. Although I've never previously talked about many of these events, I include them all here because I feel they have shaped the person I have become.

Talking about myself has never been easy so this has been a difficult book for me to write – I'm used to presenting the story, not *being* the story. It seemed to me a little self-indulgent to write a book about myself, but I slowly came round to the view that it was time for me to tell my story.

But perhaps you will bear with me as I revisit some of the most important and formative experiences in my life to date...

I

Prologue

Do you remember a time before Google, a time when computers were huge and mysterious, and encyclopaedias were the best – and one of the only – sources of reference we had? I remember that time in my life vividly – the analogue age, you might call it. And I can recall with great clarity sitting in my classroom one day when I was about six or seven and seeing a picture of some cavemen in an encyclopaedia. I thought it was *fantastic*. I was completely bowled over by it but I had a project to be getting on with, so the encyclopaedia went back on the shelf and I continued with my work.

A few months later I'd forgotten all about it, until there it was again. That encyclopaedia had reappeared and was perched on the edge of a desk next to me. I've no idea how, but the book started to slide off the desk. Instinctively I reached out to grab it, but gravity had it in its grip, and the hardback cover and spine had turned turtle. My hand found only a single page . . .

'No, no!' cried the teacher. 'Don't grab it, you'll tear it.'

But she was too late. As my fingers gripped the paper, the weight of this fountain of knowledge was more than my reflexes could handle. The book hit the classroom floor with a dull thud and I was left holding a single page from within it. And can you guess which one it was? Yep, the one with the image of the cavemen. I was both devastated and elated. I've always

3

loved books, so the damage the fall caused upset me – but on the other hand, I was able to take this fascinating image home with me. I think it's true to say, that picture awakened something within me that has defined my whole life. I firmly believe it was the spark that ignited my passion for the natural world around me.

And so began my journey, travelling along a path that has led directly to my interest in, and knowledge of, bushcraft and everything it encompasses. It's been amazing and has taken me all over the world, learning skills and techniques that have been handed down over generations – in some instances from man's earliest days on Planet Earth. But I'm getting ahead of myself. This is where it all began . . .

2

From Little Acorns . . .

The first two years of my life were spent in Lagos, Nigeria. My father Leslie was a printer by trade, and by the time I came along he was working for De La Rue, a company that specialises in printing banknotes. He'd done quite well there, and he and my mother Dorothy worked overseas a lot – as a manager he'd worked in Japan and Pakistan in the 50s so they were very well travelled, especially for those days. Mum found work in the various British High Commissions near where they were based.

Shortly after I was born, on 7 February 1964, we moved to Lagos where my father had been appointed to manage the banknote printing works. I can still remember a few things from those early days – I can picture the car we had, and our home there. I remember the chickens, and some of the sights and scenes of Lagos. It seemed permanently chaotic and busy, but I have memories of the relative calm and serenity of the pool at the hotel my parents used as a retreat. That was lovely.

We returned to England just after my second birthday. De La Rue had moved to Peterborough and Mum and Dad had no desire to live there – they were Londoners – so Dad left the company and got the next best job in printing: working on newspapers in Fleet Street. He took a job working nights on *The Times*.

My paternal grandfather died when my father was very

young and, to put it mildly, my dad had a tough childhood. His stepfather was very hard on him and I remember Dad telling me a story about how he'd made a Spitfire out of wood during the war. His stepfather took one look at it, told him the wings weren't straight and snapped them off. He then told him he had to make them again.

Mum's lovely and has been a great influence on my life. She's always been a great cook and I have fond memories of her dinners, particularly her roasts. In fact, I think it's fair to say that there is nothing she cooks that isn't good. When she was a young girl, she had an affinity for the outdoors and used to play in the woods, so I wonder sometimes if perhaps that had an influence on the direction my life has taken. Her mum died while we were living in Lagos, and she brought me back to London with her for the funeral when I was just a year old. I was an accomplished walker by then – I took my first steps at nine months and was walking well by the time I was a year old. Even then there was no stopping me. Apparently, I kept a great many of the passengers on our return flight to Lagos entertained for most of the journey, and one of them said to Mum, 'He'll travel a lot when he's older, that one.' Prophetic words indeed!

We lived briefly in Purley, on the southern edge of London, before settling in Kenley, a suburb on the border between London and Surrey. It's right in the middle of the green belt, and it's where I think of as home. It was a great place, surrounded by loads of open space, and I look back fondly on the late 60s and early 70s as a magical time in which to grow up. They were undoubtedly tough times for adults – Britain was going through a great deal of change in those years and there were power and food shortages, unreliable cars, seemingly endless strikes, rampant inflation and the Cold War, but who cares about all of that when you're a kid? To me, it was a time of the sort of freedoms that would leave a lot of

today's youngsters reeling. It was a great time to grow up because we didn't have computer games, or homes – and come to think of it, lives – dominated by technology. Everything in the world was on a slightly different scale. There was more space, more room to develop.

Today's youngsters are part of a digital generation, whereas back then everything was analogue and I like that – I feel enormously fortunate to be part of that last generation that experienced an analogue youth. We went 'out to play', unfettered by the bounds of smartphones, which today mean worried parents can track their children and delve into their Internet use. You made your own entertainment, and you made things.

It was a great time to be young. And the area that I grew up in was really lovely. There were a lot of trees and open space, and people seemed to have a lot more time to lavish on their gardens and their environment in a way that today's overworked and over-stressed commuters don't seem to have, sadly. It's true to say life has changed dramatically since those low-tech years.

My parents wanted me to have a good education so they sent me to a lovely prep school called Downside Lodge, and then later to Downside School, in the leafy suburb of Purley. It was a special place, one I recall as a 'summery' place rather than a 'wintry' one. It may have given its students an old-fashioned education, but it was good one, helped by the fact that class sizes were small and the teachers could teach you things that interested them. We were encouraged to read, and to take an interest in, and understand, all the things around us. We learned to be patriotic; we were taught to be loyal and self-sacrificing as well. It was a traditional way of teaching, almost Edwardian in its outlook, but that was all good – well, all except for Latin, which I detested.

There were some old stocks on the village green. They were a hangover from the past – a law was passed in 1405 that

required every town and village to have a set, which were usually placed by the side of a public highway or village green. When I was at Downside, they were pressed into use for whoever came last when we did cross-country running, although there was one particular boy who must have enjoyed them a little too much; he always seemed to put extra effort into making sure he was last through the gate after a run.

Before we broke up for the summer holidays, we would be given four books to read and there was always a quiz when we got back. The quiz wasn't the point though – the important thing was reading the books, and the ones they chose were always very good. It didn't matter what age you were, the four novels you were given would be suitable for you – books like *The Eagle of the Ninth* and *The Silver Sword*; we were given some excellent titles to read. And so I developed a passion for reading. I still read obsessively now.

The ability to read is so very important in life although, sadly, there's not enough emphasis placed on that today. I despair sometimes at the poor grammar that I hear around me these days. Youngsters don't read anymore but the fault doesn't lie with them, it lies with their parents, with society at large and even the schools to some extent – or perhaps it's the fact that we haven't given the teachers the tools they need to be able to teach and maintain discipline in the classroom. I mean, if you have a classroom with no discipline, to me that's a form of child abuse. It's that serious – children simply *must* have the opportunity to learn. They need clearly defined and enforced rules at school so they can learn the pathway from which they can step out into the world.

The schooling I had was very formal and old-fashioned; we were taught to write nicely with a fountain pen – you got into trouble if you used a Biro. We were treated as individuals, whereas today's 'one-size-fits-all' education seems to be more about how to pass the exams rather than understanding the

topics. It's a very different approach – I was taught to take an interest in life, the world and everything around it, and I feel blessed for that experience.

I didn't spend all of my childhood with my head buried in a good book though – far from it. For as much as I loved reading, bicycles also played quite a large part in my young life. I got my first bike for my third birthday and took to it really quickly. Once I left the Lodge and went up to Downside School, I used to ride the few miles to and from school. We didn't have BMXs or mountain bikes in those days, but we did have the Raleigh Chopper. I remember getting a little over-zealous with the front brake on one occasion as I rode down a very steep road; the front wheel locked up, I went head-first over the handlebars and knocked myself clean out. I ended up walking home semi-conscious. Still, it was all part of the learning curve. To me, bikes were all about fun. I used to tear around on the common with friends, chasing each other on our bikes. Once I reached my teens, it was like an American Express card – I never left home without it.

Not long after that day when I tore the page out of the encyclopaedia, I remember our teacher giving us the task of painting a scout. I think she had Baden-Powell in mind, but I knew nothing about Baden-Powell way back then – or the Scouting Movement that he established. So, I did a picture of a North-West Canadian Mounted Police Scout from the period of the Riel Rebellion, but I have no idea how on earth I knew anything about *that*.

Anyway, the teacher asked me what it was and I said, 'It's a scout from the North-West Frontier of course.' I must say, I've often wondered what the teacher thought – everyone else had drawn these boys in shorts and funny hats.

Perhaps in some strange way, fate chose me for this life. Looking back, I think I strolled into the woods one day and nature saw me and said, 'Walk this way.' I think something

similar happens to most of us in life. We don't choose our path, it chooses us – like that page from the encyclopaedia.

My interests back then were never in make-believe; they were always firmly rooted in the real world. The films that captured my attention were the films about pioneers and the great frontiers. When I watched Westerns I wasn't at all interested in the cowboys – I always thought the Indians were better. To me, they were much cooler.

———◆◆◆———

The most life-defining element of my schooling occurred while I was at Downside and it was all down to the simple fact that judo was an integral element of the curriculum. Judo would go on to create ripples that extend all the way through to my present. For it was through judo, at the age of eight, that I met the man who would become a great friend and mentor, and who encouraged me in the outdoor life that has become my lifelong quest. That man was Kingsley Hopkins and he was to become a very important figure in my life.

Today we think of judo in the Olympic sense – as a sport – but it's more than that; it's a way of life. We were exceptionally lucky though, in that we learned judo as a martial art and a life skill – not as a sport. The word 'judo' means 'the gentle way' but it's inaccurately named really because there's not much that's gentle about judo. However, it does teach you to think in a certain way. Judo is like chess – if you've never done judo, it may be difficult for you to understand what I mean by that, but any *judoka* would understand exactly what I'm talking about. Judo teaches you a certain way of dealing with things and it's a very healthy process because you can never get too big for your boots – there is always someone better at it, or more skillful than you . . . If you lose your temper on the judo mat you'll get turned over, so it teaches you to focus

your energy in the appropriate direction and, if something's not working, to immediately abandon it and try something else. It teaches you to be perceptually aware of what's going on around you, but it also gifts you determination, strength, toughness and the knowledge that technique is more important than size. Really, it teaches a whole range of things – it's a great philosophy for life, as well as showing you how to fall over without hurting yourself.

Judo was compulsory for all pupils between the ages of eight and thirteen, and was taught on Saturdays – we had Saturday school at Downside. Kingsley taught it and I liked him from the off. There was a steeliness about him, but he also had a gentleness that emanated from his very core. He'd fought behind enemy lines in Burma during World War II and it showed in his strength of character.

He was an interesting man; the Kingsley I knew as a judo teacher at Downside was a man who'd lost his wife, who studied Sanskrit and who took a great interest in the world. As I said, he was to be a mentor and friend to me for many years.

Kingsley was a great judo teacher, one of the absolute best – probably because he learned it himself from one of the martial art's masters. He'd started judo when he was sixteen but his learning was cut short by World War II. He told me that his parents had asked him about his service upon his return and they were horrified when he'd described how he took off a Japanese soldier's head with a shovel that he'd 'liberated' from another Japanese soldier. Apparently, this shovel had been made from very good steel that you could have sharpened a pencil with, and he used to bemoan the loss of the shovel. He'd lent it to an Australian soldier to dig a trench a short while after and he'd never got it back.

When the war was over, his interest in judo was reignited. He was taught by Gunji Koizumi (known as GK) who had in

turn learned from Jigoro Kano – the founder of Kodokan judo. GK was a Japanese master of judo and he introduced this martial art to the United Kingdom, so by learning from Kingsley, I was only two degrees of separation from the man who invented it.

Jigoro Kano founded judo in the 1880s by reformulating jujitsu. In jujitsu, there are many techniques for self-defence that are dangerous and potentially harmful, even in practice. Jigoro Kano reworked it, taking the dangerous techniques and putting them to one side – he didn't remove them, he just *moved* them from ordinary practice so you could practise using full power without necessarily hurting each other. His great genius lay in understanding that the most important thing was not necessarily just the technique itself but what the technique developed and required. The Japanese call it *tai sabaki* (body movement); Kano built judo so that you could develop strong *tai sabaki* and then just pick up any of the dangerous techniques as you needed them.

Judo is a wonderful thing for the human spirit because it's cerebral and physical all in the same moment. It's a very healthful practice because two people can go hell for leather, trying to smash one another to pieces, and then smile and laugh about it afterwards. Kingsley said that the ultimate goal is never to have to use it. But he was quite clear that in a crisis, if someone took the initiative, we should finish it for them.

I remember when I went up to grammar school, I was running along and one of the older children tripped me up. He starting laughing – but it was a little prematurely, because I didn't fall on my face as he expected. Instead I instinctively went into a forward roll and came up on my feet. *That* wiped the smile from his face.

Over the years, judo has helped me out of a number of tight corners. Occasionally you bump into people who want to throw their weight around; you know, the guy who uses his fists to

send a message because his vocabulary doesn't allow him to articulate whatever he wants to say. Judo can be quite, er . . . disarming under the right circumstances. In judo, you don't hit somebody with your fists; you hit them with the ground. It's a very, very powerful and useful skill set to possess.

Kingsley was 'old school', and the judo I learned from him was old-fashioned. That's not to say it was out of date; far from it. It was pure, unadulterated. I really enjoyed it and I found a freedom in it that's hard to convey. The philosophy behind it was important to me. I read a lot on Shintoism, and the history of the martial arts; I read the Japanese creation myth and many other classic samurai texts, including *The Book of the Five Rings* (a text on kenjutsu or Japanese swordsmanship, and the martial arts in general, written by the swordsman Miyamoto Musashi circa 1645). I was a willing student of judo and immersed myself in it, keen to master its knowledge.

Kingsley and GK had become good friends and after GK died, he left Kingsley his black belt. At eighty, GK felt that his mind had started to go and he wasn't as sharp as he would have liked to have been. He wanted to be remembered at his best and he felt it was important not to be a burden on others. So, as is the way of the samurai, he put his affairs in order and took his own life. He succeeded in his aim because everyone who knew him remembered him at his sharpest. That black belt he left Kingsley was given to GK by Jigoro Kano, and Kingsley in turn left it to me.

When I was thirteen, Kingsley took me to the Budokwai for the first time. The Budokwai is the judo club where he'd learned the martial art and it's in Fulham, London. Actually, 'judo club' doesn't really cover it. It's a proper *dōjō* (a formal gathering place where martial arts students conduct training) and it's the oldest and most famous Japanese martial arts club in Europe.

The club is housed in what was once a Victorian school building with a wood-beamed roof and when you go through the door to the changing area you immediately see a picture of GK on the wall. He founded the club in 1918.

Going to the Budokwai took me into an old world of judo, full of masters of the art. People like Richard 'Dickie' Bowen, who is sadly no longer with us. Dickie had studied in Japan and was married to a Japanese lady. He was an exceptionally skilled exponent of judo and he followed a traditional attitude to it which dictated that he refuse higher *dan* gradings because he thought them unnecessary. In the old days, all belts were white but you never washed them so, as you became more experienced, your belt would get grubbier and grubbier until eventually it turned black. And that's the way that I was taught – belts weren't important. That was the way at the Budokwai – the colour of the belt wasn't the be all and end all in terms of achievement. It was useful in that if someone of a high grade was carrying an injury, they would wear a belt of a lower grade. Somebody might walk on to the mat there in a white belt, but he'd be competing at national level. It was a very healthy place, the Budokwai, a place where a lot of egos were remodelled.

During my time, two Japanese champions taught there: Katsuhiko Kashiwazaki, who was a master of sacrifice techniques, a real technician; and perhaps the person who most impressed me, Yasuhiro Yamashita, who's arguably the most successful judo competitor of all time. He won five international gold medals and 203 consecutive victories up until his retirement. He was unbeaten from 1977 to 1985 and nine times all-Japan champion. Yamashita's dedication to technique, his thoroughness in training and preparation, is something I have tried to learn from and build into everything that I do. I'd love to meet him again someday – his judo was just magnificent.

I was really lucky to practise with Neil Adams too – he won

Olympic silver at both the Moscow and Los Angeles games and then found a gear no one else had and went on to become world champion. When he came on to the mat, he'd get people to walk up in a handstand and I'm certain nobody could have done it if he hadn't been there; his presence on the mat had a galvanising effect. He was truly inspirational to me and a great many others. His judo was very acrobatic – he'd have you in an arm lock halfway to the ground. That said, his timekeeping was dreadful, so when it was announced that he was leaving to coach in France, they handcuffed a giant alarm clock to his wrist.

In what other sport do you get to practise with world champions? If you're learning tennis, you can't exactly rock up at your local court and play a few games with Andy Murray or Roger Federer, can you? But in judo you can do that, and it means experience and knowledge are easily accessible to anyone willing to put the time in. That's both instructive and inspirational.

The Budokwai was a very important waypoint in my life. It really gave me an extra dimension and I still miss the place. As I grew older, though, my life was taking me into the woods. However, judo meant that I carried both the lessons I'd learned and the judo philosophy with me always.

———— ◆ ◆ ◆ ————

He was a very thoughtful man, Kingsley; he was very interested in the world. The time I spent with him was my university – he was very good at encouraging free thought and he was a very profound man. He encouraged me to always look for the source of information, to try to understand the root of the teaching, and test it out – always test what you're being taught and if it's true it will stand up but if it's not you will find out – and that was to prove important later on.

Kingsley was something of a paradox – he was gentle, but

he was as hard as nails too, and a little eccentric. I remember one night when he dislocated his shoulder doing judo – he just ran into the wall to relocate it. He loved motorbikes and had one that he rode everywhere, rain or shine. He was out on it one winter's day when I was much older, and his accelerator froze; unable to slow down, the bike reared up, he came off and the bike came down on his hand, crushing one of his fingers. I remember I hadn't heard from him for a few weeks, which was quite unusual, so I rang him to ask if he was all right.

'Yeah I'm fine,' he said, 'but I can't talk now, I'm heating a chisel on the stove.'

Kingsley was a craftsman; I mean this guy used to make beautiful chess sets and carve the individual pieces by hand, so the thought of heating a chisel was anathema to him – he'd feel like he was ruining it.

'Why on earth are you doing that?' I asked.

And he said this like it was the most natural thing in the world:

'Well, my finger's starting to smell a little, so I'm going to cut it off.'

And he would have. Had I not called when I did, had I not talked him into going to hospital, he would have cut his finger off. So he went to the local A&E with this finger that was crushed to a pulp and he didn't say a word, he just sat there while everyone else was being dealt with. That was him all over. When they took his glove off, his finger just disintegrated on the desk in front of the doctor. He was of that generation, I guess, when men seemed to be hewn from different material. He'd done stuff in his life and he'd seen and known true hardship; he knew himself in a way that most people today could never hope to achieve.

Kingsley was an awkward person to do judo with, as many people would discover to their cost. As he got older he wasn't

able to turn people over in the way he could when he was a bit younger, but neither could anyone easily turn him over. He'd learned how not to be thrown and perhaps that was the more important skill. He had mastered this business of turning energy against you, making it feel like you were fighting a piece of wrought iron.

It was a privilege to train with him.

3

The Call of the Wild

As you might have gathered by now, judo played a huge role right through my childhood and into my early twenties. It shaped the person I've become and its philosophy – alongside the sage advice I got from Kingsley – has meant that I've been equipped to deal with a lot of what life has thrown at me.

But another strand was inextricably intertwined with the judo and my relationship with Kingsley, bound in a Gordian knot of destiny, and that was my love of the outdoors. Judo and my outdoor life ran like a train track through my formative years, each one forming a rail running parallel to the other, propelling me to where I wanted to go.

Yes, that image of the cavemen was indeed what sparked my passion for nature but it was fanned and set alight when I was about eight years old and I became fascinated by foxes. My parents gave me a book called *Animal Tracks and Signs* by Preben Bang and Preben Dahlstrøm. It was truly wonderful. In fact, my life spent as a student of bushcraft can be traced back to that one book. It's still in print and has been the model for every similar kind of book that's followed since.

I think I read it in two days, and when I was done I was determined to go out and put some of the lessons I'd learned into practice. However, an afternoon tracking foxes wasn't enough for me. I wanted to stay out at night too, but I didn't

have any camping equipment and I couldn't really afford to buy any, not on the pocket money I was on.

I mentioned this to Kingsley.

'Well Raymond,' he replied, 'when I was behind enemy lines during the war, we had only the clothes we were wearing, plus our weapons and basic kit.

'A knife did everything else for us. With a sharp knife and the trees and plants around you, you can fashion whatever it is you need.

'We had nothing else; we had no tents, no camping equipment, nothing like that. We didn't need it. Neither do you.'

'Tell me more . . .'

'I managed to get hold of a spare set of mess tins so I always used one as a lid to keep the flies out of my food. That meant I never fell ill.'

'But Kingsley, where did you sleep?'

'We made our own shelters, Raymond. We utilised natural features and vegetation, but we were always comfortable. We survived quite comfortably with none of the equipment that people use today when they go camping.'

I listened in rapt attention as he went on to share with me some of the skills he'd used to survive behind enemy lines. He explained how I could find shelter, stay dry and keep warm. I was enthralled.

He told me, 'Raymond, you don't need camping equipment, you need these skills.'

Little did I know that those ten words would be the blueprint of the rest of my life.

I had the naivety of youth, I suppose – to me, what I needed to do seemed simple enough, and Kingsley had breathed life into the prospect of my staying out overnight by simplifying it still further. He had shared with me some of his own experiences behind Japanese lines and made what I wanted to do sound so . . . well . . . easy. I was lucky, too, in that I also had

wonderful parents who were very supportive of me. Good parenting is a real skill and, I have to say, they were very good. I had a great childhood and I'm very proud of that fact.

One of my earliest 'proper expeditions' took place with a friend, out on that distant, desolate, exotic land that is . . . the North Downs. It wasn't particularly memorable for what we did, and I'm not even sure how far we went, but I've never forgotten that feeling of being out overnight for the first time on our own with no one to support us and nothing but the knowledge we carried with us (which really wasn't a lot at that time, if I'm being honest).

Neither of us had sleeping bags, although I'd bought one of those orange survival bags that never really worked. We didn't have Karrimats either (those wonderful, lightweight mats that insulate you from the ground) as they hadn't really been invented then – I don't recall seeing them until I was about fifteen. For all that we didn't have, though, we never felt disheartened or like we were missing out on anything. There is so much that we take for granted today. I'm amazed at the amount of kit that young people who are starting to stay outdoors take with them these days. What on earth is it all for? I wouldn't want to carry all that even now, and the fact is, it's not all necessary. We had none of that stuff and I never minded because, ultimately, you have to manage – and you can't miss what you've never had. We certainly didn't have a camping stove or cooking utensils; my first cooking pot was a simple old Jacob's biscuit tin. I did have an Army surplus poncho, however, and I felt lucky because I had that. It was an expensive purchase – probably around £14 or something, which was a lot of money in those days. My rucksack was awful, though – it was one of those ghastly dayglo orange things, made from cheap nylon fabric with a very open weave. I painted it olive green; it looked much better then and the paint even gave it a degree of waterproofing.

I do remember we didn't have enough food with us on that first expedition (a minor oversight) but I don't recall feeling any great hardship, just a wonderful sense of achievement and independence. I made a note to myself there and then though, that I needed to learn how to find food for myself from the land. I recall sitting around a fire that we'd lit and looking down on the town of Oxted from my high vantage point and thinking, 'I'd rather be here than down there indoors watching TV.'

On that trip, we used matches to light that fire but it didn't feel right to me – it felt like I was cheating. So, I soon set out to learn how to make fire in the traditional manner and read every book I could find on the subject, although I do recall that my first attempts weren't very successful . . .

Another early trip took place on a snowy winter's night – a friend and I were trying to make a fire without matches without much success. I was using sparks to ignite some clematis seed heads wrapped up in finely shredded clematis bark. I had a couple of Oxo cubes with me, so we boiled up some water and made Oxo drinks to warm us up. We'd taken a sledge out with us – not to play on, but to carry our 'kit' (comprising a couple of small, virtually empty rucksacks). It felt like we were on our own little mini Arctic expedition and we took it very seriously. Oh, the power of imagination when you're young.

I have to say, my parents were really great about it all, considering I was still at primary school. I do remember occasions when they'd go looking for me on the common, but then, as parents, I guess it was only natural for them to feel a little concerned about me, although I can't recall that they ever *really* worried about me while I was out. Mum always said that I seemed to know what I was doing and she and my dad were happy to let me forge my own path. Maybe having played in

the woods herself when she was younger had a role in that, but who knows? She says I was always confident in my abilities when I was younger; perhaps that confidence was misplaced, but what I was doing never felt dangerous to me. It's said that the past is a foreign country – they do things differently there – and it's so true. Looking back, England *was* a foreign country compared to today: the population density wasn't anything like it is now, and it felt like a much safer place.

Besides, I had an old World War I bayonet that I used to tuck down my wellington boot. Eventually I'd use it to dig up edible roots and make fire with, but in those days it was just part of the childish adventure. I never thought of it as a weapon with which I could threaten anybody – I never felt scared being out, so that was the last thing on my mind. In fact, I felt that if there were any problems, I could deal with them. The woods were swiftly becoming my world, after all.

I'd started small and built up my experience and knowledge gradually and, for me, that's exactly how these things should start. It's very important that if someone wants to learn to go to remote parts of the world and travel in safety they should start small, and start young. You need to learn progressively, starting with the basics and working your way up from there. It really bothers me that there are some people today who don't go in for that sort of preparation. They have this idea to go somewhere, they have the money, but they haven't got the wherewithal, self-knowledge or experience to know what they're doing. The danger is that if something goes wrong, there's a good chance they could be overwhelmed by it.

———◆———

I'm sure most people feel that they were lucky to grow up when they did, and I'm no exception – the 70s were great. I loved that analogue side of life – the way that, if you couldn't

find what you needed, you'd try and make it. My dad, like many of his generation, was very good with his hands and he passed that on to me.

'Come here, Raymond,' he'd say as he changed a fuse, or wired a new plug. 'Watch how I do this.'

In turn, I was forever asking him questions.

'Dad, how do I do this?' I'd say when confronted with something that vexed my young mind.

'Raymond, watch me solder this and then you can try,' he'd say whenever he had some to do.

He was a patient man and he always had time to show me something, or to explain how it worked.

He had a lathe in the shed, which he used as often as some people use the kettle; he was always making, repairing, shaping or just generally 'lathing' – he used to make all sorts of things, but then that was indicative of the time. Unless the house was falling down, or your car was destroyed by fire, people did what they could themselves and if they couldn't, they'd learn through trial and error. A leaky tap? You'd fix it. Car needs an oil change? You'd do it yourself. The first course of action for many young adults now is to call a plumber when a tap leaks. And it seems many drivers don't even know how to change a wheel. Back then, you had to develop a reliance on yourself and it taught you valuable lessons.

When I was thirteen, the time came for me to leave Downside and move up to Reigate Grammar School. It had an excellent reputation and I remember it as a good school; it didn't matter what your interests were, it had a place for you. It was at Reigate that I met Mark Bailey and Adrian Braham. We got on well from the off and soon became firm friends.

Although I was now at a different school, those books we

were given at Downside to read over the summer holidays paid dividends for me as I got older and my passion for books grew. I became a regular visitor to the local library. I'd go straight to the reference section and read everything I could find on the outdoors. And the more I learned, the more I wanted to know. I wanted to know what things you could eat in the wild; which plants were edible and which ones weren't; which mushrooms and other fungi you could eat, and which ones would kill you. I found a book that told me everything I needed to know, packed with photographs of wild plants and captions loaded with information. The first wild plant I ever ate was wood sorrel, which tastes like apple peel, and once I tasted that, there was no looking back – I was hooked for life.

As well as the local library, I could often be found in the school library too. I loved the books they had there, and it was somewhere away from the cut and thrust of school life – well, most of the time. I remember this one day there, when I was about fourteen, the memory of which has stayed with me ever since. I was messing around in the library with some friends when a teacher walked in and suddenly – you know what it's like – everyone grabbed the nearest chair and sat down, pretending to read.

I sat there like everyone else, grabbed the book closest to me and started reading on a random page . . . and immediately stopped. I was completely blown away by what I read – so much so that I went straight to the beginning and started reading from the first page. I was so engrossed in this book that I completely missed the next two lessons. That book was *The Forest People* by Colin Turnbull, and it had a massive influence on me in the years ahead. Turnbull was an anthropologist and he'd written about the year he spent living among the BaMbuti Pygmies of the Ituri rainforest. I was utterly captivated – by Turnbull's writing, by what he'd done and,

most of all, by the BaMbuti Pygmies. Having read about them, I wanted more than anything to meet them.

———◆———

You can probably see a pattern developing here – as a young teenager, I was either out in the wilds of the North Downs, practising judo with Kingsley and the others at the Budokwai, or I was in the library. I spent a lot of time reading; reading and then going out and 'doing'. I think learning what I could eat outdoors was just the next step in the process. I read all the 'survival' books I could find; survival was the thing then – there was no bushcraft. Even so, the collected knowledge on survival back then was somewhat limited; its practice was developed and shared by a small group of people, and the status quo was rarely questioned. Information existed in something of a vacuum, so most of the books on the subject weren't very good. Even then, they were out of date.

These days I can put the survival studies of the time into context. Of course, the people who had the real knowledge back then were the military. There was the survival training that the Royal Air Force had responsibility for, which focused on escape and evasion for aircrew – if they were shot down, they needed to survive until they were picked up. The other type of survival training was that given to our Special Forces, who were much more likely to have to get themselves home – there was no rescue plan in place for them. The instructors were really good but, for obvious reasons, they weren't accessible to the public – even to as willing and committed a student of bushcraft as me. Back then, the relevant knowledge was kept within the military – just as it should be.

The first survival instructor of any note was Eddie McGee, and he really shook up the nascent survival industry. He'd enjoyed a long career in the Parachute Regiment and, after

twenty-two years of service, he left to establish the National School of Survival, near Harrogate in North Yorkshire. He single-handedly knocked the industry into shape, and he was prolific. He wrote a number of books on the subject, and one of them – *No Need To Die* – was regarded as a bible at the time by survival enthusiasts.

Eddie had spent time living with pygmy groups in Africa, and among Australia's indigenous Aboriginal people, from whom he learned about tracking. I was about fifteen when I first met him, after attending one of his courses, and I learned some valuable skills from him. Eddie had been involved in tracking the multiple murderer Barry Prudom, who had shot and killed two police officers and a man he'd taken hostage. In the summer of 1982, McGee was brought in by police in North Yorkshire to help in the search. He picked up the trail after finding footprints in the early morning dew, and tracked Prudom to his hideout in Malton, North Yorkshire, where, surrounded by police, Prudom shot himself.

———◆◆◆———

Having done the survival course that Eddie ran, I realised I was pulling away from the social groups at school that everyone else seemed to belong to. Given my interests and the pursuits I was involved in, it was perhaps inevitable that I wouldn't fit in with my peers at school.

I have always been a bit of a loner, so I looked forward to the weekends when I could head out into the woods – I had no restrictions, nothing to tether me, so I would wander off in whichever direction I fancied. Initially I'd go to the common, but over time the lure of the North Downs always caught me. It felt to me like it had its own gravity, reeling me in across the five or six miles that I'd hike to get there.

I loved the Downs' wide open space but it was its forest

that was the real allure. I'd started to really feel a part of that forest; I knew it intimately and felt a real connection to the forest environment that has remained with me to this day. I'm equally comfortable in Arctic, jungle, desert or urban environments, but it's the forest where I feel *really* at home. Sometimes I'd sit in the woods and just watch things happen; I used to love the time I spent there.

I learned tracking by following foxes and, as with any skill, I started with the easy stuff. Initially, I'd see their paw prints in the snow and follow them. When the snow melted, I found I could follow their tracks in the mud and so I just kept on going.

I started to look for other clues when the paw prints became hard to spot. When foxes carry a kill in their mouth, they have to stop for a rest periodically because it's hard on their neck. Often, when they drop a freshly killed pigeon, the bird will leave a downy feather or two. I'd notice these, and it started to colour in the picture I was seeing. Foxes like trails, so they would often run along the trails through the woods in the North Downs. There are hawthorn woods there, and in spring the hawthorn blossom would stick to the soles of their pads. As they left the area where the blossom was, there'd be traces of it on the forest floor where it had fallen off their pads. Sometimes I'd find where they'd cached the pigeon, because I'd see a pigeon's foot sticking out of the ground. It was fantastic to the young me, and a brilliant education in learning how to track.

When I started tracking there were gaps in my knowledge but I didn't worry about them. As a kid you don't worry about what you don't know. Over time, the gaps got smaller and smaller. I learned how to piece things together because I was always observing what was going on around me and becoming more 'at one' with my surroundings. It was almost like learning through osmosis, as my subconscious became more and more

finely attuned to the environment and I'd start noticing signs that I wasn't able to spot before. The forest became a book and I learned to read not just what I could see but, perhaps more importantly, what I couldn't – the absence of the expected. Gradually I got better and better, until one day I just felt completely at home there. Being so in tune with my environment in the forest meant that I'd become quite an accomplished tracker.

I especially liked to go into the woods when it was raining because then I'd have them to myself – the rain kept everyone else away so there'd be absolutely nobody else around. I'd push myself into a holly bush on a rainy day, and use that for shelter or I'd seek out a yew tree. I learned early on that no matter how cold and wet it was, once I had a fire going and I had shelter I could stay warm and dry. I'd always make a fire, and I'd cook up an Oxo cube in an Army mug. I'd become quite adept at making fire without matches. By then, I used to carry cotton wool in a plastic bag with me, and I carried a piece of artificial flint that I used as a rod – scraping a knife down it created hot sparks. I kept it in a metal tube along with a piece of magnesium that I'd scrape for tinder. I made a habit of going out in the worst conditions again and again in order to hone my ability to make fire. Being able to make fire at will is an invaluable skill in the wild because it is a real game changer, particularly when it's cold and wet. A supply of hot drinks and food creates a paradigm shift in morale, and when I had all of that, I felt like I could stay in the forest forever.

Being able to feel at home somewhere is all well and good, but it's not much use if you don't know where you are, or how to get from point A to point B, so I taught myself to navigate – first via a map and compass, then by using the night sky. I learned quickly because I had a thirst for the knowledge, and the information I consumed was like ice-cold water to a parched throat.

I learned navigation indirectly from a *Warlord* annual one year. It told you how to use a Silva compass, so I asked my parents to get me one and they delivered in style by giving me a lovely Silva Polaris and an Ordnance Survey map (which I still have) covering the South and North Downs. I set myself targets with them; the first time I used them, I decided to go out and search for something so I opened the map up and found a spring marked somewhere in the Downs, and I thought, 'Right, I'm going to find the spring and fill my water bottle from it.' And that's exactly how I started. I'll never forget that spring because it was so hard to find – it was deep down through very tall, thick nettles and I got stung to blazes trying to get there – but I did it and I filled my empty water bottle from it. Every time I fill my water bottle now, wherever I am in the world, it makes me think of that spring.

I derived a tremendous sense of satisfaction from that little navigation mission. I'd set myself a task, one I had no idea whether I'd be able to do, and in the end I'd managed it. It's so important to step outside your comfort zone because that's usually when you learn best. I think it's really important that you do things like that for yourself – no adult with you, just you and your own self-belief. Sadly, I think many parents would be too afraid to let their children make a journey like that these days.

Having started to really enjoy navigating with my map and compass, I quickly moved on to learning to navigate via the night sky, which in many ways is just a map that's accessible for twelve hours out of every twenty-four (or thereabouts). I was really interested in all that – not just navigating by stars, but mastering and ramping up every skill I acquired. I got all the information from books, and honed the skills and techniques I learned by going out and putting them into practice. There's no substitute for doing things, ever – practice beats theory every time.

I also surveyed my own maps of all the little trails through the woods that I used to use by pacing out compass bearings and mapping the pathways. When I teach people how to navigate now, I don't let them have daylight for the first few days. Because they learn to navigate at night, they learn to trust their compass – that's how you become really good.

———◆◆◆———

It should come as no surprise that Reigate Grammar School's long-established Combined Cadet Force (CCF) had acted like a magnet on me ever since I'd been a wide-eyed new pupil. The prospect of learning to climb, shoot, acquire military tactics and live and sleep outdoors in all weathers – and on school time – didn't just appeal to me, it all but consumed me. This offered nirvana – everything I loved, plus the prospect of sponsorship by the armed services through sixth form college and university and, ultimately, a commission into my chosen branch as a junior officer.

Finally, after three long years of waiting, I was able to join at the beginning of the fourth form. I opted to join the Navy section instead of the Army or RAF sections because the Navy published a list of all its available courses at the beginning of the year whereas the Army and RAF published theirs piecemeal throughout the year, so you could never really plan ahead. The Navy section included a course with the Royal Marines, which was where I wanted to end up ultimately – a career as a Royal Marines officer seemed to offer everything I wanted in life at that stage.

The first course I did with the CCF was weapons handling, which included live firing on the range at Shorncliffe using the Mk 4 Lee-Enfield. I loved that, so I really got a lot out of it. The next course was run by the Navy – more shooting on the ranges at HMS *Excellent* shooting SLRs and SMGs, but we

stayed on board a ship for the duration, which was great fun. The best elements for me, though, were the courses I did with the Royal Marines down at the Commando Training Centre in Lympstone. They included being dropped off a rigid raiding craft and marching across Dartmoor, killing your own chicken for dinner and abseiling down Foggin Tor. It was absolutely brilliant and everything I saw and experienced there just re-affirmed my commitment to a career as a Royal Marines officer. I ate, slept and breathed Marines. I honestly couldn't get enough.

I think it was while I was in the CCF that my love of the outdoors hit home. I was never scared of the dark and I've always loved wild places. I've been very lucky in my life to be able to know myself: I know that I get bored unless there's a real challenge. If it's difficult, that's when I find I'm at my best. If there's a crisis, I'll try to find a solution to the problem. I can focus on what needs doing; it's not that I don't feel fear, I can just push it out of my mind and I think that's something I learned from Kingsley. The wilder a place is, the more I like it. Every page of Colin Turnbull's book resonated with me every time I went out, and I was growing in confidence with each trip. I positively ached to undertake something bigger – like a jungle expedition as Turnbull had, rather than just my regular forays into the forest. And as I gained experience, the kit that I carried with me changed. I replaced the World War I bayonet with a British Army machete, known as a Golock – a much more effective tool. What I really wanted, though, was what Kingsley had: a rather large knife that he called a 'Dymtah'. He'd acquired it in Burma, and it had been made from a lorry spring. He used to carry it around his neck with the cord wrapped around its wooden sheath so that it rested on his chest at an angle of 45°.

Anyway, I was listening to the radio one day in 1981 – I'd have been about sixteen or seventeen then – when I heard the

presenter talking to a guest who was organising an expedition to the Arctic and looking for volunteers. I thought this offered a real opportunity so I talked to my mates Mark and Adrian about it and they agreed to travel up to the Lake District with me to look into it. As it transpired, we were to be disappointed – the guy planning the expedition was big on ideas, but had nothing lined up in the way of backing, so I thought: *chalk that one up to experience.*

It wasn't a total write-off though – in fact, we ended up pulling victory from the jaws of defeat because off the back of the expedition-that-wasn't we got to climb Skiddaw in the company of Geoff Somers. Geoff was a big name in the British Antarctic Survey at the time, and he'd also been at the meeting with the expedition planner. He offered to take those of us who were there climbing on Skiddaw, so we leapt at the invitation.

On the way down, I asked Geoff if we could stop for a few minutes to watch a kestrel that was below us; I'd never been above a kestrel before. Well, five minutes became half an hour (that's become something of a theme for me ever since). I went on to climb the Alps when I was in my twenties, but even then I never subscribed to the 'Let's rush to the top, climb that one, and then rush on to the next one' mantra. I like to stop and take it all in; I need to know why I've been there. As far as I'm concerned, that's what is important.

For me, the challenge of the outdoors is not about whether you can cope, whether you can overcome nature, do it bigger, higher, faster or further than anyone else. I'm not interested in crossing a continent on foot, or doing it in record time, or any of that stuff; to me it's all artificial. Don't get me wrong – I'm not against people who do that. It just doesn't appeal to *me*. What interests me is becoming more attuned to the environment: understanding it, how it fits together, and what our place in it is. It's about how to work *with* an environment

so that you bolster each other and don't feel threatened, and that's what I was learning.

We're all different though, and I really have no problem with people who have different motivations. Take Ranulph Fiennes; I like him as an individual, and I have huge respect for him and what he's achieved. I think, in terms of what he does, he really understands why he's doing it – I don't think there's any doubt about that. He's got it in perspective. But I think British society is very immature in its attitude to exploration. It's all about conquering this, conquering that, but the important thing to remember is that you *never* conquer nature. If you get to the top of a mountain, it's because you did all the right things and nature said yes, OK, you can get there. But twenty-four hours later, nature might well feel differently, and you could die trying. You can never beat nature; you have to learn to work with her.

If you are able to devote all of your time to focusing on tuning in to nature, you develop a sense, a feeling for when things aren't right on any given day. It's very hard to explain; sometimes you just develop an instinct – some people call it a sixth sense – but you can develop it to an extraordinary degree. Part of my education has been to learn to recognise the signs, to attune myself to the flow of nature so that I better understand what's going on. It can mean the difference between life and death.

Sometimes when I was tracking as a youngster, I would get drawn to things and I'd often find a sign *after* the event, when I was wandering home. It's as if something had been leading me there, when the reality was that I was seeing a sign but not consciously noticing it. I think the fact that I did this when I was so young played a huge part in my acquiring the skills I have, because when you're young you're unfettered by responsibilities so your mind is free to wander in a way that is all but impossible as an adult. Some people might call it

daydreaming, but it's not that – you're allowing your mind the freedom to explore the world in its own way. I think it's interesting that Einstein had a lot of his thoughts in a similar way – not that I'm comparing myself to him! I just believe that letting the mind have free rein early on is absolutely key. As you get older, your responsibilities get in the way and they cloud your vision.

A Canadian Indian once told me that his goal in life was to be a person of power. By that he didn't mean power in terms of wealth or importance in his tribe, but rather in the sense of what we would call a 'medicine man'. That said, he would never want to be called a medicine man – someone of that nature in that society would never put themselves forward as such.

'I want to be a person in tune with nature so that nature will treat me and my clan well,' he said to me. Is it nature responding to him, or is it his reading of nature? Who knows, but the net effect is the same and that is that he's attuned to nature.

4

Transition

I can't overstate the remarkable effect Colin Turnbull's book had on me. It had a profound role in dictating the path I would take through life and my all-consuming interest in bushcraft and expeditions. It opened my eyes to the world like never before and my fascination for it knew no bounds; throughout my mid-teens, my curiosity and thirst for knowledge was like an itch I couldn't scratch.

The course I'd done with Eddie McGee played a pivotal role, too. As well as giving me a whole host of vital survival skills, Eddie had told me about the Royal Geographical Society (RGS). I learned soon after my first visit there that the Society was intending to run a course entitled 'How to Plan an Expedition to a Tropical Rainforest'. There was no way I was going to miss that, so I threw caution to the wind and enrolled. I raided the piggy bank and, at fifteen, I was the youngest person on the course. All the others were postgraduates, or proper adults with established credentials and hundreds of thousands of miles of global travel under their belts, and all of them planning to go off to interesting places. And then there was me – a wide-eyed fifteen-year-old with a dream and an insatiable drive to learn everything.

It could have been a disaster – I mean, what did I know? Would I be out of my depth? Would everyone else there look at me like I shouldn't be there? But it wasn't like that at all;

it was wonderful. I went with an open mind and a single objective: to learn all I could. The seminar was run by an incredible man, Major Roger Chapman, and he brought together some of the most experienced rainforest explorers of the time. We learned about rations, how to live in the jungle, how to navigate in the rainforest – all sorts of things. Chapman gave the most amazing lecture about an expedition he'd made for Operation Drake up the Strickland River in Papua New Guinea. I was sitting there, listening, watching, drinking in every word, and the hairs on the back of my neck were standing on end as if I'd been plugged into the mains. I'd heard of Operation Drake, which was named after Sir Francis Drake, who had circumnavigated the world on the *Golden Hind* some four hundred years earlier. Operation Drake ran between 1978 and 1980 and was a round-the-world voyage that was divided into nine ocean-based and one land-based phase, each lasting about three months. On each phase, a number of young volunteers aged between seventeen and twenty-four, who had been selected from countries all over the world, worked together on a series of scientific explorations, research and community projects. I had heard there was something new in the pipeline but details were scarce. All I knew for sure was that Roger Chapman would be involved and that it would be called Operation Raleigh. I also knew beyond a shadow of a doubt that I wanted to be involved.

That course at the RGS gave me so much – a much better understanding of the jungle for a start, and great reading lists. I started to hunt down and digest everything I could find on rainforests and it was all valuable knowledge – although it was to be a long while before I could put it to use. But that's the beauty of knowledge: it doesn't go off, and the best thing about it is that it doesn't weigh anything, so you can carry it with you wherever you go.

While I wasn't able to immediately put the lessons I'd learned

on expedition planning to use, the course did confer other benefits on me. It had a galvanising effect and really focused my interests. It also woke me up to the fact that there were other organisations out there that I'd want to mesh with, organisations I could learn from and that could help me. The course was invaluable and well worth every penny.

I was still heavily involved with the CCF at school and keener than ever to join the Royal Marines as an officer – for the young me, at fifteen, it felt like that was my destiny. The Royal Marines felt like my ideal home, combining so much of what interests and drives me. But that dream was to come crashing down around my ears because of something so fundamental, so out of my control, I would be powerless to resolve it: my eyesight.

I wore glasses when I was a child and my visual acuity was outside of the accepted parameters laid down by the Marines. I knew all along that you didn't need perfect sight to join, so I'd always assumed that I would sail through that particular hurdle. Apparently not. There were degrees of imperfect vision that were acceptable, and mine fell on the wrong side of the line. I was told it wouldn't even be worth my while applying. These were the days before laser surgery was an option. There was nothing I could do, no right of appeal. That aspiration was over before it had even started.

At a rational level, I understood it. But it was still a crushing disappointment nonetheless and I think that the rejection – for that's what it was, when you get down to it – sapped a lot of energy from me, because for once in my life I felt completely helpless. Had it been my academic results, I could have worked harder. Had I not been fit enough, I could have trained harder. But my vision? It seems daft when viewed through the lens of hindsight – and given how things have turned out for me, it's not as if it matters now – but to the teenage me it was a big thing, and for a while I felt anchorless.

So, at fifteen, suddenly I was left with no plan. I sleepwalked through my O-levels, but my results were good enough for me to stay on and do A-levels, which only served to delay the inevitable. I quite literally didn't know what to do next. I felt frustrated because I couldn't find anything that I really wanted to study at university; neither of my parents had been so they didn't really understand how it all worked, and I didn't think there was anything there for someone with my interests.

For most people, university is a world of opportunity, but none of the usual subjects interested me and nobody ever said to me: 'Why don't you look into anthropology or ethno-botany, or any of those things?' Consequently, I didn't know it was possible to study them. There were lots of subjects I could have done – and would have loved to have studied – but I didn't know they existed.

In the seemingly endless summer holidays after my O-levels, I did another course with Eddie McGee that involved living out in the open for a week. By then I was very capable and living outdoors held no difficulties for me. The course involved feeding yourself and sleeping out with very little equipment – we ended up sleeping in a cave on the Yorkshire Moors. For warmth, we made blankets from bracken, which we wove with fibre that we got from brambles. It wouldn't be my choice now – there are other natural materials in abundance that are far more effective, comfortable and hold heat better – but that's what was taught on that particular course. Making the blankets was challenging enough for most of those on the course with me, but for me it felt as if we weren't even scratching the surface. I wanted more. I wanted to know how native people did things. Also, I had begun to feel that survival wasn't the whole story. Survival is just the shorthand of bushcraft – bushcraft is the bigger subject. It's more about how you live within an environment rather than just exist. And the great thing about bushcraft is that wherever you go, the skills go with you.

I didn't quite understand that then, but I knew that I wanted
– no, *needed* – to know more. The problem I had was finding
enough literature on the subject. There were lots of books out
there, but not enough from trustworthy, reliable sources, so I
had to sort out which books were good and which weren't. It
was trial and error and I digested a hell of a lot of material
in the process. It was tedious work at times, but ultimately it
was time well spent because I came across some valuable
information in the process. And let's be honest, nothing valuable is easy to come by. Among the rough, I found a couple
of books that became my bibles – *Woodcraft and Camping*
by Bernard S. Mason, and *Bushcraft* by Richard Graves; they
were very good and well-written and everything in them
worked.

When I wanted to learn about fungi, I contacted the best
authority I could find – although my quest could have been
over before it began. I'd been watching a TV series called *The
Good Food Show* and they had a mushroom expert on: the
late Dr Derek Reid. He ran courses on fungi, so I made a note
of his name, tracked down a number for him and rang him
up. I explained that I was a student of bushcraft and survival
and that I wanted to take one of his courses . . . and he put
the phone down on me. Then I met somebody else at one of
the lectures I attended who was also an expert on fungi, so I
made arrangements to go and see her. She gave me some
instruction and then told me that if I wanted to go further
I should really go and do Derek Reid's course. Of course I
laughed when she told me that, and I explained what had
happened when I called him. She said, 'Oh, don't worry about
that. Just book in on his course but don't tell him what it is
you're interested in.'

So I did just that. He was as amiable as can be and I arranged to go and attend one of his evening classes, which he held at Kew Gardens. He was more than just an expert though – it turned out that he was no less than the head of mycology at the Royal Botanic Gardens, and an acknowledged world authority on the classification and identification of mushrooms, toadstools and the like. As a mycologist, he had an unrivalled general knowledge of fungal habitats and taxonomy.

His courses were fourteen weeks long and he had all of Britain's top amateurs among his students. New faces would get one hour's instruction from him on the microscopic properties of fungi and afterwards we'd go into another room where all the old hands had been and they would bring out fungi which they identified and labelled and then laid on the table according to their spore colour. Derek would then go around explaining any mistakes they'd made. I attended these wonderful courses for the last four years that they ran.

His students included some very serious, semi-professional mycologists so, between them, they might have collected some three or four hundred different fungi there of an evening – an astonishing range really. Derek would go round, look at them and identify them all by eye. At the end, I would select all the edible ones and put them side by side with those that they could be confused with, and pore over them. In later years, Derek and I became very good friends, ironically enough, and we eventually ended up running some courses together because I had studied the different uses of fungi, including for food. There's a special knowledge not just in being able to identify which fungi are edible and what to do with them, but also in being able to find edible fungi in reliable quantities, and that's a skill that I developed.

The courses I did, however, were a mixed bag. Some, like those I did with Dr Derek Reid and Eddie McGee, and the one at the RGS, were invaluable. The others, however, didn't

stretch me. That said, they were all good experiences because I took something away from each of them and learned more about my own abilities. But I still wanted more; I *needed* adventure.

I had learned to make fire by friction on one of the courses, although I ended up working it out for myself as the instructor who taught it knew all the theory but couldn't put it into practice. He was using the wrong sort of wood for the drill and the hearth, and the dimensions of the drill were all wrong so if he'd tried forever and a day, he'd never have made fire. For all I know, he's still trying.

Again, I learned an invaluable lesson from that because it taught me never to bullshit, and it's something I carry with me to this day – if you don't know something, *say* you don't know it. I feel very strongly about that and I've built Woodlore up on that basis. If anyone who works for me bullshits, they won't be there long. If you don't know, say so – then go and find out. Do otherwise and you lose all credibility.

———◆———

My relationship with Kingsley was stronger than ever when I started my A-levels. I was still going to the Budokwai on a regular basis, so judo still played a major role in my life, but I was seeing a lot of Kingsley outside of judo as well. He was very much a sage for me, and the time I spent with him at this stage was like a series of tutorials with an exceptionally good lecturer at a top-tier university. He was a very clever man, very bright. What I really liked, though, was that he took an interest in *my* interests. And his advice didn't conflict with my parents' influence on my life – quite the opposite really. As a parent you are bound by certain concerns; if you are an adult outside of that relationship, you can be nurturing in a different way. He filled that role perfectly, and I valued our friendship greatly.

Looking back, I'm grateful that my parents didn't worry unduly about my increasing knowledge of bushcraft and the way I would go about teaching myself new skills by 'doing' and staying out. By this point I was making bows and arrows, making flint into arrowheads. I used to make my own knives; I could make a knife out of an old saw – cut it out in the vice with a cold chisel and then grind it. I cut an old cutlass down and put a plastic handle on it from an old bow. It looked a bit Tarzan-ish, but really I was inhibited only by my own imagination and it was running wild. I made my own karabiner; I abseiled down an 80ft cliff using that thing. Looking back, I'm probably lucky to be alive.

I wanted to know how to be a native of my own country and that, for the next few years, was to be an important focus. Instead of walking across the common with a cricket bat and stump like other youngsters, I was walking across it with a spear and a spear thrower, bows and arrows and fire sticks. I must have looked like an Aborigine to anyone who saw me.

Mum and Dad were very supportive. They never got at me or criticised what I was doing, and consequently their trust reinforced my self-belief. That said, they must have been a little bit annoyed at times because the freezer may have housed the odd deer head and a dead animal or two, and the house was always full of sticks, flora and fauna. But hey, when you're interested in these things, that's what happens.

When you have a formal education, there's a structure, a framework for what you do, but I didn't have that with what I was doing. In some ways I was evolving something new, so I just followed my interests, flitting from one subject or skill to another, like a bee to a flower, gathering what I could to store and make use of later. There was never any great master plan or end point to what I was doing. Even after forty years of studying bushcraft, I'm still learning new things and new skills, so really there is no end to the subject. It expands, and you have

to keep up. Anyone who thinks they've mastered it is deluding themselves – it's like running for the horizon: you're never going to reach it because the closer you get, the further away it is.

Fortunately for me, I was going from one little thing to another all those years ago, and somehow it all meshed together into a coherent narrative. It was informative and useful so I look back on it as quite a good way of doing things. Now though, if someone wanted to learn the subject I'd structure it for them, but that structure wasn't available for me so I had to find my own way through it, which is quite an eighteenth-century approach to things, really. In the Age of Enlightenment, if people wanted to know something they tried to work it out for themselves. It was a time when people saw for themselves. It's my belief that if you have an interest, you should explore it. I would encourage everyone to do that.

The exploration of my subject took me to the most wonderful museum in London: the Museum of Mankind. It's closed now, which is a crying shame because it was a dedicated museum of anthropology and they displayed the most amazing exhibits there. It was a really important and useful resource to me because of the range of materials on show: all sorts of bark, clothing artefacts made of birch bark from Norway and Scandinavia, rainforest longhouses . . . you name it, they had it. One of my favourite exhibitions there was called 'The Thunderbird and Lightning Exhibition' which was about the Woodland Indians of North-East America. There was a period of my life where I was in there all the time and I'd be poring over the exhibits, drawing them, making them, having a go – I wanted to understand everything about them.

Alongside my insatiable lust for knowledge on bushcraft and the outdoors, I had also developed quite an interest in photography. Being a printer, my dad appreciated the way that photography recorded history and that interest was passed on to me aged about ten when he gave me a complicated 35mm

SLR camera. I was far too young to fully appreciate it, and I wasn't too hot initially on how to use it, but my dad's enthusiasm was infectious and I gradually started to get to grips with it. It would be fair to say that as my interest in bushcraft grew, so too did my interest in photography. In fact, by the time I was in my early twenties I'd reach a fork in the road whereby I could have ended up as a professional photographer rather than a specialist in bushcraft and the outdoors. Photography has remained a big part of my life to this day, but I'll come on to that.

I sleepwalked through my A-levels in much the same way as I had with my O-Levels but then I really was in a quandary: the Royal Marines wasn't an option, I couldn't earn a living by being able to live in the wild and although I was good at judo, I was never at a level where I could turn pro. That said, I wouldn't have wanted to even if I could. For as much as I loved judo, my heart lay in the outdoors, but I had no idea at that time how I could possibly turn that interest into a revenue stream and make it pay. I had a clutch of exam passes but I was just another school-leaver in a crowd of people looking for something worthwhile to do with their lives. Given that I was unable to do what I wanted to, I followed the only path open to me and tried to find some work of a more conventional nature so that I could at least get some money behind me.

That's how I found myself in the most unlikely role possible: going to work in a suit and driving a desk in the City. I don't really understand what I did – and it's not age or a foggy memory affecting my recall. Truly, I don't even think I knew back then. Picture it: I worked in an office with thirty people, twenty-seven of whom smoked – and this in the days when you could smoke at your desk, inside buildings, on aeroplanes and, yes, on the London Underground. I hated it.

Although I wasn't sure what I wanted to do, I knew what

I *didn't* want to do and perversely it was exactly the job I found myself doing. I knew from early on that I wasn't destined for a conventional career. I think I've always been a fighter – I'm not one to be pushed down, and back in my earliest days at school, I almost always won when we played British Bulldog. If someone tries to stop me from doing something, then I'll find another way to do it. I'm very single-minded and certainly a loner. I don't want to be a part of a herd. The moment someone tries to put me in a pen with everybody else, that's the moment I can guarantee I won't be there. I'll slip the fence and be somewhere else doing something else. I don't want to be pigeonholed in any way. I'm my own person.

Consequently, I felt trapped from the off, and not just because I was constrained in a suit and wedged behind a desk inside four very smoky (and consequently yellowing) walls. I enjoyed the money I earned, and I loved the freedom of adult life, but whatever it was I did that earned me the money, it was terribly boring. I also seem to recall that whatever my job was, I wasn't very good at it. I felt like I was staring down the barrel of a gun and I didn't like what I saw at the end of it: a loan for a car, a mortgage for a flat, weekly shopping, trips to the cinema and living for the weekends. They were all metaphors for a set of handcuffs, chaining me to the monotony of a job I hated, in an office where I didn't belong, in a life that wasn't mine. I had to get out before the job sucked me in. So that's what I did. I stuck it for a year and then left.

Do I regret it? Not a bit. Like everything in my life, I learned something as a result of working there. I gained a respect for other people's interests. I knew then, but even more so now, that I had a very unusual interest to pursue – and I've been privileged, and very lucky, that I've made a career out of it. But when I meet people who work in the City, I have enormous respect for them. I couldn't do what they do. We all have different skills and I have tremendous respect for everyone who

is a part of that, regardless of what they do to earn their money.

As things transpired, my resignation from my City job was somewhat serendipitous; just a few weeks later, I was invited by Roger Chapman to join Operation Raleigh. And with that, I took the first step along the road to where I am now. Although I couldn't have known it then, Operation Raleigh was to play a very positive part in everything that has followed. Without it, Woodlore would never have existed.

5

Raleigh Point

Operation Raleigh was established in 1982 by Colonel John Blashford-Snell as a successor to his previous project, Operation Drake. The origins of the two projects dated back to 1978 when Blashford-Snell and HRH Prince Charles had a shared vision of giving young people a chance to explore the world and, by doing so, discover their potential as leaders and members of a team working together to make a difference. In essence, the concept behind Op Drake and Op Raleigh was to give those who were selected the challenge of war in a peace-time situation.

I was almost nineteen when I started there towards the end of 1982, a year that was dominated by news of the battle for the Falkland Islands. We were based in a building that harked back to a much earlier conflict: our team occupied rooms 440, 441 and 442 of the old War Office building in Whitehall. I sometimes wonder if JK Rowling had ever been there because when I look back, our working environment bore more than a passing resemblance to her imagined world of Gringotts Wizarding Bank as realised in the Harry Potter films.

There was very little organisation initially, just a group of us with a willingness to help out, a belief in the objective and a desire to see it succeed. There were twelve of us at the start, divided into two groups of six – they wanted to call us the Young Lions but we were having none of that. In the

end, we became known as the Selection Weekend and Administrative Team or 'SWAT Team' for short. It was never planned, but we weren't too disappointed with the acronym and enjoyed the play on words. Our job was to design, set up and run the selection process. Age-wise it was a repeat performance of the seminar at RGS where I'd first met Roger Chapman – I was far and away the youngest; all the others were postgrads.

Working on Operation Raleigh was a real life-shaping experience for me, a fascinating time in which we were all doing something really worthwhile, and I met some amazing people through it. Roger Chapman was the great unsung hero. He always worked away in the background – it was never *about* him. There was also the inspirational Wandy Swales, one of the great old-school explorers and Op Raleigh's chief of staff – No.2 to Colonel John Blashford-Snell. He was a truly wonderful man, a larger-than-life character with tremendous people skills. There were a great many other people who helped make it such a worthwhile project, and I think that's part of what made it really special.

A week or so after I started, I found myself abseiling down a 300ft-high block of flats in London's Shepherds Bush. It was typical of the kind of things we got involved in with Operation Raleigh, and I loved it. There was a 5ft wall around the edge of the roof which, having clipped on to the rope, we had to climb over. On the other side was a 300ft sheer drop; that focused the mind somewhat. I got a real buzz from that; it was just the sort of thing I enjoyed doing.

The first role for those of us on the selection team was designing the presentations that would be given by the county co-ordinators – a network of people across the UK who would be responsible for organising the interviews for the expedition. In the end, they interviewed in excess of 8,000 young people from which to select the candidates, each one of whom needed

to raise at least £2,500 in sponsorship for a place on the expedition. I was tasked with writing the reference notes on how to interview people. That was interesting – back then, what I knew about interviewing could have been written on a postage stamp with room left over for *War and Peace*. But I wanted to contribute, so I did some research and worked it out for myself.

That was good; I liked that because it was a real challenge and it was way outside of my comfort zone. So I learned a lot of really useful things: I learned about interviewing; I learned about putting presentations together. And I was working with the operation's professional photographer – that was really interesting as well. I learned a lot about photography then, and moving images; it was really helpful stuff.

My role at Operation Raleigh came along at just the right time in my life, although some of the challenges I faced, such as organising a schedule of events and liaising with different organisations, stretched me. We were given responsibility, and that required a degree of growth on my part. Fortunately, those I was working with all had different skills to me – whereas I'd always been on my own in the outdoors, I was now in a team with two very good mountaineers, a couple of guys who'd become alpine guides, a guy who had been into sailing and another who was into canoeing, plus someone who'd been the president of the Cambridge University Exploration Society. They were a fascinating and really interesting group of people.

Eventually, due to cost constraints, our team of twelve became six and we were split into two teams of three – a Northern team and a Southern team. I was really very lucky to be in the North; we had to travel further than our counterparts in the Southern team so it meant we were away from the office for longer, and that I was getting to see parts of the country I'd never been to before.

Our role now was to set up and run the selection weekends. I was working with Arthur Collins, who is now one of the foremost mountaineers in the world. He taught me to climb, so I feel really fortunate to have learned from the best. The other member of my team was Jonathan Raper (the ex-president of the Cambridge Exploration Society); he's now a professor of geomorphology. They were two very intelligent and capable men, real doers, and it was a privilege to work with them. We're all of us an amalgam of everyone we've met, worked with, loved or lost, and here I was, nineteen years old, with the 'people' equivalent of a jackpot win. How lucky was that?

We each took responsibility for two selection sites, which we would then co-ordinate and run. And on the selection weekends, it was our job to get those candidates in our charge very wet, cold and tired so that a team of judges could attempt to discover their 'core' personalities. Each of us has a face we present to the world, but it's only under stress that the real person is seen. It was hard work, but enjoyable and interesting. And we had a lot of laughs – we worked hard and we played hard.

There was a really special expedition atmosphere within Raleigh, even at that fledgling stage, and even when we were back in the office. Given that we only had three rooms in what was essentially a building at the heart of government in Whitehall, it made for some interesting times. It was like the centre of the civil service universe outside our small enclave, with civil servants straight from Central Casting striding purposefully along dark-panelled corridors with folders under their arms, desperately trying to look important.

I remember a young guy – we'll call him 'Mike' to save him embarrassment – who'd had the enviable job of travelling the globe in a search for countries and locations suitable for Operation Raleigh to run its expeditions. He'd not long been

back from an overseas reconnaissance trip and he'd written a report on his findings, but let's just say that he hadn't been very tactful when writing about some of the people that he'd met on his travels.

Someone told him, 'Mike, you really can't circulate this to everyone. Given its content, you'd best keep it confidential and be selective about who you give it to.'

However, he was very proud of what he'd written and wanted to share it. So he went out one afternoon and, unbeknown to anybody, had twenty or so copies of his report printed and bound. Just for good measure, he stopped off and bought a 'Confidential' stamp and some red ink. Then he carefully stamped the cover of each copy of the report with the word 'Confidential' and when everybody had gone home for the night, he called back in to the office and placed a copy on everybody's desk.

In his excitement, he'd obviously forgotten that we shared the building with civil servants so we had to abide by the same rules as they did. Perhaps unsurprisingly, given their role in government, those rules included a 'Clear Desk' policy. At some stage after the last person had left for the evening, the security team had gone in to do their usual nightly inspection and they must have had a collective fit at what they assumed was a major security breach because when we got to work the next morning, we found Special Branch officers crawling all over the place. It was incredibly funny. Well, *we* thought it was funny – I'm sure they saw the funny side . . . eventually.

Another day that stands out was the birthday of one of the women on our admin team. Someone had bought her one of those helium-filled balloons and, as it was a quiet day, the inevitable happened: a small hole was made and the balloon was passed round for us all to breathe in a lungful of helium. Cue all of us talking like Mickey Mouse and everybody present

laughing like it was the funniest thing they'd ever seen or heard (some party tricks never get old). Just as we were in full flow, there was a knock on the door and who should walk in but the Governor of Papua New Guinea. Luckily for us, he was a really cool dude rather than some stuffed-shirt career diplomat and he immediately started laughing; he even ended up joining in. For us, though, it was just another day in the office . . .

On Operation Drake, they'd come up with a selection test that involved them using a real gorilla. They had it in a room, and candidates would have to open the door, walk in and take its chest measurement. It was as much about their reaction once they opened the door as it was anything else, but the idea was novel and also very successful. Of course, somebody on our team suggested we should also have a gorilla in one of the selection tests. We'd found one who had been taught to hug people in return for a chocolate biscuit, but in the end we couldn't afford a real one, so we went for the next best thing – a darkened room containing a member of the team in a gorilla suit. No, really! And oh, the laughs we had with that suit. There was a serious side though: the person in the gorilla suit learned a great deal about the behaviour of the candidates from how they approached the 'animal'.

The ruse was so good that word got out and, before we knew it, the national media started reporting allegations that Operation Raleigh was abusing this gorilla. The whole thing blew up out of all proportion and there was a story about it running in the *Telegraph* for ages, with campaigns to have the poor animal freed, and everybody very indignant and up in arms about it. There were the usual 'Mr Angry of Tunbridge Wells' letters to the editor, along the lines of: 'Oh, it's disgusting how this poor gorilla is being treated . . .' and of course it was all nonsense. We dined out on that for ages.

I remember we were invited out on one night to a party in

Killingworth, at that time a really depressed sink estate in Newcastle; it was razed to the ground not long after. Those were interesting times in Britain; it was a period of great social change and we saw a lot of it at first hand. Leaving London one day, we were delayed by the siege at the Libyan Embassy following the fatal shooting of WPC Yvonne Fletcher. We left London only to arrive at a different siege in the North, which pitted police officers against striking miners. The dichotomy was evident; there was a real North–South divide back then. We met lots of people from different walks of life and backgrounds: the well-off and well-heeled, the disadvantaged, people with learning difficulties, as well as people with other disabilities and those who work with them. It was very interesting, and seeing it all gave me a great faith in humanity. Although the world news is full of depressing tales of humankind and the terrible things we do, there is another side that you don't hear about very often and that's the remarkable work carried on across the board by people who want to make the world a better place. Those of us involved in Operation Raleigh really got a sense of that first-hand.

It was evident right from the off that some of those who attended the selection weekends belonged to an organisation that involved outdoor pursuits; this gave them the edge over those who hadn't. These candidates came from various organisations, like the Scouting Movement, the Boys' Brigade and the Cadet Forces, but they all held a massive advantage over those who hadn't been a part of something similar, simply because of the knowledge, skills and self-confidence those groups conferred. It really drove home how important those organisations are, and how great their contribution is to society at large. We saw a tangible difference in those who had been a part of one of those groups: they were more self-aware, more rounded and deeper individuals than others who had come straight from day-to-day life. I think that all young

people today should try and find a club, society or organisation of that nature to join, even if it's only for a short while, because it will enrich them in a way that will benefit both them and society for the rest of their lives.

———•◆•———

I was very fortunate in that part of my role at Op Raleigh involved me visiting outdoor centres and undertaking some of their courses to get a feel for what their instructors were teaching. I remember one survival course I did where I'd get up each morning and pick mushrooms that I'd cook for breakfast. The instructors were horrified. They had no idea which ones were poisonous and which ones weren't, and consequently thought I didn't either. Meanwhile, I'm thinking, 'How can you run a survival course and not know how to do this?' Even though my knowledge of fungi was relatively basic at that point, I think that was the first time I realised that my skills and knowledge of the outdoors were more comprehensive and better developed than some of the people who were making a living out of teaching survival.

I also learned that if people are *sent* on a course, it's nothing special to them, but if they've *chosen* to be there and put their own money down, then they're going to be a whole lot more committed. That's when I first thought that I might stand a chance of making a living out of what I knew and loved. It was a moment of clarity. I really felt I had something that could be marketed, although I knew even then that while I might know more than those who had instructed me, I didn't know everything. I think that this is a recurring theme in the world of bushcraft and survival courses – too many people start too soon. In an ideal world, I would have taken a few more years to prepare myself, but back then that simply wasn't an option – there was nowhere I could have gone to learn the

things that would plug the gap in my knowledge, whereas today there are lots of options.

On one of the first courses I ran for Operation Raleigh, I was working alongside a chap called Philip Wells. We had a similar outlook and got along famously, and I confided in him about my plans. I wanted to come up with a name that I could use to market my skills. It was 1983, the era of the Rambo films, and the word 'survival' had terrible connotations, conjuring up images of people running around in combat clothing with headbands and carrying big, ugly knives. I wanted to break away from that, but it would take time to reclaim the word, so I didn't want 'survival' to appear anywhere in my company or trading name. It was Phil and his family who came up with the name 'Woodlore'. I loved it the first time I heard it; I knew it was the right one.

The very first course I ran under the Woodlore name came off the back of a selection weekend that I'd held for Operation Raleigh in Birmingham. One of the judges on that selection, Terry Lewis, had a day job as an Army officer. He told me that the unit he commanded was responsible for despatching Special Forces via Hercules and he thought they might benefit from some survival training.

'Raymond, are there any things one might eat in the countryside?' he asked me.

'Sure,' I said, looking around. Nearby, I spotted the telltale leaves of the pignut.

'Terry, if you look over there,' I said pointing, 'you'll see some leaves that resemble those you get with carrots.'

Terry nodded, and we walked over to them together.

Pignuts were a major source of calories in mankind's distant past. It's the underground part of the plant that we're most interested in – the root, or tuber. I dug some up, cleaned them, and handed one to Terry.

'Here, try this,' I said.

'Pignuts are one of the more palatable wild foods. You can eat the tuber raw, it's really tasty. The flavour and consistency is reminiscent of celery heart crossed with raw hazelnut or sweet chestnut.'

Terry tried it. 'There's a spicy aftertaste too – similar to what you'd get from radishes or watercress?'

I smiled. That was all it took to secure Woodlore's first paid gig.

A few weeks later, I took Terry and twenty or so of his men to a very wet Elan Valley, in Mid-Wales, to teach them some survival skills over a four-day period. I really enjoyed working with them; it was my first experience of teaching the military and I learned very early on that they'd be great to work with. They have a lot of energy and professionalism, they love acquiring new skills and, crucially, they have a great sense of humour. I think I earned £200, but it meant so much more to me than that. It was what it represented – and that, to me, was priceless.

I taught the men how to snare, butcher and cook rabbit, and I then had them rubbing sticks together to make fire by friction. I taught them survival skills – basic things like shelter, fire, and finding water and food. I had a pretty good idea of how to go about doing these things, but in the time since, I've really been able to refine those skills. This is largely thanks to the success of Woodlore and to all the students who have made it successful. Students are far and away the best teachers; the questions they ask are the best guide as to what they should be learning. I had enough knowledge in terms of timber then to get a weak flame going, but the knowledge I've acquired over the years since is what's turned that flame into a fire.

I learned a great deal from that first course, but not from the things that went right; it's more from what *didn't* go so right. Even if I have a general feeling that things have gone

well, I'm never happy with how I've done; I never have been. There are some things you can pat yourself on the back for, but I'm always focused on what didn't work or what I could have done better. *That's* how you learn, that's how you hone your knowledge and that's how you make something work properly. Generally, it's better to be critical about what you've done, the things that didn't work, and the things that could have gone better. That's how you improve your performance and grow.

6

Photographic Memory

I left Operation Raleigh in 1984 having completed what I'd been recruited to do; we'd run the assessment weekends and all the candidates had been selected for the first expedition and were making preparations to leave. I'd had a brilliant time, made some great connections, learned some valuable lessons and acquired new skills but I wanted to build on them, and develop and hone my knowledge still further. I wanted to see what I could do with Woodlore.

After a short period of consolidation back at home, I set off for the US. I'd made contact with some Native Americans before I left and I wanted to spend some time with them, learning about their traditional skills. I also spent time in the desert; that was great. In those days you could light fires in the back country, although recently the rules and regulations on camp fires have been tightened. It's a shame because it's a special thing to hike into the back country, collect a couple of mullein sticks which I'd rub against alligator juniper and make fire by friction in the evening – it's an experience that's not so easy to have now, unless you break the rules.

One night, not long after I arrived back, I was practising at the Budokwai when I noticed Kingsley lying down on the side of the mat. He looked very pale and unwell and somebody was standing beside him fanning him with a towel. I rushed over and I could see immediately that it was serious. I called

an ambulance and he was rushed across the road to St Stephen's Hospital. It transpired that he'd had a massive heart attack and he passed away peacefully the following morning. He was seventy-three when he died and I'd known him for almost twenty years by then. I felt his loss terribly – my mentor, my friend. I miss him still.

His loss had a galvanising effect on me and it crystallised the fact that I felt I was drifting. His death was the catalyst for me to do something and take control, so I did something decisive and threw myself into writing for a magazine. It was a part-work on survival, and although it wasn't what I wanted to do, I couldn't afford to be choosy – it paid the bills. I'd realised that no matter how much I believed in myself and my abilities, it was going to be difficult to support myself solely by running courses on bushcraft when nobody knew what it was, so I needed another string to my bow. The magazine used to send a photographer out with me on assignments and I realised very quickly that his images were nothing to write home about; I thought I could do better, so I started to take my own. I enjoyed it, I was reasonably good at it (and learning all the time) and I thought, 'Well, maybe I'll try photography.' I was still seeking the right path and trying to find myself, really.

So, I joined a photographic society – I wanted to improve, so I was casting around for ways in which I could gather new techniques. The society had a newsletter and one of the first editions I received had some useful advice on how to make a living as a photographer. It was pretty simple, common-sense advice but effective nonetheless. It suggested browsing magazines, picking the ones with the best images in, and then ringing the editors up to arrange a meeting so you could show your portfolio.

I'm a practical man – I much prefer to do rather than just read theory – so I went to WH Smith and was immediately

drawn to *National Geographic* which, from a photographic perspective, was my favourite magazine. I thought that might be a little bit out of my league, but I noticed a brand new publication called *World*, which appeared to have a similar remit and was essentially a glossy British version of the venerable US periodical. Being new, I thought they might be looking for photographers, so I put a call in to the editor, an Italian gentleman called Mark Ausenda. I was more than a little surprised when I was put straight through to him.

'Hi, my name is Ray Mears, I'm a photographer [yeah, right!], and I'd like to show you my portfolio.'

He said, 'Yeah, sure,' and gave me a date to meet with him. It was as simple as that.

Then I put the phone down and thought, 'Ah, maybe I'd better put a portfolio together.'

I already knew the kind of transparencies that *World* wanted so I selected my best images, put them together in a slide sheet and off I went to meet with Mark. I arrived at the magazine's offices in Kensington. Mark met me in the foyer, held my slide sheet up to the light and said, 'Really, these aren't good enough, but thank you for coming.'

I did a double take. I didn't think he'd looked at them closely enough. I was incensed, but he'd been very polite to me, so I asked him what was wrong with them. He sat down (a positive sign, I thought) and explained to me that they weren't sharp enough. He also said there wasn't enough depth of field and they weren't colourful enough.

'Thanks,' I said. 'I'll be back.'

He didn't look convinced.

It hadn't gone quite how I'd expected but I wasn't put off; I was still high on the success of actually talking to an editor, so I went into town and bought a wonderful book called *The 35mm Photographer's Handbook*. It was very concise – there were no words wasted – and what text there was in that book

absolutely banged the nail on the head. It made me realise I couldn't carry on using the kit I had – a Canon AE1 programme camera and cheap telephoto zoom lens – so I sold it all and raided my piggy bank again. That gave me enough to invest in my first serious camera, a manual-only Nikon FM2 and a 35–105mm lens. Then I spent six months teaching myself to take better pictures.

I went up to see Mark again. He came out to the foyer, took the slide sheets from me, held them up to the light and looked at them again. I wasn't very happy with the time he spent on them but it didn't change what he said.

'No, they're still not good enough.'

And then he looked at me and said, 'But come back and see me again.'

That was quite encouraging, but I had no idea what to do next. So I went away and thought, *Right, back to the beginning. Start again.* I gathered up every copy of *National Geographic* I could find and looked for images that stood out to me. They were all stunning, but I couldn't see any pictures of stone tools. I'd become quite adept at making stone tools and I knew about them, so I decided to shoot my own.

I made some flint arrowheads and a few bone needles. Several things stood out about the *National Geographic* images. They were very sharp, they had strong colour in the background and they were artistically lit.

So I got some coloured paper, some glass and some bricks, plus two rolls of Kodachrome 25, the sharpest film you could buy. Then I put the stone tools on the glass so I could backlight them, hired another flash gun to front light them so I could capture the facets, and I put different coloured paper behind them. I shot images with a number of different coloured backgrounds, put them on a slide sheet and went back to see Mark.

Again, he came down to the foyer and had a look at what I'd shot.

I was half expecting to hear the same, 'Thanks, but no thanks,' but this time he said, 'Yeah, come with me.' We went into his office and he put the slide sheet on his light box and then called in Rachel Horner who was his assistant editor. He asked her what she thought.

'Wow, the sharpness, the colour. Pretty good.'

And I walked out of there with my first assignment for *World* magazine.

A week later, I was taking photos of some of Britain's most precious fossils behind the scenes at the British Museum. Of course, I didn't really know what I was doing but what a great way to learn on the job!

Using a manual SLR camera was instructive, so from a technical perspective it was one of the best things I could have done because I had to learn how to do everything the hard way rather than relying on a program or automatic function to take care of the settings for me. I was fortunate enough to be able to consult with the photographic legend that was the late Terry Donovan. Of course, to certain sections of high society and the media back then he had almost mythical status. Along with David Bailey and Brian Duffy, Donovan captured, and in many ways helped create, the Swinging London of the 1960s. To me, though, he was just 'Terence', someone I knew and had become friends with as we practised judo together on a regular basis at the Budokwai.

I also immersed myself in different photographic techniques such as flash formulas, reciprocity failure and colour correction, all of which were vital back then. With today's multi-function digital SLRs you can literally point and shoot straight from the box and get half-decent results, so I think having to do things manually would scare a lot of budding photographers now.

It's like many things – if the conditions are OK, then you don't encounter too many problems, but it's when they are at

their worst that photographers really earn their money. If the camera can't cope with the conditions, you can visualise the image all you like but recording that image is a different thing entirely. That job at *World* magazine was very good training for me because I simply couldn't go back to Mark with nothing.

Mark was demanding as an editor – he was a perfectionist and he wanted the best, and I learned a lot from that. I was, yet again, outside of my comfort zone, which is where you need to be because you don't learn anything when you're inside it. It takes a lot of practice before you develop the ability to release the shutter at the right moment and, even now, that's a concept that escapes a lot of people. There's this notion now with digital cameras that if you just keep shooting you'll eventually get the shot you want. I don't shoot that way – I'm much more selective than that.

The assignments were tough, too. Some of them could take weeks to complete and I really had to be inventive sometimes to get the shot required. One of my assignments was to shoot some images for a piece on smuggling in the eighteenth century. Now, how the hell do you photograph something like that? And it was winter, so it was a real challenge.

First off, I read up on the topic, and I learned that smuggling then wasn't based out of Cornwall as I'd assumed, it was focused on a part of the coast near Deal, in Kent. The smugglers used certain techniques and equipment, and I thought that I might be able to make a good image of some of the kit they used, but I didn't know if any of it still existed.

I rang Customs and Excise and eventually I got through to someone there who was quite interested in that area of history, to the point that he was involved in re-enacting eighteenth-century smuggling. How's that for luck? I arranged to take photographs at his office, thinking it might be some grand Georgian building by the Thames.

What I was hoping for was a nice Georgian window that I

could lay things out beside, with a nice bit of natural light streaming through. But you hope for the best and prepare for the worst so I took along an old tent and some rope, just to be on the safe side. When I arrived at the location, I wasn't entirely surprised to discover it was a modern office building with no windows. But as I had come prepared with the canvas and rope, I managed to make it work.

I arranged afterwards to get some images of the re-enactment guys in a specific eighteenth-century scenario, so I started to give some thought to a venue for the shoot. I'd been running some courses for the Countryside Education Trust down at Beaulieu in Hampshire, and there's a historic maritime museum near there called Bucklers Hard on the edge of the New Forest, with lots of seventeenth- and eighteenth-century buildings. I arranged to meet the guys there, and when I got there, I found an old white rowing boat, so some ideas started to come together. I had various concepts: one was the Kipling poem, 'A Smugglers Song', and I felt that was the right one for the job. I put the guys in the boat and took them upriver, dressed in their eighteenth-century clothing, and equipped with muskets and old lanterns. It was a bit of a Heath Robinson approach but I got some great imagery from that shoot. Those were the sorts of challenges I was up against. It was never straightforward.

And that's how my career as a photographer started. Every couple of weeks or so, I went into the *World* offices and collected a big case of Kodachrome 25. That was unusual, but wonderful – before digital cameras, film was the biggest expense for all photographers, and the reason that all but a few high-end photographers had to choose their shots carefully. *World* was very demanding as a magazine – they wanted quality images with maximum depth of field, absolute clarity and sharpness, lots of colour and creativity, and they knew that meant providing the best quality film, unlike most other magazines whose photographers had to buy their own. *World* wanted

the best and that forced me to up my game, by schooling myself in all of photography's different techniques.

But I loved it. I felt very lucky to be doing something I enjoyed, something that was a hobby for so many people, and I was not only being sent on some fascinating assignments, I was getting paid for it too. I ploughed all the money I made back into lenses and cameras, and kept on developing and expanding my repertoire.

Now I was working and doing something I enjoyed, the opportunities for teaching bushcraft were few and far between. Also, I had no time or energy to spend on marketing myself. That's not to say that my love for the outdoors took a back seat. I still headed out to the forest whenever I could – how I could I not? It felt like home to me, after all. Something had to give though, and it was judo that fell by the wayside. As much as I loved it, my outdoor life won every time and I simply couldn't commit to both as I got older.

Photography suited me as a way to make a living and I think it's fair to say that at that time, in terms of whether I made bushcraft my future or taking pictures, it was in the balance which way I would go.

I don't think I ever made a conscious decision about the direction my future would take. I was still young and I had my whole life in front of me, so all I was concerned about at the time was enjoying myself and earning a decent wage. I think rather than choose between bushcraft and photography, I deferred the decision at a subconscious level and maybe I thought fate would take care of it for me. And I guess it did, given how things have turned out. Even today, photography is still a big part of my life, but I see the two interests as running side by side. It's healthy to have more than one interest – if you do just that one thing in life, you can get stale.

My passion for photography has run like a thread right

through my life and it's enabled me to record all the things I've seen, the places I've been, the things I've done and the people I've met. In many respects, it's created a visual diary of my life. Some of the cultures and ways of life that I have covered no longer exist so, to me, that makes having a photographic record all the more vital.

———◦◦◦———

Alongside working for *World* magazine, I was enjoying life. Having climbed Skiddaw in my mid-teens, I wanted to learn more, but it was only now that I had the independence and money to do so. I'd been fortunate to do some climbing with Arthur and Nick Parks, two of the mountain guides at Op Raleigh, but I really wanted to tackle the Alps. I wanted to become a good climber. It was important to me, and if that's how I feel about something then I'll put my heart and soul into it. That's how I've always been.

So I did tackle the Alps; however, I never became an expert in climbing because first and foremost the trip reaffirmed for me my love of the forest. It showed me that forests are more exciting – you go up a mountain, reach the summit and then you come back down again, but when you enter one of the world's great forests, you go in one side and you come out somewhere different. Sometimes, you go in and come out and *you're* different. And that's what rocked my world the most.

That's not to say I didn't enjoy climbing; I did, and it's almost as if some unseen hand was guiding me because it conferred on me lots of skills and experience that translate to bushcraft, so it was a vital part of the learning curve I'd carved out for myself. Thanks to my Alpine climbs, I acquired lots of experience of working with ropes, so I'm now pretty good with them. I can do everything from splicing to advanced rope-working. If there was a caving ladder that needed to be

thrown over a high branch, you can bet your bottom dollar that I'd be there. I particularly enjoyed winter climbing because of having to use the ice axe. I'd become accomplished using axes in the forest, so I felt there was a kinship between my bushcraft and mountaineering.

It was while climbing in the Alps that I first encountered the Therm-a-Rest. What a wonderful device it is. It's a sealed, self-inflating foam mattress. Like all the best inventions, it was produced by people with a skill in the right discipline, to help facilitate a passion they had. In this case, the inventors were two former Boeing engineers who were avid backpackers. The Therm-a-Rest is a must-have piece of kit because it's light, portable and effective – it insulates you from cold ground and retains warmth, so it's really useful when you're sleeping out. If you're sleeping in the wild, wherever that might be, you need to be as comfortable as possible. A lot of people, when they start out, don't have a good enough sleeping bag but it's absolutely vital to have the best possible. A good one keeps you sufficiently warm, is large enough for you to be comfortable in, and is as lightweight and compact as science allows. A good sleeping bag and a Therm-a-Rest are two small things that make a huge difference.

Working for *World* magazine did give me some time to do other things. I wasn't out doing commissions for the magazine every day, so it allowed Woodlore to tick over in the background, and for me to run the odd course now and then. The RGS course all those years earlier was really paying dividends now. I'd gone back from time to time, and eventually undertook one or two lectures there myself. I kept in touch with a number of people I'd met there – yes, we'd all gone our own separate ways, but we had common interests in a niche market so we called on one another from time to time.

It was at one of these lectures that I met a couple of guys

from a company called Survival Aids. It had started out in the early 80s when the threat of nuclear annihilation was at its peak and the phrase Mutually-Assured Destruction (MAD) was part of the everyday lexicon. As well as selling things like filters for your nuclear fall-out shelter and other assorted goodies, the company started a club and they asked me if I could organise a few courses for them. That's when Woodlore really started to gather some momentum.

My first car was a humble Peugeot 104. Having the car enabled me to travel further quicker and I'd do things on a whim. Sometimes I'd head off to the New Forest and hone my tracking ability, only instead of just tracking animals, I taught myself how to track people. The principles are the same but by following people, my tracking skills really leaped ahead.

There's only so much you can learn in terms of tracking animals; after a while, it becomes tricky. It all depends on the season, and the ground – if you're in desert areas and you're following animals, or in snowy places, you can follow them over a considerable distance because their tracks are easy to see. I loved it when it was snowy; I'd get a pair of skis on and follow fox tracks for miles. But a lot of the time when they're travelling through wood and the ground is hard, they're so light, they leave virtually no sign. It becomes too slow to be able to follow them effectively. But following people is a different story. People are much heavier on their feet, and they leave a more noticeable sign on the ground, especially if they're running. I'd look for a footprint and follow it – that's all there was to it. I found I could often follow people all day, and eventually I'd get to a point where I would see the person I'd been tracking. I would watch them and they never knew a thing about it.

I'd been so wrapped up in my interests that the opposite sex hadn't really figured too prominently in my life up to that point. I'd had girlfriends, but there was never anyone serious, and unlike a lot of my peers I wasn't going off to pubs and clubs at the weekend, so opportunities to meet girls were limited. However, I wasn't exactly a hermit – I was out all the time, and I was running lectures on what I'd learned, so I suppose it was inevitable that I'd find someone eventually.

It was a few months later, in early 1990, that I met a young lady who caught my attention. I'd been presenting a lecture on bushcraft up at the RGS in London and this blonde girl came up to me and said, 'Hi, my name's Ffyona Campbell, I'm walking around the world.'

Quite frankly, I didn't believe her. You meet people all the time who make bold claims and most don't come to anything. I realised she was serious a few months later, though, when she came to one of my courses to learn some bushcraft to help her on the African stage of her trip.

She was a charismatic young woman with a drive and determination that were readily apparent and, after talking to her at length, it wasn't difficult to see where her wanderlust originated. Her father, Colin, was a Royal Marine officer whose postings sometimes lasted as little as six months, so she grew up on the move. By the time she was fifteen, they'd moved home some twenty-four times and Ffyona and her sister had been to seventeen different schools. She walked from John o' Groats to Land's End at sixteen, raising some £25,000 for the Royal Marsden Cancer Hospital in the process.

At eighteen, she set her sights on crossing America and left New York to walk to Los Angeles, and by the time she was twenty-one, she had walked the 3,000-odd miles across Australia, beating the world-record time set by a man. She'd written a book about the journey called *Feet of Clay*, which was published a short time after we met.

There was an obvious connection between us and we quickly became an item. I'd been living at home up until that point but I was spending an increasing amount of time away and I'd outgrown the nest. Ffyona and I started looking for flats in South-West London; we were lucky because we found a one-bedroom flat in Wandsworth that was perfect for us, and we moved in together a few weeks later.

Life was good. We had fun, and while most of my work revolved around Mark and the magazine, I was running an increasing number of courses, too. I did the odd lecture up at the RGS, and whenever I was at home I'd help Ffyona while she planned her African expedition. I have to admit, I found her project intoxicating – perhaps it enhanced the attraction. Every Friday, I'd throw everything in the back of the car and Ffyona and I would head out of town somewhere – it didn't matter where, as long as it was outside of London. We'd try to beat the rush out and we'd head down the A3 out of Wandsworth and find some countryside and go camping.

Having made the jump from living at home to living in a flat, money was tight at first and we were really just scraping by. I was running courses for the Countryside Education Trust, so that brought in a bit, and the odd lecture helped. There was no business plan or strategy on my part – I just took what I could find and did what I enjoyed. I was learning so much in the process, and really loving what I was doing. And all the while I was meeting people who had skills I wanted to learn and vice versa, so we'd barter and swap. I've always tried to find the best teachers if I need to learn something. I wanted to learn how to work flint so I tracked down the foremost authority on flint working in the UK, John Lord.

We traded skills – I taught him to light fire by friction and he taught me to work flint. I'd be sat in the flat in Wandsworth breaking pieces of flint to make an axe head and our landlord would be constantly sticking his nose in to see what the noise

was – looking back, I suppose it sounded a bit like breaking glass so no wonder he was a little concerned.

When I was younger and I'd first started to make tools, it was very difficult. I was looking up archaeological books and looking at drawings and they didn't explain the *how*. They'd be illustrated with conceptual drawings but they don't exactly show you how it's done.

You have to strike the flint in a certain way. Flint's an igneous rock and when it breaks it does so with a conchoidal fracture, a muscle-shell shaped fracture, which means that if you hit it straight down, the shock waves go out on the angles of the cone at 120°, so if you wanted to break a piece off you have to hit it at 120° from the direction that you want the shock waves to go and you also have to make sure the platform that you strike is strong enough to take the force that you're imparting.

Once you learn those two things you're off and away; that's it, in essence, but of course then there are other processes involved. The advances in flint-working technology from the very earliest tools to the very latest tools that were still being made during the metal era, during the Bronze Age, are massive. Those conceptual leaps represent the development of the human brain. People look down their noses at Neanderthals and I've never understood that, because actually they were incredibly skilful people – they were able to live through an Ice Age, after all. We still joke about Neanderthals even though we now know that they are among us, that we have integrated with them. They survived on this planet as a species longer than us fully modern humans have; we are not yet in a position to make that judgement. And that irritates me. I have a great respect for them because I have learned to do the things that they knew how to do, and I can tell you how difficult they are.

Woodlore was really starting to gain ground now. I met

someone through one of my courses who said that his family owned some land in Hampshire that might be suitable as a venue for me to operate from. It was on Lord Selborne's estate in Blackmoor and it was perfect – acres of empty fields near a hill with woods nearby. It was everything I'd been looking for.

With the rent on the flat and Selborne, and running the car, it felt like I was barely making a living sometimes. I was doing such an eclectic mix of things but I was happy. I was young, and none of it mattered to me because I knew I was on to something. I just knew it was all going to turn around at some point. I honestly don't know where the feeling came from – it was that old sixth sense again – but it was unshakeable. I felt like I'd reached a point of critical mass; I was consuming so much knowledge on the one hand, and on the other giving out, educating others in the skills required to live outdoors. I'd really got to grips with the technical side of photography, the commissions were coming in, Mark was happy with what I was producing and everything combined to make me feel that I could do anything. That was all down to the days I'd spent in the open, the time I'd invested in the libraries, the courses, and the way I'd listened to and learned skills from people I met.

Then I landed a commission from Haynes Publishing to write a *Survival Handbook* for them. I got a small advance for that and wrote the manuscript quickly against the backdrop of everything else that was going on. They were happy with what I produced and, soon after, I landed a commission from Random House to write another book. Life was good, the money was coming in and I was also spending an increasing amount of time helping Ffyona make her preparations for Africa, which was the penultimate leg in her round-the-world hike. It also represented by far the longest, and potentially most dangerous, sector of her project – she was facing a

monumental 10,000 mile trek south–north from Cape Town to Tangiers. There was a lot to plan, sponsorship to arrange, and she was also in the middle of a book tour, undertaking interviews to promote *Feet of Clay*.

It took a Herculean effort but eventually everything was in place for her to leave for Africa. The date was set for 2 April 1991, just six months after she'd attended the course I'd run. The day she was due to leave for Cape Town clashed with the start of another bushcraft course that I was running under the aegis of Woodlore, so we said our goodbyes by spending the night before in the woods, alone. I had commissioned a carbon-steel knife for her from Wilkinson Sword and had made her a sheath and an antler-horn handle for it, so I presented that to her as her going-away present. We'd agreed to wait for one another while she undertook her walk, but it was a promise born of the optimism and naivety of our youth. We didn't know it as we said our goodbye, but it was the last time we'd do so as a couple.

7

Walking in Africa

'*I never knew of a morning in Africa when I woke up that I was not happy.*'

Ernest Hemingway said that and, having been there many times over the past ten years, I can understand why. I spent a few years as a child in Africa, when my dad was posted out there through work, I still have some memories of it, but who knows the impact something like that has on shaping you as an infant? I don't – other than that I've always felt a connection with the continent. When Ffyona flew to Cape Town to start her walk, little did I know that I'd be joining her, renewing some connections but losing others . . .

I knew instantly that things had changed between us when she phoned me a month or so into the walk. I could tell by the tone of her voice before she said as much – there was a distance there and it wasn't the 9,000 miles between us.

'Raymond, I've had a lot of time to think and my feelings for you have changed.' And that was that.

We agreed to stay in touch – what's the saying? 'Just good friends', isn't it? But I don't think either of us expected to hear from the other ever again. I can't say that it came as a huge surprise to me but it hurt all the same. Still, they say the best thing to do is pick yourself up, dust yourself off and carry on. And that's exactly what I did – I gave notice on our flat in London and I moved back home. There, I knuckled down to

finish the book on survival I'd been working on for Random House.

While I was busy in London, Ffyona had been making good progress in Africa – right up to the point when she arrived in Zaire (now known as the Democratic Republic of Congo). Her timing was immaculate; in May 1990, Zaire's President Mobutu had agreed to the principle of a multi-party political system with elections and a constitution, but he delayed in setting out details of the reforms. Ffyona was about halfway through the country when its soldiers began looting Kinshasa in protest at their unpaid wages. Things unravelled very quickly after that, to the extent that over 2,000 French and Belgian troops, plus elements of the Foreign Legion, arrived to evacuate some 20,000 endangered foreign nationals. Ffyona was one of them, and she and her team were forced to abandon both their Land Rover support vehicle and the project in the city of Kisangani and head home to England.

She'd been back in London some two weeks when she called me again. It was the morning of 14 October 1991. She was, as ever, straight and to the point.

'Ray, do you want to come to Africa with me and walk unsupported? I want to get back to my walk but I don't think the support vehicle will still be there. Will you come and help and take care of me? I think you're the only person who can.'

By this point, things had settled down a little – both in Africa, and between us. I didn't hesitate. I had some clear time ahead so I could afford to devote a few months to her project. She said she'd pay me, but even before I knew that I'd already said yes. It would have made no sense for me to undertake an expedition like that for my own benefit, but to use my skills for someone else's? Absolutely. It felt like a vindication of everything I'd learned. She needed someone who knew bushcraft, someone who knew their way around

a camera, someone who understood her and what she was doing and who supported it. I fitted the bill.

At that time, Zaire was still too dangerous for her to return to, so we decided to pick up her walk in the Central African Republic (CAR) which was the nearest northern border to where she'd abandoned the attempt at the end of September. The Guinness Book of Records said that was acceptable and so we went. We flew out of Heathrow a week later and after a short layover in Lagos, where we waited for our connecting flight, we arrived in Bangui, CAR's capital.

I'd known before we left London that it was going to be impossible to continue the walk with everything we had to carry. Even if everything had fitted comfortably into two over-sized rucksacks – and the medical kit alone would have taken up more than one – carrying that amount of weight in the African heat over such a long distance would have been a reach too far. I'd decided to look for solutions once we arrived and one presented itself almost straight away.

I noticed that the locals used carts – battered metal panels that were welded together to form a rectangular box. The box was then mounted on a couple of wheels and towed behind a bicycle. I bought us one of these – it comfortably swallowed all of our gear with room to spare, but instead of trailing it behind a bike, I decided to push it along. As it transpired, I didn't have to push it far – we had arranged a lift from one of Ffyona's contacts who took us as far as Bangassou on CAR's south-eastern border with Zaire.

We were both tired from the journey and our feet hadn't touched the ground so we needed a cheap hotel, somewhere to dump our stuff and get some sleep. There wasn't much to choose from so we selected the one that looked the best of a bad bunch. But best is a relative term – our room was the sort of place where you would want to pitch a tent on the bed. The mattress had so many suspect stains it probably had its

own ecosystem. It was truly awful but the fan worked, so we cleared space on the floor and slept there. We were up and away first thing the following morning; I pushed the handcart and Ffyona's walk was on.

I wasn't in the best place, physically – two or so days in and I'd already picked up some sort of bug. I had a really bad case of the runs, which is bad enough when you're in the comfort of your own home and you've access to your own bathroom. In the African bush, it makes life, er . . . interesting, to say the least. Despite this, we settled down into a comfortable rhythm, and we were making good time – we covered over 300 miles in the first ten days.

There isn't much you can plan for on an expedition like this – again, it's very much about the journey rather than the destination, so we'd sleep in the bush at night and strike out again shortly after first light. I was just taking everything in, watching, listening and learning – getting acclimatised. We were reactive, rather than proactive, just taking everything in our stride.

I realised quite early on that it was going to be difficult to sleep in the bush on a regular basis, if only because the locals would descend from nowhere, telling us, 'You can't stay here, it's dangerous. Come stay in our village.' From our perspective that prospect didn't make us feel any safer, but after a few nights of repelling offers of accommodation we talked it over and agreed to give it a try – we both wanted to embrace and learn as much of the local customs and culture as we could and we were never going to do that if we disengaged and spent every night in the bush. So we established a pattern. Towards the end of a day, we'd arrive at a village and ask to stay under the chief's protection. That was really interesting because it was a really good learning curve and each morning, invariably, some of the villagers would want to help us by pushing the cart, which was just marvellous and really took some of the pressure off.

We were making good progress but there was no question that the loss of Ffyona's Land Rover left her feeling vulnerable and me a bit concerned. The whole point of me being there was to protect her, keep her safe and ensure she came to no harm. This would have been easier with a vehicle, as then I could have gone up ahead of her when I felt it was necessary or hung in behind her to keep watch. There was no telling where the Land Rover ended up, so there seemed little point in lamenting its loss, and on the plus side walking did give me a huge insight into how the locals lived. Walking through those villages, we met generous people with a great deal of humility. They had nothing really, but would invite us to share what little food they had and they'd cook for us. It was truly humbling.

We were approaching Bambari when providence shone on us in the form of an Exodus overland truck. The overland trucks are a frequent sight in Africa and represent the cheapest way for most independent travellers to cross the continent. They're like a cross between a coach and a truck – a truck with a coach-style body instead of an ISO container or other type of cargo platform. Travellers all muck in, cooking, digging the vehicle out if it gets bogged down, and accommodation is generally in tents out in the bush. It's completely informal and it puts continent crossing in reach of most of those with a dream. Although there's an ultimate destination for each truck, it's not about that; it's all about the journey. Consequently, if the drivers see other travellers walking, broken down or otherwise stuck, they'll often stop to offer assistance.

Unusually, at first the truck rumbled past us, leaving behind a pall of dust from the track, but then we saw brake lights come on and it started to back up. The driver wound down his window and said he didn't stop when he first saw us because he thought we were missionaries. And what was it about our appearance that made him think that? 'It was because you

81

both looked so clean.' (We'd made a point of keeping clean – I run a tidy camp when I'm out and about because I think that it's bad admin to walk around all muddy and dirty.)

We really struck gold with the truck. The driver explained to us that he was heading across the border and back to Zaire and his was the first overland truck to make the attempt since the riots. Things had settled down somewhat since Ffyona had been evacuated. He told us that he'd be driving as far as Bumba on the Zaire River (now the Congo River) before heading east and on to Uganda. Ffyona wanted to get back to Kisangani – it had been eating at her since we arrived back in Africa and she was determined, if at all possible, to pick her walk up right where she'd been forced to abandon it. The truck wasn't going there, but it was going in vaguely the right direction, so we accepted the driver's offer to take us as far as the town of Bumba.

One thing struck Ffyona and I immediately as we drove back along the road we'd just spent so many days walking. We couldn't believe how different the Africans looked and acted as we passed them. They were the same individuals who had accommodated us, but gone were the helpful, dignified, proud people who'd given us charity, invited us as guests into their villages – we were on a truck now, so as far as they were concerned, we were a different tribe. It was instructive to say the least. As we passed, they slouched peasant-like and begged the truck, and in turn, all of us in it. I was shocked and dumbstruck. This was a very different Africa to the one we'd seen; it was all but unrecognisable. By virtue of the fact that we were on the bus, they saw us as wealthy and that made them, in turn, feel poor.

That said, it's an aspect of life in Africa that I'd never have seen had I not initially accompanied Ffyona on foot – it's a perspective that's denied so many, and it remains for me one of the most profound experiences of my life. There was so

much that happened in those first 300 miles, but more than that, it was an acclimatisation. The trip gave me a really helpful insight into the African psyche.

By the time we arrived in Bumba, our two had become four. Among the ragtag group of paying tourists on that truck, we struck up an immediate affinity with two independent travellers: Michael Duffy, an American national and former Marine who was trying to cycle across Africa, and Johann Sundblatt, a huge, hairy young Swedish guy with a long, straggly beard. Meeting those guys was typical of Africa at that time. So many people were trying to cross it, but their journeys were fraught with difficulty on a good day, danger on a bad one; it was a volatile continent and trouble would suddenly erupt any time, any place, anywhere. Wars were commonplace in countries with unstable military governments and corrupt police and border officials were a fact of life. It all added up to myriad travellers from across the globe all in the same place, trying to find alternative routes to where they wanted to be.

Mike and Johann were both heading in similar directions to us so they both decided to come as far as Kisangani with us. We found another filthy hotel and took two rooms there but it was a bizarre place. Everywhere you looked there were Art Deco lanterns that the Belgians had brought in when they annexed the Congo as a colony – they must be worth an absolute fortune. You couldn't get them out though – they're an integral part of the great expanse of the peeling, dilapidated concrete structure that was our hotel. They were true works of art and so incongruous given where we were. As I was learning though, Africa is like that – a litany of things that you just couldn't make up.

The following morning, we said goodbye to the driver and the other passengers and the truck left to continue on its journey to Uganda, minus Ffyona and me, Mike and Johann. There was a definite air of intimidation around us in Bumba,

a really tense atmosphere that you could have cut with a knife. Due to the violence and uncertainty that had led to foreign nationals being evacuated, all financial aid to Zaire had been suspended. The locals were really in a bad way financially – they were desperate. They all wanted our trade because it meant cash for them – *we* represented cash to them, and I guess we felt it so palpably because the four of us were the first 'tourists' since the trouble had ended. Travelling in Africa is nothing like travelling in a place that's 'safe', such as Australia or Europe. And this part of Africa most definitely *wasn't* safe – people were saying to us, 'Your lives are in danger – you should leave here.' That really didn't instil confidence in us.

We decided to head towards Kisangani upriver so we hired a *pirogue*, which was easier said than done, mainly due to the fact that I didn't know the first thing about African negotiations. I just bulldozed my way through and doubtless provided great entertainment for the locals. We got there eventually and ended up with two *pirogues* that we chained together. We also hired some locals to crew the boat and a captain – Joseph – to look after it all. Eventually, we loaded up and set off down the Zaire River, into the great unknown.

———◆———

When we were on the move along the river, we could get to the stuff in our rucksacks, but realised they would present a potentially lucrative target to any light-fingered locals if we went ashore, so we'd bought some big grain sacks in Bumba. They proved to be an inexpensive but wise investment; we placed our rucksacks inside them to make them appear a little less 'interesting'. It was a practical and simple solution to a potential problem, rendering our luggage invisible to prying eyes. The only time we really stopped was to cook on the shore, although on a couple of occasions we'd go to a local

village and prepare food. We'd learned while we were walking to cook rice the way the locals cooked it. You take palm oil and heat it in your pot and then add to that washed and rinsed rice. You don't spill a single grain – coat them all in hot oil and then add the water. We'd mix it up sometimes, add tomato paste or pineapple to make it interesting, and it always went down well.

We had one worrying moment on the journey when, at a stop for provisions, a local guy tried to buy his way onto the boat. We'd made it perfectly clear to Joseph when we hired the *pirogue* and crew that there were to be no passengers. This was because we would easily be overwhelmed with people and there would be a good chance that the boat would sink. So when this guy realised he wasn't getting anywhere, he tried to play the crowd against us. He was getting them increasingly agitated and the crowd seemed to multiply exponentially; there was a real air of menace and things felt like they could turn ugly any minute. We were balancing on a knife edge.

Suddenly, one of the crew – a big burly guy, like an African Bill Sikes – turned to the guy who was causing all the trouble. He grabbed him and said in a tone that brooked no argument, 'Get away from the boat or I'll break your head.' That was all he said. No drama, no histrionics, no idle threat . . . and that was it. As quickly as things ramped up, they dissipated again. The guy realised he was beaten, so he turned around and walked away. With him gone, the crowd dispersed and we continued on our way. But it was just one more example of how unpredictable Africa could be.

Our trip along the river lasted four days. And then we were there: Kisangani. Being among the vanguard of outsiders returning to the town, we had no idea what to expect. As it turned out, we weren't the first – we were the twelfth, thirteenth, fourteenth and fifteenth white people to hit Kisangani

after the riots. I know this because we were told by a Portuguese man we met on the riverbank as we struggled ashore.

'Is it safe here?' I asked.

'Yes, yes, it's fine now. The rage has disappeared; people only want to rebuild their lives and businesses now. The army is still here – the very same people who started the riots, only now they're policing the town.'

That really cheered us up.

Ffyona asked him about the main hotel – this had been something of a landmark, a beacon to all the travellers and overlanders who had been making their way across Zaire before the army rebelled.

'It's open but it's no longer a hotel – it's er . . . it's now a brothel.'

There were a couple of rooms that the hotel made available to us and, as it was almost luxurious compared to where we'd stayed so far, we took them. We may have been sleeping in a brothel but at least the rooms were clean. We decided to make camp there while we gathered ourselves and made plans.

Now she was back in Kisangani, Ffyona was obviously curious as to what had happened to her Land Rover. She'd left it at a Catholic Mission on the outskirts of town. We knew it was a long shot, but we had time so she and I set off to the Mission to see what we could ascertain. It didn't take much detective work on our part – as we walked into the compound, Ffyona let out a squeal.

'I don't believe it! It's still here! Oh my God, it's exactly where I left it, Raymond. It hasn't moved.'

She was visibly delighted and, if I'm honest, my spirits lifted somewhat too, although I counselled caution.

'That's brilliant news, Ffyona, but don't get your hopes up too much – let's see if it's OK first, shall we?'

I have to say, I was amazed when I inspected it; it had a flat battery (unsurprisingly, given that it had sat there under the

baking hot sun for some five or six weeks). It needed a service, and its fluids needed a top up, but otherwise it was fine; oh, aside from the ants' nest in the driver's footwell. We found a mechanic locally who did all the work there and then for the princely sum of £2.50 for the lot. He was as delighted with the 50p tip we gave him as we were at having got the vehicle back and working again. It was against all the odds, but it meant Ffyona's walk was back on with a vengeance; and we could leave behind the handcart.

When we got back to the hotel, we decided to take a few days to recharge our own batteries. While we'd been gone, Mike and Johann had learned of a beer truck that would be leaving at the end of the week for Uganda. They'd managed to get themselves space on the roof of that, so we'd be saying farewell to them and going our separate ways. That was to come though; in the meantime we had time, space and freedom, so we cleaned out the Land Rover, sorted out the kit and drank beer in the evenings.

I started work on getting the Land Rover properly set up for the expedition when I got back because I was horrified at how it had been set up previously. I'd be driving it now in support of Ffyona and I had my own way of making sure everything was shipshape.

One morning, we went down river by canoe about five miles back the way we'd come. I was interested in traditional skills and while we'd been on the boat, one of the crewmen had told me about a man he knew of who made fire using a fire plough. I'd heard of this, but had never seen it done before so I drove to the village where I'd been told I might find this man, and there he was. There are very few places in the world where people still use a fire plough – a piece of wood with a groove along its length, in which the tip of a stick is rubbed up and down – so it was amazing to actually find someone who was still using that ancient method of creating fire. Afterwards,

the villagers insisted we head into the forest to drink beer – it was their way of saying thank you to the forest for its gifts. I liked that.

I remember trying to buy some dammar resin from one of the locals – it's combustible, so they use it to light their fires. I'd managed to get some from a young guy in the village but as we were concluding our trade, some old crone came out of nowhere and started bashing him over the head with a piece of burning firewood before snatching the dammar resin back. It had obviously taken her months to collect, and there's her son selling it off for the price of a beer.

I had a look through Kisangani's market, which isn't exactly your average place to go shopping as it's on the river. There's a market in the main square that most travellers headed to, but the best one to go to was just past the town's brewery. You look upstream from the riverbank and there are hundreds and hundreds of dugout canoes all chained together. Each one forms both part of the walkway from one to another, and an open display of the goods on offer – from food to plastic goods, every conceivable item that you might find in any market. What really stood out for me was the massive bunches of giant land snails that were tied together through holes that had been made in their shells. They're huge – a giant land snail will fill the palm of your hand, and they're a good source of protein to many in Africa. That market was a real eye-opener, a really fascinating place to explore.

Ffyona and I decided to head out and see if we could find her last camp site, which she thought was about three days' walk away. There'd been heavy rains since she'd been forced to leave the country so the landscape had changed massively and we weren't optimistic – bamboo can grow more than 3ft in a day there, and there was a lot of bamboo in that region. But it was important to her, and I was there to support her, so we looked. We were a long way out from Kisangani when

My mum and dad on
their wedding day.

My dad in typical
relaxed mood.

My mum stands proudly
by the car she was
learning to drive in.
You can see from the
vegetation – and the
sunlight – that it was in
Karachi, not England!

With my dad in the cockpit of a Spitfire at Biggin Hill Air Show. He taught me to appreciate the people who fought in World War II – and to admire beautiful machines like the Spitfire.

This bike gave me my first bit of independence – it was my third birthday present and the stabilsers weren't on it for very long!

I was never very keen on team sports but I enjoyed rugby. I'm on the far left, with all the hair.

Judo became – and has remained – a very important part of my life. The Budokwai in London was where I learned most of my judo skills. It's a temple to judo and other martial arts.

My teacher Kingsley Hopkins being thrown by Gunji Koizumi, who introduced judo to the United Kingdom.

Dickie Bowen (standing) was an exceptionally skilled exponent of judo – he studied in Japan and was an old-school practictioner.

Kingsley Hopkins, my mentor and friend – I took this photo of him when I was about 15 years old.

Mark Asuenda, editor of *World* magazine, who gave me my first big break as a photographer. Like all Italians he had an insatiable appetite for fungi!

Another big career break was filming my first TV programme, *Wild Tracks*, in 1994.

My first wife Rachel,
who died in 2006.

We set up Woodlore
together and she was
very much at home
in the outdoors – this
picture was taken in
British Columbia.

With Ewan McGregor in the Amazon. I really enjoyed working with him because he was such an able student and a good person. As he learned, comfort in the jungle is a matter of mastering a thousand tiny skills – like how to put up your shelter.

For me, being with indigenous peoples has always been as much about listening as anything else. That way you can learn so much and start to earn their respect.

Making a birch bark canoe with Pinnock Smith and then paddling it myself was a dream come true.

I had to really fight to get the television people to make a series which would bring
the story of the Telemark raid in World War II to a much wider audience,
so it was a special privilege to meet five surviving members of that secret mission
and visit the memorial to the bravery of the saboteurs at Vemork in Norway.

something caught Ffyona's eye. I stopped and she jumped out and ran through thick vegetation and into a gravel pit; she was searching for any evidence pointing to her having made her last camp there before leaving for the UK, and almost unbelievably she found it. There among the undergrowth was a damp, faded piece of paper – the packet of a used Sainsbury's chicken soup. We were right back where she'd left off.

The following morning, she started walking back to Kisangani and I trailed behind her in the Land Rover. She would walk what she termed 'quarters', each representing 16kms, and she'd aim to walk three quarters each day. I'd follow in the vehicle most of the time and generally look after her. Sometimes, I'd go a little way ahead, stopping at some of the villages on our route to engage with the locals. I'd make a point of talking to people, asking them about the trees and the plants nearby and what they used them for. I learned so much by doing that. There's a particular type of tree – they called it *kamba*, which is the Swahili for 'cord' – and its wood makes it a really useful medium for fire sticks. Almost all of the villages used it for that purpose, but it's a massively versatile plant and I talked to people on that journey who had all utilised it for a different purpose. In some villages they used its leaves as toilet paper; some used it for its medicinal properties . . . they even used the bark to make string.

It took us three or four days to get back to Kisangani but Ffyona was delighted because it meant she had picked up her walk from exactly where she had left off when she was evacuated. It also gave us a good opportunity to warm up for the walk proper and establish a rhythm, a routine with me in the support vehicle. We hit Kisangani on the Saturday morning, and that afternoon we bade a fond farewell to Mike and Johann who went off to join their ride – sitting on the roof of a beer truck to Uganda. We vowed to keep in touch and I was really sad to see them go – you form a close bond on expeditions

like that, a really strong sense of camaraderie that is born out of shared experiences.

———◆———

That night, we woke to a loud banging on the door. That was highly unusual, so I was immediately on guard. I remember there was a huge tropical storm raging outside and the air was heavy. I quickly pulled some clothes on and guardedly opened the door.

In front of me was Johann, covered in blood.

'Christ, Johann, what's happened? Where's Mike?'

I shepherded him inside and he went straight to the bathroom where he threw up. We cleaned him up as best we could, tending to his wounds and then he sat on the bed:

'Guys, it was awful. We were on top of the beer truck with ten or so other passengers and assorted luggage. I think the driver had been sampling the merchandise because he was driving way too fast. The truck was completely top heavy, and we had to hang on to the sides every time we went round a corner.

'There was one particular corner that the driver was never going to clear; he'd been driving at 60 or 70mph and as he turned in, we knew we were never going to make it. I had a sick feeling in my stomach because we knew the truck was going to go over and I really thought that was it for me. Everything happened in a split second. I felt us going, and suddenly we were hurled to the ground among all the crates, tyres and assorted freight that had been stowed up on the roof with us.'

As he talked, he painted a vivid picture of the carnage that he'd witnessed. One guy had compound fractures of both his femurs, and a pregnant woman lost her baby in the most horrific way imaginable. Several of the passengers were killed.

Johann had been knocked unconscious when he landed and his back was absolutely peppered with glass shards. Mike had been hurt really badly; one of the spare wheels that had been up on the roof had broken one of his ankles when it hit him as he lay on the ground, and he'd also dislocated his shoulder. Johann had gradually swum back to consciousness and, under guidance from Mike, had relocated his arm for him – the pain from that would have been horrendous. With that done, Johann promptly dropped unconscious again. While this was happening, nearby villagers swarmed across the wreckage, running off with crates of beer that were strewn across the debris field.

Luckily for the wounded, word reached a nearby logging camp and a team from there with at least one medic arrived on the scene. They loaded the most seriously injured, including Mike, into a van and drove through the night to reach the hospital in Kisangani but there was little the doctors there could do to help as all the medicines had been looted during the rioting. They were on sale in the market place – grouped by colour, which was absolute madness. I'd seen a witch doctor ask for 'a red one and a yellow one'. Who knows how many people died after being administered lethal drugs simply because the witch doctor liked their colour?

We spent the rest of the night watching over Johann, pulling the glass out of his back and tending his wounds. The following morning, we found Mike amongst the filth in a local clinic, awaiting an X-ray on a rather enlarged, blue-coloured ankle that was the size of a basketball. After waiting an age, he was seen and it was no surprise to any of us that his ankle needed setting, but again, because of the rioting, all the plaster had been looted; there was none to be had anywhere in the clinic.

We couldn't leave Mike like that, so I fired up the Land Rover and headed through the town to try and locate some. Once again, fortune was on our side – I found some on sale in the market, and Mike's leg was set. That done, we did

the best thing we could for him: we got him out of that dirty hole and into a French restaurant that – and you couldn't make this up – was serving frogs' legs, pizza and wine . . . on white linen table cloths. So we had an impromptu party. Mike probably thought he'd died and gone to heaven.

We were in the run up to Christmas by now, and just to complicate things further, we had to leave our hotel because they needed our rooms to expand the brothel. At least business was booming somewhere in Kisangani. Reluctantly, we packed up and moved to the main hotel in town, where we all spent a very merry Christmas together. But time was marching on and Ffyona's walk wasn't going to do itself, so a few days later, we said a big goodbye to Mike, who planned on remaining in the hotel until his leg had healed. Then with Johann, who had opted to come with us, we loaded up the Land Rover and set off to start Ffyona's walk proper.

———◆———

We soon established a rhythm: Ffyona would go on ahead, with Johann and me following in the Land Rover, and we made steady progress. I was the first up every morning and the last to bed because I had a responsibility to Ffyona – and I felt to Johann too – so it was my job to make sure everything ran smoothly and that we all got through safely.

Food wasn't always easy to come by, but we managed – sometimes only just though. At one stage, nobody would sell us chickens because the birds were just too scrawny, and I had to buy a tortoise so I could kill it and we'd have something to eat. Tortoises are an integral part of the diet in that part of Africa. It kept the three of us going for two or three days.

I was in my element because I learned things I could never have gleaned through any book. How much knowledge I

acquired varied from village to village, but I always came away with some new skill or a piece of information to fill the gaps in what I knew. Seeing how people cooked things, the medicines, the plants, how they built and made things, and dealt with the tropical rain, it was all fascinating stuff. In some places I'd go to fill a jerry can from a river where the locals got theirs and the water would be crystal clear. In others, I'd do the same, but I'd look up stream a few yards and there'd be a guy washing his body in the water beside me. Sometimes, we'd come across entire villages that were deserted and I'd wonder what happened there. Was there a cholera epidemic? Had a massacre taken place?

I keep a tidy camp so I insisted that no matter how tired we were, we'd find time to wash both ourselves and our clothes each day. Johann and I would go down to the river at the same time as the men. We'd pick a point where they were washing, take our clothes off, and wash with them. They'd have a little stone there that you'd wash your clothes on. Of course, just when I thought we had a system going, I got it wrong one day and went down to the washing stone when the women were washing and I suddenly found myself surrounded by lots of men wielding spears. I had to play the 'I'm Johnny Foreigner' card to get out of that one.

———————◆———————

On 31 December 1990 we crossed the Aruwimi River – where Tarzan lived, according to the novel by Edgar Rice Burroughs. That place sticks in my mind because Livingstone had a man speared to death there. Also, in the 1960s the daughter of a missionary family living there had come out from boarding school to stay with them, and one night she'd seen her whole family massacred by rebels. She was given a choice: become the bride of the rebel leader, or die. She bravely chose to die,

suffering a horrific death after the rebels threw her to the crocodiles.

We didn't feel very safe that New Year's Eve because the local people tend to get very drunk, and things, perhaps unsurprisingly, were still a bit wild. On New Year's Day – 1 January 1991 – we stopped to stock up on food and provisions, and there were a lot of youths milling around. They'd run out of alcohol – they made their own from palm oil but once it was all gone, they'd be on the hunt for more. It's a pretty familiar scenario the world over, I guess. They started to surround the Land Rover while Ffyona was outside and I felt distinctly uncomfortable. They were drunk and unpredictable, and you could have cut the air with a knife. One of them, who I assumed was the leader, approached my door and made it quite clear that he wanted to have sex with her.

There's no easy way to deal with a situation like that but you have to seize the initiative because events are balanced on a knife edge. There's a crowd of them, Ffyona's outside, and there's just Johann and myself inside; we're already at a disadvantage before we start. I'd learned a bit about how to deal with the locals when we'd walked earlier, so I invited the leader of the guys to come closer. I had my window down and as he leaned in, I showed him the machete that I held in my hand down by the door.

'If you want to sleep with her, you'll sleep with this first,' I said, smiling as I looked him straight in the eye.

He got the message loud and clear because he backed off and walked away. Importantly for him, I'd allowed him to save face because the rest of the group neither heard what I said or saw what I had in my hand.

That resolved that – you have to know when to be firm but just as importantly you need to know *how* firm to be. That's the difficult thing and a lot of people make the mistake of not being firm from the off. If you do that, you've shown weakness

and weakness will be exploited. One of the key things in Africa though is that you have to allow people to save face. There's an equilibrium that has to be maintained, so you tread gently. We learned very quickly that we needed to be constantly aware of and sensitive to the background at all times.

8

Heart of Darkness

There were many occasions when there were difficulties. We frequently found people trying to break into the vehicle – both when we were outside it, and sometimes inside. Sometimes things unravelled very quickly, and it got down to us having to beat them off physically with sticks. I always made sure that I had an escalating level of force available – from my fists, through to sticks and ultimately, a very sharp and fearsome-looking machete. We did a good job of looking after Ffyona, although in an environment like that, unless we were walking alongside her at all times, armed with a gun, we could never entirely guarantee her safety. There was one occasion when I was a matter of yards behind her and someone punched her in the face because they wanted to steal her sunglasses. It was that desperate. You couldn't drop your guard at all, not for a second.

We were in unknown territory so, while there were a few things that we could anticipate, most of what we did was just thinking on our feet. There was no book to refer to because Ffyona was the first – no woman had ever walked across Africa before, and I have to say she was brilliant. Her planning was excellent; she did very, very well and she was incredibly brave. Most of the time, she got on famously with everyone she met but there were always these unpredictable scenarios and we never knew what would happen, so we simply couldn't legislate

for it. One thing we had agreed from the off was that we wouldn't pay any bribes; that was a given.

Nobody tells you the truth before you get to Africa – all I'd heard before I got there was the good stuff: the beautiful scenery, the pared down existence of the people who lived there and how stoically they coped with having almost nothing to their names. I didn't know anything about the aggression we'd find, the sheer bloody-mindedness, the *violence*. You'd walk through the villages on a Sunday and all the men would go to church. Afterwards, they'd go to a little *shebeen*, which invariably consisted of a hut and a bench to sit on, and they'd drink their palm beer. They'd get very drunk and then the beer would run out. Come the evening, all you would hear was the sound of children crying because the drunken fathers had come home and beaten their children. I met missionaries who couldn't stand it. Nobody tells you these things; nobody mentions the bad stuff, the things you have to do.

There was one very dark period that lasted about three weeks where we were quite literally attacked every single day. People were either attacking Ffyona or they were trying to get into the vehicle and attacking that. Most of the time, we were crawling along at no more than 10 to 15mph. To keep Ffyona in sight, and be within easy reach of her, I was driving at the sort of slow speeds where we could have been overtaken by continental drift, so we were an easy target.

There was one particularly nasty scene in Aketi. We knew there were problems there because we'd met a few overland trucks coming through and they'd all had issues there with corrupt officials who had tried to get money out of them by saying that everyone needed to have their profession shown in their passports, which is complete nonsense – maybe thirty years ago they would have done, but that disappeared in the early 80s.

We decided that we'd aim to reach Aketi at around 13:00hrs because at that time, everyone's enjoying a siesta. We planned

on Johann and I holding back in the Land Rover, with Ffyona walking through the town, then we'd come through separately and we'd be gone. It wasn't perfect, but it was our best option.

There was a bridge as we approached Aketi and as we got closer, we saw another Land Rover approaching from the other side. It was occupied by two independent travellers like ourselves, so we pulled alongside to talk with them. It transpired that as they'd driven through Aketi they had seen a barrier erected across the road; for some reason or another, they hadn't stopped – they'd actually crashed through it, and they were worried they'd get arrested. This worried me because I could see us heading into a storm that wasn't of our making. They were driving away from the mess they'd created; we were heading straight into it, in a vehicle that looked just like theirs.

Aketi looks like a town straight out of the Wild West. As we drove in, it was deserted; there was only one woman on the streets and she had a little fire going on which she was cooking dough balls. Ffyona had seen them too – ahead of us, she pointed and mouthed, 'Get some,' so I pulled up.

Ffyona carried on – she had to turn right, cross a railway line, and up to a roundabout. Johann hopped out and went over to buy some dough balls but as the woman was bagging them, he realised he didn't have any small change. So what should have been a quick, simple transaction felt like watching infinite monkeys as they tried to produce the full works of Shakespeare. While Johann was trying to sort it out, I noticed a man in a green uniform approaching. He looked vaguely official but when I looked at him, something struck me as odd. Then I realised what it was: there was no insignia on his uniform.

Johann arrived back at the Land Rover and climbed in just as the man in the green uniform arrived at my open window and started waving a pink chit at me. He looked slightly deranged and I felt immediately on edge. The last thing I wanted to do was to get bogged down in some long,

drawn-out argument so I pretended I couldn't speak French. Then I adopted the classic Englishman abroad stance, shouting, 'Jolly nice to meet you, old chap. Sorry, can't stop, places to go, people to see,' and with that, I shoved the gear lever into first and went to pull away – which is when he upped the ante and grabbed the steering wheel.

I was younger then and a bit more hotheaded but I felt seriously threatened by him doing that. How dare he try and take control of the car? So I pulled my arm fully back and slammed him in the face with my elbow. He went down and I floored the accelerator, trying to make a break for it. We flew across the railway lines at speed, causing everything in the back that wasn't strapped down to become temporarily weightless and float for a second before unceremoniously crashing back down. Ffyona heard us and looked back as I signalled at her to up her pace a bit. Then I backed off – I wanted it to look as if we were nothing to do with her. Then I heard a squeaking sound; as I looked round, it was the man in green again, trying to catch us on a rickety old bike. So I started shouting in French, trying to raise a commotion.

'*Voleur, voleur, voleur!*' I said, pointing. *Thief, thief, thief!*

That elicited no more than a disinterested look from the few locals who woke up at my shout; their faces said, 'Yeah, and so what?'

As I turned the corner, ahead of us was a military base with an armed soldier at the front. I shouted at him, 'Arrest this man, arrest this man, he's a thief. I insist you arrest him.' That's when I looked ahead and saw Ffyona being chased by a group of people.

Suddenly, out of nowhere, more people crowded around the vehicle so I floored the accelerator again. Just as we shot forward, Johann shouted, 'There's a guy on the roof!' so I slammed hard on the brake, pulling up on the handbrake to bring us to a sudden stop more quickly. Physics took over then

and the guy who was on our roof suddenly learned how to fly without wings, shooting forwards like an Exocet missile and falling to the ground some 10ft ahead of us.

Ffyona had started to run, so I accelerated after her, which is when I noticed a man run out from a hut along the edge of the military base with a brick in each hand. He pulled his arm back, making as if to throw one at us through our windscreen, and then I did something that tends to work in Africa – I looked him in the eye and extended my arm to point at him.

For some reason, Africans really don't like that so he froze on the spot and I immediately turned the wheel to drive at him, forcing him to jump out of the way.

While this was going on, the man in the green uniform had somehow overtaken us on his rickety bike and as I looked ahead, he had caught up with Ffyona and was wrestling with her. This was beyond ridiculous – we only stopped to get some dough balls. The man in green had broken away to move in on Ffyona so I seized the opportunity and accelerated. I used the Land Rover to push him against a fence and pinned him there; that was him dealt with at least.

Then someone who appeared to be the head honcho came over to my window. I looked him in the eye and told him, 'This has gone far enough. Back off! We're just trying to leave this place.'

He insisted we go to the police station a short distance away (in reality, just another hut). So Ffyona, Johann and I, the head honcho and the man in the green uniform all made our way there. When we arrived, someone decided they wanted to search our vehicle. I knew this was happening because of the trouble they'd had earlier with the guys in the *other* Land Rover that we'd spoken to as we crossed the bridge to Aketi. For some reason – mistaken identity, or merely the fact we were all white too, and we had the same make of vehicle – the locals took all their frustration out on us.

It transpired that the guy in the green uniform was a police officer. So I said to him, 'If you're a police officer, why do you have no badges on your uniform identifying you as such?'

His response?

'I'm a secret policeman'!

Honestly, you couldn't make this stuff up.

In the end, they let us go in return for a bar of soap – because Ffyona had apparently 'dirtied the guy's uniform' when he wrestled with her – plus an umbrella and two aspirin. No, I've no idea why the umbrella, either. But the aspirin? They were 'for the headache you've caused.'

Our 'adventure' in Aketi was like a low-rent, poor man's version of Indiana Jones, written by Kafka and acted out by idiots. It was really very funny when we looked back on it. Whatever they'd thought when we arrived, by the time we drove out of Aketi, people were waving at us. I think they were sorry to see us go. We weren't sorry to be leaving.

All joking aside, the incident in Aketi could so easily have turned serious. Like so many of the incidents that we were involved in, it could just as easily have fallen the wrong side of the knife edge and who knows how things would have finished? That wasn't the only 'incident' to befall us on the walk, although some, such as the following account, were mere annoyances by comparison. This one took place in Gemena, near Zaire's borders with CAR and Congo.

As we drove into town, we were once again stopped by a 'police officer' who asked me for our papers. We'd been given a letter to present for incidents such as this by the British Consul in Kisangani. It said that we were in Zaire as the guests of the government for Ffyona's world record attempt and we should not be delayed by any persons, but afforded any assistance we required. I thought it might be a good time to present it, but I had an idea of what we would be up against as soon as I handed it to him – he held the letter upside down. He

couldn't read. I interrupted him and said, '*Écoutez-moi!*' and pointed at Ffyona. 'This woman is very important and she is here under the protection or your embassy in London. She's *extremely* important and when she returns, she will be asked, "Did you have any problems in Zaire?"' and Ffyona piped up and said, 'Yes, Gemena!'

And the guy couldn't get away fast enough. He all but saluted us as he left, but it was a prima-facie example of just another day in Africa. So much faux authority; the best way to deal with it was through bluff, smoke and mirrors. It meant we were living on our wits throughout the trip, which is enormously tiring on its own without even taking into account everything else we had to deal with. It became part of the background noise, just something we had to do each day to survive – a bit like eating or drinking.

Don't get me wrong, I have a very healthy respect for the African people we met but the corruption that we – and they – had to deal with felt really pernicious. It destabilises everything and reaches into every stratum of society, so it's like a cancer eating away at respect for authority. Most of the people we met were lovely, really hospitable, humble and full of warmth. On the occasions where we'd driven ahead of Ffyona, we'd go into the backstreets of villages, into the real back edges of towns that most travellers never get to see. These are the places where they grow the plants and herbs they need for midwifery; I saw funerals, and people driving their cars into rivers to wash them – all the bits of African life that you never usually get to see. I found that really interesting, really educational and enriching.

———◆◆◆———

We'd made good progress and soon it was time to leave Zaire for CAR. There's a border river crossing at Zongo that takes

you across to Bangui and it was here that I learned the rules of a popular game in the African heartland which is called 'Try to Make the White Man Go Red in the Face'. It seemed that whenever we tried to do anything in Africa, a crowd would quickly gather. It's amazing what passes for entertainment there and I guess we were a break from the norm – something for the locals to look at, and laugh at. I was trying to reverse our Land Rover onto the ferry but every time the crewman tried to give me directions, the crowd would shout and drown him out. And I quickly realised they were trying to get me to blow a fuse so they'd see me lose my temper. That was the aim; so I stopped, got out and laughed at them. They laughed, and then we got on much better.

Once we landed at Bangui we had to clear customs and immigration, so Ffyona went in to deal with the paperwork while Johann and I stood outside by the vehicle. We'd heard there was often trouble while you waited for clearance, so we'd both got out armed with sticks, and in retrospect I'm glad we did.

We'd been warned beforehand that there are groups of thieves who hang around outside the border control offices in Bangui. They prey on the unwary, stealing their vehicles or otherwise disabling them while their owners are inside the offices dealing with paperwork. Their brazenness was astonishing, given that Johann and I were both standing beside our Land Rover – there was a group of between ten and twenty people milling around and the aggression coming off them was incredible. One of them broke away from the crowd and, calm as you like, approached us. Given his stance – and the tools he had with him – it was clear that he was determined to break into our vehicle. He must not have seen me, because he gave Johann a wide berth and made for the driver's side of the car, which was where I'd stationed myself. Both Johann and I adopted an aggressive stance and pointed our sticks at

this guy, threatening him. He realised he was beaten, so he slunk back into the crowd.

If we thought that was an end to it though, we had another think coming. As the crowd absorbed the aggressor, they started drawing their fingers across their throats and ratcheting up the aggression. It felt like they'd have happily killed us, given the opportunity. It didn't help that Bangui was a Foreign Legion garrison so the level of violence there was of an order several times higher than elsewhere. All we could do was brazen it out. You cannot afford to show any weakness whatsoever. We stood there on the corner of the vehicle pointing our sticks at individuals in the group and shouting, 'You!' again and again at various people. They hate that; it's really intimidating to them, so they kept their distance.

A short time later, Ffyona left the office with our clearance and got in to the passenger side of the car. I thought that was it, but as I went to pull away, one of the gang obviously decided he wanted to show how brave he was to the crowd. He ran at the passenger side at full tilt and tried to slash at the tyre with a razor blade. He was easily dealt with – I turned the wheel towards him and accelerated. It's difficult to focus on anything other than getting out of the way when you've got two-and-a-half tons of Land Rover bearing down on you.

Although we escaped the border point at Bangui with our vehicle – and our lives – intact, the trek came to a halt when we reached the town proper. Bangui became our temporary home for seven weeks while we waited for the next tranche of Ffyona's sponsorship funding to come through.

There was one occasion not long after we arrived that Ffyona had to go to the Sofitel on the other side of town to use the phone. Sadly for us, this meant going past the checkpoint at the border crossing again, so we deliberately chose a time of day when we knew it would be quietest – generally, the locals siesta in the afternoon, so many of them would be asleep.

But again, after Ffyona got back in the car, one of the guys ran at us, and this time he reached through my open window. I was in no mood to negotiate so I grabbed his arm and put him in a wristlock. He wasn't expecting that, and I held him in place for a few seconds, and then quickly wound the window up, trapping his arm at the top. Then I hit the accelerator and drove off. I soon left him behind.

We found out later that the trees near this border checkpoint have razor blades embedded in the bark so that the thieves always have them to hand. Their plan is simple, and in most cases effective: while the vehicle is unattended, or your attention is diverted, they slash your tyres. Then, while you're occupied changing the wheel, they'll rob you. The police are in on it, so if you call them to report what's happened, they'll find some non-existent or invented infringement and then they'll rob you too. Twice at this border point was enough – after that trip to the Sofitel, we found another place where Ffyona could make phone calls. We weren't going to put ourselves in the firing line if we could possibly help it.

While we waited for the funding to come through, we planned the rest of her walk. She wanted to take the expedition up through Chad and on through Libya, which was the quickest, easiest and most direct route north. It wasn't without its risks though, so I started to analyse exactly what they were.

9
Out of Africa

Chad was well-known for its Zaghawas insurgents. They'd made a number of attacks on people over the previous year, so I made a point of plotting the locations of all the attacks on a map. Having done so, I could see a pattern emerging. They were coming into the CAR down the river and then attacking people along the roads either side, morning and evening, but always leaving themselves plenty of time to escape back the way they'd come.

My questions soon attracted the attention of a certain US intelligence agency. After all my hard work plotting and planning, I was called in to the US Embassy to meet with the CIA's head of station, who wanted to know what I'd discovered. In the process of tracking down the intelligence I needed to draw conclusions about the best time for us to travel and avoid the Zaghawas, I'd been asking questions all over town, so I guess the CIA soon got to hear about it – intelligence is its business after all, and there's a massive interest in that part of Africa due to Zaire's vast untapped mineral wealth. The French had a huge embassy there, too. Back then, Africa was a great big chessboard where the Cold War was played out.

After meeting with the CIA head, I managed to secure a meeting with General Canal, the then commander of French forces in Africa, because I thought he may be able to help with information on how we might get into Libya. He explained

there were secret roads into the country and showed me where they were. Afterwards, I paid a visit to the Libyan Embassy and I was told we'd be safe in Libya (but then, they would say that, wouldn't they?). They said that the road was metalled for most of the way and we'd be taken care of. Finally, with the money due any day now, it looked like everything was falling into place.

But as if to prove that in Africa you can't take anything for granted, the French performed a complete about face two days later. I was called in again by General Canal and told that if we tried to go through Libya, we'd be arrested. The Lockerbie bombing was still all over the news and there was a very real prospect that if we went ahead we'd become hostages and the Embassy didn't want that to happen – let's face it, Libya was having enough bad press. So after all that hard work and planning, we were forced to reroute through Cameroon.

Finally, the last tranche of Ffyona's sponsorship funding came through, so once again we loaded up the Land Rover and travelled up through CAR. Because of the Zaghawas' attacks, I decided that it would be safest for us to travel at night and hide the vehicle in the bush by day, so that's what we did. We travelled in the cool of the night and tried to rest and sleep in the heat of the day. It was tough going, but it was different, and it worked – our drive through CAR was largely uneventful.

———◆———

Did you know that you always, always, shake hands *with* respect in Africa? To do that, you place one hand over your wrist as you extend your other hand forwards. It was one of the subtlest and perhaps most important things I learned while I was there. Very few visitors to the continent know anything about it, but it's important that you always shake hands in

that way, to show respect. It's all about being polite, friendly and genuine with people.

One day in CAR we had no food and, in desperation, I drove ahead of Ffyona a short distance and stopped at a village at the foot of a hill. Looking around, I saw a man who had some chickens, but they were scrawny and I knew from previous experience that he'd probably be too ashamed of them to sell one to a Westerner. So I went up to him and shook his hand in the traditional, polite African way, placing one hand over my wrist, and he seemed genuinely moved by that. I asked him if I could buy one and he agreed. I know for sure had I not shook his hand in the way I did he'd have said no; that's why it's so important to find out local customs and traditions before setting out on any kind of expedition.

But while I was paying him, I became aware of a noise behind me. When I looked, it was Ffyona and she looked distraught as she ran over to the vehicle.

She was in such a state; her T-shirt was torn, she had scratches on her face and arm and she was struggling to get the words out, but eventually I heard, 'Ray, somebody just tried to rape me.'

I was frozen in horror at the enormity of what she was saying, but all I could do was hold her until she stopped shaking, telling her it was all right now, she was with me and she was safe.

After a few minutes, she told me what had happened and that she'd managed to get away from her attacker. I'd heard of this kind of thing but had never had any kind of experience of it. I immediately took control; first, I'd need to find somewhere she could sit quietly, away from the general hubbub so she could collect her thoughts. The man with the chickens asked what happened, so I told him in French what Ffyona had told me. He was horrified as I explained it all and quickly organised a group of the villagers to try and find the

perpetrator. He also had one of his huts cleaned out so that she'd have somewhere private to sit and recover from her ordeal as it was quite clear she was in shock. It was a very kind thing for this stranger to do for us, and a short time later he came back to ask me if she was OK. As he approached me, he extended his closed hand forwards and opened it, palm up in the respectful manner. Secreted inside was an onion; a tiny onion about the size of a shallot. He was giving it to us; it was his gift. I mean, what would that mean here in the West? Nothing? Less than nothing? There though, it wasn't what he was offering, it was the gesture. And in that context, the gesture was enormous, his gift to us was massively significant, and I believe it was all down to that handshake when we first met.

This whole episode epitomises African life and to be close to that means we got to understand it in a very African way. Tourists who travel to Africa have never had these experiences so, in essence, they can't really *know* that side of the continent. Those kind of experiences colour and inform your understanding at a fundamental level and when you work that intimately with African people, if you've had these experiences, they feel it and they understand that you know something more of their world and so there's a certain respect for you; they treat you differently.

Sadly, we never did find the man who'd attacked Ffyona, and it was just one more incident that she had to chalk up to experience. It is a mark of her strength that she shrugged it off and the following day was back on the walk, each step putting distance between her and what had happened, each stride taking her closer and closer to her objective. Yet again, Africa had humbled us and shocked us in turns. Yet again, violence and aggression had come from nowhere. To me, each attack, each incident highlighted just how much bigger Ffyona's task was than just the miles she had to walk to cross Africa. It was an expedition fraught with danger.

Finally, we crossed the border into Cameroon. My time with Ffyona and Johann was coming to an end because I had to get back to London for the publication of my second book. I had mixed emotions about leaving: I was loving my new relationships with Africa and Johann, and I knew I'd miss my relationship with Ffyona. We were together over a year and while we hadn't rekindled our romantic relationship during the trek across this wonderfully diverse continent, we'd shared something special. That said, all good things come to an end; that aspect of my life was over and I knew it. Life had to go on and I had my book launch to think about, so when we reached Douala I bid them all a fond farewell and caught a flight back to England.

That trip with Ffyona took almost seven months of my life, and it was a hell of an expedition with experiences and lessons that had a huge impact in shaping the man I've become.

Ffyona went on to complete her challenge, which was an amazing feat – a truly incredible achievement. However, she was treated abominably by the press on her return – castigated and censured when she should have been praised and held up as an inspiration. I think the press set her up. They saw her as a spoilt rich kid because she spoke nicely and was the product of a private education, but what difference does any of that make? Considering the upheaval of her childhood, I don't think her background conferred any advantage on her at all. None of it lessens or otherwise tarnishes what was a stunning triumph.

A lot of the animosity she faced stemmed from the previous trip that took her across the US, during which she had some awful problems. She became ill and was in danger of missing media calls set up by her sponsors – an astonishingly busy schedule of media appearances that would have stretched her when fit, let alone sick. Because she felt obligated, and because she didn't want to let her sponsors down, she ill-advisedly

accepted a number of short lifts from her support driver – 15 miles a time, three or four times over a 1,000 mile stretch of her walk. She felt guilty about it so she went back and walked across America again, then wrote about all of it in her third book. She was attacked by the press for her admission. Had she been American, she may well have been criticised but it wouldn't have overshadowed her achievement. Here in the UK, though, people seem to want to knock anyone who aspires to be better, anyone who achieves success.

Looking back, I learned several things on that trip. One of them was knowing when to be firm. I think this is something a lot of people who travel like that don't understand – they want to be all things to all people and you can't; you have to know where to draw the line, when to be firm, when to be friendly, how to be polite and respectful towards the people you meet.

They say the people you meet colour, shape and inform you – change you in certain ways – and in that regard I feel lucky to have met both Johann and Mike. Johann had this saying, which always made me laugh. If something went wrong, or if something broke, he'd say, 'Ah, it's OK, it wasn't a good one, anyway,' and I've hung on to that. He had a great sense of humour, and he was a really solid guy, a good man to have on your team. That made the man from Malmö a brilliant partner to travel with. In fact, it was a privilege.

As for Mike, I learned when I got back to England that he'd got his bike, which had been severely bent up in the crash, and repaired and welded it back together. You can do that sort of thing in Africa – there's always someone able to do whatever it is you need. Then he cut off the plaster because it was 'bothering him', put a bandage around his ankle and cycled

to Uganda. There, he had his ankle re-broken and reset. I met up with him in England a few years later and it was really good to see him; we had a lot of laughs. Johann, though, dropped off the radar and I never saw him again after Africa. I often wonder what became of him.

The downsides? There weren't many, and even the incidents, the aggression and violence we encountered were all instructive in some way. Bad as they were at the time, we came through each one unscathed and somewhat wiser. I think it's also important to view them in context. When I joined Ffyona on her walk, we were going through some of the most unstable regions of the African continent, and working our way through countries riven by years of violence and unrest. We were considerably younger than we are now, and we were both perhaps rather more naive than the people we've become. Despite the trouble we encountered in the heart of Africa, my overwhelming memory is of a beautiful place that would call to me and draw me back countless times in the years ahead, and of those wonderful local people of modest means who went so far out of their way to help us and show us kindness.

Oh, and how could I forget malaria – I contracted it not once but twice, both times when we were in the absolute middle of nowhere. It's really not pleasant at the best of times but there, in the wilds of Africa, was just the worst experience. It's truly nasty – I felt like I'd been beaten up by a Rugby team and I was running a temperature of 103. Waking up in the middle of the night with the runs when you're sleeping in the bush is an experience I don't really want to repeat. The worst thing for me, though, was that I could hear life going on around me but I was unable to take part.

We did have medicine – Halofantrine – with us to treat the disease. This consisted of a course of six tablets; the first two stabilise your temperature; six hours later you take the second pair, which bring your temperature down, and once you take

the third two a few hours later you're starting to feel you can communicate with people again. Over the course of the following week, you feel better every time you go to the toilet. When I got to Zaire at the start of the expedition I weighed thirteen stone; when I left Africa seven months later, I was half the man I used to be – almost literally. I weighed just eight stone.

In terms of my future, probably the best aspect of that expedition for me was that it clarified my feelings about the direction I wanted to take in life, and I realised how much I'd enjoyed talking about, and learning, new bushcraft skills. It was such an education but also it validated so much of what I'd already learned, and legitimised it too. Things like knowing how to get safe drinking water, how to cook in the bush, how to take care of yourself – they were all vital skills but now I had seen them in their true context. As much as anything, it was also a test of me, personally. On that front, at least, I felt I could hold my head high.

10

Changes

When I left England for Africa in 1990, I was at a turning point – one of those forks in the road of life that confront you every now and then. When I arrived in Africa, I still wasn't sure whether I wanted to devote my life to photography or whether to focus on the bushcraft, but there were no two ways about it – when I got there, I was undoubtedly a photojournalist but I knew as soon as I hit British soil on my return that things were different.

When I came back in the autumn of 1991, I learned that *World* magazine had changed hands and Mark had moved on. Mentally, so had I – I'd been so close to the outdoors for so long that, even though I still took photos, I no longer felt like a photojournalist. *World* had ultimately become a victim of its own success; it was bought out by the BBC, which appointed a new editor who wanted to make his mark on the magazine. He started to employ people like Sebastião Salgado to do assignments for the magazine and it started to lose sales because Salgado's fine art photography wasn't what the audience wanted; they wanted a home-grown version of *National Geographic*. *World* and I parted ways.

———◆◆———

The publication of my book for Random House went OK, but it coincided with the peak of the recession that hit Britain

in the early 90s, so sales were disappointing. Ironically, sales of the survival handbook I'd written for Haynes were rather healthier, although by the end of its first year in print it had been stolen from almost every library in the UK – perhaps it was down to the recession starting to bite. The Random House book was something of a slow burner though, because it's still in print now.

While I'd been in Africa, all of the things I'd been teaching had proved incredibly useful, so I came away with a renewed interest in the culture of the outdoors. I was hungry to build on that, so Woodlore became my sole focus.

I met Rachel on a foundation course that I ran quite soon after my return to England, and I just *knew*. We hit it off from the beginning. She was a scuba diver – she worked for a company that specialised in teaching people to dive in Israel's Red Sea – and she was really keen to learn new skills. She had my attention from the off. She was one of those people who lit up a room, so it was inevitable really; she had her own gravity, so people were drawn to her.

She had this wonderful dark curly hair but she wore it short and it suited her. She had the most amazing smile, just wondrous; she'd smile and it was like being bathed in sunlight. She had these beautiful, deep hazel eyes, and a really sharp wit – a great sense of humour. She was always up to mischief! We got on like a house on fire. And though I didn't know it, she was almost nine years older than me – not that you would have known by looking at her.

We took things easy at first – we were just good friends initially, but it was a feint really. We both knew how we felt about one another, so why pretend? A few months after we first met, we decided to go to France together and I guess that's where it became official – we cemented our relationship there and when we came back to England, we were a couple.

We went to Normandy and I remember we'd forgotten to

change the lights on the car so we blinded everybody coming towards us. We didn't bother with camp sites, so ended up camping on the banks of the River Seine and in the Brotonne Forest, while avoiding *gendarmes* with their mobile headlight-testing kits who were looking for cars just like ours. It was beautiful. We went to Paris for a few days and it was just magical. It was a great place to forge the bond between us – just incredibly romantic. We had a great time together.

Not long after we returned, we made a home together in Eastbourne; it was Rachel and me, plus her two young children, Nathan aged seven and Ellie aged five. Our house was on the coast, so the South-East of England where the bulk of my work with Woodlore took place was easily accessible. Then Rachel fell ill with a throat infection and the company she worked for got really uppity about it; they were concerned at how long it would keep her off work and kept pestering her to return long before she was ready. We were both really annoyed by this – she'd given everything to that company, she'd never let them down or so much as taken a day sick before, so it felt really petty for them to treat her so badly, and it soured things somewhat. On a whim, I suggested that she resign and come and work for me, running Woodlore from a bedroom at our house, taking care of the admin. That way, I could devote all of my time to running courses while she ran the business. She loved the idea and resigned the same day. And we never looked back.

I know not every couple is able to work together, but it came easily to us. We trusted one another implicitly and it was all just very, very relaxed and easy. Rachel was dynamic, and she was really good for me; a lot of things fell into place. I've never been motivated by money, but I appreciate you can't get very far without it. What makes the business work – and this is something I learned at the beginning – is that I don't chase the money, I chase my interests. If you chase the money as

well as your interests, you break the spell, so it's always best to have someone else sort out the finances. From the day she started working with me, Rachel always looked after that side of things, which left me free to concentrate on my strengths – being outside and furthering my knowledge. After she joined, Woodlore started to grow really quickly. Before I knew it I was taking courses back-to-back. The company grew and became more successful because I had the energy to devote to it, and the belief was there. Rachel brought order and direction to the chaos. We were the perfect combination.

Things were ticking along nicely, and within a year or so I became the subject of a television documentary – I'd given a lecture and I was approached by someone in the audience who was a producer for TVS. I quite enjoyed making the documentary, and it brought in more business, but it also gave me an idea. As Woodlore had to support both Rachel, the children and myself, I needed to find a way to boost its income and TV looked like the perfect medium. So in late 1993, I found an agent to represent me and he organised a meeting with Collette Foster, a TV producer at the BBC's Pebble Mill studios, in Edgbaston.

I liked Collette immediately. She was warm and approachable, and had a good track record. She'd produced the BBC's massively successful *The Clothes Show* and had an idea for a magazine-style series on the outdoors. She thought I might be able to present three five-minute items within that series, so I did a screen test. It took place in the Malvern Hills and the director, Kath Moore, asked me if I could find three things to make or eat using natural resources within 100m, and talk to the camera about them. Thanks to my bushcraft skills, and the lectures I'd done, it wasn't too difficult. In the end I got the job and I've never looked back. The cameraman who shot that section was Barrie Foster, who was Collette's husband. Kath directed me, and the sound recordist was Sam Cox. In years to come, we all worked together regularly on various commissions.

Kath clearly liked what I did because instead of three five-minute things I ended up being commissioned to do six ten-minute pieces. That is how my first ever TV series, *Tracks*, was born and I took to it like a baby takes to water. First broadcast in 1994, *Tracks* was a great success and ran for six series. It was made at Pebble Mill under the guardianship of John King. I liked John a lot; he was a very intelligent man, one of several very capable TV executives in the BBC at that time who had an innate understanding of their business and made it work. John was something of a wizard at the Beeb in those days and, rather appropriately, he liked to dress completely in white – I called him 'Zeus'.

Tracks was well received, it paid reasonably well and I enjoyed doing it. Not because it was TV – I've never quite understood the whole concept of people being 'famous' simply because they're on TV. To me, TV is a medium, the same as books, newspapers, magazines and the Internet. It's just a more efficient and effective medium for getting a message out which, for me, means sharing the knowledge and skills that I've acquired with the widest audience possible. It was also good fun because I was lucky enough to team up with a director, Paul Watson, who I really enjoyed working with.

I was keen to do another programme and the BBC was keen to work with me again, but which vehicle? *Tracks* had been set in and around the UK but the Beeb wanted me to do something more adventurous so they pitched the idea of dropping me into remote places so I could show how to survive in them. The problem was that what viewers would have seen would have been me killing and eating things, which would have been a bit gratuitous and unnecessary just for the sake of television. Of course, several other networks have since gone down that path but I wasn't comfortable doing it so I declined.

Then I suggested we go and film indigenous people around

the world – the real masters of living in the bush – engage with them and really get a feel for how they lived. We played with the idea, refined it a little and settled on filming in these places when they would be at their most inhospitable – at a time when no other film crew would even consider venturing there. I liked that idea and it found favour with the higher-ups at the BBC so we got the green light.

What we produced was broadcast as *World of Survival* – two series of six thirty-minute programmes filmed in some of the world's most extreme places. Those series were broadcast in 1997 and 1999 and we had literally weeks to make each film. Television was a different business then and, in the context of today's programmes, it was a simply unbelievable amount of time to invest in each episode. What it did do was enable us to really get each one absolutely right.

Having a budget that enabled me to do what I had been longing to do was a tremendous opportunity for me. My focus was on making sure I did a good job for the viewer. I wanted to make sure I did a good job of honouring the indigenous people that I went to see. But it was also an opportunity for me to go and meet people and ask questions that I didn't believe were being asked by anthropologists. I had a practical interest in the way they lived in the bush. Dr Johnston said that those who go in search of knowledge must first acquire it. To my mind, if you don't know anything about the lives of the people you meet then they will be inclined to treat you like a child, but if you can hunt, if you can make fire, if you can make shelter and you know how to take care of yourself, they see this; they know the time it takes to acquire those skills and they will treat you as an adult. From that, they might involve you in conversations that you would not otherwise have. That is what I wanted to try to tap into.

I don't think there's anything worse than a presenter going somewhere and acting like a complete idiot. It's a peculiarly

British disease and it's disrespectful of the people they're reporting on. But at the same time I didn't want to appear to be too pompous or too macho; I wanted to make the subject accessible to people.

World of Survival was great, a very special series to make. Through my involvement in it, I learned a lot about myself, a lot about television and a lot about what's needed to make films in remote places. All of the different hunter-gatherer groups that I ended up working with gave me the most amazing education. Looking back now, with over twenty years of television under my belt, I think somebody at the BBC was really smart in green-lighting that project, but at the time I just didn't realise how special it would be. Those programmes documented cultures that have now all but disappeared. The elders we filmed were the last flickers from an ancient fire. Because what we didn't realise then, was that the indigenous people we'd end up filming were, in many cases, part of societies and cultures that sat right on the precipice of change. In the years following, many of them made the step into a more modern world, and the changes that occurred were irreversible. Some skills that had endured for millennia were lost within a generation.

Making those sorts of programmes is incredibly complex so it's absolutely essential that you have the right people in the crew. I was lucky in that Kath Moore, who'd directed me in my screen test, was the series producer for *World of Survival*, so I trusted her and she got where I was coming from. I said to Kath right from the start that when we went into these communities it would be a two-way exchange. We'd be taking something away, but we would also be leaving something of ourselves behind so it was imperative to choose crews that were sensitive to that, because television can be very harsh; it can walk in and trample over everybody. Kath listened; she was brilliant and we selected our team accordingly. It's

interesting that the two cameramen we chose – Barrie Foster, who'd also been involved in my screen test, and Alan Duxbury – were the two cameramen I'd work with on almost every programme I made over the following sixteen years.

Barrie was as accomplished as they came; a consummate professional prepared to take risks; there was nothing he couldn't achieve in filming terms. Alan Duxbury was also one of the best cameramen I'd ever work with – he was known as 'Steady Al' because he could hand-hold the sort of shots that most other cameramen used a tripod for. Alan would go to the ends of the earth to get the right shot. He was as hardy as hell, prepared to endure everything that the weather and the environment could throw at him if it meant he could film exactly what he needed. Both Barrie and Alan were very special people and we would go on to become firm friends in the coming years. We would soon realise that *World of Survival* was to be a real learning curve for us all.

For the first series, we filmed between late 1995 and early 1997 and we focused on six locations and their indigenous people. Episode one took us to Baffin Island with the Inuit for a film about the Arctic; episode two took us to Arnhem Land to meet the Aborigines who live in Northern Australia, with its high temperatures and humidity. For episode three, we travelled to Siberia to meet the Evenki nomadic reindeer herders of the Taiga Forest. Episode four looked at life on the island of Savai'i in Western Samoa. For episode five we travelled to Namibia to see the survival skills of the Jo'hansi bushmen, and for the final film we looked at the Spice Islands of Indonesia and went to the island of Seram where we filmed the Nuaulu, a rainforest people who are historically head-hunters.

All of the trips were memorable for different reasons, though some more than others. The travel we undertook, and the places we stayed at to research and make each thirty-minute

episode, made each film an expedition in its own right. The planning, the logistics, the difficulties we encountered just in getting to each remote location and the inherent risk in being there made them some of the toughest expeditions I've done to date. But putting ourselves in some of the world's most hostile and isolated environments when nobody else would go there made it some of the best stuff I've ever done. In part, that's down to timing; it was a perfect storm in TV terms, benefiting from generous budgets, time and forward-thinking producers who were prepared to take risks in pursuit of really good television. When you endure – and sometimes suffer – the same privations and hardships as the indigenous people you are filming, you develop a bond that is quite unique. It becomes something special, a 'happening'.

I learned so much in making each programme, not just in terms of bushcraft – the new skills and knowledge I acquired from these indigenous people could fill a book themselves – but in terms of what I learned about TV. There's a lot of maturing, a lot of learning and growing in the world of television, particularly with the sort of programmes we were making. There was no training course – nobody teaches you to do TV, you have to learn on the job. I didn't mind that because it's how I learn everything really – by doing.

What was really wonderful for me was that we were making principled films; we knew what we were doing, what we wanted to convey, and ultimately the people we were filming came first. I'm not sure that everything that came later was like that. *World of Survival* is without doubt, one of the highlights of my TV career.

It was tough on Rachel, though, with me spending so much time away either through filming commitments, or running Woodlore courses, so it was always going to be hard for us in that respect, but it's just the way it was. That said, neither of us was particularly clingy – we were a strong couple but we

were both independent people and we got used to it. We always made the most of the time we did have together, and whenever I was away filming, we always had a sat-phone with us, so that helped too.

What follows are my accounts of some of the episodes from *World of Survival* that really stood out for me. Whether it's the people, the place, the smells, the ease with which the programmes came together – it doesn't really matter. These are the events that have their own special place in my head and my heart.

II

40 Below

We travelled to Baffin Island in February 1996. Baffin Island straddles the Arctic Circle and lies in the Canadian territory of Nunavut. There was a crew of four on this trip – Barrie Foster; Dennis Jarvis, the director; Sam Cox; and myself, which back then was the absolute minimum number required if you want to get the job done. Today, TV executives think you can do it with a single cameraman who'll direct, record the sound and film at the same time. You can't – at least, not if you care about standards. I firmly believe that these same television executives consistently underestimate the intelligence of their audience. Viewers are smarter than they realise, and will always see through shoddy production.

That trip was a real eye-opener for all of us. In planning the programme, I'd invested considerable time talking to people on Baffin Island, trying to establish which of the communities had the best traditional skills, particularly igloo building. At that time, there was a particular group of very skilled old men at Pond Inlet, on the northernmost tip, so it was a simple choice as to where we would go to make the film.

We flew from London to Toronto and from there we were due to catch our connecting flight to Pond Inlet. The weather had closed in though, and we ended up diverting to Iqaluit on the island's southern tip, where we got stuck for the night. We

found a hotel and, after we'd checked in and dumped our kit, Dennis and I thought we might go to the hotel bar for a drink or two. We approached the receptionist and Dennis asked if she could direct us to the bar, but her response wasn't quite what we expected.

'You don't want to go to the bar, sir.'

'Sorry, let me rephrase that. We'd like a drink in the hotel bar, could you point us in the right direction please?'

'No sir, you really don't want to go to the bar!'

Dennis, who had, among other programmes, directed *Top Gear*, wasn't having any of that.

'Actually, we DO want to go to the bar!'

'Sir, I can't make this any plainer: you really don't want to go there. But if you insist, it's that way,' she said, pointing to a corridor. So we thanked her, and walked down this corridor where we came to a door, except this wasn't your average door – it was made of solid metal and was the sort of portal you'd find on a heavily stocked armoury rather than a bar. That should have served as warning enough, but we were thirsty for a beer so we knocked.

When it swung open to admit us, we were ushered in by a bouncer and one quick glance at him told us all we needed to know. Dennis and I looked at one another; the bouncer was 7ft tall and dressed in the armour that American football players use to protect themselves on the field. And behind him was the strangest bar I'd ever seen: the beer – in fact, all the alcohol – was kept inside a safe behind the counter.

It was packed in there but it didn't have the welcoming, gentle hubbub you'd find in your average village pub in Britain. Nor the jolly, well-fuelled revelry of your typical Irish pub or US bar. No, there was a distinct edginess to this place and the local people who were its denizens looked a rough and ready crowd. It was too warm by far; the humidity of so many bodies in one place was palpable, the view

through the small windows obscured by condensation. It was also very smoky.

Still, it was too late to back out now, so we headed in and placed our order. We wanted beer, but they didn't have any of that, so we had to settle for a Budweiser. While we were waiting for our drinks to be drawn from inside the safe, somebody walked past us carrying a very large and very drunk Inuit woman on his shoulders. Sadly, alcohol is a real issue for many indigenous people around the world, partly because communities have often been relocated and some don't have the genetic make up to process alcohol efficiently. So alcoholism is a disease that blights many indigenous communities.

We soon received our drinks, but we'd no sooner taken a sip when we sensed, then saw, that the attention of the bar's customers had fallen on us. It was like someone had thrown a switch; whatever conversation or entertainment had been going on previously, suddenly we were the focus. The tension in the air was palpable. The receptionist was right. We *didn't* want to go to the bar after all.

I looked at Dennis. He looked at me.

'I think we'll drink up and leave, shall we? Like, now?' he said.

I took a quick look around the room. To be honest, even if we hadn't suddenly become the centre of attention, it wasn't the sort of place we'd have hung around in. I nodded.

'Good idea, Dennis. Let's do that.'

We swallowed our Budweisers and walked out. We didn't look back.

———◆———

At least nobody had a hangover to contend with when we awoke the following morning to bright sunshine and clear skies. Our flight to Pond Inlet was confirmed, so we headed

to the airport. The check-in girl asked us where we were going, and when I said Pond Inlet she said, 'Oh, you're flying long haul.' I'm thinking, 'Long haul? It's only the other end of the island!' but then I remembered that the flight was six hours long – you could fly London to New York in that time. I think that's the first time it hit me just how big Canada truly is. You see it on a map and yes, it's large, but there's no context. When you're there, its diversity and sheer scale dominate. It's astonishing.

Things were just as bizarre on the flight; when the Inuit women boarded, a lot of them had babies with them which they carried in their *amauti* parkas, and they were all carrying kettles in their hands. The *amauti* is a unique garment: a huge windproof anorak with a built-in baby pouch just below the hood. The women were walking down the aisle to their seats and, as they sat down, almost every one of them banged their baby's head on the overhead compartment. Predictably, the babies made quite a racket as a result of this, although they very quickly settled down afterwards as if this was a regular occurrence. It was all rather charming – it was so different to anything you'd experience anywhere else and really quite lovely in a strange way.

When the cabin crew walked down the aisle with the drinks service, I asked what they had, and the steward winked and said, 'Would you like one of our special hot chocolates?' Apparently, the special hot chocolate is laced very potently with rum – it's their antidote to the fact that Pond Inlet is a dry community. I have to say, it was a great service.

We knew that Pond Inlet would be a difficult environment to work in the minute we stepped off the plane. It wasn't so much the temperature (at -30°C, it was actually quite balmy for February) but more the extraordinarily strong north wind that was blowing. We were lucky because temperatures in winter often reach as low as -50°C – that's 30° colder than

your average home freezer. Despite this, and despite it being one of the most inhospitable areas on the face of the Earth, people had lived off the land there for over 4,000 years, using traditional knowledge.

We were met by Ham Kadloo, a lovely old Inuit fellow who we'd be working with, and I took an instant liking to him. He took us straight off to get kitted out in proper Inuit clothing, made from caribou skins. It was a nice touch, them dressing us in their clothes.

We had planned to spend two days or so filming on Bylot Island, which lies just off the coast of Pond Inlet. There's no permanent settlement there, but there is a seasonal hunting camp, so after a five- or six-hour crossing of the frozen sea ice by snowmobile we ended up in a hunters' cabin. I'll never forget it because some Inuit with a great sense of humour had written on one of the beams in the ceiling: 'O J Simpson was here on the night of the murder and that's the truth!'

The journey out by snowmobile was fascinating. I already had quite a bit of experience of riding snowmobiles but over nothing like the distance we had to cover here. The journey was tedious in the extreme as the sea ice was covered in pressure ridges that gave you a jolt every time you hit one. When the Inuit travel on snowmobiles, they have a sledge attached to the back that they call a *komatik*, and on top of that they build what is effectively an oversized dog kennel. Inside each dog kennel is a large mattress, and instead of sitting on the pillion seat of the snowmobile, whoever isn't riding it lies down in the kennel where they're protected from the wind. It's a great idea. Every 90 minutes or so, you stop and change riders – whoever was in the kennel takes over, and the rider gets to lay down in the warm.

I made a mistake on this expedition of assuming that the entire film crew would know how to take care of themselves, and that included the director. Now, some directors are very

good at the logistics and organising side of things, whereas others are creative-minded and logistics, let's say, may not be their strong suit. But I think it's fair to expect anyone going on any kind of expedition to have the common sense to take enough food with them for the length of time they'd be there, plus some extra in case of an emergency. You certainly wouldn't dream of going out to the Arctic for two days with just a Thermos flask of chicken soup now, would you . . . ? (I still laugh about that.)

Fortunately, the Inuit had a plentiful supply of seals for food – they'd just go out to the sea ice and shoot one when necessary. Inside the cabin, there was a thin sheet of cardboard on the floor and atop it was a seal that had been sliced open. As we were working with them, they invited us to share their food, so we helped ourselves whenever we needed to. You'd just cut a piece of meat off when you were hungry, dip it in blood and eat it. It was great fuel for keeping you fired up and warm. They also made a delicious seal stew – I'd brought some ingredients with me, so they made liberal use of the Oxo cubes I had on me.

I learned quickly on that expedition that there was a difference between me going places on my own as I had in the past, and going as an integral part of a film crew. Dennis asked me to walk along the edge of the frozen ice to do a piece to camera. That was never going to happen – not before I'd asked an Inuit to test it with a harpoon to determine the thickness. While I was waiting for him to do so, one of the other Inuit guides, Jaco, walked over to where I was standing and pointed to where Dennis had asked me to walk two minutes earlier.

'Whoa, don't stand there,' he said. 'That ice is rotten!' That was a stark reminder that ultimately I would have to make my own choices when it came to what I'd do for the camera – an extremely important lesson.

One of my favourite aspects of that whole trip was the time

we spent with old Ham Kadloo. Most Inuit can build an igloo very well. It's part of their cultural identity so they have the skill but, just as in any culture, there are certain individuals that have a higher degree of ability. Ham was one of these individuals. It all stemmed from when he was a young boy, and he'd go hunting with the men. He was very lithe and they would get him to put the top block on an igloo – because Ham was thin and light and wouldn't break the ice blocks when he stood on them, he was able to make a slightly bigger igloo than all the others. I guess this sparked a desire to learn more, and over the years he became exceptionally skilled at building igloos.

We were going out daily to film with the old men on the sea ice and then coming back to our accommodation. Our hotel had a central congregation area similar to the main reception at a mainstream hotel, except this one was adapted for heavy-duty cold weather gear. I had one of those bizarre moments when I looked at us all sitting there one afternoon and laughed because the first thing everyone did when they got back was to remove their caribou jackets. So they'd be standing around in their caribou trousers, which were held up with braces, and it'd look for all the world like we were part of a convention for the rear end of pantomime horses.

Some young Inuit (and by 'young' I mean in their thirties) who were the hunters for the community we were staying in asked: 'Why are you interested in all this old stuff? We don't use igloos any more; we use tents and we've got Colman stoves and petrol lighters.'

'Well,' I said, 'I'm interested in that too. But it's important to me that we record the knowledge and the skills that the old guys have. When they die, a lot of what they know will die with them and those skills will disappear forever.'

They got that; they understood exactly what I meant, and it had an impact on them because they came over and joined

us, and when we left to go to our rooms, they were in deep conversation with the old-timers about the skills they had that the younger generation didn't. That moved me; it all goes back to what I'd said to Kath about the two-way trade of information – that we take something away of them, but we leave something of ourselves too.

We went back on the ice later that day to film a piece with Ham on the use of a *koodlik* (a seal blubber lantern) and another piece with me dog-sledging. That was an amazing experience, although I did have a *bit* of a problem . . . obviously, with us being with the Inuit, the dogs only understood commands in Inuktitut, the Inuit language. Well, I could make the dogs go and I could make them stop. I could recall the command that Ham had given me to make them go left too, but out on the sea ice at full pelt, my Inuktitut pronunciation wasn't good enough to make them turn right. This had all the Inuit killing themselves with laughter because to get back to where they were on the right, I had to make a huge circle to the left. Eventually though, I managed to arrive back where I needed to be and we all had a good laugh about my pronunciation.

As we were standing there chatting with Ham, we heard the sound of snowmobiles heading towards us from the town. When the newcomers arrived and dismounted, we saw it was the same young guys we'd been talking to at the hotel – they'd seen us out on the ice and after what we'd talked about earlier, they'd come out to see what the older guys were up to and have a chat about it.

The old men were holding court and they were really in their element because suddenly, the younger generation were expressing an interest in what they knew. I watched Ham show them how he could make a quick snow-block wall to shelter himself if he was fishing or hunting for seal. When the Inuit usually build an igloo, they'd chink the gaps between the

blocks, but here Ham was showing them a way of making the wall where no chinking was necessary; it was 'ready-chinked' as he made it. Even the old men with him had never seen that done, but the younger guys stood there in awe.

'Who showed you this?' asked one. 'When did you learn this?'

He told them how he'd learned as a boy, and that the older generation that had taught him skills and given him knowledge were effectively dying out even back then. It appeared that Ham was the last exponent of what he was showing them.

'Really, did he show you this? I didn't know that,' said another of the young guys. Just by being there, we had started a dialogue, bridging the gap between these two generations. I was amazed and humbled. It was tremendously important because while we were recording stuff, we had also created an opportunity for people within the community to remember lost elders and discuss skills that might otherwise have been lost to them forever. That was perhaps the most fulfilling aspect of the whole trip and it really affirmed what we were doing.

As well as seal, the Inuit's diet contains fish, but to go fishing in a freshwater lake in the Arctic means hacking your way through 6–8ft of rock-hard ice. It takes hours of back-breaking labour. The hole has to be about the width of a man's shoulders, and once you get past a certain depth, the only way to clear the ice is by standing in the hole you've dug. The breakthrough, when it comes, is quick – so you have to judge it just right and climb out to chip away at that last inch or so. When you break through, the water all but erupts and then settles as it equalises with the surface. If you're fishing on your own, you have your double-pronged kakivak spear at the ready and then dangle a lure of antler in the water to attract the Arctic char.

If there's a group of Inuit men fishing to feed their families,

nets are used, and there are different methods used to cast them. One consists of cutting a series of holes in the ice and passing a line from one to the next, often by means of a long, straight pole. The line is then used to pull through a rope that, in turn, is used to extend the net beneath the ice. Another method uses an ice creep called a jigger, which is a sled-like wooden device that slides along the underside of the ice. The jigger is launched under the ice, towing a rope. When the rope is pulled, a lever is raised; when the rope is released, the lever springs back in such a way that it pushes against the ice and jerks the jigger forward. Another Inuit then listens for the sound as it creeps under the ice and, when it's gone far enough – a hundred metres or so – you clear the snow and then pour hot water or lick the ice with your tongue to defrost the surface. The ice is so pure that the Inuit can see the jigger through 8ft of it. All they have to do then is to repeat what they did at the start – i.e. dig another backbreaking hole to get to it. Once that's done, they can then thread their nets through the two holes and leave them there for six or seven hours overnight. If they're lucky, there might be as many as thirty or forty fish in the morning. If they're unlucky, there will be none and they'll have to repeat the whole thing at another location.

Because of the ambient temperature, the Inuit need to set up a tent for shelter, and a stove to heat food and drinks. It was fascinating to watch – not just the act of catching fish but how the Inuit organised themselves to provide the life-support system necessary to conduct the tasks. The patience required, their whole demeanour and the way they took every-thing that the Arctic could throw at them was truly amazing to behold. The Inuit are very different to us – it was like stepping into a totally different world.

That trip was special for a number of reasons, but being the first one we did, we all learned a few lessons over the time we spent with the Inuit. I knew Barrie was a good cameraman,

but this trip really put his skills in perspective. It's an exceptionally difficult job to do in cold conditions because he'd have one hand holding the camera and the other supporting the lens. The lens is made of brass, which is a brilliant conductor for the intense cold, so for most of the time he was in pain while working out there.

We went out hunting for caribou with Jaco at one point and Barrie wanted to get a shot of him looking down the sight of his hunting rifle and swinging it round so that the barrel ended up pointing straight down the lens. I thought it might be a good idea to check that the rifle wasn't loaded and I got a rather indignant look back from Jaco when I asked him. 'Of course it's unloaded!' he said. I said that regardless, I'd still be happier if he just checked so he opened the breech and I heard him say, 'Oh my God, there's one up the spout!' If we'd carried out what we planned to do without checking, Barrie would have been looking down the wrong end of a loaded gun.

Some of what I learned was fascinating, but as ever, it's the small details that are most vivid. When Jaco shot and butchered the caribou, I saw how he pushed his knife into the meat when he wasn't using it – the snow is so deep that if he'd put his knife down on it, he'd have lost it. Nothing of the animal is wasted – not even its body heat. I watched Jaco take the stomach and fill it with snow. He then knotted the top and put the stomach back into the caribou's carcass while he butchered it. As he did so, the warmth of the carcass melted the snow. It was thirsty work, so that when he was finished, he took the stomach and put two small blocks of snow in it, which absorbed the water. He then sucked on the snow, which acted as a natural filter as he drank the water through it. It was absolutely fascinating to watch.

My interest has always been in traditional skills and knowledge. I want to know how you live in any given environment.

I wasn't there because I was writing some anthropological thesis or a doctorate study; I was there because of a specific interest. I was asking questions of the Inuit that others didn't ask and it was a shame I didn't have longer, really – I could happily have spent months with them.

12

Mud, Sweat and Mears

The *World of Survival* series took us down under to focus on the Aboriginal people in Australia's Arnhem Land, which has been occupied by indigenous people for more than 50,000 years. They were still living a Stone Age existence until as recently as the 1930s. Its native Aboriginals are one of the oldest living cultures actively maintaining their traditional life in the world today.

The Arnhem Land Region is situated in the north-eastern corner of Australia's Northern Territory, about 300 miles from the territory capital of Darwin, and is truly remote. How do you measure that kind of remoteness? Well, in parts of Europe you might lose your way for a few hours; in America it might be a few days; but in Arnhem Land you could wander for months without seeing any sign of civilisation. That puts 'remote' into perspective and also explains how the Aborigines who live there can be so unaffected by Western life.

So, from this vast expanse we were focusing on a very, very small outstation called Jibalbal, which had only about fourteen people in it. They had broken away from the community at Maningrida, the nearest large neighbour, which had a population of around 2,000 people, because they felt that their traditional way of life was being diluted and becoming 'too Westernised' – spoiled by the effect of alcoholism.

We'd arranged to work with this particular group, but just

prior to our departure they decided they didn't want us to make the film because they were worried about the impact it would have on their community – I could completely understand where they were coming from. We were committed at that point though. After a protracted negotiation with them, I went on ahead with Joe Ahearne – the director – and Jayne Simons, an anthropologist.

We drove into Arnhem Land, and what an amazing journey that was: an eighteen-hour trek off-road and across rivers, with no maps of any particular worth. It was also my first off-road driving experience in Australia and while it wasn't quite as challenging as the drive across Zaire in support of Ffyona's walk, it wasn't far off. I loved it; hard off-road Land Rover driving is wonderful.

After being greeted on arrival at Jibalbal, I asked if there was somewhere we could set up camp. They showed us to a suitable location nearby and I then asked them where we could find some decent sticks that we could use to support our tarpaulins. They said the best place was a short drive away, so they jumped into a pick-up truck and asked us to follow them. We ended up driving through grassland where the grass was higher than our vehicle's roof – it was a good job we kept them in sight because I had no idea where we were. After a short drive, we arrived at a spot where we were told we'd find some good sticks.

The next thing, we were up to our waists in swamp following an Aborigine ahead of us armed with a shotgun that was so rusty, the whole thing looked like it had been painted scarlet. I immediately realised we were in danger, but Joe didn't seem to know why we needed the guy with the shotgun, so he asked me. His face was a picture when I told him we were wading in crocodile territory.

Fortunately, no crocs impeded us and we were able to gather up the sticks we needed so we went back and made camp. The community's chief came over and we shared the contents of

our billycan with him, which was the beginning of the two days we spent forging our friendship. That was a very special time; building a rapport with these people was the most important thing we did, and it was real – not just for the cameras. Lots of films have been made since then but because time is money in TV, you often don't have time to do this and it really is a shame. But we'd made a genuine connection and really got to know the people in the community we were filming. The corollary of that is that the indigenous people were much more forthcoming in terms of what they were prepared to share, and that meant I could do an honest job in depicting their lives, which was important to me. It's not about what we're taking, but what we're leaving of their world. In order to work this way, you need a crew made up of people who are worldly enough and humble enough to understand that if you give, then you receive; if you just take, you get nothing back. We had that in Barrie, Alan Duxbury, Andy Morton and Sam Cox, which is why we collaborated on so many programmes over the years. Hopefully the results speak for themselves.

While we were forging this bond with the local community, the rest of the crew had the most horrendous journey out to join us. They flew from Britain to Darwin, which in itself is a hell of a journey. It's an exceptionally long flight, and they'd arrived in the early hours of the morning and transferred to the old Darwin Hotel (let's just say it doesn't exist any longer and nobody who stayed there at that time will have mourned its passing). Barrie and Sam had eighteen silver boxes of gear with them and they were exhausted after husbanding it all the way from the UK – they just wanted to get some sleep.

Two hours after dropping off, they were awoken by a knock on their door by Rafferty Finn. Rafferty is a superb guy, one of the best local guides and fixers I've ever worked with. He was going to bring them out to join us and I think Barrie and Sam were just so tired, they didn't know what day it was so

they just went along with it when Rafferty said to load their gear into his 4x4 so they could drive over to join us. I think they assumed the journey would only be an hour at most, so you can just imagine the look on their faces after Sam asked how long it would take to get to the camp and Rafferty replied, 'Oh, only eighteen hours or so . . .'

It was fully dark when they arrived and I remember there were so many insects buzzing in the beam from the headlamps that if you'd taken a bucket and pulled it along the beam you'd have filled it. There were Aborigines coughing, dogs being sick, and the air was so thick with mosquitoes you almost had to cut your way through them. Actually, the mosquitoes in Arnhem Land are like nothing I've ever encountered before – they can bite through the thick hide of a buffalo and can get at humans through two layers of clothing. They're really something else.

Barrie and Sam looked in a state of shock as they crawled under their mosquito nets, delirious with tiredness and needing sleep like a junkie needs a fix. They can't have been best pleased when they were awakened by the rising sun just a few hours later, accompanied by the sound of kookaburras calling above their heads. I did feel for them, I have to confess, but it was quite funny from afar. The point wasn't lost on me though that while for me it was all a great adventure – and my *raison d'être* – they were a professional film crew and the organisation could have been better. To be fully effective, they needed to be rested so, again, it was all part of the learning curve for us.

Each morning we'd go down to a billabong to wash – it was a case of jumping in quick and jumping straight back out again in case of errant crocodiles. Then in the evenings, the Aborigines would go down to the creek and catch *yabbies* (crayfish). I noticed two of the youngsters using a bow and arrow, which was just the tool for the job (although it most

definitely *isn't* a traditional Aboriginal tool). I asked them where they'd learned about the bow and arrow and one of them ran off. He came back a few moments later with an English book containing the story of Robin Hood. These two Aboriginal youngsters had read it, adapted the concept, and made a bow and arrow to catch *yabbies*. I found that truly remarkable.

The time I spent with the Aborigines at Jibalbal was like a university education in terms of the breadth and depth of what I learned from them. They taught me how to make the traditional spear shafts that they use; how to use a spear thrower; what plants you could eat; and what sticks you could use to make fire. I made fire there with a man whose advanced age meant he struggled to do it using a traditional hand drill because he couldn't get to the best sticks. They were out of reach to him because the flood waters hadn't receded following the wet season so he was forced to use these 'B' class sticks, if you like. I offered to get some for him and there was a group of three or more younger Aborigines nearby. 'No, don't let the Balanda (white man) help you, Grandfather,' one of them said. 'We are the ones who should be helping you to do this.'

The old man looked sagely at me. Then he turned to them and barked at them in his language, 'You had the chance to learn this and you chose not to. He can do this. You can't.'

In letting me help him over his own kin, he was sending them a strong statement that instead of listening to their Bob Marley records, they should have been learning their traditional skills. I felt humbled to have been included in that experience; it was a very great privilege.

The Aboriginals also took us to the mangrove swamp. Mangrove trees have roots which extend above ground, so crossing the swamp is like climbing over giant wooden spaghetti that can come up as high as your chest. The Aboriginals persevere though because mangroves are also teeming with

food. And one of their favourites is the *teredo*, or mangrove worm – possibly the weirdest thing I've ever eaten. *Teredo* worms live inside wood rather than in the mud. Also known as naval shipworms, they tunnel into underwater piers and pilings and they're a major cause of damage to underwater timber structures and the hulls of wooden boats. In the eighteenth century, the Royal Navy resorted to covering the bottom of its ships with copper to prevent the damage caused by these worms, which is where the saying 'copper-bottomed' originates.

They're actually molluscs rather than worms – a species of saltwater clam – and in these mangrove swamps, they bore their way into rotten logs. They don't look terribly appealing – like a long, slimy, pallid grey worm. I thought they'd taste revolting but they are actually quite nice with a flavour somewhere between crab pâté and smoky clam. They're a delicacy to the Aborigines, and they're also very popular in Asia.

Being there with the Aborigines, being welcomed into their community the way I was, was both humbling and remarkable; remarkable insofar as it was just like stepping back in time. I guess it's the closest thing we've got to time-travel at the moment. There were many events that made me think this, but one of the things I witnessed was how, when they used tools, it sometimes looked as if they didn't know how to use them. Take a knife, for instance. Hard as it is to believe, Arnhem Land has only had metal for the past 200 years, so the Aborigines might hold it by the wrong part and use the sole of their foot as a sort of chopping board to cut down onto. It struck me that when I was watching them demonstrate a skill or show me the way they do something, they were doing so according to their cultural practice, which is, de facto, their law. In effect, there is only one way of doing something for them and that's the way it's *always* been done. When I was being given a survival skills demonstration, for example, it took me a while to fully realise the implications of what I was

witnessing. I was seeing how their people had always done it, in many cases for tens of thousands of years. I've seen this many times since in Australia and it's like you're pushing the 'replay' button on the way it was done the very first time. I'm not sure I fully understood that in the beginning.

There was one trip I did with one of the elder men in the community – a lovely man with a huge shock of snow-white hair on his head. I can't use his real Aboriginal name because he's no longer with us and once their people have passed away, it's seen as disrespectful to use their names, so I'll call him John. Besides, Aboriginals often have a 'white' name as well as it's easier for us to pronounce, and in most dealings with people, they prefer to use their white name rather than their Aboriginal name.

Anyway, I'd been out with John and his wife digging up edible yams. We were driving back, and they were sitting in the back of the truck talking away for ages in their native tongue when John suddenly said, 'Ain't that right, Ray?' like I'd been involved in their conversation all along.

'What's that, John?' I said, using his Aborigine name.

'Ray, you've got the same story as us – you know, about the man in the moon?'

While it's true they do have the story about the face in the moon, it's slightly different from ours – even so, it was a cultural connection. Those were really charming moments, the moments when you realise how closely we all are tied by the things that bind us together rather than separate us. That to me was profound, because when I started making that series, I was convinced that what I would see were the things that made us all so different.

Another funny moment when we were filming with John happened while we were on the coast looking for mud crabs. John was poking in muddy holes with an Aborigine crabbing hook, which is rather like what the Cornish fishermen use.

The sun was setting and the whole scene was beautifully filmed; it all looked rather romantic. Every time John looked for a crab in the hole he would come up with nothing. This happened over and over again to the point where we thought we'd have to stop filming. However, his wife and children were watching and decided to have a go themselves. Lo and behold, each time one of them poked in the same hole as he did, they'd pull out a crab. It was quite remarkable and genuinely funny. Aboriginal people have a finely developed sense of humour very similar to our own and they enjoy taking the mickey out of one another.

Eventually we made fire, and sat round it cooking the crabs with the sun setting behind us. Although the camera was rolling we were all aware of the beauty and significance of the scene and I was in another world to the camera crew. To me it was a 'real' experience with this man and his family, and it was the same for them, too. Once the camera stopped rolling, John's wife took a couple of crabs, wrapped them in some leaves and gave them to me. I was very touched by it.

We were welcomed with open arms into the homes of the people of Jibalbal and I found it really hard to leave. They were very special people. We spent just under three weeks there in total. Today, to make the same programme, we'd be lucky to have five days.

On our way back to Darwin our 4x4 broke down, so Barrie and Sam got back ahead of Joe and me. They'd also booked themselves into a much swankier hotel without telling us, so when they eventually got to town, instead of heading for the old Darwin Hotel, they were dropped at the Grand Marble, replete with gold door and air-conditioning, while Joe and I eventually rolled up at the nightmare that was the old Darwin.

When we arrived a party was in full swing but we were told it would finish at 1 a.m.; however, it was still rocking the building at 4 a.m. I got to my room and turned on the air-conditioning – it didn't work. So I went to turn on the fan and it made a terrible clunking sound as it turned. 'I know, I'll have a shower,' I thought – it was broken. So I sat on the bed and, just when you think things can't get any worse, I heard a creak and a groan . . . and it collapsed under me, throwing me onto the floor. So there I am, in abject misery after this horrendous journey back from the bush, thinking about Barrie and Sam in their palatial luxury, feeling oh so sorry for myself. I looked over at the dressing-room table and there was a comments card in my room saying, 'We know that the old Darwin Hotel – the "Raffles of Australia" – is some-what the worse for wear but please help us to rectify things by telling us what you found.' So looking for some humour to tranquilise the discomfort, I wrote: 'You should bulldoze it to the ground and rebuild it.'

The funny thing is that a year or so later, that's exactly what they did. What I didn't know then though, was that things hadn't exactly gone to plan for the camera crew, as we learned when we left for the airport the next day. Barrie and Sam got to their air-conditioned hotel and got all their gear out. They were smelling their lovely soaps and feeling their soft fluffy towels and marvelling at the walk-in power showers, thinking how great it all was that they could have a proper wash, no doubt enjoying the fact that we were back in the Darwin Hotel. They cleaned up, relaxed and had just settled down to a good night's sleep in their respective rooms when the fire alarm went off and they were paraded out into the street in their dressing gowns. They didn't get back to sleep that night, so there was justice after all. As I told them, it's those sorts of experiences that bond a team.

13

South Pacific

Our next shoot in the series took us to Savai'i, Western Samoa. We thought it best to take the same approach as when we first met with the Aborigines in Australia – Joe and I went in first to establish a relationship with the community while Barrie and Sam would follow on later.

Western Samoa is about as far from Britain as it's possible to get; it's one of the tiny Polynesian islands out in the Pacific Ocean, way east of Australia. In my quest to find traditional survival skills, I was headed to the tiny coastal village of Falealupo, situated at the west end of Savai'i island, about 20 miles from the International Date Line. Due to its location, it was often described as the last village in the world to see the sunset each day – although since then, the International Date Line has been moved so it no longer has that particular claim to fame.

The islands have only been settled for about the last 1,000 years and, despite the stunning scenery and location, the environment is far harsher than it looks. The Pacific Ocean breaks on the island's coast with terrifying ferocity and there are treacherous currents just offshore. Cyclones regularly sweep through – there'd been one shortly before we arrived and it had flattened a concrete church completely – so it made good sense for the community on the islands to retain their traditional skills, although these are a curious marriage between

the traditional and the modern, as they've integrated electric ovens and chainsaws into their old ways.

The Samoans are a very proud and self-reliant people. They work on the principle that while ships and aircraft arrive with supplies on a semi-regular basis, the prospect always remains that maybe one day they won't. So it helps to have fall-back skills and experience.

A good example of this is in the traditional houses they live in, called *fales*. *Fales* are designed to stand up to cyclones, torrential rain and strong sun. They're the most common house-type in the village, built straight from the forest. A simple yet effective design, each house is supported by several hibiscus uprights and open-sided, with the frame and rafters tied together with the bark of one of the trees used in its construction. Coral from the beach is used to make the floor, which is then covered with woven coconut leaves to make it hygienic, and also to keep the sand out. Woven coconut leaves are also used for the roof – two layers provide waterproofing, and their natural curvature (side on, they look like the cross section of a wing) allows rain water to drain away. They can be used to make an effective drop-down blind for the open sides too, keeping the wind out on a blowy day.

When the recent cyclone struck, traditional *fales* stood up better than most of the modern houses; the open sides allow the air pressure inside to equalise when a shockwave hits, whereas most closed structures just explode.

The Samoans live from the sea, but they make plentiful use of the forested centre of the island, and the incredibly useful coconut palm trees (known by Samoans as the Tree of Life) that delineate the edge of the forest. These provide fronds for roofing, flooring, baskets, plates, hats, beds, roofs, and have a million and one other uses including a water supply, in the form of unripe coconuts, or food and milk when the coconuts mature. The Samoans on Savai'i make their living

from the island and there is nothing they don't know how to use.

One of the first things that struck me on arrival was the melodic singing. If you want to really hear singing, then you need to go to a church in Samoa and listen. It stems back from when the first people arrived there – they knew they'd found paradise and they've been singing about it ever since. It is just the most beautiful place with the most beautiful people.

A few days after Barrie arrived, he and I had a bit of a falling out. I'd spent the day building a canoe with the islanders – whether it's a traditional house or a canoe, they like to complete everything in a single day.

With a project like a canoe or a *fale*, every able-bodied member of the community works together to get the job done. We had gone down in the morning with a chainsaw, cut down a tree and run back to the village with it on our shoulders. I was helping and they were all shouting at me. I thought they were saying something to do with me not carrying my weight and wanting me to carry more but what they were actually saying was, 'Bend down a bit, we can't all share the weight because you are taking too much.' Anyway, we'd made this canoe and I was paddling it along. Barrie had wanted to put the setting sun behind the boat, but I couldn't place it where he wanted because what he couldn't see from his position on the shore was that there was a reef there and no depth of water for me to clear it. He thought I was being awkward, and once I got back to land we ended up having a bit of a set-to.

We were both trying really hard at the end of what had been a long, hot day to do the right thing, so tempers were a little stretched and we went back to the accommodation not speaking to one another. It shows the measure of the man though, because half an hour later there was a knock at my door and when I opened it, there was Barrie, standing with a

perfectly mixed gin and tonic in each hand. I'd had it in my head to go and see him to sort it all out too, so I knew right then and there that we would be able to work together for years to come, because he understood that tempers may flare but the bigger picture is more important. I've never forgotten that – with people like Barrie in the crew you can achieve anything.

Diving for clams was one of the most amazing things we did there. To swim past the razor-sharp reef and out into the deep sea, the locals 'read' the waves and wait for just the right one to come along. I wouldn't know it – you have to have local knowledge to do this. When they said: 'Now!' that was the signal for us to jump into the right wave. Next they grabbed their T-shirts at the neck and trapped air underneath, enabling them to float out on the wave until they were somewhere between a quarter and a half a mile offshore. Then they'd dive down and collect the clams from the sea bed, resurface, and eat them raw as they bobbed in the ocean. I joined in. Eating clams in this way is an experience I would like to do again. Watching them do this was incredible – the clams were buried under rocks 60ft or more below the surface. I was in awe. And they can go deeper. In just a pair of hand-made wooden goggles into which they glued a piece of glass, and a T-shirt, the deepest I watched one of them dive on that afternoon was an astonishing 70ft. Whatever the depth though, they don't seem to be in any sort of hurry, having the astonishing lung capacity which can only be built up over years.

When we got back to shore we stopped in a volcanic pool filled with rainwater. We took a couple of leaves from a fisao plant which, when rubbed on the rocks, produces a lather, and so we washed the sea salt out of our hair.

On leaving Savai'i we were escorted by Va'asilifiti Moelagi Jackson, a lovely woman who had been our guide while we were on the island. She was a real character. We were on a ferry travelling to the neighbouring island of Upolu when all

of a sudden there was a massive rush of passengers to one side of the boat. When I say a massive rush, it was enough people that it caused the boat to list, so you get the idea. They'd moved because a school of dolphins was swimming alongside us. Va'asilifiti turned to me and said, 'When our people used to travel by canoe, they felt a connection, a relationship, with the dolphin because they were very close to them in the water. That connection is lost now because our lifestyle has changed, but the people still long for it. That's why everyone moved – they had gone to talk to the dolphins.'

As we watched, a couple of dolphins within the school jumped out of the water and turned round to face us. That was a very profound moment.

'Historically,' she said, 'our canoes weren't as developed as those on some of the other Polynesian Islands because our island was bigger, meaning we didn't need to travel as much as others.'

The practice of making long canoe journeys across the Pacific ended in the 1950s due to the number of people killed in the rough seas. Va'asilifiti told us about a centenary celebration that her grandfather was involved in when she was a little girl. He was crossing to Fiji – the mere thought of that is astonishing – and at some point, he'd dropped his paddle in the water. The others on the canoe had laughed and joked, saying, 'Ha, go and get your paddle,' and, although he didn't really want to, he felt pressured and had to save face. So he jumped in and retrieved it, but as he was swimming back to the canoe, unfortunately he was attacked by a shark. But what a brave man.

She also told us that on long crossings, they'd shout praise at the helmsman to keep him awake. You can just imagine being on a long, tedious journey across the ocean and someone in the back shouting out: 'Well steered, sir!' in Samoan. It worked though, as I can personally attest, as she would often shout it out while I was driving around the island.

According to local protocol we exchanged gifts with our hosts before we left and as the gifts were made, a man announced what they were in a very loud voice. You can imagine our astonishment when we discovered that we had been gifted an enormous pig, which had been roasted in a ground oven. This posed the problem of what to do with it; I couldn't imagine the airline flying us home would have allowed us to take it on board as hand luggage, after all. So we loaded it into the Transit van we were using as a production vehicle and left the rear doors open to accommodate the oversized pig's legs. We then drove around the island distributing meat to its many communities.

———◆———

There are lots of incidents that never made it into the film and generally, the most amusing anecdotes took place off-camera. In television, sometimes you have to ask people to repeat what they do because there are myriad issues that can mean reshooting a particular scene – maybe someone messes up, the sound doesn't record, the camera isn't in focus or it may be that you need to shoot from another angle. Anyway, we were filming one of the guys chopping some hibiscus wood as a segment to go with the footage of the *fale* being built, and Barrie wanted to get a shot of this guy coming towards the camera, but he had to stop and ask him to do it again because he was moving too fast. So the guy went back to the starting position, Barrie started filming again, only this time the guy moved even quicker. So we asked him to do it again and he got faster still. By the fourth time the guy looked like a Whirling Dervish whistling past the cameraman with his machete. Barrie didn't even try to film it then – he was too busy taking cover behind his camera. It turns out the man had thought he'd look weak and less manly because we'd

asked him to slow down, so he sped up instead. You just can't win sometimes.

There was another amusing incident after we'd been diving for clams. We were back on shore and Barrie wanted to check the footage to see what he'd got, because he'd been shooting underwater. It was a very bright day, so we put the tape into a unit on the Transit van. Sadly, we couldn't see the monitor that the tape was being played back on because a huge Samoan man who'd been diving with us was completely blocking the gap at the side door so that he was the only one that could see the screen. We found out later that he hadn't been wearing any underwear when he dived and he was just checking the film to make sure that nothing was on show that shouldn't be.

14
63°N 96°E

For me, the film that we made in Siberia for the fourth episode is one of the best films we ever made. It's hard to say why, exactly, but there was something magical about both the remote location we were in and the Evenki, the people we'd come to make the film about. I was also working with a new crew – Alan Duxbury was my cameraman, a genius behind the lens who was willing to get his hands dirty and do whatever was required to get the shot he wanted, plus Andy Morton as the sound recordist and Ian Paul directing. This programme came about largely due to the expertise of the late Thomas Johansson, a Swedish expert on primitive technologies I knew. His knowledge of the Siberian boreal forest and its indigenous people was unrivalled. Those of us who knew him miss him dearly.

I knew that Siberia was big, but after travelling for four days to get there, and flying over it for four hours, I started to realise just *how* big. It covers five million square miles, is one and a half times larger than Europe and encompasses a million lakes and 53,000 rivers. And trees – millions and millions and millions of trees. To reach it, we'd travelled in three aircraft and a helicopter, which delivered us to a truly remote spot not marked on any map.

The journey itself was like a mini-expedition. We'd flown from London to Moscow, where we spent a couple of days

before catching another flight from Moscow to Novosibirsk and then on to Krasnoyarsk, which had been a closed city until four years earlier – it was where the USSR manufactured some of its nuclear arsenal. We then boarded a small cargo aircraft that dropped us in Tura, a real frontier town. We spent the night there, as the helicopter taking us to our eventual destination wasn't leaving until the following morning, so that night we were taken to a bar where one of the locals was having a birthday party. The vodka flowed, the crew started dancing – which was very popular with the women there because the Russian men don't like to dance – and then suddenly they were surrounded by said Russian men who were all getting very agitated. We were then told that if we didn't leave then, we might not leave with our lives. A very quick exodus ensued.

The next morning we went to the airport to get a helicopter to our final destination, where we discovered that our pilot was one of the revellers from the night before and was *definitely* the worse for wear. That didn't exactly fill us with confidence, but then we discovered he was navigating with a Michelin road map of Asia! I do sometimes wonder how we ever made it. Alan got to film out the open door as we flew. Now normally when you do this, the cameraman is restrained via a harness. In this case though, one of the crew had hold of the back of Alan's belt. Rather him than me.

I was there to meet with the traditional Evenki people – nomadic reindeer herders who live deep in the Siberian forest and whose lifestyle has remained virtually unchanged for the past 800 years. They live in family groups, or 'brigades', and we'd be spending two weeks living with the brigade Gyalski in their traditional *chums* (pronounced 'chooms') or tepees.

The Siberians have the *chum*, the Native Americans have the wigwam and Scandinavia's Sami people have the *lavvu* – they're all variations on a theme but they share the same DNA, as it were.

However, the Siberian version is not to be confused with the Plains tip which is constructed with twelve poles on a tripod with two short, one long pole – so it sits into the wind. The *chum* that the Evenki use in Siberia is the Asian version of the North Woods tepee, which is symmetrical – its conical shape means it's easily constructed and covered, and the top part allows for the drying of clothes or meat. North Woods tepees are used throughout the open boreal arctic forest – and the culture has remained the same because all of its inhabitants are related in one way or another. The boreal forest (or *taiga* – a Russian word meaning 'barren place') stretches around the northernmost part of the globe like a blanket, and is the largest land biome on the planet. It takes its name from Boreas, the Greek god of the northern wind. I've been to most corners of it and it's absolutely fascinating – I love it.

There are only six Evenki brigades left in Siberia, and their whole lives revolve around the reindeer. The herds provide transport, milk, clothing and most of the Evenki's food. I was there to learn the skills that have allowed them to live and flourish in such a huge, harsh, barren land.

The community had put aside one of their *chums* for me and the crew to live in. It was heated inside by a wood-burning stove that did a great job of combating the relatively balmy September temperature of -8°C.

We soon got into a rhythm, and having taught Alan how to make feather sticks and fire, he was always up first, getting the fire going every morning. In fact, we all became really well integrated with the brigade and I loved how Andrew, Alan and Ian all developed their own rapport with the Evenki, each one of them contributing something unique to the overall experience, making it really special.

All the expeditions we did together were special, though, because they were all so far removed from the life we lived back home. In some cases, it was easy to forget just how

different life was, even at the most basic level.

As an example, on most expeditions, we got in the habit of bringing various small toys with us to give to the children in each community, and on this trip we'd brought some of those really bouncy small rubber balls. One of the guys – I think it was Alan – gave one to one of the girls and she looked at it as if to say, 'What on earth am I supposed to do with this?' Then we realised that there was no hard surface anywhere for over 1,000 miles; it was just moss everywhere. There was nothing to bounce it on, but you don't think of those things.

We'd go out into the forest with the local people to film each day, which of course I loved because the forest is my environment. To keep their reindeer from wandering off, the Evenki build a really effective and simple fence, which they put up incredibly quickly (they erected over 100m in just twenty minutes). They chop down only the trees they need, and the fence is a series of interlocking poles. No tools are required other than an axe to fell the trees and chop them to size; the supports push easily into the soft ground and no nails or other fixings are required as the cross bars just sit across the interlocking sticks.

Evenki skills may look easy, but they're incredibly precise. They kill the reindeer with a swift, single knife thrust to the spinal cord and death is instantaneous. The reindeer are communal property so the meat gets shared among the entire brigade. The carcass is skinned with great care because everything has a use; nothing is wasted. In winter the temperature dips to -70°C or below, and the warmest clothes are made from reindeer skins stitched together. The intestines are used to make soup. The meat from one piece of a leg can feed one man for four days. Once the sinew is dried, it makes the best natural thread there is. The fur makes socks, hats, boots . . . it's all used.

They lay fish nets in a nearby lake and go out twice a day

to check for the catch, but it's a precarious task. Vitally and Vadim, the two brigade members who took me out with them, made their way out to the middle of the lake on the most unstable, rickety, home-made raft I've ever seen. The water is so cold that if they fell in, they'd only have minutes to reach the shore before hypothermia would set in. That would be somewhat academic in their case though – they told me after they returned to shore that neither of them could swim. There's a reason for that: the water is always too cold to learn.

The fish are a valuable supplement to the brigade's diet and make a pleasant change from reindeer. And like so many of Siberia's resources, the Evenki don't seem to make even a dent in the stocks. But then, with one person for every 600 square kilometres, that's hardly surprising.

They have to be self-sufficient because the handouts that they used to get – and on which they depended – evaporated almost overnight with the collapse of the old Soviet system. Under the communist regime, a helicopter would fly in once a week and the Evenki could send pelts and furs to sell in the local town, buying tools and summer clothes with the money they made. Back then, the helicopters were free but with the introduction of Siberia's market economy, they now need to pay – and the flights are hugely expensive. The good thing is, though, because they've retained the skills to live in the forest, the Evenki will survive whatever happens in Russia. That said, it's not an easy life; although the forest may look benevolent, the reality is that it's semi-barren and the ground is gripped by permafrost, solid ice just a few inches beneath the moss-covered floor. So yes, life is really hard for the Evenki, but they're Russian people – they're tough. Let's face it, what else can they do?

Reindeer, as with all grazing animals, eat everything in sight, and because of this they need careful management. Their diet

is lichen, which grows incredibly slowly but the Evenki have become masters at knowing just when to move their herds on. On average, each nomadic brigade has to pack up and find a new location every month, so they're masters at doing so – as I watched, it took an hour from start to finish to dismantle and pack up their whole existence, ready to move to pastures new.

───────◆───────

When the time came for us to leave, it snowed very heavily and it occurred to me that if it snowed a little bit more, we would be stuck there for weeks. I have to say, the prospect didn't daunt me at all, but a betting man wouldn't have liked the odds on the crew's feelings on the subject.

As it was, I was the first to hear the helicopter coming to get us, and it was so quiet where we were, so remote, that I heard it forty-five minutes before it arrived. There's no ambient noise, none of the background aural wallpaper that defines life in an urban environment or even in the English countryside. This is the sort of quiet that you only get in truly remote places. On the sub-Arctic forest edge, on a cold winter day, sound travels for miles. The Evenki are a very tight-knit community of people literally out in the middle of nowhere – their nearest 'shop' was over 300 miles away. The nearest hospital was a week's journey by reindeer, so they almost never get sick. Just as well, really.

It's a very honest way to live: chopping firewood and bringing it back to the stove; no mortgage because you build your own house wherever you stop, from the wooden poles you chop from the forest; your reindeer provide transport, food, milk, clothes, thread, covers for the *chum* . . . The forest provides wood, lichen to eat, flora and fauna. The lakes are filled with pike and other fish, which offer a much-needed change from

reindeer. The Evenki are almost entirely self-sufficient in one of the earth's most hostile, barren environments. That alone is incredible. That's very much how I try to live when I teach courses, so I felt very at home there.

All of us loved that trip and we felt that we'd forged a very special bond with the family we stayed with. Making a film like that is like an iceberg: out of how we live, what we do for each episode and what we experience, only about a third – maybe less – ever goes into each programme. There's so much you never see on camera – the singing in the evening, the rapport with the people.

Just before we left, Alan decided to put up a tarp to make a rudimentary cinema. We put a monitor under it and ran the tape to show the family some of what we'd been filming. As the film was running, one of the little girls came over. She looked at herself on screen and said, 'Who's that? Who's that there?'

Andy said, 'That's you.'

'No, no, that's not me,' she replied. She'd never seen her own reflection and didn't know what she looked like. 'Who's that little girl? I've never seen her.' She got all upset and she just couldn't accept that it was her.

I learned so much too, just by being there. We could always tell how many Evenki men are in a *chum* because they all left their axes outside – if there were three axes in the log outside, then there were three men inside. They never went anywhere without their axes. They make their own knives too – they have a single bevelled edge, and the Evenki have a special way of cutting where they'll have the knife in front of their knee and they'll pull the wood towards the knife. They have a very special way of tanning the reindeer skins too, using the soft, rotting, punky wood from larch trees. They're a very adaptable and capable people.

I remember Alan had brought a pack of cards with him,

but we never got to use them. That said, someone was using them . . . We'd go out each day filming and each evening when we got back, we noticed the cards were getting dirtier and dirtier but they were always exactly as he'd left them. Eventually we asked Sacha, the head of the family, and it turned out that every time we left the camp the children had been going in and playing cards. Of course, after that we got roped into playing their particular card game and I think Alan ended up losing everything but his shirt. To me, the way the children treated the cards was typical of their gentleness, the way they put everything back exactly as it was.

15

The Red Centre

I've always worked very hard at increasing my knowledge. Thanks to a combination of my formal education, parental input and Kingsley's mentoring, I learned to take a subject apart, look at the nuts and bolts, and then rebuild it. That's the only way you can really understand how something works. You have to *really* study your subject to know it inside out. And it's what I've always done, and still do. I've never stopped because there's always something new to learn. So I'll attack an area of knowledge that I want to become familiar with and I mean really attack it – a peripheral acquisition of knowledge is never enough. Once I've done that, I'll think about it from the perspective of my own particular requirements and then re-evaluate whether I've got the information I need to answer the questions that I'm asking. If I have, then I'll look very carefully at it, reformulate the knowledge that exists to suit the need that I have, test it, and if I'm happy I'll move on to the next thing. There is *always* something; I'm never idle in that regard.

One of the limitations of TV is that you can only ever show the tiniest fraction of whatever subject you are trying to tackle. That applies to any skills that I have too; having been a student of bushcraft for over forty years, there's only so much of my repertoire that I can present in a thirty-minute film. But, by going back several times to make a series about the same place,

I can bring to bear different aspects of my skills and knowledge. More importantly, my underlying understanding of a culture improves massively so I can ask better questions when I'm there. Nowhere is this more evident than the time I've spent working with Australian Aborigines.

We were lucky to have had the length of time we did in order to make the film about them for the first series of *World of Survival*. These days, we're always under pressure to make a film in the shortest time possible – that's all down to budgetary constraints. But the time we invested in the early days of my TV career paid dividends in enabling me to build relationships and to better understand the people we were filming.

For the last episode of the second and final series of *World of Survival*, we returned to Australia, this time to its Central Desert. This is the red heart of the continent, some 200 miles south-west of Uluru – or what we in the West know as Ayers Rock. It's indicative of the vastness of Australia that the coastal rains hardly ever reach there, so drought is common. Don't be fooled by the trees and shrubs that dot the landscape – they're specially adapted to desert conditions. The same goes for the Pitjantjatjara Aborigines, or Anangu as they refer to themselves, who inhabit this part of Australia; they've had over 40,000 years to acclimatise.

The earliest explorers of Australia were astonished by the Anangu's ability to travel with impunity across land that they believed to be devoid of water. The secret was that their elders had told them stories about the landscape from childhood, detailing the location of every source of water to be found. That said, if those early explorers had been standing on top of the water, they might never have known it; many of the water sources are below ground. The water they contain seeped off the landscape when there were rains and ran down the rock into a sort of basin under the desert floor. The basins are filled with sand, which protects the water from evaporation

by the sun. When you dig down to the rock, the water starts to bubble up through the soil. The Anangu place grass over it, which acts as a filter. What they collect at first is a brownish colour but once this is done, the well begins to produce crystal-clear, perfectly clean water.

We were there with the Pitjantjatjara because I wanted to focus on their spiritual and religious beliefs, something that, despite our best efforts, we weren't able to do in the first programme. There were several reasons for this: firstly, the interests of the director of that film didn't seem to lie in that direction. If you're not interested, it comes through in the end product. This is an important and often overlooked factor; the director *has* to have an interest in the subject for the film to be effective. You see that in movies all the time. If you look at the work of my favourite movie directors, the Coen brothers, the depth of detail in their films, the deep characterisation and the mood they build is a result of their own personal interest in them. And the same is true in television.

Another reason we had trouble was that, in Arnhem Land, modern Australia is largely shut out. Contact with the outside world is controlled by the Aboriginal people themselves and this has enabled them to retain their culture. They're exceptionally protective of it, so they are reticent about even discussing their belief system with outsiders. In fact, the law by which they abide – their tribal and cultural law – prevents them from doing so.

By contrast, the Pitjantjatjara have had much more frequent contact with white Australia over the years and, because of that, they have had to confront the issue of how to communicate their belief systems with outsiders. I thought that gave us a much greater chance of recording this information and we'd also be able to show the viewer a different Aboriginal people in a different place. Too often, people think Native Americans and Aborigines are all the same, and of course

they're not – they're very diverse and very individual and for me it's very important to show that.

I was keen that we should avoid, wherever possible, using 'white' words to describe the Aboriginal belief system while we were there. This was important because I had come to realise that almost every description of Aboriginal beliefs was constructed by Western societies and that none of the terms seemed to do justice to the complexity of what they were describing. In the past, people covering this have spoken about 'song lines' and 'dreaming tracks' and 'the dreamtime' but I was very keen to avoid such clichéd terms because they're meaningless, really. Those words don't portray anything of what's involved in how indigenous Australians live their lives. We were very lucky in that we worked with a group of people there who were able to provide definitions for concepts, in English, that they were happy with. That said, when I'm trying to tell a Westerner about it, it's sometimes helpful to call it something 'white' for ease of reference. It's a shame that I have to do this, but often we just don't have a word or phrase that truly explains it, so 'as-near-as' has to suffice.

Very early on in our stay I had a conversation with one of the elders of the community. I explained that I'd worked with Aboriginals previously, and he knew the name of the tiny outstation in Arnhem Land where I'd filmed the earlier episode. But he wasn't finished.

'That oul fella der?' he asked, in the strange but rather delightful pidgin English that they use.

'Yes,' I replied, amazed. He actually knew the name of one of the old men we'd worked with there. I was astonished. This man was of a different tribe, thousands of miles away, in the tiniest community I'd ever come across anywhere. It was the equivalent of me knowing the names of everyone in the phone book for the Isle of Arran. I was completely blown away. As incredible as this was, it also helped because once the elder

realised I'd worked with another tribe, he was different with me. It was like kicking off from where I'd left off in Arnhem Land, so I didn't have to start building a rapport right from the beginning.

————◆————

The Pitjantjatjara have lands that cover an area of almost 40,000 square miles, and a population of 3,500. We were filming among the 500-strong community of Amata who, while they still fiercely maintain their religion, are also forward-thinking. They have a clinic and a school because they want the younger generation to benefit from healthcare and education. But, conversely, Anangu families still return to the bush because of their religion. They believe that at the beginning of time, creatures both human and animal wandered over the land, shaping it. They believe that the landscape they inhabit – the hills, the rocks, the lakes, the pools, the canyons . . . everything – was created in the 'Dreaming' (to the Anangu it's known as the *Tjukurrpa*) by ancestral beings (or ancestral spirits). In most stories, these beings came to earth in human form and invented everything, not just the rocks, animals and plants but also the relationships between groups and individuals to the land, animals and other people.

Once this 'Creation' was done, the ancestral spirits became trees, stars, rocks, watering holes and other objects that are the 'sacred places' of Aboriginal culture and hold special properties. This means that the ancestors never disappear but remain on these sacred sites, linking past and present, people and land.

As an example, you might look at a cave on a hillside and this might be where a particular ancestor slept one night; then three days' walking distance further along you'd see a cluster of large boulders where this ancestor may have eaten too many

onions and vomited them out. These stories are very, very important and are tremendously significant to Aboriginal people. They pass on vital knowledge, cultural values and belief systems to later generations and it's done through story-telling, song, dance and art.

And they have so many meanings and uses. One of the things that the community use them for is to navigate. This is their map, so if you're an Aboriginal person in your tribal territory you will know the stories of your spirit ancestors in your territory; you will know where all the sacred sites are and where not to linger in case you might fall ill. Traditionally, each sacred site will have a caretaker – a responsibility handed down from their ancestors – and this is as much a part of their way of life as is breathing. I remember reading a quote somewhere and I think it was from a clan elder. It went something like: 'Our story is in the land . . . it is written in those sacred places . . . My children will look after those places. That is the law.'

There will be some stories in your territory for which you are the traditional owner, and you will have the responsibility for looking after the animals associated with those stories and the ceremonies and the songs that go with it. You will pass down what you were taught and what you have learned to your children, and so it goes on.

Traditionally, Aboriginal people would migrate through the country, moving in an annual round – or biannual sometimes, if the distances were too long – travelling from site to site to site, performing rituals and ceremonies to ensure stories of the Creation and the Dreaming stayed alive, living off the land as they went.

Finding food is a complex thing in Australia – it isn't like finding it in Europe. In Europe and most of the Western world you can predict by season and by habitat where you'll find a blackberry or where you'll find a sloe berry, but in many parts

of Australia this is very difficult. A bush in one area might be ripe while the same bush nearby might not be. So it's traditional, long-held experience and the knowledge of the elders that enabled the Pitjantjatjara to move to the right place at the right time. There's a very subtle relationship between the landscape and their lifestyle; being settled in one place for too long could break that connection.

So, as you can see, the *Tjukurrpa* is absolutely fundamental to Anangu life. It contains the knowledge of how to survive in their country and is the law that binds them both physically and spiritually to the land. Law is a 'white' word though – in Pitjantjatjara terms, it means so much more.

It's such a hard thing for us in the West to comprehend, because these stories depict the very essence of existence for these wonderful people. They are all-encompassing: traditional knowledge, education, religion, responsibilities, behaviour, law – it's all in there. The *Tjukurrpa* is their law and their tradition; it's their heritage, and it's a concept, and it's more expansive than any word we have in our lexicon. *Tjukurrpa* is the spiritual focus of the people, their spiritual guidance; it's also their history; it's their very essence, really, and it's multi-dimensional. Notice I said it's partly the 'law'; by that I mean if you break any of its tenets, the consequences are severe and potentially life-changing. Respect for the *Tjukurrpa* is so strong, it can be a struggle for some Anangu to even talk about it. Given that breaking it can mean they or their family may be ritually speared and killed, it's no surprise really.

When I was working with them, I'd say: 'I want to ask you a question now. If you are unable to answer this question because of your responsibilities, just say you can't answer and I will try to rephrase it in a way that you can.'

And so with a great amount of very painstaking effort, we would have conversations that could then be recorded to enable

us to capture something of the essence. It's very difficult because television is a medium that was created by 'us', in 'our' world, and my experience of working with the Australian Aboriginal people is that they see the world in a multi-dimensional way – that's the only way I can describe it. Time is a more fluid concept for Aborigines than it is for us. Maybe they're string theorists, but I think that modern physical theory regarding the concept of time certainly has some resonance with an Aboriginal perspective.

When we were making that programme, there was an old woman (who's passed away now, so I cannot use her name) who was very concerned that the young weren't taking on the knowledge of the past. So she was more willing to talk to people outside of her culture who were interested because she was worried that the knowledge would disappear.

Anyway, this old woman enabled us to go down what we might previously have called call a song line or dream track; it's a pathway, a story pathway left by a very important ancestral spirit. One of the places we went to told the story of the Perentie lizard man. The Perentie lizard is a big monitor lizard with round circular markings on its body, and we followed this story. For me, it's important to engross myself in these things in an Aboriginal way and not question or try to put the story in a Western context. I find even talking about it now is difficult because I have to use our words to describe something that is much more than our words are capable of describing.

Anyway, she took us down this track, we filmed it and we eventually came to a place where there was some bedrock – about the size of a breeze block – sticking out of the sand. To find that in the desert, even with the benefit of eight-figure GPS co-ordinates, would be tricky enough. At this rock she wanted to perform a regeneration ceremony and she asked me to perform the act of rubbing this rock. On its side, it had the same marking that you find on the Perentie lizard. It wasn't made by people, it was a geological formation, but this to

them was the Perentie lizard man and, by rubbing it with another rock, there would be a regeneration of a part of the story that was associated with an edible mistletoe that is found in the desert there. We could not stay there for more than twenty minutes, or she said we would fall ill.

So it was a one-take special. We did our bit, I said what I was expected to say to the camera – under her direction (for which I got a thumbs up) – and we left. Part of the purpose of these regeneration ceremonies is to ensure the continuous abundance of the resources associated with them, and about three days later, when we were filming again, I had a little bit of time where I wasn't involved. I just happened to be looking to my right when I realised I was looking at a mistletoe bush and realised it had just come into fruit in the time we had been there. Of course, I made the connection between this and the regeneration ceremony. And then I looked to my left and there was this old woman watching me, and she smiled and just gave me the thumbs up again, almost as if to say, 'You understand.' That was a very special moment for me.

———◆———

There were many times when we were filming that our hosts would take us to sacred sites of significance. Initially, they'd tell us we couldn't film but they'd add that they'd like to involve us, as it was about getting the message across. This is one of the reasons why I feel it's so important to have the right crew on these films – people like Barrie and Sam, who were with me on this trip, or Alan and Andy; people who would respect these privileges, who wouldn't laugh about them and who wouldn't in any way denigrate them. In taking part, we were then better able to communicate what they were actually trying to show us. As budgets and time constraints narrow, film crews are less and less able to connect in this way.

Leaving the Anangu was a bittersweet moment for me, and I think for Barrie and Sam too. With them, the other crew of Alan and Andy, and Kath Moore, who produced both series, I'd forged a strong bond. We'd been on a journey together that was as spiritual as it was physical. We'd racked up hundreds of thousands of air miles over the course of the two years it took us to make both series, and while I was on a learning curve that filled in some of the gaps in my knowledge of bushcraft, so too were they; they were learning a great many outdoor skills through osmosis – often without them realising. Our strength as a team would see us all the way through to the present day.

16

Reflections

After twenty-six hours of flying, three planes, a Jeep, a hydrofoil and finally a canoe trip, we arrived in Seram for the Spice Islands episode in the second series of *World of Survival*. Seram was home to the Nuaulu, the most feared tribe of headhunters in the world. The Dutch ran these islands for over two hundred years, all the while trying to pacify the warrior peoples of the jungle interior, and the Nuaulu eventually stopped taking the heads of their victims. That was the theory anyway; in reality, the current chief was in jail for beheading someone during an argument just four years previously.

When we finally arrived in the rainforest, it took us most of the afternoon to set up camp. We rigged our hammocks about a mile from the village we were filming in and, just as it was getting dark, our interpreter showed up to tell us there was a problem.

As the chief was in jail, a man from the village was nominated as his stand-in. This upset the chief's brother who felt that *he* should have been appointed as interim leader, especially as we were paying the Nuaulu for allowing us to film them. He'd come to the village and was threatening to find us and 'have a word'. The interpreter said he couldn't quite understand the brother's intentions, due to the nuances of the Nuaulu language, but he suggested it might be advisable for us if we

didn't camp out as the brother had been drinking heavily. He was also armed, as all Nuaulu usually are, with a razor-sharp machete.

The interpreter wasn't panicking; in fact he was very calm, which made it worse in many ways. He very calmly told us there was a risk that we might be attacked by machete in the middle of the night.

It took us less than five minutes to de-rig, load up the vehicles and get out of there. Luckily, we established good relations with the brother the following day and moved back into the jungle. It wasn't the most auspicious start to that episode, though.

Alan filmed the Nuaulu collecting palm grubs that were burrowing in a rotting sago palm. They're a popular food for the Nuaulu, packed with protein. The director asked me to eat one, which I did, but I didn't want it to make the final film because I didn't want to get a reputation as someone who is famous just for eating strange foods for the sake of it. I was always very selective about which bush foods I'd eat, simply because I think there's a propensity to show gratuitous 'bug eating' which doesn't add anything or inform the viewer – it's all about entertainment, and to me that's never good because it drowns out whatever message you're trying to get across.

———◆———

Another episode of the second series saw us filming in Tanzania, where we were making a film about the Hadza who live in the Great Rift Valley. This enormous fissure is visible from space and extends over 6,000 miles, all the way from Mozambique, through East Africa and into Turkey. Numbering fewer than a thousand people, the Hadza are one of the last remaining tribes of true hunter-gatherers left anywhere in the world.

We'd followed some of the Hadza boys to get some footage of them practising their hunting skills, shooting at birds and lizards with their bows and arrows. On returning to the vehicles, Annette Martin who was directing, leapt in to our Land Rover and locked the door when it was pointed out that there was a snake on the path directly by her feet. I love the fact she instinctively locked the door after her – as if the snake could have opened it when it was unlocked! One of the boys shot at the snake, but he missed. Ever the director and always thinking of the next shot, Annette wound down the window:

'Alan, why don't you move the arrow so you can film it?' she said, pointing to the arrow lying just a few inches from the snake.

Alan had no idea whether the snake was poisonous or not but, given our location and the numerous poisonous snakes in the region, I suspected he wasn't about to take any chances.

'You're much closer than I am, so if you want to move the arrow, I'll be more than happy to get the footage.'

That made her think twice. Strangely, she decided that particular clip wasn't so important after all . . .

Then there was another moment when Gudo, who was the main Hadza contributor, was demonstrating how to make poison for his arrows. He did this by mashing up desert rose root, squeezing the juice from it into my mug, and heating it to concentrate the liquid. Gudo got the juice boiling then walked away, leaving Alan to film a close up of the liquid bubbling away. As he moved in, the interpreter came over.

'Alan, be careful!'

He said that the fumes are more poisonous than the paste that's left behind!

Sometimes, it's nice to know these things in advance.

One of the things that struck me about that was that after they'd boiled the liquid up in my mug and given it back to me, they told me that not only had they washed it out, they'd

also tested it by drinking from it to make doubly sure that it was now safe to use. I was really touched by that.

Before we left, I presented Gudo with a bow and some arrows that I'd had made by Christopher Boyton, my old friend and perhaps the world's greatest living bowyer. Gudo was delighted with it and sang to it as he carried it away, patting it by his side. He returned a short time later and said it shot like a rifle, and that it was much more powerful than their native bows. I was over the moon that he was so pleased with it, although I felt a little deflated the next day when we learnt that he'd sold it to buy some beer. Alan and Andy had a good laugh at that. Me? I was sanguine about it because even if Gudo wasn't using it for hunting, somebody somewhere sure was.

That reminds me of an incident when we went on to film with the Maasai for another episode in the series. I built a temporary *boma* from thorn branches for us to sleep in overnight. The thorns were huge; I actually had one pierce my hand and come out the other side, but that was one of the reasons we used them – their sharpness and size meant that they afforded a degree of protection to us against predators of the night.

There were two Maasai guys with us and one of them was dressed in traditional Maasai robes so he really looked the part. The other Maasai was a ranger and so was dressed in the appropriate uniform and carried a rifle and rucksack. Something was lost in translation though because for some reason the Maasai in traditional robes thought I'd built the *boma* for fun; he was quite taken aback when I told him we would be sleeping there because although he looked the part, he was completely unequipped to sleep out.

For a further episode of *World of Survival*'s second series, we also filmed in the Amazon rainforest with the Sanema, who

live in the jungle near the headwaters of the Orinoco, close to Venezuela's border with Brazil. The Sanema are hunter-gatherers and their lifestyle has remained almost unchanged for over 10,000 years. Their only concession to modernity is that they've incorporated agriculture into their way of life and cassava has become their staple food.

We had to take a small plane from Ciudad Bolivar to the Sanema's settlement and missionary station, and I'd flown in with director J.P. Davidson ahead of Alan and Andy. Alan was very excitable when they arrived a few days later.

'We had to leave some of our kit behind, Ray,' he told me.

'Oh?' I asked.

'Yeah, when Andy and I got to the airport the pilot looked at our equipment and told us we'd need to leave some of it behind. I know you think we carry too much with us, but we actually travel about as light as is possible for a film crew. Everything in the excess baggage that we travel with on each expedition is necessary.'

I smiled. 'Go on . . .'

'In the end, I had to leave some camera batteries behind as well as the monitor so we won't be able to watch the footage back. The pilot said that the landing strip we were using also doubles as a football pitch for the local villagers, who remove the goal posts whenever a plane needs to land. The strip is on a bit of a slope, and to take off the aircraft has to accelerate down the slope and then make a sharp left once airborne to avoid a ridge immediately to the front and across the river. If we hadn't left some of our kit behind, we wouldn't have been able to gain enough height to clear the ridge. To ram the point home, as we took off, the pilot pointed out the broken aluminium fuselage – complete with grass growing through it – of a plane that didn't make it.' Obviously, travelling light has its advantages.

As it happened, towards the end of our time with the Sanema, J.P. wanted to play back to the villagers some of what we'd captured during our stay, but as Alan had had to leave the monitor behind all we had was a 2x3 inch square LCD screen that we used to check colour. One of my enduring memories from that trip is J.P. inside a hut before some sixty or more villagers. They were all looking up, trying to see the tiny screen he was holding aloft in his hand, and it looked for all the world like he was some kind of alien god and they were all looking towards him for guidance.

Some god! Somewhat ill-advisedly, J.P. had a tendency to wear sneakers in the jungle and he ended up with an infection in his foot. It turned out to be jiggers, which are tiny parasites that burrow into the skin and lay their eggs. Removing them is relatively straightforward and painless and involves using a needle in much the same way that you would to remove a splinter just beneath the skin. I know the sole of your foot is sensitive, but even so I was a little surprised that J.P. yelped as I held his foot to hook the egg sack away. Especially as I hadn't started yet. That really made Alan and Andy laugh. J.P. saw the funny side too . . . eventually.

We got in the habit of bathing in the river and using an eco-friendly soap that we'd brought with us. There was a young Sanema boy who followed us everywhere. We nicknamed him 'Chatterbox' as he would talk to us constantly even though we had no common language between us. He'd also stand in the doorway of our hut giving a running commentary to the rest of the village; he never, ever shut up. Then one day, he asked us for some of our soap while we were bathing in the river, and before long it seemed like every boy from the village was in the water with us, washing. The soap we were using lathered up really well and all the boys started sporting foam beehives on their heads. It had

us in hysterics because they looked for all the world like Marge Simpson.

———◆———

Whereas every other film we made focused on remote indigenous people, we did a film in India for the second series that was unique in that it focused on a rather congested area. We were filming on the Coromandel Coast on India's Bay of Bengal and what's different here is the degree of intimacy in terms of how people live. This is the heart of the caste system and every person in the village has a single skill. They all live cheek-by-jowl on the beach, sandwiched between the sea on one side and a main road on the other. Conditions weren't great – there was no privacy whatsoever and we were watched constantly day and night.

There was a short opportunity before sunrise to go to the toilet without too much attention down by the water's edge. Unfortunately, everyone else goes there too, so when Alan was out filming the fishing boats being launched, he said he would sometimes be aware of something in the surf running across his foot. It would invariably be a human turd gently rolling along in the waves.

———◆———

I'd really enjoyed my work on *World of Survival*, so I was delighted when the BBC offered me the chance to make a series called *Extreme Survival*. This reunited me with Alan, Barrie, Sam and Andy on a number of shoots that took us, once again, all round the world to some of its most remote and little-known locations. The series was broadcast in the run-up to the new millennium and, after we were back in England and settled, I invited Alan and Barrie round one evening for dinner. It's all

well and good reflecting on the stand-out moments on your own, but together we'd often trigger other memories in each other as we talked. Fed and watered, we retired to my lounge with some fine whisky.

———◆◆◆———

Alan kicks things off, and the conversation goes something like this:

'Remember when we were in Alaska filming the story of the Wortman family at Rose Inlet?'

'Yeah, I remember that,' I say. 'That was on the site of a dilapidated, remote canning factory from Victorian times. We stayed on a boat and were able to go out on the dinghy to fish at the end of each day and have a beer or two.'

'That's it!' Alan says. 'That was where I caught that large salmon that you cooked for us on camera in your own inimitable way. Remember, Dan, the captain would say, "It doesn't get any better than this . . ."?'

'Yes,' I interrupt, 'except it did. The next day we saw a bear by the water's edge and Dan said, "It doesn't get better than this," and it became something of a mantra. Every day it *did* seem to get better, but I don't think anything topped us seeing a whale dive a couple of times, raising its tail out of the water. That was something really special.'

'Barrie,' says Al. 'When Ray and I did the expedition in Costa Rica, the director wanted me to film a sequence with Ray using his *parang* to hack his way through the rainforest.'

I laugh as he says this. 'It was completely ridiculous because nobody ever hacks through the jungle like that – it's the sort of thing Bogart might have done in the movies back in the 1940s. Neither do you walk through the rainforest with your face spattered with mud. You look for game trails and walk through them, not hack your own path through

the vegetation! Honestly, the things we have to do to make an image.'

'So he did it in the end, Barrie,' Al continues. 'He's walking through the vegetation with a razor-sharp *parang* in his hand cutting and slashing the thick vines and branches as he goes. Sam and I had climbed up a slope slightly ahead of Ray and the plan was for him to stop as he got to us.'

'Yeah, I know,' I say sheepishly. 'You told me to stop after I'd made several strokes but you suddenly shouted out, "Ray, watch out! That's Sam's audio cab . . ." and you said it just as I brought the blade down and cut what I thought was another vine in two.'

'Yeah, except it wasn't another vine, it was the cable from Sam's portable mixer to his headphones. Ray looks up and there's Sam looking baffled and twiddling knobs on the mixer because he couldn't hear anything!'

'It looked just like a vine,' I say defensively, 'and he *did* have a spare.' Barrie and Al laugh at the recollection.

'I did a shoot with Ray in Arctic Sweden,' says Barrie, 'and it was one of their coldest winters. It was -40°C and I was shooting from a helicopter in the usual position, door open, feet on the skids.'

'It must have been -70°C with the wind chill,' I tell him. 'Wasn't that when my Ski-Doo packed up? It was just as well, as I recall, because your head cover had slipped and you had mild frostbite on your face!'

'That was painful, but you know us, Ray . . . anything to get the shot!'

'Wasn't that the gig where it was Ray's birthday in the middle of the trip?' asks Alan.

'It was. We were there to follow the Swedish Army Survival instructors' final test, where they have to survive for a week with just a sleeping bag and the means to light a fire,' I say.

'That's right,' Barrie offers, 'and afterwards, you were snug

in the warmth of a Sami tepee interviewing your great friend Lars.'

'Yes,' I say, 'I thought it was strange that you had the camera mounted on the tripod – you'd have normally hand-held for something like that.'

'And you know why, don't you?' says Barrie mischievously. I smile.

'I had the camera favouring Lars, but with Ray in shot,' Barrie tells Alan. 'Rachel had told me it was his birthday before we left and she asked me to give him her present. That was why I asked Ray to cheat his eye line away from the camera slightly and then asked him to look straight down the lens. It was that moment that I pushed the custard pie in his face . . .'

'And said "Happy Birthday from Rachel!"' I say, laughing.

'I thought you took it quite well, mate, considering,' says Barrie.

Alan grins. 'Closer to home, one of my favourite memories is from when we were filming in the Forest of Dean. Do you remember, Ray?'

'Yes, I do. We went to a pub for our evening meal, and the place was empty until about five to eight when it suddenly filled up. We were playing darts and had to grab a table because it was quiz night.'

'That's it,' laughs Alan. 'We did quite well, Barrie, and we were in second place halfway through. The last round was via TV, with us watching a cartoon clip and answering questions about it afterwards. Because of our different disciplines we all noticed different things and scored full marks, winning a bottle of wine and four Snickers bars.'

'Yes, as I recall, the team next to us had been leading and were most put out.'

Alan laughed out loud: 'Yes, they asked us if we were coming again the following week in a tone that said we most definitely wouldn't be welcome!'

I look at them both. 'One of the things I like about working with you guys is how you're not afraid to roll up your sleeves and get involved in the nitty-gritty. Including, Barrie, your willingness to try most of the edible offerings I've tried.'

'Yes, you do enjoy your food, Ray,' Barrie replies. 'I think I've probably eaten everything that's been offered, including witchetty grubs – although I couldn't have done that with them alive and raw as the Aborigines do. They weren't too bad cooked.'

'Rather you than me,' Alan says. 'They're not my cup of tea at all.'

'I've eaten various insects,' Barrie continues, 'but the honey ants are my favourite. That sweet liquid that swells their abdomens is delicious. I'm trying to think what else I've eaten . . . there was porcupine, raw seal, emu, iguana – I was happy to try them all.

'However I did refuse one offer when we were filming Ray's first series in Arnhem Land. One of the Aborigines' favourite delicacies – you know, the teredo worm that lives in rotten wood in saltwater areas. I filmed Ray with the locals digging them out, taking hold of the head and biting off the raw white slimy body.'

'That's right, it's delicious – it tastes like crab pâté.'

'In your dreams, Mears!' is Barrie's retort.

When I finish laughing, he carries on, 'Hey Ray, remember the first shoot you ever did with Ben [Southwell]?'

'Yeah, *Tracks* wasn't it?'

'That's right,' says Barrie. 'He had just finished working on *The Clothes Show*, Al, and Ray told him that this was different – it was nature and he couldn't control it so he'd just have to go with the flow. We were filming fire lighting with a bow drill and of course at the crucial moment he got me to stop filming so that I could reposition the camera.'

'I'd forgotten that,' I say, smiling. 'The ember was lost and I pointed out that the hearth was now exhausted. Ben said

something along the lines of, "Surely we could just get another bit of wood from around us?"'

'Yeah, we were in the middle of a wood, but hearths need certain types of wood to work, as you know, and there was no tree of that type anywhere near us. Ben ended up running all the way back to the vehicles to get a replacement hearth,' says Barrie.

I chuckle at the recollection: 'I think he was worried it could have been the end there and then, but we're still working together. What's that? Twelve years now?'

'One of my favourite memories,' Alan says, 'was when we were filming in Venezuela. We were right in the middle of nowhere and Matt, who was the associate producer for that programme, spotted a team of scientists studying the rainforest.'

'That's right, they were being resupplied and he got them to bring a cool box to us filled with chilled beers,' I add.

'Aye,' says Alan, 'that was quite something. Several days into a trip in the heart of the rainforest and we were able to have a few cold beers in the evening. Now *that's* perfection!'

'I forget where we were when we did this but Ben wanted a showroom dummy for a sequence to show the type of clothes you'd wear in the mountains,' Barrie says.

'I remember that,' I tell him. 'The dummy had a bendy wire frame so we doubled it over and bound it up so we could send it via the aircraft's hold. When we got back into Heathrow, everyone in the baggage hall took a sharp intake of breath because when it came out, it looked like there was a body on the luggage carousel.'

'Hey Barrie, did Andy ever tell you about when we played *Who Wants to be a Millionaire* in Morocco?' says Alan.

'No, I don't think he did.'

'It was funny really. It was really big on TV then and one of the guys – I think it was Matt, one of the researchers – had

brought the *Who Wants to be a Millionaire* book with him for us to play round the fire in the evenings.

'Half of the book had the relatively easy questions in – you know, the £50, £100, £250, £500 ones and the last three pages of the book contained the £1,000,000 questions. We'd agreed among ourselves before we played that you'd have to take the first question on whichever page you turned to for that particular round – there'd be no scanning down the page looking for questions you knew the answer to.

'So we're sat around the fire one evening playing *Who Wants to be a Millionaire* and taking it in turns. You could ask the audience, which basically meant everyone around the camp fire, or phone a friend, which meant picking one person who you thought might know the answer. Matt knew about football, so if it was a football question, you'd ask him.

'Old Mears here just didn't want to know, though, did you?!'

'I was happy to play a part and answer as a friend or part of the audience,' I protest.

'Yeah, but that was in name only, generally,' Barrie replies. He goes on, turning to Alan: 'He didn't answer at all as I recall, and this went on for a couple of nights. Eventually I said, "Look, it's only a bit of fun – I mean Andy could only just about answer: 'Mary had a little . . . what?' so it's not like we're taking it at all seriously." Anyway, eventually Ray said he'd have a go, didn't you?'

I nod sheepishly.

'I kind of wish we hadn't bothered, to be honest,' says Alan laughing, 'because of course, you got all the way through to the £500,000 question and the first question on the page was "What's the Latin for hazelnut?" and of course, Ray knows most of the Latin names for all the flora and fauna so he went straight on to the £1,000,000 question.'

'Don't tell me . . .' says Barrie.

'Yep,' says Alan. 'The first question on the page was for

the Latin name of some obscure plant or other and he knew what that was so he went straight through and won the million! We'd been playing for three days and hadn't got anywhere near the top, and then Ray jumps in at the last minute and bang!'

'It was luck more than anything else,' I say. And it was really – I mean, what are the chances of the two last questions both being related to any area of the outdoors like that? If they'd been about popular culture or something, I'd have fallen flat on my face.

'Anyway,' says Barrie, looking wistfully at his empty glass. 'Who's for another one?'

I can see this evening isn't going to be ending anytime soon . . .

17

The Jedi in the Jungle

In 2001, the BBC invited me to make a one-off programme called *Trips Money Can't Buy*, which would involve me taking a 'celebrity' into some remote and faintly exotic wilderness. I wasn't keen on the concept, because I didn't want to propagate the myth that nature's harsh, and that therefore whoever I took with me was going to struggle. In reality, that's not how nature works. Yes, it can be harsh, but all you need are the skills to survive. What they had in mind was, I think, more about entertainment than education and I'm not a showman – I do TV because, as I've said, it's the most effective medium for me to teach and educate those viewers who are interested in bushcraft. I wanted no part in a programme that would take somebody well known out of their comfort zone and into the jungle so that they could be laughed at. That's exactly the sort of television show that I dislike.

That said, I considered how we might turn it around and still make an interesting programme and I thought, 'OK, these are intelligent people. If I give them proper tuition, they'll have a rich and enjoyable experience.' And I put forward the proposal that we should take a movie star to the jungle – it would be a tough trip but whoever we took would learn a lot.

Cue my agent Jackie. I first came across Jackie when she did some publicity for me. It also turned out she'd gone to the girls' school less than a mile from Downside, my prep school,

so our paths may even have crossed when we were much younger. I'd had some agents previously but nobody who represented me as skilfully as Jackie. Over the years, she has become a dear friend.

Most people, including me, are somewhat naive when they first get into television. I'm sure the world thinks that you're taught to be a TV presenter, but of course you're not. Jackie's background was perfect – she grew up in television and has a long family involvement in that media. She's also a very nice person, very straight, and she has a clear sense of right and wrong and fair play. She is not a short-term player; she's there because she wants to make some sort of long-term contribution to the whole process. You hear of some agents out there who think that to be effective they have to be horribly aggressive and nasty. Jackie isn't like that. She's a lovely person, dedicated and very professional She also has great ideas . . .

Cue Ewan McGregor – Jackie got in contact with him and he was up for it right from the off, which was brilliant. We couldn't have picked anyone better.

It's important for me that I get across there was no artifice here; I don't do pretence – things are what they are, so I deal with whatever an expedition confronts me with, and that goes for anyone who is with me, so everything is done for real. And that's one of the things I loved about Ewan – he didn't gripe, there were no airs and graces on his part, no ego. He really bought into the whole experience and from the minute he agreed to take part, he just threw himself into it 100 per cent.

We met at my old stamping ground the Royal Geographical Society in Kensington and I guess he must have felt a sense of trepidation but if so, it was never noticeable – he really engaged. I thought it was a bold move for him – he was then, and remains today, a big box-office A-list actor. At the time, he'd just made *Moulin Rouge* and *Star Wars* so he was a hugely bankable star. He had no idea at the time how doing this gig

would affect his reputation, but then I think that's one of the things about him that sets him apart from his peers. To him, acting's just a job much like any other, and he's got no interest in the red carpet stuff, the fame and the trappings. I think he sees himself as a regular guy whose job is making films. He enjoys it, but it's work, and when he's finished he goes back home to his wife Eve and their children, and he lives his life. I like that.

It was important to me that we weren't trying to catch him out; quite the opposite in fact. Also, it wasn't TV work for me, it was just another expedition, so I never felt like I was making a programme and maybe that comes across. I just felt like I was doing my job, which in that case was to take care of Ewan and make sure that he had the best experience possible.

There was a point to the programme – it wasn't just about Ewan and me walking through the jungle while Alan filmed us. We would be on the trail of the remains of an ancient civilisation so the journey would fall into two halves – down river into the heart of the rainforest to the site of some ancient artefacts, and then a three-day trek to a newly discovered archaeological site. For poor old Ewan, there was only one way out and that was forwards. We would have ten days to reach the helicopter landing site on the far side of the jungle, and they would prove to be ten eventful days, to say the least.

I was working with Ben Southwell, a director who is absolutely top rate, and a very, very talented guy. He's creative, he's got a strong visual style and a good editorial mind, so he brings all the tools that are needed for good, effective film-making. He's decisive so he always has a clear vision of the film he wants to make. He doesn't overshoot, he's very good on logistics and also very good with people. He doesn't have an ego that gets in the way – he's a real team player. It's not an easy job, directing, but it was a pleasure working with him.

Like any film of this nature, it's essential that you undertake

a reconnaissance trip before you make the actual programme, in order to iron out any potential problems and get some idea of the sort of obstacles that you're likely to come up against. The bottom line was that, whether he likes it or not, Ewan's a valuable commodity, so in effect we were undertaking a risk assessment.

We flew out about five weeks before filming the actual programme – Ben, Alan, Andy and me – and did the trip exactly as we were planning to do it with Ewan. I chose Honduras for the expedition into the heart of the rainforest. It's a prickly sort of rainforest because cyclones are a regular occurrence and they disturb the forest, making it more 'spiky'. It's a tough environment to be in.

The weather was awful when we got there. It was very cold, which is not what you generally expect in the jungle. Ben suffered terribly and was verging on hypothermia at one point so we had to stick him in his hammock while I built a fire, and Alan and Andy fed him a steady stream of hot orange squash. It was a bit of a baptism of fire for Ben and also, I guess, something of a rite of passage in terms of him learning how to take care of himself in the jungle and how to stay warm. It's not something you'd generally expect to do in Honduran rainforest. It was a tough old journey.

We encountered several dangerous snakes, too. I was walking up a steep trail beside a waterfall at one point and there was a local guide called Racendo in front of me. Suddenly, he jumped while shouting, 'Aie, aie aie!' and as he was in mid-air he pulled his machete out, span round and there between us was this very large and angry fer-de-lance (a venomous pit viper). Pit vipers get their name from a pit organ between their eyes that sees in infrared so they are able to detect the heat signature of their prey in complete darkness. They then strike with deadly accuracy and it's one of the reasons you don't wander around in the jungle after dark. It doesn't have a rattle,

but it shakes its tail in the leaves when it's annoyed – this is one snake you don't mess with.

That was a red flag for me, and a good heads up on what we could expect when we came back with Ewan. I could just imagine what would have happened if we'd had an A-list actor, halfway through filming the newest *Star Wars* movie, coming to grief by a venomous snake. So I made a note to make sure we brought our own anti-venom with us. Using anti-venom is never straightforward because it's not uncommon for complications to arise. These are far easier to deal with in the confines of a hospital, but not so simple when you're on a muddy trail in the middle of the jungle. The dose of the anti-venom we had with us meant you'd need sixteen separate 30ml injections into the thigh to combat a fer-de-lance bite. That's one very serious snake. In the jungle we'd be at least several days away from rescue once we started the expedition proper so we had to take all that into consideration. You have to ensure you've got literally everything you would need for every eventuality with you.

Ben was putting up his hammock one night and I shouted 'STOP!' – initially because he was going to use the 'wrong' tree but also because I'd looked up and realised there was an eyelash viper right where he was about to place his hands. There are a lot of snakes in Central America and this was just another warning that we'd have to be on our guard. It was things like this that made the fact-finding trip so vital; once we knew what we were going to be up against, we could plan for it to a degree. Forewarned is always forearmed.

It rained heavily for almost the whole time we were there and I remember one night being suddenly awakened by a noise that sounded like a tidal wave hurtling towards us. You know that strange semi-conscious world you inhabit on waking suddenly? I knew in my head that it couldn't possibly have been a tidal wave but semi-awake thought is no respecter of

logic when your mind is seeking a rational explanation. It sounded just like a tsunami and the noise lasted for ages and seemed to be getting closer and closer . . . and then it just stopped. The next morning when we left the camp, we discovered a giant tree in the rainforest had come down and the noise was caused by all the vines breaking as it fell to the ground. When I say it was giant, it truly was – it took us an hour to cut a trail around it.

We were supposed to be extracted by helicopter but the weather was still so bad that it couldn't fly. We ended up staying in a small village in the middle of nowhere and spent days standing at the landing area listening intently for the whirring sound of rotor blades. We were running out of time because I had another commitment to undertake back in England and eventually we could wait no longer. A dugout canoe was found to take us down river where a float plane would pick us up and fly us back to the Honduran capital, Tegucigalpa. Of course, no sooner were we heading down river in the canoe and settling in for a journey of many hours when our helicopter buzzed over the boat, before landing on a pebble bank in a bend in the river. The way that the helicopter just appeared out of nowhere and landed in the middle of the river felt like something straight from a James Bond movie.

Five weeks later, we were back with Ewan. We'd established a good relationship on the journey over and I'd seen flashes of his sense of humour on the flight, but I really knew we'd get on while we were waiting to have our equipment checked through US Customs so we could catch our onward flight to Tegucigalpa. Ewan was at the back of the queue with Alan and me, and apropos of nothing, he adopted the voice of Alec Guinness as Obi-Wan Kenobi in *Star Wars* and said: 'These

are not the men you are looking for. They can go about their business, move along, move along.'

He had perfect comic timing, but it was the way he said it so drily and without warning. It was just perfect and I knew for certain at that moment that Ewan and I would get on famously.

When we finally got to Tegucigalpa, it was just like the start of any other expedition. There's a kind of surreal atmosphere that exists around the preparations because, even with prior reconnaissance, until you've got mud on your boots you're never really sure what you're going to be dealing with. The other thing is, you can't make a programme like this on your own – it's like a full-on expedition except with cameras, so when the helicopter dropped us off at the start site, we were met by a team of helpers and guides, all with experience of the Honduran jungles. They were waiting for us with rafts. And unlike when we'd been there previously on the recce, the sun was shining in a blue sky when we set off down river.

My plan was to make a base camp about twenty minutes downstream so Ewan could acclimatise for a couple of days. It was a nerve-wracking time because some people find the rainforest very claustrophobic and don't get on with it at all, but Ewan was brilliant – he embraced it from the off, really threw his heart and soul into it – and you could tell that he was looking forward to the journey that lay ahead of us.

The white-water rafting was great; Ewan loved that. I think it was about our third day on the river, and both Alan and Andy were in my boat trying to get some footage of Ewan in one of the others. As we were heading down the river, I could see a large rock ahead of us, protruding through the top of the water and, in the time it took for the thought to form in my head and for me to go to warn them, we'd already hit it. Suddenly Alan was six feet up in the air, camera in hand, with Andy not far behind. Alan landed first, but by the time Andy

landed, the boat's forward momentum meant it wasn't there beneath him anymore. I turned round to look just as Andy hit the water. He struggled valiantly to keep his microphone aloft but it was a battle he was never going to win – he was in too deep and his boom mic and sound mixer disappeared beneath the surface with him. For anyone who's up on their Arthurian legends, it was like watching Excalibur disappear into the lake.

It was pointless carrying on at that point so I suggested we stop to allow Andy and his kit to dry out and then we could re-assess. Experience has taught me that normally if you have a problem like that, very often there'll be another problem you haven't noticed. When we took everything apart, a lot of the gear had got wet – the seals on our waterproof cases weren't all as intact as they might have been – and so we spent most of the following day drying our kit out under the sun. We got off pretty lightly, although some of Andy's microphones were banjaxed. We were all pretty accomplished at dealing with problems, although that one was about as bad as it gets: a day lost – as well as some mics.

When we eventually reached our destination, we hiked through the rainforest to some Mayan ruins. We had a Mayan archaeologist with us, from Arkansas, who'd been with us on the reconnaissance and he spoke just like the characters in the film *Deliverance*. Luckily, we'd all swotted up on lines from the film so the poor guy had a miserable journey as we went along with us all shouting out, 'Ain't he got a pretty mouth?' and 'Boy, you gone do some prayin' fo' me,' with a bit of 'Squeal like a piggy' and 'Looks like we got us a sow rather than a boar' thrown in for good measure. He was a great guy and took it all in good heart. He was a real asset in the rainforest – he knew how to take care of himself and I say that without equivocation.

On the pre-expedition trip, we had come across some people cutting down trees in the rainforest in a World Heritage site on the Mosquito Coast. We'd been shocked then; they were turning

it into a coffee plantation. What really surprised and saddened me when we arrived at the same point with Ewan was that in the five or so weeks since we were last there, they'd cut acres and acres of it down and there were men armed with AK-47s guarding it all. The depletion of our rainforests is a real concern and to see it first-hand that day was a shock that upset us all.

Still, we were there for a purpose and had a job to do, and at least the sun was shining, but I'd a feeling it wouldn't be shining for much longer. By day four, the weather returned to what we'd experienced on the reconnaissance trip. Once again, the rainforest was very cold and very wet – the weather was highly unusual but Ewan was brilliant and took it all in his stride. The only moment where he had any difficulty was when Alan wanted to film him cutting up some wood from a carbon tree. It's unusual because you can cut it 'green' and it will still burn but there's a particular way of cutting it with a machete that is difficult even for someone experienced – it's a really skilful job. That said, Ewan was a quick learner, really skilled in fact, but he struggled with this and it frustrated him, so much so, in fact, that he dashed off into the forest and hacked away at a few things. I sat there patiently by my fire, waiting for him to come back and I said to him, 'Ewan, remember there are things out there that can bite,' although perhaps I should have done a Yoda and said, 'Ewan, things out there, bite! They can!'

'Yeah, good point!'

And he looked down at his feet and that was when he realised he'd cut through his boot. There was literally one thread of sock left between his bare foot and where the honed, razor-sharp edge of the machete had last been. That *really* got his attention – the machete I'd given him could have sliced off his foot before he felt it. Luck was really on his side that night. For me, it simply reinforced the fact that '*parang* rash' is far more common than snake bites.

Each night we'd stop to rig our camp about an hour before dusk, and Alan would film Ewan and I setting up, but that meant that invariably he and Andy had to put their hammocks up in the dark. Alan had lashed his hammock to a tall tree, which, unbeknownst to us all, was utterly dead. The roots had completely rotted so there was nothing to hold it up, which meant that when Alan sat in his hammock later that evening, the tree toppled over and he was rather unceremoniously plonked on the ground while the vines and lianas pulled against the canopy. It made quite a noise . . . as did our laughter.

———◆◆———

One afternoon, a couple of days in, a thought struck me that we must have crossed the same river about fifty times as we moved through the jungle. There were mules a bit of a distance behind us carrying our generator and some other equipment, and as we were crossing the river yet again, they must have seen us crossing further up and decided to join us. Unfortunately there was a rapid between us, and we watched them stumble and lose their footing. Of course, the generator slipped off and the next thing we saw it was floating past us down the river. Luckily, the assistant director was an ex-Para and he dived in and managed to recover it.

There was another surreal moment a day or two later when we stopped in a clearing in the rainforest and Ewan used the satellite phone to take a phone call from Ridley Scott, who was calling to offer him the part of John Grimes in *Black Hawk Down*. That was kind of weird, the way our two worlds collided in that moment.

For all that though, Ewan didn't once act the film star. He was just Ewan, and a pleasure to be with. He pulled his weight and had real endurance. In fact, I think one incident really underlines the sort of guy he is and it's indicative of how far

he'd bought into the whole thing. We were at a point where Alan had filmed loads – more than enough to make the programme. So Ben said to him, 'Look Ewan, we've got everything we need, you're more than welcome to put your pack on a mule – that's what they're there for, mate.'

And Ewan didn't even need to think. He was straight back, 'Thanks Ben, but I'm fine carrying it.'

And he did – right up to the very end, which only deepened the respect we'd all come to feel for him. Both Alan and Andy carried all their own kit too and that's hard, especially in a rainforest. Their own packs, plus camera kit and lenses for Alan, sound mixer and mics for Andy – that's a lot to haul around, all the more so given how slippery and muddy it was on that gig. We climbed something like 4,000 metres too, so it was one hell of a tough expedition and I was really impressed with how everyone dug in and engaged.

Eventually, we reached our extraction point and the helicopter came. I have to say, it was really tough saying goodbye to the jungle at the end. It was a really emotional experience for Ewan too, I think – he had tears in his eyes, which told me that while he was glad to be leaving, he was sad about it too. He really got a lot out of it. Obviously he wasn't sure at the beginning how we would treat the whole thing, but he relaxed into it very quickly and I really enjoyed working with him.

He and I were the first out when the helicopter arrived and it felt very strange because we'd been in the jungle for twelve days and we were caked in mud; we must have stank to high heaven and we climbed into this lovely, luxurious cabin of the Squirrel helicopter with its white leather seats. Talk about feeling out of place!

It eventually put us down back on the apron at Tegucigalpa,

and we came out of a side gate at the airfield; it was weird – one minute we were in the middle of the rainforest, soaked through, muddy, living rough, avoiding snakes, and the next we're stood among the full fury of Tegucigalpa during rush hour. That was bizarre. There we were stinking, wet, stood in our green kit with our machetes and people were looking at us wondering, 'Are you mercenaries? Are you with the CIA?'

When Alan, Andy and Ben joined us, we hailed a cab back to our hotel. Of course, it was the height of luxury with a black and white tiled floor that we squelched across with mud oozing out of the drainage holes in our jungle boots. Picture the scene: five guys in the same jungle clothing that we'd had on for the last ten days or so, all unshaven, muddy and generally filthy. It wasn't a pretty picture. The receptionist later told us he thought there'd been a coup d'état and we were there to take over the hotel.

When I got into my room, I walked straight to the bathroom, switched on the shower and stepped into it, hat, rucksack, clothes, boots . . . the lot. I tipped my rucksack out into the water, socks off and into the bin – they could have walked there all by themselves – and then stood under a hot shower for the best part of fifteen minutes. It was delicious.

———◆———

It was a good trip, and I think that Ewan had come to understand the rainforest. A trip like that – a good, honest trip – can have a lasting, profound impact on a person. For me, it was just another day at the office, but for him it was a massive step to go from Hollywood into the snake-filled Honduran rainforest. I'll always have a deep respect for him for that.

18

Looking Up

I feel incredibly privileged that my work over the years has brought me into contact with so many amazing people. There are so many who stand out, and they cover every stratum of society and every age group.

We have an incredibly rich vein of young people out there and they're a long way from the myth perpetuated by some doom-mongering newspapers that paint a dystopian picture of a diaspora of teenagers in hoodies kicking around and causing trouble. Society has always had those, but they represent a minority. The ones you never see mentioned are the polar opposite and they are nowhere better exemplified than by those who aspire to the Duke of Edinburgh Award Scheme.

I've been asked to hand out Gold Awards three times and it humbles me; the stories are truly heart-warming. Presenting those awards is nerve-wracking for me because it's such a big thing for the recipients who have all made such a massive investment to get there. The organisation itself is remarkable in what it has achieved and I have the highest respect for the Duke of Edinburgh himself because his commitment to the award scheme that bears his name is astonishing.

What I love about it is that you don't even have to win an award to benefit. Of course, that's not to detract from those who've won the Gold Award and crossed the finishing line – it's a brilliant achievement – but like many things in life, it's

the journey that's important. There are many who take part but don't necessarily finish but they are still enriched by the process and enjoy the time they spend on it. Yes, they may get a few blisters, but they learn something about themselves that they can draw on at other times and in other circumstances. I believe it helps to give these young adults confidence, which is a wonderful thing. The Scout Association, the Boys' Brigade, the Cadet Force – any organisation that empowers young people to take responsibility for themselves and support themselves engenders something unique to the greater benefit of society.

All the people I've given awards to stand out because they are all amazing. Even if it were possible, I think it's dangerous to single out people for any reason, because inevitably there are certain organisations that will look for somebody who's come from the most appalling and disadvantaged circumstances. As far as I'm concerned, their achievement is no less and no greater than that of someone from another part of society. Anybody who achieves a Bronze, Silver or Gold Award achieves it, and that's it. To my mind they are all amazing.

The Duke of Edinburgh's scheme is incredibly well run. The organisation of awards ceremonies at St James's Palace is truly spectacular and performs like a well-oiled machine in a way that only the Palace can do. The staff there are selflessness personified. The contribution they make and the demands made upon them are quite astonishing. As far as the monarchy is concerned, I do understand where the republicans are coming from, but I think they have departed from the path of wisdom because that part of our heritage isn't something that, if you change your mind, you can recreate. The overall cost of the Royal Family is minuscule compared to how much is gained; it's unquantifiable. You could see from the mood of the people during London 2012 that as a nation we are quite clearly massively pro-Royal, and I think that it's a measure of our

democracy that we are prepared to listen to voices of dissent and give them space.

———◆———

Someone else who graces my amazing person's list is one of our greatest unsung heroes. You know the type: someone who has done a wonderful thing for his country or mankind, but has lived their lives quietly, away from the glare of the media spotlight, and who you have to work very hard to track down. Well, the late Jim Bradley was one such man. I was lucky enough to meet and interview him, and when I did, he was the last man alive who had escaped from the Burma Railroad during World War II. He was a lieutenant in the Royal Engineers and, in the confusion of the early days of the Occupation of Singapore, he had made some escape preparations, just in case. He'd managed to get hold of an escape compass that was disguised as a collar stud and he had a false bottom welded into an Army water canteen of the day, inside which he secreted a prismatic marching compass. When Singapore fell to the Japanese, Jim was sent up the Burma Railroad as a prisoner of war and put to work on the project. At the time, the Japanese engineers who were in charge of the project were killing the labour force through overwork and starvation.

Cholera swept through the camp where Jim was based and he learned he was a carrier of the disease. As soon as this was discovered, he was put behind wire in a different part of the camp with other victims. There were no huts, no beds, and he and others were made to lie on the ground. When they awoke the following morning, they found they'd been sleeping on the partially cremated remains of other cholera victims. Can you imagine the horror? He was then given the job of organising cremation parties for those soldiers in the camp

who succumbed to disease and died. He said he couldn't recall a single day during that period where there were less than four victims; sometimes he'd see men chopping wood in the morning and then being cremated on the wood they'd cut that same evening because they'd have died later that day. It was decided that word had to be got out so Jim and nine others managed to escape into the jungle. Weak, and with no food or other equipment and no survival training, they made their way deeper and deeper inside the jungle until some eight weeks later, when Jim and four others stumbled out alive. They built a raft and went down river but the raft broke up in rapids. They were rescued by local villagers who fed them, looked after them and promptly sold them back to the Japanese.

The Japanese had said they'd execute anyone who escaped, but Jim's life was saved by a British senior officer who could speak Japanese. He intervened on Jim's behalf and explained to the Japanese military that they couldn't execute him because it would be contrary to the code of *Bushido* (a Japanese concept derived from the samurai moral code encompassing frugality, loyalty and honour unto death). He invoked *Bushido* because, he argued, Jim had overcome the jungle which is something even the Japanese soldiers hadn't managed. That meant it would be seen as disrespectful to execute Jim. Instead, they sent him to Outram Road prison, which was the Kempeitai (the Japanese Secret Police) headquarters, and they tortured him. He couldn't describe what they did to him but it must have been terrible.

There were two occasions on which they went too far and expected him to die, so rather than have his death on their conscience, they sent him to Changi Prison, a hellhole where prisoners preyed upon each other just to survive. Word of Jim's exploits had reached there before him and, against the odds, he survived – both times. And both times he was sent back to the Secret Police. Jim became something of a legend at Changi

because he held out against the Kempeitai. It's a remarkable story of endurance and stoicism.

When the war ended and the Japanese surrendered, Jim managed to get home in three days because his story had reached a lot of people: this is the man who was in the hands of the Kempeitai and told them nothing. What kept him alive throughout was the thought of seeing his wife and daughter again. That was his motivation. But what makes him even more remarkable is that he bore no grudges; he had no hatred for the Japanese who did so many terrible things to him. He even met some of his captors after the war. I find that remarkable. I also think, in some strange way, he'd won. I'm sure he'd disagree with me but I still believe he'd won because, despite their best efforts during the war, the Japanese couldn't even make him hate them. He was a truly remarkable individual. As with other remarkable people I've met, a light burned in Jim's eyes.

Which leads me on to another heroic story. Before I went to Arnhem Land for the first time, I read a book called *Whispering Wind* by Syd Kyle-Little, who was the first policeman to go into Arnhem Land at a time when the Aboriginal people were still quite warlike and would fight those who made them feel threatened, using stone-tipped spears. In the 1950s, he was sent in to track down a man wanted for murder. Anyway, the place we were filming was the same place that Syd went to and he had founded a police station when he arrived which became the centre point of a town that sprung up around it – that's Maningrida, one of the most important towns in the area. It's a fascinating story; Syd turns up and he's forgotten to bring a bedroll. There's just him and his two Aboriginal trackers in very hostile terrain. He describes how he injured his foot, which became infected and an Aborigine told him to put his foot in one of the billabongs where the little fish would come and eat away the infected flesh. He did this, and it worked. When we

washed in the rivers there, that's exactly what happened – the fish come up and nibble away the dead skin on your feet. I believe there are places in England where you can pay to experience this now, without risk of crocodile attack.

That brought what Syd had written alive for me and I thought how much I'd love to meet him, but I assumed he was dead. He wasn't though, which was something I only found out many years later when I was back in Australia making another film. I was lucky enough to meet and interview him the day before he moved into a home for the elderly. What a man. He was like a tower of strength even then and he showed me some incredible photographs that he'd taken of the people that he travelled with, like his trackers and one of the medicine men that he'd worked with. Syd had always been a very fair lawman back in the day – he didn't use handcuffs and he told the Aborigines he arrested, 'If you run off, I'll shoot you.' He demonstrated that he could shoot straight, so they respected him for that.

He was one of those old-fashioned policemen, as stiff as if someone had put a broom up his backside, but he'd been absolutely true to his word, so he was the perfect representative of the State to work with Aboriginal people. Previously, white men had always looked down on the Aborigines as though they were somehow a lesser form of humanity but Syd didn't see them like that at all and dealt with them as equals. He administered the law fairly and equitably and treated the Aborigines as he wanted to be treated himself.

What I found interesting was that, on a personal level, it was the right time for me to meet him; if I'd met him on the first journey it would have been meaningless, but because I'd been to Arnhem Land several times before, when I finally got to interview him I knew about the places he was talking about and I'd worked with the descendants of the people he knew, so there was a real meeting of minds. He was a good bushman

and he'd crossed Arnhem Land's Stone Country as well, which is an unbelievable feat.

Syd described receiving a phone call from one of his Aboriginal trackers who was on his deathbed; as soon as the tracker put the phone down, he passed away. He'd phoned to say goodbye, which really emphasises the regard in which Syd was held. I still find it strange that Syd never received more credit for his achievements; to me, he was one of the last pioneers of the Australian frontier. In 2012, Syd packed his swag and rifle for the final time and left the old people's home he'd been staying at, and this life, forever. I am certain that on the other side his trackers were waiting for him beside a burning camp fire at a billabong and, young again, they now travel the trails of the Arnhemland bush once more.

———◆———

Reading this back, I can see there are some common traits that all the wonderful people I've met share, but the ones that stand out for me are fortitude, selflessness and understatedness – these are the qualities I like in people. I've recognised another trait too that's common to all those I've met who have done amazing things: stoicism. They don't moan about the everyday hassle of mosquitoes or cold or whatever – there are bigger things occupying their minds; they have a strong flame burning inside them.

Another truly impressive man I was lucky enough to interview, this time for an episode of *Bushcraft Survival*, was Chuck Klusmann. Chuck was the first American jet pilot shot down in the Vietnam conflict. He flew US Navy fighter bombers from an aircraft carrier and after his aircraft was hit on 7 June 1964, he ended up ejecting over Laos where, upon landing, he dislocated his leg and damaged his arm. So he did what anyone would do – he simply wedged his leg in between some trees and pulled it back into position. What a guy!

When the Carrier force with which Chuck had been based learned of his ejection, they hit a wall; quite unbelievably, they had no plans in place for the recovery of downed aviators and I honestly think they didn't expect to be taking casualties of that nature. So, as US forces weren't supposed to be in Laos, they had to ring the White House, which had to get a Secret Service agent to wake Lyndon B. Johnson, the US President: 'Er . . . Mr President, one of our men is down.'

We wanted to film in Laos at the point where he'd landed, but the risk assessment wouldn't have got out of the starting blocks for that one – there were too many mines still there, which was a great pity. We ended up setting up camp in the jungle of Northern Thailand – about the closest we could get to Laos. I brought in a friend of mine, Tom Lutyens, who had been a survival instructor in the US Air Force during that period, to give us some contextual information.

We invited Chuck to join us in the jungle and tell us his story and I have to confess, my heart sank when I saw him arriving. He'd had quite an arduous trek into the mountains and when we'd arranged for him to join us, I hadn't really taken into account his advanced age; I was worried that the effort of getting to our camp might have given him a heart attack. But he's a tough bird, and he came out to the jungle just a little out of breath. So, we set him up, made him comfortable and that night he sat down by the fire and we started to record him. We didn't have to prompt him or ask him any questions; the story just poured from him like water from a tap – being there, the atmosphere of the jungle, the humidity, the sounds, the smells brought it all back for him in glorious Technicolor and we captured it all on film. It was incredible.

To rescue him, LBJ sent in helicopters belonging to Air America, the CIA's covertly owned and operated US passenger and cargo airline. That offered the US a face-saving clause of 'deniability' but the rescue bid was a

disaster. Communist Pathet Lao fighters who were loyal to Vietnam (Laos was involved in a civil war in the 1960s and 70s) got to Chuck first, captured him and then shot at Air America's rescue helicopters, hitting one of the pilots in the head (fortunately, the round just creased his skull and he survived).

Chuck wasn't the sort of guy to just sit and take whatever punishment the Pathet Lao had lined up for him, so he tried (unsuccessfully) to escape. After that, his captors took his boots away; that wasn't too great a hardship for him though – it was so wet and muddy in the Laotian jungle that he couldn't run in his boots anyway because the design of the soles meant they didn't offer any grip. Fortunately for Chuck, he was aided by a Laotian prisoner who was sympathetic to his plight. He helped Chuck get his boots back and when he had them, he cut grooves into the soles to help give them grip. Then, with the Laotian prisoner's help, he managed to escape. Luck was on his side this time and Air America was able to launch a successful bid to rescue him. After he'd been extracted to a safe house, he realised he'd left some clothing behind on the helicopter.

The team that Air America despatched included one particular doctor who'd been a captain in the Marine Corps on D-Day; he was a real go-getter, a proper dyed-in-the-wool American Marine. This was the real deal, a granite-hard, crewcut Marine captain who'd been through the hell of the Normandy Landings. So he secured Chuck's clothing and kit from the helicopter and then he went to the safe house where Chuck was and knocked on the door. A big CIA spook with sunglasses on opened the door and said, 'Yeah, whaddya want?'

'I've brought these things for the guy who you brought here earlier.'

'There's no one here,' was the reply, and with that, the door was shut in his face.

So the Marine started hammering on the door – Bang! Bang! Bang! – and CIA Spook opened it again, but before he even opened his mouth, the Marine slammed his fist into the guy's chest and said, 'This is for the guy who isn't here.'

He went in and after giving Chuck his kit, he disappeared and Chuck never saw him again. But guess what? We tracked him down – he was living in Northern Thailand – and we were able to reconnect these two remarkable men who had played such a fleeting, but significant, role in one another's lives.

When Chuck eventually got back to Washington, he was invited to the Pentagon to give a talk about his experiences so that some of the US military's most senior officers could learn from them. As he was being cued up to go into the theatre and deliver his lecture, an Army captain came up to him and said: 'Can I just grab you here for one minute? I just want to know is there anything from your escape that could be of any use to other servicemen serving in theatre – is there anything you can tell me that might help us?'

'Well, actually, there is. I had a real problem with my boots so I had to cut these big grooves in the soles . . .'

Which is how jungle boots ended up with the panama sole with the grooves, because of Chuck's escape.

One of the things I remember most about Chuck is his sense of humour. Alan was filming for this programme and he's got a very dry and quick wit too. I like Tom Lutyens a lot but I was surprised by how very much in awe of Chuck he was. You know how it is in Britain, we have a bit of a chuckle and pull each other's legs a bit, but it's not like that in the US – they tend to look up to their heroes and Chuck was kind of uncomfortable with that. I'd made a table and a candelabra out of bamboo at the camp and so, this one night, we were all sat round it just kicking back.

'I've been to America a few times. I went to Memphis and I met Elvis,' Alan said apropos of nothing.

'Did you really?' Chuck asked.

And adopting his best Elvis impression, Alan says: 'Ah-huh-huh . . .'!

Chuck loved that. We all roared with laughter – except for Tom. Tom is a hard-core survival instructor who is absolutely uncompromising in his attitude to his chosen field. His training has undoubtedly enabled many US servicemen to return to their country and families alive, and with honour. Consequently, I think he just felt a bit awkward because he was so in awe of Chuck.

'C'mon Tom, you really ought to loosen up a bit there, fella,' Chuck said to him – and it clearly had the desired effect because from that point on, whenever anyone asked Tom anything, he'd reply, 'Ah-huh-huh . . .'!

19

Mission Impossible

The men who carried out the attack on the heavy water factory of Vemork in Norway during World War II had long fascinated me and I was keen to make a TV documentary about their exploits. Fortunately, I found a sympathetic ear in 2002 when I made a pitch to the BBC for a commission to do just that, so I was delighted when they green-lighted the idea. We tracked down the surviving members of the Norwegian Special Forces squad that showed extreme courage in a raid against the odds, and in early 2003 we flew to Norway to begin filming what became *The Real Heroes of Telemark*. The story is well rehearsed but no less remarkable for that, so I think it bears repeating. It was arguably the Allies' most important and longest-running mission of World War II.

Prior to the war, the Germans took an interest in producing a nuclear weapon but they failed in their attempts because they couldn't produce graphite that was pure enough for the necessary reaction. They worked out that they needed deuterium oxide – or 'heavy water'. It occurs naturally in nature but only in minuscule proportions, but the Germans found out it was being produced in a Norwegian factory as a by-product of an electrical process involving hydropower. The factory took its name, 'Vemork', from its location, near the town of Rjukan, at the foot of the Hardangervidda (which is the Telemark Plateau). It was situated in a very narrow gorge

that today is a Mecca for ice climbers. Because no sun reaches the valley floor in winter and the waterfalls freeze solid, the darkness in the valley was serious enough that the Vemork factory had installed a cable car to transport workers out to the Hardangervidda to experience sunshine during the winter.

When the Germans invaded Norway in 1940, they had their eye on Vemork from the off and they seized control of the plant almost immediately. Churchill was aware of their plans beforehand though, and had arranged for all the heavy water that had been stored at Vemork to be secretly transported out of Norway and into the safekeeping of the Marie Curie Institute in Paris. Then, when the Germans invaded France, it was moved to Bordeaux from where it was sent to Scotland on the last boat before the port closed.

After the heavy water came an exodus of loyal Norwegians who left the country by any means they could and made their way to Britain, bringing with them all their outdoor clothing and equipment. The Nazis then forbade the possession of winter-proof clothing and outdoor equipment because they knew the Norwegians were so accomplished at travelling around in the mountains. They wanted the population where they could see them rather than in the mountains where they couldn't, and there were very severe penalties if you didn't do as you were told.

Once they arrived in Britain, the Norwegians were vetted by the security services to make sure there were no German spies among them and then all the outdoor equipment was gathered in and stored centrally. The fittest and most capable men were selected to join Kompani Linge, the Norwegian Special Forces, and sent to the West Coast of Scotland for training. There was a worker at Vemork named Einar Skinnerland who was owed some leave and, as he wanted to escape the German occupation, he left a short time later under the guise of taking a break and made his way to Scotland on

a ferry. He was swiftly identified by Allied Intelligence as a significant potential asset and when he arrived, he was asked if he would go back to the factory and act as an agent for the Allies. When he agreed, he was given rushed training and two days later he parachuted back into occupied Norway and made his way back to the factory.

The Allies knew they had to do something to stop the Germans producing significant quantities of heavy water, but they didn't know what. There were real problems because any opportunity to carry out aerial operations in Norway was severely limited by the weather, so this made conventional operations very difficult. Also, the factory was so well defended by its position in the gorge that attacks from the air would be ineffective, and so the task fell to Combined Operations, who came up with the concept of a commando raid on the factory to destroy it.

They looked to the Norwegian Kompani Linge for men they could put on to the ground to act as a receiving committee for whatever mission they put together. So before they even had a plan, four men, known as the 'Grouse' party, were parachuted into the area: Jens Anton Poulsson was in charge; Klaus Helberg was an accomplished skier; Knut Haugland was the radio operator; and Kasper Idland was a strong all-rounder.

Combined Operations then trained two teams to be taken in by glider and dropped on to the Hardangervidda and then make their way down to the factory and destroy it. Everyone knew it was likely to be a one-way trip – as escape and extraction afterwards were thought to be too difficult, the only option the guys had was to try and make their own way out by any means possible. It was quite desperate.

The two teams had been trained on a mock-up of the factory and awaited the signal to go. When it came, they boarded two gliders that were towed by Halifax bombers. Sadly, the weather turned once they reached Norway and both gliders, plus one

of the Halifaxes, crashed. The lucky ones died instantly; those who survived fell into German hands and were either executed on the spot, or passed into the custody of the SS who made them suffer appalling torture before killing them and throwing their weighted bodies into a fjord. One group were sent to Grini Concentration Camp and later bound with barbed wire before being shot on Hitler's order.

The waiting Grouse party had laid out a landing strip in the mountains and were told by Combined Operations simply to lie low for the time being and 'go into hiding'. When I interviewed him, Haugland said to me, 'How? With what? We had no food left. We had nothing. It was easy for them to say, but what were we to do?'

The Hardangervidda covers an area of about 2,500 square miles, at an average elevation of 3,500ft. The barren, treeless landscape is dominated by rocky terrain and the temperature can drop as low as -30°C, so you can imagine how horrendous the conditions for these guys were. They ended up moving to a hut called Svensbu that's really remote and well hidden, and for the next few months that's where they stayed – with no food other than what they could scavenge from their desolate surroundings. That's what really interested me; I wanted to make a film purely about the survival side of the story. Eventually Combined Operations washed their hands of the whole affair, saying it was beyond their level of expertise, and it was taken over by the Norwegian Section of the Special Operations Executive (SOE), run by Colonel Wilson.

SOE looked at Kompani Linge and selected nine men to form a team who would go in on a mission known as Operation Gunnerside. They were led by Joachim Rønneberg with Knut Haukelid as the unit's second in command or 2 I/C. (I'd have loved to have met Knut because he ultimately finished the mission, but sadly he died before I had the chance.) The men were parachuted in, landing 18 miles from where they were

meant to be, and Rønneberg had to hold it all together while they linked up with the Grouse party.

Despite all the obstacles, the two teams did eventually find one another and this brought renewed impetus to the mission, re-energising the whole thing. They undertook a reconnaissance of the bridge that goes across the river at the bottom of the ravine and into the factory. Not long afterwards, they climbed down into the gorge, got into the factory undetected and blew up the heavy water apparatus. Quite unbelievably, the Germans didn't even notice – the team set 30-second fuses on the explosives and Haukelid later said that the noise of the explosion 'was like two or three cars crashing at Piccadilly Circus and nobody noticed'. He later received a Mention in Despatches for having a Nazi soldier in his sights within three feet and not pulling the trigger; rather than risk alerting the Germans by taking the shot, he instead waited for the soldier to move away, demonstrating remarkable coolness under pressure, given the circumstances.

Astonishingly, the whole team got away – they re-crossed the gorge, made their way to the cable car and climbed the mountain underneath it. They reached the summit just as dawn was breaking and I had the privilege of taking the surviving men from that mission back up to the cable car. Every one of them had a wistful look in his eye as he beheld the view, remembering a mackerel sky clearing from the east. I knew that this was a sight they never thought they would see again. At the time, they had no idea how serious the mission was; they knew it was special but they didn't know just how special it was, or realise the full importance of it, until after the war had ended.

Once the Germans discovered what had happened, they realised the site at Vemork was simply too hot for them to continue to produce heavy water there, and intelligence reached the Allies that the Nazis were going to transfer the heavy water

that they'd produced to date to a safer facility in Austria. To do that, though, they first had to get it out of Norway and that meant putting it on a train out of Vemork and down on to a ferry across Lake Tinnsjå from where it would be transferred to a ship and on to the Fatherland.

Of the original Operation Gunnerside team, most of them got out through Norway across the mountains. Only Haukelid remained locally on the Hardangervidda to watch over the factory. It was he who eventually planted a time bomb against the hull of the ferry on which the Germans were transporting the heavy water. When it exploded, it sank the ferry, taking the heavy water down to the deepest part of the lake. Had he not succeeded in his mission, there were several other sabotage teams waiting further down the line; there was even a submarine waiting to tackle the cargo if it had made it as far as the sea. Whatever else happened, that heavy water was never going to get to Germany.

Every single member of that team was exceptional; they were very remarkable men, each and every one. Klaus Helberg was well known in Norway for his work for the Norwegian Mountain Hut organisation, the DNT. In fact there is even a statue of him because of it. The Norwegians have a mountain huts system rather like our youth hostels and this is what he did as a job. He did it before the war and he felt that the Germans had taken away what, for him, was the best job in the world. He wanted it back, which was part of his motivation. Meeting Rønneberg and Poulsson was special; Poulsson, who kept the men of the Grouse party together for those months when there was no food, had gone out on a daily basis hunting for reindeer. He didn't manage to shoot one until 23 December and even then he missed with his first shot but eventually that day he managed to shoot a calf. He drank the blood from the carcass to give him enough energy to carry it back, and that Christmas they tuned in to the World Service

on their radio, put their headphones on a plate as an amplifier and dined on venison. That was a Christmas dinner like no other.

Poulsson truly was remarkable. I asked him, 'Tell me about your time in Scotland when you were training there,' and he told me some of the tales of what they did. He said they used to catch salmon, which interested me.

'Did you spin, or fly-fish to catch them?' I asked him.

'Neither,' he replied. 'We threw hand grenades into the water.'

And it's true. Even on the estate today, water baillifs are still dredging unexploded hand grenades from the bottom of the loch.

They were all incredible men but Rønneberg was the one who seriously impressed me. He led the final assault. We were at the factory filming on the eve of the sixtieth anniversary of the raid and there was a reception in the factory for the men, but he wasn't with them; he was climbing the gorge again that day. Afterwards, he joined me and his eyes were aflame with the memories of that night.

These Norwegians were something else; their determination, their courage, their selflessness, their readiness to sacrifice themselves for their country – it was quite unique. You have to remember that Norway is even now just over a hundred years old. It was a young country then, but they were immensely proud of their independence and, as Rønneberg very eloquently said to me, 'In Britain, you never really understood what it meant to be occupied. We did, and we would have given our lives willingly to get our country back.'

When we hosted the men for dinner, he said something else that's stayed with me: 'I want to say something. It's important. When we were in Scotland training, we felt we were free Norwegians. We longed to be back in Norway. When we got back to Norway in the mountains, we felt we were British.'

That's how warm a welcome they had been given when they arrived here after escaping. That for me showed us at our best; it was a wonderful piece of wartime co-operation, and sixty years later, it was very moving to be around people like that.

20

Blade Runner

As I've grown older, one of the things I've noticed is how the public's perception of knives has changed. It hasn't so much evolved as reached a dead end. As society has become increasingly urban, the humble knife has been hijacked by miscreant youths from deprived city areas and used as a weapon to target other young people who they believe are guilty of 'disrespecting them'. Just because some young idiot wants to carry a knife and stab somebody, that shouldn't tar those of us who need to use one for legitimate purposes with the same brush.

When I first started running courses under the Woodlore banner on a regular basis, knives were an issue that came up again and again – except it was for a different reason back then. A knife is a vital tool in the woods because you can use it to make so many things. In fact, without one you're as good as helpless, so I'd ask students attending my courses to bring a knife with them. One of the first courses I ran was for some Adventure Scouts and Scout Leaders, and none of their knives were sharp enough or suitable for the tasks involved. It meant that my students weren't able to do some of the things I wanted to teach them, no matter how hard they tried, because they didn't have a tool capable of doing the job.

This was a real issue so I started to scour the UK market for a suitable knife and what I found really surprised me: there

just wasn't one available – anywhere. There were lots of knives but they were the wrong shape and size, or they weren't sharp enough. What I was looking for was a small, sharp, strong and well-made knife with a blade no longer than the width of my hand. But I couldn't find one.

I'd had some involvement with Wilkinson Sword when I was first starting out and I managed to get a piece of sword steel from them; I set about designing exactly what I needed and then made a sample. It was a very simple knife with a very simple shape and an antler handle. Sword steel is very straight-forward to use and I had enough to experiment a little, so once I had the sample, I refined the design and made several others – one with a classic style of edge, another with a flat ground edge, and one that had a slightly convex grind which was very tough. They were very good and worked very well.

But as I used them, I came to realise that the design would work better if the blade had a slight drop for a guard at the front of the grip. I changed the blade shape to one that would be more suitable and eventually settled on what I call a flat, bevelled grind, which is typical of Scandinavian knives. I came across a couple of Scandinavian knives that students brought to my courses that cut really well, but the blades weren't thick enough and weren't as strong as I would like.

Having settled on a design that worked, I commissioned knife-maker Alan Wood to make me the first batch. Alan's an artisan – his work is flawless and the quality is second to none. I met him through Kingsley, strangely enough, at a fair in London and he was – and remains – the best knife-maker in the country. What he produced for me is what became known as the Woodlore knife and it's since been copied all around the world.

Alan can only make small numbers – as an artisan he doesn't like mass-producing things, which is fair enough because I think they'd lose something if that were to happen. I have

commissioned some other experts to make them too, so we can meet demand without compromising on quality. Over the years, we've done various editions of the original design – for our twenty-fifth anniversary, for instance, we had a Swedish blacksmith Julius Patterson design a special version of it.

Of all the things I've designed and used over the years, the Woodlore knife is the one I'm most proud of because it's so perfect for what it's required to do. These knives are exceptionally strong, razor sharp and versatile because they have to be: one minute you could be cutting something to hang your pot over the fire with, and the next you could be carving a canoe paddle – it is able to take all of that in its stride. Despite there having been a twenty-five-year span since its initial design, I still haven't found a knife I like better. Anyone who knows me knows that I would happily abandon my own version if I found one that was an improvement on mine because all I'm interested in is the best tool for the job – and currently, that's the Woodlore knife.

I designed it so that the back of the blade has a slight curvature so that when you're splitting bark from trees, you're able to keep the tip of the blade out of the wood. You can also easily control the depth to which you push the blade so you can strip the bark off very easily. It also helps when you're skinning. The curvature at the tip is quite important; it has a gentle radius to stop it slipping off if the turn at the end of a cut is too sharp. I learned that the hard way while testing one of my prototypes, and I have a scar on my leg to show for it. Another beneficial aspect of that design is that as you sharpen the blade, it will retain its useful shape; in fact, the edge shape will improve as you sharpen it. Its strength means you can split wood with it, or hammer it through wood to split it and you can pry with it – it doesn't shift at all.

We only make the knives with the antler handle for instructors at Woodlore because they're heavier; when they receive

one of these knives, we tell them that it's a weight of responsibility that comes with the job.

———————◆◆◆———————

There are many things in the world of bushcraft that are easily accessible and people take for granted today, but those things just weren't around when I first started out. We use a folding saw, for example, and those first came out in 1995. We lend saws to students on one of the Woodlore courses, and over the years I don't think we've ever had a blade break – handles yes, but never a blade – they're that strong. And the folding saw makes life so much easier in the woods. There are many things you can do with it and although it can't replace an axe in every given situation, in many cases it's enough.

Over the years I have used a lot of axes and although there are some exceptionally good ones out there, none were perfect – at least, not perfect enough for what I was looking for, so again, I designed my own. As with the knife, I didn't design it because I wanted to sell it; I designed it because I needed a decent bit of kit. A few years back I came across an axe firm in Sweden called Gransfors Bruks Axes and back then, the company was unknown in Britain. I started to use their Small Forest Axe, which is a lovely size of axe and I liked it a lot. I'd previously been using a much lighter, Tomahawk-style axe when I was in the woods or a small felling axe and the Gransfors fitted in somewhere between the two. You could use it one handed, or two if push came to shove, so it was a great axe.

I used it for many years, but in doing so I noticed that it was weak in a couple of areas. I say weak, but it does what it does and it does it very well. Sometimes though, you want a different axe, something that will behave slightly differently in a given situation, or you could do with something a little longer, with a head that's a fraction heavier. The way Gransfors

grind their axe heads means that sometimes, when you're splitting with them, they will stick in the wood. A few years ago, I met the owner of the company and he said: 'If you ever have any ideas for a different axe, let me know.'

And I said, 'Well, actually, I do.'

So I came up with a modification to the Small Forest Axe. I liked the shape and size of its head, but I wanted it heavier so the one I designed is slightly thicker and stronger, which means that you can use the back of it to hammer with greater security. The head has a slightly more obtuse edge angle – as axes used to have – and it's heavy behind the edge so it will split better.

If you're going to use an axe, as I do, for carving, you need to put magic into the edge and by that I mean you have to sharpen the edge back a little to give a better bite. You have to put the right edge on for whatever task you're doing, which is the right way because if you live in an area where you're only cutting softwood, you want a fine edge, and if you're in an area where there's knotty wood or tougher wood, then you want a stronger, more obtuse edge, so that's left up to the user. I don't believe you can make an axe for a beginner to use, in truth. The one I designed is not meant for beginners, it's meant for experienced users and they will know how to file on the angle as required.

The axe, the knife and the saw are the tools of my trade and the rest is all to do with nature. These are the things that make life possible on the trail. You can't just cut anything – you need to know which trees to cut and why so that you don't harm the forest. But these are the tools that enable us to go into wild places and to live there. We might carry heavier tools than some people, but we can carry fewer other things because we'll use nature to help us. And that's wonderful. It's a very organic experience. Bushcraft is an organic thing. Really, with a knife, a saw and an axe, you can do absolutely everything

you need to. The only other thing that's good to have is a needle – you can manage without and make them from bone but metal needles are much better.

If you could see all the things I've made over the years – if I could mount it all up – we'd have a catacomb filled to the top. Many of the things I make get thrown on to the fire later on, so there's nothing tangible left behind, so perhaps people don't really realise the extent of investment we make towards learning at Woodlore. For the first fifteen years I ran the majority of the courses, living outdoors for an average of 250 nights a year. Today that responsibilty has passed on to my team. I don't think there's any other company that has their team out as frequently as we do at Woodlore and that's what makes us special. We have a real understanding of the craft. And I still find it all really interesting. I'm still learning. I think that's the joy of the subject. One of the things I can truly say about bushcraft as a whole is that the more I learn, the more I realise I don't know. The more you undo it, the more you find. It's like an onion – there are always more layers to be found within.

It seems to me that people today are in love with the idea of being an 'expert'. Personally, I would rather continue to be a student and keep learning than consider myself in that light. There aren't the same expectations placed on a student – in fact, your only expectation is to learn, and there are few subjects where there comes a point when there's nothing left for you to assimilate. There's always something to learn because life moves on and things evolve.

When you climb the ladder of knowledge in bushcraft, as with any other field, the rungs are fairly close together initially, and you make good progress. You can look out from your elevated position of knowledge as you climb, but the further you get up the ladder the further apart those rungs become, so the harder it is to progress. That's when you really start to

see those who have the staying power and those who haven't. Every step up gives you a view back over the scenery before and sometimes you find quicker ways and easier ways of doing things, and sometimes you think, well, those rungs are strong and they're reliable but we can avoid those and take a big step past them if we do this instead. And that's the joy of climbing higher. But you should never rush the journey because to have a ladder with a bit missing is not safe.

I think the maxim 'it's about the journey, not the destination' is everything in this field. If people are starting out, they shouldn't try to know it all too soon but just enjoy the process, and enjoy what they're learning as they progress; if you're too busy focusing on what's over there, you miss what's here. And it's the here and now that's important in this subject.

Bushcraft takes a lot of dedication. It's a big subject to learn, in terms of edible plants, fungi and skills. One of the difficulties we've had, especially over the last few years, is that there have been a lot of people coming on courses who've been taught to eat this, that or the other, and there are people eating things that, in many cases, aren't edible. That's an aspect that's really changed because when I first started teaching bushcraft, you couldn't get people to eat anything – they were scared to. Whereas now the fear has gone to the wind and they think they can eat everything; and of course that's not true either. I'm afraid the reality lies in that boring, grey middle ground of learning what's edible and what's not. I've always been very careful about what I eat.

These are old-fashioned skills. Many of the early authors on bushcraft were North Americans writing in the late 1800s about how to live in the woods. There's a great following today, I think, among people who have rediscovered some of these old texts. But when you actually look at the skills described in some of these books, they describe what we would know as recreational camping. They don't describe the skills of the

pioneers or the local communities. I know the woods very well; I have had to live on the trail and I've worked closely with indigenous people, and I see very little of the native skills represented in these early books.

Sadly, I think this is typical with the subject – people will over-complicate things for the sake of a woodcraft camp rather than keeping it elegant and simple, which is usually the native way of doing things. The earliest book I've found written on bushcraft, although they don't use that term, was one written by two Britons in 1875 and has the wonderful title of *Shifts and Expedients of Camp Life, Travel & Exploration*. The authors, W.B. Lord of the Royal Artillery and T. Baines of the Royal Geographical Society, were two extremely experienced explorers and their book remains one of the very best about the subject. They write well, and they'd been all over, so it's truly fascinating. Interestingly enough, Sir David Attenborough chose that very book to take with him on *Desert Island Discs*.

21

Close Encounters

When it comes to what you see, wildlife documentaries on TV have much in common with icebergs: what's visible is about a third of the whole. It's a risky business working with wild animals, and I don't mean from a TV executive's perspective. When all the risk assessments have been done, what it comes down to is man against beast and the greatest threat doesn't always come from where you'd think.

Whenever I make a film about dangerous wild animals you'll probably see me on screen armed with a rifle, and there's a simple reason for that. It's because when I'm tracking in the wild, it's real. We're not faking anything. I'll be moving very quietly and going wherever the tracks go. If the tracks go into thick cover, I go into thick cover and if I bump into a leopard, a lion or a black rhino, for instance, I need to be able to defend myself; if there's a problem, then me having someone beside me with a rifle is no good to me. A person beside me with a rifle is a person too far away to be effective.

I believe that when I make a TV programme, it's imperative that what you see on the screen is, wherever possible, completely honest and transparent. What I don't like are wildlife documentaries where the presenters don't have a visible means to defend themselves but they'll have someone with a rifle or some other weapon behind the camera to protect them. I don't think that's appropriate for a number of reasons, but

principally because it's dishonest. It paints a false picture to viewers, who may go away under the impression that if they're ever in the bush, they can just bimble around without risk; they can't. Take Africa for instance; sure, the wild animals in some of the areas where documentaries are made are well acclimatised to the presence of humans, but in other parts of the continent it's a completely different story.

For me, a rifle is the most appropriate means of defence, and it needs to be a very heavy calibre. My own choice of calibre for self-defence is a .416 Remington Magnum. That strikes at a force of about five tons. And don't believe everything you see in the movies; if you're defending yourself against dangerous game, just about the worst thing you can do is to fire a warning shot. If you make the decision to pull the trigger, you're shooting to kill. So far, I've never had to, and I hope I never will, but you never know what's in the next bush.

Unfortunately we don't live in a Utopian world, and as beautiful as she is, nature isn't always friendly. You will never know whether the animal you bump into has just had an encounter with another animal and its blood is up, its adrenaline is flowing, and it's angry, fearful or annoyed. If you bump into an elephant, how can you know if it's got toothache? We get grumpy and irritable when we're in constant pain, and so do animals. The fact is, there are many influences – both physiological and environmental – that can change or affect a wild animal's nature, which means you can *never* truly predict its mood.

As with most things, the best option is to try to mitigate risk wherever you can. Prevention is better than cure and, yes, it's a cliché and it's oft-quoted, but it's no less true for that. I will always try to ensure that when I'm working in the wild with animals, I've done everything I can to avoid a confrontation. If I'm tracking, I have the welfare of the people with me to consider, so if we are moving into cover, I'm sharp and

alert to any threat. However low the chances are of suddenly encountering a dangerous animal, it's imperative that should I need to, I have the means to take action. When I'm around bears I don't carry a firearm of any sort unless we're in the Arctic and there's a threat of polar bears. That's a whole different ball game because a polar bear will stalk you, hunt you and eat you. We're just an hors d'oeuvre to them.

It's not an easy thing to defend yourself with a rifle, so you need to feel comfortable with whatever weapon you're carrying. At close quarters, people tend to imagine that'd you use a pistol. However, with the sort of animals I'm likely to encounter, a pistol just wouldn't be effective. Firing a pistol at a charging rhino or elephant would be about as effective as spitting at it.

The rifle that I choose to use is a Blaser R8 made in Austria. It is an extremely accurate weapon and you can interchange the barrels so it fires different calibre rounds. That's important because the overriding factor when you use a weapon is the appropriate use of force. Many people choose to use a .375 Holland & Holland Magnum round which is perfectly good for some things, but it's not as reliable against a charging rhino or elephant as a .416 Remington Magnum, even though both rounds have a similar range.

The Blaser R8 has a short, synthetic stock, which is easy to carry, and a straight pull bolt, which means you can reload very quickly. It's almost the perfect hunting rifle. It's a beautifully engineered and manufactured weapon – you can dismantle it, reassemble it and it holds zero, for instance, which is astonishing. I use Schmidt & Bender optics for hunting – their Sniper Scope 3-12 x 50 is probably the most popular sniper scope in the world for that; it has superb accuracy and that's what you want. One shot; one kill. But if I'm using the rifle for self-defence in the bush, I use Aimpoint, which is a red dot sight that enables you to respond

quickly to a moving target. It's extremely good; the batteries will last, turned on, for five years.

I'm not geeky about the axes, knives or firearms I have – to me, they are just tools. And as you've probably gathered, I don't just use the rifle for self-defence – I hunt too. Why? Well, it's not for pleasure. Let's look at deer. Firstly, I believe in management and control for the welfare of the deer population, which is increasing in Britain. Deer produce 25 per cent to 30 per cent more young than they actually need every year, and the traffic on our roads doesn't take out anything like the number that's required to keep the population under control.

We have to intervene because we've removed the predators from the ecosystem. If you have an area of land where the owner doesn't want the deer stalked, this allows the deer to breed uncontrollably and you end up exceeding the carrying capacity of the land, which leads to a subsequent decline in the animal's condition.

I have DSC (Deer Stalking Certificate) Level 1 and 2 and I have a Professional Deer Manager's qualification. Here in Britain we have the best education in the world when it comes to deer stalking. I was a Trustee of the British Deer Society for three years, so I'm very keen that we should manage our deer population, not just with the bullet but by other means as well, for the welfare of the herd.

Managing deer is an important part of looking after their welfare and British deerstalkers who have undergone Level 1 training are taught to inspect the animal for any signs of disease or ill health. In this way we have constant sampling of the whole deer population happening on a regular and ongoing basis. Generally speaking, it's a very healthy species but it needs to be monitored. In my experience, deerstalkers are some of the nicest and most mature people you'll meet in society. Deerstalking isn't like shooting pheasants. You can't just throw

them in the boot of the car. It's a big effort, it's a lot of work to recover the animal at the end of the day, and of course, it's wonderful eating. I love deer; most of the people I know really respect the animals they hunt.

———◆◆———

When it comes to dangerous animals, there's something of a hierarchy in the animal kingdom and, as I've said, there are some surprises when it comes to the biggest threat. To use another cliché, 'it's always the quiet ones'. Well, at least some of the time. These are often the ones you can't legislate for.

I've been stung by a scorpion, and a rifle isn't much good in that regard! I was just brushing past a tent in France, of all places. That was painful; they sting with arachnid venom, which is a neurotoxin that they use to paralyse or kill. This makes it safe for them to feed on prey, without the risk of a struggle, but it's a bit inconvenient to say the least for the human that's just been stung. There's a fair bit of swelling around the site of the sting but it also really messes with your mind; other venoms don't do that.

Not all of the animals that people think are dangerous pose a threat. I'm thinking here particularly of the wolf. It's such a magnificent animal but it gets the most appalling press and that really bugs me. To me, the wolf is a brother of the wild, an incredibly successful predator and a social animal. To the native inhabitants of the Americas, for instance, the wolf was a creature of power to be admired and to learn from. But to the European settlers, the wolf was an evil creature to be feared.

I was asked to track a pack of wolves in Idaho for a TV documentary that I made with ITV. In 1995, thirty-five Canadian wolves were released into the Sawtooth Mountains and by 2009 there were estimated to be over 800 of them. The release had been sponsored by the Nez Percé Indians, and when

I interviewed them, they said that for thousands of years their ancestors had lived alongside wolves, in direct competition with them for food, but they didn't hate wolves; they revered them. They recognised their strength and qualities as a social animal and they respected them for that. They also respected the wolf's skill as a hunter.

Wolves are perfectly evolved. They're not dogs, they're wild hunters – the super predators – and perhaps this is what we don't like about them. After us, wolves are our planet's top mammalian land predator. They're an effective species because they work as a team and it is team effort that's key. Although some cats, such as lions, have learned to hunt co-operatively, they're not in the same league as wolves. A wolf pack will chase a herd of caribou; two wolves will start the chase and when they tire, there will be two more waiting to take over from them and so on. When the caribou are starting to slow, the pack is ready to pounce and finish them off. Then, the wolves that were there in the beginning will rejoin the pack and share in the spoils. They work through concerted effort.

There's more and more evidence that shows that wolves play an important role in the ecosystem. They have the ability to tell whether ungulates are ill by studying their posture. Scientists also believe that wolves can tell from the breath of their prey whether they are ill or diseased in much the same way as some domestic dogs can sniff out cancers in humans. They have found increasing numbers of cases where wolves have killed ungulates but not consumed them. When they've subsequently performed autopsies, they've discovered that the dead animals were in fact diseased. So it appears that wolves are in some way programmed instinctively, to act as a regulating force in nature. People ask why wolves kill sheep and then don't eat them all: if there are too many ungulates, wolves will kill without eating so they're just performing their regulatory role in nature.

One day in our schedule was set aside for aerial filming, so as I was not involved I set off on foot to explore a quiet canyon where I had seen tracks from an alpha male. I took some forensic plaster with me to cast the track, and after six miles I found really fresh ones and set to casting them. The plaster was supposed to harden in ten minutes but it took thirty, so I sat down in the sage brush to wait quietly; I could sense the air was full of possibility. After twenty minutes I felt a presence; peering carefully over the sage brush, I saw that there, just twenty metres away, was the alpha male standing alone, sniffing the air. In complete silence and not moving a muscle, I watched him for five minutes until suddenly he looked me straight in the eye. When a wolf looks, it does so in a different way to other animals; it looks deep into your very soul. It wants to know what you are from the inside out in a way that no other animal I have encountered does. I felt no fear, no threat, just respect. We stood looking into each other in this strange encounter for what seemed like an age but it was probably only two or three minutes. Then I smiled and the wolf, with great dignity, despite my having had the drop on him, departed. I consider that moment to have been of great significance; it was as if he understood my mission. I still have the cast I made that day and it shows that alpha male's track perfectly; it's the same size as a large human hand. I am told that since then all the members of that pack have been shot – by hunters whose hearts are filled with hatred rather than respect.

At the other extreme are the animals that pose a genuine threat, and crocodiles are, as you would probably expect, a huge hazard. I remember being told when we were filming in Costa Rica that there were no crocodiles in the mangrove swamps.

Well, in my experience, there aren't too many mangrove swamps where there *aren't* any crocodiles or alligators – they're kind of synonymous with one another. Anyway, I'd built a raft out of giant bamboo and the director wanted to get a helicopter shot of me sitting on it in the mangrove swamp. So there I am on this raft, waiting for the pilot to fly overhead, completely unaware that the film crew had been delayed and the helicopter hadn't even taken off yet. And guess what pops up beside me? Yes, a crocodile. So much for there not being any.

That reminds me of another close encounter with a crocodile I had when we were filming an episode of *Extreme Survival* in Arnhem Land, Northern Australia. We were telling the story of a medical flight in World War II that had crashed near the coast of Arnhem Land, and the crew had ended up building a raft to take them to Elcho Island. I knew there were likely to be a lot of crocodiles there so the threat was real and I was wary. We filmed on this beach – there were very high tides at the time so the width of the beach was very narrow and, while we were there, I saw a rather large crocodile cruising up and down watching us. With crocs, anything above three metres or so in length will think about having a pop at you, and this one was about four to five metres long. It didn't trouble us while we were filming, so eventually we moved off.

That night, I was awoken by a noise and I instantly sat up – alert and on guard. We had a couple of snorers in the crew and I have trouble sleeping when there's snoring, so I'd moved my mosquito net a bit further along the beach, a few yards away from the main camp. I lay quietly for a few minutes and then I heard the noise again. As I looked over to my left, there was the same bloody great crocodile that had been watching us earlier. He walked past me slowly, but he was very close. I was lying prone on the ground, looking up at its body. You realise just how athletic they are when you see them like that. I lay there absolutely still with my hand on my machete. There

wasn't a lot else I could do but I'd decided that if it made a move for me it was going to get it on the nose. Luckily, it ambled past and went on its way. Believe me, that's a position I never want to be in again.

Earlier in the day, I'd killed a stingray with a spear and spear thrower that one of the Aborigines had lent me, and along with some other fish and molluscs I'd cooked it up on a nice fire on the beach; we all sat round and had a great evening. I would have much preferred to cook it all in the shade behind the beach but the director insisted that we move instead to the water's edge. And the one thing about crocodiles is that they've got an amazingly good sense of smell, so cooking seafood on an open fire in the middle of our camp on the beach was probably not the brightest thing to do. It's a cardinal lesson, though, that one of the really important things you need to know about dangerous animals is: what's their sensory ability? What are the things that attract them? With crocodiles, it's their exceptional sense of smell. Of all the large animals on the planet, the salt-water crocodile is, for me, the most dangerous. Bizarrely, it's not the most dangerous *life form* on earth – that would most likely be a microbe or a mosquito. But I'm splitting hairs here – you need to take very, very great care with salt-water crocodiles, so you regulate your behaviour when they're around. If you're in crocodile country, you don't go and get water from the same place twice. And if you're collecting water from a river, you put the bucket on a rope and throw it in.

When we were filming for that same programme, we were going in and out of the mangrove swamp by boat every day, and because the tidal range is so high, there was a mud gulley that we had to push the boat up and down to get into the water. We'd been doing this for several days so there we were on the third or fourth day and, as we were speeding up to get up the gulley, the propeller hit what we thought was a log. It

wasn't though. Of course it wasn't – it was another crocodile that had come looking for us. It had seen us moving and thought, 'I'll have some of that.' When you're on the water, what you need to look for are bubbles coming up in parallel lines. You have to be very careful though, because crocodiles are so quick; they're an ambush predator so they're infinitely patient. Often, they will sneak up on you and you won't see them coming. Not exactly my favourite animal, that.

———◆—◆———

Dangerous animals vary, and a lot depends on what continent you're on. In Africa, there are several threats that you have to consider; firstly, if you're in buffalo country, you could be in a lot of trouble. Believe it or not, the Cape buffalo is a very, very dangerous animal. It looks at you with absolute hatred; get close enough to look one in the eye and you'll see it's full of menace. As a species, it's not had a very good experience of humankind so we're not on its Christmas card list. I'm always wary when I'm tracking in the bush in buffalo country, and I wouldn't think of not having my rifle with me, although even with the right round, if you don't shoot it in the right place, the buffalo would still be a threat because when its adrenaline is up, it's unlikely to stay down. To eliminate the threat, you have to hit it in the nervous system – either a round to the brain or the spine. And when it drops, you have to immediately fire a follow-up shot to kill it.

Elephants can be very dangerous too. They can be very quiet; in fact, you can be close to an elephant and not realise it. They are wonderful creatures, full of personality, but they can have terrible temper tantrums. They're like over-tired two-year-olds in that regard, except with the power of a locomotive, and if they have had a bad day, they will want to show off and that's when they can be very aggressive. You have to be

very, very careful. When bull elephants enter musth, they're a real threat. Musth is a periodic condition which is characterised by highly aggressive behaviour and caused by a huge rise in reproductive hormones – a bull elephant's testosterone levels when it's in musth can be as much as sixty times greater than normal. There are signs if you know what to look for; one of them is that they discharge a thick tar-like secretion from their temporal glands.

Animals have an invisible boundary system – a comfort zone, if you like – and these zones are not fixed, they are flexible according to the circumstances. But it's imperative that you're aware of them. We tend to think that they're visual zones, but for many animals they involve more than just their sense of sight. It's important to be aware of the distinction as this will impact on how you use the wind when you're moving through the bush, because of how your scent carries. So if you have, say, an elephant cow with a calf, and she's standing on the edge of some mopani scrub looking out over savannah grassland, her comfort zone *towards* the grass may be quite extensive because she can see over a great distance. Her comfort zone *behind* her in the scrub will be much shorter, though, because she can't see so far, so anything that comes into this zone will pose a threat much more quickly. And if you were to walk across the savannah towards her on the grass, the first of these zones is when she becomes aware of you – we call that the sight zone; if she sees you, she can assess you and she has the chance to respond to you and move away if she feels it necessary. But let's say there's some cover and she can't see when you enter that sight zone, and then you pop out from behind a bush and you're a little bit closer – you have then moved into her flight zone, which means that if she sees you and has sufficient time, she'll run away. Alternatively, you might be walking through the bush behind her and the first time she becomes aware of you is when you're very close. If she senses,

or mistakenly perceives, that you are a threat to her or her calf, you'll find that you've entered her fight zone and, believe me, that's somewhere you really do not want to be.

———◆———

You're probably wondering why I haven't mentioned lions. Well here's where they turn up. Lions have killed more people than any other animal on the planet because, unlike say Cape buffalo or elephants, which attack when threatened, lions are predators. They hunt, then they kill, and they eat what they kill. So if you want to stay out of their food chain, you need to be aware. The lion really is the king of jungle and is by far the most dangerous of all the cats. I get really irritated when I watch documentaries and in the voiceover or narration, the presenter describes them as being 'lazy'. If you were to take a camera and film a human being at 3 o'clock in the morning while they're in their bed, you'd probably say the same. In the mid part of the day, you might find that they're a short-order chef in a busy restaurant in London and in fact they're anything but lazy, and the same is true of lions.

At night, lions are at least four times more dangerous than they are in daylight. A lion wants to kill. It's a hunter, a predator, and it's built to do just that. It's a masterpiece of engineering and nothing is wasted. Every cell in a lion's body is there to make it an incredibly powerful, capable and successful killer, and it's just perfection to watch. If you look at the skeleton of a lion, there's a big head full of teeth, with a high-powered engine behind it. A lion bringing down an elephant, for example, is not an uncommon event. Very often wildlife documentaries will say that something is very unusual, but it's not – it's only unusual in TV terms because it might be the first time it's been caught on camera.

Of all the big cats, though, the leopard is my favourite; it's

a truly wonderful animal. Leopards are very beautiful creatures and very brave, too. If you threaten a leopard, it will attack, so if you get close to one, it's important not to make eye contact with it because it may just think that you want to have a go. That said, I have done just that with one and I remember thinking at the time, 'I really shouldn't be staring into your eyes like this.' It was looking back at me as if to say, 'Maybe I'll take a pop at you . . . maybe I won't . . . Let's just see who looks away first . . .' They have so much personality and they're very complex creatures. I find them absolutely fascinating. I really enjoy tracking leopards – probably because it's such a challenge. They have the perfect camouflage in the scrub and they're most active after dark. When you find a track to follow, you see how they move through a landscape and you get a sense of their identity and personalities. That said, tracking doesn't tell you everything – going out and observing them is the only way to fill in the gaps.

If there are lions about, leopards have to be careful because there's really no contest – a lion will kill a leopard without breaking a sweat. They don't have dominance in the bush like lions do, so they need to resort to guile and stay hidden wherever possible. They'll use gullies to get around, and when you track them you can see which side of the gully they've moved down, where and when they chose to cross, what they sniff, what they're looking at, and what they've scent-marked – it truly is fascinating. Occasionally you might find a place where females have been with their cubs, but that's a novelty – usually that side of their life is well hidden.

A few years ago, ITV had asked me to go to Namibia, to the Erindi Game Reserve, just east of the Erongo Mountains, to look for a specific leopard. The game reserve used to be a hunting ground, but in 2007 it was transformed into a nature conservation venture, and this elusive leopard who'd been named Houdini because he'd survived the hunting era had

been the older dominant male at one time, but I thought it unlikely that he would have still retained his dominance.

He had a very big track; by that I mean his front right foot. Some people measure length but I use width and anything from 9cm and over is on the large side. Houdini's was about 11–12cm. He fascinated me because he didn't skulk like the other leopards and he was, against all expectations, still the dominant leopard, so any other male coming into his territory would have to be careful. There is ongoing research into this, but the theory for leopard behaviour in this area shows that you have a series of females that each have their own territories and they are all contained within the territory of a single male. This dominant male will do a circuit, visiting all of them, so he's always on the move. The females will hive off part of their territory if they have a daughter – that will then become hers, but a male cub gets pushed out once he's independent, and he then has to find his own territory. I'm sure in time we will discover more things. There is wonderful research going on now to try to establish the animal's behaviour patterns.

Houdini was quite happy to move in the open but we had great difficulty filming him; he was a very elusive character. We had specialist film crews working with us, and eventually we managed to get some footage of him with night-vision equipment while he was visiting a waterhole that already had some lions drinking from it. He was completely nonplussed and just walked up without a care in the world, gave them a look as if to say, 'I'm going to take a drink. What are you going to do about it?' took his fill and left. That's one pretty bold leopard.

***

Of all the animals I've tracked, studied or encountered, though, one of the most amazing experiences I've had in my life was getting up close and personal with a grizzly bear. I was running

a trip in British Columbia to watch and study bears in 2003. Rachel had joined me for this trip and we were living on a yacht with two clients and two of the boat's crew. When you live on a boat, space is at a premium because you have to carry a lot of food and we were sailing a long way – along the Nass River from Prince Rupert up to the border with Alaska. After a few days we had quite a few empty boxes that we needed to get rid of, and the easiest way to do that was to take them ashore and burn them. I looked along the shore for a gravel bar so that I could make a fire and not set anything else, like nearby trees, alight. Having found one, myself and the client built the fire and threw the boxes on. They were burning nicely – and that was when I heard a crackling sound beside me.

I turned to my right and there he was: a male grizzly stepping into the river right beside me. He was stood upright and he measured in at around 8ft, so he was pretty big. He stopped and looked at me. Now I wasn't completely unarmed – I had some pepper spray on my belt that was specifically for defending yourself against bears – but he didn't look like he was going to attack me, so I just stood still and watched.

All the conventional wisdom says you should never stare a bear in the eye – and it's sound advice, but inordinately difficult to carry out because their eyes are absolutely hypnotic. But I managed to pull my gaze away from the bear and I said to my client, 'Whatever you do, don't stare at the bear. We're just going to back off very slowly and move away.'

So I turned my back on the bear – which was a very difficult thing to do because it's counter-intuitive, but it's vital because it's imperative that you appear non-threatening. I gently moved away, but when I was at a safe distance and looked back, I saw that the client was absolutely frozen to the spot. I don't know whether it was from fear or the excitement of the encounter but, regardless, he needed to get away, so I had to very carefully retrace my steps and grab him. Funnily enough, though,

as I got to him the bear backed off. He took a few paces backwards, and then lay down and went to sleep, as if to say, 'Oh for goodness sake, leave me alone to rest here in peace.' So we did. That really was one of the high points of my life – just an amazing experience.

Sadly, bear encounters don't always end as well as ours did. I remember a series I made a few years ago about bears, wolves and leopards where I interviewed a lady from Alberta who had been attacked by a grizzly bear. She'd been out hunting with her husband and, for whatever reason, he was into shooting animals from a long distance. He used a .300 Winchester Magnum rifle, which is a fairly pokey weapon to use; he'd shot at an elk and wounded the animal and then shot again but hadn't seen it go down so he assumed he'd missed and it had gone into some willows. He'd arranged with his wife, who was also a keen hunter, that he would stay where he was at his vantage point so that if the elk showed up again he would finish it off, while she would go down to the willows and look for it. And that's what she did. She was also armed with a .300 Winchester Magnum rifle – however, she'd never got on with it.

Bears are quite canny creatures and in the area that they were hunting, the bears had learned to run towards the sound of the fall of the shot because they would often get a free meal; the hunter would do the work and before he could get there to recover the spoils, a bear would have beaten him to it. Well in this case, the man's wife never found the elk but she did find a grizzly with her cub running towards her. She stopped to chamber a round in her rifle but the chamber was empty. So then she was stood there, fumbling for rounds to load into a rifle she didn't like, and of course as she looked

up the bear was right there in front of her.

She described the bear's eyes to me; she told me how hypnotic they were and how she couldn't help but stare into them. To a bear, though, that's a sign of aggression and the bear did just what bears do when they feel threatened. Most people assume that a bear would swipe you with its paw, but its primary means of attack is to use its mouth. The grizzly stood fully upright, placed its paws on the woman's rifle, and then bit her in the face. It then went for her breast, and as she dropped to the ground, the bear took a bite out of her hip. That's when she realised that she had to play dead to survive, so, struggling with excruciating pain, she lay stock-still. The bear then walked away with its cub and left her alone.

I imagine you think that the bear was trying to kill her, but that would be wrong; it was only trying to warn her off, so it did what it normally does with other bears and bit her. When a bear bites another bear, it's almost never fatal because it's really only issuing a warning and so not using all its strength. Also, a bear's skin is tough like old leather, whereas by comparison ours is like tissue paper. The lady was badly mauled and has since had very successful reconstructive surgery. She doesn't dislike bears, although her husband does. I look at the aftermath of that situation and the obvious thing is that if her husband hadn't shot the elk from such a ridiculous range, he would have killed it with one shot and, in all likelihood, nobody would have been hurt. Also, if his wife had been using a rifle that she felt comfortable with, perhaps she'd have been able to chamber a round more easily. Really, she should have had a round already in there with the safety on; an unchambered rifle is just a club where dangerous animals are concerned.

The .300 Magnum rifle that her husband was using was a powerful weapon to use against an elk, but not from where he was shooting. Also, it has a lot of recoil and his wife was

small, which may well have been why she didn't like it. If she'd had her own rifle – a .243 – with her and had loaded it with an appropriate solid copper bullet, she would have had the means of slowing that bear down and would probably not have been injured. Just having the rifle chambered would have made a difference. The bear would have perceived the situation differently because her posture would have changed. So lots of lessons to be learned there.

Grizzly bears have quite a bad reputation that I don't believe they deserve. I think black bears are rather more dangerous because they're more gregarious and much more likely to sneak up on you. If a black bear was hungry, it would deliberately stalk you and try to eat you. With grizzlies you really have to go out of your way to upset one; they'll let you know if they don't want you around.

22

Dark Clouds

In 2002, Rachel, Nathan, Ellie and I moved house. We'd outgrown the property in Eastbourne that we'd built our first home in, and Woodlore was really taking off, so we needed somewhere suitable both as a home and a place from which we could run the business. I was still having to go away a lot, either with filming commitments, lectures or running courses for Woodlore students – although, because there are only so many hours in the day, I'd had to recruit people to run some courses in my absence. I had also started to offer courses further afield – in the Arctic, and in the rainforests.

Rachel found a bungalow with some land on the edge of a beautiful forested part of England, on the border between East Sussex and Kent, and it's where the four of us made our home. On the first morning after we moved, Rachel ran outside and did cartwheels on the lawn – in her pyjamas. We were happy there for a while, but eventually the bungalow had to go because it started subsiding, so over the next year or so we designed, and then built, our perfect home.

It was a good move. By early 2003, things were going well for Rachel and me, and for Woodlore – the company that I created but which we'd built up together. When I think back to its inauspicious beginnings, forged in the crucible of Operation Raleigh, it's hard to believe that things were going

along so smoothly then. When I set out, it felt like I was the only person in the UK with an interest in bushcraft, and when Woodlore started, that was all there was. Yes, there were survival schools – but they didn't do what we did.

During the first twelve years of the company, I spent a lot of time developing my technical skills. I was experimenting with everything to try to find out what was real, what wasn't, what was the creation of woodcraft camps and what was genuine bushcraft, real native bushcraft from the wilds. That took a lot of sorting out, but by 2003 I really felt I was getting somewhere. Rather than teach thirty ways of doing something, I would rather teach five that people can use anywhere; five skills that are bombproof.

In terms of my personal life, things couldn't have been better. On the TV front, I was happy with where my career was going. I had several series to my name, and I felt that I'd started to get my message out. People were watching, and learning. I'd travelled the world making programmes that I hoped were of interest to the viewing public, but in doing so I'd also acquired a much better knowledge and understanding of indigenous cultures, and the skills used by their people to survive – in one or two cases, skills that had withstood the test of 10,000 years or more.

In July 2003, I had a commitment in London to do some voice recordings. It was a rare day off in many respects – a few hours in a studio recording the narration to one of my TV documentaries, but otherwise I had time on my hands, so Rachel came with me and we booked into a gorgeous hotel. The plan was to go out for dinner when I finished, a few drinks and then back to the hotel. A nice big breakfast the following morning – the full works – and then off to a travel agency to book the trip of a lifetime.

For years we'd talked about planning our own trip to Australia. It had been a long-held dream but it had to take a

back seat while we built the company and established ourselves. Sure, I'd been there a number of times making TV documentaries, but I'd never had a holiday there and Rachel had never been to the continent. So we had made a decision. After lots of prevaricating, we'd settled on a holiday: just the two of us, in a country that I knew intimately and loved. We'd been putting it off and putting it off but something changed and on a whim I said, 'Look, let's just do this. Let's make it happen.'

So I went to London to work, and the next day we were going to book the trip. The voice recording had gone really well and Rachel met me straight from the studio. We walked back to the hotel together, but she didn't seem herself. It was when we got back to our room that everything changed. I shut the door; she sat on the bed.

'Come here. I've got something to tell you.'

'I've got something to tell you.' Think on that for a moment. Six words. But they're loaded; it's one of those phrases that you never, ever want to hear, isn't it? Those six words almost never presage anything good. My blood ran cold. My stomach flipped. I don't know what I expected her to say, but whatever it was, it wasn't what she said next.

'Ray . . . Ray, I've got breast cancer.'

And it was like the world stopped turning on its axis. Suddenly everything changed; everything was different – in an instant. Just like that. Four words. And everything changed. Forever.

It was as if I'd been hit by a sledgehammer. The room began to spin a little and for a moment I couldn't function. My head didn't feel like mine because there was nothing there. No words came, no actions came, because I'd no idea what to do or say. I just sat there, looking at her. I remember putting my arms around her but I couldn't tell you if I spoke. Actually, I don't think I did for a few more minutes.

The news left me reeling because I'd had absolutely no idea.

Not a clue. I didn't even know she'd found a lump. She had obviously suspected something, but she'd kept it to herself. She'd even delayed seeing anyone about it for a week because she wanted to see a female doctor. She had seen her that morning while I was in the studio.

We didn't stay in London that night – how could we? We checked out of the hotel straight away, the bed as pristine as when we'd arrived, and headed home. We'd come up on the train and I remember the journey back as if it happened yesterday. There was a terrific storm – thunder and the most extraordinary lightning. It was as if the earth was angry too; like it was mirroring how I felt.

The train was packed, so we took seats in First Class because there was nowhere else to sit. A ticket inspector approached us and got very aggressive when I told him we didn't have tickets for First Class, but were quite happy to pay whatever the fare was. But he was having none of it. That's when I lost control and let him have it. Poor guy, it wasn't his fault – but I told him in pretty clear terms that my partner had had some really bad news and to just take the money, give us the tickets, and clear off. It did the trick because he backed off and never said another word.

I was in the middle of filming a series of *Bushcraft Survival* the day our lives changed, and was due in Canada a few weeks later, but I don't remember much of what we did in the immediate aftermath. I put my own anger, my own feelings aside and did everything I could to reassure Rachel. She was a fighter, and between us we were determined to beat this horrible disease, but in the meantime we were stuck in limbo with no clear path ahead and no way of knowing whatever the future held. Woodlore and my filming commitments placed demands on us both that we couldn't escape, so it was with a heavy heart that I bade her farewell in early August and headed to Northern Ontario.

The filming went OK but my heart wasn't really in it – for

the first time I was looking forward to it ending so I could get back to Rachel. Towards the latter end of our time there, Ben Southwell, the director, suddenly changed the venue for the next shoot, saying he wanted to bring forward a scene he wanted to wrap now instead of later. So I did what he asked and found myself canoeing along the Missinaibi River, when I noticed a float plane circling overhead. As I watched, it made a final turn and began its descent, landing a few hundred yards downstream of me. I paddled towards it and realised he'd landed in some rapids, which I thought was bizarre. Then the door opened and I heard the pilot shout, 'I've come to pick you up.' I immediately thought he meant all of us, but then why on earth would he do that when we were in the middle of filming? I quickly realised the aircraft could only take two people at a time, plus one canoe, so I said, 'OK, but take the others first. I'm more at home in the bush so it makes more sense to come back for me last.'

'Are you the presenter?' he asked.

'Yes, I am.'

'Then it's you I've come for; get in.'

At that point I started to wonder what the hell was going on but I climbed in, took the seat next to him and, as I settled, he handed me a Thermos flask.

'Here, have some coffee.'

Except it wasn't just coffee; it had Baileys in it. And then I knew something really wasn't right. That's when I started to panic; Rachel, it had to be Rachel. Something must have happened and she needed to get in touch. The pilot handed me a satellite phone.

'Raymond?'

For a moment, I was completely thrown. It wasn't Rachel; it was my mum, the absolute last person I'd expected.

'Mum? Is everything OK?'

'Raymond, it's your father. He's been rushed into hospital.'

After that, everything seemed to happen in a blur. Within two hours of climbing aboard that float plane I was on a jet starting my journey home. I left all my gear – Ben and the rest of the crew brought that back for me.

And that's when I learned that my father had terminal lung cancer.

Dad's 'mistake' was being young at a time when smoking was so trendy. Back in the 40s and 50s everyone smoked – all the movie stars, the glamorous women, the icons, and so everyone emulated that. He smoked a pipe; he was part of that generation for whom, I guess, it was cool to smoke. He'd been ill for some time, so I can't say the cancer came as a great surprise but it was still a shock to realise that our long-held fears had come true. We'd always warned him about it.

The prognosis wasn't good. They gave him a year.

23

Down to Earth

What with my father's lung cancer and Rachel's diagnosis with breast cancer, it's difficult to see clearly through the fog that blanketed much of what I did over this period. The entire family seemed to exist by mechanically plodding onwards from one thing to the next without thinking about the future too much. It truly was a very difficult time. However, when it came to my work, I had no choice but to step outside of myself and wear a mask that I could present to the world. There's one day though, even through the all-enveloping fog, that remains crystal clear in my mind's eye. I can even remember the date: Monday 23 August 2004. I can be certain about the date because it's the day that I almost died.

———◆◆◆———

It's early morning, Wyoming, USA. I'm in a town called Riverton. I push through the door of the faceless chain hotel that's been home for the past couple of days and out into the street. It's a grey day – low cloud, light precipitation with very strong gusts of wind. That could be a problem; we've chartered a helicopter for this afternoon to use as a platform for some aerial filming.

I hear the door open again behind me, and Alan Duxbury steps out.

'Not the best weather for flying, is it?' I say.

'Touch-and-go I reckon, mate,' is Al's reply. 'I'll get Matt to give the pilot a call, find out where we stand.'

That'll be Matt Brandon, the series director who heads up the film crew for the episode of *Bushcraft Survival* that we're here in Wyoming to make. There's also our sound recordist Andy Morton, production manager Cassie Walking and researcher Mary Albion. They'll be out too any moment.

We're making a programme about local legend Jim Bridger. For me, Bridger was undoubtedly *the* most notable of all the mountain men, trappers, scouts and guides who explored and trapped the Western United States between 1820 and 1850. His was a fascinating story. He was a really interesting guy who, unusually, didn't die with an arrow in his back – it was old age that killed him. He managed this unusual feat because he understood the Native Americans and there was a mutual respect between them.

He also had a reputation as a great storyteller and one of his favourite yarns had him being pursued by more than a hundred Cheyenne warriors. He'd recount how, after being chased for several miles, he'd found himself at the end of a box canyon, with the Indians bearing down on him. At this point, he'd go silent, prompting his listener to ask, 'What happened then, Mr Bridger?' He'd reply, 'Why, they killed me!'

───────◆───────

The others step outside into the chilly August weather. I hear Al speaking to Matt about calling the pilot and watch as Matt steps away to make the call.

Al turns to me: 'That guy we filmed yesterday was amazing, wasn't he? What was his name?'

'Ah, Jake Korell,' I say.

'Yeah, that's him – "Trapper Jake".'

Korell is in his late 90s and another fascinating figure who still worked trapping beavers and shooting coyotes for the ranchers in the area. One of the reasons we'd filmed him was because as a boy he'd known people who had met some of the legends of the West such as Calamity Jane and Annie Oakley, so he was a living link with history. After we'd finished filming, the old-timer cooked for us all over an open fire in the bush, finishing off with a peach cobbler that really hit the spot.

'Days like that are priceless,' Al says, 'a real privilege.'

Just then, Matt comes across: 'OK, I've spoken with the pilot – his name is Lionel Lester. He says that provided the rain holds off, we should be OK. He's got to fuel up later, so he'll reassess then. If it's dry, he'll meet with us as arranged. If not, he'll call me from his satellite phone and turn back.

'What I suggest is that we head to Lander and meet Jeremy Washakie this morning as planned. We can wrap up filming some of Ray's pieces to camera and some of the more basic shots.'

Lander is a small town up in the mountains and the famed Oregon Trail runs east–west near there; the wheel ruts from the old wagon trains are still clearly visible and we wanted to get some aerial shots to illustrate that. Calamity Jane lived in it back in the day – apparently she had a whorehouse on one side of the main street in Lander and a dress shop on the other. As Jake put it, 'She was making money on both sides of the street!'

Jeremy Washakie is the great-grandson of Chief Washakie, a Shoshone chief who was another contemporary of Jim Bridger. Jeremy is a one-off – a Native American Indian who is also a cowboy. It means he's an excellent rider, which is one of the reasons we are meeting him.

We spent some time the previous week filming me on horseback in Yellowstone National Park. Now horse-riding isn't a skill I've ever had to acquire before this series, so I

had to learn before the shoot. I feel privileged to have been taught by a Shoshone Indian, but I could hardly claim to be experienced.

We need some aerial footage of someone riding a horse by the Oregon Trail. Bring on Jeremy – the plan is to film some long lens shots of him riding.

Now until this point, things have really been going our way, even to the point of us filming wolves in Yellowstone when we'd been told emphatically that none were around. Despite all the problems back home, this was turning out to be a great shoot.

So, onwards to Lander where I spend most of the morning doing pieces to camera. There is still a large amount of cloud overhead, with exceptionally high winds and the odd bit of rain but we carry on regardless. It's only weather – you deal with it.

When we finish, Mary and Cassie go back to our hotel to organise our luggage for the move to our next location. When they come back, they bring some food so we all break for lunch and kick our heels waiting for the helicopter to arrive.

It's about 13:30hrs when I first hear the familiar whirring of blades, then watch as the helicopter settles into the hover and lands. The pilot shuts down the aircraft – a Bell 206B JetRanger – and walks over to us. He extends a hand.

'Hi, I'm Lionel. Nice to meet you.'

I return the compliment and we all introduce ourselves.

'Have you done any aerial filming before?' Alan asks.

'Yeah, a fair bit. I did two tours in Vietnam, logged over 16,000 hours on various helicopters, so whatever you want to do is fine by me, just so long as it's within the physical capabilities of the aircraft – and my own.'

I've no idea where it comes from but I'm struck by a feeling that something isn't right. It's not something I can put my finger on – call it a sixth sense – but I have a definite feeling that

something is wrong. I can't articulate it any better than that. Events overtake us though, and conscious concerns overrule my subconscious. The feeling is buried.

'Obviously, it's exceptionally windy today,' Lionel says. 'For that reason, it'll be better if you film when I'm flying *into* the wind because I can control our speed better. If the wind is behind us, then we're going to be flying a lot faster and the aircraft won't be as stable a filming platform as it could be. Clear?'

Alan nods, and explains what we're looking to achieve:

'OK, if you've filmed before, you'll be familiar with this, but what I want to do is to get some footage of Jeremy – he's the guy on the horse over there – riding along the ridge.'

Lionel nods, and Alan carries on talking through the list of shots that he wants to achieve, while Lionel interjects with affirmatives and the odd, 'Sure, that's not a problem.' Lionel is affable enough – he appears to be exceptionally pleasant and seems keen to help us get the shots we want.

'I understand you want to take the door off,' Lionel says to Alan.

'Yeah, the left one ideally – I can just sit the camera on my lap and still see the viewfinder.'

'Ah, OK. Really, I'd prefer we ditched the right one so I've got you sat directly behind me.'

Alan demurs – at the end of the day, the pilot's the captain of his ship and wherever there's a conflict between what we, as passengers, want and what the pilot says is preferable, his decisions trump everything else.

Sitting on the right isn't ideal for Alan because it means that he has to twist round to see out of the viewfinder, but ultimately you have to play the hand you're dealt. It makes things more difficult, but not impossible – life's all about compromise.

Lionel removes the door and we agree between us who will sit where. Lionel is flying from the front right seat, so Alan

will sit behind him. I want to shoot some stills, so I sit next to Al on the left side. Matt has never done an aerial shoot before, so we suggest he sits in the front left seat with his monitor so he can review what Alan is shooting. He'll also be able to hear Alan talking to the pilot, so it will all be useful in the future if Matt's to be involved in other aerial shoots.

Alan is wearing a five-point harness with a karabiner, which he uses to secure himself to the inside of the cabin – it's an additional layer of safety when shooting through an open door so he can lean outside without any worry of falling. Alan looks at me: 'Ray, if anything happens, this is where I'm anchored, just in case I'm trapped or unable to release myself.'

'It won't come to that. Come on, how many times have we done this?'

We both laugh.

'Lionel, if I ask you to do anything that you consider too stupid, unsafe or you're simply not happy about it, then don't do it. Just tell me and we'll find another way to achieve what we need. OK?'

'Affirmative to that.'

It's something I've heard Alan say to every pilot who's flown us – a tacit admission that he recognises that the pilot's word on any matter is final, Ultimately it's just Alan's way of saying, 'I know how this works.'

Lionel gives us a standard safety briefing and then fires up the Bell's engine. I watch him as he takes the controls, and within seconds we lift gracefully into the afternoon sky.

First off, Alan wants to get some shots of Jeremy riding across the plain. We accomplish this without too much drama, although initially Lionel is worried about spooking the horse, so makes a pass quite a long way out, thus making life difficult for Alan who has to shoot right on the limits of the lens'

capabilities. Eventually, Lionel flies closer to the ridge and Alan gets the shots he wants.

The next shot on the list is for a close-up of Jeremy which Alan will then pull slowly outwards to reveal that Jeremy's sat on a horse. As he pulls back to the end of the lens, the shot will encompass Jeremy on the horse and show the whole of the plain with the mountains behind, the sky and the surrounding topography. It's a classic 'reveal' shot that gives the viewer a frame of reference.

Alan's contorting himself with one leg folded underneath him in an attempt to get the best position for the shot, and I'm sitting upright, watching everything around me, when Lionel makes his next pass. It's too quick.

'Can we make that pass again, Lionel?' Al asks over the intercom.

'Sure can, but it'll be at a similar sort of speed,' says Lionel. 'That wind's pretty gusty so I'm not able to fly as slow as I might. And I'll have to fly downwind.'

'Not a problem for me,' Alan replies. 'Now I know, I can set the shot up.'

The fact that Lionel says he has to fly downwind means nothing to us. None of us are pilots, nor are we particularly 'air-minded' so we don't realise that it means the aircraft will need more power to stay aloft, power that is in short supply as, unbeknown to us, the aircraft is within 1 per cent of its maximum weight given the full complement of passengers and our equipment, plus an almost full fuel load.

That sort of weight figure isn't a problem if you're flying point A to point B at altitude, but if you're flying any sort of manoeuvres – such as those required in aerial filming – then you need power in hand. This particular manoeuvre turns out to be a grave mistake that will have serious ramifications for all of us. And it's born of the fact that most of Lionel's 16,000 hours' flying experience has been garnered at sea level, flying

to and from oil rigs. As it transpires, he's only recently started flying in the mountains, where the air is thinner. That has an impact on how aircraft perform.

Singularly, none of these facts present a problem. Combined though, they come together to create a 'perfect storm' that whips up all too soon.

Lionel makes the approach. We're 40ft or so from a ridge that forms the edge of the plain that Jeremy is on; I notice the altitude indicator on the instrument panel and do a double take – we're flying at just 20ft above the deck. I glance at the airspeed indicator – it reads 70 knots. The thought occurs to me that, with the fact we're flying downwind, our groundspeed is going to be somewhat higher than 70 knots.

Lionel makes a violent turn that leaves me utterly disorientated. I look out of my window and at first I can't work out where we are relative to Jeremy. Then I notice the ridge seems to be a lot closer than on our last pass. It occurs to me that the ground beneath us rises in a gentle incline – and we don't seem to have the altitude to clear it.

I sense we're drifting – there's a definite list towards my side, the left-hand side of the aircraft – but all of this is happening so quickly, almost simultaneously.

I see the ground beneath us and it's rushing towards me.

The thought, when it comes, is calm and rational: 'We're going to hit.'

As I think it, I hear an alarm going off in the cockpit. With it comes the chilling, certain knowledge that I'm about to die.

'Shit, this doesn't look very good,' is the last thing I remember thinking.

———◆◆———

Nobody in their forties lives without sometimes confronting the uncomfortable knowledge of their own mortality. I've often

wondered how I'd die – I guess it's fair to say I've had a few close shaves before now, but none of them ever got to the point where I thought without doubt, 'This really is the end.' Always, in the aftermath, I'd think about how my death might pan out and the things I might do as my impending doom unfolded – maybe I'd pour myself a huge drink, listen to some music and make some calls as I readied myself for the moment. Author Chris Ayres says in his book *War Reporting for Cowards*, 'If drunk-dialling is bad, imagine death-dialling – that could really get you into some trouble in the morning if you were unlucky enough to survive whatever you thought was going to kill you,' so perhaps on reflection, I'd ditch the phone calls.

But I don't get a chance to do any of that.

Inside the helicopter, everything changes in an instant and a subconscious thought prompts me to adopt the brace position. I do so without thinking and I feel like a giant hand is forcing us down.

The skid on my side of the aircraft strikes the ground. The force is immense.

We bounce up, and I have the sense that we're almost clawing at the air. The tail rotor strikes the ground and shears off with the boom and I'm vaguely aware of it flying past me, past the cockpit, at great speed.

Then suddenly, we're upended and we pitch forwards, nose down. The Bell's rotor blades – the sole means of keeping us aloft – spin their last. They strike the earth ahead of us, then dig in and shear off with terrific force.

People in car accidents and other severe traumas talk about time becoming elastic and slowing down, but in this case it feels like the polar opposite. Time seems to *accelerate*. It is so, so violent – like nothing I've ever experienced before. The energy is phenomenal – like having hold of a giant elastic band at full stretch before letting go. The mass of

energy, the torque that's involved in a jet-engined helicopter, is something to behold. There's an aphorism that says that a helicopter is really just 10,000 totally unrelated moving parts, bent on self-destruction, flying in relatively close formation. Let loose, those moving parts exert a force that's all but beyond words.

The cabin, by now orphaned from the other components that made up the helicopter we'd been flying in just a few seconds before, somersaults three times. We are inverted and I reach out to grab Alan, but as soon as my hand approaches him, massively violent g-forces snatch it back and we tumble over and over again, impacting the ground before finally, thankfully, sliding to a halt.

Gone is the iconic shape of the Bell; we're now suspended upside down in what from the outside must resemble a random collection of mangled, twisted metal. The debris field is huge, bits of our helicopter strewn across the plain like discarded litter. Even now, I can still hear the sound of the aluminium body as we crash, and it's a sound like the earth screaming. I can hear the gravel death-rattling as we slide along it at an altitude no aircraft should ever be in. It's a sound I never want to hear again.

———◆———

We've stopped and all I can hear is silence – it's deafening. It's as if the twisting, scraping, nails-on-a-blackboard noises that define the crash have created a vacuum in their wake.

My brain sends out questions to the furthest reaches of my body, and my nerves convey signals back that answer: 'All present and correct.' I feel all right, but surely I can't have survived that completely unscathed?

A thought: 'Maybe I'm injured but I don't realise it.' But no, I'm really OK.

I've survived. I thought I was dead but I'm alive. I'm filled with a sense of euphoria.

At that moment, I feel Alan move beside me. My sense of euphoria increases as I realise I'm not the only one alive; Alan is too.

'I'm alive, but my legs are broken,' he says. My heart sinks. I look across to him and his right leg is at a horrific angle, the bottom half at 90° to the horizontal. His feet hang uselessly from broken ankles, with all the rigidity of a rag doll. The tibia and fibula in both legs are smashed. He must be in agony.

'Don't move,' I say to him. 'You'll be fine. I'll get you out.'

My survival instinct immediately kicks in. I know exactly what to do. I fumble for my seat belt release.

And that's when something ruptures above us and we're immediately drenched. I smell it even before it soaks me. It's jet fuel – 250 litres of it.

We're trapped in the wreckage, soaked in fuel with no idea what to do next. This is what *real* terror feels like.

24

Zanshin

As I'm hanging there, soaked in fuel, a thought occurs to me and I remember something that Kingsley had said to me so many years before. He told me, 'Ray, if you're ever in an accident, try to relax. You're less likely to be hurt if you're relaxed.' What he said is a fundamental element of judo – you always try to fall relaxed rather than stiff, and that's what I did as we came down. I adopted the brace position, just trying to absorb it, and it appears to have paid off. I feel OK.

I release my seat belt and drop gently to what had previously been the helicopter's ceiling but is now the floor. I clear my head. I need to focus; I'm the only one that I know for certain has escaped this crash without a scratch. I need to free Alan; he's my first priority.

I exit the aircraft through a hole that has been opened up in the impact. I'm wearing a new pair of buckskin gloves that I bought locally; it turns out they're absolutely perfect for wiping jet fuel from your eyes, as they are incredibly absorbent. Who knew?

I get to Alan.

'Alright mate, I'm here. I'm going to get you out.'

I brace myself as I undo his seat belt; Alan's a big guy and I'm worried he'll fall back *into* the wreckage and on to something sharp. I grab hold of him but nothing happens. He's stuck.

'Ray, I know we're close but can we save the hugs until later?' he jokes. 'I'm wearing my safety harness, remember?'

My small folding knife is in my pocket. I take it out, unfold the blade and cut Al free with one hand, while supporting him with my other. He's 6'2", but I have so much adrenaline pumping I'm able to hold him by myself. That's when I notice Matt is stood beside me with Lionel, our pilot. I can't quite believe we've all survived.

'Here, let me help,' says Matt, and together, we remove Alan and carry him to what I assume is a safe distance. We place him gently on the ground. His courage and stoicism are amazing; I can see his left foot and ankle are all mashed up, and his right leg is still at an alarming 90° angle to where it should be. The pain must be excruciating but he's still making the odd joke. He barely complains. He has a cut on his head – there's always a lot of blood with those because of the number of tiny blood vessels in the skin there.

'I'm sorry,' says Lionel. 'I don't know what to say. I've no idea what happened.'

'Are you OK?' I ask him and Matt.

Matt says he's OK, bar a few scratches. I'm worried about Lionel though; he appears to be in profound shock. He's also stooping; he looks like he's injured in some way. However, it's Alan who's the most badly injured and it's him I need to deal with first.

Jeremy Washakie rides over the hill on horseback and Matt shouts to him: 'Jeremy, we're OK. Can you ride over to the girls and tell them what's happened?'

He nods and, turning the horse around, gallops over towards Cassie, Mary and Andy who are with the cars about half a mile away.

Matt and I make Alan comfortable. I put a coat under his head and use my knife to cut his trousers open from their hem up to the knees. He has a major deformity to his right leg above his boot; his tibia and fibula are clearly broken. His left

foot is damaged too but his boot's providing support so I leave it in place. I check his pupils; no dilation.

While I'm doing this, I hear the production cars pull up. Andy, Mary and Cassie get out and come over. I can see the shock on their faces.

Matt walks over to greet them. I watch them walk towards the cars and return with some Pelican cases. I use them to make a windbreak to shelter Alan.

I'm worried about Lionel. His stoop has worsened. He appears to be in pain.

'Lionel, come on. Why don't you lie down?' I suggest. We need to keep him prone until help arrives.

I get the first-aid kit from one of the production cars. As it transpires, it's really poorly packed and as good as useless. I'm angry. A few years ago, I asked the BBC to put together a proper expedition medical kit, but of course it went off on other trips and never came back, so we're stuck with a bog standard one which isn't majorly different to what you'd get off the shelf in your local Boots store.

I end up using some gaffer tape and a Karrimat and I improvise some splints to immobilise Alan's legs. We can't put him in traction – the pain would be too much for him to bear – so I very carefully straighten his legs out and then wrap them. That way he's afforded at least a degree of protection.

Cassie and Mary are just brilliant. I get Cassie to make a list of the injuries that I've identified, and ask Mary to contact the emergency services on 911. As she's talking, it appears from what I can hear of her end of the conversation that they don't believe her – I mean it's probably not the sort of occurrence they're used to dealing with every day.

She hands the phone to me and I explain what's happened to the girl on the end of the line. 'Look, we've been in a heli-copter crash. Everyone is alive but it was a serious crash with a lot of energy involved. There's one seriously injured person

so we'll need an air ambulance to recover him – he has two broken legs and other injuries, including possible internal injuries. We also have one man complaining of back pain.'

I have a Garmin Geko GPS device in my jacket and feel for it; it's still there. I was worried it had been dislodged in the impact. I take it out and give the emergency operator a six-figure grid reference for our exact location. I then ask her to read it back to me, which she does. She confirms that help is on its way and then I end the call.

When I walk over to Alan, somewhat typically for a cameraman, he's only concerned with the tape in his camera and I hear him shout to Andy, 'Mate, get the tape out, get the tape out,' which Andy does. Then I remember I've left my cameras – a Mamiya 7 and a Leica M7 in the wreckage too. I recover them. The two filters I put on the lenses have both been smashed in the impact but, incredibly, the bodies themselves and the lenses appear to be in working order. I take some images of the crash site, as does Mary.

Things start happening pretty rapidly after that. First to turn up is the sheriff, who doesn't really seem to know what to do. Hardly surprising really; I can't imagine he's seen many helicopter crashes up to that point. So in lieu of doing nothing, he resorts to that law enforcement officer's favourite stand-by and starts taking everyone's name and address. Next, some 'amateur' paramedics arrive – one of them kicks Alan's leg, so you can imagine how well that went down. I don't really need to say a thing, though – Alan does *all* the talking needed. I have to say, I had no idea his repertoire of swear words was so vast.

Then a fire engine turns up. It looks utterly incongruous given our location in the middle of a great expanse of open plain. The crew look immensely disappointed that there's no fire. A short time later, a much more professional team of paramedics arrive and administer some much-needed analgesia

to Alan. Lionel is placed on a spinal board with his neck immobilised and then he's taken off to hospital.

It's only when I see the air ambulance making its approach a few minutes later that it suddenly occurs to me that perhaps another helicopter isn't the best thing for Alan from a psychological perspective. It's no more than a passing thought though; he's severely injured, and a helicopter represents his best chance of getting to the appropriate level of medical care in the fastest time possible. The crew are a model of professionalism. They ensure Alan is comfortable, load him up and that's it, they are gone.

It's only now that everyone has been dealt with that I relinquish control and responsibility for the accident site; I find doing so really, really difficult because as long as I was co-ordinating the rescue, I was occupied and in control. Handing it all over means becoming a casualty myself. It has to be done though, and then I too am taken off to hospital, along with Matt, to be checked over.

Looking back now, I remember that in the immediate aftermath of the accident, my overwhelming feeling was simply one of shock. For someone like me, that's massively frustrating because I just want to get on with whatever I have to do, but after the crash all bets were off. I felt completely discombobulated and out of sorts.

Almost unbelievably, aside from a few bruises, both Matt and I escaped injury. Lionel chipped a tooth and fractured a vertebrae in his back, and was in hospital for a week or so, but poor Alan remained in hospital for over two weeks receiving treatment and was eventually repatriated to the UK, where he was admitted to a top Birmingham hospital for more operations and rehabilitation. Unfortunately, although he did

eventually go back to work, it didn't last – the legacy of that trip was that he was no longer able to work. It was terribly sad because he was a first-rate cameraman and a key member of the team on so many expeditions. He is also a good friend and I know that even now, he still feels the loss of his career.

Both he and Barrie are really special, just brilliant guys. I know other cameramen used to wonder why they got all the jobs, but it was simply because they were really good at what they did. Nothing was too much trouble for Alan and he never seemed to get tired. Before the accident he had boundless energy, and to see that stripped away from him by the ineptitude of our pilot that day makes me angry.

When you fly with good pilots, you *know*. I didn't feel that with Lionel. He had supposedly done two tours of Vietnam – although it later transpired that he wasn't out there as a pilot; he'd been a Chief Tech, so there's a massive difference. On paper, he appeared to be one of the best around – he had over 16,000 hours logged, which is a simply huge amount for any pilot. Sadly for us, he was completely inexperienced in both mountain flying, which was what we needed him for on the day, and perhaps just as crucially, filming – he'd done almost none.

I'm still angry about that, although in my more contemplative moments I do recognise that we're all enormously lucky to have survived that crash. We were lucky too where the fuel cloud was concerned. I mean we were all covered in it, but because of the way it landed on us – almost like a mist – we all breathed it into our lungs too and if it had gone up, we'd have burned from the inside out. It doesn't bear thinking about.

———— ◆ ————

Sadly, for me, the accident wasn't the worst aspect of that trip to Wyoming. And although it's the day that I almost died and

I remember it for that, the following day delivered another massive blow.

It's the day I found out my father had died.

The morning after the crash, I hadn't long woken up and was in my hotel room, looking at my camera and wondering how salvageable it was and whether I'd be able to shake out all the broken glass and other debris from the crash.

The phone rang. I picked it up.

'Ray, hi. It's Dick Colthurst [the series producer]. I'm afraid I have some very bad news for you. It's your father – he died yesterday.'

However much you expect to hear news like that, it still knocks you for six. And while his death wasn't unexpected, it still felt like the bottom had fallen out of my world. The only plus for me was that he never knew about the crash and he died without knowing that Rachel too was battling cancer.

My dad; my lovely, patient, wonderful, warm and caring dad. Such a lovely man.

He lost a finger when he was a young man; it got caught on a rag when he was cleaning one of the printing presses and got crushed, but it didn't slow him down. His zest for life knew no bounds and he was extraordinarily patient. He was something of an engineer as I guess a lot of men from his generation were – I once saw him convert a friction-feed printing press to suction feed, and he made *everything* involved in that. He made the device that he connected to the gearing system to control the suction device; he machined the pistons and he even made the rubber suckers to go on those pistons. With friction feed you have a bar that moves forward over a stack of paper and pushes a single sheet in, but what his suction-feed machine had was two pistons that would pick up the paper and feed it into the printing press. That's not an easy thing to create, especially in a garden shed. He did that

so that he could print envelopes with greater accuracy. He was a very, very clever man.

While he was at News International, he became embroiled in the bitter dispute that occurred when Rupert Murdoch abruptly moved his printing operation to a non-union plant in Wapping. My father kept his integrity and fought, but it was a hopeless battle that sadly the guys were never going to win. Murdoch had covered all his bases and he broke the unionisation that had dominated Fleet Street for decades. When the strike broke, my dad started his own printing business. It was very successful and he retired happy and content.

I still really miss him.

25

Into the Dark

After her diagnosis, Rachel was advised to have a mastectomy. That was when time became an issue: if her lymph nodes were clear, then they'd do reconstructive surgery then and there, and she'd be in theatre for a number of hours; if, however, she was in theatre for only a short time, that was a different matter altogether and something I didn't want to think about.

The day of the operation came around much too quickly, but it was imperative we knew what was happening. Sadly she wasn't in theatre for very long. The news was as bleak as we could have feared: the cancer was terminal. I heard the words coming out of the consultant's mouth but they didn't compute. It was like having one of those out-of-body experiences people talk about; like I was watching this from afar and it was happening to somebody else. Rachel? Terminal cancer? How on earth could that be true?

The trauma of learning that the woman I loved was going to die – and that we almost knew the date – was devastating and it affected my eyesight. I don't know how or why, and I can't explain it any more eloquently, but it temporarily damaged my eyesight.

She had two years. Two years. Twenty-four months. Seven hundred and thirty days. That was all it took. Two years to go from full health, a picture of vitality, to her death. We

thought we'd book that once-in-a lifetime trip to Australia that we never got round to arranging when we went to London. But the most mundane of things put paid to that idea and it never left the ground. We never got to travel to Australia together and it was all down to travel insurance. One of the things we learned quite quickly is that once you're seriously ill, you can't get health insurance to travel. How cruel is that? You've got limited time to live, so you think, 'I know, I'm going to go to that paradise I've always wanted to go to with the one I love. Sod the consequences.' But you can't.

The cruellest twist of all, though, was how quickly Rachel fell ill. There are different forms of breast cancer and Rachel had the most aggressive. Her decline was as painful to witness as it was rapid. She was amazing in how she dealt with it, just amazing. She was so, so brave. Immediately after we found out it was terminal, she seized the bull by the horns and got straight down to business. She'd never made a will; she had one drawn up the very next day. Then we sort of came up with a strategy to fight it. Terminal? She wasn't going to just give up, she went down fighting and she fought like a tiger right to the bitter end.

It's almost like you're living in a parallel universe after the diagnosis, as if you've been hived off from the real world. You start going to these clinics and you meet all these different people with all these different types of cancer, all different degrees, and they're all fighting this battle and it's a whole world that most people, thankfully, don't know anything about. There's a whole new language and shorthand to learn – it's like a secret landscape within Britain, complete with its own population.

My memories of that time have taken on a strange ethereal quality, and there are periods where I just can't remember anything – it's almost as if it's just too painful and my brain's shut those memories down and denied me access to them.

Rachel underwent both chemo and radiotherapy – the chemo in particular was awful. But there was a wonderful period of sunshine where she seemed to be a lot better. Sadly, it turned out to be false hope.

Rachel was a proud woman. She wanted life to continue as normal for everyone else around her, so she hid the fact that she was in a lot of pain. I remember her taking Nathan to the airport one day and she held it all in until she got home, where she subsequently collapsed and I ended up rushing her to hospital. The staff in A&E were fantastic, just fantastic. She was admitted straight away and that's where her care came undone. She had private healthcare so she was under an oncologist, but the hospital consultant didn't notify him. He was a bully, this consultant – a real bully. And when he realised how far her cancer had progressed, he sent a junior doctor to tell Rachel that she was dying. If I were ever unfortunate enough to be admitted under his care, I'd pull the lines out of my arm and crawl out rather than allow him to treat me.

I drove Rachel out of the hospital and took her over the South Downs – I thought if she was going to die we needed to spend some quality time together out of the hospital environment, and it's what she wanted. She hated being in hospital. I think that was on the Friday. Anyway, come Monday I managed to get word to her oncologist and he was furious. He had her admitted to a private ward and he took control again. Your first reaction is to complain and boy, did I want to fight. I wanted to go down and give that bully of a consultant a hiding. I thought of getting the press involved – there were so many different ways I was going to show him – but in the end I realised what was important, and energy spent on fights like that is energy you don't have to deal with the real battle.

Terminal cancer – anything like that, something life-changing, something that is going to take away the person you love more than anything in the whole world – teaches its own lessons. There's a paradigm shift in how you see and experience life. But you have to survive; life has to go on because, ultimately, there's no alternative. You still need to get up in the morning; eat, pay bills, buy shopping . . . it's the sheer mundanity of it all, the realisation that it's the minutiae of life that keeps you going. And in some ways, I guess, it's a good thing – the routine, the structure. It's its own form of support because if you're not careful, something like that can utterly overwhelm you. It's such a big thing to deal with, I'm not entirely sure you actually *cope* – you seem to more blunder through like a ball in a pinball machine, bumping from one problem to the next. As for the pain, the fear – I think I've blotted it all out. I really don't have a strong memory of that time.

All I can say is that when you are confronted with something so enormous, there's a profound challenge to your personal philosophy. You only survive if you've invested sufficiently in that philosophy because I think at that point you're on auto-pilot – you're no longer able to have control of anything. You become a passenger to some extent and life just carries you along. You have ups and you have downs but . . . how can I put this? You learn to swim, and at a time like this you are in rapids – occasionally you rise above the surface and take a gulp of air, but most of the time you feel like you're breathing water and drowning. All you can hope is that you'll eventually find the strength that enables you to swim out of the current.

In my case, I was my own support network. I trust myself. I trust my own judgement. I can deal with things. That's how I am. I don't really get lonely. I've always enjoyed solo trips into the bush but when Rachel was ill, I didn't want to leave her.

Fifteen years we'd been together; fifteen years in which we'd ribbed one another mercilessly about getting married. It became 'our thing', we joked and teased one another about it all the time. I'd ask her to marry me, and she'd say no. She'd ask me and I'd say the same. Because we never needed to. We were so together, we had consummate, utter trust in one another and we were in love. We didn't need to be married; it didn't matter, it wasn't important.

It didn't matter. Didn't. Past tense. Then suddenly, it took on huge importance. Nothing else mattered. It became the most important thing in the world. We married at Eastbourne Register Office.

Lars Fält, a close friend from Sweden, was my best man. And the date? It was 7 July, 2005 – 7/7 the day of the London bombings.

And then, a short time later, everything unravelled. Suddenly, being married didn't seem important. We had a vision of the end, and I would have given everything I had to delay the inevitable. I'd sworn to protect her. And I couldn't. I wanted to mend her, make everything better. All my knowledge, everything I'd learned, and there was nothing, *nothing,* I could do.

───────◆◆◆───────

We'd been sat in the lounge on the afternoon that everything started to spiral downwards; the day that flimsy wall we'd erected around ourselves crumbled to the ground and her illness unveiled itself before us in the most pitiless manner. There were a couple of steps at the end of the lounge, and another couple that led up into the kitchen. She had just got up to make a cup of tea; how mundane is that? And she tripped. I saw it happen, but it wasn't a normal trip like you or I would do if we got to a step and missed our footing. I could *see* – and her legs just didn't seem to be working properly. And I knew. I just knew something wasn't right.

Rachel rang her doctor and told him how she was feeling. Then I spoke to him and that's when he explained to me that the cancer had reached her brain. Sadly, medicine hasn't yet developed an effective way of delivering therapeutic agents across the blood–brain barrier to treat that type of cancer. That really marked the beginning of the end; we both knew that there was no way back from there.

The really awful thing about a terminal disease like Rachel's is that those left behind have time to prepare. There's an end point, a demarcation zone, a line in the sand. A part of you knows there's life on the other side for *you* but not for your loved one, yet your brain doesn't want to acknowledge it. It's an awful thing to say, but while Rachel deteriorated I had time to try – and try is all I could do – to come to terms with everything. You know that death is going to be a form of release for the person dying, but you don't want to let them go. My mind was awhirl with so many conflicting emotions, and for me it was one of the worst things because you can't help focusing on the end even though you feel awful doing so – it feels disloyal, like a betrayal of some kind.

There's no way Rachel was going to go into a hospice. I've nothing against them, but she wanted to be at home and I wanted her to be where I could take care of her, so that's what we did. I'm not even going to try and describe the last few days. She was aware, but she couldn't communicate by that stage so it was indescribably difficult. When she finally passed away, Nathan, Ellie and I were all there with her; the whole family was there in fact. It was 16 May 2006.

Afterwards, I was in a really strange place. It affects everybody differently, the aftermath. I really wasn't in a very good place at all. Losing Rachel was almost unbearable. I spent two years

caring for her and all of a sudden there was a void there, this Rachel-shaped vacuum where the person I loved, worshipped, used to exist. For the whole of that two years, we hadn't had a normal relationship but that's how it is – when the person you love and care about more than anyone else in the world is dying, you stop caring about yourself. For me, there was only her and I let myself go. I fell apart – physically as well as mentally. I wasn't important – she was. And then all of a sudden, I was on my own. Sadly, the immense strain of the whole ordeal, and the way that the effects of grief affect everybody, eventually tore the family apart.

I had so much resentment, frustration and anger inside me. I was angry at the world for taking her away. I felt lost. There was so much negative, poisonous emotion bubbling within me, yet I couldn't take it to the forest, which would have been my normal escape. It would have been wrong to take all that into the wilderness and get rid of it, almost like contaminating something beautiful. You have to rediscover your longing to go out again and so to take a problem outdoors would be to infect the outdoor experience with that problem.

I had to find another way to let it all flow out of me. After she died, I cried for three days solid. You have to let it out; you can't hold on to it. You have to let go. It's like in judo – if something's not working for you, you have to let it go, do something else. Judo philosophy is very powerful in that regard and it's a matter of finding a focus. You have to find a lifeline to grab hold of. And I found it, after a few months of floundering, in the gym.

The gym allowed me to create a routine, find myself something to do in the times when my mind was idle, when it would dwell on the things it shouldn't. It was very helpful – because it's so physical, it forces your body to produce endorphins and endorphins make you feel good and then you wear out as well, so you sleep, because otherwise you don't

sleep. *That* was really important. The weights, the cardiovascular equipment, became the focus of my existence for a while and I took all the bitterness, the hurt and, the anger into the gym with me. I wore myself out and in the process, got myself fit – both mentally and physically. Mentally, because I had the time and space to process everything in my head, and physically because it was my body that benefited from the training.

I had something to get up for every day, and very gradually I started to feel better. It was good for me – you just have to cope, but you need a focus and that was mine. Coping is something I teach people on my courses – I teach them to cope in the wilderness, so I had to take some of my own medicine and turn those skills inward. I had to cope with the loss. Also, it got me out of the house; memories of Rachel screamed from every room so it was good for me to get out. And to be around people again. I don't mind being on my own, but the isolation you feel when your soul mate dies is just so traumatic. It's horrible.

Her death changed me in countless ways. I can't watch a soppy TV programme or film now without a tear coming to my eye – things like that never affected me before. It's made me a lot more empathetic. But the biggest change is in how I see the world and how I don't believe in wasting a single second of life. Filming involves a lot of standing around and kicking your heels and I get really frustrated by all of that these days. I want to do something with the time, so I'll say to directors, 'If you don't need me in the next hour, tell me because I can do something with that time.' I don't want to stand around – time is too precious.

In the aftermath, I had to close the door on my old life – the life I had with Rachel. I had to accept that it was over and the best way for me to honour her memory was to start something new – a new life. Life goes on. I decided I'd do all

the things that I had denied myself before. If I was invited to any functions or events, I'd go – previously, I turned them all down.

I started a new chapter and was clear in my mind that I wouldn't make comparisons – what was before was before; everything that followed would be different. There is clear blue water between the two. I had to draw a line and it was important to me that I never made comparisons – either good or bad, between my old life and the new life I was leading. I needed to become a new person and to do that I needed clothes – clothes suitable for doing all the things I'd never done before. I didn't know anything about this – previously, I'd just worn green, all my attire was geared towards my outdoor life, my woodsman's life. That's still who I really was at heart, but I thought I should start doing all these other things too.

The irony is, I was doing publicity for a new TV series so it was the usual round of journalist interviews. One of the broadsheets wanted to talk to me, and the journalist – I won't name her, but she knows who she is – wanted to meet me in London, so I thought I'd dress appropriately for once. Instead of my usual greens and a fleece or outdoor jacket, I dressed in a good shirt with cufflinks, a smart jacket and slacks – you know, smart clothes, just what you'd wear for a decent hotel or bar in the capital. And the journalist made some snide reference in her copy about how I was dressed for the city rather than the woods. That was really hurtful and actually a bit of a cheap shot. She even had a dig at the fact that I didn't have a survival knife or emergency flares in my rucksack. The whole concept of dressing for, and carrying, what's appropriate for your environment seemed a bit lost on her. It was as if the clothes I was wearing detracted from who I am. Does dressing in a shirt really negate the fact I've dedicated my life to what I do?

I had bent over backwards to make myself available for

that interview. I don't court the press – but when you write books and present TV programmes you accept that you have to do a certain degree of publicity. It's something I'd rather not have to do – I really don't enjoy it – but I'd gone out of my way to accommodate her and it felt like a slap in the face. Funnily enough, I bumped into her again at the launch for the Range Rover Evoque. The look on her face when she saw me was a picture.

———◆———

Eventually, you have to get back on the horse. Life goes on. Suddenly, I was single again after fifteen years of sharing my life with someone, so I found that all very strange. You form relationships with people and it's all part of the healing process – it's just a very strange place to be.

The most difficult thing of all came much later. I'd reached a point where the constant reminders – Rachel's clothes in the wardrobe, her perfume, her stuff, the physical possessions that were imbued with her personality – were holding me back. What do you keep? What do you get rid of? What is a person when they're gone? Rachel existed now only inside of me, not in the physical possessions she had acquired over her lifetime. But still I found it all but impossible to do and in the end, I needed help in doing it. And do you know what? The hardest thing of all was her shoes; that almost killed me. Because for the longest time while she was ill, I'd had to put her shoes on for her – she was so weak, she couldn't do it herself.

One thing I did hold on to was a voice message from her that had been on my mobile phone from way back. It meant the world to me and I'd been careful to keep it. In fact, I would probably still have it, only someone stole my phone. It's strange, but it felt like losing her all over again.

I've always been fascinated by the history of the American West, both from the point of view of the settlers and the native peoples who were there already.

Whenever I look at these pictures of the helicopter crash in Wyoming in 2005 I ink it's extraordinary no one was killed. As you can see, it looks more like a squashed metal box han a helicopter. The wer picture is unclear because there was aviation fuel on the lens of my camera.

Gordon Hillman, archeo-botanist who knows as much about plants, their origins and their uses as anyone.

Lars Falt, one of the great old men of the northern frontier and a real expert in the ways of the north.

With Syd Kyle-Little, bush policeman, one of the last pioneers of the Australian frontier, who died in 2012.

Working and travelling in the northern wilderness is always special for me. Making snow-shoes with Pinnock Smith and building an igloo were a great part of creating the television series.

With my wife, Ruth (below, on our wedding day) and I took this picture (right) in the Arctic.

The search for Raoul Moat involved some intensive days tracking in Northumbria, during which I worked with the Metropolitan Police Fire Arms Squad.

Encounters with animals (and fish). This photo (top) may look as if it's not real, but I can assure you it is! This wolf had been specially reared to be comfortable around humans so scientists could learn more about the habit and behaviours of its wild brethren. The dog fish looks rightly pretty keen to return to its own environment, the sea.

With Her Majesty the Queen.

Working with young people is something I enjoy very much – and introducing them to the art of fire-making is always special. Empowerment is the secret of proper bushcraft instruction – it takes the fear away if you teach people simple techniques they can use themselves.

That said, I realised there was nothing I could do. The phone was gone and so was she.

Rachel was a very special person. Hardworking, full of life, full of energy, and very bright. She lit up a room when she walked in. She had a very good sense of humour and was really generous; she was always helping people out. For several years after she died, I was still receiving letters from people and I'd discover that she'd been helping or advising them and nobody had known anything about it. She was like that; she just wanted to contribute to the world and make it a better place – and she did.

26

The Light of My Life

Ihonestly did not think that I would ever find love in my life again, so I threw myself into my work to cope. I managed to function, I was still undertaking filming commitments and, on camera, I was the same as always. I was running courses for Woodlore and to all intents and purposes I had returned to the world of the living. But there was a difference and, if I am honest, I was running on auto pilot and my internal flame was very low. Thinking back, I am not even sure that I was aware of it myself until someone burst through and rekindled that flame with the warmth of her amazing personality.

That someone is my wonderful wife Ruth.

One day towards the end of 2007, I was on the final few dates of a lecture tour. It had been a packed itinerary and I found myself in a huge theatre in Newcastle. The lecture had gone well and I was finishing up, as I normally do, with a book-signing. Support staff were busy dismantling equipment, and I was just sorting myself out prior to going outside where I was going to do the book-signing. A few members of the audience were milling around and chatting in groups, as if waiting for the official instruction to form an orderly line.

Suddenly, from out of nowhere, Ruth appeared. She had a beautiful radiant smile on her face as she held her arm aloft, wielding one of my books in her hand.

'Excuse me, would you please sign my book for me?' She arrived with such energy she quite literally knocked me off my feet; I fell to the ground.

And when I got up, I felt completely different; there was just this instant connection. The chemistry was right there from the start. I've no idea how, but she broke through the fog that had been surrounding me. It was love at first sight. But of course I didn't tell her that. I said, 'The signing is outside in ten minutes and yes I'd love to sign it for you.'

Ruth was there with a group of friends who had persuaded her to come along because, as one of them had said, 'Oh, you're quite outdoorsy, aren't you Ruth?' which I later found out was true. Ruth was reading Geography, Archaeology and Social Science at Durham University as a mature student. It turned out she was into mountain biking, running and camping. So yes, she was a bit 'outdoorsy'.

She'd been given one of my books for her birthday, but she hadn't read it and when she got to the front of the queue outside, she walked up to me and said, 'There's one question nobody has asked you yet, so can I ask?' and she just came out with it: 'Are you married?'

It kind of floored me for a second, but I recovered my composure, looked at her and said, 'Actually, my wife passed away,' and as I said it, I thought, 'Brilliant Ray, nice work. That's really going to put her at ease.'

All things considered though, I thought she handled it brilliantly, even if she probably did feel like she wanted the ground to open up and swallow her whole. She touched my arm and it was like a bolt of electricity had passed between us. She looked me in the eye and said, 'Oh I'm so sorry; I feel awful. Would you like another one?' She has an excellent sense of humour. But there was magic in the air.

My heart missed a beat. She was gorgeous. I liked her – a lot. I said, 'Why, are you asking?'

She laughed, and then the people in the queue behind started getting restless, so she moved aside to join her friends. They all stayed around for ten minutes or so afterwards taking photographs and one thing and another, and I meant to ask her for an email address or phone number, but I got tied up talking to someone and when I next looked up, she'd gone. To say I was disappointed would be an understatement, but there wasn't much I could do. That was when one of the security girls came up to me.

'Oh, Mr Mears,' she said, handing me a scrap of paper, 'a man gave this to me and asked if I could pass it on to you.'

I thanked her and looked at it; it was Ruth's email address.

Apparently, she'd told one of her friends that she really liked me but was so mortified that she'd asked about me being married that she'd left. However, unbeknown to her, another friend had written her email address down and passed it on to my security team.

I didn't want to appear too keen so I'd planned to email her a few days later, but I still had a couple of dates left on the tour and it wasn't until I arrived back home three weeks later that I realised I had forgotten. So I wrote to her, saying how much I'd enjoyed meeting her and that I hoped we might meet up again. The reply I received was cool to say the least, so I assumed she was making me pay for having taken so long in getting in touch. After playing email tennis a couple of times I called her, though it didn't exactly go as planned . . .

'Hello?'

'Hi Ruth, it's Ray.'

'Oh, I'm sorry. I don't know anyone called Ray. How did you get this number?'

That was me put in my place, then!

'Ruth, it's Ray Mears.'

Then there was silence. And I could almost hear the penny drop.

'Oh, Ray! I'm so sorry!'

Well with that cleared up we talked and talked; there was no stopping us and we arranged to meet up. Ruth was to be off from university around Christmas but she wanted to spend the time in the run-up to the 25th with her young son Kristian. Christmas day was the earliest that we could meet that suited both of us.

So she drove down to meet me and we got on famously. It was as if we'd known each other for years. I knew she was the one and I asked her to marry me. She said yes. Two weeks later, she thought she had better return to see her son, who was enjoying staying with her grandmother. Eighteen months after that we married. It was a discreet affair with seventy guests at a small castle; it was just lovely. I never dreamed I would be this happy again, but Ruth has changed everything and meeting her and her son Kristian was the best thing that's ever happened to me. They both moved in with me and, with our Labrador who joined us as a puppy in 2010, we are as happy as can be.

I love Kristian very much. He was twelve when we first met and I really enjoyed getting to know him as an individual. We have a fantastic relationship, which is built upon love and trust. He is a remarkably gifted and intelligent young man and I am really excited to see what he contributes to the world.

There are so many lovely things about Ruth, we share many of the same interests. Music, taste in food, the great outdoors. We spend a lot of time out watching wildlife together and whenever she is able, she accompanies me on overseas expeditions. She is wonderful and brightens the world around her.

It was shortly after Ruth and I married that I was finally diagnosed and cured of a disease that had dogged me for some sixteen years but which I didn't even know I had. My health had suffered massively and I'd put on weight, but over time it became like background noise. It had always been there, and I learned to live with it and work around it.

I'd been overweight for most of my TV career but I'd always put it down to the fact that I couldn't exercise because I suffered from severe back trouble. Over time, it started to affect what I could do. In my line of work, where I spend so much time outdoors, my being unfit was making me hesitant to do things – to go somewhere, to climb something, to cross something – and that's not healthy.

I thought I just had a bad back but it transpired I'd had long-term Lyme disease. Lyme disease manifests itself with myriad symptoms – in my case, a bad back and weight gain – and it would appear that I picked it up when I came back from filming in Samoa for *World of Survival* in 1996. At first I simply thought I was suffering from a trapped nerve and the pain was intermittent. I didn't really think anything of it, but it got worse and worse and eventually I was filming in Venezuela one year and the pain was so bad I had to fly home. I had a scan when I got back and it showed I had two discs that were worn out and were pressing on the sciatic nerve, causing my back to go into spasm. I was given morphine-based painkillers, anti-inflammatories and muscle relaxants and told I had to stay fit.

Talking with others who have suffered from Lyme disease it seems that quite frequently it exploits or exacerbates an existing physical weakness, which makes it difficult to diagnose. Throughout this period I also made frequent trips to the tropics and it is likely that the anti-malarial medication which I was using had masked the symptoms. The painkillers helped to sort it out to a degree but it was only ever a temporary fix

because they were treating the symptoms and not the cause. It was only about five years ago – shortly after Ruth and I married – that I realised it was something altogether more serious than a bad back. I went to the dentist because I thought I needed some work done but it turned out I didn't – the jaw pain I was experiencing was just another symptom of Lyme disease. I spoke to a naval doctor friend and he emailed me a list of symptoms for it and when I looked through it, I realised that I ticked almost every one. So I went to see my doctor, who treated me with anti-biotics, and I have been fine ever since. I'd had it for about sixteen years and never realised. Being pain-free and healthy again has given me a new lease of life, and it's made my life with Ruth much brighter.

<hr />

I feel blessed to have been able to find such profound love. Ruth and I are inseparable. Every year since we met she has been by my side in Lapland where I teach Arctic bushcraft, we have tracked and watched African wildlife together and paddled by canoe in the Canadian wilderness. While going solo is magical, travelling in remote areas and sharing those unforgettable experiences with your wife cannot be beaten.

Ruth is the love of my life, and I can honestly say that I am the happiest I have ever been. This is a new and exciting chapter in my life.

27

Going Solo

Canoeing is one of those things that I love doing more than anything else. In fact, I'd go further and say that I think the canoe is one of humankind's greatest inventions. It became popular in Canada in its earliest days because of the relative ease with which a canoe could be built, usually requiring no more in its construction than what could be secured from cutting down one of Canada's millions of birch trees. Travel by water was one of early Canada's quickest means of transportation, particularly in its more remote regions, because there was no access by rail, car or horse.

A canoe is an amazing thing – it floats on water like a leaf, and you can travel across a continent with it, because when you can't paddle, you can lift it up and carry it. You can load it heavily if you need to. It feels as if you live on the surface tension of the water, caught between the current and the wind, and you harmonise and choreograph the process to travel in a specific direction; it's like a dance.

Canoes played a major role in the fur trade, which is an area I wanted to cover when I made the TV documentary *Northern Wilderness* in 2009. This programme focused on Samuel Hearne who, for me, was one of Britain's greatest explorers. He joined the Royal Navy and went to sea at the age of twelve as a captain's assistant, and went to war. When the Seven Years War ended, he secured a position in the

Hudson's Bay Company. He threw himself into life there and learned to snowshoe, and how to hunt. He learned to speak Inuktitut and other languages, and in 1769 he went off in search of a possible copper mine.

What set Hearne apart was his commitment. He learned to travel like a local and he did it so well that the locals respected him and treated him as an equal. He proved that the only way to travel across Canada was by travelling in the manner of the Indians, adopting their strategies, skills and equipment – particularly the use of snowshoes, toboggan and canoe for transport. He set an example that everyone who came later was influenced by. He trained David Thompson, who went on to map three-and-a-half million miles of Canada. It was his example that Dr John Rae – who discovered the Northwest Passage – followed. Going there made me realise just how stunning Hearne's achievement was. You can't ever really get to grips with just how vast Canada is, but following Hearne's route was astonishing. To go there and realise your budget will only take you so far on that route just puts it all in perspective.

There were two aspects of canoeing involved in the documentary. One was the small canoe of the *coureur des bois* (runners of the woods) – the guys who ventured into the woods to trade European items for furs – so we had one made from birch bark and I paddled that through rapids. I also told Ben Southwell, who was producing the programme, that I needed a *canot du maître*. The fur trade depended on these canoes, which were as long as 12m and carried six to twelve crew and a load of 2,300kg. I told him it had to be the real deal – not a plastic canoe *painted* to look like birch bark.

The BBC had kittens about that – there were murmurings about health and safety, insurance, the whole nine yards, but a saviour came forward in the guise of Jeremy Ward, the curator of the Canadian Canoe Museum at Peterborough, in

Ontario. He took one of their *canot du maître* canoes apart, then reconstructed it again a week before we needed it to make it river-worthy. Then we took this 36ft canoe down the river. That was important – a plastic canoe wouldn't have had the same atmosphere, the same smell, feel and sound of the boat. It's a small detail, but it's an important one. The devil, as they say, is in the detail. Always.

I was so grateful to the Canoe Museum for going that extra mile for us. Their passion for the canoe – which for me is the true symbol of Canada – their championing of it, was truly special. It was symbiotic, the way that so many things came together for *Northern Wilderness*. A TV film like that is so much bigger than any one person, because it connects so many people who are passionate about their subject and they all bring their own unique quality to it. It becomes bigger than the sum of all its parts.

For me, what's instructive is the dichotomy between what we had logistically, and what Canada's earliest explorers and settlers such as Samuel Hearne, Dr John Rae and Donald Thompson had. I'm not complaining because in every way we had it easy, but it makes you stop and think. We had cars, trucks, planes, float planes, powerboats – every means of transport conceivable to get us to where we needed to be. Those whose stories we were telling had horses and canoes, hardship and starvation. Interesting, isn't it?

As fascinating as Hearne, Rae and Thompson were, personally, one of the best aspects of making that film was that it allowed me to canoe along some of Canada's beautiful rivers. If the forest is where I'm most at home, being on the water in the vast openness of the Canadian wilderness runs a close second. Given the chance to do that solo – with no camera crew, nobody in support, completely alone – is my all-time favourite pastimes. Going solo is a large part of the appeal because the value of travelling alone in remote wilderness is

how it allows you to connect both with yourself and the environment. We have so many distractions in daily life; firstly our constant stream of connections to one another and the wider world via the omnipresent Internet. Then there's the telephone and the traffic. The chance to escape all of that and get out into the wilderness is one of the things I live for.

Now please don't think that I'm proposing that we should all travel alone in the wilderness all the time. In fact nothing could be farther from the truth, for travelling with friends is one of the greatest joys life has to offer – particularly when you travel in good company with a common purpose and outlook. No, my suggestion is that just once in a while we should turn our back on our community and step into the wild to benefit from a unique set of experiences that cannot be felt in any other way – experiences that will enhance our lives and strengthen us for the journeys we make in company.

Let me paint you a picture of what it's like and just why it feels so magical.

As I begin to prepare for a solo trip, I'll think about the purpose of my journey. My intent is not 'exploration' or 'adventure travel' where mind and muscles are pitted against the wild to, in some way, demonstrate human dominion over nature; you may have worked out by now that this is something I have little time for. In the days before the world was mapped, great feats of endurance were certainly achieved during the exploration of the uncharted regions of our globe. But today I believe such genuine goals to be few and far between. The purpose of my journeys is to engage with a landscape and its wildlife, to better know and understand them. To understand nature so that it will accept me. A conceptual view of nature which, when made, seemed rather abstruse, but which in light of new discoveries in nature seems to be astonishingly insightful, was posited by chemist and zoologist Davey Rhoades in 1979. He demonstrated that in some yet poorly understood way, trees

could detect damage in their neighbours and react by generating stronger chemical defences. From this I have learned that how I interact with nature can also influence how nature interacts with me.

Join me as I draw on my memories to describe a solo trip into the North Woods of Canada by canoe.

———◆———

There is an old Army saying: 'Proper Preparation Prevents Poor Performance', and so it is here. Preparation is vital and sufficient time must be allowed for it. Travelling in any remote wilderness requires a set of key skills. First of all, I must be able to navigate with map and compass (call me old-fashioned if you like, but while GPS is a wonderful tool for navigation, it will always come second in my mind to those old woodsman's friends). Secondly, I must have a high degree of first-aid training, not only because I must care for myself but also because it is the best way to develop a sober head regarding the consequences of rash decision-making. Thirdly, I shall of course need to know how to take care of myself in the wild: make fires, find shelter, get food, etc. This is one of the largest skill sets to learn and many wilderness trippers pay the least regard to these skills. Bush skills do more than dispel fear and make us safe: they greatly enhance our understanding and knowledge of local flora and fauna and show us the difference between existing poorly in a landscape and living there in comfort.

Fourthly, as I am travelling by canoe I shall of course have to know how to paddle. It is important that you learn this skill – unlike the viewers who decided to set out on their own Canadian canoe adventure with no canoeing ability whatsoever. Reading the credits at the end of my Canadian programme, they engaged the outfitters that my production team had

employed and hired an Indian guide, who it turned out could hardly speak English. After a couple of days they misunderstood their guide and merrily paddled into a set of rapids that even experienced canoeists would consider walking past. The net result was a terrifying capsize, which resulted in the destruction of one canoe and a sobering near miss.

Fifthly, some investigative skills are required because mapping for the area I intend to traverse will need to be sourced and ordered well ahead of departure, which today is usually easily achieved through the Internet. Guide books, if available, will need to be consulted to establish how serious the rapids I will encounter are likely to be. They may also provide a useful reading list to improve my knowledge of the region, its flora, fauna and cultural history. I like to mark my maps with useful information. Fortunately I have made many such trips so when it comes to packing lists it is all simply a process of recital.

So, can you feel it? My journey has already begun.

But what of the dangers I might face? Well, they are all pretty apparent really: bad weather, drowning, getting lost, losing my canoe, strong winds, rapids, cold, injury, forest fire and bears, so really, without any backup, I just have to be extra careful. The truth is, there is no shortcut to gaining sufficient experience, so don't do any of this unless you have the skill sets to cope. Perhaps the one unique hazard the solo traveller faces, though, is unfamiliarity with being alone. If you are not comfortable with your own company, it's advisable to build up gradually to a long and remote journey.

Now I can contact a local outfitter, organise my transfers and hire of equipment. We will discuss make, length and material of the canoes available and water levels, and I will be able to test the feasibility of my intended route. Attention to detail is everything at this stage. A good outfitter is invaluable, but beware because they are not all good.

Fishing permits can usually be purchased ahead of time

over the Internet. One surprise may be to discover that even in remote Canada there can be rivers and lakes where there are pollutants that limit the number of any given fish species that you can consume safely in a month. Guide books in which you can look up the waterways you will be travelling on can usually be downloaded prior to departure.

Here's the outline of my journey. I am going to join a river that I have been reading about for several years. But rather than start at its source, I am going to access it from a series of lakes and rivers to its east. I shall begin by paddling up a large lake, to a river that connects via a chain of small lakes to another large lake. From its north-west corner, I shall join the river I intend to explore. This I plan to paddle down in eight days, allowing three days to lay over, fish and explore.

The joy of travelling by canoe is that it is an incredibly versatile craft that can be paddled, poled, and even sailed. Relatively light, it is capable of transporting considerable loads and, where the water is too forceful or too shallow for passage, it can be emptied and carried overland – a process that retains its name from the fur trade: portage.

In fact, my journey will begin in earnest with a long portage, but rather than carry it on my shoulders, the canoe will be strapped to the float of a bush plane – a de Havilland Canada Beaver DHC-2. It's a wonderful aircraft, a real workhorse that is so respected that its appearance has become an integral part of the North Woods aesthetic and as much of an icon in Canada as the Spitfire is here. Despite the fact that production stopped in 1967, these specialised short take-off and landing aircraft are still plying the waterways of the far North, providing a vital lifeline for remote communities, logging and mining camps.

The flight in provides a bird's-eye view of the forests, lakes and rivers that are my destination; as much as I enjoy the view, I can't wait to be on the water. Eventually the

plane will circle and, with practised ease, the pilot will glide smoothly on to the lake. I'll unhitch the canoe, load it with packs and take my place inside. There's a unique sound to it – the sound of the canoe banging against the aluminium float of the plane, the water lapping against the side, the pilot walking on the float. He says, 'OK, you take good care now,' and waves. I start to paddle away; with a buzz and a splutter, the engine starts up and he flies away, back to the world of electric lighting, the Internet and 24-hour non-stop noise and consumerism. As he climbs, he looks down and I look up. Then it's just quiet until a few minutes later the wildlife starts up – they fell silent with the plane's arrival but with its departure they're in full voice again.

With the plane gone, there's just me and my inner voice. I paddle to shore and set up camp for the night on a small island where I take stock. Now my life is reduced to its simplest form. As the sun sets, I sit beside my fire drinking in the quietude but not yet becoming a part of the scene. I feel I'm being watched, being judged by suspicious eyes all around me. I feel free from the rigid strictures of preparation, and I can relax now, yet I feel a reluctance to do so. Is this what a captive-bred animal feels when released into the wild: a reluctance to leave the familiarity of the cage? A hot chocolate liberally laced with rum will help get me off to sleep.

After waking on the first morning, I allow myself some time to get properly organised. On my body I carry my knife, saw and fire-starter. In the canoe I have four packs: my clothing and equipment pack, my food pack, my day pack and my camera case. All are stowed to provide proper trim and balance. I am using a beavertail paddle and a copy of an Iroquois paddle from 1800 that I have carved especially for this journey. My compass is set with the first bearing and rests atop the canoe pack in front of me.

I pull on the paddle; the canoe resists at first, heavily laden

as it is with my supplies for the journey. Two more strokes though and I am away, the compass directing me as the canoe swings on to the correct heading. In an hour my paddling has settled into a comfortable rhythm and the canoe is eating up the kilometres. The long preparations seem insignificant now and I am overwhelmed by the beauty of the lake. The first day under way is important – it is a time to settle, for muscles to adjust to the loading, for the mind to adjust to the lack of distraction from modern life and the continuous traffic from within.

It is now that the real benefit of preparation pays off. With all concerns accounted for, life is greatly simplified and with distractions removed, the mind starts to empty further with every passing hour. By an empty mind, I don't mean any loss of intelligence; with the trivia and worries of day-to-day life forgotten, there is in its place an increased awareness of the external stimuli of the environment. Consider if you will that your brain is a computer, running many applications simultaneously; now it need only run one application so all of its capacity is liberated to concentrate on the present. In short, you become more open to things – more alert, more intuitive and more observant of minutiae.

My camp site on the second night is not the best – the ground is sloping and lumpy so I'm awake and away early on the third day to allow plenty of time at day's end to choose somewhere more suitable that night. It's a frustrating day – several portages mean little distance gained and, on one occasion, time lost as I spend an hour locating the portage trail. But at the last trail there is the reward of fresh wolf tracks.

By mid-afternoon I am traversing a long lake that runs west to east. Halfway across there is a spit of land that juts out from the eastern shore. It is a perfect camp site with a well-used fire circle, nice level ground and a large pine tree with a good sturdy branch from which my food sack can be hung,

out of the reach of nosey bears. The only thing in short supply is firewood, but that is easily remedied when I paddle to a fallen dead tree 200 metres or so across the channel. I take what I need using my folding saw and axe; in fact, I probably have enough to leave a small stock for the next visitor. I enjoy a wonderful evening. A calm settles over the water as the sun falls in the sky and I watch, hands clasped round my mug, as in the very last minutes of the day a loon calls across the mirror-calm water. Then, with the camp in good order, sleep draws me into my tent.

Sadly, the peace is not to last. Just after midnight I am awoken by a gale-force, howling wind. At daybreak, I find it is still blowing hard from the south but, looking at the waves in the lee of the spit, I believe I can handle the conditions and reason that, with the canoe packs lashed for buoyancy, should I capsize I will be able to get myself and my kit to shore. I decide to break the journey into small sections and take them one at a time. No heroics – if conditions prove to be unmanageable I'll head back and try to wait it out. As it happens though, my heavily laden canoe shucks the wind better than expected and my beavertail paddle provides just the right contact with the water to enable me to keep the nose into the wind. With the cheek of a pilgrim begging a life, I use the wind to ferry across to the far shore and tick along close in until I'm in the wind's shadow at the head of the lake.

I celebrate with a handful of gorp; also known as trail mix, it's an acronym of Good Old Raisins and Peanuts. It's a combination of dried fruit, grains, nuts and sometimes chocolate, and it's the ideal snack on an expedition because it's tasty, lightweight, easy to store, and nutritious – you get a quick boost from the carbohydrates in the dried fruit and granola, and sustained energy from the fats in nuts. You can buy it ready-made but I prefer to choose my own ingredients and make it myself.

Sated, I set to on a three-kilometre portage trail to the last large lake that will take me to the river. This will be the acid test – if the gale is whipping up that lake, I'll have no choice but to try and wait things out. The wind conditions on the far side are manageable but the trail is blocked by windblown trees. Well, they say that fortune favours the bold, so my axe and saw prove their worth once again, and after considerable effort I savour the moment when my canoe sits on the waters of this new lake. After all the exertion, I need sustenance again so I moor up and enjoy a well-earned lunch. Focused on the gale I find I have slipped without noticing into a new state of mind and I am now living totally in the moment. My mind enjoys the challenges. I find that decision-making and decisiveness come easily to me now. In the normal world, we support each other constantly in decision-making. Even walking into a coffee shop in company the decisions are shared – 'Where shall we sit?' or 'What'll I have?' Here though, all decisions are mine, as are the mistakes. I love it because it brings a certain clarity of vision. Perhaps all CEOs should make such a journey like this once in a while.

I sniff the wind like a veteran and feel the weather lifting. As I paddle away I feel the breeze. It is steady, with occasional gusts that I see on the water as they race towards me. I am alert but relaxed; my canoe is part of me and I settle into a steady, strong paddle rhythm. It will be hard going all the way to the head of the lake where my maps show me there are islands and the possibility of shelter, but I'm up for it. Five minutes before I find a camp site, the wind drops altogether. I feel that I have been tested and have passed. A swim before dinner and an early night.

My routine keeps the journey tidy. I fill a Thermos with hot water last thing each night so there is no need for a fire in the morning. In this way I get away early – the best paddling is

always in the first half of the day. Mid-afternoon, I find a camp site, set up the tarp, swing the kettle and go fishing.

Now I am happy in my own company and I have joined the wildlife around me; we share a secret: the secret of silence. It's beautiful. As I travel, I enjoy the company of wild creatures that somehow sense that I pose them no threat. I play with a family of otters who swim just ahead of me, blowing air noisily through their nostrils in my direction. While I am fishing I watch beavers bringing back branches for the food cache beside their lodge. I thank them for their dams that have kept water in the river for me this late in the summer. I sidle up to a moose while its head is submerged in search of sedge bulbs. I could easily forget what day it is, and in truth I must admit that I have indeed done that several times already. It's only at the last minute that I realise I must paddle hard to make my rendezvous with an outfitter.

It isn't all plain sailing; it's easy to injure yourself when shifting heavy loads over slippery rocks. But what is there to do but get on with it? There is no one to complain to but yourself, and self-pity has no place here. Now one learns the true meaning of the stoic Indian. In time, and with enough experience, stoicism becomes a tool you can employ to deal with hardships. Out of this stoic persona is born the equanimity of the master bushman. Like a rock in the rapids you become a place of stability from which others can gain strength.

As I reach the final day I know that my journey will soon end as abruptly as it began. My paddle moves with the hint of reluctance but still I must follow my course. There ahead of me on the far shore is a huge black bear, the biggest I have ever seen, large enough to give a grizzly a run for his money. I paddle towards him, but with a telling glance he takes cover and I know that I will not see him again. No bear grows that large in these parts without being very wary of humans. Somehow, that thought brings me back to earth. I turn the

canoe for home and overhead two bald eagles glide past. I call out a greeting to them and they break their glide in surprise as they circle, scrutinising me from above. One of them calls back to me. I smile, give a wave, and as they settle back on their original course, so too do I. In that moment I can see nature; I feel it intuitively and I understand what cannot be written. That is when I know my journey is complete.

At the rendezvous, my outfitter meets me. It is a six-hour drive back to his base – a little time to readjust to the whirligig world of today. We have covered only a few miles before the claustrophobic warmth of the pick-up sends me to sleep.

28
Manhunt

It's a perfect day for driving – warm and balmy with bright sunshine and clear blue skies. Mid-afternoon in early July and I'm heading up the M1 in my Land Rover Discovery. A heat haze rises from the tarmac ahead.

The sun's rays on the windscreen turn the Discovery into a greenhouse. Ruth sits beside me as I drive, and we're both enjoying the respite of the cold air from the air-con. With a heavy foot on the accelerator and a clear road in view, we make rapid progress but as I pilot us along the motorway, a thought occurs to me – I'm probably the only person in the country who is wishing for dark skies and heavy rain.

I have no wish to ruin this perfect summer's day for the population of England; sadly, a man called Raoul Moat has already done that in Northumbria and it's both the man and the place that are the focus of my journey. Moat is also the reason I want rain instead of sun.

Like most people, I was horrified as I became aware of the developing situation through the news reports. Thirty-seven-year-old former bouncer Raoul Moat had been released from Durham Prison on 1 July after serving a sentence for assault. Two days later he went round to the house of his ex-girlfriend Samantha Stobbart with a sawn-off shotgun. There, he shot Chris Brown, her new boyfriend, killing him instantly. Then he shot Samantha in the stomach before fleeing the scene.

He wasn't finished though – far from it. On the following day, Sunday 4 July, he walked up to police officer David Rathband's Volvo patrol car, which was parked in a lay-by. Calmly Moat levelled the sawn-off shotgun at him through the passenger-side window and blasted him twice in the face and chest, leaving him totally blind and with horrific injuries. Moat then disappeared, only to surface the following evening to rob a fish and chip shop in Seaton Delaval at gunpoint. On Tuesday 6 July, he went on the run.

At that stage, the police were using conventional methods to track Moat – triangulation of his mobile phone signal, closing off streets and specific areas to deny him possible avenues of escape. They got an early break when they received a reported sighting of the Black Lexus he'd been using. It had been found by a member of the public parked on an industrial estate and when police arrived, they arrested two men – Khuram Awan and Karl Ness – who it transpired were two of Moat's accomplices. Both were later charged with conspiracy to murder and sentenced to life imprisonment. Fortuitously for him, Moat had taken off into some nearby woods before the police arrived and that was it, he went to ground.

That's when I began to think I might be able to offer some assistance. I have unique experience in tracking. It's a perishable skill, so unless you use it constantly, you lose it. Fortuitously, I'd been uncharacteristically busy over the previous couple of years tracking leopards and bears, and all sorts of wildlife. It was a skill I'd used almost constantly and I was at a really high pitch; I knew I was at the top of my game.

Six years previously I'd been invited up to the Police National Search Centre (PNSC) to give a lecture on tracking and its capabilities as a means of search, so I put a call in to Chief Inspector Phil Thomas, a police search advisor there who I'd kept in touch with. Even as I dialled, I felt a little apprehensive. I'd tracked literally hundreds of animals over the course of

my career and numerous men when training, but this would be the first time I'd ever tracked an armed and dangerous fugitive. It was within my skill set, but outside of my comfort zone. Phil answered on the first ring.

'Hi Phil, it's Ray Mears.' After the initial 'hellos' and 'how are yous' I made the proposal.

'Look, this Raoul Moat thing – there's a possibility I could help. If I come up, I think I could let you know pretty quickly whether I can or not.'

'You'll get no argument from me there, Ray. I'll put a call in to Gold Command up at Ponteland [Northumbria Police's HQ] and someone will be in touch.'

Someone did get in touch, but not for a few days. A lot happened in that time so I'll always regret not going up there and then. A few hours after we spoke the police located a camp site that Moat had established, and that would have been the perfect starting point for me to begin tracking from. If you can locate your quarry's starting point, it makes life so much easier. Sadly, in the hours and days that followed, the police trampled all over it in their search for clues, and members of the press were given access, leaving no stone unturned. So by the time I eventually got there, any signs that might have given me an advantage were lost. Was a golden opportunity missed? What might I have found at the camp site? Could the whole incident have been brought to a speedier conclusion? These questions linger to this day but I'll never know the answers. What happened is what happened.

I imagine it was difficult for the police to make a snap decision to use me. In a situation like this, I'm probably not the first person that springs to mind; tracking just doesn't fall within the normal remit of what the police do, even for search specialists. I think that, initially, it was too obscure an idea for them to live with and I can empathise because the pressure they were under to get a result was absolutely massive.

In any event, I didn't hear a thing until the morning of Thursday 8 July. I was in London for a meeting with my publisher, Rupert Lancaster, when my phone rang.

'Ray, it's Phil Thomas. It's on; can you come straight up to Newcastle?'

I signal to Rupert that I have to take this call and walk out of his office to the corridor.

'I can, Phil, but I'm in London at the moment.' My brain kicks in and I think out loud: 'Get back home, pack some kit . . . it's probably best I drive because I don't want to draw attention to myself by flying or taking the train. There's enough media attention on this as it is; I don't think my involvement being reported is going to be helpful. Call it a few hours; I'll be with you later on tonight.'

Phil was happy with that, so I made my excuses to Rupert and caught a train back to Kent. When I explained everything to Ruth, she immediately said she wanted to come with me. She's from Durham so she could spend time with her family while also being close to me. I think most people can understand that – she didn't really want me to go, given the perceived risk, but for all that she understood and was totally supportive. So we loaded the Discovery up and headed off, which is how I found myself driving up the M1 towards Northumbria, blinded by sunshine but wishing for rain.

Why rain? Quite simply, rain would give me a far greater chance of bringing Moat down. If it's dry, he can relax; the weather is one less thing for him to worry about, meaning he has more mental capacity to focus on staying one step ahead and remaining hidden. Heavy rain on the other hand would make him cold and wet. His will to carry on would be diminished so he'd be much more liable to make mistakes; he'd want shelter; it'd get inside his head and defeat him. He'd also leave more signs for me to follow. The conditions were perfect for Moat, but an absolute nightmare for me.

There were some positives, however. Moat might well be armed and dangerous, and dry, but he was thought to be in the woods and the woods are *my* world. Having taught people to live off the land for thirty years, I know what happens to them psychologically. I understand the difficulties they face; I know the signs they leave behind and I know what will break them. I was hungry to go head-to-head. This wasn't Man vs. Wild, or even Man vs. Man; this was *my* world and Moat had come crashing into it, so the balance was uneven. It was a real-life hunt; he'd crossed a line, and now it was going to end.

———◆———

It's gone 22:00hrs when I reach Newcastle. I'd called ahead to Phil Thomas who had moved up to Northumbria Police HQ at Ponteland a couple of days earlier and we meet just outside the city centre. I jump into his car with him while Ruth takes the Discovery and heads for her parents' house. As I settle down for the drive to Ponteland, Phil updates me on what's happening on the ground, and gives me some idea of the political situation I'm walking into.

I had no idea there'd been something of a storm going on behind the scenes over whether or not to engage my services. With any major incident or disaster, the police utilise a Gold / Silver / Bronze command structure to establish a hierarchical framework for command and control. Gold Command is in overall control of resources and is usually based off-site at a distant control room – in this case, at Ponteland. The Gold Command team formulates strategy and has ultimate responsibility, reporting at government level to 'Platinum Command' in the guise of the Cabinet Office Briefing Rooms (COBR – the government's crisis response committee). Silver Command manages strategic direction from Gold and formulates tactics to achieve the desired result. Bronze Command implements

the tactics and directly controls resources at the scene. In this case, Gold Command comprised Northumbria Police's Chief Constable Sue Sim working with the then Deputy Chief Constables (DCC) Jim Campbell and Steve Ashman.

Silver Command had been reticent about using me from the off, based on the fact they'd be putting me, an unarmed civilian, into an environment where firearms were involved. A Chief Superintendent told Phil, 'We've carried out a full risk assessment and it ain't happening.'

'What about Prince Charles? He's surrounded by an armed police close-protection team every time he goes out. I don't see that this is any different,' countered Phil.

But there was no arguing until Phil stepped out of the room and literally bumped into DCC Campbell, who asked how things were going. Phil related the conversation he'd had with Silver Command, causing the DCC to say something along the lines of, 'This is ridiculous, I want Ray here,' so that was that.

———◆———

On arrival at Ponteland, I'm introduced to the team and briefed by a Police Search Advisor (POLSA) from Northumbria Police who is part of Bronze Command. He's a real asset and I'm massively impressed by his professionalism and knowledge as he gives me some really useful background and detailed intelligence on everything they know. The night before, they'd foiled an attempt by two of Moat's accomplices to get a car and a firearm to him and I'm told about them having found his car and the tent he'd been using, both of which were in the small market town of Rothbury. Police have established a five-mile, 5,000ft air-exclusion and a two-mile ground-exclusion zone around the town.

Bronze command decides it's worth me seeing Rothbury

first-hand and I'm driven there in a squad car on 'blues and twos' by colleagues of David Rathband, the traffic officer that Moat had shot. When we get there it's dark – it's close to midnight – but still I'm stunned by what I see. It's like I've stepped out of the patrol car and straight into a war zone.

The manhunt for Moat is perhaps the largest in modern British history, and Rothbury seems to have become the physical embodiment of that. Bright lights are set up everywhere, turning night into day and giving the immediate area the look of a Hollywood film set. It's all a bit surreal. Over 160 armed officers are involved from eight of the UK's police forces, including almost fifty from the Metropolitan Police, along with eight of the Met's London-based Armed Response Vehicles (ARVs). Ten armoured Land Rovers from the PSNI have been shipped over on a ferry from Northern Ireland and an RAF Tornado GR4 jet has been made available to undertake reconnaissance sorties. Specialist police snipers are also on hand, along with helicopters and countless police dogs. The armed officers are standing around in groups, dressed in black coveralls. They all wear body armour with ceramic chest plates and Kevlar helmets, and are armed with an assortment of weapons – H&K MP5 9mm carbines and Glock 17 sidearms along with percussion grenades. As if I needed a reminder, it brings home to me the gravity of the situation.

I'm escorted into the local police station. It's a hive of activity and I acquaint myself with the latest reports and news through osmosis. I learn that Moat has reloaded his sawn-off shotgun with large-gauge ball-bearings, which do terrible damage at close range. I find out where they'd had sightings of him and the locations where they've picked up various items of his. They'd recovered several mobile phones he'd used – it shows he's not stupid and is obviously clued up on police procedures and how they might track him via conventional means. The police have done well so far, they've really closed

him down and reduced the number of avenues of escape open to him, but he's now gone off the radar and it's my job to find him.

I look at a map of Rothbury and immediately see how much woodland there is in the surrounding area. It's known as the Cragside Estate and encompasses some incredibly dense forest. I pick up an envelope and start to sketch out an assessment of the situation as I know it so that I can start putting together a plan.

———◆—◆———

Point one: the weather – it's in Moat's favour. It had been dry since he'd gone on the run, which is bad for me in terms of him leaving signs, but good for him.

Point two: has he taken any hostages? It's not like it is in the movies; most people on the run end up taking hostages by accident rather than design. They'll take the easiest option, which generally means a building, but where you find buildings you normally find people and if you add a man with a gun to that scenario, those people become hostages. I want to know if he's done that – there are lots of outlying farms around the area, so I ask the police if they'd checked them. They hadn't, so they send officers round to knock on the doors.

———◆—◆———

It's becoming increasingly obvious to me that the Cragside Estate is where Moat is most likely to be. I know he's been in there already because the northern extremity is where the police recovered his mobile phone and his camp site is located at the south-west corner. It was by a river bank, which immediately suggests to me that he's been using the River Coquet as a point

of communication with his accomplices. It's a dark, shadowy river at night, which rises in the surrounding mountains and runs through the town of Rothbury. It's the perfect place for someone who wants to move without being seen.

Moat's a fisherman so he'll know this river. To move around at night without a torch in an area with no natural lighting, you're going to need something to serve as a handrail to guide you. A river bank would fulfil that role, as would natural features in the landscape. There's no point my going to the point where he's discarded one of his phones; the terrain in that area has been heavily trampled by the police firearms team that found it.

The Cragside Estate bothers me; it's huge, exceptionally dense wooded forest with few natural trails, so it's perfect for someone who wants to remain hidden. There's just so much natural cover there. That suits Moat. At night, as long as he's there, he's under no pressure. I want to change that. I want to remove any sense of sanctuary from him, because then he'll make a mistake. He'll have to get up and run. And if he does that, I'll track him or flush him right into the police net.

Perhaps the biggest obstacle for me is the press. I understand that they have a job to do but there are certain members of the media who have gone too far. The police have requested that certain details be withheld as it's felt that revealing them could help Moat. At least one household news organisation hasn't honoured that request. Police have found various letters that Moat had left, and from these it's clear that he has a radio and that he's monitoring what the press are saying. Northumbria police are doing a brilliant job but they're being hampered by the media. They've asked that they hold back on reporting elements of Moat's private life as he has threatened to kill a member of the public every time there's an inaccurate report. I believe the police should have a legal power to exclude the press in situations like this. It's the curse of 24-hour rolling news coverage . . . it hates a void so you end up with reporters

speculating, imagining, even inventing facts to fill the gap. This helps nobody.

An important aspect for me is that I don't want the press reporting that I'm involved. Firstly, I'm not doing it for recognition; I don't need to establish myself or build a reputation. I have the skills to assist and I feel duty-bound to use them. Secondly, I don't want Moat to know I'm there. I want the element of surprise on my side because I need every break I can get, especially as I have no starting point to track from, so I'm going to have to find one. This is the worst possible situation for a tracker and it's made worse by the fact that the area he's likely to be hiding in is big. There's no getting away from it – the odds are stacked in Moat's favour.

Ordinarily, I would have used his camp site as a starting point, but that had been compromised from a forensic point of view by Sky News having been given access to it shortly after it had been found. They'd taken in two people who'd claimed to be 'trackers' and they'd trampled all over it. Even if there was anything of use to me there (and it seems highly unlikely), I'd be seen by the press, so I make a decision to focus on Cragside. I look at the map and work out the places that would be of most interest to me if I were in Moat's place. I prioritise them and start walking through them all in my mind, area by area. I've nothing firm to go on but you need to be bold sometimes, and with the benefit of hindsight, I think what I did was right.

We drive back to Ponteland shortly after, and I present my findings to Gold Command, with the caveat that I want to leave at first light. There's a path that works its way north–south in Cragside; I want to start tracking along that. I'd start at the southern tip where it comes down to the river. That river interests me greatly, but if I begin there, I'll be showing my hand too soon. I want to get at least one day's tracking in without Moat knowing I'm there.

The Gold Command team agree with all my suggestions, so we have the makings of a plan. It's late and I think I should try to get some sleep. I'm staying in a bungalow within the police compound here at Ponteland and I literally just drop my kit and lay down on the bed as soon as I'm through the door. It's been an exceptionally long day and a very busy one. I need to be sharp for the track tomorrow morning so it's imperative I get some rest. But my mind is racing – analysing the plan I've come up with, looking for flaws and other ways of doing things. It's going to be a long night.

I'm awake as the sun comes up and a hot shower makes me feel a little more human. I dress quickly and make my way over to the canteen in the main building. It's exactly how I imagine police canteens up and down the country to be: a long, rectangular room lit with fluorescent lighting, and natural light from windows along one side of the rectangle. Along the opposite side there's a counter with an array of hot food, sandwiches and the like on offer, cooked and served up by civilian staff. Two vending machines sit along the far wall offering a range of canned drinks, plus another selling high-energy 'junk' food – Mars bars, crisps etc.

However, there's one element that sets it apart from most police canteens and that's the sheer number of weapons lying around. Sniper rifles, H&K MP5s, G3s lie on the floor and against walls. Every seat is taken by the 'Men in Black' – firearms officers from seemingly every force in the UK, all dressed in black coveralls that give them a distinctly paramilitary look. From a distance, they appear indistinguishable from the SAS team that stormed the Iranian Embassy at Princes Gate in 1980.

Phil ushers me towards a group of officers from the Metropolitan Police's specialist firearms unit SO19. I'm

introduced to their tactical advisor, Mark; Derek, a team leader; and to his sergeant Paul. They've come up from London as a self-contained unit along with forty or so of their colleagues, six firearms support dogs with their handlers, and SO19's unique silver-coloured BMW 5 series ARVs. They also have all the kit and weapons they might need to cover 'the worst-case scenario'. The cars look a little out of place in Northumbria, decked out with their Met Police decals declaring 'Working Together for a Safer London'.

I'm eager to get going and implement the plan I presented before retiring the previous night, but there's a problem. There have been 'heated debates' prior to my arrival over exactly how they are going to keep me safe. They've reached the conclusion that, assuming they can get me out on the ground, I won't be able to track from the front because they can't keep me safe there. The issue is still unresolved.

'Look,' I say, 'there's no point in my even going out if I can't track from the front.'

I'm met with stony faces and the absurdity of it hits me: there's a manhunt on for a fugitive who is armed and represents a clear and present danger, and there are more armed police officers on hand than you can count. My frustration is growing.

'Look, just give me a gun if that's the issue and I'll go out and get him for you.'

It breaks the ice. They laugh. It also breaks the deadlock.

'Look, let's make this happen,' says Mark. 'If we can protect the Royal Family when they're out and about, we can protect Ray. I really don't see what the issue is here.'

'I need to be at the front,' I repeat. 'But how about if there's anywhere I can't see, your guys can check it out first?'

'I think that could work,' offers Paul. 'We've got the firearms support dogs so let's use them too. We'd normally use

one for a job like this but we've got six so let's use all of them.'

They issue me with black coveralls, body armour, a Kevlar helmet and ballistic goggles so, visually, I am identical to the others except for the fact I'm not armed with a weapon. I consider taking something to defend myself, and then decide against it. The Met's SO19 firearms unit is rightly regarded as one of the best in the world. There's an innate self-belief about the guys born of the fact they don't talk about what they do, they don't brag – they just do it and their reputation goes ahead of them. I feel both safe in their care, and confident in their ability to get the job done. No, if it comes down to him or me, he's going down.

As well as affording me protection, my clothing and kit means I won't be noticed by the press, who have staked out the gate to Police HQ at Ponteland and are filming every vehicle going in and out. First off Derek conducts a briefing for everyone involved in the team that will be out on the ground with me, so we all move into an anteroom off the canteen. He goes over everything known about Moat, and 'Actions on Contact'. The objective is clear: if found, all steps are to be taken to ensure he's brought in alive so that he can be tried in court.

There are nine Met Police firearms officers in the team that will be looking after me and helping me in the hunt for Moat, and we will be travelling from Ponteland to Rothbury in the Met's ARVs. In the first car will be Derek and an officer called Nigel who will drive, with Paul and me in the back. I am quickly introduced to the six other members of the team. Finally we are joined by six of the Met's dog handlers who each have one firearms support dog.

We move to the car park and take our places in the vehicles. Once we're strapped in, Nigel edges out into the rush-hour traffic on the main road away from Ponteland. As soon as

we're moving, Derek hits the blue lights followed by the Tri-Sound siren. Our car is now a moving symphony of '*son et lumière*' signalling our presence to other road users.

The traffic along the main road is a solid mass, one long snaking line of frustrated commuters. Driving on the offside of the white centre line, Nigel seeks a clear view of the road ahead. We're travelling at a fair pace and it occurs to me that the concentration required must be immense. I'm immersed in an alien environment but surrounded by the basics of familiarity. I've spent several decades driving in heavy urban traffic, but it was nothing like this. Here, the road noise is mixed with the constant stream of radio traffic, fighting for prominence with the muted sound (to those of us inside the car) of the 200dB siren focused ahead of us.

As we press on, I notice a set of traffic lights at a junction ahead of us turn red; my foot instinctively reaches for a brake pedal that isn't there. Nigel scrubs off some speed and then runs the red light – properly; not a shade after it's turned or a furtive dash for the other side, but a full ten seconds after, with cross traffic at its height. Traffic is still heavy, but we're making progress and I check our speed – 80mph in a 30mph limit.

Over a roundabout, around the wrong side of a traffic island, and we're heading towards oncoming traffic. I watch it part miraculously before us, our progress unimpeded despite the number of vehicles approaching us. My adrenaline on fast-feed, we pass through another two red-lit junctions, and onto the dual carriageway. A Gatso camera ahead of us catches us – 95mph in a 50 zone with no prospect whatsoever of a ticket being despatched. I could get used to this.

The road clears ahead and Nigel really opens it up. I watch the needle on the BMW's speedo start to climb over the ton . . . 110, 120, 130, 140mph and still it rises. There's a sense of urgency about events, made real by the strobing of the car's

blue lights on road signs and the rise and fall of the siren. It is 25 miles from Ponteland to Rothbury and according to Google maps the drive should take forty-five minutes. We do it in fifteen.

We stop in a lay-by close to the outskirts of Rothbury so that we can get everyone together and kill the lights and sirens. Then we drive to our 'jumping off' point, the car park of a nearby quarry on the east of Cragside Woods. In this way, we're able to deploy together, and with the minimum of fuss – no easy task when you're in a group sixteen strong, with six German Shepherd firearms support dogs along for support.

———◆———

Tracking is almost as old as mankind itself. When humans first started to eat meat, they had to learn to track their prey. Man tracking followed shortly after – it is a natural extension of hunting both animals and people. It is physically impossible for a person (or animal) to traverse ground without leaving *some* sort of telltale sign. 'Sign' in this context is the physical evidence of any disturbance of the environment left behind by animals, humans or objects. The detection of this sign is called *sign cutting*. My job as a tracker is to identify, interpret and follow signs.

When most people think of tracking, they usually think of following footprints. But a tracker looks for far more. I'm looking for soil depressions, kicked-over rocks, clothing fibres snagged on brambles, changes in vegetation, changes in the environment, ambient noise or lack thereof. I look for the disturbance – the sign – left behind by the target being tracked. In this case, it's me against Moat. Everything else falls away.

I start as soon as we dismount the vehicles. The adrenaline's pumping, I can feel my heart racing and there's a metallic taste at the back of my throat. It's not fear so much – not fear of

Moat, anyway. It's fear of failing. There's so much riding on this; I know the police have taken a risk in using me and I don't want to let anyone down. The Northumbria Force and Sue Sim, its Chief Constable, are under intense pressure. Mine is self-imposed, but no less real. I've come into this with my eyes wide open and I want to deliver.

My plan is to cut for sign in likely areas; my intention is to take the initiative, employ the tactics of surprise and aggression. This is a hunt, and I'm determined we'll get our man. It's often said that no battle plan survives first contact with the enemy and in this case, the woods are both my ally *and* my enemy. It's clear to me immediately on surveying the environment that this will be the most difficult tracking I've ever undertaken. I have never seen forest and vegetation as dense as confronts me here. It's so thick as to appear impenetrable at first sight. The ground is dry and heathery. It holds almost no sign whatsoever. The woods are so tight, so thick, that visibility is close to zero. This is going to be like wading through treacle.

I think about the track and have a picture in my head of pushing through the forest and suddenly stumbling upon Moat, equipped with his sawn-off shotgun, and me standing directly in front of him. I turn to Paul who is immediately behind me, Derek alongside him.

'Er . . . if you see me duck out of the way, you'll know I'm close!' They laugh, and the mood lightens.

I'm sure it must be difficult for them and the rest of the guys who have to protect me but they're peerless in what they do; I feel totally at ease with them. We start off by sending the dogs ahead to check things out. Because firearms are involved, the option of using bloodhounds to sniff out Moat's location is denied to us. Firearms support dogs are trained for one purpose and one purpose only: to search for and confront armed criminals and to bark on finding them. Firearms support

dogs train with the specialist firearms teams so are desensitised to gunfire.

Their handlers release the dogs, send them forward, and the dogs return quickly without signalling, so we know it is safe to move forwards. I take point, looking, searching . . . tracking.

I have the utmost respect for our police, who do a difficult, dangerous and often thankless job. They spend a lot of their time dealing with the worst excesses of society and experience things that most people fortunately never have to. Police officers can be cynical, but coppers up and down the country share a love of banter and generally cope with events thanks to a dark sense of humour. I'm impressed as soon as we get out on the ground though, because once I start tracking, they're strictly businesslike and professional. The good-natured banter and piss-taking I've observed takes a back seat and it's all about getting the job done.

I start to move. It's easy to get bogged down when you're cutting for sign and you don't find any. It's easy to think that you're walking along a dead end (metaphorically speaking) so it's important to remind yourself that what you don't find is also a form of sign. If you find nothing, it's a sign that you can discount an area, so there's a positive there.

Almost immediately, something catches my eye. I put my hand up so the guys behind me know that I'm stopping – it's a pretty universal sign, that hand signal. I crouch down for a closer look but I'm immediately sure of what I find.

'I know he was here in the last twenty-four hours. I know what way he was travelling,' I say pointing. 'He slept here.'

Paul is immediately behind me. 'What?' he says. 'There's nothing there. Nothing.'

'Look closer. Here,' I say, pointing to a rudimentarily constructed pile of brushwood. I can clearly see that somebody has spent the night on it. I teach people how to make these things on my courses so I know what they look like. I've slept

on them often enough, so I know that simply by laying on one you compress it and it takes on a definable shape.

I hear Paul whistle, almost imperceptibly, like he's suddenly got it. 'Amazing,' he says. 'Amazing.'

As we're walking along, I'm reporting everything to Paul and Derek. They in turn pass it down the line – you have to remember the woods are so thick, it's impossible for us to walk in a group so we're stretched out in single file, some sixteen men and six dogs. Derek is reporting everything back to Gold Command over the radio, so there's a constant stream of verbiage backwards and forwards, one long chain of information.

I push forward a little further and after about twenty minutes I stop again, raising my hand to signal to the team. What I've found are bits of dried wood – lying on a bed of heather. They don't belong where they are. They aren't in a place you'd choose to walk but that's where the trail goes. It looks like Moat has stumbled and dropped the sticks. I can see him in my mind . . . he'd been collecting firewood for cooking but in the darkness with no way to see where he was going, with no handholds to guide him, he's stumbled in the heather and let slip these few pieces from an armful.

That one tiny detail lifts me. Picture it. He's been amassing the wood for some time, working hard to find what he wants. He's got everything he needs, he's making his way to wherever he has in mind to set up camp and he's tripped and dropped some of his cache. He wouldn't even have noticed it go. Insignificant and invisible to him. Hugely significant and noticeable to me.

I notice that there is a trail, disturbances going through the heather to my left, like he's stumbled that way and headed off in that direction after dropping the firewood. Now when I say a trail, I don't mean a trail as in a footpath as you might imagine one. To me, trail is a sign that somebody has been there. The trail leads down into some thickets, but I can't see

ahead to what is there, so the handlers send the dogs forward again.

When they come back, two of the six seem to be giving an indication. I can't put my finger on it but they aren't barking as they would have had they found someone. But they are agitated, like they've seen something of interest. The guys feel it is safe for me to move forwards so I head on, and about 30ft down the trail I find some empty food tins on the forest floor: tuna, something he could have opened, eaten straight out of the tins which he'd then discarded. Small cans pack 32g of protein at a time, about 120 calories, so he'd loaded up on just what his body needed to keep him going. Every little detail adds to and colours the picture I'm building of our quarry. I take nothing away from the fact he's simply discarded the tins. It doesn't indicate carelessness on his part or anything like that. He'd been so far into the dense woods no normal person would ever have stumbled across them. He was where he felt safe – way, way off the beaten track.

I decide to walk back along the trail I've found, and a little further on I find some signs that suggest that somebody has been moving around at night in both directions. That in itself tells me a lot: in daylight you avoid bumping into things; at night, you blunder into things that otherwise would be visible. There are a couple of rocks disturbed from their original position. The way in which a rock is disturbed gives one an indication of direction. And we had sign going in both directions.

I'm left with the impression that he might have been wandering backwards and forwards in a state of confusion. He clearly would have felt safe so deep in the thicket but he doesn't seem to realise that he's leaving sign everywhere.

We get to a slight bend and the dogs give an indication that there might be someone up ahead. As they come back, they stop and their ears prick up. I can hear something too but just

as I'm about to focus on the sound, a report goes out over the radio and I'm distracted by it. But I *know* I heard something move off toward the north-east. The handlers send the dogs forward to investigate again. They go far further than previously, but they come back with nothing. What I'd have given then for a live rewind button; I know I heard something, and I'm convinced the dogs sensed it too, but whoever or whatever it was has gone. It's him; it has to be. There's nobody else here; the woods have been cordoned off.

We carry on and I again notice sign in the area where I'd heard him moving. There are recent disturbances, but not through the bracken. What I'm following is a trail left by somebody who clearly didn't want to be followed. It's recent because at night it would have been impossible to walk down that trail without leaving obvious, clearly visible sign. What I'm seeing is the merest token hint of disturbance. It's very faint – like a snowy TV picture you can't tune in – just some slight areas of flattening *between* the bracken. It can only have been caused by someone carefully picking their way through it. Someone with a level of counter-tracking awareness; someone who clearly wants to remain hidden. It's yet another indication that I'm on the right track.

No matter how careful you are, there will *always* be sign to be found if you traverse ground; always. It's just a matter of knowing what to look for. And I know. I can see tiny little birch sticks, thinner than matchsticks, that have been broken. When you break birch sticks, they go grey over time, but to start with they're quite bright with a clear yellow hue to them. These are yellow so they tell me that Moat's walked through here very recently. I'm talking about the faintest sign, almost invisible to me, completely so to the untrained eye. Paul and the others, who clearly started out sceptical of my bringing anything to the party, have become almost evangelical in their conversion but, try as I might, I can't get Paul to see what I

am seeing. It is there, a consistent pattern of sign passing between the bracken. This trail is the freshest of anything I've seen so far, but even so it's frustratingly non-committal. It tells me he was here very recently, but without something else to anchor it, I can't say exactly when. Following it is taking every bit of focus I have and it's immensely tiring.

Eventually I find another lying-up position – somewhere somebody has stepped off the trail into the heather and lay down. I imagine they've lain down for some time, but it doesn't indicate an overnight stay. It's in a part of the woods where the canopy lets in the sun so the ground would have been warm. It's the perfect spot for someone who was cold last night to lie down and warm themselves in the sun's rays earlier this morning.

I carry on following the sign and eventually it leads to a main track, a gravel path that runs west–east. There's a building adjacent to where the track comes out, a boathouse. It stands at the edge of what in Victorian times had been a lake, but the water has long since been drained so it looks a little bizarre standing in the middle of open land. It stands high off the ground – when the lake was there, its base would have touched the waterline but with the water gone it looks misplaced, like it's been picked up by a giant hand and moved from somewhere else.

I'm keen to go and investigate it but we are forced to hold off as a succession of frustrating incidents occurs. We hear across the radio that members of the press have been trying to get into the woods to see what is going on, so we go to ground while the police at Rothbury send a team of blues and twos to chase them off. While that's going on, the force helicopter is flying overhead taking photographs of the ground so that we'll have a better idea of the terrain ahead of us for the following day, but that has to depart at short notice because the Tornado GR4 that the RAF made available has deployed on a sortie over Cragside to search the area with its Raptor

reconnaissance pod, which is so advanced it's capable of reading the time on Big Ben from the Isle of Wight. We watch as that goes screaming overhead.

Once we're cleared to move out of cover, the team organise themselves and move ahead of me to clear the building. Once again, I'm impressed by their professionalism in very testing circumstances. The dogs are sent on ahead. When they return without incident, the team move in to perform a tactical clearance. After a short time, they pronounce the building clear. Then I'm beckoned forward to investigate the boathouse interior.

It's hot and dusty inside. It's gloomy, the only light coming from some high windows that are dirty and smeared with the detritus of time. The floor is rough, consisting of heavy railway-grade gravel. There's a raised platform towards the far end of the building about four or five feet off the ground.

'He's been here,' I tell Paul, 'probably in the last couple of hours would be my best guess.'

I point to the disturbances that indicate two very definite footprints below us in the gravel. We know Moat's height, his weight, everything available about him, and it's obvious to me from the depth and clarity of the footprints that they're his. It appears that he has jumped down from the platform, landing firmly at that spot in the gravel. The frustration is palpable. I feel that we're within touching distance of him but he remains one step ahead, elusive. He's just out of reach.

By the time we leave the boathouse, we've been on the ground for over eight hours. Eight hours of moving methodically, slowly, tactically through dense forest. Eight hours of being silent, on alert, focused and aware. Tracking, at times, in close proximity to Moat. The dogs are exhausted and a snap poll reveals that all of us are in a similar state. Everyone says that they're happy to carry on, but the law of diminishing returns applies. None of us is half as effective as we were just a few

hours earlier. But I tell Paul and Derek that I'm happy to continue, that if I find fresh sign I'll carry on until we find Moat and flush him out. As it turns out, the decision is made for us; Gold Command wants us to return to Ponteland for an extensive debrief.

As we walk back to the vehicles and mount up, I tell the team of my plans for the following day, Saturday 10 July. My favoured time to strike out is first light and I expect a chorus of groans to greet this news, but to a man the team is enthusiastic. I'm buoyed, there's a real sense of cohesiveness about us and I feel that every member of the team has my back and has bought into the mission.

As we drive back, I feel a sense of a job well done. When we set out this morning, I had nothing more to guide me than experience and intuition. There was no prima-facie starting position, only my informed guesses. It was like looking for a needle in a haystack, and against the odds I've pricked my finger and drawn blood. It's not just me; the others feel it too. There's an energy about the guys.

'Nice work, Ray,' says Paul. 'I'll be the first to put my hand up and admit to being sceptical, but you had me on board from the very first sign when you found his bed. Pretty amazing.'

We arrive at Ponteland and I start to put my thoughts in order, making sense of the day's events so I can relate them to Gold Command. All of the sign that I've found has been pointing towards the west and the north-west, so that gives me a pretty good indication of where he is. I ask the guys in the team what they think and without exception, they tell me that they think we bumped Moat; we disturbed him. I felt we'd got very close to him. Whether it was in one of the two areas where the dogs had given an indication or whether it was the boathouse, I can't say for certain. My money would be on him being near to the boathouse. Given that we were

delayed coming out of the trail and exploring that building, there was more than enough time for him to make an escape. I'm convinced he was somewhere in that area. We all are.

I'm in the process of relating all of this to Gold Command when I become aware of a change of tempo in the room. Something's happening and then it comes over the radio:

'There's an IC1 [the police identity code for white Caucasian] male matching Moat's description, we've got him running out of the Coplish [a large culvert that leads into the drainage system under Rothbury] at the bottom of Blaeberry Hill. Standby . . .'

Over the radio, we can hear officers shouting, 'Armed police; stand still . . . STAND STILL!'

The information comes in thick and fast. It *is* Moat. He's surrounded. Armed police from the Northumberland Force are engaged in a stand-off with him and he is kneeling at the edge of a grass bank with his sawn-off gun pointed at his temple while negotiators attempt to calm him down and resolve the situation peacefully. Paul and Derek look at me, and it's clear we're all thinking the same thing. The timing is bizarre. We're convinced we got in close to him, harried him, and within minutes of us withdrawing and arriving back at Ponteland he comes out into the open and into the arms of the police.

Gold Command invite us into the control room and I watch in amazement as events unfold live from the feed on the police helicopter that is overhead, monitoring the stand-off. Eventually though, it becomes clear that nothing is going to be resolved in the short term, so I withdraw and make my way back to the accommodation. It's been an exceptionally long and exhausting day. Despite my exhaustion, I'm beyond sleep; it's been almost forty-eight hours since I had any decent rest yet I feel wired, my mind a maelstrom of thoughts.

I learn when I arise early on the following morning, Saturday 10 July, that the longest manhunt in modern British criminal history officially ended at 01:15hrs earlier that morning when Moat fired a single shot to his head. He was officially declared dead at 02:20hrs by doctors at Newcastle General Hospital, shortly after arrival.

So, in hindsight, was the operation a success? Even though Moat took his own life and would never stand trial, I'm convinced it was. Clearly Gold Command did too – one of my most treasured reminders is the thank-you letter I received from Chief Constable Sue Sim shortly after I returned home. This is what I feel we achieved: we established that Moat was still in the vicinity; we took the search to the fugitive, and more than likely disturbed him; we established an effective plan for the way forward. The SO19 team told me that they believed Moat's emergence from hiding just minutes after we left the scene was a direct result of our presence.

I've heard since that when specialist firearms officers from Northumbria Police were negotiating with Moat on the river bank, he told them that he'd been visited by a police dog while he was in hiding. The dog looked at him and then left without barking. Given our position at the time the police dogs were left off the lead, we would have been within 20ft of him and he either had to have seen some sight of us or, at the very least, been aware of our presence. He'd have been enormously disturbed by that because he'd have known the game was up. We'd found his trail, we knew where he'd been and that would have got inside his head and really upset him, because he would have known that nowhere was safe. We'd denied him sanctuary. We could follow him where he believed that nobody could. I take immense satisfaction from that.

When all's said and done though, perhaps the last word should go to Mark, Derek, Paul and every one of the Metropolitan Police team from SO19 who took such great

pains to ensure my safety on the operation. Their skill and professionalism were evident throughout the time I spent with them and I came away greatly impressed by their coolness under pressure.

Of course at the end of the day they're still coppers, so I shouldn't have been surprised when I bid them all goodbye before leaving Ponteland for the last time and they shouted as one, 'Thanks for everything, Bear; it's been a pleasure!'

29

No Stone Unturned

I mentioned that when I was brought in to assist in the hunt for Raoul Moat, I felt that I was at the top of my game in terms of tracking skills, but let me give you an insight into how it works. You might recall from the beginning of this book that it was my desire to track foxes that opened the gateway to a life spent as a student of bushcraft. My confidence that I could help the police was born of my long years of learning, then honing the skills required. As I've said, it's a skill set that goes off quickly; you never forget the theory, but unless it's practised on a regular basis, you quickly become rusty in its application.

Unfortunately, because not much is known about tracking outside of those of us who practise it regularly, a little bit of ability can appear impressive to the uninitiated. There are a great many people claiming to be experienced and capable who, quite frankly, are barely beginners. Sadly, honesty in this business is severely lacking in certain quarters. You have to know and acknowledge your own shortcomings because you do nobody any good if you over-inflate your ability.

I was approached by a police force twenty-five years ago, with a request to help them with tracking. It sounded interesting so I thought I'd have a chat with them and see exactly what it was they needed. So, we met and talked, and I very quickly realised I couldn't help because, at the time, I just wasn't good enough. What they wanted was outside of my

capabilities and experience so, being honest with myself, the only course of action for me was to walk away.

I've studied bushcraft for almost forty years and I've learned from the very best. In the run-up to the hunt for Raoul Moat, I'd been tracking almost constantly, so my skills were recent and fresh, which meant I was sharp. But there are still indigenous people out there, like the Kalahari bushmen, whose ability in terms of tracking makes me look strictly second-rate by comparison.

We'd made a programme on them a few years previously and we'd ended up filming in a year of drought; it was searingly hot – around 57°C in the shade, if you could find any. The Kalahari bushmen are a fascinating group of people, and their tracking ability is exceptional. I'd been back to see them again fairly recently when I was out there tracking big cats and I found some droppings that I was convinced were from a leopard. I said this to the bushmen and they said, 'Oh, they're not leopard droppings.' And of course, they were right; they're *nearly* always right. But I said, 'What are they?' and – this is one of the things about them I really like – they couldn't tell me straight away; they had to stop and think about it. So they had a good look and a poke around, they pulled the droppings apart and analysed them, and after about ten minutes, they said rather resolutely, 'Ah, these are genet droppings.'

'How do you know that?' I asked.

'Well, these are owl feathers,' one of them said pointing, 'and only a genet would eat an owl.'

It's that kind of knowledge, that eye for detail, that makes them so good.

I remember filming with two bushmen in particular and one day we came back to their village. It was a large village in terms of numbers – there were a lot of people living there. Also, it was at the end of the day, so there were a lot of footprints in the dust; there must have been thousands of them

and all of a sudden, one of the bushmen said, 'Stop! Stop a moment.'

He jumped forward and I watched him study the ground ahead of us for several seconds – he was looking to see if his wife was at home. He was able to pick out her footprint from all of the others. *That's* how good they are.

———◆◆◆———

There's a certain type of magic you feel when you're tracking; your senses are heightened, it's almost like you exist in a different state of sensory awareness when you're focused on finding a target, and there is a definite frisson in your inter-action with the natural world. There's nothing quite like the feeling you get when you're following tracks and you get to see the personality of the animal reflected through their trail.

You have to start small though; my own tracking ability grew from me finding fox tracks in the snow. I'd go out and follow them, and then when the snow melted I'd follow them in the mud. When the mud hardened, I'd follow them in the dust and my tracking ability evolved and grew from that. Mostly it's about becoming hyper-attuned to your environment. You always leave trace, even if you can't see it. It's a matter of degrees – a bloodhound can follow a few cells that have come off your body as you walk.

I also learned by working with indigenous people who have grown up with tracking and have been using the skills all of their lives. That's good because it shows you what's possible. It opens up doors in your own mind that you might otherwise have shut because if they can do it there, I used to think, then why can't I do it here? And I started to. I learned a lot just from knowing what's possible.

Usually, that means looking further afield than within our own shores and some of the best trackers I've ever come across

were the Ovambo people in Namibia. During the war on the Angolan border Ovambo army trackers were so good that when they slept out in the bush, they didn't bother putting out sentries – they'd have a barbecue. Their enemies had learned the hard way very quickly because if they ever ambushed the Ovambo and didn't kill every single one of them, they were never able to get far enough away that the Ovambo trackers couldn't catch up with them. When the Ovambo tracked, they *ran* and they would shout, 'We're coming to get you!'

Terrain makes a difference. Some terrain lends itself to tracking, as in Namibia and much of the rest of Africa. Cities and major conurbations, such as you find in England, are much harder. The terrain varies massively and there are other variables: more vegetation; more disturbances; other people coming along; the weather. It all makes life more difficult. On the plus side, however, it's all good training for when you go to other places. Hardest first – that's the way to do things. The conventional wisdom says that when you launch a business, the time to do it is in a recession – if you can make a success of it in the tough times then you'll find things much easier in the boom times. If you learn to track here in the UK, you can track just about anywhere.

Sometimes I see sign when I go out normally, in much the same way that some people hear background noise all the time – the traffic sounds, the sirens, the soundtrack to living in a city. I have a visual version of that where I see sign everywhere. Ruth and I were out walking our dog one day just before last Christmas, and Ruth went one way with the dog while I went the other. She tried to sneak ahead but she'd left sign without realising it. As soon as I saw her footprint, that was it – I found her.

Tracking animals is different to tracking people. Tracking people is, in some ways, more interesting but when you're tracking an animal, you generally have more options simply

because what you can do is very much determined by the nature of the ground. In urban areas, which is where most people live, there aren't as many clues. Take Africa, for example: depending on where you are, the ground can be very sandy so it can hold a lot of detail – all the more so if there has been recent light rainfall, or there's moisture in the ground. In other places, the ground might be more granular, consisting of coarse gravel, so it will hold sign, but not the fine detail that makes life easier.

When you begin tracking for a specific animal, the first thing you're looking for is fresh sign. That will allow you to establish details such as the size of the animal, any distinguishing marks in its tracks. Next, you want to establish the direction that it's moving towards, and look at the landscape. You do this to visualise how the animal – let's say a leopard – saw that landscape; was he moving at night, for example, and if so, what did he see? You need to work out the age of the tracks, identify when they were laid down; you can make a mark beside them to see how a fresh mark looks in comparison. The size of the track may give an indication of the size of the animal and its age – that information will allow you to assess whether he's the dominant male or not. Knowing that, you can then predict his likely behaviour.

When I was tracking Houdini the leopard in Namibia, in 2007, I also found tracks of another male who was visiting the area and we managed to put up a trail camera to catch it on film. When we reviewed the footage, he'd behaved and moved exactly as I had described and that felt great because it's so rare that you get to see the leopard that you're tracking. Moments like that make it so rewarding. It's a form of validation; as I say, it's all well and good knowing the theory, but it's nice to get confirmation that you're on target every now and again.

The whole point of tracking is to locate the animal you're

hoping to find, or to ascertain what the animal has been doing, where it's come from, its nature, how it behaves. These are all things that you can discern from its tracks.

Animals can be quite predictable in that they will generally follow game trails; they are interested in food; they are interested in sex; they want to drive out territory invaders; so in a way, it can be a little predictable. Don't get me wrong, it's still really exciting to follow and the reward is the same when you finally locate the animal, or have your suspicions on a certain aspect of its behaviour confirmed. In 2012 I ran a tracking course in Erindi and I gave my students the task of establishing which female leopard was the mother of some cubs. To do that, they had to find the cubs' track, see if they could find a leopard associated with them and, if so, establish which one was the mother. That was quite a challenge, but they accomplished it successfully, so they felt an enormous sense of achievement.

I find following people much more interesting though. People do crazy things; they're a lot less predictable than many animals, so it's much more of a challenge. That said, they are the animals that we understand the best so they're predictable to a degree; you could argue that people are also interested in food, sex, etc. just as big cats or game animals are, but we do a great many other things as well. It's bizarre what you can discern sometimes. But the principles of tracking humans are, of course, exactly the same: the way you use the light, identify the sign, establish direction, and so on. The same basic principles apply – it's the same process.

What many people don't realise is how effective a technique tracking is – it can be used in many, many environments and it works very well in Britain. I think there is a general belief here, especially in the search and rescue community, that tracking has limited uses. That's actually not true at all. The problem is, those people who work with genuine trackers very often impose some sort of limitation; the tracker should always

be the one determining what is and what isn't possible, with regards to the capability of tracking.

So, tracking in a rural environment is great but when it comes to people and an urban environment, although it's nigh on impossible to track them through the heart of a city and over a long distance, you can discern a lot of other information. You might find, for example, where somebody has been moving on waste ground around a lockup, which might lead you to the garage where they're storing stolen goods. You might be able to identify when a potential thief has been checking out a place, or determine where he's entered and exited places – there are opportunities, and many of them can be linked to forensic evidence.

I've found that those who are best at tracking are those who are constantly immersed in the natural environment. There are, as I've said, numerous people purporting to be 'experts' and while they may be experts in theory, having read lots of books, and formulated lots of ideas about the subject, that is a million miles away from actually being able to find that crucial, usually really tiny, piece of evidence. And I'm not talking about footprints here – I'm talking about the tiniest disturbances in leaf litter, or a bent or bruised piece of vegetation, which might be invisible to the unpractised eye. Being able to do this is hugely significant as it is generally the linking piece of evidence that solves the tracking problem. It takes *years* to learn and I get very irritated when I hear some of the nonsense that's being spouted forth by these various 'experts' who do more harm than good.

So how do you grade tracking ability?

There's a whole list of qualities that all trackers must have, but to my mind the key thing is that they must be honest with themselves so that if they can't see something they say so; that is the single most important skill. They must be patient and have perseverance, determination and tenacity. So, if you have

a person with the right traits, and you teach them a proven system that they then practise, they will successfully find and follow sign. Expertise comes through long-term application of the skills in circumstances that range from straightforward to complex.

I have experimented and honed different methods of teaching tracking over the last thirty years and I've largely settled on a system akin to the method used by the military. We use their terminology so the two systems are comparative across the board – things like 'last definite sign', 'trail axis' and so on – but we do things slightly differently, in that we put an emphasis on different areas. When you do something for a very long while, you are able to assess the importance of certain aspects because you have a better understanding of what's important.

Tracking Raoul Moat was the most difficult tracking I've ever done. The sign was very vague and there was one point on the trail where he had deliberately hidden his sign, stepping carefully over the bracken, so it was extremely difficult to spot. But even the most cautious quarry leaves a trail – if you know what to look for.

I think Moat was massively spooked by the fact that we'd followed his trail and all of a sudden he was having to hide from armed cops and dogs. He knew we were hunting him and he knew he was prey. We'd denied him the freedom of the woods and forced him out into the open.

This man had murdered; he had attempted other murders and he had told the world he was going to murder again. He was in the woods, effectively saying, 'Come and get me.' There was only one thing to do at that point and that was to get him before he was able to kill again. There is no question in my mind that whatever the reasons for his murderous spree, once he'd crossed the Rubicon there was only one possible response and that was to find him. What he did was a game changer for

me. I have a persona when I teach that is distinct from what the world sees when I'm on TV, but I'm a different person in other circumstances too, such as the hunt for Raoul Moat. He'd stepped into my world, and he'd committed violence. There was only ever going to be one of two outcomes: he'd have been found and sent to trial, or he'd be cornered and he would die. It was his choice to evade justice by ending his life.

I debated long and hard about whether to talk about the role I played in tracking Raoul Moat in this book. I know there was speculation as to my involvement in the media around the time of the events but that was only because there was an information vacuum, so there were all sorts of rumours flying around. I could have lived with that, but what I don't like are wannabe 'trackers' going around the circuit claiming they were there, that they were involved, in an effort to bolster their credibility. I've even been told of one particular individual who opens his 'lectures' by throwing down a plaster cast that he claims is an imprint of one of Moat's boots. I'd love to know how he could possibly have come by that, given that the only cast that was ever taken was made by the police forensic team in the aftermath – and they still have it.

What happened was tragic for everyone concerned and I think it's immoral to try and claim some involvement in bringing Moat down for reasons of personal gain, or from some misguided and perverse idea that it'd bring some sort of 'glamour' by association.

As I say, I felt honour- and duty-bound to offer my services to the agencies involved in the hunt for Moat because I believe that if you have the tracking skill and something like that occurs, you can't stand by and do nothing. Maybe I couldn't join the Forces, but it's still nice to be able to contribute to my country in some way. At the end of the day, this is what I'd trained for and anybody who trains for many years wants to put the skills they've acquired to use.

I'd be lying if I said I didn't feel a great sense of achievement tracking Raoul Moat but what I find infinitely more satisfying is the fact that from my earliest days, I've wanted to introduce people to bushcraft – the proper subject, not shorthand survival – and I've done that. I've no problem with survival training – it's very important and has its place, but it's only a part of bushcraft. I wanted to introduce people to this much larger subject and take it away from people who want to wield big knives, the Rambo-types, and make it healthy and wholesome, which it is. I really do believe that I've done what I set out to do. I think it's a very good way to introduce people to nature because it's not just about remembering the proper names for flora and fauna. Nature has practical values and when plants and animals become your friends and allies you want to cherish them, you want to take care of these things, and I've spent a lifetime learning how to do that.

30
Thirty Years On

It's hard to believe that this year marks Woodlore's thirtieth year in business. It's also my fiftieth year on this planet, and 2013 also marks the twentieth anniversary of my running courses in the Arctic, so there's a nice symmetry in those figures. Yet in many respects I feel as if I'm only just beginning.

Never in the furthest reaches of my imagination did I ever dream my life would follow the path it has. I never set out to make bushcraft my career, and neither did I have any great desire or plan to have a twenty-year career in television, but that's just the way things have panned out. It has felt at times like I am a passenger on a train; I'm loving the journey but I'm not at the controls, so I just go where the engines take me. It's never felt like work; how can it when I've spent my life doing something I love? It's been a lifelong exploration of a subject that fascinated and inspired me, even as a child, and the best part of all is that I've been able to share some of the knowledge I've acquired with a wide audience through my books, courses, lectures and television documentaries.

It's been an enormous privilege to travel the world as widely as I have, spending time learning about and from the numerous indigenous people that are dotted across the planet. And I've felt humbled to be invited to train members of our armed forces and equip them with tracking skills that are saving lives

in Afghanistan by enabling soldiers to find and identify IEDs. I spent nearly a decade training the members of 22 SAS Regiment in survival techniques, and have delivered lectures to our police on a number of areas of interest. I've been trusted to do that, and listened to, which truly is an honour. Ultimately, I didn't learn any of what I teach on a course, or at university. Despite searching there was no school for me to attend that could teach me what I wanted to know and, aside from a few small pieces of the puzzle, it wasn't written down in manuals or books. What I've learned, I have learned from the forests, the mountains and the deserts of our planet. I guess I'm fortunate in that I don't remember the hardships, just the high notes.

I was immensely lucky to find a friend and mentor in Kingsley Hopkins, a man with the patience and desire to teach me what he knew. For the first twenty years of my life, he shaped, informed and coloured my interest in the outdoors and brought to bear sage advice and wisdom acquired in one of the most testing environments in recent history – on the front lines during World War II. I still miss him and the influence and counsel he provided me with, but his legacy is something that lives on within me.

In the way that Kingsley was there in the first twenty years of my life, Lars Fält has been there for the past thirty. I feel fortunate and privileged to count him as a friend and he has played a major role in shaping one aspect of Woodlore with me. Lars Fält is a household name in Sweden, the founder of the Swedish Army Survival School and in reality the father of Swedish Survival. He is a former Parachute Ranger who, throughout his long military career, had a reputation for being a 'hard soldier', cut from the cloth that only airborne troops

really understand. His thoroughness in training reflected his heartfelt dedication to the welfare of his students. Lars cared deeply that, when tested, his troops would survive against the odds and return with honour. Knowing that he would not be at their side, he drilled them hard in the lessons of survival.

But there is another side to Lars; behind his craggy exterior is a warm-hearted family man with a sense of humour that's even sharper than his axe. The Lars I know is a passionate woodsman and a consummate professional. He retired from the military in 2001 and, since passing on the baton of responsibility for military survival, he has been able to express the quieter, more philosophical side of his nature. While he is always up to date with the latest technological advances, it is his passion for older knowledge and native tradition that inspires his own bushcraft.

For twenty years now Lars and I have worked together in Swedish Lapland teaching Arctic survival and bushcraft. We have shared good times and bad, weathered extreme cold and dried our socks at the same fire in years of abnormal warmth. I trust him implicitly, and his judgement is totally reliable. With a telepathy built on shared hardships, I can predict with 100 per cent accuracy his response to a crisis, as he can mine. Lars would say that we drink from the same cup. We have both travelled to remote areas of the Arctic and had the privilege of living for a time with various bands of First Nations. But what unites us most strongly is the belief that traditional knowledge and skills are only validated by testing them on the trail, on real journeys.

Lars has been a very important person in both my own history and that of Woodlore. We first met in the early 80s when he attended a lecture that I was giving about survival at the Royal Geographical Society. There were a lot of people in the audience but Lars stood out from the crowd. After the lecture, a delegate came up to me, saying I hadn't made fire by friction correctly in my demonstration; of course, he was

talking out of his bottom. So I asked him to demonstrate what he was talking about and he replied rather arrogantly, 'No, I am only here to observe,' and made a quick getaway before his bluff was any further exposed. The subject of survival and now bushcraft have sadly always attracted Walter Mitty characters such as this, that have read much and done little. Overly willing to impress the gullible with their self-professed 'expertise' they can cause no end of confusion. Fortunately for me, his departure provided the opportunity for Lars to introduce himself and we talked for a few minutes, and when he left he gave me a copy of a book he'd written, together with his business card, and we went our different ways.

At that point he was a captain in the Swedish Army, running its survival school. At the beginning of the 1980s, the Swedish Army realised that none of its conscripts had the rural skills of twenty years earlier; society had become more urban and people had lost the traditional knowledge of how to take care of themselves. The army wanted to redress this situation and their solution was survival training. The search was on for someone with the skills to run the course and somebody suggested Lars, saying, 'He's a pain because he never stops talking about survival, but he's your man.'

And he was – he was just perfect for the job. Lars was passionate about survival as a subject. The bulk of his military career was spent at the height of the Cold War when the threat of invasion or war with the Soviet Union was very real, so survival training was an absolute priority. After appointing Lars to write and run the course, he was sent around the world to spend time with allied armies on their own survival courses. He came to the UK and did the SAS course in 1982 and then went back to Sweden to establish the Swedish Army Survival School. I'd heard about the school but it was only after I came back from the Africa walk that I made the connection and realised it was Lars who was running it, so I dug out his

business card and made contact. When I went over to see him, I noticed that his house was just like mine inside – chock-full of knives and survival gadgets with a great library on survival. He was definitely a kindred spirit and we hit it off straight away.

Eventually I set up a Woodlore course with Lars and we ran our first one together in Lapland in 1993. We've been collaborating ever since, making Lars Woodlore's longest-standing instructor aside from myself. We run two courses each year at the height of Swedish Lapland's winter, and through all those experiences we've come to know each other very well. That's a very special thing because it's so rare in an industry where anyone can set themselves up as an 'expert' without necessarily having the judgement that can only come from walking the path. He's walked that path and back again, so I know that in a crisis we can depend upon each other absolutely. It's people like Lars that make the world tick for me.

Closer to home, Gordon Hillman is another man I feel privileged to know. Gordon is Honorary Visiting Professor in Archaeobotany at the Institute of Archaeology, University College London, and someone who has shaped and informed another aspect of bushcraft for me. Archaeobotany is the study of how people used plants in the past and there is nobody more knowledgeable than Gordon on this immensely wide-ranging topic. From the moment that we first met it was obvious that we had the same passion for plants and were asking similar questions about their edibility. It was inevitable that we would collaborate in the pursuit of our shared interest. That said, it's his personality that makes him shine; he's one of the nicest fellows I've ever had the good fortune of knowing and a pretty remarkable human being.

Gordon's greatest work as an archaeobotanist was at a site called Abu Hureyra on the Euphrates, which is widely accepted as the place where mankind made the transition from hunting and gathering to farming. He did a massive amount of work there, although most of my dealings with him were much more parochial, and we spent a great deal of time in Scotland, where Woodlore runs advanced courses that teach students to live off the land. Having Gordon there with me helped to share the pressure of teaching, and it gave the students a different perspective. If I had to head off somewhere, I'd say to him, 'Gordon, remember, they'll only really remember ten plants,' yet I knew that when I got back there would be a hundred or more plants laid out, which was his way. His love for his subject is infectious and the students can't get enough of him. He's quite the most wonderful man, a real Gandalfian character in appearance with his white hair and trademark chinstrap beard, and whatever the weather, he'd always take a skinny dip in the loch.

Sadly, now in his later years, Gordon suffers from Parkinson's disease. It's such a hideous disease, so cruel. I could see that the outdoor life was becoming more and more difficult for him to cope with, so it was no surprise when he eventually told me one night that he wouldn't be able to join me in Scotland any more. We sat by the fire afterwards and it was one of the saddest moments of my life. It felt very strange knowing we'd never be able to share the experiences we had again.

As well as running courses with me over the years, Gordon and I also worked together on the BBC TV programme *Wild Food*. This series rode on the back of ten years' research we had made, investigating the wild foods that Britain's last pre-farming hunter gatherers may have eaten at the end of the British Mesolithic. Many of the plants we needed to experiment with are now considered as arable weeds and consequently in very short supply. At Enoch Dhu near Glenlivet in Scotland we came

across a field choked with Hemp Nettle, a plant whose seed we needed in quantity for an experiment. To collect these seeds Gordon had improvised a rather Heath Robinson collecting apparatus that involved the frame and handle of a carp fishing net attached to a hand-stitched canvas bag and a child's purple and pink tennis racket. He did look a sight as he went into this field beating the heads of the plants to knock the seeds into his bag. It's one of the funniest things I think I've ever seen.

We had a lot of laughs like that. I remember on another occasion we were trying to cook some roots. My contribution was my knowledge of the Aboriginal approach to cooking. Gordon's contribution was his incredible understanding of the genetic relationships between species – for example, you might have one plant species that is genetically similar to another, and perhaps some of the edible qualities will be inherited because of their similarity. Anyway, we were sitting there cooking a particular root that he'd theorised would probably be safe to eat, although I was a little more sceptical than him. When they were cooked and we'd started to eat them, I looked at him and said: 'Gordon, are you sure this is edible?'

'Oh yes. Theoretically it should be fine.'

'So why is my mouth swelling up?'

Bang goes the theory then. That was the nearest I've ever come to poisoning myself and it was a good reminder that even specialists sometimes get things wrong. I miss working with him even now, although whenever I walk across those same landscapes, they evoke wonderful memories and I'm enormously thankful for them. Some things you don't forget.

━━━◆━◆━━━

Both Lars and Gordon have added immeasurably to the success of Woodlore. It's vital to me that everything and everyone connected with the operation reflects the same high standards

that they have set. This is not easy as we search for specialists who are not just authorities in their fields but also people with a humble demeanour who gain their reward from seeing their students acquire new skills, confidence and aspirations.

At the end of the day it all comes down to people – having the right people in the team. I am proud to say I work with the most amazingly dedicated and talented team at Woodlore it is a tight knit-team. There is a 'can do, will do' expedition ethic that drives the business. As a business we believe that we can help make the world a better place and strive to do so. It is hard to believe how it all started when I see the professional and energetic team carrying on the work I began thirty years ago. Through the last thirty years I have had the privilege to lead courses and expeditions to many of the most remote and fascinating environments on the planet. The ultimate goal, to inspire respect and appreciation of our natural world. The best part though, is hearing our clients tell of their successes, the challenges they have overcome and what they are planning to do with their newly acquired skills.

———◆———

In terms of bushcraft, I'm still learning new skills and there remain things I want to develop. As you learn more, you ask more questions and those questions lead to more learning, and I still have a long list of questions for which I need answers. A long time ago, I came to the realisation that one lifetime is simply not enough.

Also, there are a great many places I haven't visited yet, so there is work still to do. I have maps on the walls on which I plot where I've been and I've marked places I've been to many times such as Africa, Australia, Canada and the globe's various rainforests. I've never been to Japan though, and that remains a long-held ambition. With the influence that judo has had

throughout my life, I'm very interested in the culture, the traditions and crafts – and also the wildlife. Japan is a very wooded country with bears and a host of other interesting creatures, all of which intrigues me.

My life to date has been pretty varied and fantastic but I've never become complacent and never rested on my laurels. Nothing should ever be taken for granted; I've never done that and I don't intend to start now. I'm grateful for every opportunity presented to me, for all the wonderful people I've had the privilege to meet and for the truly special experiences I've had along the way. But there's so much more to learn and do, so many tracks to be discovered and places in which to immerse oneself. I just hope Father Time is kind to me because I have a long road ahead of me still to travel, and a wonderful wife with whom to share those experiences.

Acknowledgements

No book is ever the work of a single person; my name may be on the cover, but it stands as testament to the industriousness and efforts of a whole team of people, each of whom has been essential to the project's existence.

First and foremost, I'd like to thank my wife Ruth, and son Kristian, for their steadfast love and support, endless patience and belief in me. You make my world complete, thank you.

Also to Jackie Gill, my long-standing friend and agent. Jackie – I couldn't have done this without you.

Also, my heartfelt thanks go to Steve Gurney, my right hand man who over the years has become a friend as well as a very important part of Woodlore. Also Jane Mitchell, Steven Bullen, Diana Taylor, Daniel Hume, Keith Whitehead, Rebecca Brewster, Harvey Taylor-Meek and the rest of the outdoors team at Woodlore; you are the bedrock on which our success is built. As much a family as a team it is a continuing privilege to skipper such a brilliant crew.

I would like to pay tribute to the calm professionalism and efficiency of Rupert Lancaster and his team at Hodder & Stoughton who have worked so hard in recent years on all of my books. To Rupert must go my foremost editorial thanks – he has lived with this book, and many others, for as long as I have. His delightful assistant Kate Miles has been wonderful throughout. I'd like to thank all at Hodder for their support over the years. Thanks too, to Tara Gladden for polishing the

manuscript, and to Rose Alexander for casting a watchful eye over it – you both did a really sterling job.

To Ben Southwell, Barrie Foster, Paul Watson, Alan Duxbury, Andy Morton, Sam Cox and Tim Green – thanks for making the journey so much fun. And to Collette Foster who first saw something in me and encouraged me on my first steps into the world of television.

I'm indebted to all of the elders and the many indigenous people who have given up their time over the years to so generously share their wisdom and experience with me and who remind us all what it means to be part of the human family.

To Lars Fält, friend of the northern trail; thank you.

Lord and Lady Selborne who first provided me with access to land to experiment with the techniques of my profession and to establish the courses which still set the standard for Bushcraft education within the UK today.

The many students who have attended the Woodlore courses, without your patronage none of this would have been possible. Teaching is a two way street you have taught me so much and greatly broadened my outlook, thank you.

Thank you also to the Seventh Purley Scout Troop and my friends in the British Deer Society.

Sally – thank you for being there when I needed you.

Edward Cadogan for being the truest friend. Dr David Campbell for providing astute advice regarding the medical hazards of my more exotic expeditions. The Grey Family for their continuing inspiration and support.

Peter Fincham, Alison Sharman, Diana Howie, Puiey, Phil Coles and everyone at ITV for giving me such a warm welcome.

Finally thanks to my many friends, in all branches of the armed forces, for whom survival skills are a necessity. I have the deepest respect for the selfless service you provide. Your, very often appalling, sense of humor in the face of adversity continues to be the most powerful lesson in survival.

Picture Acknowledgements

M ost of the photographs are from the author's personal collection.

Additional photographs: © Mary Albion: 9 (top & middle). © Ed Bagnall: 16 (bottom). © BBC: 4 (bottom), 12 (top right). © The Bowen Collection, University of Bath Archives: 3 (middle left and right). © Phil Coles: 15 (top). By kind permission of Joe Hill: 11 (top). © ITV: 15 (bottom). © victoria-kaye.co.uk: 13 (bottom left). By kind permission of the Metropolitan Police/ photo author collection: 14 (bottom). © Martin Pailthorpe: 8 (bottom). © Rex Features: 3 (top left), 14 (top), 16 (top). © Ben Southwell: 12 (top left and bottom).

Every reasonable effort has been made to contact the copyright holders but if there are any errors or omissions, Hodder & Stoughton will be pleased to insert the appropriate acknowledgement in any subsequent printing of this publication.

Index

NORTHERN WILDERNESS

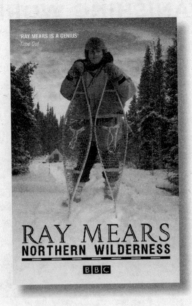

'Amazing scenery, fascinating history and
oodles of good old-fashioned scouting skills'
Daily Telegraph

'NORTHERN WILDERNESS is different, grown-up,
wider ranging, a trip through the Canadian tundra
in the snow show tracks of the early explorers . . .
effortlessly beguiling'
Sunday Times

This book is rich in bushcraft, as Ray explains the
unique survival techniques of the Native Canadians
and the Inuit, as well as how the prospectors in the
gold rush used bushcraft skills to survive in this
inhospitable but awesome landscape.

HODDER

RAY MEARS
VANISHING WORLD

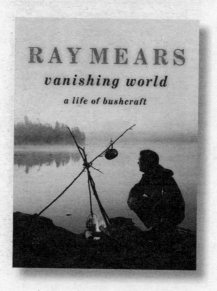

Ray Mears reflects on his experiences in some of the most remote and beautiful places on Earth along with his own stunning photographs of the landscapes and people he's encountered.

Fascinated by photography from an early age, each of Ray's pictures captures an instant of life, a powerful experience he has compared to releasing the trigger on a rifle when hunting.

This book reveals our dramatically changing planet and inspires us to look more closely at the changes around us. See our vanishing world through the eyes, ears and camera lens of Ray Mears.

HODDER

WILD FOOD

Ray Mears has travelled the world discovering how native people manage to live on just what nature provides. What has always frustrated him is not knowing how our own ancestors fed themselves and what we could learn about our own diet.

We know they were hunter-gatherers, but no-one has been able to tell what they ate day-to-day. How did they find their calories, week in week out throughout the year? What were their staple foods? Where did they get their vitamins? How did they ensure their bodies received enough variety?

In this book he travels back ten thousand years to a time before farming to learn how our ancestors found, prepared and cooked their food.

HODDER

BUSHCRAFT SURVIVAL

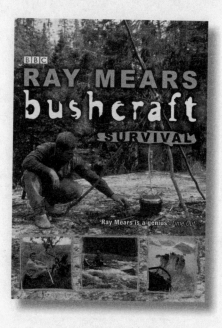

In BUSHCRAFT SURVIVAL Ray Mears travels to some of the most remote and beautiful wildernesses in the world, and experiences first hand the survival techniques of different indigenous cultures.

From the Hudson Bay in Canada, via Tanzania and the jungles of Venezuela, to the moors and highlands of Britain, BUSHCRAFT SURVIVAL explores a range of locations and techniques from indigenous peoples. Drawing on centuries of knowledge as well as his own experience, Ray demonstrates how our enjoyment of the wilderness comes through respect for our surroundings and the people, plants and animals that live there.

HODDER

ESSENTIAL BUSHCRAFT

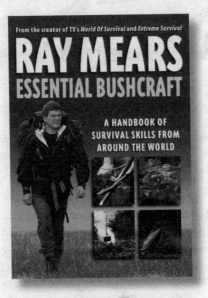

From the creator of TV's *World Of Survival* and *Extreme Survival*

RAY MEARS
ESSENTIAL BUSHCRAFT

A HANDBOOK OF SURVIVAL SKILLS FROM AROUND THE WORLD

Ray Mears is well known to millions of television viewers through his acclaimed series *Tracks, Ray Mears World of Survival* and *Ray Mears Extreme Survival*. Now, based on the bestselling BUSHCRAFT, he has created a handy portable compendium of vital survival skills and wisdom from around the world. Packed with essential wilderness techniques, this book is an invaluable companion on any expedition.

H

HODDER